Thank you
and Virginia for your
help to make this a success.

Pat Peterson

# The Chatelaine Connection

## By

## Patricia E. Peterson

authorHOUSE™

1663 LIBERTY DRIVE, SUITE 200
BLOOMINGTON, INDIANA 47403
(800) 839-8640
WWW.AUTHORHOUSE.COM

First published by AuthorHouse 06/20/05

ISBN: 1-4208-1864-3 (sc)
ISBN: 1-4208-1865-1 (dj)

Library of Congress Control Number: 2005901667

Printed in the United States of America
Bloomington, Indiana

This book is printed on acid-free paper.

Color photograph of Patricia E. Peterson taken by Morin's Studio of Milford, Massachusetts.

The cover artwork was designed by artist, Martin Poole of West Midlands, England, who is well known on both sides of the Atlantic for his watercolor art. Many of his paintings depicting scenes from Scotland, Wales and Norfolk are displayed in galleries and exhibitions.

I dedicate this book to those dearest to me—my family. Though some are no longer physically present with me, they all provided me with a treasure of wonderful memories that contributed to my desire to create something unique. There is nothing quite so wonderful as to see one's secret aspirations—once just pebbles of ideas—evolve into a tangible creation that can be shared with so many others.

**Writing this book gave truth to the words:**

"The significance of man is not what he attains, but rather what he longs to attain."

**Kahlil Gibran**

# ACKNOWLEDGEMENT

First, I especially want to acknowledge and express my deepest gratitude to my very best friend and lifetime soul mate, my husband, Paul. His quiet patience, endearing encouragement, firm inner strength, and never-ending technical computer assistance has made it possible for me to accomplish my first literary aspiration.

Secondly, I want to thank my children, Norman and Douglas, for their unfailing encouragement, love, and kindness shown to me during this long process.

Thirdly, I know my dearest daughter, Brenda, who is no longer physically with us, is an indefinable part of my success in this accomplishment.

I love you all.

# PROLOGUE

*SILENCE.*

First light. The darkened distant hills appear to hold back the slowly rising sun; the dew of the night glistens timidly in the first morning rays; the blackness of the night evolves to subtle shades of gray, merging gradually into the cinematic colors of daylight.

*SHE SLEEPS.*

Distant noises taunt her to open her eyes to chase the sounds. Thoughts bombard her consciousness as her sense of vision gains a hold. "It's so dark...so dark." Turning toward the single shaft of light filtering through a window...barely able to focus on the light beam, "I see...dancing flecks...in the distant light...can't make out shapes...too many dark shadows concealing... I'm not sure...is it first light? Or is this just another one of my kaleidoscopic dreams... not real, playing another game with my memory? Can't shake off these stuporous feelings; can't will my body and mind to work together!" Nervously rubbing her eyes and head to wipe away the muddled scene, she focuses again and speaks out.

"Aye! The images are becoming clearer and more vivid to me! I feel...something...urging my senses to work...What is this place?...Can my eyes deceive me!" Slowly, the slight figure raises her head to a position to glimpse her surroundings... "This moment feels so real…like it's actually happening to me now…Yes! I think *it is* real…It's really happening now and not a dream…this time…this place is real!" There's a hint of excitement in her voice! To capture this real mental instant, she speaks—breaking the surrounding silence, "I *cannot…will not* let this moment fade away like…my past dreams!"

A rush of cool air comes from somewhere out in the gray dawn, and her skin tingles with a sense of fear! "My thoughts are so jumbled… disconnected…so confused! What's happening to me and why? My feelings…so muddled…like clouds of shapeless images that I don't understand! Why does my body feel strangely heavy…weak?" Desperately straining to raise herself up, she manages to overcome the paralytic weakness throughout her body. Suddenly,  a  sharp, pungent odor overtakes her sense of smell, forcing her to cover her face with her hands to hold back a caustic, burning nasal sensation.

"Ach! That smell…so acrid!" Her mind can't relate this experience to these surroundings—nor does the pungent smell immediately conjure up a clear, familiar past experience. After several minutes of trying to remember *anything*… "*It does* have a similar offensive odor that I've smelled before somewhere…remember! Try to remember! Yes! I smelled it in a laboratory…*a chemical laboratory*." Vivid mental images of a *laboratory,* filled with flasks giving off astringent odors of acids, are clear in her mind!

"At least I have some connection of things past!" As quickly as the odorous whiff comes, it dissipates into the cool dawn draft.

The room's soft lighting reveals an enormous canopied bed with four wooden bedposts intricately carved in disparity to the rough-hewn gray stone walls. Atop the bedside table, a candle sputters; the wick flickers and dies out in the bottom of a pool of ashen wax. A small wooden stool is nearby.

"What *is* this place?"

Unexpectedly, an icy chill makes her body shudder, and that same frightening feeling overtakes her again!

"I can't think why I'm here, or what has happened to me! I've got to make my mind and feelings search out why I'm in this place. Yet, nothing's familiar…recognizable, to give me a single hint to my past!" Rapidly, her eyes dart around to capture a familiar object.

"I recognize nothing!" In exasperation, she throws off the bed covers to get out of bed, but an overwhelming weakness makes it so painful and slow to stand. Panic overcomes her, making her heart race faster! The morning light in the room is brighter, making it easier to explore, to search for familiar objects…something…anything to give her a hint of recognition what is this place!

Her gait is slow and each step deliberately placed to keep from falling…Weakness makes it difficult to walk without support from some nearby object. "My legs feel so strange…weak…numb; I can't seem to feel my feet on the stone floor." Her eyes glance down to her dressing gown. Feeling the cool, plain white garment against her skin, she senses her body trembling from the cold air; the hostile air grips her like a sharp vice! Grabbing the blanket off the bed, she wraps it tightly around her before taking a few more steps towards the shafts of light spewing through the windows. The floor feels icy cold to her bare feet.

"Why do my arms and legs feel drained, so heavy and slow to move? What has happened to me make me feel like this?" Mumbling, "It's as if my body hasn't done something as simple as walk in a long time!" Loudly, she calls out, "Please? Is anyone here?" The echo of silence is frightening as she struggles to hold back the tears.

*SILENCE.*

Her eyes scan the large room for a familiar object—nothing. Touching the few pieces of furniture—a wooden chair—a large table covered with intricately made lace cloth—sparsely placed furniture around the room conveys no familiarity either. Nothing! No hint of recognition.

"I must have a past!" Rationalizing…"It isn't in this place?" Covering her eyes in a desperate gesture to jar a thought, thoughts flee through her mind…a memory…a picture…when a cloud-like veil shrouds her psyche and blankness returns. Despondent she assumed, "If I belong here—then something in this place would tell me that!" Overwhelmed with frustration, she said, "It's like I'm seeing everything for the first time, but how can that be? How long have I been in this place?" She hears her voice trembling…echoing her questions again…fighting back her tears…no answers come.

*SILENCE.*

The sun's rays are vividly dazzling now, slowly shifting around the room to lighten the darkened areas. The illuminating glow first strikes the ceiling and then slithers down onto the walls. Her senses are clear now as she slowly surveys her prison-like structure. The room appears immense with four feudal stone walls; two covered with various old-world tapestries. The high, narrow windows are set with clear and stained glass panes, allowing the sun's rays to spew into kaleidoscopically radiant colors throughout the room; none allow a view outside—to a tall tree bough twisting or straining against the fury of the wind.

"If I could only see outside, I might recognize a familiar sight!"

The furnishings look sparse, old, and singularly unique. On one of the walls, hangs a large, heavily framed picture of a man dressed in a seventeenth or eighteenth century costume. At the farthest end of the room, over a great stone hearth, hangs a large wooden crucifix, secured by a heavy link chain bolted into the stone ceiling. The light diffuses into shadows to change the room's composition. Her attention is hypnotically drawn to watch the prism's colors slink down from the ceiling onto the walls…to the stone floor, revealing everything in its path. Her vision shifts to the fireplace filled with ashen embers.

"This place has a certain rustic old-world feel to it. I'd say it belongs in some medieval stone stronghold somewhere in history past!" Instantaneously, she realized her memory recognized a bit from her past! "Now, how did I know this place could belong in a historical setting? I *do* remember some things…but why just that?" Slowly, she continued to explore the room, mumbling her thoughts aloud as if she were talking to another in the room. "Who brought me to this place? Why here? There must be someone aware of my presence here who can answer my questions!" In a panicky loud voice, she calls out, "Please, can anyone hear me?"

*SILENCE.*

The ominous stillness is broken! Startled, she moves to a darkened corner as a loud metallic noise comes from the distant end of the room. Keeping her eyes riveted on the huge wooden door slowly opening inward, she sees a shapeless figure that glides noiselessly towards the bed, carrying a covered tray, and setting it down aside the bed.

"My dear, you are awake. I hope you are hungry. This serving of food...for you."

The visitor's hands gesture to sample the food. The voice is light, softly pitched, reassuring and encouraging her to come closer. Her visitor is a young woman speaking English with a foreign accent.

Cautiously walking towards the stranger, still wrapped in the blanket, she sees the uncovered tray's simple meal. Curls of steam waft upward from the bowl into the cold air, giving off a sweet aroma. With a corner of her apron, the visitor grasps hold of the pot handle and pours a hot drink into a beaker half-filled with a milky liquid. Next, she watches the delicate hands break the bread to offer her a piece. Hesitantly, she accepts the morsel and accepts the warm bowl in her trembling, frail hands; all the time, the stranger bids her to taste the steaming contents. Almost fearfully, she hears her urging and obeys.

"Do not be frightened. Please...for you? It will make you feel... strong."

Accepting the warm bowl of food, she cannot take her eyes off of her visitor. The bowl of gruel is thick, sweet, and warm. Her hunger surges, and she takes pleasure in eating the fare. Slowly, the warm food begins to dissipate the chill inside her, at least for a little while.

Her thoughts are, "Dare I ask this stranger my haunting questions? I'm so hungry..." Quietly, she continues to consume each morsel, never releasing her gaze from the figure next to her. The hot mug cupped in her hands lets the heat penetrate her icy fingers. Its sweet aroma entices her to drink its contents...the taste is unusually sweet, but she consumes all of it before setting the empty beaker back on the tray. Her attention is fully focused on this "companion" seated next to her on the bedside stool.

Straining to see the face under the large-brimmed hat atop a black scarf headdress, which is wrapped completely around her guest's head, she could only make out her pale delicate features. A long, white sleeveless apron covers her dark oversized dress. The garb looks like a costume. Her large, clear dark eyes emit sadness; her pale complexion gives her a youthful appearance…a child's look of innocence! Her oversized clothing bares only her hands, which work with deliberate and gentle motions, complimenting the gentle voice and tenderness in her saddened eyes.

"Do I know you?"

"No, I am Compangnia."

"Thank you, Compangnia, for all of this…It tasted very good."

"Compangnia, what is this place? How did I get here? How long have I been here? Do *you* live here? Do you know *my* name?" She looks pleadingly into her eyes for answers to her bombardment of queries.

"*Si*, I live here…but I'm just one of the servants." She knew she had answered her last question truthfully.

"Then who does own this place…and who else lives here?"

"This place belongs to the *old family*, the same family has owned and lived here for many generations," Compangnia replied in her soft voice with her slight accent. She was captivated by her presence and observed her rise from the stool and noiselessly walk across the room to the hearth to clean out the burnt embers.

"This family…what is the name of this family? And how do you know me? Please, can't you tell me why I am here?"

Her questions only drift off into the silence as Compangnia moves throughout the room snuffing out the remnants of burning candles from the night; tasks she seems to perform with familiarity. She observes her movements, as Compangnia next pours a bucket of coal and arranges the wooden logs in the fireplace to bring back a bright flickering flame.

Pleadingly, she asks, "Please, Compangnia, how did I get here and why am I here?" She feels her silence is deliberate as she places the dishes on the tray to take them away.

"I know you want to understand everything… to learn answers, but for now, you must be patient…trust me…all your questions… you will have answers soon." Taking hold of the bedding as a sign for me to return to the bed, she gently smooths the bedcovers around me.

"Here…fresh water for you, but now you must rest!" Grasping her hands in mine…her eyes…so pleading, she says, "There is nothing…to fear here…all of your questions will have answers…in time." Her words…it was as if she was trying to make me understand something other than what her words expressed…it was in her eyes!

There *were* so many questions that I needed answers for, but I knew *Compangnia would not tell—or did not* have the *answers.* Her words, "nothing to fear here,"—not so…there *is* something to fear here!

Picking up the tray and looking directly at her charge, Compangnia remarked, "Feel…as if you are home." Her words, *"feel at home,"* stunned me! That single word, *"home,"* echoed in my mind! I faltered to find the words to ask what she meant by *"home?"*

"Compangnia, why do you say I should feel at *home?"* The question…too late! Across the room, Compangnia disappeared on the other side of the large, heavy wooden door swinging it shut and sending an echoing thud throughout the room…the door's metal latch turned…it was locked!

*SILENCE.*

Once again…alone. The diminutive figure in the large canopied bed appeared lost within the dungeon-like walls. The hearth's fire glowed brightly with crackling embers, radiating its warmth throughout the room.

"I feel so cold…so terribly cold."

No matter how strong the fire roared to spread its heat, it would never relieve *her* kind of icy coldness! Drawing the blankets tighter to keep the icy feeling at bay, she waited alone. But waited for what? Fighting to remember…an identity? A past? What kind of life she had before …this place? No answers came…the bright light in the room grew dim…dimmer…

"The drink…so warm…too sweet…please…noo…"

*SHE SLEEPS.*

# BRITAIN-LONDON-SOHO

# CHAPTER ONE

London's dawn is breaking over Parliament, etching its massive ebony outline against the purplish-gray tones of the eastern sky, painting a pseudo-palate of russet browns on the ancient stone structure.

Daybreak, seen from the high-rise office adjacent to Piccadilly Circus, reveals the beginning of a classic spring day in London. Layers of shapeless distant clouds settle on the land, shrouding the sharp definition of the nearby towers of London Bridge. Wisps of vapor float aimlessly, creating strange ephemeral shapes; flashing glints of water from the Thames blink back through the drifting mist. The slow, lifting cloud layer gives way to a stratum of light in the east, not an unusual greeting to a quiet London dawn. Likened to a painting's first non-descript etching, first the outline, then dabbing from a palate of purples, browns, and grays—finally evolving into bright, vibrant colors seen in a Van Gogh masterpiece filled with urban sights and sounds. Emma had worked through the night at her desk, strewn with case files piled high. Not realizing the lateness of the night hour, she succumbed to sleep slumped over the stack of files.

A soft distant noise awakens her. Slowly rousing from a semi-stuporous state, she looks toward the direction of the sound while moving in a discernible way to adjust her rumpled garb and to shake off the overwhelming stiffness in her arms and legs. Her attention focuses on the office door. It's only Peter entering with a hot steaming cup of tea and a fresh-baked pastry—his morning ritual upon her early arrival.

"Is it that time already, Peter?" she murmurs, as the events of last night flood her memory with reasons why she was here in the office so early this morning.

Peter is Emma's secretary, more accurately her "aide-de-camp." A young man who knows her habits and peculiarities so well, he has the uncanny ability to instinctively anticipate her thoughts and needs. Some people have even commented, "Peter mothers Emma," which doesn't make her feel uncomfortable at all, even though he's her junior. In fact, she's grateful for it!

"Another night in the trenches? How many does that make this week? Don't tell me, I already know the answer to my queries!" Peter carefully placed the steaming cup of tea and the pastry on the desk, not allowing Emma time to rearrange the piles of documents carefully stacked.

"Yes! And I can't even tell you why I did what I did!"

Staring at the stacks of files piled on the desk, she picks up a document. "Doesn't make any more sense to me at this early hour than it did last night." Sipping the hot tea, she attempts to explain what happened last night.

"Whatever are you talking about?" Peter asked while readying the office for the day's work, drawing the drapes open and turning out the lights.

"Yesterday, after office hours, I went to the Royal Court of Justice to research transcripts of cases similar in standing with the Bufford case…you know, the case that's coming up for trial in several weeks? I needed to find similar cases in standing to support my arguments, and preferred to view transcripts in bound volumes rather than recorded tapes—it's easier to read the actual court transcriptions rather than view them on tape monitors." Emma explained while savoring her first cup of morning tea—the best of the work day.

"Old files are now stored in the rear of the basement in the court house." Rubbing off the layer of thick dust on the box next to her desk, she said, "These thick layers of dust give testimony that that area of the stacks rarely sees an inquisitive eye searching for files! Neither is there any decent lighting in that part of the basement, making archive searching so laborious—not to mention reading the material in those conditions is impossible! Something should be said to improve such unpleasant surroundings for solicitors to work in! Why anyone would delegate the rear part of the basement for box storage as adequate should be challenged! Not a place anyone would deliberately choose to remain for any length of time—at least, not if they could help it! Alone down there...I found it dark...eerie and a little unsettling!"

Kicking off her shoes, she chose to sit in front of the fire Peter was lighting.

"Worst of all, I never did find all of the case files I originally searched for...I was distracted by that dusty box wedged into the deepest part of a rear shelf," she said, pointing to the files stacked on her desk. Peter walked over to the desk to examine the multiple stacks of neatly arranged envelopes.

"Once I was able to retrieve the box and opened it, I realized it wasn't anything related to the case...Instead, it's an old box containing envelopes—each envelope is carefully labeled; some are partially open...you can see the sealant had dried out, and this tweaked my curiosity to look inside at the contents! I opened one particularly large envelope and a transcript fell out! If you look closely...you can see the transcript is neatly typed in a foreign language...not English. Now my curiosity was really there! The original transcript language looks like it's in Italian, but there are handwritten English translations...annotations in the margins! Once I started reading the transcript, I randomly translated a few familiar words that made me want to read further...examine it more thoroughly. So, that's when I decided to sign out the entire case file and bring the box back to the office where I could study the contents more closely!"

Emma's voice changed to a meditative tone, "Something about the name of this file nudged my memory...urging me to discover more facts about the case...but I can't seem to remember exactly what it is that nags me!"

As an afterthought, she said, "By the time I reached the office with the box of files, everyone had gone home."

"What is the name of the file?" Peter asked.

Emma walked over to the desk to show Peter how much she had accomplished up to the moment she fell asleep. Picking up the stack numbered "*Uno—Vinticinque,*" she handed the top page to Peter.

"I first sorted the contents according to the numbers on the outside of each envelope and then chose one to start reading, hoping to translate the contents from the envelope marked "*Uno,*" into my own personal notes. The late hour combined with my selective Italian vocabulary made translating slow and difficult; it just set the stage for sleep to set in—which is exactly where you found me this morning." Handing Peter her notepad with the few scribbled transcribed entries, she said, "As you can see, the extent of my Italian vocabulary is limited to conversational expressions. Needless to say, it all went very slowly, and I must concede, for all my efforts and interest, I didn't accomplish very much."

"Tell me the name of the case you found?" Peter queried, looking at her brief transcription notes.

"The contents are all labeled 'The Chatelaine Case'." The box has no distinguishing marks outside or inside, which is very odd!" Inspecting the box again in the full light, she said, "Daylight doesn't reveal that I missed any script on the box to suggest the file's name or contents...or why it was placed to the rear of the shelving... almost as if someone wanted to keep it hidden!" Her last phrase was added as an afterthought. "Peter, do you remember a case called 'Chatelaine,' or was it before your time?"

"No," Peter paused thoughtfully, "'Chatelaine' is not a name or a case I remember. The word, *chatelaine,* it's a French word for 'mistress of the castle'...'keeper of the castle'." How is a French title connected to Italian transcriptions?"

"That's one of the questions I asked myself last night! It's an enigma!" For a few seconds a thoughtful silence hung in the room.

"That name...*Chatelaine...Chatelaine*...somewhere, I have a memory of the name...it may have been a case litigated on the continent several years ago that I vaguely recall. But I can't remember any specifics—if indeed, it is the same case I'm thinking about..." she mused, speaking her thoughts out loud to Peter.

"I really didn't have a legitimate reason for signing out the box of records...except that I have this overwhelming desire to learn more about this case, what it's about, where the trial took place and the outcome." Contemplatively casting her attention to the pile of records, Emma started leafing through the stack to locate an envelope partially opened.

"Peter, does this phrase here refer to a kidnapping?" Handing Peter the transcript, Emma pointed to a list of citations listing names and crimes.

"Yes, that's a possible translation, but let me look it up in the computer's legal thesaurus to get the most accurate translation."

"Now, why would transcripts of a case from a trial apparently tried in the Italian courts be stored in the basement of an English court justice building? AND hidden, I might add! If I hadn't started moving file boxes around in the older stacks, I would never have found it!" Verbalizing a rhetorical conclusion, she said, "The way someone marked these margins with English notations tells me someone was interested enough in the *Chatelaine* trial transcripts to make pertinent references—in English—to certain facts from the transcript! *Then why store—or hide them—away in the basement of the London justice court? Why not just take them...as I did and make a copy?"*

Peter closely checked the outside of the box.

"I doubt you'll find anything...I took the time to examine the box closely before I left the library stacks. There's no catalogue file number on the box or on any of the envelopes, which means the case file is not filed in the court's system...or someone removed that information deliberately after it was catalogued in, and then attempted to conceal it to avoid easy discovery! But why?" Neither had an answer.

"I had to promise the curator I would return the file in one week on penalty of losing my privileges there!"

"If someone wanted to discourage anyone from looking further than the outside of the box, *they* would deliberately remove all catalogue information to dampen anyone's interest. They didn't count on *you!*" Peter remarked while inspecting the pile of records, fingering through the different numbered folders.

"I still have a respectable understanding of Italian. Do you remember me telling you I did a paralegal internship in Naples for a year? Well, I still have a respectable memory of Italian legal phrases…if you wish, I'd like a try at translating the files into a case memorandum for you…it'll make easier reading. Is this matter a priority?" he asked while scooping up the files.

"No, I can't say it is, Peter. Too much else on my plate now! Still…it's just… my inquisitiveness wants to say, 'yes'! Can you do it without delaying your other work?" Casting a grateful smile to him, she said, "Thanks Peter." She watched him slip out of the office carrying the dusty box of files in his arms.

* * *

The history of Peter Hobart has an unusual beginning at E.G. Llewelyn, Ltd.

Peter came to work for Emma nearly four years ago, replacing Mrs. Tibitts, her first office assistant, who started working for her when the first office opened in Soho. With her hiring Mrs. Tibitts, Emma became very dependent on her, and viewed her as a permanent, integral part of the firm! Surprisingly, within several months, their case load doubled. It was a startling realization for Emma when Mrs. Tibitts dropped the word "retirement"! Oh, occasionally, she would slip in a word here and there, and a few remarks about a replacement, usually at the oddest of times, prompting Emma to consider the real possibility that her retirement may be sooner than she realized—or wanted!

Shying away from any open discussions about it, one day, out of the blue, Mrs. Tibitts announced she was "relinquishing her secretarial reins." As many times as Emma subtly tried to discuss the issue of retirement with Mrs. Tibitts, her reaction was to turn and walk out of the office, leaving Emma to think she shunned the thought of ever really leaving the firm! But now! Hearing her speak the words "relinquishing her secretarial reins" gave Emma a sinking feeling that made it hard to cover up her deep sense of loss.

Emma composed herself to confront her, "Mrs. Tibitts, I had no idea"… Abruptly, she stopped speaking in mid-sentence, after hearing Mrs. Tibitts's words, "not to worry," her attention quickly turned to Mrs. Tibitts's explanation. "I have a most suitable and reliable replacement for you!" Emma was aghast with this totally unexpected piece of information. For a few moments, she couldn't speak.

"Mrs. Tibitts, I have complete confidence in you choosing a replacement and without my assistance of course, but I would be only too glad to help in this matter." Emma knew it was futile to query her further…Mrs. Tibitts really ran the firm, and she would know exactly the kind of person needed to replace her. Emma accepted that fact and acknowledged Mrs. Tibitts's ability to select her replacement without Emma's assistance. There was nothing she could do or say…except to just wait and see how it all worked out!

Emma viewed that day as the "changing of the guard at Llewelyn, Ltd." On the day of reckoning, Emma arrived very early that morning to clear her desk of last minute dictation before Mrs. Tibitts's successor arrived. With no idea what to expect, Emma knew for Mrs. Tibitts to give her stamp of approval, her replacement would have *her* same high ethical standards. At nine o'clock sharp, the office door opened to show a young, fine-looking man with curly brown hair, dressed in a conservative gray suit and a dark blue tie. He approached Emma with hand extended in a warm friendly greeting and a broad disarming smile. P. Hobart, Legal Assistant, walked into the office to report for work. Any reservations she had as to his suitability immediately vanished.

"Ms. Llewelyn, I'm Peter Hobart, Mrs. Tibitts's nephew. You were expecting me?"

At that moment, Emma knew Mrs. Tibitts had made the right choice, but with a second revelation, Peter was her nephew! Welcoming him, she thought, "Why did she never confide she had a nephew whom she was priming to take her place, knowing all the while he would make a most suitable replacement when she retired!

"Yes, I'm Emma Llewelyn, and I'm most pleased to have you aboard, Peter Hobart."

Directed by her unknown *real* superior, Mrs. Tibitts carried out her directive to groom Peter to take over her position as Emma's assistant, and the change would occur when Mrs. Tibitts felt the time was right. Retirement was not a topic for any discussion until she—Mrs. Tibitts—decided Peter was completely geared up! With

Peter now at the helm, the office continued to run as smoothly as if Mrs. Tibitts's was still present!

"I like the way Peter keeps one step ahead of me in my cases; keeping me focused on each case at the proper time. Yes! Peter Hobart is exactly the right replacement for E.G. Llewelyn, Ltd!"

\* \* \*

Shrugging off reminisces of Peter's secretarial beginnings, Emma finished the tea and the raisin scone. Time was short this particular morning, and there was no opportunity for Emma to return home for a change of clothes and arrive back in time for her first scheduled morning appointment. Recalling she'd been in these same clothes for nearly two days, she headed to her adjoining private quarters to clean up to appear as if she just freshly arrived at the office.

Long ago, Emma made a promise that when she relocated from Soho to Covent Gardens, the new office would meet two mandatory requisites: First, it would have a large bank of windows overlooking the Thames, and secondly, there would be ample storage area. She managed to have the large office with lots of windows overlooking the Thames and the majestic Parliament buildings in the distance. However, compromise was necessary with the second objective. She had to settle for a small adjacent room for storage. Still, it served the firm well the first year as the box room. In no time, it outgrew its capacity and files were no longer retrievable! Peter had a way of putting a double meaning to the phrase, "Old files have the uncanny ability to multiply when no one is around!" This was Peter's convincing argument to relocate the box room to another part of the office suite.

With the practice growing quickly since the move to the new larger office in the center of London, Emma was putting in longer days that included a daily routine to integrate part of her lunch hour with daily exercise. Over time, her daily run took a familiar route through Covent Garden up to Ludgate Hill, preferring familiar scenery, and then circle back for an hour of rigorous exercise. Running was her stress-reducing activity! After such an activity, she needed facilities at the office to freshen up and change before she could meet her afternoon clients. That's when she made the decision to convert the old box room into private quarters. Since it already had bathing facilities, small but adequate, the rest of the transformation was left to the carpenters and decorators to give it the feel and look of personal quarters. Small as it was, it served as the perfect refuge for Emma for those times when her schedule wouldn't allow a trip home. Today was one of those times.

Checking today's calendar date, Emma saw her entry—this was the day she had scheduled an afternoon meeting with a new client. "This new client is someone unique!" When Emma took that call, she recognized her client's name immediately—someone well-known on the continent, her name frequently seen in newsprint in London's papers, too. Thinking aloud, Emma remarked, "What really intrigues me is why is *she* in London asking for an appointment with *me*! I *do* want to make a good impression...so let's see, what to wear?" Checking her wardrobe, she thought, something conservative—but chic—for today's meeting!

"Yes! The pinstripe gray suit is perfect!" Making a few last minute adjustments in the mirror, she said, "Yes, it's doable!"

Walking out to the front office to check with Peter, the thought came—the Chatelaine Case files should stay out of sight to anyone passing Peter's desk.

"Peter, when you're finished with the Chatelaine transcription, please see that the files are locked in the office safe until I can study their contents more." Picking up her morning mail, she saw her partner, Olivia Grimshaw, Associate Barrister, come through the front office doors with her arms fully loaded.

"Hi, Liv. How's your schedule today? Think we could arrange lunch together?"

"It sounds like a wonderful reprieve to me! Yes, I definitely will arrange my schedule for us to lunch!" she remarked, while trying to hold a scone in her mouth and balance a cup of tea on her briefcase without too much success. Liv seldom missed a lunch—one of her favorite times of the day she'd say. Finally, she mumbled audibly, "I'm late for my nine o'clock, and it's only the first of many clients today! Em, lunch sounds great...I'll buzz you later...or is there something you need to discuss now?"

"No, nothing special...I'll catch you later." Emma was about to confide to Liv the name of her special client expected this afternoon.

Waving back to Liv, Emma returned to her office. *"I really should learn what this new client wants of me first, **before** I speak with anyone about our meeting."*

# CHAPTER TWO

Emma Gray Llewelyn is a strikingly beautiful young woman whose beauty and poise commands attention alone or in a crowd.

Simple, shoulder-length raven-colored hair frames the sculpted oval face that accents her bisque-like complexion. Her most entrancing natural beauty are her intense dark brown eyes, which convey a languid, mesmerizing quality! Her finely boned cheeks, aquiline nose, and sensuous mouth enhance her sensual and playful smile. There's no detection of added blush highlighting her delicate porcelain skin, no lip cream needed to enhance the natural red color of her lips, definite physical traits of the MacKenna women. In the legal arena, her physical presentation is even more impressive. Emma draws her dark hair back in a twist under her barrister's wig and with her regal black robe commands an air of professionalism and dignity in chambers her counterparts find fairly disarming.

An idiosyncratic trait inborn in all of the MacKenna progeny is a strong innate ability to sense the truth or a lie when a question is posed. History records evidence of this extraordinary peculiarity long found in past generations, a few clan folk possessing an outstanding, high degree of proficiency, in this *Cymry* clan. Of old—anyone confronted by a MacKenna called out, *"Lwe dda,"* meaning you needed "good luck" to escape from the truth. Emma's unusual gift gives her an edge over her counterparts in the legal field, both with clients and peers. She uses this superior quality when she directly queries her listeners; the direction of the listener's eyes speaks the answer; a look to the left with no eye contact, a psychological clue they are lying! If their eyes deviate to the right, more likely they are telling a truth. Likewise, she watches how the iris muscle contracts when deceit is spoken—and the subtle change in manner. Emma inherently relies on this attribute to discover the truth. And it has never failed her! Her distinguished Welsh brogue validates her *Cymry* ancestry, and her peers are captivated by her distinctive features in her eloquent soliloquies in court chambers!

* * *

Emma was born in Wales where she spent most of her early years with her grandfather, Cyrus MacKenna of Llandrindod Wells, in County Powys, Wales.

A time past recalls when Cyrus and Caitlyn moved into Lyn Brienne as a young couple, a youthful girl named Margaret Mack joined them, first to help part-time—in time, over years, she became the devoted housekeeper, known as "Maggie." Her devotion to this couple earned her a permanent place in the family. Caitlyn came to rely on Maggie for her excellent direction and worldly wisdom in helping to make the kind of home she and Cyrus planned, overseeing their life at Lyn Brienne in the valley called *Ty*. Years later when Michael Llewelyn made his painful decision to let his only child, Emma, remain at Lyn Brienne with Cyrus and Maggie—Caitlyn dead long ago—it was Maggie who assumed the motherly role—her Magere—and Cyrus became Emma's Papa.

Cyrus MacKenna spent those first married years acquiring pure racing bloodlines for his stables; breeding them selectively to produce some of the British Isles' most famous racing lineages. Competition was especially keen among international racing circles to own a foal or stallion from his stable of superior lineage. He had the final decision who this year's buyers would be to acquire one of his limited number of foals—giving just a few breeders cause to boast in racing circles about their acquisition from Lyn Brienne! The fierce competitor and shrewd businessman he became fostered his reputation as he traveled throughout Britain and the Continent. Today, the breed from the Clan of MacKenna still holds that distinction.

The name, Cyrus MacKenna, draws spoken accolades from other outside arenas—international, political, and legal communities.

Today, this Welsh icon is viewed as that elderly tall, handsome, indomitable man with intense deeply-set brown eyes—a spellbinding quality, a quick wit, a disarming smile indicative of a warm embracing personality that hides an intuitive, challenging intellect—all traits making him a formidable competitor–be it in a small or large assembly. His silver-gray hair and full beard propose the confident figure of an experienced statesman. The clear, deep resonant voice, with a thick Welsh brogue, captivates a room's assemblage, forcing them to listen intently as the crescendo verbage proves his point. But the most awesome quality of Cyrus MacKenna is the fearsome trait his adversaries are quick to discover. When put to a question, he has the uncanny awareness to distinguish the truth or falsehood answered by his challenger. Relentless to discover the truth from his opponents, they sense this unfettered sagacity and feel compelled to answer truthfully—to avoid a position of embarrassment. Unless, of course, they are willing to accept the consequences of deceit. This quality has always been one of his strongest wiles.

* * *

It was in Emma's fourteenth year at Lyn Brienne that Cyrus and Michael Llewelyn agreed Emma's life would change. She would travel to the United States to live in New England with her widowed father. Years before, Michael Llewelyn had chosen to return to Connecticut after the death of Emma's mother, Katherine MacKenna Llewelyn. The loss of his beloved Katherine had been too painful for Michael to remain in Wales after her untimely death during childbirth. The time and memories of their life together at Kittery Cottage were too painful to put behind him—if he chose to stay. Michael's family lived in the States, and it was this family tie that weighted his decision to start another life in Greenwich, Connecticut. He rationalized that, "Greenwich is a good place to live and work…to start again…Someday, Emma will come to live with me to discover the other half of her ancestral heritage."

So, Emma's teenage years were spent in Greenwich, Connecticut with Michael Llewelyn and her extended family, giving her the opportunity to understand just how deeply her father really loved her when he made that fateful decision in her first year to leave her, knowing she'd have a better start in a family with Cyrus and Maggie. Those teen years spent with Michael did evolve into a strong father-daughter bond that allowed their relationship to flourish, grow, and shape a meaningful part of her future.

In Greenwich, the Llewelyn family life was so very different to that which Emma had known at Lyn Brienne. Here, she was part of a much larger family, which gave her the opportunity to Americanize her knowledge and customs. It was during those years spent in Greenwich near the sea that Emma began to appreciate her father's love of the sea. Michael taught Emma how to sail his two-masted schooner *The Welsh Maiden.* As often as his work allowed, they'd go off together to sail the *Maiden,* and in no time, Emma became a seasoned sailor and scuba diver to match her father's skills. Those years in Greenwich were busy, happy, and full, not allowing her much time for feelings of loneliness—for what she left at Lyn Brienne—Papa, Magere, and Ddu Kate.

Still, the summers were meant for Lyn Brienne. Anticipation would begin to build weeks before that last day of school, knowing she would return to Wales, to Papa, to Magere, and to her beloved mare, Ddu Kate. It was to be those early years spent at Lyn Brienne that would indelibly figure and shape major decisions in Emma's future life, events she could never fully imagine. Deeply proud of her Welsh heritage, it was never more evident than when she spoke of her Papa! The MacKenna heritage would have the greatest power over her destiny!

Emma's talent for horsemanship was definably her real passion, inherited from her mother, Katherine—ultimately a gift from her grandmother, Caitlyn. Llandrindod Well's past is filled with tales about Caitlyn, the black-haired Irish maiden, a Welsh horsewoman for men and woman to set their standards against—the beautiful black-haired equestrian lass.

The summers in Wales brought opportunities for Emma to revive her equestrian skills, and in her own right, she gained national fame just like her predecessors—matriarchs of the MacKenna Clan. Emma and Maggie would single out the different fairs she would enroll in, given what time would allow—she easily earned most of the winnings. Maggie made it her personal task to collect all the news printings from the summer derbies, carefully placing each account in her "Magere" Book. Every time she recorded an event in her tome, she would brag to Emma, "Some day lass, this book 'ill be for yur children, Luv, for them's to see ther' famous mother's winnin's!"

Emma savored those summer days she spent with Ddu Kate— her spirit mate. Here was an extraordinarily magical union between rider and horse. A unique relationship few would ever experience or understand. Seated atop her black mare at full gallop, she rode through green hilly pasture fields fearlessly, effortlessly jumping stone walls, creating a sight for travelers on country roads that compelled them to pause to view the distant rider with reins firmly gripped. The mare's mane fluidly intertwined with Emma's own ebony hair, making it hard to distinguish where one ended and the other began—a wild panoramic scene! At summer's end, a silent sadness would permeate the farm and cottage, knowing the Welsh lass would soon be gone from Lyn Brienne for another school year back in Greenwich.

Autumn brought an unspoken emptiness to Lyn Brienne for Cyrus, Maggie, and Andrew Masters, the farm manager for many years and Cyrus's most trusted confidant. Even Ddu Kate sensed Emma's absence. Though Emma loved her father, not without several of his own international racing champions, most dearly, that strong, deep MacKenna connection with Papa and Ddu Kate was never duplicated nor replaced. Secretly, Emma felt Lyn Brienne was *the* only one *real home* in her life.

In the cold of winter days, Cyrus was often seen riding Ddu Kate on his early morning rides instead of his champion golden stallion, *Aur Cymru*, "Welsh Gold"—as if riding Ddu Kate brought her closer to him. Even the mare sensed Cyrus was the rider, not Emma, and held back the urge to race with the wind as she did with her.

From a young age, quite a different trait emerged in Emma's character. She exhibited an unusual curiosity and interest in the law. A very noticeable and insatiable curiosity developed in her very early years, something Cyrus approved of and purposely fostered. Cyrus's

17

greatest enjoyment was challenging Emma to speak her opinions and matching his skills with her reasoning, all the while teaching her to strive for the highest intellectual accomplishments. In those early years, with Emma sitting in his lap, Cyrus chose a topic to provoke a thoughtful discussion with her to impress on her the importance of "how to listen intently"—"learn the facts"—then argue and speak her mind to query an opponent. Many a night, before the hearth in the Great Room, the two sparred with words; each presenting forceful, common-sense but different points of view—Cyrus schooling Emma in using a logical, rational, intellectual process to find the truth—and Emma confidently challenging Cyrus to defend his position against her issues. Those special evenings spent before the Great Hearth was the best part of the day.

"Facts are to be queried and challenged; never assume their truthfulness!" was his frequent admonition to her.

As a young girl, Emma noticed that the farm business kept Papa away—and often Andrew, from Lyn Brienne for seemingly long periods of time, sometimes lasting over a month or two. Instinctively, she never fully accepted Papa's reasons for his lengthy absences. It never occurred to her there could be any other reason, other than horse breeding business, for him to be away from the farm...not until she returned from Connecticut to live in Wales.

Emma's total fascination was with international law, and Cyrus watched her develop a deep understanding about human rights and societies' laws. He made it his mission to return from his long trips always with a surprise for her and started her on a book collection with gifts of books from the different countries to which he traveled. During Cyrus's long absences, Emma looked to Andrew Masters as his substitute. Andrew had been at Lyn Brienne when Emma was born and often assumed the role of her instructor in equestrian skills when Cyrus was absent. He was considered an integral part of the family, seeing her grow from that little child into a strong-willed girl, to emerge into a successful woman with a reputation in London as a distinguished barrister in international law. Their relationship was more like big brother and little sister—a bond never mentioned—but it was always there. One day, she would come to know just how important Andrew Masters was in her life.

Emma's last year at Westerly Academy in Connecticut presented no difficulty in deciding her career choice. It was always the law. Drawn to attend undergraduate school at Yale University, when it came time to choose a school of law, Yale Law was her only choice, and without disappointment, she was accepted at the prestigious American school of law. In her third year of studies, Emma made the decision she would return to England to pursue her career in London—establish her own law firm.

Once she learned that she had successfully passed the American bar exam, she had to tell her father the rest of the news. Later that special evening during the celebration, Michael commented to her, "Emma, we're all so proud of you! Our first lawyer in the Llewelyn family!" It was an occasion for celebration and the whole Llewelyn clan gathered to commemorate—boasting her accolades!

Knowing no easy way to say the words, she blurted them out loud in the midst of the frivolity, "Father...I've decided to return to England to meet the requirements for my barristers' degree!"

The room went silent. "I want...to start my own law practice in London to establish my name in the English courts of justice as a barrister of international law." Emma cast her eyes downward, waiting for someone to break the silence. Michael heard the determination in her words, and while this news came as no real surprise to him, he was deeply disappointed. He always knew someday her strong Welsh origin would call her back...now that occasion was here... her dream...to return to her birthplace.

"Emma, I've always wanted what you wanted in your life... whatever makes you happy makes me happy. I know one day you'll reach your dream...remain focused like your mother was...she is very proud of you at this moment...as I am!" Taking her tenderly in his arms, they embraced each other for that brief encounter meant only for a father and daughter. The silence in the room embodied the emotions felt.

Applying immediately to Cambridge University, she was accepted and began her English studies that very fall. It wasn't long before she completed the requirements and petitioned the English bar. The barrister's examinations came and went, and Emma waited patiently at Lyn Brienne to hear the outcome; the English counterpart of the American Bar accreditor's moved much slower.

This particular morning Emma was out riding Ddu Kate, allowing the mare to take the reins, feeling the mare take the lead. This day the mare took the rider to the farthest meadow, to Kittery Cottage. This was happening more frequently each time Emma gave the mare her head. There, poised on the crest of the Bern, the two stood viewing the deserted cottage down below... She could only imagine how it once held happy memories for her mother and father...*but it was never her home!!* Each time Emma viewed the cottage, she'd experience troubling emotions and confusion about her lost life at Kittery Cottage. The darkened house and wild shrubs and trees grown too tall gave the dwelling a desolate, melancholic appearance. It seared a poignant image into her memory. Emma found herself softly saying, *"Someday, Mother, I would like to unlock that cottage door, but I'm not ready to do it yet—not today."* With a quick tug of the reins, she turned the mare and raced to Lyn Brienne. Just as they reached the paddock, Maggie came running out of the cottage waving her hand. "It's 'ere! It's 'ere, Emma!"

That night Cyrus called the farm, as was his usual task, to hear an excited Emma give him the good news. Even before she spoke, he knew what her excitement was about.

"Papa, I passed! I passed the barrister exams! I'm a Queen's Counsel!"

"I never expected anything less of you, Lass! We'll celebrate your success in high fashion when I return. I've been away much too long...I expect to arrive within the next day. Tell Maggs to prepare her best dishes for a feast! We must celebrate a MacKenna's new success—for Barrister Llewelyn, Queen's Counsel!"

Cyrus was enormously proud of Emma's achievements, but secretly he knew the hard road ahead for her was just beginning. The longer he waited to tell her *his* truth about everything...the harder it became for him...as it would be for her, too, to understand and accept it. He must tell her everything, his secret truth, very soon— the longer he put it off the greater the chance she would find out from another source!

**"No! She must learn the truth from ME...no one else!** *Will there ever be a right time to tell her what my life has really been all about?"*

# CHAPTER THREE

Emma's first legal position was as a junior solicitor in a large successful firm in London, at "Kavanaugh & Associates, Ltd".

To anyone who asked about her position and duties at the firm, she described it as an assistant to an assistant to an assistant. Many of the firm's young solicitors found Emma's passion for work unnerving. To her, no job was too menial or too small to go after; rather, her work ethic sought out opportunities to gain experience and exposure in the legal community. Her pace of work didn't allow her many opportunities to return to the farm, but whenever it did, she'd first make certain Cyrus was there.

On those infrequent occasions home, Maggie loved to fuss, putting extra effort to make Emma's visits special—always a time of real family celebration—Papa, Magere, and Andrew! As expected, the evening meal ended in the Great Room, predictably the conversations turned to the past. Nothing was more important to Cyrus than spending time with Emma, finding her energy invigorating and her enthusiasm reassuring and rewarding. Often, when Emma would recount an experience she encountered, Cyrus found his thoughts wondering. It was at these times a haunting fear would overshadow his thoughts and feelings about his hidden life and the dangers it posed to him—and to his family. *"How long can I keep the secret from her?"*

Reflecting back to how "it" all came about, he'd capture a happy picture of his only love, Caitlyn O'Hara—then, as quickly as it came, the memory of her face would fade—and great sadness overtook him. In its place, he saw himself back to that time, brooding her loss, becoming isolated, self-contained, and useless as a man. He needed to reach out to commiserate with others; he needed to do something to help others—to help himself—there had to be something meaningful to fill the deep void of her absence—something more in his life than just a tiny babe to care for. Thus, began his clandestine life! Now, after years of mystery, it was becoming more and more difficult to conceal the truth from the most precious thing in his life! And yet, he had no idea how he would tell her what his life was really all about outside Lyn Brienne! Would she understand and accept his reasons for not sharing this other life with her all these years? He made the solemn promise, *"Someday, very soon, I must reveal the complete truth to her, but will she understand? I cannot take that chance yet—not today!"* The sound of Emma's spirited voice in the background drew his thoughts back to the present—with relief.

Her question caught him unaware. "Papa, why does your business take you away for such long periods of time? Surely, it's not *just* the business of purchasing new stock for the farm? If it is farm business, why can't Andrew make some of these trips for you? He knows as much as you do about the farm business, and he could consult with you before making any decisions! Then you'd have more time to spend at *Lyn Brienne* with Magere and me."

Cyrus deliberately focused his complete attention on Emma to frustrate her skill to detect his untruth. Knowing her keen perception to interpret the truth in his answer, he needed to deceive her.

"You have a valid point, Emma! Andrew does know the business of the farm—and very well, I might add. There's nothing that I don't feel he could do as well as me…maybe even better. That idea has crossed my mind in the past—and who knows—that day may not be far in the future." He fully realized she doubted his explanations and was searching for other answers. Indeed, Emma was trying to distinguish whether he was using *his* skills to deliberately mislead and confuse her to misinterpret his answer.

"Papa is telling me the truth—but not all of it," Emma thought. She didn't like doing this to him, intentionally posing questions to test for truthfulness, but there were times she knew Papa deliberately avoided telling her certain *whole* truths. She needed to know WHY? *Two strong MacKennas—rivaling against each other's inbred gift one to hide the truth—the other to learn the truth!*

\* \* \*

That night she returned to London from the farm, Emma went directly to the law office to finish a difficult and complex brief her counselor needed in the morning. Big Ben was chiming the midnight hour, when the most senior barrister, Jonathan Kavanaugh, QC., walked into her small corner office with a brief in hand.

"Are you Ms. Llewelyn?" He asked in his most authoritative voice. Emma rose from her chair as he stood next to her desk.

"Yes, I'm Emma Llewelyn."

"Is this your work?" he said, handing her the brief to examine.

"Yes, this is my brief," she answered, feeling anxious, her hands sweating.

In a low soft voice, he said, "It's a remarkable piece of work for so young a barrister," and seated himself in the client's chair next to her desk as if speaking to a peer.

"Tell me how long have you been with us?" he asked with directness.

"Sir, I've been here almost two years. I did my graduate law at Yale in the States, and then returned to Cambridge to complete the requirements for the barrister's exam. Since then, I've been employed at this firm." Quickly, she added, "I like the work very much here!"

"Yes, I can tell…your thoroughness shows in your work. I've had my eye on you for some time, and I'd like you to come to work under my sponsorship as one of *my* junior counselors. Do you have any objections to that?" He slowly rose out of the chair.

The proposal was a complete surprise, and she faltered for words. "No sir…rather, yes sir…I'm honored with your proposal! It would be a privilege to work under your tutelage…but I need time to finish my work here…I could be available in a few days…if that's acceptable with you?"

"Fine, I'll have Mrs. Schuster ready the cases I want you to handle." He turned and walked out the door. Emma watched his stately, portly figure stride down the hall to the lifts, still feeling overwhelmed by what had just happened to her. Slowly sitting down, Emma heard herself saying in a disbelieving manner, "Jonathan Kavanaugh made a personal effort to follow *my* work!" Out came a jubilant, "Yes!"

Jonathan Kavanaugh continued to observe and assess Emma's performance, taking a singular interest to criticize her—always with the purpose of challenging her potential abilities to new levels in her work. Clearly, he saw in her, a woman barrister with the greatest potential from the pool of junior counselors under his sponsorship. Eventually, Jonathan assigned Emma to work with him on his important, high-profile cases. He enjoyed coaching her to new levels of confidence, amazed at the depth and quality of her effort, never fleeing from any critique or challenge. Out of this professional relationship, grew a deep respect for each other—first, employer and staffer and then, into mentor and friend.

On a routine workday, Emma finished her assignment in the library stacks and returned to her cubby to find a memorandum on her desk with a red flag indicating important mail. Upon opening it, she immediately read, "new assignment." Reading the counselors' names, there was one she never expected. Her counterparts of young barristers vied with one another for this very assignment; she gave it no thought because she knew it would never happen for her. In spite of the improbability, it did happen! Q.C. Kavanaugh assigned this case to *Emma Llewelyn, Esq., First Counsel*! Thinking that she read a typographical mistake, she immediately consulted with Jonathan's secretary.

"Mrs. Schuster, this document…this motion on my desk, it lists me as first counsel. This must be an error."

"No, Emma. It's no mistake! Mr. Kavanaugh chose you! You had best get your gown 'n bib and right-new hairpiece ready for the high court." Mrs. Schuster smiled, seeing the disbelief on Emma's face.

"Congratulations, Emma, you deserve it!"

Now that day was here! A day she worked so hard towards—to be first counsel. She had been to court chambers many times as counsel's clerk, and then junior counsel, but today was entirely different! Donning her black robe and wig, fashioned with rows of gray curls signifying Senior Counselor for the defendant, she consciously walked with confidence and pride into the chambers of the high court to the *first chair* for defense counselors. Chief Justice called the court to order, commanding Defense Counsel to begin deliberations. Without hesitation, Emma rose up from her chair and stood quietly, taking the advantage to wait for the gallery din to fade to silence. Carefully commanding the court's attention with a few pregnant moments of silence, all eyes gave way to a hushed respect, and with the fluid ease of an experienced and seasoned professional barrister, she began her opening presentation to the court. That case was Emma's defining moment in time. From that day on, her reputation as a formidable opponent to beat was cast. For Emma, it was a doubly great feeling when the jury verdict came back, "Not Guilty!" She had won!

Unable to contain her emotions for winning her first major legal victory, she hurried back to the firm and raced up the stairs too eager to wait for the lift, to tell Jonathan of her first big success in high court! Without knocking, she dashed into Jonathan's office. "Jonathan...Jona...". Total surprise reflected on her face. From the sea of faces came a sudden clamor of applause as she felt the flush rise on her cheeks and broke into a big radiant smile. Jonathan was standing in front of the group with a raised glass of champagne.

"To our newest successful barrister, Emma Llewelyn, Q.C., I'm proud to have her with Kavanaugh, Limited."

"Here—here," the accolades resounded throughout the room. From that day forward, Emma kept her sights on her real goal. It was not many more months later that Emma informed Jonathan Kavanaugh she was leaving Kavanaugh, Ltd. to start "E.G. Llewelyn Ltd".

\* \* \*

Moving day had arrived! Packing her legal books into boxes, bidding friends and colleagues brief farewells at Kavanaugh, Ltd., she drove to her office in the Soho district of London. Carrying her new barrister shingle which Andrew made for her, she unlocked the door and paused. Despite its smallness, it was *her* firm! Looking out of one of the two windows in the single room, the scene in the near distance were the Courts of Justice near Piccadilly Circus. *SOMEDAY...Covent Gardens and Piccadilly! For now—Soho!*

Soho is a unique section of London, with its boundaries a stone's throw from Piccadilly Circus. Evidence of its old reputation for seedy establishments, once reminiscent of a raunchy and lively lifestyle, was now gone. Instead, everywhere were signs of renovation with new up-scale facades for its newest tenants—sleek new chic style shops, fashionable restaurants, and international pubs. Soho was experiencing an awakening for young professionals launching new enterprises. Today, Emma could only afford the rent for this one-room office, but she rationalized that the site and accessibility would be easy for her clients. This was her first giant step on the ladder toward her ultimate dream—*She willed that one day her law practice would be located in a large office with lots of windows looking out to the center of London with its majestic panoramic view of Parliament and the Tower Bridge.*

It was the excitement of the present moment that overtook Emma's revelries. "For now...my first chore is to hang my new brass sign!" Finding hammer and hook, she hung her barrister shingle on the door directly under the light—easy for all to see. "Andrew, it is so lovely and thoughtful!" Thinking about her father, Michael, she knew he would be so proud of her. But it was not Michael who captivated all of Emma's thoughts, rather it was Cyrus who had the bigger role in Emma's life, and now it was Papa who captured most of her feelings on this day.

*No. This is just a milestone in my dream!* Today, nothing could take away her joyous celebration!

*On that day, Emma had no insight just how much this single decision would influence her future choices, inexplicably bringing risks and danger to her and to those she loved!*

# CHAPTER FOUR

Her reputation traveled quickly in the next two months in Soho…
and even farther—this meant her caseload increased sufficiently to
give her financial stability to advertise for a legal secretary.

She set about placing her notice in the *Evening Post* and *London
Herald* papers to run for a week. The advert had barely been posted,
when a pleasant, elderly professional-looking woman entered the
office with the new advert section in hand. It had to be more than plain
luck that a candidate responded immediately to her newly placed
query! She was thinking, this candidate is probably only inquiring
about my secretarial position and won't be seriously interested when
she learns the job particulars and the wages.

"Good afternoon, I'm here to see about the secretarial position
to Barrister E.G. Llewelyn."

"I'm Emma G. Llewelyn. The G stands for Gray."

"So pleased to meet you, Ms. Llewelyn. My name is Mrs.
Margaret Tibitts, but I prefer to be called Mrs. Tibitts."

Motioning her to a seat, Emma remarked, "Mrs. Tibitts, I'm
looking for a legal secretarial assistant to work for me," indicating
the stacks of filing materials on her desk. "Presently, I'm the only
attorney—and employee, in my firm, and I've been performing all
aspects of law and office work, as you can see. My law specialty is
international criminal law. But of late, I've been involved more in
civil cases…until I am more established. Have you ever worked for
a new solicitor just starting up a new office?" Emma asked.

"Most assuredly," she said and handed Emma her Curriculum Vitae, which she read with incredulity.

"This is most impressive, Mrs. Tibitts! I can see you indeed have extensive legal experience with a long background in law, both public and private employment. Surely, someone with your expertise and background in the legal field must realize I don't have the financial resources to compete with the income from these more established employers? The payment here would be considerably less than what I imagine you're used to receiving."

"Yes, I understand your situation, but you see I am somewhat financially stable, and enjoy my work; therefore, I can be selective with the kind of employment and employer I prefer," she said with deliberate clarification.

Emma wanted her with such eagerness. "Then I would be most pleased to have you join my firm, Mrs. Tibitts. The starting earnings are fifty pounds a week, but when my case numbers increase, I will be happy to renegotiate a wage increase with you."

"A most satisfying contract, Ms. Llewelyn. I can start tomorrow, if that is agreeable with you? What are the exact working hours?"

"I would expect you in the office from nine to five o'clock, but I often come into the office much earlier and leave much later."

"Then I shall see you tomorrow at nine o'clock." Mrs. Tibitts turned and walked quietly out the door. It was all very matter-of-fact and the whole process only took minutes. Emma just sat for several minutes to digest what had just transpired when a certain relief overcame her.

"I think I just hired the most experienced woman in the whole legal profession!" She realized she had a secretary! Not just any secretary, but a well-experienced professional one. "Eureka! I have an assistant!"

"Now, how do you think that came about?" she queried herself. Emma knew a person with such qualifications would be a tremendous addition to her firm but wondered why such a highly qualified person with an exceptional C.V. applied for a secretarial position with a new barrister, especially a new barrister just starting a law practice. It didn't make sense... "It was all so easy...clearly, it was not the income that attracted Mrs. Tibitts to my position." This only further evoked Emma's curiosity about Mrs. Tibitts's reasons for joining E.G. Llewelyn Law Firm. She couldn't put aside the idea. "Cyrus could have had something to do with Mrs. Tibitts's application for this secretarial job." Recalling that she arrived with the edition of the advertisement in hand and that the advert had been posted only for a few hours made it hard to believe Mrs. Tibitts was searching for such a notice and came right over for the interview. Emma recalled her words to her during the meeting, "A friend of mine told me about this position opening up, I checked the adverts and I came directly over".

During the interview, Emma felt compelled to ask Mrs. Tibitts if she knew a Cyrus MacKenna, but thought better of the idea and decided to wait until they had established a good working relationship. The question persistently nagged at her. "Why would such a highly qualified person apply for *this* job?" Over time, a few opportunities did arise to approach the question to both Mrs. Tibitts and Cyrus, but each time Emma suppressed the urge. "It's best not to chase after answers that I know will never come," and the subject was put to rest—but not forgotten.

The small workplace was physically divided into the "Reception-front office" area and the barrister's rear office area. Mrs. Tibitts took the front corner nearest the door and converted her secretarial furnishings into a very professional arrangement, signifying to new clients entering, they first had to greet the firm's legal assistant if they wished to speak with the barrister. Mrs. Tibitts had a keen eye and instinct about clients and knew how to speedily get to the nub of the issue that brought them to a law firm. Her practice was to screen all clients before they met with Emma. To accomplish this, she would first interview the client and instruct them to take a seat next to her desk and wait. This gave Emma time to appraise the client's demeanor. As the scenario played out, Mrs. Tibitts then consulted Emma, "Ms. Llewelyn, you have a client wishing to speak with you," all within ear's hearing for the client.

"Yes, thank you, Mrs. Tibitts, please bring them over." In a most commanding confident manner, she escorted them to the attorney's desk with her usual professional introduction. It was clear to the client who was in charge. Emma made it a rule never to turn any clients away until she first learned their reason for seeking legal counsel.

The small firm had all the professionalism and character of a Covent Gardens up-scale firm—but without the physical parody! With purpose, Mrs. Tibitts kept a keen eye on Emma and her clients, making periodic comprehensive reports to her real private employer—*as this was her **prime directive** for assuming the position.*

# CYMRY-LEGACY

# CHAPTER FIVE

## *TIMES PAST...*

Llandrindod Wells is one of the many historical small towns located in central Wales in the county of Powys.

History's earlier periods dates back centuries, to the Victorian and Edwardian influences, to where the name "Clan of MacKenna" was first known. As history records, there were many clan wars in the *Combe Tywi* fighting for the right to win claim and possession of the *Caer* of Llandrindod Wells—the castle of Llandrindod Wells. As seen today, the same emblazoned tartan flag of black, red, and green of the Clan MacKenna has flown in the *caer* tower in Llandrindod Wells for nearly two hundred years. Past those early centuries into a more contemporary life today, the town's folk saw an advantage to promote the county's fresh water springs, The Chalybeate Springs. These natural springs widely known for their healing properties, trace back to the seventh century—and possibly even earlier— when inhabitants made claims that the Springs cured any sickness. Eventual arrival of a new method of transportation, the railroad, Llandrindod Wells grew quickly and prospered into a small inland resort around the Chalybeate Springs. In its present day, the town is best known for The Llandrindod Wells Victorian Festival that's held annually each August—most importantly for its prestigious horse race, the Wells Prefecta.

* * *

The ancestry of Wales's MacKenna Tribe spans many centuries and gives validation to its deep roots and beginnings up to the present generations still living in the *Combe Tywi*. A historically powerful, renowned clansman was Angus MacKenna. During his reign as *Pen,* head of this tribe, he was recognized to be a very shrewd chief, but more importantly, a man who bore many sons during his period of power, that propagated the traits and qualities of the MacKenna Clan far and wide. A prophecy often heard was, "Many sons strengthen the power of the Pen!"

Cyrus Colin MacKenna was the second born to Angus and Moira MacKenna at Brent-Bern, the farm in the smiling valley of *Tywi*. Cyrus grew into a striking, strong, and forceful lad who developed a great inquisitiveness about life outside the *Combe Tywi*, something his brothers did not always appreciate. As were the ways of Welsh men, the time came for Cyrus to marry and receive claim to his portion of his father's land—a parcel selected by Angus for each son, bestowed to the couple in the marrying ceremony. The farthest and greenest acreage of Brent-Bern went to Cyrus and his bride, Caitlyn O'Hara, on his marrying day.

The history of this couple's beginnings goes back to earlier years when Cyrus first laid eyes on an Irish beauty named Caitlyn O'Hara. The O'Haras moved to Llandrindod Wells from Cork when Ian O'Hara found work in the nearby marble quarries. Caitlyn was the oldest girl in a family of three sons and three daughters; as always, the first daughter had the hardest position to win a hand in marriage, that must first be approved by the family patriarch.

This one cold, wintry day a robust young Cyrus was working with his brother, Colm MacKenna on the stone wall in Karney's pasture—so named for his brother's land—which needed completion before the worst of winter set upon them. Cold winds were blowing hard from the North Sea trying to spit out contradictory signs of an approaching weather front. The cold winds didn't keep the sweat from Cyrus's brow on this cold day. Pausing from the heavy masonry work to wipe the moisture from his brow, he caught his first glimpse of a fair, dark-haired lass off in the distance wearing a hooded cloak no longer covering her long black tresses. Caitlyn

O'Hara was riding home from the nearby marble quarry mine after taking her father his hot lunch—her daily chore. Only this day, she chose to take a different path. In the past, he had seen a similar rider a far distance without raising his interest. On this day, he was drawn to the sight of a beautiful young lass riding bareback on a *pure white* steed. Intently, Cyrus watched her steed reach the crest of the far Bern, fiercely racing the wind without fear of tripping or falling, demonstrating the lass's complete command of horse. Captivated by the scene, he stood motionless following her movements as she descended down the Bern, through the pasture and drew closer to him. Cantering the graceful white stallion until she was but a few meters away, she had his complete attention.

"Such a magnificent black-Irish beauty!" he thought. Mesmerized by her presence so close, he held his thoughts in silence. With only an exchange of glances, she signaled the horse to go forward. Cyrus deliberately took a step into their path forcing the rider to rein the stallion to a complete halt. A long silent gaze passed between them. Suddenly, pulling on the reins, she quickly pushed the mount forward, brushing past Cyrus, signaling her steed to go up to the top crest of the next Bern. Atop the crags, she stopped, turned, and looked down to the valley pasture. With the light behind her, silhouetting her fragile frame against the summit of the Bern, Cyrus strained to see her face. He managed to detect a smile on her delicate features, and he returned the same, thinking, "Who is this black beauty of a lass?"

"I see you've finally 'ad your 'ead turned by a lass, Cyrus!" his brother Colm mockingly said to him.

"Aye! That's the young woman I'll one day marr'," he told Colm.

"Ah, don't be daft, brother! She'll not give ye a second look! A beaut' like that 'as better suitors seekin' 'er 'and than ye!" Colm retorted in admonition to his younger brother's prediction, drawing his attention back to the task of building the stone wall. Cyrus promised he'd prove his brother wrong. Within a year's time, Cyrus MacKenna and Caitlyn O'Hara were married.

In keeping with the Welsh tradition, Angus MacKenna bestowed a parcel of land to his second son on his wedding day. It was a prime section of the hills outside Llandrindod Wells near the river Ithon in the deep winding *combe*—the valley. Angus took the new couple aside to speak.

"Tis the time for ye to make ye mark on the land, Cyrus, the land 'as be'en waitin' for ye to give it life, so 'ere's the deed."

Plans were drawn to build their cottage, which was more like a baronial great-stone house with turrets and towers atop the several floors. It was to be the great house for the many *mabs* and *merches* to be born there. In time, the stable for the horses would come to be erected. Before the change of seasons that first year, Cyrus and Caitlyn moved into their great stone cottage, eager to start their dream of having their own horse farm in the *Glyn of Tywi*. They named their home Lyn Brienne. The first year saw unusually cold, mean weather taking great tolls on the crops planted. The setback only delayed their decision to purchase the first mare after the next year's harvest. It only made for determination that one day they *would* have a large family of children and a stable of thoroughbred stallions and mares in keeping with Welsh traditions.

Good fortune changed the next year, and the whole valley reaped a generous harvest. With the gathering of families from the *Tywi Valley* to celebrate the abundant harvest, Caitlyn told Cyrus her exciting news. She was pregnant with their first child. "Our *newydd mab* will be born with the next lambing." Cyrus knew this was the beginning of his and Caitlyn's dream to have the large family of children to "noisy up the cottage." All the while, Cyrus secretly saved his earnings that year to purchase his first prized mare, Siobhan Tudor. The mare was his gift to Caitlyn, hoping one day Siobhan's foal would be the pony for his first-born child, *a mab!*

The time for the new spring lambing was fast approaching. The day Caitlyn told Cyrus she felt signs of labor, he rode the distance to town to get the doctor and midwife for the birth at Lyn Brienne. Cyrus cautioned Dr. MacOwen, "We'd best be hurryin' back! The *glyn* is settin' up for a fierce storm with those black clouds comin' near'r!"

Hurrying the horses as fast as he dared, it didn't keep the fearsome thunderstorm from reaching them. Winds toppled trees and scattered debris while thick white sheets of rain made it barely possible to see the road ahead. Cyrus was forced to make frequent stops along the way to clear the road delaying the trip back. When Dr. MacOwen was able to examine Caitlyn, he found her in advanced labor.

"It's been 'ard for 'er...it'll be an' time now," he told Cyrus.

During the long labor without medical attendance, Caitlyn had lost a significant amount of blood, gravely weakening her condition. Dr. MacOwen wrapped a small lively baby girl and placed her in Caitlyn's arms.

Pale and weak but with so much pride, she turned to Cyrus in exhaustion and whispered, "Cyrus, I've thought long 'bout a title if it be a *merch*, and I'd like to name 'er "Katherine".

Cyrus always thought he would have his son, a *mab*, first, and never considered a name for a daughter—his *merch*. He hesitantly took the tiny bundle, cradled her in his arms and softly began to sing his own mother's lullaby to his new daughter, "Katherine MacKenna."

Over the ensuing weeks, Caitlyn's weakened condition continued to decline, growing weaker every day despite Maggie's attentive care and concern. Cyrus could see the unhealthy paleness in her worsen, until one day, he was not able to awaken her to feed Katherine. Everything changed for Cyrus. All he ever cherished in his life was gone, their dreams and plans for a life together. Left in its place was this tiny bundle of life—a *fach merch*. Nothing could diminish his overwhelming feelings of emptiness, despair and pain after Caitlyn died. Neither the business of the farm nor the care of Katherine relieved his loneliness on those long days and even longer cold, empty nights. Maggie Mack tried hard to interest Cyrus in Katherine's life but without much success. Several months passed since he laid Caitlyn in the ground, and still he had no release from his pain...until unexpectedly, an old friend, Sir Colin MacEachen called upon Cyrus at Lyn Brienne.

"I've come to express me grief to an ol' friend." True, he wanted to comfort his friend, but there was another hidden agenda he had in mind to speak about. Colin MacEachen made his proposal to Cyrus that day.

Colin MacEachen was a titled Scotsman of the Crown known to have ties to certain British governmental agencies. For some time, he kept Cyrus MacKenna's name on a slip of paper on his desk with a question mark next to it. This very morning, he was seated at his desk when he picked up the well-worn slip of paper and deliberately read the name out loud.

"Now," he thought, "'is the best time to visit an ol' friend." That evening, Sir Colin MacEachen commiserated with Cyrus, knowing well the deep torment and pain he was living, hoping a small change in his life might lessen his grief. "This way...both win." He uttered.

"Cyrus, I've got a proposition for you. Don't turn me down now 'til ye 'ear it all—just you think 'bout it first! I'm in need of a favor from you...could be a somewhat dangerous favor! And possibl'...there may be more future opportunities to use your singular expertise...if you agree to it." The men talked for a long time, drinking Scotch while Cyrus listened intently to his friend's explanation and request.

"I'm in need of a man I can completely trust in every way—someone not known in an' intelligence communit'. There's a mission on the continent in the intelligence field for a man with the kind of 'xpertise you 'ave. We need to get an 'xpert out of a Russian gulag, and our last two attempts ended in failure. As a result of our failures, our man is now kept in triple securit' in a Siberian gulag, deep underground, near Minsk. Yo'r reputation on the continent is well known to be a shrewd businessman, and yo'r presence in Minsk wouldn't raise questions from the establishment. You know the sayin', 'Put the key out in sight where no one will see it.' I feel your skills would give us one last chance at savin' this bloke...if you should agree. I 'ave the 'spects all worked out...with your approval, of course...we reall' need to get 'im out. What say ye?"

The words Colin proposed did not sound unduly dangerous to Cyrus; rather he felt this might be the opportunity he needed to start a new path in his life, a new direction in his life. Secretly, he hoped if he accepted this assignment, this new venture wouldn't allow him time to dwell on the past or what could have been!

"I see no reason not to give you my answer now, Colin. I'll be up to your office in two days to discuss the details of the assignment." The two men raised glasses to toast one another. This was the beginning of a secret life away from Lyn Brienne. Cyrus rationalized that Katherine would always be safe in the hands of Maggs during his trips away from the farm—wherever this new venture took him. Maggie Mack's grief was as deep as Cyrus's for she dearly loved Caitlyn as if she were her own kin. But now Maggie realized her duty was to care for Cyrus and even greater for Katherine. She felt a special duty to Cyrus's child, without her real mother to love and care for her, the role of Katherine's mother became hers alone.

Whenever Cyrus's business trips took him away for long periods of time, sometimes for weeks, Maggie singularly had the daily care of Katherine and a strong bond grew between them. Each time Cyrus returned from one of his extended business trips, he came to notice how much Katherine was growing to look like Caitlyn, definitely possessing the dark-Irish side of her heritage.

"Katherine holds strong the dark-Irish beauty of her mother," Cyrus would comment to Maggie upon his return each time. Katherine looked upon Maggie as her own mother rather than a nanny and named her *"Magere,"* a combination of Maggie and mother to the child. Over the years, the three figures were often seen at the local fairs with Katherine in tow between Cyrus and her Magere, a handsome family sight.

The years passed and Katherine grew into a strikingly beautiful woman demonstrating her Irish/Welsh ancestry—the Black Irish. The curly, dark, shining hair, matched by deep dark-brown eyes accenting the whiteness of her complexion, and richness of her mouth, she was often taken for the young Caitlyn. To Cyrus and Maggie, it seemed only a blink of an eye and the woman was here. Her name and beauty became familiar throughout Llandrindod Wells. Seeing her grow into a woman gave him so much pride seeing the 'liking of his Caitlyn in her,' but this would bring on a feeling of deep fear…*What if he ever lost her!* Always in the back of his mind, the thought resided that the dangers of his clandestine work could reach out to his family! This forced Cyrus to take the greatest precautions, never to permit his clandestine life touch his family or life at Lyn Brienne.

Cyrus repeatedly pledged, *"I must never let anything happen to me family…the most important persons in me life…nothing must ever touch Katherine!"* But never did he feel the need to abandon his secret life!

# CHAPTER SIX

## *THE LAST FAIR...*

A new young veterinarian was seen working the summer fair in Llandrindod Wells.

Michael Llewelyn was a fine-looking young man, tall and thin of stature with fair, sandy hair and gentle light-blue eyes. It was more his gentle manner with the animals that first captured her attention. Today, his job was to examine the animals in the show pens before the auctions started. Michael became aware of Katherine's presence from afar, but not until he reached the last pen, did he notice she was a young Welsh beauty, carefully observing him while trying to look indifferently away. Without acknowledging her presence, he kept on working until he completed his final inspection of the sheep herd. Surprising her, he turned to the girl sitting on the fence—his eyes meeting her glance with a mutual smile passing between them. The pregnant, silent pause lasted a few seconds before he went inside the pen where she was sitting atop the rail. As he was passing beside her, she felt a quickening of her heartbeat, bringing a blush to her cheeks. Katherine knew...just as her mother and father had known their destiny at first sight... "This is the man I will one day marry!" As if making a promise! Without a word spoken between them, she raced back to Maggie to tell her what she felt.

"Aye...yo'r MacKenna 'eart is tellin' you who yo'r mate 'ill be...listen to it, me lass."

It was a special day when Katherine and Maggie convinced Cyrus to meet this man, who had turned his daughter's head and seemingly captured her heart. It wasn't long before Cyrus realized this man was someone different from the others, and someone special to Katherine. Calling to mind a past scene, *a young girl called Caitlyn O'Hara on the white steed racing past him to the crest of a hill...* In the year's time and with Maggie's ceaseless urging, Cyrus gave his permission to Michael to marry Katherine. Long ago, Cyrus put aside a portion of land in the MacKenna tradition for the marrying ceremonial gift, his gift to his heir, once thought was to be a son, instead was a daughter.

## THE WEDDING DAY...

Very early that morn with the sun bathing the room in its brilliant white rays, Cyrus stood before the hearth in the Great Room gazing out to the green pastures still ringing with memories of the laughter of a young girl racing on her horse. Recalling milestones of years passed, a rustling behind him distracted his thoughts back to the present. Turning toward the rustling sound, Katherine walked over to him next to the hearth with Magere carrying her train of veiling. The image he saw standing next to him overwhelmed him. Fighting to hide his emotions, he couldn't keep back the tears as he embraced Katherine as *his daughter* for the last time. In the same wedding dress Caitlyn had worn eighteen years earlier, Katherine took on the countenance of her mother. For that fleeting moment, *it was as if Caitlyn was standing with him on their wedding day!* All the memories of their brief life together came flooding back. In that brief instant of time, a lost life and love was felt *again!*

On that beautiful, crisp, clear fall day, Cyrus drove the horse-drawn cart with Katherine at his side to the *Llan* on the hill, St. Michael's Church. The *Llan* was a centuries old church on the slope above the river Ithon. They rode the distance in silence. All had been said earlier. The marrying ceremony did not last long. Each had written and recited their vows to one another ending with the vicar's blessing. Cyrus met the couple outside the doors and embraced the newlyweds with his gift.

"As is the custom after the marryin' rite, my gift to you...for much happiness and..." with his words trailing off in a silent blessing, he handed them the deed to the land for the east-end pastures— hopefully their new home. No discussions were necessary. Michael and Katherine knew this was the only place for their new home. By the next spring lambing season, the new cottage was ready. They christened it Kittery Cottage.

Gone from Lyn Brienne were noises of a child. The darkness and stillness closed in around Cyrus. The only evidence of life heard was the flickering, crackling flames from the hearth in the Great Room where he sat alone. Maggie stood silently in the doorway watching the melancholy man seated in his chair. Moving toward him, he roused from his thoughts as she sat down at his feet placing her head on his lap. Neither looked at one another nor spoke...the warm tears were telling all. She, too, shared his deep feelings of loneliness tonight.

That day Dr. MacOwen examined Katherine, he confirmed she was definitely pregnant. She dashed home to tell Michael. "We'll have our first child by the Christmas season," she blurted out when she arrived at the door to his office.

Cyrus and Andy helped set up the new nursery, moving some of Katherine's old baby furniture from Lyn Brienne to Kittery Cottage. The *grib* was the first to be placed in the nursery room—a gift from Grandfather, Angus MacKenna, made for Katherine; now decorated with a soft sheepskin pillow and handmade woolen blankets for the new *mab* or *merch*. Maggie's bright yellow curtains hung in the nursery for the "Bonnie Prince," as she called the baby.

"This is our beginning," Michael spoke to Katherine as they beheld the completed nursery. "This child will one day have many brothers and sisters to play with!"

It was an exceptional day when Katherine told Cyrus he would soon become a *"Papa,"* her endearing term for grandfather. His silence was puzzling to her...thinking her words would be received with gladness. He was thinking, *Would not a mother want to hear these precious words from her daughter?* This only deepened his realization and sorrow that Caitlyn was not there to share this special moment with him. After hearing her message, he quickly turned to

Katherine and took her in his arms, "I've been wondering, lass, how long I'd have to wait to have that title bestowed on me!" Holding Katherine in his arms to hide his tearful pain, "I'm very happy for the both of you…as your mother would be…were she here!"

Always the same deep fear was with him whenever he thought of Katherine bearing this child! Remembering how he lost Caitlyn soon after her birth, he never let on to Katherine or Michael his ominous, unexplained fear he felt for them. Cyrus's intuitive gift often brought great fear about something to pass. As Katherine's due date was drawing closer, Cyrus found it harder to cope with the nearness of the birth. His visits to Kittery became less frequent, using farm business as an excuse to stay away for longer periods of time. Katherine knew her father loved Lyn Brienne, but there were times she felt there was another part of his life taking him away from her for long unexplained periods of time that had nothing to do with the business of horses or the farm. Whenever Katherine asked her father for details about these trips, he would just take her into his arms and say, "It's just business, my lass. Not to worr'!" Then he'd kiss her forehead to keep their eyes apart. But Katherine was her father's daughter with the trait to read his thoughts to recognize truth. His answers always had some truth to them, but his demeanor and deliberate evasion of her eyes told her more—he didn't want to be caught in a deceit. She had a realization, *there was a secret side of her father's life that did not include her!* For whatever reason, he did not share it with her. Begrudgingly, she came to accept this hidden part in his life, always hoping one day he would make her a part of that hidden life, too.

The pain was very sharp and sudden, Too early to show signs of labor! Still the contractions had begun and were increasing with time. The day began bright with high thin clouds on the horizon. Now, that all changed. The weather became cold and blustery with dark storm clouds closing in on the horizon. Michael knew with the storm approaching he must hurry Katherine to hospital, *ysbyty,* in town in Llandrindod Wells before nightfall. The winds were blowing at their backs as the drive began down the winding, hilly roads. Stronger gusts of wind followed with the darker storm clouds seen with frequent flashes of lightening! Michael drove as quickly as he dared, as he made his way down through the twisting roads in the valley into town. When they finally reached St. Mark's, the storm clouds opened up, releasing a relentless cold driving rain.

Cyrus had just returned to the farm from one of his long trips and walked into the house, calling out to Maggie. "Maggs...I'm back and I'm hungry!"

Not hearing Maggie call back to him he continued down the hall, "Tis a bad, black night that's comin' with this storm!" Putting his bags down in the hall, he walked through to the kitchen.

Maggie blurted out, "It's Katherine's time, Cyrus!" Stopping in his footsteps, not waiting for Maggie to say more, he knew what she was going to say, he ran back through the hall. Grabbing his coat, he ran out the door through the drenching rain to the car. Maggie ran after him calling out, "Michael took Katherine to hospital several 'ours ago, and I've not 'eard a word since!" Maggie cried out to Cyrus, "You must call me...I must know what's 'apping to me luv!" She stood watching him drive down the rain-swept lane, her tears not distinguishable from the torrents of rain on her face. *Driving through the rainy darkness...all the while flashes of white lightening lighting up the hills...the wind...rain..."must reach Caitlyn at Lyn Brienne! No—no, it's Katherine's time!"*

Fighting his fears and the storm, Cyrus finally reached the hospital and ran through the torrential rains to the entrance to St. Mark's. Walking quickly down the hall, he saw a sister whisking away a tiny bundle toward the nursery. The sister recognized Cyrus and stopped to open the blanket. In her arms, he saw a pink, dark-eyed, tiny little girl, with the blackest hair he had ever seen on a baby, wiggling and looking back up at him!

"She's doing fine, sir, and I'm taking her to the nursery for a clean," Sister said.

Cyrus continued down the hall to the waiting room. At the door, he caught sight of the doctor speaking to Michael in a hushed tone. In that instant, a deep gut-wrenching pain grabbed at him inside... again...the same deep pain he felt many years ago when he found Caitlyn dead after Katherine's birth. The image of finding his Caitlyn lifeless in the bed next to him flashed before his eyes, and that same cold sinking feeling completely overtook him. Slowly, Cyrus walked over to Michael, afraid to draw near to the men speaking in hushed whispers. Standing silently, he heard the words the doctor spoke to Michael…and somehow he knew what he was saying. Something was very wrong!

"This can't be happenin' again," he thought. Not daring to speak, to break the ill-omened silence, Michael turned to Cyrus and he saw the tears streaming from Michael's eyes. He heard the words.

"I'm so very sorry. We tried everything medically and humanly possible to save her. Nothing we did helped…we couldn't reverse the bleeding. She was never in any pain."

Once again, hearing the unbearable expressions of finality, the doctor turned and walked away, leaving the two men to accept their meaning. The words echoed again and again in Cyrus's mind. *"Couldn't reverse the bleeding!"* An unfathomable pain reached deep into the soul of each man—forever inescapable, that pain would forever be an unspoken part of each man's life.

*One of these two men will be the driving influence in this new child's life! It will depend on one man's decision—for that man, will his decision be the right choice? Years later, that answer will be instantly understood!*

# CHAPTER SEVEN

## *THE BEGINNING...*

Tradition followed with the birth of this new little babe—the MacKenna heritage will go on.

This time it was not Cyrus's decision where this child lived her life! He had no right to speak or impose his thoughts or wishes... even though deep inside, he knew what would be best for Michael and his child! This was Michael's decision alone to make! Return to Kittery Cottage with his new daughter...or follow another path? Michael Llewelyn never spoke outwardly about the deep loneliness he was experiencing whenever his thoughts turned to Kittery Cottage, imagining life with only his daughter...and not Katherine. The day came for him to bring his new daughter home from hospital. Cyrus empathized with Michael's conflicts, experiencing mixed emotions of happiness and pain, memories of a life he once spent with a loving woman at the cottage they built, now empty.

"Michael, consider Lyn Brienne your home for as long as you want or need to be a part of it. There's no rush to decide your path."

Hearing those words made it easy for Michael to accept the offer to return to Lyn Brienne, with Emma, Cyrus, and Maggie, instead of Kittery Cottage. This decision was easy, but he knew at some later time, he would have to make a more permanent choice about

Emma's life. Would he be able to do that? Make the most important decision in his life—for his daughter?

The first night spent at the farm, Michael recounted to Cyrus there were times Katherine would call to the baby, "'Emma Gray— that was a good kick!' Why she never called it by another name is still puzzling…it's as if she knew it was a girl." Michael was reticent for several minutes before he shared his thoughts.

"I'm not even sure why she chose to call the baby Emma…I think this was her way of telling me she wanted a girl! I've given it a lot of thought these past days…been thinking more about that name, *Emma,* and I'd like to name her Emma Gray Llewelyn. "

Michael looked to Cyrus for his opinion but heard none. Emphasizing his statement, he reiterated again, "The more I thought about it, the more I knew Katherine would like the name, too."

Cyrus heard everything Michael had said. He walked over to the cradle by the hearth in the Great Room and gazed into the child's sleeping countenance, so much like her mother. Taking the tiny hand into his, "Aye, it does seem to suit her…Emma…Emma Gray. I, too, like it, Michael. Aye! She'll be known as "Emma Gray Llewelyn". Michael felt a joyous relief for a brief second.

From that time on, the days and weeks passed slowly, both men focusing their thoughts and attention on the care of this new little girl. It was easy to show their love for Emma, for the sake of the other, their demonstrable efforts hid each man's real emotional pain.

It was a time of celebration; Emma had turned two months old, and Maggie made a festive supper. When all were seated at the table, Michael made his announcement.

"I've come to a decision!"

Cyrus heard the finality in his tone and looked up with a feeling of dread. Pushing his plate aside, he wasn't prepared for this moment he hoped would never come.

In a soft tone, Michael spoke, "Cyrus, Maggie, I've done a lot of thinking of late, and there's something I must do and do it now! Katherine was everything to me…my whole life…I feel the time is right now…for me to get on with my life…but I first need to give Emma some stability in hers." Neither Cyrus nor Maggie spoke or looked at Michael, fearing the words to come.

"Cyrus, I'm very grateful to you and Maggie...for your help and hospitality all this time, but I've been giving my life a long hard look to the future. Now, I must think about what is best for Emma. She needs a mother in her life...and I can't give her that." Cyrus tried hard not to look stunned or pained! Seeing the bewildered look on Cyrus's face, Michael quickly said, "Hear me out first! My family now lives in the States...in Connecticut, and I've decided to leave Lyn Brienne for a new life in Greenwich. I want to make a new beginning...start up my veterinary practice again." A long pause of silence fell over the group—no one daring to meet Michael's gaze.

"My sisters have all married and settled there with their families. I need somewhere different to start over...there's too many painful memories here...Kittery..." his voice cracked with emotion and trailed off. The minutes of awkward silence made it more difficult for Michael to continue...he would have to let them know everything! Tense with heartache, Cyrus and Maggie quietly listened to Michael discuss his plans to start his life in Greenwich, Connecticut near his family. That could only mean Emma would not be apart of their lives at Lyn Brienne.

Cyrus tried to focus on Michael's words, but his thoughts were elsewhere—somewhere in the past. Placing his hands in tented fashion to his face to hide his dejected countenance, all he could think was Emma would not know the measure of his love; not share this life on the farm as her mother had done! Supper ended and without uttering a word, Cyrus rose and walked to the Great Room. Standing by the large window, looking out into the valley pastures, he barely heard the words Michael spoke to him from behind. A deafening pause of silence forced Cyrus's consciousness back to hear Michael ask again, "Cyrus, do you think Emma could remain here...with you? She needs the kind of care Maggie gives her...and she loves her as her own...I'd return as much as possible to see her...and the rest of family here, of course."

Cyrus was so engrossed in his own thoughts he barely heard the words, "Emma remain with you." Disbelieving what he heard, he turned to look at Michael for assurance that the words he spoke were true! He did hear right! Michael was asking Cyrus to raise Emma at Lyn Brienne! The rest of his words just drifted off... He could not

believe what Michael was asking him! Finally, Cyrus hesitated to
find the words to answer.

"Aye…of course…yes, of course…Emma can stay here with me
and Maggs! Maggie and I will do just fine by her! Michael, you
know you are always welcome here…whenever and as often as
you can return. Emma will always be *your daughter*—nothing can
ever change that! I see you have given this great deal of thought…
weighing the consequences…and what the future may hold…for
both of you…to come to this decision. Michael, is there nothing I
could add to make it easier for you? We are your family! You must
know how deeply we'll miss you here…but you deserve a chance to
live your life, too, I understand that. I hope you will always think of
Lyn Brienne as your home…us…your family, too!"

"Yes, Cyrus, you and Maggie have done so much to make
this time easy for me here. I truly believe this decision is best for
Emma…no matter what the future holds for me."

Each man found it too complicated to speak further about his
true thoughts. One man would know happiness while caring for this
small child. The other would only know a deep, empty loss. Cyrus
thought, "Which of us will have the better life for the decisions
made today?"

The day arrived for Michael to leave for Connecticut by ship
from the Port of Aberystwyth. Breakfast was unusually quiet and
strained, with Maggie continually wiping her eyes to conceal her
tears from Michael.

"I've packed a lunch for ye…the trip is long and this'll 'elp," she
said, handing Michael a basket of his favorites carefully arranged and
secured. Michael embraced Maggie as if he were saying goodbye to
his own mother, her sobs no longer quiet and restrained. Cyrus was
in the Great Room standing in front of the hearth with his back to
the door. He heard Michael's footsteps in the hall, and he dreaded
what was to come. He wanted so much to tell Michael he was the
nearest he had to a son of his own…but the words he dearly wanted
to speak silently stuck in his throat! Turning to face Michael, it was
Michael who spoke first.

"I think it best if I just leave quickly…best for everyone…I
can't thank you enough, Cyrus, for everything you and Maggie have

done to make this decision easier for me." Grasping Michael in his arms, the two men understood there was nothing left to be said. The tenderness of the embrace spoke their silent thoughts.

Michael picked up his valise and knelt by the cradle next to the hearth to see Emma sleeping. Taking her tiny pink hand in his, he kissed her as she slept whispering…

"Be good for Papa. I love ye, little one, and I'll be back as I promised—*Hwyl.*" Quickly, he walked out the door, daring not to look back for fear someone would see his tear-stained face. Cyrus stood and watched out the window in deep silence for a long time while the ambient light from the most distant hill and surrounding fields became nothing more than a cloak of gray in keeping with the solemnity of the occasion. Except for the soft ticking of the old mantel clock nothing broke the silence in the Great Room.

"God be with your footsteps, Michael Llewelyn," he said softly, watching him drive down the winding road until the car was a mere dot in the distance.

Michael returned to Lyn Brienne every summer and each Christmas holiday to be with his Welsh family—Emma, Cyrus and Maggie. Each trip back, it became a little easier for him to openly share his memories of Katherine with Emma. But he never, again, set foot inside the darkened countenance of Kittery Cottage. Kittery Cottage would remain dark and locked for many years. Life at Kittery Cottage abruptly stopped the day Emma was born.

* * *

Cyrus doted on his beautiful Welsh granddaughter—with all the characteristics of her mother and grandmother, she had the MacKenna features and traits. The passing years found her growing into the lovely image of her mother, dominated with the black-Irish qualities. Like Katherine MacKenna and Caitlyn O'Hara, it was those distinguishable traits of natural beauty and quick wit that dominated her personality. The features of dark ebony hair, large dark brown eyes—at times almost fiery black—accented her white flawless complexion framing a full mouth that was quick to show a captivating smile. Most importantly, she possessed that unique intellectual quality in its purest form. She was endowed with one of the keenest superior, intuitive abilities to sense truth and dishonesty in anyone who challenged her.

It was Emma's sixth birthday anniversary. That late fall morning, Cyrus led Emma by the hand out to the barn saying, "Em, 'tis time you rode with me to check the horses and pastures."

Until now, Emma had not been allowed to accompany Papa on these early morning rides. As usual, the cold north wind blew straight down the valley. The sun's rays had not yet warmed the air, and Emma saw white clouds of moisture rise in the air from each breath. By the time they reached the post where the saddled horses were tied, there were small puddles of ice still hidden from the sun's rays. Emma saw *Aur Cymru* tethered next to a new chestnut pony. Cyrus's attention was on Emma, as her eyes grew big.

"This is a new pony…is he mine, Papa?"

"'e's just yours, Em. Happ' Birthday! What will you call him, Em?"

Without the least hesitation, she answered, "I'd like to name him…*Brenin*—for a king! Do you like the name, Papa?"

"I like it fine," he said. Soon the two of them—pony and girl—were a familiar sight to spectators. No matter the weather, for many years Cyrus and Emma rode out together those pre-dawn mornings to check the pastures and herds, before Emma had to leave for school…but only when Cyrus was home!

\* \* \*

Years later, it was another cold but sunny morning. As usual, Cyrus and Emma went out together to the stables in the early morning dawn, as was their routine. Only on this day, the stall where the mare, Mary Tudor, was stabled was empty. Emma looked puzzled at finding the stall empty. Taking her by the hand, Cyrus led her to the farthest stall in the stable where a beautiful ebony black mare stood. The black mare and Emma were instantly captivated by each other. As Emma slowly opened the stall door, the mare walked over to her, giving her a gentle nudge and trying to pry into her pocket. Emma knew the mare smelled the carrot and offered it to her, caressing her long shiny ebony mane.

"She's so beautiful, Papa!" she said, stroking her cold nose.

"She's yours, Em. Happ' Birthday! What will you name her?"

Emma thought, "Papa, I'd like to name her Katherine, but I'd call her *Ddu Kate*—'Black Kate'?" She has the color of my mother's hair, does she not?" Emma asked while stroking the long, thick black mane and softly whispering to the mare in *Cymraeg*.

"We'll call her Ddu Kate then," Cyrus echoed.

In the paddock, Andrew held the reins of the black mare and hoisted Emma into the saddle, remembering how he was there with her years earlier, helping the small girl atop her new pony. Emma held an extraordinary place in Andrew Mc Master's life. He doted on her...always there whenever Cyrus was away.

"Papa, she is so beautiful...I love you very much and thank you!"

Aur Cymru and Ddu Kate with man and young girl trotted out past the gates to the pastures, and then, in a full gallop, the two raced across the hills in unison. Neither had any idea how deeply these treasured memories would later influence how their lives affected one another—or that a time would come when their very lives would depend solely on each other's strengths and bonds of love. Lyn Brienne remained the center of Emma's life and Emma the center of Cyrus's life!

\* \* \*

For Emma's fourteenth birthday, her father, Michael, returned to celebrate the occasion as he had done every year. Only on this visit, Michael surprised Cyrus with a request he didn't anticipate.

"Cyrus, each year I return and I find a daughter no longer a child, but a young woman that I deeply miss. With your permission, I'd like Emma to come live with me and attend a private school in Connecticut. What few years she has left for schooling, I'd like to be part of that." Michael wanted Emma to understand why he made that decision to let her remain at Lyn Brienne as an infant while he traveled to the United States.

Cyrus understood his request and his need to spend more time with her to become the father she never really had. He found the words, "Michael, Emma is your daughter in every way. I think it's a good idea for the two of you to get to know one another…and for Emma to learn and understand everything about her heritage."

Emma knew her father loved her deeply, and she experienced emptiness after he returned to the States. Secretly, she always wanted to understand what prompted him to leave her and travel to the States; she even dreamed what it was like to have a big family with lots of brothers, sisters, aunts, and uncles. So, when Michael told her about leaving Lyn Brienne to live with him, she didn't understand why she had such ambivalent feelings…pleased to live with her father…but gravely saddened to leave Papa, Maggie, and Ddu Kate. Her only consolation was that she knew she would return each year to spend summers at Lyn Brienne. The school year seemed overly long and lonely at Lyn Brienne for Cyrus and Maggie—waiting for those summers to come.

The legacy of the Llewelyns was never in competition with the Clan of MacKenna. The bonds of the clan inherently bound Emma and Cyrus together in a strong, unique way that no other kind of relationship could ever surpass. In an unimaginable way, one day their roles would be reversed…*when their very lives would depend on each other's special traits and the strengths of the MacKenna Clan.*

# CHAPTER EIGHT

Cyrus counseled his solicitor to change his Will when Emma was born; Katherine's trust was assigned to Emma Gray Llewelyn— effective in her twenty-fifth year.

On her twenty-fifth birthday, the trust was exactly what she needed to start her own law firm in Soho. Once established, it wasn't long before word spread accounts of her successes within the legal community. Barrister Llewelyn had a flourishing law practice in international criminal law. It was a Tuesday when she first hung her law shingle, and it was on a Tuesday that first important, prestigious client walked into her tiny Soho office requesting her services.

* * *

Sir Colin MacEachen was a tall, energetic, muscular man with slightly graying dark red hair and dark, cold blue eyes that conveyed authority when he spoke. Like most prestigious-looking Scots, he sported a thick red mustache and wore a black suit, white shirt with sartorial tartan tie, colors of his Scottish ancestors. A man of character and nobility, he referred to himself as the average man. Emma observed him when sat speaking with Mrs. Tibitts. Watching the scene play out in the front office, Mrs. Tibitts excused herself to approach Emma. She was thoroughly orchestrating the whole scenario for *his* benefit. Emma rose to greet him; she noticed that he definitely had an imposing figure of a man as he walked toward her desk.

"I'm called Colin MacEachen and I've come to ask ye to look into a ver' personal matter involvin' me family…It concerns me son." He said in a booming voice with a thick Scottish accent. Extending her hand, he grasped it firmly.

"How can I help you, Sir MacEachen?" Motioning him to be seated directly across from her, she explained it was her policy to tape a new client's first interview, which was usually lengthy and fact-laden.

"It saves me time if I don't have to write the facts during our meeting." With his consent, she started recording a most interesting but tragic story.

"Six years ago, me on'y son, Dougal MacEachen, then thirteen years old, was attendin' a private school in Edinburg' in his first year at St. Anselm's Preparator' School for Young Men. It was that spring term, the 'ead Master notified me, 'Master Dougal was nowher' to be found on the school premises!' Despite a tho'ough search of the grounds and buildin's no evidence of 'im was found! The 'ead Master's call was to ask if Dougal 'ad returned 'ome unexpected'y?" The Scot's demeanor indicated great emotional control while explaining facts with directness, not wasting words.

"Aye. "E 'ad no reason to come back 'ome, Mr. Whittens,' I told 'im. I asked for another tho'ough search of the school, but the results were the same—*Dougal was nowher' to be found and there was no sign where he went!*" Without hesitancy, he stated, "Of course, I 'ad my house and grounds folk search the estate…several times over several days, but we found nothin'!" Despite his masterful self-control, I saw an emotional chink in his deportment, and let him tell his story at his pace.

"I contacted the local police and even 'ired a prestigious private agenc' to find me son. I gave this matter my full and individual attention for months. The police, the private agenc', I 'ired, e'en me own personal contacts—and resources, all failed to come up with a clue of 'is whereabouts…or with an' reason why Dougal disappeared without a 'int or trace of 'im! None of the boys at his school admitted they saw or 'eard an'thing unusual before 'is absence was discovered.

'Is mates last saw 'im goin' into the librar' and ne'er saw sight of 'im leave! Ne'er a ransom note or communication from any source askin' for monies for his return!"

Emma jotted down on her pad, *??? Private agencies...personal contacts??? Neglected to identify names.* When Colin MacEachen did clarify the different agencies he worked with, his voice changed when he uttered the words, *"e'en me own private contacts and resources."* Was it done purposely to avoid my questioning him further about this part of the investigation? Or did he deliberately want to withhold certain facts? What she did note was that Sir MacEachen had already done an exhaustive investigation with no results...What did he hope I could do?

Watching Colin MacEachen's body language change from a father controlling his emotions to an angry frustrated man, gave Emma insight that this man had a dual task in this matter. He presented an excellent account of facts that occurred several years ago. You could see how he knew every facet of information to give a logical and factual account in a well-organized manner. Emma surmised, "This man had developed this kind of trait somewhere in his past."

"I 'ad not given up 'ope Dougal would be found. The media lost interest in the story after several months and the 'ole incident seemed to be forgotte'. The few leads me investigators did come up with led to Ital'. But Ital' proved to be all dead ends!"

Her instinctual insight of this man gave her the answer...*Here was someone who was in British government, MI-5 or another covert department...who'd done a thorough job trying to locate his son, but without success...and now was coming to a solicitor to see if I could find something they missed!*

"I never saw or 'eard from Dougal for the next five years," he said matter-of-factly. At this point, his exterior deportment changed.

"It's not a day I'll ever forget! Five years 'ad passed and then this day...a young man showed up at the estate gate, givin' 'is name as *Dougal MacEache'*, claimin' to be me son! Aye! The moment I laid eyes on 'im I knew he was me son! I questioned 'im man' times but 'e 'ad only a memor' of 'is name and family residence. Of course, I 'ad his DNA tested for authentication...along with other methods of ID, too. There's no doubt—'e's me son! To this day, he can tell me no more than 'is last recollection of a day at St. Anselm's—goin' to the Library and then—findin' 'is way 'ome to Cardiff from the Scottish boarder." Emma turned the tape recorder off.

Emma remembered reading newspaper accounts about this case, but some of this information given today was never reported. Recalling the actual printed headline, *"Son of prominent MacEachen family with ties to British government, mysteriously disappears."* Initially, the press included daily reports of the MacEachen family tragedy, but when there was no more new information, the story soon became an occasional news item relegated to the back page of the *London Times*. The whole matter resurfaced again when Dougal MacEachen's sensational return home occurred after five years disappearance. No one could forget the last caption: *"The boy from the past! Gone five years? Why?"*

Emma remembered that when Sir MacEachen first introduced himself today, he briefly mentioned he knew Cyrus.

"How do you know my grandfather, Cyrus MacKenna?"

Colin casually offered his explanation, "We 'ave some mutual business interests..." His response didn't—or he wouldn't—elaborate in detail what that "mutual business interest" was. Emma knew he was evading the truth...and didn't believe "mutual business interests" meant horse breeding! She kept this to herself...for now.

While listening to his scenario, she rationalized, if I accept this case, I'd have more opportunities to find out from Cyrus about their 'mutual interests.' Something was different about this man. Definitely, there were more unexplained facts he didn't speak about to her. What he did tell me was forthright for the most part, making direct eye contact gave credibility to his statements...it was as if he knew I was evaluating the integrity of his answers and facts. I have an unmistakable sense there's much more important information he's not telling me!

Her original query was still not answered: *"Why is Sir MacEachen coming to me for legal assistance, when there are many more prestigious firms, with well-known investigators, in England to choose from?"*

"Sir MacEachen, I'm troubled. Why are you here today asking for *my* help, when Dougal is home, and the police and your private sources were not able to find reasons and answers for his disappearance?" As an afterthought, she added, "Does your son have any residual affects from his alleged kidnapping?"

"Ms. Llewelyn, I know of your reputation in international law, and I think a fresh new approach into this matter is warranted. Please understand, I'm grateful Dougal is 'ome, but the perpetrators are still out there...at large and I mean to find 'hem! I cannot explain all of me reasons at this time, but I want someone not direct'y associated with all the past investigative agencies to bring a fresh mind to this case. A clean start may uncover somethin' we missed."

He was asking for someone not associated with the family or past law enforcement agencies to find out what really happened during those five years his son was missing! He was asking *her* to discover who was behind it and make them pay according to whatever international law was applicable. Emma realized it was a major undertaking and a very difficult case...the case facts were cold...and any good leads have long disappeared.

"Sir MacEachen, I need time to think about this case before I can give you a definite decision to accept or reject the case. If I do agree to look into the matter, there can be no guarantees as to the kind of results I find." Rising and walking around to him, she said, "Can you leave a number with Mrs. Tibitts where I can reach you? Say within two days time, I will give you my answer. If I do agree to investigate, I will use my own resources in the investigation."

"I total'y understand. I'll wait your decision and telephone call."

Emma carefully observed him as he returned to Mrs. Tibitts's desk to leave the necessary information she requested. Her mind was mulling all the great concerns about this case, but she felt she first needed to weigh the facts and not allow her feelings to dominate her decision. She desperately wanted to accept this case, even knowing how impossible the odds were for any positive outcome..."If I could find something new...any thread of a lead that everyone else missed...it could be *the case* I need to make it to Covent Gardens!

Still, I might find some small piece of information that's new…who knows!"

The following day, she telephoned Sir Colin MacEachen to inform she would accept the case! Determined to find answers around Dougal's five-year disappearance, she had to first find a good reputable and dependable investigator to work with her. That was the beginning of the relationship between Emma G. Llewelyn, Ltd and Private Investigator, Sean Dillon O'Rourke!

\* \* \*

Emma's first encounter with Dillon O'Rourke came about shortly after joining Kavanaugh Ltd, when she delivered a court summons to him. In her travels to locate him, she found his so-called improvised office. That's when she discovered Mr. O'Rourke had many connections to influential people in all positions… private, governmental, and political positions throughout the United Kingdom, and even ties to the Continent. Still, all of this information offered very little personal knowledge about the man called Dillon O'Rourke, a man possessing good insight and knowledge about people. After a few encounters with Dillon, Emma had her own insight into the mystery man with the means to strip away that hard façade and find beneath it, a man with the best of qualities: honesty, loyalty, and commitment. Exactly the kind of man she needed on her team, especially in this new high-profile case!

Dillon ran his office from the back booth at the "Black Swan Pub." Their first encounter was a psychological confrontation between two strong intellects. Dillon took an immediate liking to Emma, perceiving her tireless energy and determined effort in working her cases. He saw her purposeful energies were to get results for *the clients*. Dillon liked that. It was the way she'd put her questions to Dillon. With such directness, he knew she was judging him in every capacity, and he answered with only the truth—meeting her resolve face-to-face and eye-to eye…she didn't detect even the slightest deviant mistruth in his remarks. Nor did he resist an opportunity for a quick-witted comment! Mentally, she did consider, "Does he have a method to outwit me or is it just mere luck—or is he just a painfully truthful man? No, what I see and hear is what this man is all about," Emma concealed her thoughts.

Their ensuing work together in the MacEachen case had some minor successes, proving Dougal MacEachen spent time during those lost five years in Italy, but nothing was ever discovered about exactly why he was abducted, and where he spent those five years. Emma and Dillon did learn the name of the Italian family who was thought to have been associated with Dougal in Italy during those five years of absence. The investigation led them to a family in Venicia. Disappointingly, they discovered the family left the area several years ago. Coincidentally, the date of their disappearance from Venicia matched the date Dougal returned to Scotland. This was the only fact Colin MacEachen and his team hadn't learned. Every other piece of information Emma and Dillon uncovered, had been found by the previous investigation.

Physically, Dougal had been well cared for those five years—but why didn't he remember any part of what happened to him during those years? Medical doctors called it a form of amnesia—encouraging his family to have patience; counseling often the passage of time brings back lost memories. After undergoing a long period of therapy, Dougal MacEachen never did regain his memory from those five lost years. Ultimately, the bigger question was never solved. *Why was he abducted—and then allowed to return home, apparently unharmed? This is not the usual method of kidnappers who steal children for labor or ransom money!* This one fact is why this case is so different—which is why Emma and Dillon never officially closed this case file even though they knew the more time passed, the harder it would be to ever find new answers.

It was Dillon who revealed certain facts to Emma about Sir MacEachen's true background with his ties to influential government positions he held.

"MacEachen is a name frequently associated with a government level of MI-5—strictly classified intelligence work."

Learning this fact only increased Emma's curiosity to search for the real reason Colin MacEachen asked for her help when he probably had the entire English government working on his case.

"WHY ME NOW?" she asked Dillon. "If there is truth to the fact that he holds a high level position in the government, then why come to me for answers when all the resources of the Yard, Police, and probably his own MI 5 people failed to produce results? There's more secrecy to this case than I've been told—and I trust my instincts more than I trust Colin MacEachen!" she told Dillon.

If Dillon knew more about this titled Scot, he was not going to confide all of it to her.

"No reason to give any more details now," he thought.

Even though the case appeared officially closed, Dillon continued to work tirelessly on his own, meticulously following every bit of information he discovered, it always ended the same way—in a dead end! Each time a lead fizzled out, Emma noticed how despondent he became for a time. This wasn't like the Dillon she knew. It was as if this case had some hidden personal agenda in it for him. She cautiously let him know she was aware of his driving force in this matter.

"Dillon…sometimes there are cases with no logical answers out there… and that fact becomes the answer we have to accept." Emma made a mental note at some future time she would talk about this case again with Dillon, but instincts told her this is not the right time to further pursue it. If there's something concealed in his past to make him feel this way about this particular case, I need to find out just what that is. Despite the negative case outcome, Emma received a handsome fee for her work from Colin MacEachen. It was the case that turned the tide and made it possible for her move to the new office—her ultimate goal.

The big new office with glass windows overlooking Parliament and the Tower Bridge was located in the well-known Winthrop building in the center of London near Grosvenor's Square. Her new address for E.G. Llewelyn, Ltd.was Suite One-Hundred Five, Ten Berkeley Place, London.".

* * *

The move from Soho to Berkeley Place, London brought a bigger caseload to the firm with so many more demands on her and her new junior partner, Olivia Grimshaw. Telephone calls replaced trips to Lyn Brienne. When she did manage a weekend trip to the farm, Maggie would fuss and splurge making each visit special. More than anything else, it was those early morning rides with Cyrus that meant the most to Emma. Just being together in each other's company again was her pleasure. Though infrequent, those trips away from the law practice to the farm were a source of rejuvenation to Emma—and to Cyrus.

"How are things going at the new place?" Cyrus asked.

"Busy and demanding! We've had a significant increase in our caseload. If it continues, Olivia and I will have to consider a third partner. Some of my cases have taken me to Italy and France over the past year. This leaves only Liv at the office alone, another reason to consider bringing in a third partner."

Emma never discussed the outcome to the MacEachen case with Cyrus. She was not certain why she didn't.

"Any good paying clients lately?" Cyrus asked specifically to see if she would mention the MacEachen case.

"Yes…a while ago, I did have one good client…the case had less than satisfactory results." Cyrus knew her reference was to the MacEachen boy—*She can't know my involvement…She'd want to know all the details, and I can't afford that now!*

"Have you been back to Milan since your last visit?" Cyrus asked.

"No…not in eight months. Why do you ask, Papa?"

"No particular reason. I remember you spending holiday time there and how much you liked it—until your last visit. It's puzzling… when you came home you seem to bury yourself in your work, as if the trip wasn't pleasurable, and you just wanted to forget!" Cyrus remarked to her, remembering the time he could not locate her for several weeks—a frightful worry to him. It was not like Emma, she made no response to his observation and comments. Whenever that particular event was discussed, she'd feel a frightening fear…with no idea why! *She had no memory of that trip to Italy! Just total blankness! Yet it had to have happened—Cyrus was not the only one person who occasionally referred to it…then why doesn't she have any memory of the trip?.*

"When do you think you'll get back to the farm again?"

"I'm not sure Papa. My schedule is very full when I get back." The horses were becoming restless while Cyrus and Emma walked them.

"We best start back. Storm clouds blowin' in from the north," Cyrus commented, and both turned the horses pressing to a full gallop back across the pastures. With a slight hesitation Cyrus held Aur Cymru back to let Emma and Ddu Kate take the lead ahead. He missed seeing her ride with the winds whipping at her, both mare and rider appearing freer than the air. It always evoked a similar past scene…when he first saw *Caitlyn crest the Bern and they exchanged a smile!* Eventually catching up with Emma they entered the enclosure gate together. Reaching the paddock, Andrew was there to meet them, taking the horses for a cool down.

"We both enjoyed that ride, Andrew, alluding to her and Dhu Kate. She'll appreciate a good rub." Andrew Masters confided to Emma how Ddu Kate would know days in advance she was coming back to the farm. Those were the times the stable became too confining for her, and he had to put her out to the pasture to vent her vitality. Emma understood what Andrew was saying. Many times when she'd arrive at Lyn Brienne, Ddu Kate *was* out in the pasture, and hearing the approach of the car motor, the mare immediately jumped the fence and trotted to the cottage door to meet her, a re-union of soul mates.

"She's got a second sight for you! Tis like she has the MacKenna understandin'—she knows your comin' back. No one tells her you're commin'—she just knows! *The MacKenna insight!"*

# BRITAIN-HERITAGE

# CHAPTER NINE

Emma had finished changing into the light gray flannel suit and garnet-colored sweater to meet her newest 'client'.

She felt comfortable for the day's schedule ahead—that important day circled on her calendar! Walking back to the desk, she attached her gold watch, her graduation gift from Michael. Only two days ago, a woman, of international prominence in a distinguished Italian family, personally phoned Emma to ask for an immediate appointment to meet with her in London. The urgency of the woman's request lent mystery to the meeting!

Emma secretly hoped this day's schedule would be light and checked with Peter for the list of clients expected.

"Not making it home last night, I don't want this to be another late day at the office. Good, only three scheduled clients."

It was the third one listed who was the potential new client. First, consultations took up a good part of her day, which is why Emma personally rearranged her schedule to accommodate the client's trip to London. Peter blocked off the whole afternoon on her calendar for this new client.

"I wonder why *she's* coming to see *me?*"

The buzzer on the intercom sounded; it was Peter saying her first client, Mr. Moore, was in the waiting room. Peter and Emma worked out a system of communication not requiring lengthy verbal messages of explanation; different coded buzzes meant a special communication. Retrieving the client's case file from the IN tray,

Emma quickly perused it. There were two more quick buzzes, and Peter escorted the client into the office.

"Good morning, Mr. Moore. It's always a pleasure to see you again. I hope you have been well."

"Thank you, Barrister Llewelyn, and yes, I'm very well. It was nice of you to see me on short notice, but I am in great need of your assistance in this matter," he said with anxious conviction.

Mr. Moore was one of Emma's old clients from the Soho office. He, too, had a most unusual case never resolved successfully, and that, too, still gave Emma troublesome feelings about how the case ended. It was another case Dillon worked on with her, and both felt they missed something important—something they should have discovered before the case ended. When the case was officially closed, Mr. Moore had a melancholyness that followed him today. After the firm moved to the Winthrop office, Emma continued to make herself available to him whenever he asked for counsel.

He was a thin, tall, mustached man, impeccably attired, as was the case today. Dressed in a black pinstriped suit, white shirt, and a brilliant turquoise tie which was held in place with a diamond stick tiepin, he seated himself in his usual chair. Mr. Moore was meticulous, always following the same routines even in the choice of seat he took in the office. Emma couldn't help notice that today he seemed particularly anxious, exhibiting more than his usual uneasiness. Casting furtive glances around the room without making eye contact, it was as if he was anticipating something unexpected to occur, not quite trusting in the moment or the place.

"How can I help you today, Mr. Moore?"

With a slight hesitation, he began to speak in a rapid rhythm explaining his reason for their meeting, not allowing for interruptions. Emma listened intently to his account, but her concentration started wondering to the case files she found in the stacks yesterday, the Italian transcripts of The Chatelaine Case. *Why am I so taken with this Chatelaine Case?* She thought. Hearing Mr. Moore's voice in the background, she turned her attention quickly back to hear him summarize his thoughts into the question that brought him to see her today.

Reflecting on the facts in his case, Mr. Moore's young son disappeared under mysterious circumstances without a trace. Originally, it was thought to be abduction for ransom money, but no ransom note or contact from the abductors was ever received. Edgar Moore was twelve years old at the time of his disappearance from the private boarding school in Staffordshire. It seemed one day Edgar just vanished from his school without leaving any clues or traces. Mr. Moore heard that Emma represented Sir MacEachen concerning Dougal MacEachen's disappearance and purported return home. Thinking she had something to do with his return, he came to her shortly after Edgar's disappearance, asking for Emma's help to find his son. This was another child disappearance case that Dillon and she worked closely together on, but neither of them found a traceable lead that gave them any significant information about Edgar's disappearance or his present whereabouts. Dillon's failure to find real answers to such a tragedy once more affected him in a personally depressing manner. Again, Emma couldn't help but notice the driven Dillon, working tirelessly to find a rational answer to Edgar's disappearance. To this day, Dillon still occasionally remarks about the information discovered—"leads to dead ends." Emma began to sense a pattern in Dillon. Each time he spoke about these kinds of cases…about disappearing children…his voice betrayed more than his frustrations. It was not until much later that she learned a startling truth about Dillon's personal life, why he exhibited a driving force to find these lost children.

Mr. Moore confided that his one single hope was that Edgar will return home one day in the image of a handsome young man, since his disappearance happened years ago. But today, this meeting with her was to discuss his will and testament status asking for information about adding a codicil to his will in the event Edgar should return after his death. If this were to ever happen, Mr. Moore wanted his son to receive all of his rightful inheritance.

J.D. Fenimore, Q.C. had been Mr. Moore's solicitor in these matters until his recent death. As such, Mr. Moore now turned to me for advice and encouragement in these matters, despite knowing my practice of law was not testate law. Because of the failed outcome, I felt a certain obligation to help him as he clearly had trouble placing his trust in people.

"Mr. Moore, I cannot advise you how to go about setting up a codicil in your will, but I will contact a very reputable colleague for you to speak with at your convenience. We'll do it expeditiously." He clearly seemed relieved, having had this discussion with me, as we walked out of the office to Peter's desk.

"Peter, contact Brian Cooper, of Cooper, Whitcomb & Berkeley and ask Brian to see Mr. Moore as soon as he can as a favor to me. Just tell Brian it's about making a codicil trust to Mr. Moore's Will." Peter was speaking to Mr. Moore about a scheduled time and date to meet with the Cooper Law firm, when she saw Peter's preliminary work on the computer screen on the Chatelaine files. Reading from his memorandum, she was surprised to find out one of the defendants was a well-known physician from Calais, France. Reading from the transcript,

**"The Chatelaine case first litigated in Rome with charges of kidnapping against families in Milano, Perugia, and Napoli as well charges against individuals from France, Germany, and England. One defendant, Emile de Brera, was apprehended in Naples with evidence found in his home belonging to some of the kidnapped victims, indicating some of the victims were held there at various times. Further evidence alleges the defendants are tied to a *"continental kidnapping organization."* Subsequent trials for other defendants were transferred to Firenze."**

"Who were the attorneys representing these defendants?" Emma wondered. With no more time to read the rest of Peter's transcription, she glanced to see Mr. Moore exit the office into the outer rotunda area, turning to wave, as was his routine. At the same time, exiting the lift car was Mrs. Blaine, her next appointment. She always arrived early for her sessions.

"Be with you in a few minutes, Mrs. Blaine," Emma said and motioned to her to be seated in the outer office.

Finishing her final entry in the Moore file, Emma place in it in the OUT tray. As Emma was retrieving Mrs. Blaine's file, the office door opened with Peter ushering her in. Peter was most solicitous and remembered each client's individual needs and preferences—in Mrs. Blaine case she preferred a large cup of tea prior to our discussions. Mrs. Blaine remained one of Emma's clients after she defended her husband, Edward Blaine, five years ago in Scotland. Edward was one of several defendants on trial for smuggling Ancient Celtic artifacts out of the Isles to the Continent. He received the lightest sentence when he testified against his mates. His release from prison was coming up within the next year or two. Since his imprisonment, Emma continued to keep tabs on the family for the sake of the six children.

Preferring to conduct their meetings in the sitting area, Mrs. Blaine usually seated herself in the larger armchair nearest the hearth with her back to the windows. Her manner indicated she was eager to speak about her problem that brought her there today.

"It's me dole cheques," she said. "I 'aven't been gettin' 'em now for a month, and I've 'ad trouble payin' me bills. Collectors callin' at all hours for their monies! And I 'ave none, a fine muck 'bout," she said, wiping tears away from her eyes.

"How long has this been going on, Mrs. Blaine?"

"Nearly t'ree months now!"

For some unknown reason, Mrs. Blaine had not been receiving her state financial aid, with no knowledge why the cheques stopped coming. Discovering nothing had changed in her government status, Emma made a list of facts and questions to ask the Social Department about her cheques. Besides this income, she took in a small laundry clientele to supplement her government cheques. Emma saw no legal reason why the cheques stopped, and reassured her they would track down the reason this was happening. Reassuring her, Emma said, "Mrs. Blaine, I'll get to the bottom of this dilemma, and your cheques will come this next month." She had a feeling Mrs. Blaine's cheques were snipped—stolen—before she retrieved them at the letterbox.

Emma saw relief in her face with the tears gone, knowing someone was doing something about her situation. She instructed

Peter to make a few calls, first to the Social Department, but Peter had a better idea and arranged to change her post address and set about a plan with the Postal Service to catch the perpetrator—if this was the case.

"Mrs. Blaine, Peter has set the wheels in motion to make certain you receive your cheque this month, and he will explain the changes he's made to you." Bidding her good-bye, Emma returned to her office.

The clock chimed twelve on the mantle in the office. Just thinking about lunch whetted her appetite for the food at the nearby pub. Looking out at the thick dark heavy clouds collecting outside the window—all indications a North Sea storm was heading their way—Emma grabbed her raincoat. Liv left Emma a message saying she couldn't make lunch today..."It's best...I need more time to finish some other work before the new client arrives."

Working on the tenth floor of the Winthrop building made it easy to see approaching weather and springtime was notorious for North Sea storms. Rain was definitely in the forecast. On her way out, Emma checked the time Peter blocked out for the new client.

"Peter, I'm going to the Blackthorn Pub and Tavern around the corner for early tiffin..." Before she finished, he handed her a stack of messages to review making it a working lunch.

"I'll be back before the *signora* arrives," Emma said softly.

Exiting the building, she noticed that the wind was already gusting with a cold snap. Tightening her coat to keep warm, Emma briskly hurried to reach the pub before the deluge started. Entering the Blackthorn Pub and Tavern, Emma saw hostess Molly Thornbird who greeted her. Molly and Camille Thornbird sunk all their savings into the business three years ago. Now they own one of the most popular pubs, attracting a large professional crowd. Camille was a reknowned chef with extensive restaurateur experience at several well-known Continental restaurants in the Bordeaux region in France before moving to London and taking on this enterprise. The pub's ambience felt like a century-old tavern catering to wayfarers. The old-world décor attracted the working class near Piccadilly Square in London for some of the finest cuisine. Each table was artfully decorated in different motifs and set for a sumptuous fare. The bar was located in a separate cove-like area, enclosed as if it were a galley and sumptuously stocked. The tavern was usually filled with professionals for lunch daily. Molly understood if Emma was alone for lunch, it was usually a working tiffin and showed her to a corner table out of the din from the bar and traffic.

"What's the stew today, Molly?"

"It's Camille's special rice and fresh vegetables, and exceptionally fine today. I watched him make it myself this morning so I know it's one of his best and very fresh," she replied.

"Then I'll have a bowl of the stew with house cheese and crackers. Top it off with a pot of tea. I've had my quota of coffee for today." Taking out the stack of memos Peter handed her, she started reviewing them. Peter knew how to manage the many interruptions that came during client conferences and gave her only the important messages to review.

Emma used all the time to work and enjoy her lunch, oblivious to a single lone patron seated nearby, intently watching her every movement in a surreptious way while appearing to enjoy his own meal, oblivious to his surroundings.

*"Ah, she is still as beautiful as always, "* he mused, taking delight in his thoughts and the direct view he had of her across the way.

With lunch finished, Emma finished reading the memos, making the necessary responses on each one for Peter. It was nearly two o'clock. The new client was scheduled for this hour. Hastily paying the tick, she said, "Molly, please tell Camille his luncheon fare was one of his best!"

Still completely oblivious to the chap seated at the nearby table, who was now standing directly behind her, she made her way through the crowd to reach the front entrance. The dark, swarthy man made certain they'd not make any physical contact, but with the crowd propelling them closer they ended up next to each other. For a fleeting second, their eyes met, without any signs of recognition. Buttoning her coat collar tightly and readying her umbrella, she exited the pub. Rain was pummeling down hard. The portable gamp was no match for this storm as she darted back to the Winthrop.

Outside, the stranger pulled his coat collar up and his hat down firmly against the battering rain and wind as he followed her out among the scurrying crowds. Emma shown no outward sign of recognition of the swarthy-looking man at that chance encounter. Despite the wind-driven rain, he sauntered in the opposite direction from the Winthrop with a single thought; *she has no memory of us!*

*Glancing back for a last look, he smiled and walked to the corner and hailed a cabbie.*

# CHAPTER TEN

The lift went directly to the tenth floor without stopping.

Exiting the lift, Emma realized she left her briefcase at the pub with all the memos for Peter. "Peter, I apologize, but in my eagerness to return before my two o'clock appointment arrived, I left my briefcase on the pub seat with your memos and instructions." Checking her watch, she said, "I don't have time to get it myself, would you please run down to the pub and get it for me?"

"Just let me put the phone on auto and I'll retrieve it." Peter first called Molly to inquire if it was still where I left it. "Molly found it. It's exactly where you left it," Peter said rushing out the door toward the lift. I watched him enter the lift. Simultaneously, the adjacent lift door opened and an extraordinarily attractive, well-dressed, young woman exited, pausing to take notice of the direction she wanted to go. Not waiting to see which direction she took, Emma returned to her office.

Sounds of softly rushing air came from the outer office. Emma recognized the sounds of the glass doors quietly opening in the foyer. Knowing Peter was on her errand, she went out to see who had entered. Standing in the outer office was the same strikingly beautiful woman who captured her attention just moments before. She was meticulously dressed in a light cream-colored tailored suit with all the right trendy accessories. Her eyes were as green as emeralds and her striking golden-red hair accented her flawless complexion. Approaching her, Emma extended her hand to greet her, explaining that her secretary was on a brief errand and would return momentarily. So this is the new client. Emma motioned for her to enter her office.

"Please come in…is it *Signora Rudolphi*?"

She nodded and smiled.

"I'm Emma Llewelyn, senior barrister at the firm," Emma said, extending her hand, "and I'm so very delighted to meet you. Please, call me Emma."

"*Grazie,* and I am *Lucinda Magdalena Sophia Rudolphi.*"

"Are you related to the Rudolphi Family from Milano?" Emma asked, escorting her to the sitting area close to the warmth from the fireplace. With the cold storm outside, Peter had the gas fire lit while at lunch to offset the dampness.

"*Si,* I am Giuseppe Rudolphi's daughter-in-law. You've heard of the Rudolphi family?"

"Yes, in a manner of speaking. I've *read* about the Rudolphi Winery. I know they have a fine reputation, especially for their famous Italian champagnes."

"*Si,* I am married to Marcus Rudolphi five years now, and we live outside of Milano in the Villa del Christianna." She spoke freely and fluently in English with just a hint of an Italian accent.

"Have you ever been to Milano?" Lucinda asked.

"Oh, yes. On several occasions. I spent past holidays in the Umbrian-Tuscany regions, and every time I return, I reaffirm how much I enjoy that region! The pace of life in Tuscany is so naturally unhurried without the stresses of big city life. Tuscany makes me feel like I had a life there a very long time ago! Italy is a large beautiful country. But Tuscany is one of my favorite areas."

Emma motioned for Lucinda to be seated in the sitting area. She chose the chair nearest the fireplace opposite the natural bright window light, giving Emma the opportunity to closely assess her behavior during their meeting.

The longer Emma watched her, the more striking Lucinda Rudolphi's beauty became evident. Her deep, languid green eyes were like agate pools set wide apart but lacking that expected sparkle. Rather, they expressed a haunting sadness. The paleness of her nearly lucent complexion gave her an appearance of fragility.

Her full lips had a sumptuous quality but without a smile. Her golden red hair was swept back and carefully quaffed tightly in the back with an attractive hair clasp. Small emerald earrings accented her eyes. A single large gold band was the only adornment on her left hand. A delicate emerald and gold bracelet dangled from her wrist. Her manner was gracious with a quality of demureness. Her very presence radiated the stature of a *la signora nobile.*

"Do you have any objection to me recording this meeting?" I asked Lucinda.

"No, none at all."

"I like to revisit the case facts initially discussed, and this way I can devote my full attention to the whole story and recall the exact sequence of details at a later time. Do not be worried; everything recorded is a work product and cannot be disseminated without your consent. Everything we discuss today is held in client privilege."

Turning the recorder on, Emma asked, "You are *Signora* Lucinda Rudolphi?"

"*Si,* I am. Please call me Lucinda,*"* she said, pronouncing her name with a slight Italian inflection. "I am aware of the fine work your firm has done and of *your* reputation! Your law firm is well known in Italy and elsewhere on the continent, too." Placing the recorder between them, Emma asked her why she wanted to see her. Lucinda began an account of a most implausible story!

"I am not certain how much you know about my family, Emma, but the Rudolphi family is well known on the continent for producing some of the finest wines in Italy and is very philanthropic. The land and vineyards have been in the family for many generations. Signore Giuseppe Rudolphi, my father-in-law and patriarch of the family, came from a very old Italian family dating back to the seventeenth century. History records that the Rudolphi family were the first settlers to plant the sweet grapes for the vineyards that began producing the earliest known wines in Tuscany." Her deportment became more relaxed as she continued to articulate a story.

"I first met Marcus on a trip to Milano about seven years ago, as I am originally from Napoli. We married two years later and moved into our very large and beautiful home we call the Villa del Christianna, located on the northern part of the Rudolphi estate. Ever since I have known Marcus, he has been part of his father's wine business. It is only the past several years he has assumed more responsibilities in the business—taking up all of his days. He's been very successful to make the Rudolphi Winery what it is today. Recently, he was named *il presidente superiore* in the business but still reports directly to his *padre*. His brothers have other, lesser positions in the business, too. This position of senior *presidente* takes up all of his time now—away from our home...away from me. With so much time alone, I try to keep myself busy managing and overseeing the villa and servants, still there are many times I am alone. Because of Marcus's position in the family business, we entertain many clients in our home." Here Lucinda paused with her thoughts before continuing.

"Of late, I have found Marcus spending most of his days and even nights away from the villa, and when I ask him why, he just passes it off lightly as if he does not want to share with me his reasons. I feel he has become—how shall I say it—*piu secret*...more secretive.*" Emma must have had a puzzled look on her face.

"I can see this is puzzling to you. Let me explain," Lucinda said.

"When we first married, Marcus and I would meet several times each week for lunch to share the day's events with each other. It was a very happy time for us! Soon these luncheon meetings came to be once a month...now...no more. One day not too long ago, I asked Marcus to meet me this day for lunch at one of our favorite *ristorantes* where we often dined together in the past. What alarmed me was his response! He became very angry, even defensive, when I pressed to find out why he was behaving so badly to me! He gave me no reason why he was angry with me for asking to meet with him. Marcus is really a gentle man, and this change in him—well, it is very disturbing and hurtful to me." Hearing her voice tremble and seeing her hands tightly clasped in her lap told Emma that this was difficult for her to speak about. She deliberately didn't interrupt her account of facts.

"Whenever I try to persuade him to make time for us to be together...he becomes angry and leaves the house...angry with me. So many different times I have tried to arrange time together with him—a time for us to share and hopefully regain...something that I feel we have lost. But he is always too busy! This different Marcus... is not the same Marcus I married. It is as if something inside him has changed—something inside possessing him to change, and he will not talk to me about it! There must be something else... or someone else...who has taken over his life...preoccupying his energies and his life totally now! *It is not me he wants."* Pausing with downcast eyes, Lucinda spoke softly, "I want to believe this change is...it is not because of me."

"Have you discussed his behavior with any other member of the family?" Emma asked.

"Oh, no! No one else!" Lucinda said with finality. "I'm afraid to speak to *Il Padre* about it! Giuseppe and I have had our differences in the past, and besides, he would only think there is no *il problema*... but only in my mind! Giuseppe holds Marcus in the highest esteem of all his sons. I have a feeling if I mentioned this to his brothers, they would only go back to Marcus and tell him. Marcus would become extremely angry with me for speaking behind his back. No! They all have allegiance to Marcus and would not keep my confidence. The Rudolphis are very loyal to each other, especially to Marcus! Her emotions betrayed a fragile and simple woman wanting only the love of her husband.

"Now...these days, when he returns home later and later...he never offers to explain his late return...so I have stopped asking him to explain." Lucinda cast her eyes toward the window. Clearly, they were tearful and deeply sad.

"I have stopped asking him for explanations...Now we are two separate people living in the same *casa*...but our lives are distantly apart." Her eyes misted while recounting these events, expressing the pain she was experiencing. The sadness only deepened her eyes to a darker green, and her appearance changed to melancholiness. Emma let her articulate her story without interruption, even when there were long noticeable pauses, but she could not help but wonder just where this tale was leading to and why she was here to listen. Sensing Lucinda had more to tell her, Emma turned the tape over to be certain she had a complete record of her narrative.

"It is what I have found out this past week...*that brings me to you today,"* she said, raising her eyes to meet mine. "You see, I know of your reputation…this gives me the courage to come here to see you today. Emma, I need your kind of help, but I'm afraid to seek local counsel or speak to anyone associated with the family in Italia! The Rudolphis' influence and allegiances reach to many people in Milano and in all of Italia! This meeting with you, Emma, must remain most confidential—no one must know I have spoken to you—or asked for your help!" Lucinda pleaded passionately, almost fearfully.

"I told Marcus I was coming to London to do some shopping for spring clothes at my couturier, which he's aware I have done in the past, and didn't pose questions about my trip." Here her manner changed to anxiousness. "It's what happened in the past weeks that brings me here today!"

At this point, Emma felt she was about to learn the reason for this meeting.

"Normally, I do not go into Marcus's library or touch his desk when he is not present—he adamantly forbids it…to me and to the servants! However, on this particular night, while preparing for bed, I discovered I had lost a very valuable earring. We had dinner guests that evening and during the whole evening of our *la festa di cena* our dinner guests, *le signore* went into the Great Room for cappuccino or liquors, while *gli uomini* retired to the library with Marcus. After the last guest left, Marcus went out…I was alone. I retraced my steps to the areas in the house thinking, I may have lost the earring in the library when I entered it to give Marcus an important telephone message. Usually Marcus locks the library, even when he is working there and always when he leaves. This time, when I tried the door, I found it unlocked. Marcus began locking the library several years ago, explaining he did not want the servants in there. Now I am considered a servant, too!" Lucinda was becoming candid.

"While carefully searching the study for the earring, for some reason that I cannot explain, I opened Marcus's cabinet box. This is an antique box on a table behind his desk, I have seen him lock journals and computer discs in it. I was curious to learn why he kept the box locked inside a locked study. Marcus is meticulously careful about this antique box…It is one of his favorite pieces! I was very surprised to find the key in the lock—the box unlocked!" Lucinda spoke her thoughts clearly and deliberately.

"Though I knew my earring would not be in the box, I was curious to learn what Marcus kept inside that was so important to keep it locked from my eyes! Inside, were several logs…journals with handwritten entries on pages of lists…like files…journals of information…I did not understand what the contents meant. There were some computer discs marked in a code of numbers and letters… maybe Greek letters." Lucinda's excitement grew in her voice. "One file-book contained hundreds of names in it. There were some names I recognized as prominent people from different countries all over Europe…even Americans, French and German names…along with oriental titles from different Asian countries. Among them, I read several well-known English Lords listed; I know this because some of these people have been to our villa for special dinner events!" Here Lucinda paused seemingly to decide whether she should continue. "I was very surprised when I saw this one particular name written down."

"Please continue, Lucinda. We have complete privacy here."

"I had read about your successes in the international criminal field." At this juncture, Lucinda paused. When she continued, her voice conveyed definite fear, "It was your name, **Emma Gray Llewelyn of London**, which I read in the journal. It was written in Marcus's handwriting!"

Emma must have looked stunned at hearing her words. Lucinda hesitated to watch her reaction before continuing, "Next to your name were symbols and abbreviations, none of which I understood, and I saw no explanation given to understand what the different symbols meant. Many of the other printed surnames had similar symbols with Marcus's handwritten notations next to them. Checking another diary, I found a different kind of file…this journal had handwritten entries in Italian—not in Marcus's writing—with names and dates going backs five years or longer. Another book was a list of doctor's names—or maybe they were scientists…I think they are men in science! All of them had professional titles next to their name. Some were people who had been guests in our home at one time or another…" Pausing before continuing her thoughts, she added, "What was most revealing was the name Dr. Ennio Carruchi, who is our family's personal physician. Recognizing his name on the outside of the journal, I did see initials, E.C., next to certain names inside the other journals. I think E.C. meant Ennio Carruchi—Dr. Ennio Carruchi. This name I know very well! Dr. Ennio Carruchi is both a close friend and physician to the family for many years. He comes to our villa frequently for meetings with Marcus and he maintains a medical practice in Milano. He is charming...charismatic and handsome, and yet...there is a secret elusiveness about him... at times almost frightening. As long as I have known him, I know nothing about his personal life," she said matter-of-factly. "He is frequently a guest in our house and on many of those occasions I asked him about his work and his family. Always he says, 'I do research mostly and have no time for love or a family...and changes the subject to another topic of conversation.' His was the only doctor's name on that one list I was sure I recognized."

Lucinda's account was extremely revealing, but most shocking when she said *Emma's* name was on a list she found locked in her husband's library! Emma took this opportunity to ask Lucinda if she would like some tea, and rang Peter to prepare a tray for them, which he quickly brought in and set on the table between them. Emma needed time to gather her composure before she listened to more. Emma said, "I'll be mother," and poured the tea which Lucinda graciously accepted.

"Do you take sugar, milk, or lemon?"

"No nothing, *grazie*." It seemed the tea break rejuvenated her and gave her energy to go on with her story. Emma was doubly glad she was taping her narrative! The details seemed overwhelming and almost incredulous, and she'd definitely need to recall every precise detail again.

"Please continue when you're ready."

A few minutes later, her manner became almost pleading. "I know all of this does not seem relevant to you, but seeing your name in that file, and then inquiring about your fine reputation...I had to come in person today to speak with you! At first, I thought I would be taking a great risk coming to see you. The more I thought about it, the more I knew you would be someone I could trust—and I had to take the risk! I had to confide my concerns to someone, and who other than you, a most reputable lawyer. Emma, do you know why your name in on the list in Marcus's study?" Her question caught Emma off guard.

"Lucinda, I have no idea why *my* name would be on a list that your husband keeps locked in his library! I have never met your husband, Marcus, or any other member of the Rudolphi family, either professionally or personally...and I know of no reason why you found it there. Can you remember any of the other professional names or titles on that list besides Dr. Carruchi?" I asked.

"Some names I have heard Marcus speak about with Giuseppe, his father, but I have no idea if they are associated with the wine business or some other professional capacity. I have never been involved in the business of the winery...and many of the people he sees are not familiar to me." Hesitating as if trying to recall a name, she said, "No—no other name I read means anything to me other than Dr. Carruchi." She sipped her tea and continued with a more profound statement.

"I guess the most important reason I am here today asking for your help is something that happened to me just last week!"

Here, Emma deliberately stopped the tape recorder and inserted a new tape—a second tape. She wanted all the information about Lucinda's findings...more importantly that her name was on a list in the Rudolphi study, recorded on a separate single tape. She felt what she was about to hear from Lucinda now what was more her true reason she came to meet with her.

"Yes, please continue on Lucinda."

"When we married, Marcus and I wanted children very much. Shortly after our marriage, I became pregnant, and we both were very happy and excited about it! I had a very good pregnancy, with no complications. The day I went into labor was one of the happiest days for Marcus and me! I did not want to be asleep for the birth, but the doctor thought I should, and my baby boy was delivered by Caesarean section. When I awoke, I was told I had a baby boy, who died shortly after he was born. Marcus thought it better I did not see him...and I never did see my baby." Lucinda said wistfully and

85

wiped her tears. Clearly, this was still a very painful story for her to recall.

"We named him Antonio Giuseppe Rudolphi. I was not able to attend his funeral with Marcus, I fell ill when I learned the baby died. Marcus felt we should not delay the burial for my sake." A deep despondent sadness overtook this beautiful woman's countenance. She was barely able to speak the tragic words.

"When my health returned, I felt this emptiness inside...never knowing what my son looked like...if only I had seen him...just for a moment...I believe it would have helped me! I had such an empty longing to know who he resembled...my sadness turned to anger toward Marcus for not allowing me to see Antonio! A day does not go by that I do not grieve his loss and frequently I go to his grave...alone and bring him my flowers. Marcus told me Antonio looked liked him but did have some of my features. He explained that he had his dark hair, his mouth with the same dimple in his chin...telling me his coloring and the shape of his eyes looked like mine. All I can do is create a picture of my baby in my mind...but never to see or touch him...!" Softly, the tears spilled down onto her cheek. It was very clear Lucinda had a great void in her heart with the loss of her child, but I sensed that there was more to her story.

Lucinda continued recounting, "I was able to become pregnant again a year after Antonio died. I thought this was wonderful that God was going to make up for my great loss! Again, I had no problems with the pregnancy, but I had to have the birth again by Caesarian delivery and was put to sleep for this birth. When I woke, I asked for my baby. The nurse told me I had a beautiful baby girl, but it was born not breathing—a stillborn, they called it. My grief became overwhelming, and I promised myself that I would *never* go through that kind of tragedy again! No, *never again* would I bear another child! It was after the loss of our second child that I noticed the greatest change in Marcus, as well as in myself. I know we still love each other, but it seems that each of us is holding something back— we...just can't go back to what we had!" she said with finality!

Feeling her sadness and not quite knowing what to say, Emma said, "Lucinda, your loss has been tremendous, and you are still grieving deeply over the loss of your two children. There is some truth that 'time' does take away some of the pain; that kind of pain never completely goes away. I know from experience the passage of time will soften your pain. You must be patient with yourself and with Marcus." Reaching out to touch her hand, it felt icy cold. "How can I help you in this matter?"

"I know you will think me strange—even mad—to say this to you, but I have this sensation...a feeling that I can't explain...that my children are not dead!" For several seconds, there was just silence in the room. Emma never expected her statement and felt shockingly speechless, because she fumbled for words.

"Not dead? Why do you say this? You say it is a sensation...there must be something triggering you to experience this feeling!"

"I often have this dream...over and over...where I see two children growing up and when I awake...it is a feeling my dream is really true! These children I see in my dream...are *my children alive somewhere.*" Her thoughts trailed off, and Emma waited for her to continue.

"I thought this was happening to me because I was never able to see my babies to say goodbye to either of them at death. I tried to dismiss these morbid feelings! But the dreams and the feelings never go away...always returning in the same way!" Noticeably, her grief turned to anxiousness with excitement in her voice as she imparted the next part of the story. Emma expected this next fact was the real reason Lucinda took the chance to come to London. What was so important to risk the anger of her husband if he found out she was seeking legal counsel in London?

"Several weeks ago I traveled to Perugia in northern Tuscany, where friends of ours have a small vineyard there. News came to me the youngest daughter of Count Majoli, Theresa Fabiano, lost twins in childbirth. Again, stillborn girls. I thought I might travel to Perugia to offer comfort or some consolation and started out early in the morning for the drive up. When I arrived at her villa, I was told she was too ill to see or speak with me. I just left a few gifts with a personal note and started my return trip back to Milano. It's what happened on the trip back to the Villa del Christianna that alarms me!" Lucinda rose out of the chair and walked over to the fireplace.

"On my way back to the Villa del Christianna, I stopped in Perugia's Piazza to get a cool drink in the early afternoon at one of the *palazzo's* cafés before setting out on the rest of the drive back…I wanted to be at home before nightfall…when Marcus usually came home. I was sitting outside on the *palazzo* with my drink, when this little boy ran out from the shop calling out *"il mio mamma."* The child looked about four or five years of age, with a large bright smile, tussles of dark brown hair and dark brown eyes. Remarkably, he had an uncanny resemblance to Marcus and me…his smile and the look—his expression in his eyes! His skin coloring was paler…like mine…his smile and brown eyes were much like Marcus's. Most importantly, there…in his chin…he had the same dimple in his chin as Marcus has. I felt I was looking into the face of Antonio…if he were alive at four years of age! The boy ran to me…friendly and playfully…he placed his head on my lap, just looking into my eyes. Suddenly, a woman in the café called his name, *'Giorgio!'* The boy ran quickly ran back to the woman. Impatiently, the woman hurried him to the rear of the café as if she did not want me to see the child." Excitedly, Lucinda continued, "I realized, if she was his mother there was no physical resemblance between them! She had black hair with very sallow, olive coloring—like the Greeks and appeared to be in her late forties or fifties! I thought—she is someone caring for him, who was not his mother. As I was settling my account, I glanced toward the back room door and there…behind a curtained door…there was a small girl about two or three years old peering out. She was so different from the little boy! She had the brightest green eyes with red hair and her smile…" Lucinda sat down on the edge of the chair opposite me, "Emma, it was as if I was looking into a mirror of myself—twenty years ago—as a child!"

Emma must have had a disbelieving look on her face, because she said, "Emma…I am rational and lucid! I am not making this up…It's all the truth…Please believe me!" Shaking her head, she said, "I can understand how you feel…hearing me say the words out loud…even I can hear how incredibly hard it is to accept them as true! As the saints are my witnesses, Emma there must be some truth to what I found. I am not a grieving insane woman!"

At that moment, Emma knew Lucinda was telling her the truthful version of what happened to her. Her manner was straight-forward and her eye contact direct.

"The rest of the way home, I thought of nothing but this little boy named Giorgio and how much he resembled both Marcus and me. Still today, I am not able to get that little boy's face out of my mind," she said wiping her eyes. "The little girl...she looked so much like me...*Neapolitan!*" With fierce determination, she said, "That woman was not her natural mother!" Pleadingly, Lucinda asked, "How could such a coincidence happen—two children who look so much like Marcus and me—and yet can belong to someone else? Is that possible in nature?"

Emma couldn't answer her question. She didn't have an answer, not even a remote possibility of how it could be true...except... Lucinda interrupted her thoughts.

"When I arrived back at the Villa del Christianna early that evening, I told Marcus about the boy, and how I felt when I saw him. He became extremely angry and annoyed with me; angrier than I had ever seen him! He paced and pounded his fists...for the first time I was truly afraid of him, afraid for myself! He commanded me 'never to mention the incident again and to forget it ever happened... forever'! He accused me of causing us both needless pain, and said I should accept that our son, Antonio, is dead and buried in our family plot on the estate. Of all people, I thought Marcus would understand me, even though there was no logical or sane explanation for what happened or why I had such feelings," she said in a quivering voice. "I dared not mention I saw the small girl, too! I was frightened of what he would do to me...thinking me crazy," she said, softly, as if fearing if she said the words too loud Marcus would hear her. With conviction, she muttered, "It was like looking into a mirror to see myself twenty years ago!" Neither of them spoke for many moments...emotions filled the silence in the room.

"I know of your work and past successes in finding out details around the disappearances of children and bringing the offenders to trial. It is because of these facts that I want to solicit your help. Please, Emma, please find this little boy called Giorgio. I want to know if the woman is his true parent...and when was he born. And if there is more information you learn, then I want to know that, too! I need to do this so I can deal with these feelings that Antonio is alive. For my sanity…somehow I must put this to rest!"

Emma turned the tape recorder off and took notice that Lucinda's countenance changed as she leaned back in the chair…as if she had a great weight lifted from her. The look in her eyes was earnest, pleading!

"Have you thoroughly thought this through? What will you do if I do find this boy, and discover he is legitimately another mother's child?"

"If I learn this child is truly the son of a family in Perugia, I will dismiss any idea he could possibly be Antonio," she said softly. "I ask myself, why do I even think Antonio is alive? I have no proof to believe anything other than that he is buried in our family cemetery with his sister Angela. We named our daughter Angela Maria Rudolphi," she said. "It is just a mother…has these feelings for a child that cannot be explained rationally! My heart tells me something is not right. I must have some kind of proof that what happened over the last four years is real…*my children are dead!* Maybe, if I had seen them…*i miei bimbi,* in death…I would not be here today. Do you understand what I am asking of you?"

"Lucinda, I am not a mother, but I do know how strong the mother-child bond is. I *am* willing to look into this matter for you, but this is a most unusual problem. I cannot promise any definite results or what the outcome will be," Emma said matter-of-factly.

"This account must remain most confidential between us," she stressed.

"No one…no one must learn I have spoken to you while I was in London—no one connected to the Rudolphis—especially not Marcus! We will need to pre-arrange a time for us to speak next before I leave today. I cannot take the chance that Marcus will learn of this matter. I'm frightened to think what he would do to…if he found out I spoke to you today! When do you think you will have something for me?" Emma sensed she was physically afraid Marcus would harm her.

"It may take several weeks to a month before I have any kind of information for you. I will need to make a trip to Milano personally.

I'll arrange a trip on the pretense I need some well-deserved 'time off,' and plan a holiday trip to one of my favorite places, Tuscany. Yes, Tuscany is a place I have traveled to in my past trips to Italy. No one should question my choice of holiday to this region...many know I prefer this region for holiday. Anyone inquiring about my reason for returning there at this time will simply be told that it is personal holiday time." This seemed to put Lucinda at ease. Checking her calendar, Emma said, "We will speak on the 20th of next month. I'm sure I will have something definite to tell you by that date. I must confide...my private secretary will be the only other person in the office privy to these facts, and I trust him implicitly. Please understand in many of my cases I use a private investigator to assist me, and he must know all of these facts, too."

Lucinda rose and again assumed the posture of the stately noble lady. The tears gone...a countenance of a beautiful woman in complete control again, completely stoic, no outward evidence she had just re-lived a traumatic emotional upheaval and painful recollection from her past!

Jotting on a blank piece of paper, Emma said, "I have an unlisted private telephone number to give you. You may reach me at any time, day or night, and I will get the message. If I must speak with you, before our pre-arranged time, I will call and say I'm your clothes designer in London speaking about an outfit I am designing for you. I will give the name of 'Lillian from London.' If you get such a message, call this private number to reach me. I advise you to memorize it and then destroy the paper before you return to Italy." She handed her the paper.

"I understand." Lucinda said. "Financially, I am independent... I have my own money, and I'll be glad to pay cash for any fees or expenses you encounter."

"I had my secretary draw up a contract for you to sign on your way out today. It will be kept in the safe-vault...not in the file notes. Please, just initial it now...no signatures. My fees and expenses can be paid after I have completed the assignment, if that is agreeable with you?"

"Yes, but I have drawn this money out of my account...to pay for new clothes on this trip to London...it is better for me to advance you this at this time." Lucinda handed Emma a sum of English pound notes. While Emma was escorting her out of the office, Lucinda graciously thanked her for her time with the composure of a woman in complete control. She knew how to wear the outward expression of a titled woman, never allowing others to perceive anything other than graciousness, while inwardly she felt an overwhelming sadness.

"We will speak again in several weeks...and *grazie*, Ms. Llewelyn."

Emma watched her exit the office in the direction of the lifts.

This was not the kind of case she usually accepted, but she had to find out why Marcus Rudolphi, a prominent Italian man, had her name on a list kept in a locked study in his villa! Especially since the name, Rudolphi, was not a familiar name to her and her only recollection of the family is what she read in newspapers! Deep in thought, she still felt a little overwhelmed at what she just heard in this meeting and conjectured to herself, "Where will this case take me?" The question conjured up dark and frightening feelings for Emma without her knowing the basis for such emotions.

"She is a remarkably beautiful woman, but there's a deep sadness in her," Peter remarked as the lift doors closed behind her.

"Peter, find Dillon O'Rourke for me and ask him to call me, please. Try the last number he gave us, and if he's not there, then leave a message at that number asking him to contact me as soon as possible?" Hearing Peter's comment about Lucinda, Emma added, "And yes, your perception of *Signora* Rudolphi is very accurate, Peter. Though I'm not at all certain I can find the kind of answers she is searching for," Emma remarked looking back toward the lifts.

"If there's a problem reaching Dillon in the next day, let me know." Handing Peter the English pound notes, she said, "Please deposit this money in a new client account under the name Antonio."

Emma slowly walked back into the office to listen, once again, to both tapes. She needed to confirm what Lucinda Rudolphi just revealed did indeed transpire. The information that Marcus Rudolphi kept her name on a list locked in a study only raised feelings of apprehension and fear. More so, did the chronicle about her dead children...and her charge to find a child in Perugia seems an insurmountable, unrealistic task.

"If anyone can do it, it's Dillon. I definitely need him with me in this matter!" she thought. Removing the tapes from the recorder, she marked them "Antonio," and placed them in the well—the special safe.

No one knows of the existence of these tapes, except me—and Peter, and we are the only ones who know of the existence of this safe we call, 'the well'.

"I have no choice in this case. I've got to find out why Emma Gray Llewelyn is a name in Marcus Rudolphi's journals! What will Dillon and I discover in Milano for me...and for Lucinda? There's no turning back here...until I have answers to *those two questions*! Dillon, are you with me?"

A sudden feeling and picture came to her mind:

*An cold icy chill...sparkling lights of color fluidly moving down the stone wall...silence...pain*

# CHAPTER ELEVEN

"Before my 'holiday' can start in Milano, I need to search out as much information as I can find about the background and history of the Rudolphi family...the Municipal Public Library would have this kind of research information I need."

Peter immediately booked Emma's travel arrangements to Italy, giving her two weeks to set a plan in this case and find Dillon O'Rourke. She instructed Peter to arrange their flights separately and hotel reservations independently at the Hotel Manin in Milano. Not certain what was ahead for them, she felt more comfortable if they traveled separately, not making it obvious to anyone interested in them that they were working together. She petitioned the courts for an extension in the Thompson case which was originally on the court docket for next week and was granted a sixty-day extension. This way, Emma could give all her attention to her newest client without neglecting or getting too far behind in her other cases.

Honoring Lucinda's request literally, Emma confided to no one at the firm, other than Peter, the real reason she was traveling to Italy. Everyone around the office, including her junior partner, Olivia Grimshaw, knew she was due for some much-needed time off. Emma instructed Peter to tell anyone who inquired about her schedule that she was going to Milano on holiday. She said, "Inform them I will be away for several weeks. Say I'll be spending time with old long lost acquaintances. If by chance it becomes known Dillon was with me, well...he's there to help me find old friends for a reunion," which was not far from the truth. The fewer who knew about this case taking her to Italy, the easier it may be for them to find answers. "I don't want to tip my hand as to my real reason for going to Milano, not just yet—not to anyone!"

Whenever she traveled abroad, she usually left her itinerary with Maggie and Cyrus. This time her inner voice told her to keep the details from them for this trip...at least for the present time. When Emma dialed the farm, Maggie answered to say Cyrus was away on one of his trips, and she didn't know when he would return.

"No, luv, he just said he'd be in touch with me and would let me know when he was returnin' to the farm."

"Magere, I'm taking a holiday myself to Italy for several weeks and wanted to let Papa and you know I'll be away. When he calls you, tell him I'll be calling you again to tell you both where I can be reached, if necessary." A stretch of the truth...with Papa away she'd have to call again...She wouldn't be able to conceal her location—as she planned.

"That's wonderful, Em, now you enjoy yo'rself, and I'll tell Cyrus you called if he rings. It's so good to hear yo'r voice, luv!" Maggie always sounded the same—surprised and eager to share any recent news concerning some of the recent additions to the farm. While Emma did want to hear about things happening on the farm, she still had so much to do before she left for Milano. "Magere...I'm in the midst of a case right now, can't talk too long—I must run...I still have so much to do before I leave. Tell Papa I'll call him when I get to Milano to give him my phone and address to reach me...and for you, too."

"I will, luv, and you 'ave a good time." Maggie hung up. Still holding the receiver, Emma had qualms about her short conversation with her, "I should have talked to her longer!" Cradling the receiver, Emma chased many queries about this whole trip: *Why do I have such an ominous feeling about this journey? And now...hearing Papa is away...on what kind of work? Why do I have these ill-omened feelings about Papa? There can be no connection...to my case and his trip!*

95

Two days passed since Peter left his message at Dillon's office before he made contact with the firm. His greeting betrayed his identity.

"Emmie, me girl, it's been too long. 'Ow 're ye?"

"Dillon, I knew it was you just from the way I heard you blow out a puff of smoke. I thought you gave up that monkey! More to the moment, how are you?"

"I 'ave, me dear! Old 'abits die 'ard! And to answer yur last question, I'm fine, thank you, and I 'ope you've been be'aving yourself, as I 'aven't read about you in the news lately!" he said lightheartedly. "No unusual cases of late?"

"For that very fact, I haven't read about your latest exploits either!" she said, letting him know she did keep tabs on his escapades.

"No reason for ye to read 'bout me, m'darlin'. I've be'n as good as a newborn babe and workin' 'ard!"

"I wish I could believe that, Dillon!" Emma said to his counter his wit.

"Now and why would ye be sayin' that, dear Emmie! What brings ye to me at this time, m'dear?" he asked out forthright. He had lost neither his thick Gaelic brogue nor his sense of humor...and Emma felt they were things she had missed...his uncanny way to buoy her spirits! No, he'd never change.

"Dillon, I'm about to start on a new and unusual case in a few days that will take me to Milano, Italy for an indefinite time... possibly several weeks. I need your help with this case. I don't want to go into details on the phone, but *trust me*"—Emma exaggerated those words—"I need your fine skills and expert contacts in this matter. I need someone with all your *connections* to help me find answers expeditiously for a client." She wasn't comfortable telling him her personal interest in this case—not yet.

"Are you available to go to Italy?" she asked—"Say, right away?"

"Sure, and it sounds like a holiday to me, Emmie. Ye' know I can never say no to the likin's of ye'. Just tell me where to meet, and I'll be there for ye!"

"Can you meet me in Milano on the thirteenth? Your flight is earlier than mine, and you're booked at the Hotel Manin on the Via d

Manin? The hotel is across the way from the public gardens, which is why I prefer that particular hotel. I had Peter arrange reservations—separately—for both of us. For now, I'd like to keep our relationship quiet…secret. So, when you check in leave a message for me, and we'll set up a meeting. I'm not certain how receptive the local folk would be towards me asking questions about one of their more popular Milanese families." Exaggerating her point, Emma said, "Now if *you're* on holiday, Dillon, I know the local folk will warm up to your curious ways of getting information from them without them knowing it. You have that natural tourist-like approach to get information." His method always got results.

"It's a gift of Irish gab, some call it!" he said coaxingly.

"Your account received funds as usual. Is your passport up-to-date and legal? No! Don't answer that last question! It's better not to know. Is the name for making reservations the same customary one?"

"Why, I'm Sean D. O'Rourke, the 'D' is for Dillon, Emmie, just a bloke visitin'… seein' the Italian countryside! And don't worry, lass, I'll be gettin' 'here on me own with no fuss. I'll be meetin' ye in 'bout three days from now. Just tell Pete to book me as Sean O'Rourke, and 'e knows me peculiar preference for a corner room nearest the first floor, or as close to it as they can arrange to 'ave."

"Peter has all your flight information at the office so contact him to arrange when to pick it up."

"I'll be sendin' ye my bill when we're finished, m' girl," he said, and the phone clicked dead.

Emma instructed Peter to transfer an additional two thousand pounds into Dillon's account in the firm to cover his personal travel expenses. In the beginning of their working association, they established unspoken guidelines to make their relationship work …somehow it had evolved into a comfortable idiosyncratic relationship for both of them.

Sean Dillon O'Rourke is a tall, muscular, good-looking middle-aged man with black wavy hair, slightly graying temples and a full mustache. Years of hard physical work kept his well-proportioned appearance of a younger bloke with considerable muscular strength. What charms most folks are his soft, clear blue eyes—penetrating and disquieting. His beguiling charm can disarm any man or woman to reveal information to him when he puts his mind to it. If this trait fails, he has his own relentless persuasive ways to find answers and information.

\* \* \*

Emma couldn't help but recall her first meeting with the Irishman.

That first meeting with S.D. O'Rourke occurred as a new attorney shortly after joining Kavanaugh, Ltd., when she served him a summons at the Black Swan Pub in Soho—the pub was Dillon's listed business address. It was never clear how that symbiotic relationship for him and the pub began, but the locals understood the rear booth in the pub was never occupied by anyone except S.D. O'Rourke. Emma expected it was because the booth was nearest the phone and rear exit. Only much later did she learn that Dillon was in the private investigator business—legitimately—and worked out of the pub.

At the time, she was searching for a reputable private investigator to assist her in the MacEachen case. It was Mrs. Tibitts, no less, who brought up his name—she put Emma on to Dillon's expertise as an curious kind of investigator with exceptional skills, good connections, and has an "inside track" to the most unexpected places.

"I don't think you'll make a mistake in using Mr. Dillon O'Rourke to help you with the MacEachen case—I've heard he gets results!" she said. Emma had some instinctual misgivings about Dillon's past, initially—queries told her his name was bandied about with the IRA as well as the Irish underground. But further investigation refuted all the rumors as groundless. Despite the unfounded rumors, Emma liked Dillon the first day she met him in the Black Swan Pub, when he invited her to sit for a drink despite her serving him a court summons. She liked his directness, the spontaneity in his queries, and the truthfulness in his answers. Dillon was exactly the private investigator she wanted to work with her.

With Mrs. Tibitts recommendation in mind, she had to consider how she would convince him to work with her. One night, Emma hatched a plan how to convince Dillon to work on the MacEachen case with her. She ventured into the Black Swan Pub to enjoy a night out. It was common practice for the locals to target a single woman—they had the propensity to target "the crack" toward the "single tarts," but Emma felt she could handle them. Once inside the pub, for some unknown reason, there were no whistles or cat-calls from the men toward her—taking their cue from the man in the rear booth. Dillon walked over to Emma and introduced himself. Immediately, they experienced a friendly interaction—as if they might have known each other before that meeting. It was Emma who remembered she once served a summons to him in this very pub. Not until a much later date did she discover that Peter, too, knew Dillon from a former employer. Emma was never able to learn how their mutual beginnings really started!

Their work together in the MacEachen case proved they were "cut from the same cloth." In spite of his earthy, abrupt manner, Dillon was a man with great integrity with an uncanny ability to quickly interpret a situation to ferret out facts, not always immediately evident to Emma. Nothing and no one intimidated him. His place of business began to grow on Emma. At first, Dillon resisted the proposition to work on the MacEachen Case, Emma thinking he resisted because she was a female attorney. That was the farthest reason from the truth. It was not until after they worked on several cases did the true reason come to light.

Dillon's commitment to the MacEachen case was undaunted. He used every connection he had from Whitehall to Downing Street, from the alleys of East End London to Rotten Row and Regent Street. It was as if he had his own personal agenda, connected, in some way, with the MacEachen's plight. Most people are never privy to a hidden part of Dillon, the real man—at least not until he put them through his kind of analysis. Only then, did he let them into his complete trust, and allow someone to penetrate that hard exterior facade to find a thoughtful, caring, and even loving Dillon. Another revealing fact Emma discovered was the scope of his numerous contacts, all on a familiar first-name basis, too, all influential entities; members of Scotland Yard, names in the National Security Department, and even members from both houses of Parliament; reinforcing her instinct that his past was dark and very private.

A year later it was Peter who confided to Emma a startling fact—Dillon was once married and had a family in his past. Peter explained that he once held a position in a government department when he was a young man…no one knew exactly—or would say— what kind of job it was—something to do with deep security with a national agency. Then it became known he just up and left his government position. He relocated to London from Ireland, living somewhere in the Soho area with the Black Swan Pub his office— and second home. His real home address was so secret no one ever knew where he went when he was not at the pub, a secret he still scrupulously guards to this very day. Emma explored the internet and other public sources looking for a listing for Dillon O'Rourke. It was as if he didn't exist in the cyberworld. Emma heard rumors that he had ties in Swinton Barrow, but this may have been a planted rumor he wanted circulated about to misdirect anyone trying to learn his real place of residence. Neither she nor Peter could help but wonder what made him go to such great security lengths about his home and privacy. Emma respected Dillon's need for privacy and never crossed that line.

Once the ground rules were known it didn't take long for Dillon to accept Emma as an equal. The only rule they agreed on—she didn't try to change him, and he didn't try to change her. For, truth be told, Emma actually felt good knowing Dillon was at her back in their cases. The MacEachen and Moore cases made the difference. Emma Llewelyn became Dillon's own private responsibility. She always thought his protectiveness toward her was because she became his surrogate family, taking the place of the one he once had.

Many times, Emma asked herself the question, "What *did* happen to his family and where are they now?"

Eventually she did learn why Dillon had such personal drive. One particular late night, Peter, Dillon and Emma were working in the office conference room going over material gathered from multiple sources associated with the Moore family, hoping to find some important piece of information they missed. A phone call came for Dillon on his mobile phone. At the end of the conversation, he left abruptly without an explanation calling out from the door, "I'll contact you tomorrow!"

It was Peter who remarked, "It was not a family call that took him away."

"Why do you say that, Peter?"

Peter repeated the facts to Emma. "I don't know all the particulars, but Dillon once had a family in Kildarggen. A wife, Maura, and a daughter, Siobhan, and the three lived outside Kildarggen, Ireland. Dillon was away on his usual government assignment, something to do with national security, when he returned home from that assignment he found his wife and daughter missing. Of course, his own government department investigated their disappearance, but nothing was ever really discovered why they just disappeared from Kildarggen. None of the townsfolk remembered seeing them for several weeks, thinking they traveled to England to see her parents while Dillon was away, as they were known to do. Dillon has spent the last five years or more searching for them in his own way. That whole thing changed him. When he left his government position he became a private investigator. This is why he works so hard on these missing person's cases with you." Peter gave me all the answers I was looking for.

\* \* \*

Her instincts about him were right on the quid then, and now she felt the same kind of confidence about the Rudolphi case. Dillon's skills and contacts were vital if they were to find answers about the Rudolphis. When she accepted the Lucinda Rudolphi case, it was done with a mental agreement that Dillon would work it with her. Because of his own personal grief, she counted on his deep commitment, again, to find answers for Lucinda and for her. *I know his kind of dedication is rare—and thank God I have him!* She thought. There was no one else she would trust to work with her to find out why Emma Llewelyn is on a list locked in Marcus Rudolphi's villa.

The Rudolphi case made Emma fully realize just how much Dillon O'Rourke was an intregral part of the firm—even more so—a special friend, and a first-rate investigator. But most importantly, Emma felt this case had some common tie that bound them together…just a feeling…with no realistic basis…but it was there.

101

Is it possible Milano may hold answers for both of us, my friend?

# CHAPTER TWELVE

Emma phoned the London Municipal Public Library to ask the curator to locate both current and past sources of information on the history of the Rudolphi Family as well as the history of the *Rudolphi International Winery in Milano*.

When she arrived at the library, the curator gave her what he selected for her. Once she collected enough information about the private lives of the Rudolphi family, and public articles about the winery, she'd make copies of everything to take with her. As she read some of the information about Tuscany, it triggered a singular memory… her last visit there. The closer the date came for the trip to Italy, the more she found her thoughts turned to Carlos…and the last time they were together.

*When I accepted this case, I knew there might be a remote possibility Carlos could be in Milano at the same time Dillon and I are there. It seems no matter how hard I try to dismiss what happened at our last meeting eight months ago…everything we last said to each other…each moment is still all so vividly clear in my mind… he's always in my thoughts!"*

That time her flight to London…alone…emotional feelings of betrayal…and anger. *Why can't I move on and forget my anger… Looking back," I must accept with banal honesty—I fell in love with the man on the hilltop!"*

*Will I be able to do my job in Italy...keep my feelings for Carlos separate? I cannot deny—there's a man I still love—and he lives in Milano!*

\* \* \*

## AN AFFAIR TO REMEMBER...

Emma found her thoughts slipping back to that experience...that glorious trip to Tuscany almost two years ago, when everything in her life changed.

Again, standing on that Umbrian hilltop, I can see that splendid spring day, and feel the soft, cool, distant ocean breezes caress me as I waited for the garage truck.

I had traveled to Tuscany before, but this time I chose to spend my spring holiday in the Umbrian hills. Tucked away on a hilltop, I found this quaint little villa on the outskirts of the sleepy town, called Gubbio. My hideaway was the Villa del Costello for the whole month of May in a mountainous corner of Umbria. The medieval lifestyle in this town is not yet well known to the outside world. With its quiet streets, this hidden jewel called Gubbio sits perched on the slopes of Monte Inguino. Because the town is actually carved into the mountain, the laddered streets are dramatically steep, not one on level ground in the whole town. The usual seasonal tourists haven't yet found this place even at the height of summer holidays, which is why the Italians give it the nickname "*La Citta del Silenzio*"—"the City of Silence."

A car is definitely a necessity out in the Italian countryside, and I rented a Porsche for my holiday stay; a model I knew would perform well on the steep and tortuous mountain roads. On my second day, it was a clear, warm spring day, and I decided on a trip, a *gita*—a little trip to *San Remo* on the east coast of *Golfo di Genova*. Rising early that morning, I informed Maria, my housekeeper, of my plans for the day trip to the coast. She willingly told me the best directions from the villa to San Remo pointing out the route to me on my map. The trip route would be an hour's drive on one of the lesser-traveled Autostradas. Tossing a few things in the back, I left very early to avoid any heavy traffic. Listening to the wind whistling down from the mountains, I was lost in the beauty of the drive while putting the car to its maneuvers on the switchback turns, when suddenly I felt the car swerve with a loud noise coming from the underside. Coaxing the car slowly off to the side of the road, I saw the tire was totally flat and punctured. With the nearest town several kilometers away, it was obvious the car would not make it into the town garage for repair without causing further damage. Feeling disappointed and rebuking myself for not learning mechanics to change a tire, my only recourse was to get help from the nearest town. Placing a call to the town garage on my mobile, I asked for repair aid.

*"Allo?* My tire is flat…I'm about ten kilometers away…Can you come fix it?"

*"Il mio pneumatico e` patteo…di dieci chilmoetre lontano. Lie lo puo reparare?"*

With a minimal understanding from the Italian-speaking mechanic, I managed to interpret that their repair truck would reach me in thirty minutes or more.

*"Si, grazie."*

What they really meant was, I would see them in an hour on the hilltop. On such a extraordinary warm spring day, I certainly wasn't going to sit and wait in the car…deciding, instead, to climb up to a small ridge on the hillside to wait for the garage truck; to a place atop the hillside where I could plainly see them coming. Leaning against the trunk of a fruit tree, I smelled the mountain's scents on the gentle breezes rolling in from the distance, conjuring up a hint of salt air coming from the distant blue ocean of San Remo. My surroundings made for a quiet, peaceful feeling on the hilltop in an *almost* perfect world, and felt less dejected.

I saw the car coming around the curve; it slowed down as it neared the Porsche.

I watched the driver park the Gia on the dirt shoulder. A tall, dark-haired young man emerged and walked over to inspect my parked car…totally unaware of my presence above him. He just stood and gazed around looking for the occupants. It was more his manner that kept my attention riveted on him as he neared the hillside. He was close enough to distinctly see his handsome features and well-tanned face. Dressed in old jeans, a sleeveless sweatshirt, and sandals, he looked like someone who worked outdoors—I noticed his tanned skin. His dark hair, tousled from the blowing wind, had a natural look. Watching him remove his sunglasses, I saw he had the softest brown eyes. The sight below me captivated me in silence for a few more minutes before I wanted to make my presence known. Then, in a quick turn of his head, he looked up. I acknowledged his look with a wave.

*He saw her up above...the sun shining on her dark hair tussled by the wind. As the image before him descended, he whispered... "Vedo stare in piedi di bellezza sul hill...in vigone fra gli alberi ed I firori!" 'I see beauty standing on the hilltop...standing among the trees and flowers.'*

Shading his eyes, he said, "I can see you need some help, *Signorina*. What happened?" He asked in English with a hint of an Italian accent. I wondered how he knew I was English-speaking without me first speaking.

"It looks like the left rear tire punctured when I hit a ditch back in the road," I said, pointing to it.

"This happens many times if you are not familiar with these hilly roads. Let me see what I can do."

I made my way back down to the roadside to the car.

"I did call the local garage—*il garage locale*, but they can't come out for an hour or more, so I was reconciled to sit and wait. I really didn't mind on such a beautiful day here on this hilltop!" I said, looking around at the expansive view to prove my point.

He made no effort to acknowledge my explanation. I repeated my explanation again, "I really was enjoying the quiet of the hillside and taking in the beautiful view of the distant hills, not paying close attention to the road conditions. There doesn't seem to be much traffic on this road, which was one reason I chose this route to San Remo. You are very kind to stop and help me."

Without uttering a word, he just smiled, hooked his sunglasses in the neck of his shirt, and headed for the boot of the car, motioning for me to follow him.

"Will you please open the boot for me"?

I did as he asked and went over to see if I could help him. I knew I wouldn't be much assistance to him and felt distinct vibes that he didn't like small talk while he was working. So I just watched silently. His muteness made me all the more determined to find out more about this man on my hilltop. He went about changing the tire as if he had done it many times before, answering my questions in monosyllables or with a simple nod. In twenty minutes, he had the tire changed, stored the flat tire in the boot, and wiped his hands on the cloth inside the boot.

"Please accept my thanks, and how can I repay you for your help?" I asked, reaching for my bag in the front seat of the car. I was prepared to pay him for his services. It was an absolute surprise when instead he took my hand and bowing gently he kissed it.

"Payment will be for you to allow me to take you to dinner tonight, *Signorina*."

His request caught me off guard…He was waiting for my response! His hands felt soft even after doing such a dirty job! Not expecting his invitation, I couldn't think of a quick reason not to accept his invitation as I faltered to answer him. My first thought was to quickly decline his invitation. My honesty told me I wanted to see him again!

"You know, I haven't been out to dinner since I arrived here in Tuscany…Yes, I'd like that very much."

At his suggestion, we agreed to meet at the *Taverna del Lupo* at eight o'clock in Gubbio. Searching for something more to say before we parted, I said, "I've heard of the Tavern of the Wolf but haven't been there to dine." I was thinking, what must he think?…I already said that to him! Quickly collecting my thoughts, I knew I wanted to drive to the *ristorante* separately; I wanted to keep my residence private, and besides, if the evening was less than expected, I could dream up an excuse and leave on my own. That way, I'd still have my privacy for the rest of my holiday…no loss…no gain.

"Yes, I'll meet you there…at eight o'clock."

"Start your engine, and I'll wait to make sure everything is running fine."

I watched him in the rearview mirror standing on the roadside as I pulled out onto the highway 'til he was almost out of sight. On last glance—he made a quick motion to his watch; he was reminding me we have an eight o'clock date. Driving home, I found myself humming…when I realized I didn't even get his name nor he mine! I felt like a schoolgirl, flushed at the thought of meeting a new young man for dinner.

"It's just a simple dinner to repay him for his kindness!" I rebuked myself. Still, I couldn't rid myself of the eager and happy feeling I felt…knowing I would see him again. I would make San Remo on another day and returned to the Villa del Costello.

Reaching the villa, I explained to Maria what had happened and decided to try another day for San Remo. The coolness inside the villa was a relief. In the kitchen, Maria was busy preparing wonderful dishes for dinner.

"Maria, I have a dinner date tonight and will be eating out. Why don't you take the evening off to spend with your family? I won't need you until breakfast."

"*Grazie, Signora. Si,* my family will appreciate me with them today. *Grazie!*"

Maria and her large family lived in a cottage at the bottom of the hill at the entrance to the Villa del Costello. The whole family participated in the keep of the villa; each assigned specific chores. Umberto, her husband, did all the gardening; Sophia, her oldest daughter, took care of the house and linens. The rest of the children all had a particular task to do each day, but most days they played in the garden, except if I was sunning in the gardens. Evidently, it was a house rule that if the guest was in the gardens, it was off-limits to the children.

I caught sight of the hot, fiery sun beginning to dip in the west behind the hills. The heat of the early spring sun was beginning to compete with the late afternoon cool breezes, now blowing stronger. Second thoughts began to nag me about this dinner agreement for tonight. *How did I get myself into this situation?* Thinking more about tonight, I thought, *Why didn't I ask his name? Stupido! How could I agree to meet a complete stranger for dinner?*

I began considering all kinds of excuses *not* to have dinner with this stranger. *How can I cancel?…I don't even know his name…or how to reach him! I'm acting more like a schoolgirl on her first date!*

I thought, rebuking myself. Trying to end my turmoil of thoughts, I decided, *Maybe a long leisurely bath would put my mind at ease, and I can think about what to wear!*

The warm bath gave me time to think about what I should wear—considering nothing formal or too casual, a dress that would suit any occasion. The sapphire-blue chiffon-hankerchief dress was cool, loose, and casual and could be considered either casual or dressy...I'll wear my hair down—the real me.

"Yes...the blue chiffon...," I said. Admonishing myself for letting simple decisions become complex ones, I exclaimed, "It's just a simple dinner, Emma!"

I finished dressing and checked the mirror once more for final approval, slipped my sandals on, and grabbed the purple silk stole in case the night became too cool. Walking through the living room, I had to take one last glance in the full-length hall mirror.

"Good choices. It's doable!" I started out down the driveway for Gubbio.

Twilight was beckoning as I drove down the hillside into town, even though I had come to know the mountain road fairly well, I was glad to have the natural light driving into town. Arriving at the *Taverna del Lupo*, I parked the car close to the entrance and saw his Gia parked nearby...Thankfully, I wasn't the first to arrive. The Tavern of the Wolf was rustic and filled with old-world charm with the most incredible smells of food and wine greeting me. Emerging from the bright evening light into the dimly lit doorway, I stopped to adjust to the dimness of the room. An elderly *cameriere*, dressed in black attire with the typical black and white striped vest, greeted me. Attempting to explain to him in Italian that I was there to meet a gentleman for dinner, he immediately knew what I was trying to say and showed me inside, instructing me to follow him.

"*Si Signora*, we've been expecting you. *Questa maniera, per favore?*"

He led me to the farthest end of the room, where the candles on the tables were the only source of light. Passing several couples already finished with their meals, I heard hushed tones of laughter.

He rose to meet me as the *cameriere* escorted me to the corner table in a small bay off the large dining room. The soft, low candlelight exaggerated the warmth in his dark eyes and his spontaneous smile made him even more handsome tonight than I remembered on the hillside. The blue chiffon dress was the perfect choice when I saw he was casually dressed; slacks, open shirt, and jacket!

"Hello again," he said, taking my hand with the usual Italian greeting, a gentlemanly kiss on each cheek.

"I must apologize for my rudeness this afternoon. I did not introduce myself to you or get your name. I am Carlos Esteves."

"Carlos, I'm Emma Llewelyn." I gave him my hand. He bent with a gentle kiss to my hand, all the while capturing my eyes in a long acknowledgement. He seated me across the candlelit table.

"I'm very glad to meet you, Emma." His warm smile and captivating charm made me feel very good about being there with him.

"After we parted this afternoon, I was afraid you would change your mind and since I did not know your name or where you lived, I thought I might never see you again. And that would be my great loss," he said softly, looking directly at me. I saw and heard honesty in this man. He ordered a bottle of Merlot wine and poured my glass.

"Did you have any trouble with the car on your way home this afternoon?"

"No, none, I actually enjoyed the ride back to the villa. I was planning on spending the day in San Remo when my tire punctured. As an omen from the Gods I decided to postpone my trip for another day and returned home instead. I'll make San Remo another day," I said laughingly.

"Be certain you do. It's a very romantic place to go. It's a lovers' resort by the sea."

Immediately, I felt at ease talking to him, and I was glad I had met this man. The evening slipped by as we sipped wine and talked about our lives—laughing a lot.

"Tell me about Carlos?" I asked.

"My family are farmers and has lived on a large farm in the Umbria region for several generations, growing olives and lemons. My father was born on that very farm and my brothers and sisters were born there, too. I was not. I was born in hospital in Firenze. My

110

mother was visiting her parents when I came along!" he laughed. "So, I am considered the black sheep in the family for this beginning."

He made me feel so comfortable; all facades gone and together we felt the ease of a singular familiarity with each other.

"To further my special family status, I was the one to leave the farm to attend college in Roma, eventually entering the diplomatic field, where I'm presently assigned to the embassy in Roma...though Milano will always be my home. I have a flat there where I go to get away from the throngs of Roma. Roma is too big! Milano? She is as big as I like a city to be!"

As he was telling me this memorable story, I couldn't help notice his little gestures. How he would look directly at me when he spoke—indicating an openness and sincerity. Touching my hand in a warm caress...I realized he was caring. Carlos explained that he had several brothers and sisters, some still living and working on the family farm, while others moved to the southern part of Italy, explaining that all of them were raising large families and making his father very happy.

"My father has all but given up on me!"

I had to ask if there was a Mrs. Esteves.

"Not yet. Someday, I hope there will be, but until I find her just Zeus and Apollo live with me, my dogs!" His gazes at me were long as if he were quietly studying me.

"I have done all the talking! Now it's your turn. Tell me about Emma Llewelyn."

I gave him a brief history of my Welsh and American upbringing. "I was born in Wales and lived my early years with my grandfather, Cyrus MacKenna, on a farm called Lyn Brienne with our housekeeper, who is like a mother to me. My mother died when I was born. My grandfather, I call him Papa, raises and races Arabian Thoroughbred horses. When I was fourteen, I traveled to live with my father in Greenwich, Connecticut, where I went to college and law school at Yale University. After passing the bar examinations there, I returned to England, studied for my barrister's degree, and I today I practice law in London."

He seemed most interested in how and when I started my law firm in London. I was surprised to learn he knew of some of my legal successes.

"I didn't realize that kind of information circulated in the diplomatic community," I told him.

"Your grandfather in Wales, does he breed and selectively sell mares and colts to those who can afford one of his prized Arabian horses?"

"Why yes! You have heard of him?"

"Most assuredly! I know of his excellent reputation here in Italy where his horses have won some very prestigious racing cups! I feel I am in the presence of one of Wales's most famous families!"

"No, not at all! We're simple, plain Welsh country folk!" I said, smiling at him.

"Then you must be a good horse rider if you grew up on a horse farm?" he stated as more of a question.

"Yes, I love to ride! Do you ride?" I asked him.

"*Si*, we had several work horses on the farm, mostly for working and tilling the land. I would take them out and ride bareback with my father trying to chase me down. I loved to ride alone out to the hills, to feel the breezes blow against me." He paused with reminiscing thoughts. "Those memories are the best ones!" he said, looking down as if to catch that same feeling again.

"Yes, I know what you mean. I have a special mare...her name is Ddu Kate. She's beautiful and ebony black. I take her out whenever I'm back on the farm, and we just ride through all the pastures— feeling free as an untamed spirit...jumping as many stone walls as we can find. I think the both of us have some gypsy in us, loving the sense of independence and oneness with the hills!"

Taking hold of my hand across the table, he said, "Maybe some day we can go riding together, Emma."

"Yes, I'd like that very much, Carlos."

Sipping our wines, our thoughts and conversation seemed to be about how much our lives had in common. Carlos ordered dinner for both of us, which turned out to be a very light and filling meal and perfect for the night. When the cappuccino came, I realized how comfortable this whole evening had been with this man. We never ran out of something to talk and laugh about—and I found myself wishing the night wouldn't end. He seemed to be as comfortable with me as I was with him.

Remembering I still had the long drive back to the villa, I said, "Carlos, I really must go now. It's late and after today's car trouble, I don't relish the idea of driving a long distance back to my villa at a very late hour. I *really* enjoyed our dinner *and* the company even more!"

Walking me to my car, he opened the door as I slipped in behind the wheel. He surprised me! Gently leaning into the car he kissed me ever so lightly…his lips soft and moist.

"May I see you again, Emma, while you're here on holiday?"

I found myself telling him, "I'm staying at the Villa del Costello for several more weeks. If you like, call me tomorrow—I have no plans cast in stone. The number is TUL88440." Slowly driving away, I glanced in my rearview mirror; he was casually standing in the shadowy light of the doorway.

*I definitely want to know more about this man! I only hoped he has the same feelings about me. Will he **really** call me tomorrow?*

*So **she's** the reason for Mac's obsessive compulsion to keep his job a mystery! What would he do if he knew **I** wanted to pursue this relationship?* Carlos thought.

# CHAPTER THIRTEEN

A loud noise suddenly jolted Emma's attention back to the present moment—back to the library!

*"I'm losing valuable time and the only opportunity I'll have to get this information before the trip! I need to stop thinking about the past—about him. It's the present that's important now—Emma concentrate on the real reason I'm going to Milano—to find answers for Lucinda and me. I can't allow Carlos to dominate my thoughts on this trip!*

At odds with herself, Emma shrugged off her reminiscent attitude and focused her thoughts on fact finding for answers for Lucinda—more importantly to find answers for herself! Still, the thought nagged her, *Why does Carlos still have this hold on me? There should be no way Carlos would know I'll be in Italy...not unless I make my presence known to him, and I'm certainly not planning on doing that!* Reassuring herself, she thought, *There won't be any reason for me to contact him, especially since he's made no effort to get in touch since that last day...over eight months ago.* "The agreement was mutual...and final! We went our separate ways. Then why do I keep hoping our paths will cross again? Will that ever really happen?" she said, softly speaking out her thoughtful questions.

With a firm resolve, she turned to start viewing film-tapes. The tapes were newspapers articles and periodicals about the Rudolphis. Emma started scanning microfilms for any mention or picture of the well-known Milanese family—hoping to see a picture of Marcus and Lucinda Rudolphi together.

"I need material on as many different members from the Rudolphi family as I can find."

Searching back several earlier years, news articles described how the whole family was involved in the wine business. More than occasionally, there were articles about social events; a society note reporting a party—listing the guests attending.

"It appears Marcus and Lucinda Rudolphi did a lot of entertaining at their Villa del Christianna. It is as Lucinda said, one single name stands out—listed in most of the social accounts—the name, Dr. Ennio Carruchi, is on all these guest lists!"

*Dr. Ennio Carruchi is one person to get as much information about as possible!* A thought came to her, *I wonder—if Dillon ever heard of this man...in his past adventures?*

Quickly reading the articles, she learned that the Rudolphi Winery was a prestigious and lucrative business within the international community—they had won many awards for prized wines.

"I had no idea this winery did such a big business—and equally internationally competitive, too!"

While printing out the articles on the Rudolphis history and their status in the wine industry, Emma continued to search for more data. So far, most of these facts appeared to be related to their successful business enterprises...What she needed was more personal information about the family members in this Milanese family! Perusing the literature, Emma discovered that the Rudolphis had controlled a very large part of the Tuscany countryside for many generations.

Looking up their genealogy, she found a whole section of personal history on the Rudolphis dating back to the seventeenth century. These are the kind of facts she needed to know—who are the people that make up the Rudolphi family today? Seeing the extent of this section, she decided it was too lengthy to read in one sitting and decided to select pages from the texts about the family to print out—making double copies for Dillon, too. To make certain she'd have an accurate and fairly complete history, Emma decided to sign out more historical reference books to take back to the office to read and copy—she had only three days to complete this research.

The curator was understandably resistant to let the tapes out of the library. Relying on her influential and professional legal standing, Emma managed to convince the curator she'd take very good care of the research tapes and promised—with her life and professional licence—she'd return them in three days without fail. Now she really began to feel apprehensive about what she still had to finish before her departure to Italy!

Replacing the rest of the tapes and books in the stacks, Emma turned and suddenly collided with a dark, swarthy looking man—knocking the book out of his hand.

"Please forgive me, I didn't mean"…In a flash, the man turned, leaving the book lying on the floor, and ran quickly out of the stacks before she could apolgize.

*I've seen that man before…but where?* Emma prodded her memory but couldn't associate details of a time or place. As she was picking up the book he dropped, a card fell out.

"*Il distributore di vecchi libri il manuscripts, Il Famoso Majoli Negozio, Milano, Italia.*

"Dealer of Old books and Manuscripts,"Emma read the card…*an Il Famoso Majoli Negozio Shoppe in Milano?* It jarred something…conjured up a scene…*a past memory?*

**somewhere long ago...an old picture hanging on a stone wall...dusty and dirty...dying embers...a large canopied bed...**

Shaking off the cold feeling of some past memory, she thought, *"Think only about Milano, Emma! You leave in four days!"* Emma placed the business card in her briefcase. *Maybe I'll inqire about the shoppe when I get to Milano.*

# ITALIA-SONATA

# CHAPTER FOURTEEN

All too quickly—the date to fly to Italy arrived!

That last day in London was spent going over details with Peter about her other cases. They reviewed the list of work he needed to do in her absence. Hurriedly packing for her trip, Emma kept telling herself if she forgot something personal she could get it in Italy. Most importantly—she made certain she packed her briefcase with all the copies of the research information, her passport, flight information, along with a recorder and a laptop, and the two tapes from Lucinda Rudolphi's meeting.

"Peter, I'll contact you as soon as I'm settled in the hotel. In an emergency, you can reach me on my mobile. Remember, to anyone who inquires, I'm on holiday!"

The drive to Heathrow Airport was uneventful; Emma left much earlier than necessary, making certain she had plenty of time to pass through the extra custom checkpoints since terrorism became top priority in these megalopolis ports. She located the long-term parking garage with ease. Taking the transport bus from the garage to the terminal, Emma still had ample time before flight boarding. Exiting the terminal bus, an eager attendant approached her to take her bags to the ticket counter. The terminal was crowded and busy and all the ticket counters were manned and working to capacity. It was spring holiday in Europe, and travelers were taking advantage, despite the heightened security—and the long departure process. She felt a rush of anticipation at the thought that she was really flying to *Italy* again! But Emma challenged her feelings—was she eager to start this new case, or was it that Milano meant she might see Carlos again?

Emma was too deep in her thoughts to notice the man in a raincoat, bowler hat, and umbrella a short distance behind her—appearing disinterested in her while reading his newspaper, but casting frequent glances toward her as she passed through customs.

Boarding Air Italia went without incident.

"At last! Italy in a few hours." To stay focused on the Rudolphi case in flight, Emma worked on the Bufford case on her computer and sent an email to Peter about last minute memoranda in the Bufford case along with additional up-dated telephone numbers if he had to contact her in Italy. Emma trusted Peter to make the necessary discreet decisions for the firm in her absence, and knew that if it was necessary to get her imput, he would contact her. Then, too, he always had Olivia to consult for unexpected emergencies.

The flight landed on time in Rome's international airport. The warm air rushed at her walking down the ramp stairs to the tarmac where the bus waited for the deplaning passengers. Rome's temperature felt like spring.

"Those poor buggers in London are still coping with the cold spring rains! Only the lucky few can get away, and I'm glad it's me! It's definitely the best time of year in Italy."

After passing through several checkpoints, Emma found the car rental agency. Peter made the arrangements, and all she had to do was pick up the keys. The Peugeot was a replica of her old one, and she was very familiar with its performance and felt comfortable tackling the mountains north to Milano. The road maps indicated the best route was up the coastal highway, revealing lush views of the countryside—from the hilltops down to the sea. History was everywhere here! Someone once told her, "To know Italy is to know its soul."

Though her heritage was *Cymru*, *Italia* captured her heart. The latest maps she purchased at the rental agency, one of Roma and another of Toscana, clearly showed the most direct route would be the Autostradas. The wait was lengthy to clear customs and retrieve her luggage which gave her a chance to make travel plans and calculate when she would arrive at the Hotel di Manini to meet Dillon. Driving out of Rome was noisy and confusing to get on the Via Parigi II, where she headed north from Roma. Once in the rural countryside, she was able to see how the land was twisted into weird shapes from the many prehistoric upheavals that took place millennia ago—making Italia what it is today. It was Carlos who told her about these seacoast towns built of the local purple-black volcanic rock.

With her mind cought up in thought, it seemed like a very short time when Emma came to Cerveteri—known for its medieval Etruscan heritage, particularly the Rocca, castle, of Orsini, owned by the prominent Ruspoli family.

Continuing up the coast, Emma passed Santa Marinella and Tarquinia, eventually reaching the part of Italia, called Toscana, in early afternoon.

"This is a good place to stop for lunch," she said, realizing her last meal was on the plane early that morning. Driving around several *piazzas* looking for a place to eat and refuel the car, she saw several churches and a small bistro right off the main *piazza* route. The sun played with casting shadows on the streets and shops—shades of purple, pink and grey. Entering the small café, Emma saw many empty tables.

"I missed the lunch crowd."

A *cameriere* suggested the special lunch pasta salad, and she left her choice up to him. At his encouragement, she had their local wine, a fine *vino blanco*, or white wine. As Emma finished the last bite, her little waiter came over to ask if he had made the right choice.

Emma replied, *"Perfecto,"* and gave him extra Euros for his attentiveness. Before leaving, she asked if she could reach Firenze, Florence, by nightfall. He assured her in his best spoken English she should drive the distance and find lodgings there before dark falls.

Once back on the northerly coastal route, the traffic noticably increased. Unaware of the silver Lamborghini, which though distinctive, remained a fair distance behind the Peugeot, Emma's concentration was on the countryside, not the rear traffic. The drive up the Via Manzoni was without incident—her thoughts carefree—unsuspecting anyone was interested in her arrival in Italy.

Her thoughts. *Everywhere in Italy there's a feeling of time eternal, merging the present and the past together. I can see why the Tuscans brag that their countryside is the finest beauty in the whole of Italia. I think I'm actually sensing a holiday spirit despite my real reason for being here is work!*

Emma enjoyed the spectacular sight—*Firenze at dusk!* Lying halfway between Roma and Milano it is the quintessence of architectural and artistic beauty, and well deserved to be called the "Cradle of the Renaissance." Firenze preserved the best features of historical Tuscany. Remembering all she had discovered about Firenze—it offered so much more culturally, historically, and architecturally than other cities in this region! Most of its inhabitants never get to see all the treasures within their city.

"I'd have to spend a lot of time seeking out its treasures to really appreciate its exceptional beauty!" She remembered Carlos's words to her, *"Firenze has culture for everyone."*

"I promise—one day I'll make a trip back to Firenze to see it as it was meant to be seen! For tonight, I am only able to appreciate a good night's lodging and get an early morning start to reach Milano—and find Dillon!"

*"She is on schedule as expected—driving north to Milano—and alone tonight in Firenze."*

The man in the raincoat and bowler hat finished his brief message and disconnected his mobile call. Watching Emma turn into the drive to the *Torre Guelfa,* the Lamborghini slowed at a safe distance behind—then sped off north toward Milano.

# CHAPTER FIFTEEN

Darkness was complete in Firenze. The streets were dimly lit.

"There's a little known hotel-like inn called *Torre Guelfa*" located on a narrow street past one of these many *piazzas* in Firenze—I remember entering through an iron gate to take a lift to the third floor lobby. Inside—you're transported back to a thirteenth century Florentine tower that captures your imagination about how life was lived centuries past. I'm certain it's in this section!"

Emma remembered Carlos telling her about its historical significance—the modern changes still kept its aged-past ambience, and the knowledgeable traveler could still find a night's lodging at a moment's notice—its reputation not yet discovered. A century past, the Torre Guelfa was under the protection of a wealthy family, the Acciaiuoli family, who transformed it into one of best small hotel inns hidden in Firenze. The small parking area in the rear of the inn isn't visible from the street, which is why motorists easily pass by it. Emma knew exactly what to look for to find the hidden entrance to the parking area. She turned into the narrow passage.

The canopy of trees along the road hid the dimly lit entrance to the parking area in the rear next to the main entrance of the stone tower. There were three parked cars all with Italian plates. Emma chose a spot closest to the inn's entrance. Grabbing her overnight bag, she locked the Peugeot and went inside. Again, she sensed that same feeling—stepping back in time, not only architecturally, but her memories of her visits here with Carlos. Those same unforgettable feelings she felt when she and Carlos walked inside for the first time—and again, the same experience now. Nothing had changed. "It's exactly as I remember it! A hidden jewel!"

At the desk, Emma requested, *"Posse avere una stanza ed un bagno per una notte?"*

An elderly woman dressed in the traditional black old-country attire led Emma upstairs to a room overlooking the *piazza*. She was glad it wasn't the room Carlos and she had been in together! The room was moderately large and overlooked the sloping street leading down to the *Piazza del Centro* where a few wandering town's folk ambled. The walls and ceiling of the room were painted stark white, creating a disorientating affect. With the lack of color, the dark baronial pieces of furniture stood out in harsh disparity—the décor simple utilitarian. The absence of color and warmth was begging to be filled with the presence of color from an occupant.

The sheer white canopy over the bed could be used as netting at night if needed. Behind a paneled wooden door was a completely white-tiled bathroom, with a claw-footed tub and adapted shower fixtures. Hot and cold running water had been a recent renovation to a large marble sink, with the old washbowl and pitcher on the side stand as a reminder of the past. Though the lighting was dim, the glare off the glossy walls and floor tiles seemed to add several degrees of illumination to the room. All the fixtures were old European brassy Baroque, highly polished, glistening and properly working.

Placing her bag on the bed, Emma locked the door and started drawing the bath water. Falling onto the bed, she felt very tired, but didn't realize how much. What she still needed to do was figure out how much farther she had to drive to reach Milano tomorrow. Studying her maps, Emma jotted down certain reference points on the map to Milano.

"First thing in the morning, I'll confirm my reservations at the Hotel Manin to give them an estimated arrival time. I hope Dillon is already checked in and his rooms are to his liking!"

Fatigue was quickly overtaking her. Undressing, she slid into the warm freesia-scented bath water, and slowly her anxiety dissipated. Her thoughts, Lucinda—*Carlos—the list—Perugia*—everything merged together. Staving off the sleepy effects of the warm bath, she toweled down, slipped on her gown and crawled into bed. Turning the small light on dim, the silken bed covers felt so cool, crisp—pure ecstasy as she sank down slowly into the feathered-down—allowing it to envelop her.

"Tomorrow I will…"

* * *

The noise from the town square drifted into the room and roused Emma before the alarm rang. Opening her eyes, the brilliant morning sun's rays streaming in through the windows triggered a vague memory.

*Sunlight…rays…reaching down to me…kaleidoscope colors…the icy cold…*

She felt a shudder from a fleeting chill—even though the sun's rays streaming into the room felt warm.

"Why do I keep having these recurring thoughts…is it a dream?"

It took her several seconds to remember where she was and why.

"Oh yes…Firenze…I need to get to Milano *pronto!*"

Jumping out of bed, the memories of last night and her plan to reach Milano came flooding back. "Yes…I still have that drive to Milano to reach the hotel…I must get there no later than mid afternoon—I need to meet Dillon!"

Showering, dressing, and thinking about all she had to do in Milano only made her anxiety return. "Dillon and I definitely have to meet today—can't afford to lose precious time! There's a lot of information I need to brief him about—I'm certain he's 'biting the bit' waiting to hear the reason we're in Milano!"

She knew that Dillon would get to the nub of things quickly— once he's given the case facts, in no time he'll have a well-formulated plan.

"I can't help thinking his finely-honed characteristic is a product of his years in past government work. After he listens to the tapes of

Lucinda's meeting, we can lay out a plan together—where to begin to find answers for Lucinda and me!"

The recorder and two tapes, along with doubles of the articles, were still undisturbed in the locked briefcase.

"He has his homework cut out for him tonight!" Stowing the maps of Firenze, Milano, and the Toscana/Umbrian region in her bag, she said, "There will be answers for us this time—not like the MacEachen and Moore cases, *failure will **not be ours again!***"

Packing the rest of her personal things in her overnight bag, Emma walked down the three flights of circular stairs to the lobby level to check out. The woman at the desk was not the same woman as last night. Emma asked if she had any messages, but then—no one knew she would be staying there either.

*"Qualungue messaggi. Paghero `il ticchettare adesso, per favore."* Settling the tick, the woman said, *"Grazia, arrivederc."*

Crossing the *piazza* to a small café for a continental breakfast, Emma ordered cappuccino and fruit with some of their freshly baked pastry. She asked for a copy of the morning local paper, and a small young boy laden with a bag of papers quickly approached the table.

*"Mi scusi, Signora."* He handed her the paper. She gave him fifty Euros, which was more than he expected by the very large smile on his face. He walked away carefully counting his cash. She finished her breakfast, always her best meal of the day, but disappointedly found nothing about the Rudolphi family in the newspaper.

"Nothing newsworthy," she said and slipped the paper into her bag to walk the short distance up the hill to the car. Before she left the Torre Guelfa, Emma checked with the manager how long it would take to drive to Milano. Her Italian was flawless with a few broken English words interspersed—she figured it was only seventy kilometers. The map's directions indicated the quickest route was the Major Autostrada II—Emma could pick it up just two kilometers north from the inn—and it went directly through *Milano* continuing further north to Verrena and Switzerland.

The Peugeot just seemed to take off on its own, and Emma was its passenger. Driving out of the city, the morning dew was still shiny on the grass, and trees glistened in the sunlight. The car hugged the road with its tortuous twists; with each switchback, Emma felt the mercury drop a degree or two from the cool winds blowing down from the hills and far mountain range. The landscape was just as beautiful as she remembered it with hillsides of sloping vineyards, undulating in endless rows. In the distance, she saw an occasional open-columned villa atop a hill. For years, the Tuscan villas were purposely built on the top of hills to catch the mountain breezes to cool the dwellings. Modern electric air conditioners were for urban residences—nature's coolant was still thought the best. Most villas had large overhead sails–canopies—on the loggias to channel the natural breezes to blow, yet offer shade on the patios from the sun's rays—some measure of respite from the sweltering temperatures. Various villas had blue-tiled pools used to relieve the summer heat, but even the pool's waters, heated by the sun, could offer little respite from the sizzling summer heat. Life in the hills represented more endurable temperatures, clearer, starrier nights, and nature's abundant scents with sounds echoing more clearly. The *villas di Firenze* rivaled any Eden image.

*I just can't help wishing this trip ended in Firenze instead of Milano! This Renaissance Firenze is meant for holidays—AND there is less chance I'd see Carlos!*

The Autrostrada signs indicated Milano was near, anticipation and excitement hurried her on to reach the hotel and find Dillon.

"This rush of excitement...is it honest to say I want to meet with Dillon ...or... is it to find out if Carlos is in Milano?"

Shortly after the noon hour, Emma was on the outskirts of Milano amidst the church bells tolling the noon-hour, and inevitably the congested traffic forced her to slow down.

"I have a vague memory the direction of the Hotel Manin is this way...across from the public gardens—I need to head northeast."

At one of the roundabouts, Emma found a *poliziotto* in his reflective vest directing traffic and asked for directions to the Via d Manin. He pointed her left of the circular fountain without breaking the rhythm of his arms directing multiple inroads of traffic all the way through the roundabout. A few more kilometers and there it was!

"He was right—only a few city blocks away!"

Driving up the circular drive to the front colonnade, Emma parked the car and let the valet remove her luggage into the hotel. Peter had requested a hotel parking slot in their garage with Emma's reservations. The valets first retrieved each guest's luggage into the hotel and then parked their cars, remembering each car's parking slot for every guest. In her eagerness to reach the Manin, Emma didn't take notice that the same silver Lamborghini traveling behind her yesterday and following at a distance today—was already parked in front of the Manin.

The Hotel's beautiful columns at the front entrances, with their many marble acanthuses were meant to impress every guest with the regality of the façade.

"Yes…the Hotel Manin is perfect—with its central location and easy access to public transportation—and if necessary—we can get out of the city, avoiding congested traffic in this area. But I'd like to think really for the Guardino Publico—the Public Gardens! It's like having your own private garden estate if your room faces the north!"

Most importantly the area maps showed the Rudolphi Estate was located on the northeast side of the city, closest to the Hotel Manin!

The Manin's lobby astonished guests as they walked through it—as it did again with Emma. The rows of great marble colonnades swept their eyes up to the large central pink marbled staircase, gracefully dividing into two staircases leading up to the mezzanine level. The bright afternoon sun shone through a wall of colored glass panes, spewing brilliant impressions of shimmering colors—dancing lights down the stairs to the lobby floor. The affect was like a child looking through a kaleidoscope. The sight captured Emma's attention…

*A dark space…kaleidoscopic colors slipping down from tinted windows panes…down to the stone…cold…the cold stone floor…silence*

*Then—gone in a flash! Why do I keep having these feelings… these pictures from some past? But where? There's a memory trying to break through a wall in my mind! Why?*

The sounds of laughter, floating down from the balcony, wrenched her attention back to the opulent grandness of polished marble walls covered with thick Turkish wall-hangings. The columns in the lobby concealed the lifts to the upper and lower floors. Echoes of music came from the lounges—on the right was one with heavy baroque doors.

"I bet that's the lounge where I'll find Dillon."

*The Machiavelli Lounge!* On the opposite side of the lobby, there was a second lounge with frosted glass doors, *The Bello Sguardo,* 'Beautiful View out to the gardens.'

"I don't think the Garden Lounge is his style—too opulent! If I were a betting woman, I'd bet Dillon would be in the Machiavelli Lounge, and that's the first place I'll look!"

The last guest left the reception desk. "*Mi, chiano Emma Llewelyn...Varrei Una stanza...*"

"*Si, Signora Llewelyn*, I have your reservation here," he said in English. "You already have several messages here," he said and handed her two sealed envelopes with her name typed on the outside.

The uniformed attendant ushered Emma to her suite on the third floor. Entering, she saw a large beautiful domed-ceiling suite with a full balcony culminating in a spectacular view of the public gardens across the Via d Manin.

"Thank you, Peter, your choice of room is the perfect selection!" Immediately throwing open the balcony doors, Emma walked out onto the balcony and breathed in the view and the air.

"Is *he* somewhere out there in Milano?"

From her balcony with the view of the public gardens, Emma felt she was viewing her personal garden—with its red, graveled walkways bordered with beds of dahlias—its perfectly manicured Bocce grass surrounding the large central terrace. The showpiece of the terrace was a blue-tiled fountain with water cascading into the blue pool completely encircled by green sculpted hedges—the whole picture vying for competition with the majestic background—the Lepontine Mountains.

"What a marvelous majestic sight!"

The rugged Lepontine Alps rose in the distance with the higher peaks still covered with glistening frozen ice. Memories flooded Emma's mind of the times Carlos and she took their picnic trips up to the secret mountain pastures. *Picnics—soft breezes—beautiful surroundings—nuances of country noises—the smells of the mountain air in the winds sweeping down from the Lepontine Mountain Range to the soft pastures below.*

A car's loud honking horn startled her thoughts back to the moment—and reality.

Upon Emma's return back inside the room, the attendant asked, "Is everything to *Signora's* liking?"

"*Si,* very much so. *Grazie!*" He handed her the room key. Her bags were all on the stands and unlocked. Before doing anything, she grabbed the briefcase and handbag, left everything else, and went out of the suite locking the door. In the hall, Emma made a mental note that her suite was located at the farthest end from the lifts with the nearest exit door to stairs at the opposite end of the corridor—thinking, there may be times she'd want to take the stairs instead of the lift to get to Dillon's room. The lift door opened and she went to look for Dillon in the lobby.

The Machiavelli Lounge was quieter now, no music, dimly lit, with only a few patrons inside. Emma felt a surge of urgency and impatience to locate Dillon—Dillon was nowhere in sight.

"I could have sworn this would be the Lounge I'd find him in!" She next checked the *Bella Sguardo Lounge* which was brightly lit up.

"Definitely not Dillon's milieu!"

Not expecting to find him there, Emma decided to return upstairs to freshen up and then leave Dillon a message.

"*MY* messages! I forgot all about them…They must still be with my luggage in the room!"

The man in the silver Lamborghini made it a point to be inside the lobby of the hotel when Emma entered the lobby. As a way of making certain she didn't recognize him, he was no longer dressed in bowler hat, coat, and umbrella, now he was casually dressed in light slacks, jacket and different sunglasses and a summer cap. "Not a twinge of recognition!"

After he watched Emma tour the lounges, he left the lobby. The Lamborghini drove away from the Manin and entered a private drive to a small shop in a suburb of Milano, parking the car in the rear he went to the single entrance. At the entrance, he punched a code on the wall panel, spoke his name, and gave a password. Robotically, the door unlatched and swung open to let him enter—alone.

# CHAPTER SIXTEEN

The two messages were still on top of her luggage—unopened.

Opening the first one, she saw it was Dillon's discreet message, "Cocktails in the **M** lounge," with no signature.

The second message was from Peter. It surprised Emma to hear from him so soon! The message had to be urgent for him to contact her as soon as she arrived—it cryptically read, "Call the firm. Peter." There was a sealed telegram letter included with Peter's phone message.

Just as she opened the telegram, a knock came at the door, *"Si, avanti...uno momento!"* It was the concierge delivering a complimentary bottle of wine with a large bouquet of fresh flowers.

"How beautiful! Who are they from?" *Peter is the only one who knows I'm staying here...Why send me these gifts here?*

"*Signora,* there is no card with the flowers, and the wine is packaged as you see in the velvet box without a card." He held the wine up for Emma to see the lavish packaging. "They were delivered to the front desk with your name on them...I have no more information. I can have the matron put the flowers in a vase for you if you wish?"

"*Si, grazie!* Leave the wine on the bar." Thanking him for his service, Emma waited until he had left before she opened Peter's telegram.

"*Grazie, Signora,*" he said, closing the door. "They must be from Peter. Who else knows I'm here at the *Manin?*" Opening the telegram message, she read,

> "*Office burgled yesterday. Inventoried—only one missing item. Case files from archives at Royal Court of Justice—original CHATELAINE files—all missing from office safe.*
> *Complete Chatelaine transcription memorandum erased from hard disc—with other data.*
> *C-Files' transcription was saved to CD discs under different label—not Chatelaine—discs not taken—still safe! Break-in reported to police, did NOT report name of stolen files—need you to advise. PLEASE CONTACT ASAP.*"
> *Peter.*

Immediately dialing the office number, Emma remembered it may be too early to find Peter at the office unless he's working late—noting London's time difference. The number rang and rang.

"No answer!" Emma disconnected before the answering machine switched on. "Peter should have his mobile phone with him—I'll call him on that number," she said and next dialed his mobile number.

"No answer again! Bloody damn! He's probably turned it off, too! Peter, where the bloody hell are you?" Dialing his home number, still no answer.

This time I'll leave a message! "Peter, received your telegram and message. Call me at Hotel *Manin* tonight—whenever you get this message—no matter the hour!"

Now, she knew it was doubly important to speak *both* with Peter and Dillon—as soon as she could locate them. Emma took out the double copies of information on the Rudolphi family from the briefcase and sorted a complete set to give to Dillon.

"I wonder how he'll react when he learns my name is on a list kept in the study of the prominent Rudolphi family! Dillon has got to know *everything* about this family if we're to be successful in the case! Nothing can be held back between us—we must be completely open and honest—it's a two-way street between us—we've got to be successful in this case!"

Again, trying Peter's home number, Emma finally reached him. "Peter, I'm so glad I found you! I just arrived in Milano, and your message was waiting for me. What has happened—and when?" she asked impatiently.

"The thieves broke in night before last—the night you left for Italy. I arrived at the office yesterday, the outer doors were locked as usual, but my desk drawers were unlocked. I saw where some of the file drawers had been pried open—the locks broken! Emma, you know I always lock my desk when I leave, and I have the only key to it—not even *you* can get into it! Immediately, I began checking all the cabinets and files and that's when I discovered the office safe had been forced opened, too! I had put the Chatelaine file in the safe as you directed—the entire Chatelaine file was gone—other files were strewn on the floor. It looked as if they were searching for just that one file! All the transcripts you took from the Court of Justice—are gone!"

Emma felt sick listening to Peter describe the extensive chaos.

"When you asked me to transcribe those documents, I decided to make back-up copies on CD discs after I completely deciphered all the files. I locked the originals in the office safe as you directed—but not the CD copies—I stored them with the 'closed cases'—since they were not one of our open cases. When it looked like the thief was only interested in taking that one file, I immediately checked the computer, and found the hard drive blank—everything gone! We've lost all the data from the drive—I've started searching other computers for those other cases—some I've found. I'm thinking I can get some of the data from the recycle bin!" Peter's voice sounded apologetic. "Don't ask me why, Emma, but when I finished transcribing the Chatelaine files and copied them to CD's, I re-named the CD's *a different title!* Now I'm doubly glad I did that! Whoever was here thinks they got all the files, because the cabinet with the CD discs had been opened and rifled—but the two discs with the Chatelaine information were still there! I gave them a file number instead of a name—which is why the thief didn't find them. For now, I stored them in the well. Whoever did this didn't look further than the cabinet files, the office safe, the disc's files, and the computer. Emma, do you think the discs are safe in the well? What if the thieves learn we still have copies of the transcriptions? They may come back to search again!" Peter's voice was pure alarm.

"Peter, if they missed them the first time, most likely they think they found and took everything! If it didn't occur to them to look for another safe or other discs with a different title—then they must think they got it all. Don't tell me, or anyone, the numbers you assigned to those discs or discuss any of this information on this line now. I don't trust this connection—especially to your hardwired phone. No more about the files—until I'm certain we have a safe line to speak. It's best that information remain just with *you* for now! I'm not certain how safe any phone lines are—here or there now that we know someone wanted everything we had from the original Chatelaine Case files. There may be a time in the future when I'll ask you to send me the discs. When I do, I'll ask for *your numbers,* and we'll work out some arrangement to get them here."

"I understand," Peter acknowledged.

"Peter, I'm so grateful to you for your quick thinking! It was absolutely the right thing to do. But why would someone want those files, and how did they know I'd taken them from the archives in the Justice Building?" Emma posed the question rhetorically.

"The theft must've happened the night I left for Milano?"

"Yes, it was that very next morning, I found the front office doors locked, but the office rifled!" Peter waited.

"Emma, what am I to tell the police? They want to know if anything specifically was taken in the burglary."

"Tell the police an undetermined amount of petty cash was taken—that we don't keep an exact count—usually under fifty pounds. Explain we keep it available for unexpected office expenses. Do *not* tell them about the *unnamed* files taken! I have this uneasy feeling there is more to this case than you or I are aware of at this time, and I don't want you or anyone there to be in any more danger—because of that case. Shred any and all evidence of it in our office—computer references, file copies, any hand-scribbled notes—anything that mentions the file's name! If you can track what additional information was deleted from the hard drive, put that on a backup discs, too. Keep everything in the well. Why did this have to happen in my absence? Who wants to keep me from learning what's in those files?" They were questions she didn't expect Peter to have answers for.

"Peter, I don't know how long this case will keep me in Milano. Dillon O'Rourke is here, but I haven't seen him yet. He left me a message to meet him, which is my next undertaking. I'll call you again tomorrow to find out if there are any more details from the police. Peter, you are to call me, day or night, if anything more develops! Use my mobile number while I'm staying in the Manin- not the hotel number. Nothing is too insignificant about this matter!" Emma was trying to impress on him to be cautious, and yet not show too much alarm in her directive.

"Now don't worry, Emma, everything else is well under control here. But I will call you if anything more happens or if I learn anything new from the police."

"What did you tell Liv about the theft?" Emma asked.

"I told her the petty cash was stolen and asked Hilly and Liv to check their offices, too. They didn't find anything out of place. Emma, as I speak, a Constable is at my door. I'll hang up now to speak with him. Don't worry, everything is doing fine now," he said, and hung up.

Emma's thoughts were a jumble of questions. *Why did something like this have to happen when I can't return to London? Who and how did someone learn I had the Chatelaine files in my office? Someone had to go to the Court Justice to learn it was I who signed out those files from the archives? OR—was there someone inside the Court who passed that information on—that I took the files? Why try to steal them, when they only had to call the office to ask me to return them to the Royal Court Archives? Unless they didn't want me to learn the identity of the person or persons who wanted those files—they needed secrecy! There's got to be information in those case files that could reveal information about a person—or persons,—who will go to great lengths to keep me from learning his identity.*

*Emma just kept thinking how astute of Peter to have his own filing system. First thing, I've got to do is get those discs from him to read the material on them. More importantly, I need to figure out a way to get them here in Milano without alerting anyone!*

The strong scent from the fresh bouquet of silver lavender roses filling the sitting area captured Emma's attention. The wine, wrapped in a white velvet sleeve engraved with an **"R."**, was still on the table. Removing it from the velvet sleeve she saw it was one of her favorite white wines a Pinot Grigio from the Rudolphi Vineyards.

"Why no card? Could it be... Carlos?" She said out loud. "No... it can't be! Yet—he's one of the few people who know my favorite rose is the rare silver lavender rose and that I prefer white wines! If he *is* the one who sent these...how did *he* learn I was here at the Manin?"

Contemplating the possibility that Carlos sent the gifts, she exclaimed, "No! It's probably Dillon—of course! His silent way of showing sentiment without having to say it! He never ceases to amaze me!" Emma felt she solved the mystery.

Placing the wine on the table next to the roses, she smelled the delicate scent—and approved of his thoughtfulness.

*If Dillon did send these gifts, he knows more about me than I realize! More than any other case we've worked together on, I'm really most grateful he's here with me on this assignment!"*

# CHAPTER SEVENTEEN

The city's sights and sounds were mesmerizing at dusk—everything emphasized how much Emma wished this trip was a "real holiday" with no secret agendas—just pure holiday pleasure!

The sun was slipping behind the hillsides, and Emma's next task was to meet Dillon in *"M"* lounge!

"First—an energizing shower and fresh clothes!" Seeing the bottle of wine on the table, she poured a glass of wine before showering. "Someone is assuming I'm on holiday, and what better way to keep up the idea than to open it and leave the remnants of an empty glass—a pleasure-pleasing moment!"

The shower energized her after the long drive—when finished she rang for a maid to finish unpacking for her.

The suite décor was restful with harmonizing colors creating a sense of opulence and tranquility. "I'm especially glad Peter requested the spacious sitting room with French doors opening onto the wrap-around balcony." The canopied bed, with its soft-feathered covering in subtle shades of pale peach, sea green, and soft almond was decadently comfortable. The view beckoned Emma outside to the surrounding scenery of the gardens below and up to the spectacular capped mountain scenes. The adjoining bath was luxuriously large, decorated with an ornate green marble tub accented with modern European brass fixtures. A full matching shower with twin marble sinks complemented the spaciousness of the room.

"This is definitely meant to relax the traveler—not suggest work! I wonder what Dillon's room is like—if it's as nice as this. Knowing him, he's not interested in the amenities of color and comfort. It's location and plain utilitarian function that's important to him!"

Choosing something casual and comfortable, she said, "I hope we can make tonight a casual dinner meeting." She added the final touches of crème and lip-gloss, and she had it all together—black linen slacks and green sweater with comfortable walking sandals. If the night air became too cool, a shawl would be perfect—Spring is unpredictable in northern Italy...Milano! Emma remembered the Manin was within walking distance to several very good ristorantes they could choose from. "I don't relish taking the car out again tonight, if Dillon agrees."

Gathering the documents and papers spread out on the bed, she slid them all into the briefcase and locked it, when a knock came at the door. It was the young maid come to finish her unpacking. She introduced herself as Napolita, polite and eager to help. Grateful she understood English, Emma informed her she was staying at the hotel for an indefinite time and wanted her things organized in the bureaus and wardrobe. Emma glanced over to see her give special attention to her things, as she placed them carefully in the drawers and cupboards. She noticed she seemed more than casually interested in the briefcase on the bed—while eyeing Emma's presence in the room. Emma took it out from under the large suitcase just as Napolita was attempting to retrieve it.

"No, not the briefcase, Napolita—this I take with me!" She acknowledged my reproach, *"Si, signorina."* Checking the briefcase and lock, Emma decided nothing looked different. Seeing Napolita's interest in it, heightened Emma's instinct about leaving any documents in the room—especially after speaking with Peter— nothing seemed safe. She left Napolita alone to finish unpacking— there was nothing left in the room to suggest anything but a guest on holiday.

The lobby was crowded with new arrivals and the noise level was much louder. Emma noticed there were actually several other smaller pub-like lounges in the hotel on different levels. Sounds from the Machiavelli lounge were much louder—and his message did read to meet him in the lounge *"M."*

"I'm certain he's there now—since it is the cocktail hour."

The lighting inside was soft and muted and already the bar was filled with clientele enjoying a small band playing in the far corner. Emma spotted Dillon at a rear table reading the paper and sipping a tall drink. She walked to the rear of the room and sat down two tables away, not outwardly acknowledging that they knew each other—not just yet.

Within a few minutes, the waiter came over and took her order for a margarita with a salted glass. The lobby shop carried an ample supply of various area newspapers, and Emma stopped to purchase several local papers, looking for any news about the Rudolphi family. Her drink arrived and now she felt pangs of hunger! Realizing she hadn't eaten since breakfast, a drink was the last thing she needed now. She knew she'd better eat soon because the combination of the hot shower, the wine, and now the margarita were all plying to totally put her in the arms of Morpheous. The *cameriere* informed her the gentleman at the next table paid for her drink. Glancing over to Dillon, she saw him raise his glass.

*"A lei manca—salute,"* he welcomed her with a big grin.

"Thank you *Signore,* you're generous."

Rising from his table, speaking softly as he passed by, he said, "Meet me at the Ristorante *Serpico* on the *Via Senato,* a short walk east from the hotel in fifteen." And he exited the lounge.

After their polite exchange, Emma finished her drink while checking the newspapers for any articles about the Rudolphi family. *"Non niente!"* Depositing the papers in the trash, she went out through the lobby taking the direction to the Serpico Ristorante and started walking. The cool evening air felt like soft caresses after the heat of the trip, and it helped clear her thoughts—walking the two blocks. Cool night breezes accentuated the scents of mountain laurel everywhere. Tonight's scene reminded her of the walks Carlos and she use to take from his flat to escape into the cool evening air— conjuring up pictures of the Via Benedeto, remembering how much they both enjoyed those late evening walks with the dogs. *We had so much in common...I thought we did! How could I have misjudged him so badly?* Deep in reverie, Emma failed to see the dark, swarthy man lingering behind her trying not to appear interested in her. The Serpico was less than ten minutes walk from the hotel, and once inside, she located Dillon. Dillon's penchant was selecting a table in the rear of the room, where he could monitor the room's occupants and remain inconspicuous to the patrons. Most of all, he always chose to sit with his back to a wall.

The swarthy complexioned man followed Emma inside but stayed well out of sight until both Emma and Dillon were seated. He requested the *cameriere* to seat him at a table in a corner nearest the door, preferring the dimness of just the table candle—with a good view of the room's rear tables.

"Em, 'tis good t' see ye with these ol' eyes. 'Ow was yur trip 'ere?" he asked while rising to greet her and reaching over to kiss her cheek tenderly.

"Dillon, you're a pleasant sight for my eyes too, and I had a good trip here from the airport, to answer your question. I drove from Firenze today and arrived here this afternoon." Emma chose to sit next to Dillon, not across from him.

"When did *you* get here? How are your accommodations at the hotel?" she asked.

"They're just fine, Em. I 'ave an end room on the second floor, 219, next to the exit stairs. Peter knows me funny quirks 'bout me quarters—and I arrived yesterday. But more to the moment, just why am I 'ere?" he asked, leaning closer to her not wasting any time to find out what this trip was all about!

"First, I want to thank you for the beautiful flowers and wine you sent to my room, Dillon. The wine is my favorite!"

"Em, me dear, I wish I could lay claim to some splendid gifts— but, me dear,—I'm not the one who sent 'hem. Now's the more I wish I did!"

"Then who…? It must have been…. never mind, it's not important now. I'll track down the sender later." She played down her curiosity to Dillon to squelch any further discussion about the sender of the gifts. But Emma couldn't squelch the persistent, uneasy feeling of not knowing that answer—*Who did send the gifts?*

"Let's order first! I'm starved and breakfast was a long time ago!"

They checked the menu, ordered a bottle of wine, and then their meal, which included several leisurely courses allowing them plenty of time to discuss the reason for their trip to Milano.

"Dillon, I need to start at the very beginning because this case is not our usual type. Then again—it has the intrigue of the MacEachen and Moore cases with a caveat!"

"Em, all yur cases are unusual! I'll agree with ye, those weren't o'r usual cases, but go ahead…tell me more 'bout this new case," he said, raising his glass to signal her to commence the telling of her story.

"It began a couple of weeks ago when a new client, Lucinda Rudolphi, walked into my office with a most unbelievable story!"

There seemed to be a flicker of recognition in his eyes when Emma mentioned her name. She wanted Dillon to understand the woman, Lucinda Rudolphi, as she saw her, to give her story the credibility she felt it needed. He had to hear the complete saga about her personal life and losses leading up to the secret she discovered in her husband's library. Emma didn't want to discuss the locked box containing the list of names until she first told him about Lucinda's problem, and gave Dillon the second recorded tape of Lucinda's conversation about the child she saw. It was that second tape she really wanted him to listen to first, handing him the recorder with the tape to take back to his room.

"First, listent to this tape back in your room tonight."

Then she gave him the packet of duplicate articles she'd made. "These are some articles I found at the library on the Rudolphi family…mostly about their successful wine business. It's background information about the history of the Rudolphi family going back several generations."

For now, Emma deliberately withheld the copy of the first tape of her meeting with Lucinda, telling her about the secret list of names kept in the library, with her name on one of the lists.

*"Dillon, have you ever heard of the Rudolphi family or their winery business here in Milano?"*

He casually commented, "I do know they 'ave been 'ere for a very long time, and their wine business puts out very good ports that 'ave won many awards. The'e 'ave been members of the family who 'ad brushes with the law, but nothin'was ev'r proven. But, then, money 'as a very long arm and a loud convincin' voice, too".

Emma knew he was speaking about money buying good legal representation for the family.

"I'm not certain what we'll find on this trip, Dillon, which is why I thought you may be the one to expeditiously get the information and answers we need; information maybe I wouldn't discover if my connection to the law were known, and the more I think about the case...the more I realize I'd never find the answers alone. What I'd like you to do is first is listen to that tape I gave you, then go through this packet of information. I may have missed something important." Emma handed him a sealed envelope with all the information she copied.

"For now, let me brief you about a few other facts. There's another tape I made during Lucinda's meeting disclosing another even more startling fact!" Here she paused. "Lucinda found my name written on a list her husband keeps in his library under lock and key. She asked me why my name was on that list. I told her I had no idea why my name is on a list secreted in the study! When I heard this fact it roused my curiosity to say the least! Dillon, I need to find out more about this list kept under lock. If my name is on the list, is it for professional reasons or for another reason? Either way—I want to find out what that reason is! And why this list is locked in a box not even Lucinda has access to? I've never met any member of the Rudolphi family—either professionally or personally—that's something I'd remember if I had! Let me keep this second tape until you've listened to the first tape about Lucinda's feelings about her children! The tape you have reveals Lucinda's request for our professional help concerning the death of her children."

"Which is the *real* reason we're 'ere, Em--for the list—or for Lucinda?" Dillon had the gift to cut to the quick in a matter without wasting time—reading Emma's thoughts like an open book. It unnerved her sometimes how he had an uncanny insight into her psyche. At times, his talent was alarming!

"**Both**! Probably the first and most important reason why I'm here *now* and why I asked you to help me with this case is to find that LIST of names. I want to see the complete list. There may be a common factor tying the names together, if I see all the names! My second reason is to find answers for Lucinda's problem. As incredible as her story is, there could be a thread of truth or a credible explanation for her unexplained feelings. Though, I'm not certain the answers we'll find are the ones she's looking for. After you play that tape, give me your opinions and thoughts about Lucinda's request. Right now, these are two different objectives…I can't possibly think they're even connected." She looked at Dillon for his reaction to her last statement.

"Em, first let me go over all of this information you gave me, and listen to this one tape. Then, I'll 'hear the second one…and set a plan to find 'ow we can get more information—on both issues. Right now? It's too soon to see where this case'll take us. We can go over ever'thing again tomor'ow. Tomor'ow's soon enough, and I'll pay attention to the second tape then."

Dillon was holding something back—He didn't want to confide his true feelings about this case to Emma yet. The facts she told him made his mental alarm bell go off—a reliable characteristic he acquired through years of prior covert work. First, he had to hear both tapes before he'd let Emma know any of his real concerns about this case…this Rudolphi family—a family name familiar to him.

"I feel my weariness tonight, Dillon, after that drive this morning. It seems like I've been traveling for two straight days. A fresh mind and body will do a lot to help clear my head! Not to change the subject, Dillon, it is good to see you, old friend, and to work with you again." Leaning closer to him to make a sincere impression, she said, "I only hope we find the answers in this case! Not the lack of answers that ended our other cases!"

He placed his hand over hers…for a long moment there was a silence…remembering…they held hands. It was his eyes! They told her, "We'll win this one!"

"'ow's 'bout breakfast, an' not that continental kind tomorr'a!" Dillon preferred the complete English breakfast.

"Maybe I can't get ban'ers or chips at that café I saw across the street from the 'otel, but I'm bettin' they do 'ave some good substitutes. Meet me at the Café Rosalia on the Via Turati...say... nine o'clock tomor'ow, and we'll set a plan. For now, an'thing new at the office?" he asked casually sipping his drink. Casting glances at Emma, Dillon was really targeting his attention to the dark swarthy man sitting at a distant table—his too casual interest betrayed his actions—their table was his real mark!

"Yes Dillon, there is! Something very troubling happened the day I left for Italy. I heard from Peter today. The day, or rather the night, I left for Milano there was a theft at the law firm!"

Dillon's countenance changed from calm to concern. "What was stolen?"

"Files I signed out from the Royal Court of Justice were stolen from my office safe. Peter told me the hard disc in the main computer with the information from those files was erased, too! The thief didn't know Peter finished the transcription and downloaded it to backup discs—which we still have in a safe place. It was the entire original Chatelaine file that was stolen from the firm's safe! The back-up discs were stored under a different title—which is why the thief missed them. You make the third person to know about their existence."

"Do ye 'ave an' idea why someone wanted those files...the Chatelaine files?" Dillon asked intriguingly.

"Not a clue. Except, the name of the files was Chatelaine, and my instinct tells me I think that case—the Chatelaine case—is connected to this Rudolphi case here," Emma said. "I believe the Chatelaine case was a kidnapping case! I wasn't able to read all of Peter's transcripts before I left for Milano, but I have this strong feeling there's a connection between that case and my coming to Milano—and the theft! If there IS a connection, I'm...we're...going to find out what it is!" In an afterthought, she asked, "Have *you* ever heard of a kidnapping case called Chatelaine?"

"Can't say I 'ave, Em. You say it's a kidnappin' case?" Dillon seemed particularly interested when he asked with his eyes downcast.

"Yes, I did manage to decipher that word in a brief view of the transcription Peter was translating into a memorandum for me. The one piece of transcription Peter completed described some of the defendants belonging to an international kidnapping ring...their victims were kidnapped from several countries."

"Do you know where the trial was held in that case?" Dillon asked tersely.

"I think the first trial was held in Roma, but subsequent trials were held in Firenze. The court transcription I read was taken in Italian with English notations handwritten in the margins. The case had connections to a castle in Italy called the Chatelaine Castle— hence the file name. Other than remembering that, I have no idea about other case facts."

"Do you think they broke in just to get that file, Em? More importantly—why?"

Dillon had a definite purpose in asking these questions because Emma saw a dark change in his demeanor and outward appearance— not giving any reasons for the change in his behavior.

"Nothing caught my eye from the short examination of the facts I read why someone would want that file... maybe it was stolen to prevent me from learning what those transcripts actually contained! Why do you ask, Dillon?"

"No one specific reason, Em. More curiosit' at the timin' it 'appened." Clearly, Dillon was not telling her the truth. He did have a specific reason for asking his questions, but he wasn't going to share his reasons with her now. So she just let the subject drop. There may be another time she could broach the *Chatelaine topic and get him to tell her his real thoughts.* Observing Dillon closely, Emma noted he chose his next words carefully.

"Then best we be extra careful 'ere, Em." Gathering up the material she gave him, he said, "I 'ave some work to do tonight, and you need to be extra war' from now on," cautioning her like Papa would—if he were there.

They left the *ristorante* and walked outside into the cool night air, not sharing their thoughts until they started walking back to the hotel. Emma noticed Dillon glancing back over his shoulder several times on their walk back to the hotel. *She* didn't see anyone particularly interested in them—loitering behind them—except…a swarthy-looking man standing outside a car across the street with his back to them. He almost looked familiar. Emma had a strange feeling—a mental image from an earlier time…*I may have seen that man before! Or am I becoming a little paranoid with Dillon's recent warning to be extra cautious because of unexplained things happening? Could he be that same man in the library…the man I bumped into…who ran away when I tried to apologize…?*

Remembering the business card she'd picked up, Emma took it out of her briefcase.

"Dillon, we need to find more about this place of business," she said and handed the card to Dillon. Emma thought, *Strange, Dillon didn't question me why I wanted that information.*

"Let me take care of it, Em. I'll track it down and let you know."

Dillon was totally aware that the man across the street was the same man from the *ristorante* and offhandedly he kept track of him across the street on their return to the hotel. His intuition told him something wasn't right, but he kept his feelings and observations to himself. *Can't alarm Em…with just me feelin's, but if I see that bloke ag'in, I'll know 'im,* Dillon thought. He took a good, long hard look at the car and man making certain he'd remember them. Just as they reached the corner, Dillon turned to say goodnight to Emma with a light embrace before he went in a different direction—not before he took a good long hard look at the street behind them.

"Dillon, I'll see you for breakfast!" Emma called after him and hurried the rest of the short distance to the Manin. Dillon stood at the corner for the longest while—waiting to see Emma enter the hotel—and to see if the swarthy man followed her inside.

Dillon had a sixth sense he'd see that car and man again in Milano—in fact, he was certain he would! He read the signs of danger around them…and they'd barely started their work in this case. The car sped away down the Via d Manin—too fast for him to get a good look at the driver—or the licence plate. Thinking, this is *my* territory, too.

*"Il mio territorio"!*

147

# CHAPTER EIGHTEEN

Until they knew more about the Rudolphi family, Emma and Dillon agreed it was better not to be seen together at the hotel—not knowing just how far the Rudolphi influence reached in Milano.

After Emma reached the hotel alone, Dillon took a detour down the *Via d I'lago.*

It was only this morning that she left Firenze, but it felt more like yesterday! Thankful to reach the lobby her feelings about the office theft were consuming her thoughts. Feeling the late hour, she decided to put off her call to Peter until tomorrow morning—she'd do it first thing. The same questions kept repeating over and over, *Why did someone want the Chatelaine case files desperately enough to break into my office and steal them? WHO knew I had them?*

In a way she was relieved to be busy with Dillon, not giving her time to think about Carlos. *No more calls from Peter means he's handling things well in London.* Walking to the lift, Emma saw the manager coming across the lobby calling out, *"Signora Llewelyn, scuzi prego!* A gentleman was here early this evening asking for you, and I told him you were out. He left no message."

"What did he look like? Can you describe him to me?" she asked anxiously.

"The gentleman was tall… and well dressed, and spoke fluent English. This is all I remember, *Signora."*

*"Grazie."* By process of elimination, Emma knew it couldn't be Dillon. Who else knew she came to Milano for holiday? When

she last spoke to Cyrus, she did tell him she was planning a trip to Milano and remembered calling it a working holiday, but she never told him where she was staying.

*If Papa's here in Milano...and discovered this is where I'm staying, he might stop to see me...but he'd leave me a message if he missed me—I'm certain! I kept reasoning out the possibilities of who would know I was here and come asking for me? Why did the clerk describe him speaking "fluent English?" Was he Italian speaking fluent English? Maybe it was Carlos!*

Reaching her suite, Emma placed a trunk call to Llandindrod Wells, remembering the two-hour earlier time difference at Lyn Brienne. If Papa is at the farm, he'd be the one to answer the phone. The phone rang once, and immediately, she heard Papa's voice.

"Papa, this is Emma, how are you? I'm calling from Milano. Did I get you away from something important?"

"Em, it's good to hear your voice,—this connection is very clear on this end. You didn't interrupt us—Maggs and I are just sitting here. How is your holiday going? Maggs mentioned it was a working holiday, and I certainly hope it's not all work and no play. Are you there alone?"

"Actually, no Papa...Dillon O'Rourke, my detective in London? He's with me. I'm hoping the two of us will get twice as much done, twice as quickly, which is why I asked him to come with me to Milano. So you needn't worry about me, Dillon is like a guardian angel." Emma paused to ask, "Papa, did you call me earlier tonight and not leave a message?"

This seemed a foolish question to ask. Emma knew full well Papa was not the man asking for her in person, but she needed to hear his answer to her question.

"No, Em I didn't. Could it have been Peter calling you from London?" he asked.

Trying not to show concern in her voice, Emma said lightheartedly, "That's probably who it was. Yes, I'll ring him tomorrow and touch base with him."

Her instinct told her not to discuss the office theft with Papa now; she didn't want to alarm him unnecessarily. She put the thought out of her mind.

"Em, I'm leaving here on a business trip tomorrow, and I'll be gone for a week or two… or possibly longer. I expect to be on the Continent, but my schedule changes a lot, so I can't give you an itinerary. I carry my cell phone with me and you have that number—if you want to reach me at any time! Let's say… I'll call you Monday next, at this same time—your time. It's a grandfather's duty to check on you."

"That sounds fine, Papa. I'll make it a point to be here at the hotel Monday next for your call."

"Emma, where are you staying in Milano?"

"I'm at the Hotel Manin on the Via d Manin."

"I'll be sure to remember that when I leave Lyn Brienne."

"Papa, when I get back to London, I'll plan a weekend trip to the farm. It's been too long. I miss our morning rides. Must run now…have to ring off…I love you, Papa."

"Be very careful, Emma." Slowly, Cyrus returned the phone to its cradle, but Emma's words lingered in his thoughts for some strange reason.

"Love you too, Em," he softly said.

Cyrus was bothered by the tone in her voice. It sounded deliberately guarded, and what she didn't say bothered him more.

"Emma, what are you *not* telling me?" He whispered.

Hearing Papa's voice from Lyn Brienne didn't clear up who the mystery person was asking for her, but she needed to *hear his* answer…to see if he sent someone else to check on her.

It wasn't Dillon…and certainly not Peter…then who?

*Could it possibly have been Carlos? How would he know I was here in Milano? If it wasn't Carlos…then who else is interested in my presence here…and knows so much about me?*

# CHAPTER NINETEEN

Sitting alone in the Great Room, Cyrus reached for a slim white cell phone and pressed a pre-set dial button.

"Colin?"

"Aye."

"Are you aware there are new developments in Milano? I just talked to Emma—she's in Milano with Dillon. Lucinda Rudolphi was in London a few weeks ago and met with Emma—she's accepted an assignment taking her to Milano. Do you know why this matter has taken her Italy-Milano, Colin?" Cyrus's words were commanding.

"Can't say for certain. It probably 'as somethin' personal to do with Lucinda and Marcus Rudolphi. Too coincidental not to be otherwise! Strikes me timely, Cyrus...the Rudolphis are 'ostin' a big charity party this weekend...could it 'ave somethin' to do with that?"

There was no response.

"If it isn't that—and I know our man Dillon—'tis a sure bet he finds a way for 'hem to attend that charity party at the Villa del Christianna. If they don't already know 'bout it, they will! Whate'er their agenda, Mac, if Emma's client is Lucinda, that party will entice 'hem to be there. I'll make some 'queires and should know more tomorrow—get a report exactly what's 'appenin' *in Milano.* Call me tomorrow night, Cyrus, same time."

"Colin? I'm leavin' nothing to chance! I'm flyin' to Milano in the morn. Don't like what I'm hearin'...I want to monitor this situation personally! You know how to reach me there if necessary. I'll call you tomorrow night…this time from Central in Milano. *Don't hold anything back from me, Colin!*" Cyrus hung up.

The fire was roaring in the great hearth when a knock came, disturbing the silence.

"Come."

Andrew softly walked in. "Mac, a coded message just came," he said and handed Cyrus the message.

**Two new faces on scene. Chatelaine mentioned. May not be long until Chatelaine and Rudolphi are connected. Observing two. ADVISE. Will not make presence known—unless authorized.**

Cyrus read the cryptic message again, crumpled it, and tossed it in the fire.

"Any reply?" Andrew asked.

"No!" Cyrus gave a command to Andrew before he left. "Andy, we're flyin' to Milano early tomorrow mornin'. Have the crew ready the plane tonight with flight plans to file with the tower by eight o'clock tomorrow mornin'. Check on the weather for a flight from Newbridge to Milano—usual air field!"

"It's alread' done, Mac."

"Thanks, Andy. See you at breakfast."

"Emma…be careful…be very careful in Milano!" Cyrus said quietly—almost prayerfully.

The next morning at breakfast, Cyrus informed Maggie about his change in plans.

"Maggs, Andrew and I will be away for a while in Milano…not sure when we'll return… you have my mobile number to reach me?" Cyrus knew Maggie would coordinate the care of the house while Ian, the assistant farm manager, would oversee the business of the farm when he and Andrew were away from Lyn Brienne. Only this time the return date to Lyn Brienne was left OPEN.

"Maggs—no one is to know where we are, or when we left, or when we will return! That includes Emma!"

That last comment surprised Maggie; it told her this trip could be different-dangerous...but for whom? In her usual confident way, Maggie assured him, "Not to worry, Cyrus! We'll be fine here. I'll call if there's a problem. You take good care of Emma," she cautioned Cyrus with motherly authority, as if she already knew he was going to Milano, too.

Cyrus hesitated and looked at Maggie for a long moment as if he was going to say something more. *She reads me like an open book!* he thought. Though he wanted to confide more to Maggs, it was for her safety, too, he did not go into details—at least for the time being.

"You take extra care, Cyrus." She gave him a long silent embrace as he tenderly held her in his arms for several long minutes. Standing at the door, she watched Andrew and Cyrus leave Lyn Brienne for Newbridge Airfield.

Flight plans were filed with the tower and they were cleared for takeoff. With Cyrus in the pilot's seat and Andrew as co-pilot, the private jet taxied the down the landing strip and waited for final clearance to take off.

"You're cleared for take-off on runway two-one...repeat runway two-one...visibility unlimited...cloud layer thirty-thousand...climb to twenty thousand then change course two-four-zero—repeat course two-four-zero."

The take-off went smoothly as the plane climbed, and Cyrus maneuvered a wide turn heading east for Milano's airport. The sky was clear with an unlimited ceiling with only a few puffy clouds off the horizon. The jet climbed to twenty thousand feet. In the co-pilot seat, Andrew tuned the radio frequency to the tower in Milano's Private Port for information about the landing conditions.

"Mac, exactly why this unplanned trip to Milano this time?" Andrew asked.

"Andy, Emma is in Milano on an assignment for a client, Lucinda Rudolphi...Marcus Rudolphi's wife! That's all I'm certain of for now. I...we need to determine what she's doing in Milano and to make certain she doesn't get caught up in *our case*. Though, I think we may already be too late for that. I think she's already dangerously involved in our case, and I aim to keep a close eye on her until she returns to London. I expect Colin will have more to report on that subject." Cyrus unbuckled his seat belt. He said, "Take the controls, Andy, I need to check out a map."

"Mac, does Emma have any idea we've been working on a matter involving surveillance of the Rudolphis for over the past two years? Why would her client ask Emma to do something that would connect *her* to our investigation? I don't see how our investigation around unusual disappearances of victims—possibly tied to kidnappings—is something Lucinda Rudolph would get involved in?"

"I seriously doubt there's any connection to our case and what Lucinda Rudolphi hired Emma to do, Andy, and that's what's frightening! She may already be in great danger without realizing it! *Just bein' in Milano—near Marcus is danger enough for her!* If what I think is true…she's tryin' to find out something specific for her client that just may put her life in greater danger than ours! And maybe also Lucinda Rudolpi's life. It's findin' answers for her client that may be more dangerous for *her* than for her client! That's why we're going to Milano—to answer your first question."

The plane was on autopilot when the control tower gave the crew an estimated time to arrive in Milano Private Port—just after twelve noon.

"Last night, I learned that Emma's staying at Hotel Manin with Dillon O'Rourke. So I'm goin' to have to stay at headquarters' safe house for now. I don't want anyone to know you or I are in Milano until I find out more information. You're to make arrangements for surveillance on those two—twenty-four/seven. I want to know everythin'—where they go, who they meet and anything else they do. Daily intelligence reports. Make certain neither knows they're bein' watched. Dillon is very sharp—so inform the agents you use they must be extra careful—rotate them in two-to-four hour blocks."

Andrew knew Cyrus was taking every precaution to protect Emma; he felt certain there was great danger to everyone involved. "Dillon won't let anything happen to her, Mac."

Cyrus heard his words but made no response.

"Colin informed me the Rudolphi's are throwing a big charity party on Sunday, and I want to find out who's on that guest list. If I know Dillon, he'll get his hands on some invitations for them to attend. I know *I* can't go, but I want someone there to be my eyes and ears!" Cyrus said. "Find out if the Marquissa de Favio is planning on attending the charity, and if so, she owes me a favor. This may be just the time to call in that favor!" Turning to Andrew, he said, "*You'll* be at that charity party too, Andy. You'll be my eyes and ears at the party."

Cyrus turned off the autopilot and took back the controls—ready for the descent pattern approaching the airport ten miles away.

"Did you bring the bag of tricks, Andy?"

"Never go without it, Mac."

"Nothing, but nothing, must be left to chance. We've worked too long and too bloody hard to jeopardize this case now. *Even more importantly, nothing must happen to Emma either!*" Cyrus turned his complete attention to the air controller's instructions coming from the control tower and started slowing the airspeed down to one hundred twenty knots.

"Lower wing flaps, Andy."

Cleared to land, the plane slowly drifted down toward the airstrip ahead, barely touching the ground with one soft bounce. The jet coasted to the farthest area of the airport into an unmarked open hanger. Once inside, Cyrus cut the engines, and the thrusters deadened. A nearby waiting car drove slowly up to the plane's door as Cyrus and Andy de-planed. A middle-aged man opened the car door for them.

"Good to see you again so soon, Biaggio, how are things going?" Cyrus asked, getting into the passenger seat.

"*Si, Mac. Things are fine here. I'm surprised to see you, too, again so soon.*"

Andrew emptied the cargo from the hold into the boot of the car and climbed in the car. Without hesitation, the car exited hanger, picking up speed to the city of Milano.

\* \* \*

After speaking with Cyrus and still with no idea who it was inquiring for her at the hotel, Emma found herself looking for reasons why it could be Carlos. Reproaching herself for wishing, she said, "There's no way Carlos could learn in one day that I'm in Milano!" As she walked out onto the balcony, the idea of seeing and speaking to him again was unsettling. The night traffic below was not so noisy that she couldn't hear the muted music from the nearby restaurant on the street level mingle with echoes of muffled laughter. The soft gentle breezes of the night air triggered memories of a similar evening she and Carlos spent together—particularly one evening much like tonight.

## *A MEMORY...*

Emma remembered...It had been a hot, sunny day in Milano—the kind of day for a hike up a mountainside up to the cool breezes on the mountaintop to get relief from the sweaty city heat. *He* knew all the best out-of-the-way places to spend an afternoon picnicking in solitude.

First, we ordered a picnic lunch packed for us at the local *trotino*. While waiting for our picnic basket, we explored the nearby shops and cafes, buying a blanket, napkins, and wine glasses. Carlos drove to an upper mountain pasture to a remote spot that would give us privacy—and a spectacular view of the valley. Parking the car at the base of the mountain, we loaded our backpacks with the fresh foodstuff and started our climb up the mountain to the highest meadow. The climb was exhausting, invigorating, and most of all-impressive! Periodically stopping to view the magnificent panoramic mountain vistas, we finally reached the uppermost meadow and chose a site at the top near a ledge to give us the best view of the snow-capped peaks of the Alps off in the distance. The green valleys below displayed serpentine rows of vineyards. In a nearby field, a grove of wild lemon trees filled the air with pungent, fragrant blossoms. The gentle breezes were a cool respite in contrast to the sultry heat of the city.

"This is a meadow I often escaped to as a boy because it's so well hidden from the road. When I wanted to get away, I'd climb up here and sit on this very ledge and think about what it was like out there...far away out there."

I watched him spread out the blanket on the far side of the pasture where it overlooked the best part of the green valley below.

How good the chilled wine, fresh cheeses, breads, and homemade meats tasted that day! I still remember the smells, the sounds, and the scenes so clearly...and everything we talked about.

"What if we decide to just stay here for the rest of our lives, to make time stand still, would you like that?" he asked, lying on his back looking up at the sky.

"Can you do that?" Lying next to him, I asked laughingly, "Can you ask the gods to stop the hour glass of time...just for us?"

"If that's what you really want, I can ask the gods anything here on my hilltop! They'll stop the pendulum of time for us! I did that as a young boy...I asked the gods to stop the pendulum from swinging for me...I think they almost did, in my child's mind!"

"Does that mean we will never run out of wine or food?" I asked, sipping the cool Vino.

"We could pretend our basket would overflow with wonderful foods and drink, for as long as we needed it," he laughed and took my body closer to his.

"Emma, every time I see you, you're more beautiful than before!" He leaned down, gently kissing me. Both of us lay next to one another on the blanket sated with wine and food; his kisses became more intense and warm with our feelings and passions intermingling. I felt his strong body over mine. His hands caressing me, his kisses warm, soft, and exploring. It was as if time *did* stand still for us, and I knew I wanted this man completely...as I knew he did me....there was no stopping our love now. Time stood still for us on that hilltop!

Suddenly, raindrops fell through the trees making soft splashing noises. The sun dimmed, and the winds blew strong and cold. Quickly packing what was left of the picnic, we ran down the mountain as fast as we could to the car just as the first crack of thunder stunned us.

"I've come to respect these mountains! Not heeding these sudden unpredictable changes in the weather could be disastrous. Local folk read all the subtle weather changes and treat them with vigilance," Carlos cautioned.

Feeling the cool rain drenching our clothes, there was no happier moment for me!

Driving back down the mountain was slow, as the torrents of rain formed rushing rivulets merging into a river of water flooding the road and making it practically impassible. Carlos turned the car into a drive to a higher level off the road. There at the end of the drive was a small residence away from the flooded road.

"There's a small sheltered porch," Carlos said and pointed to a sheltered portico. "Let's try for it!"

We madly dashed for cover under the portico. In the two to three seconds it took us to reach the portico, we were drenched again and huddled together near the door.

The door opened! It startled us; we had not realized someone was at home.

*"Bourngiorno!"* Greeting us with a warm smile was a short white-haired, bearded man with the brightest blue eyes beckoning us inside. *"Avanti!"*

Ushering us over to his warm coal stove, he motioned for us to feel the warmth. *"Caldo il loro!"*

*"Grazie."* Feeling my body shaking, I moved closer to the stove.

Carlos explained to the old man in Italian how we got caught in the rainstorm in the upper meadow and could go no further in our car because the roads flooded, but his account sounded like there was more than just a simple explanation. When the old man embraced Carlos, it was as if he was seeing a familiar old friend. For a fleeing second, I thought I saw a look of recognition and understanding between them…There had to be a familiar past between them…but from when? The old man seemed grateful for our company and encouraged us to dry our clothes near the stove. Removing my hiking shoes and sweater, I placed them near the heat to dry.

I took notice of the sparsely furnished room and the white walls covered with paintings. There were watercolor paintings and oil paintings everywhere! Carlos confided to me our elderly host was an artist; well known in the Umbrian and Tuscan regions for his countryside scenes. In our conversations, I did understand that some of his paintings were on display in different museums in Italy. Most of his art was sold to private collectors. I enjoyed listening to this gnome-like man as he animatedly explained why he didn't get much company up this far on the mountain—the reason he chose to live here.

"*Signore,* I like your work. Is your work mostly oils?" I asked.

"*Si,* only oils now," he said in broken English. One particular painting caught my attention: a costumed Roman man in a villa atop a hillside. The painting prompted an ominous feeling around something from a past memory…a picture…a scene I had seen before.

*A painting…a man in old world costume in a picture hanging on a stone wall…a large crucifix…a great hearth and mantle…a cold stone floor…*

Why this memory now?…Why here in this old farmhouse?

Listening to this old man explain in Italian and broken English how he came from a family of painters for generations, back to the Italian Renaissance period, made the time pass quickly. On one wall, there was a piece of artwork signed by the artist in eighteen hundred ten. Probably very valuable—just hanging on the wall in the old farmhouse without any security. I learned that as a young man, he went away to study in Paris with some of the later French impressionists. Over the years, his art became his life. Some paintings he sold; others he gave away. We viewed so many beautiful originals, walking from room to room; hundreds of paintings throughout the house, just stacked and stored in empty rooms! In one room, I thought I heard the hum of machinery and tried a door to the next room where the humming noise was coming from—a steel door not like the other old wooden ones—but it was locked.

"What kind of room requires a locked steel door?" I pondered when Carlos interrupted my treasure hunt.

"Carlos, who is this talented painter?" I asked as he escorted me back to the parlor. It was clear we had found a hidden cache of art far from any security-alarmed museum—but maybe something more? I sat, sated with warm tea and homemade biscuits. The storm abated and dusk was turning to nightfall. Before we left, I asked the old man if I could return to purchase one of his paintings, thinking I would like to own one of these paintings. I learned the old man's name was *Giuseppe Vittorio*. He gently shrugged his shoulders and said, "*Si, Signora,*" with that innocent twinkle lighting up his clear blue eyes.

Making the trip cautiously down the mountain road, we were both very tired and didn't speak much. I, for one, enjoyed the silence to reminisce about our visit with the old man and seeing his art collection.

"Some day, I'm going to find that house again and that little old painter! I'd like to own one of his originals to remind me of today…our picnic on the hilltop. Carlos, had you ever been to that house before?"

Carlos answered looking straight ahead, "I've been to many Italian homes in this area with my father as a boy. Why do you ask, Emma?"

"I thought the old man recognized you when we first entered his home."

The discussion ended silently. Emma knew Carlos was not going to tell her about his past relationship with this talented old painter, and Carlos understood Emma wasn't satisfied with his answer, but it was too dangerous to tell her the truth. Too precarious for her—if she knew the truth!

\* \* \*

The ringing phone jolted Emma's thoughts back to the actual moment. Hurrying inside from the balcony before the caller disconnected, she heard a light, rapid knock at the door. Deciding she needed to answer the door first, she was surprised to see Dillon standing there.

"Come in, Dillon, I have to take this call."

"*Si, Pronto*—Hello?"

# CHAPTER TWENTY

*"Pronto,* hello?"

"Emma?"

*"Si, Chi Parla?"* Emma asked.

"Emma…I wasn't certain if it was really you! It's Carlos." Emma immediately recognized his voice, even before he gave his name but tried to hide her stunned reaction.

"Carlos, how did you know I was here in Milano?" She glanced over toward Dillon to see his back turned.

Dillon knew Emma and Carlos had a serious relationship, and that something happened between them. He never spoke to Emma about those circumstances in her life. Watching Emma, he remembered how difficult it was for her during that time in her life—now, seeing her body language, he promptly concluded that she never did put that part of her life *completely* behind her. He was back in her life again—here in Milano! Dillon rose and started for the door.

Covering the phone with her hand, she said, "Wait Dillon, we need to talk about the case!"

"I know, Em, just give me a ring when you're done. I'll be in me room for the rest of the night. I 'spect you'll be 'ere too for the night?" Dillon was telling her—not asking—she was not to go out without first checking with him—not that she had to report to him. He felt he needed to know her whereabouts at all times.

"Too many funn' things happenin' with no obvious answers. It's just a plain feelin', and I a'ways listen to me funn' feelin's", he kept telling himself.

"I promise to call you as soon as I finish this call," she said, making a gesture with her hand, crossing her heart in a solemn oath to do it.

Slowly sitting down on the bed, Emma turned her full attention back to the phone call, still startled at hearing his voice, not finding the words to speak… "Carlos, how did you know I was in Milano?"

"The embassy in Roma receives daily lists from immigration, and I was assigned to review these lists…I recognized your name on one of them. Checking this immigration data is routine now since the terror threats. When I saw the name, E.G. Llewelyn—London—there could only be one E.G. Llewelyn in London," he said, making small talk to cover how he really knew she entered Italy. "I inquired at different car rental agencies in Roma. I knew you'd need a car… found your name with English license at a rental agency in Roma with destination—Milano! After that, it was routine to locate you. I know your preferences for certain places in Milano—and they haven't changed I can see. Emma, I'm just very *happy* to hear your voice!" At this point, his voice changed. It was almost apologetic. "I hope you don't mind, but I wanted to speak with you…Have I called at a bad time?"

All the time he was speaking, Emma felt her heart pounding. Trying to minimize the anxiety in her voice, she said, "No Carlos, not at all. I'm really here on business, hoping there'll be some time for a leisure holiday, too. Are you calling from here…in Milano?"

"Actually, I'm calling from Firenze, finishing some business here, and then I'm leaving for Milano shortly. I'm not due back in Roma for several more days, and I'd planned to stay at the Milano apartment for a few days. How long will you be in Milano?" he asked.

"I expect my business will take one, maybe two weeks before I return to London," she replied, crossing her fingers as she waited for his next question.

"Emma, do you think we could meet for lunch…or dinner? Say tomorrow or Friday? I'd really love to see you, Emma…It's been a long time."

Emma could hear the hesitancy in his words.

"I've had a lot of time to do some thinking…soul searching…about us—you and me." Carlos was really letting his feelings show, which took Emma by surprise. That last day together flashed momentarily before her eyes as she faltered for words. Quickly, remembering that she and Dillon still had to make plans for tomorrow, Emma knew she couldn't postpone tomorrow's plans.

"Actually, tomorrow isn't good for me, Carlos. I have commitments during the day—Friday is a better day for me," she said, trying not to show just how impatient she was to see him again.

"Great, Emma. I have nothing pressing for Friday. My plans are flexible—I may or may not return to Roma on Monday. How's dinner on Friday for you?" he asked. "I haven't been back to the Taverna del Pescatore, since our last dinner…I remember it's a *ristorante* you always enjoyed. I can meet you there…say, eight o'clock. Is that okay with you?" Carlos asked.

"Perfect for me," Emma replied, recalling the last time they were there. "It'll be nice to see you again, Carlos. I think you'll still recognize me—nothing changed there," she said offhandedly. "I have to ring off now, Carlos. I still have a few pressing things to work on tonight. Can I still reach you at your apartment if I need to… same number? Not that I will change anything… but if something unexpectedly comes up…and I'd need to let you know…" she explained, sounding clumsy while trying to make him understand exactly what she meant.

"Still the same number and address. Leave a message if you call…I know we left many things unanswered, Emma, that last day… Maybe now's the time to speak about things we should have spoken then…make a wrong a right? Wear your hair down, as I last remember you? I'll know you for sure that way. *Caio.*" The line went silent and Emma slowly hung up the phone as if she wanted the conversation to go on.

Carlos's dialogue with Emma confirmed that she had no knowledge that the Lamborghini followed her from Roma to Milano. She never made him at the Manin—but then, he took extra precautions to keep his identity hidden—neither she nor Dillon knew he was there!

Emma's mind was a whirl of questions. *Why did he make such an effort to track me down here? What did he mean when he said he had time to think—and now to make a 'wrong a right'?* Her feelings for Carlos had not changed; time didn't diminish them but only intensified them. "More than anything, I do want to see you, Carlos! Right now—it's Dillon I need to call. I'll make certain nothing will interfere with our meeting on Friday!"

Dialing Dillon's room, he immediately remarked, "Em, ever'thing okay?"

"Yes, Dillon. It was Carlos Esteves calling me. He learned I had flown into Roma several days ago. He works at the Italian Embassy where they get lists of travelers who enter Italy—by country and by passport information." Not certain just how much she should tell Dillon, Emma continued, "Carlos recognized my name on one of the lists, and he tracked me down through the car rental agency and called me. We've agreed to meet for dinner on Friday. He expects to be in Milano this weekend, returning to Roma on Monday." Quickly changing the topic to avoid answering more questions from Dillon, Emma said, "So, now WE need to make plans! How about you come to my suite? There's that second piece I want you to hear before we make any definite plans. I hope it's not too late for you?" she asked, knowing Dillon was a night owl.

"Be there in ten, Em. How 'bout we order up some food and drink for us, too?"

"Fine, anything special for you?" Emma asked.

"No, just me usual—if they 'ave it." Dillon laughed and hung up. "Doin' a good job, Carlos…you don't miss a thing…but me ole eyes still 'ave it!" Dillon shook his head, knowing full well Carlos had been to the Manin.

Emma quickly changed into something comfortable. Despite the large meal they both had earlier, she felt late night hunger pangs for something light. Expecting they'd work for several hours before the night ended, she called room service.

"Si, this is Signora Llewelyn in room 309. Please send up a tray of food—a tray of different *formagglos* with a bottle of *Vino Bianco* and *tre birro. Grazie, Caio.*"

Picking up her brief case, she found it locked just as she had left it. Laying it on the bed next to the light, something caught Emma's eye around the lock—subtle new dents—scratches around the lock! Scratches in the metal she hadn't noticed before. Sensing something was different, an internal alarm went off, and she decided not to open it until Dillon saw it, too. So much was happening at the office and now here. But why? And who? Were all of these events happening because someone was interested in her business here in Milano? *Did Marcus Rudolphi learn about Lucinda's meeting with me? Could someone have reported to the Rudolphi family her visit to the law office in London and then discovered my trip to Milano—putting the two together?* Emma continued to mull these questions in her mind, when she felt a chill and uneasiness inside.

**A chill...a fear...a feeling alone...sharp acrid smells...**

Then it was gone in a flash!

A soft rap at the door took her thoughts back to answer the door.

*"Avanti."* The door opened and Dillon walked in. Trying not to appear too alarmed, she immediately handed him the briefcase letting him sit down in the lounge chair next to the light.

"What do you make of this?" she asked, pointing to the lock on the briefcase.

Dillon carefully examined the whole case and noticed the remnants of scratches and dents around the lock.

"'ave you 'ad this case with you the w'ole time since you de-planed in Roma?" he asked.

"Yes, I think so," she answered, thinking back to the night spent in Firenze. "Once I arrived in Milano, I've had it with me at all times. I took it to the restaurant where we ate tonight to give you the materials on this case—there was a time when I was in the shower after I arrived—before we met tonight, the case was out of my sight then. But I wasn't aware someone had been in the room while I was in the shower. I dressed for dinner with you and called for a maid to remove my clothes from the suitcases and put them in the wardrobe. I was present when she arrived and did the unpacking, but I left with the briefcase to meet you before she finished unpacking." Emma recounted to Dillon.

"No wait! I'm not certain I did have it with me the first time I tried to locate you just after I arrived at the hotel. I hadn't read your message to me when I first arrived and just went to the Machiavelli Lounge on a hunch you'd be there. I'm not certain if I took it with me or not! But I was only gone about twenty minutes!"

"Then Em', we 'ave someone very interested in knowin' what we're doin' 'ere and *we* 'ave some idea they're tryin' to learn what that is from the contents of the briefcase!" Dillon laid the briefcase on the bed and started walking around the room quietly, just looking—as if scanning for something only he was aware of. He signed to Emma not to speak which made her uneasy to know that they knew something about the two of them, but she and Dillon had no idea about who it would be. Emma still had to discuss the second tape—Lucinda Rudolphi's description of the lists.

"These events happenin' changes things a bit for us, Em." Whispering he said, "I need to 'ear this other tape before we decide 'ur itinerary tomor'ow?"

Emma nodded yes. In a louder, casual voice, Dillon said, "Em, how's about some music, girl. I'd like to hear anything now—need for relaxin'!"

Emma turned the radio on loud. Dillon started playing the second tape using the earpiece so only he could hear the taped conversation. If someone was eavesdropping, he didn't want him, or her, to hear or know what he was doing. Re-playing excerpts from the two tapes over on the recorder at intervals, during certain parts, he handed her the earpiece to play parts of the conversation he was particularly interested in. Emma knew Dillon didn't trust anyone now—*and neither did she*. His actions told her others may be listening in to their conversations. He was cautious and deliberately chose his words— not mentioning the word tapes in his conversational comments.

He randomly moved about the room to confuse anyone who was triangulating his position from outside the hotel—hoping it would cause interference. Periodically, he'd check out certain areas of the suite, looking every place for a listening device, all the time he had the tapes playing in his earpiece. On a small pad, he jotted down some words and phrases, after replaying different portions of the tapes again. When he finished, he handed Emma his written pages of notes to read.

The notes contained single phrases and names: *Rudolphi family— Marcus—Dr. Ennio* Carruchi = *E.C.—Villa Del Christianna— cemetery records—Antonio and Angela—Perugia, the little boy— the study = list of names.*

Emma knew the last notation was the list Lucinda referred to in their meeting. Handing her a second note, he instructed her not to speak out loud about their plans for tomorrow until he was sure their rooms were not bugged with listening devices. He would check Emma's room in the morning. The rest of the evening they pretended to exchange verbal pleasantries, ate and drank from the tray of food, and still formulated a plan just on paper what they would do tomorrow to get started looking for answers.

Emma wrote down one question on a pad. "Dillon, do you think the Rudolphi family learned about Lucinda's meeting with me, and they're the ones keeping tabs on us, trying to learn more information?"

Dillon answered with a shrug of his shoulders, putting a finger to his lips, signaling her not to speak about this or any other important matters. Walking out on the balcony, he took out his cell phone and made several brief telephone calls to Roma and London, speaking in short, cryptic staccato-like phrases, which probably had double meanings in his conversations. None of his conversation made sense to Emma. When he hung up, he didn't share or explain to her what he did or said—and she felt too tired to pursue it.

"Em, we should see some of the countryside tomorrow and plan a trip to Firenze. I understand they have great sights to see, so in the mornin' we can plan our trip—It's gettin' late now."

167

If anyone was listening, they would think Emma and Dillon were going to Firenze. In reality they agreed, nonverbally, to return Emma's car to the rental agency in the morning and get a replacement at another agency. Dillon felt a new, clean car was safer to start their investigation and hopefully would confuse those who thought they were driving the Peugeot to Firenze.

The plan was for Emma to drop off the Peugeot while Dillon made arrangements to get a second rental car at a different agency and pick her up at a preplanned destination.

The night meeting lasted longer than Emma anticipated. She hadn't realized that she drank several glasses of wine until she saw the bottle was half gone and felt the lightness in her head. Dillon finished his beers and most of the cheese and crackers, while Emma did eat some fruit to stave off sleep. Both of them felt the effects of the long day and decided to call it quits for the night. Dillon walked over to the vase of silver roses and fingered them, he said, "Em, did you e'er find out who's yur admirer?"

She didn't answer. Thoughtfully, he rationalized aloud, "Carlos knew you were comin'? Or...did the Rudolphis know it, too?"

"Em, I'm takin' the rest of this food back to me room," he said, motioning to include the two tapes and recorder. "I'm still feelin' 'ungry for the rest of this."

Emma locked the briefcase with the rest of her notes from the library and put it next to the head of her bed, wedging it snugly between the night table and the bed. If someone tried to get it out, she'd certainly know it.

Dillon put the two tapes on the tray of food with the recorder, covered it with a napkin, and left, stopping outside the door to hear her latch the lock before he took the lift down to his room.

Alone in the room, Emma felt a little frightened. She *was* on the third floor and the suite wasn't easily accessible from the street. Not wanting to take any chances now, she kept only one balcony door open—the farthest door was slightly ajar—and locked the rest of them. She even rearranged some of the sitting room furniture into a random maze, thinking anyone coming into the room from that balcony door would have to wade through the maze of misplaced furniture to get to the bed. They'd certainly trip, and she'd hear them before they got to the bed! Taking a quick shower with the door open, Emma dressed in her gown and robe before slipping into bed. For extra security, she left a dim light on in the sitting room and placed a chair wedged under the door handle, securing it closed tightly.

The mantel clock softly chimed 2:30 a.m. Bed never felt so good—cool and soft.

Reaching down she felt the briefcase next to her...*Dillon is near...Carlos...*

*She heard nothing but the ticking of the mantel clock for several minute....*

# CHAPTER TWENTY-ONE

At six thirty, the alarm sounded softly as Emma reached to turn it off.

The sun's shining streams of light shone through the French balcony doors. Still half asleep, Emma rose and walked out on the balcony as if in a sleep-trance.

**bright streams of colored lights...from the high windows...**
*can't see out...only the sky... a dream...the door opening...*

In the few seconds it lasted, the *dream memory* was gone. The noise from the street cleaners washing and sweeping yesterday's debris sounded loud. Emma noticed a few cars maneuvering around the sweepers while shopkeepers watered the floral arrangements adorning the shop's facades. More awake and alert, Emma turned to scan the balcony and the rest of the suite to see if anything looked different from her recollection of it last night. Everything seemed as she left it. Immediately checking the side of the bed—the briefcase was still wedged in tightly. "Just as I left it!"

A soft rap on the door, *"Chi parla?"*

*"Una momento!"*

"Just me, Em." She heard Dillon's voice and unlocked the door. "What are you doing here so early, Dillon? I thought we were to meet downstairs at eight!"

"We are, me lass." Barely whispering, he said, "I checked me room and didn't find any listen' pieces there. So I guess 'hoever is interested in you may not be on to me bein' 'ere with you." Pointing to the shower, he whispered, "If you're planin' to shower, I want to go over yur room for the buggers."

Dillon turned on the radio to a loud music station as Emma started the shower. Taking a small meter device from his pocket, he started walking around the room, keeping his eye on the instrument's face of digital numbers. Emma wondered how Dillon got a bug detector here in Milano so quickly.

"No, on second thought it's better not to ask how he came by this equipment—just be grateful he has his sources!"

The shower gave Emma time to think about everything that happened yesterday. By the time she finished showering and dressing, Dillon had finished scanning the room and had found 'it'. He was sitting on the bed holding a tiny crystal device, no bigger than the head of a small nail, in his hand. Motioning to Emma that he found it under the bedside table near the phone, he carefully replaced it back into its recessed area where it couldn't be felt if you ran your hand over the surface of the wood. Taking care to return it exactly like he found it, he used a pair of Emma's tweezers to place it into its niche.

Turning up the music, he whispered, "Better leave it be! Whoe'er they are, they'll only plant another cockroach if we take that one out! We'll meet at eight o'clock at the café across the street as planned." In a throaty whisper, he said, "Bring a newspaper." Before leaving, he checked the hallway to make sure it was clear.

Emma finished dressing, deciding to wear jeans and sneakers not certain where this day would take them. She ran a brush through her hair and tied it back. Grabbing her briefcase and shoulder bag and sweater, she checked the room one last time to get a mental picture—not knowing what to expect in her absence. The violet roses caught her eye—"Still so fragrant!"

Emma locked the door and walked to the lift where several couples were waiting—none seemed particularly interested in her; rather, they were more interested in each other's company. Reaching the deserted lobby, she stopped at the gift shop to buy morning papers, then returned her keys and asked for her passport.

*"Si, grazie. Arrivederci."*

*"Che si diverta oggi."* It was a different concierge this morning.

Exiting the lobby door into the bright sunshine, Emma deliberately walked a short distance down the street past the café which was already filling up with patrons. Dillon was seated in the far corner nearest the open area with his back to the stone wall. The table next to him was empty, and she chose that one. He looked totally absorbed in reading his newspaper, appearing completely unaware of her presence, which was exactly the scene he wanted to promote. Quickly glancing towards her, he put away the paper when the waiter set his plate of breakfast before him. The aroma of strong hot coffee perked up Emma's appetite. Seeing the enticing breakfast Dillon ordered, she decided on a big breakfast too. The *cameriere* approached her, but at the last minute, she reconsidered her decision and instead ordered *succo d'arancia, pane tostato con burro, espresso con latte.* Her plate came almost immediately, not allowing her time to completely search her papers for news about the Rudolphi family.

Dillon stood to leave. Standing next to Emma, he placed his newspaper on her table, casually informing her as a friendly tourist that he was finished reading it and left it for her.

"I'm finished with this, ma'am," he said, tipping his cap as if to say good-bye.

*"Grazie!"* Thanking him, she motioned that she already had a paper. As he picked up Emma's papers in place of his; he smiled and started out the café. She finished the last of the espresso coffee, figured out the tick, put the newspaper away in her bag, and left to request the hotel valet to bring her car around to the front.

Back at the hotel, it only took the attendant a few minutes to bring her car around to the front entrance. Driving down the circular drive, she went over their plan—she was to return her car to the rental agency, but first, Dillon instructed her to drive around the corner and park with the engine running.

Hoping she looked like a frustrated tourist figuring out directions from a map to some destination, Emma opened Dillon's paper and read the message he slipped into it.

"Meet you at the bus stop on Via Verziere—nine thirty."

The nearest International Car Agency was in the center of Milano, and she estimated the trip should take half an hour. Inside, there was one other man ahead of her in line making a return. Within a matter of minutes, Emma had completed the necessary forms and was on her way to the nearest bus stop, the Via Verziere.

The sun had given way to clouds, but rain didn't appear imminent. Blue sky shone on the distant horizon. It wasn't hard locating the bus stop. Several small groups had already congregated, waiting for the next *autobus*. Taking advantage of the crowd, Emma deliberately mixed into the middle of the cluster while keeping an eye out for Dillon. A car came around the corner and stopped. It was Dillon motioning her to get in quickly.

"You have great taste in cars, Dillon." It was a new BMW wagon, and Emma knew he chose this model for its four-wheel maneuverability and reliability on the winding, hilly country roads.

"Did you have any trouble leasing the car?" she asked him.

"None at all, Em."

With Dillon driving, Emma asked, "Is this the direction to the Rudolphi Estate? This is a good place to start our search for answers."

"Em, first I want to drive 'round to see if anyone is followin' us. Then, if we're clean, I'll 'ead out of Milano—north to find the Rudolphi Winery. I know it takes up the biggest part of the Rudolphi Estate."

"According to Lucinda's account, the Villa del Christianna is located on the estate on the north side, and I'll want to see the proximity of the villa to the winery." All the while Dillon kept watching his mirrors for a tail.

"If the wine'y is open to tourin', maybe we can sample the fruits of the vine'ards!" Dillon had his way with words—a way of lightening the moment. He had the knack of being able to make Emma smile even in the worst of situations.

"Do ye 'ave a map we can check to see where we should be headin'?" he asked her.

Checking the maps of Milano and Toscana she purchased, Emma found the map key identifying the different wineries in the area. "Are we heading northeast?"

"Best I can tell we are. What's the route number we should be watchin' for?"

Emma noticed he was still keeping a close eye on the rear and side view mirrors.

"Anyone following us?" she asked.

"Don't see a bugger inte'ested in us, but I'm goin' to do an illegal turn 'ere. If someone is back there, I'll spot 'im fur certain!"

Suddenly, the car swerved and hugged the road as they made a sharp U turn into the opposite direction. Emma watched to see if a car was slowing and doing the same maneuver.

"Clean as a new babe—no sight of any tails. So, me Em, which way out of Milano?"

Slowing to the legal speed, they drove out the Via Cuneo, and finally came to the route leading directly to the Rudolphi Vineyards.

"I'd say we 'ave 'bout fifty kilometers to the estate." He looked at Emma next to him.

"Dillon, what's your opinion about Lucinda's story around the little boy she saw in Perugia, thinking it may be her own son, Antonio?"

"To be 'onest Em, if I 'ad just that one piece of information, I'd say she was a grievin' mother still. Then addin' to that, findin' yu're name in her 'usband's study gives it a 'hole different meanin'. I know it appears these two facts seem totally unconnected, but that's the point! I think there's some kind of linkage 'tween those two facts! Not clear to us at this time, but together they're two pieces of *one* puzzle. We need to find out what the rest of that puzzle is."

Dillon savored his words and often made his point known in a pictorial way—and Emma agreed with him.

"You have the copy of written references you wrote out last night after listening to the tapes? I'll be candid with you, Dillon, my foremost curiosity is your last underlined entry—*why my name is on a list kept locked in Marcus Rudolphi's study?"*

"Em, I 'ave a strong feelin' that we'll know the answer to that question when we learn the answers to all our questions 'bout this case! Somehow, it's *all tied together*, and I aim to find out *all the answers!* We 'ave to learn the lay of the land on the Rudolphi Estate, which is why we're 'eaded there. Then we 'ave to learn the names of all the family folks who live on the estate besides Marcus and Lucinda and the old man, Giuseppe Rudolphi. Lucinda mentioned other relatives…members in the family takin' part in the business?"

Dillon looked to her with his question but in the form of an answer. "I 'xpect they all must live somewhere on the estate, too. We 'ave a full tank of petrol!" Emma was aware that Dillon recalled every little detail from the tapes and carefully and logically developed a plan for today.

"First, we'll try for a look at the winery, and if they're doin' tours we'll take one. Then we'll drive around the perimeter of the estate and make us a map of the whole estate—the vineyards and the 'omes locations, markin' security. I 'ope you're good at drawin', girl," he laughed and winked.

To wit! Emma smiled at him.

*He made her feel relaxed and safe even when there was reason to be afraid of what was to come.*

# CHAPTER TWENTY-TWO

It didn't take long to find the *Via di Lecco* from Milano leading to several different vineyards in Tuscany's Wine Region.

Once out in the rural countryside, Emma and Dillon came across a familiar means of transportation for the local folk—horse-drawn carts. Dillon slowed the car, "Em, ask this farmer if this is the way to the Rudolphi Winer'?"

*"Perdonarme. Questo e' le maniera al Rudolphi Winery?"* she asked the young man.

*"Riguarda cinquecento metri avanti,"* he replied, pointing down the road to the main entrance. *"Ringraziarlo molto."*

The young man directed them to go a few more kilometers to where signs directed them to the estate grounds. Quite so, it was impossible to miss the entrance—with the column of Cypress trees aside the massive wrought-iron gates engraved with a large scrolled *"R"* announcing the Rudolphi Winery.

They joined several other cars ahead, entering through the front gate to a road leading up to the main Winery building in the distance. The road's meandering turns went for several kilometers before actually arriving at the main building's emblazoned sign, *"The Rudolphi Winery."*

Everywhere was evidence of the meticulous architectural and landscape design that went into planning the estate grounds. Plainly, the family wanted to create an effect of extravagance to impress visitors that wealth abounded. Along the two-lane road, poplar trees rose, dwarfing smaller compact fruit trees in front laden with lemons and limes ripe for the picking. The winding serpentine road ended at the uniquely distinctive architectural building—made of wood—a noticeable change from the usual stucco-stone facades seen in the distance. Entrance to a parking courtyard was through a security gate with a guard stopping to mark each vehicle with a colored card displayed on the windshield. A second guard recorded certain data— probably the license code and number of occupants in each car.

The large courtyard area surrounding the winery was already half filled, but before they could access the innermost area, each vehicle had to pass still another inspection by a third guard who questioned the occupants.

*"Che sono i suoi nomi?"*

"Aye, I'm Sean and me misses 'ere is Kate O'Malle', from Dublin." The guard nodded and directed us to a pre-chosen parking slot. So far, no evidence of any problems; no sign of recognition—but then, they had no reason to think there should be. Before starting the tour, they decided they'd use their character names, Sean and Kate O'Malley, Irish tourists here on holiday from Ireland, and followed the large group of visitors into a great open foyer room. Dillon immediately went to purchase tickets for the tour, while Emma started wandering about the huge foyer taking in its features—for a definite purpose.

No conspicuous signs of security—except a mirrored ceiling. Clearly a one-way glass from above! No doubt feigning an architectural choice to give the tourist a feeling of space, when actually, it was surveillance of the whole room and its occupants from above. One wall displayed panels of accolades and international awards received for the different kinds of wines produced over the years. Another wall displayed a pictorial history of prominent Rudolphi men with names and dates of each Rudolphi, listing their contribution to the winemaking business. Conspicuously, there were no women's pictures! All of the portraits had remarkable facial and physical resemblances. Emma looked for the names of Giuseppe or Marcus Rudolphi; neither was pictured.

"To gain a portrait—maybe you have to be dead. These past patriarchs go back a hundred years," Emma remarked to herself. To further confuse the newcomer, she counted no less than eight doors off the foyer room. Across the rear wall was a bank of lifts with several security men posted. Looking for evidence of stairs, there were no exit signs—denoting the only point of egress was the front entrance. "Lifts seem the only means to get you up-or down!"

A young, attractive, uniformed woman, whose nametag said, *Gaetana Liocci*, approached their group and introduced herself as their guide. She first spoke in Italian followed with a perfect English translation. Beginning with the introduction to the Rudolphi Winery, Gaetana gave a history lesson about how the Rudolphi Family came to own this land, going back to the fourteenth century.

"Winemaking as we think of it today actually started in this area of Toscana in the fourteenth century because its climate, altitude, and predominance of calcareous soils provided the vital ingredients for viticulture. In the early centuries, it took many years for the newly planted grapes to mature to start the process of selective diversity to make those different early wines. Those first wines bottled were few and only for personal consumption—legend states these wines became well known and were sought after by people in distant regions. Each generation of Rudolphis planted new different varieties of grapes, increasing the yield and diversifying to make singular blends of wines—the Rudolphi vineyard was among the first to plant the Merlot grape that gives us the deepest red—the best Merlot brand today.

World War II completely devastated this whole region, including the vineyards, and for decades wine production was suspended in many Italian wineries—only a few survived to produce wines during the Axis occupation. The production of wine resumed in this Winery within a decade after the Great War ended because of the foresight of Matissimo Rudolphi. Today's successful international business is the result of complete regeneration of the vineyards and new state-of-the-art facilities, along with this new larger winery, which you will shortly observe." The knowledgeable and well-spoken guide continued her comprehensive lessons—no doubt giving security generous time to view each individual in the group—and process them through the security system.

"What we see here today is the result of years of experimentation allowing us to produce many varieties of grapes, contributing to the large diversity of wines we make and sell."

Emma and Dillon listened to Gaetana explain the physical features they would be allowed to see.

"The tour through the building will take about an hour and a half, and wine sampling is available at the end of the tour in the wine shop. All of our wines and champagnes can be purchased and shipped anywhere in the world for those who make large orders."

Gaetana's last instruction was, *"The only rule for the group is no one is to leave the group at any time unless escorted by an employee."*

This told Emma they were all under careful observation during the entire tour. She wasn't sure what Dillon was specifically searching for, but she knew he had a definite purpose for taking this tour. She wanted to imprint a mental image of the each floor plan and the corridors, to remember directions the tour took, notice entrances and exits in relation to doors and windows, and observe the kind of security measures in each area. If they had to return here to find the answers they were searching for, it may have to be an illegal entry. As the group slowly followed Gaetana, everywhere, Emma saw potential evidence of security.

At the first level, security was the sheer number of uniformed personnel seen everywhere. More sophisticated levels had to be security cameras, well concealed. They hid them as a conscious decision to make visitors feel comfortable, not demonstrate that "big brother" was watching. Too, observable were the special concave glass ceiling inserts located around the ceiling lights. This arrangement most likely concealed cameras capable of three-hundred-sixty-degree surveillance in the room below, probably personnel stationed to get first-hand sight!

The tour began when they exited the lobby through the last door into a long hall that included well-lit window views. Upon closer inspection, the window scenes were false, very good images by computer technology depicting a scene from each window, giving a multi-dimensional view of the near and distant vineyards. Their guide said, "You can see a view of the vineyards from this spot!" The door at the end of the first long corridor opened into a large room with a glass wall for viewing a mechanical conveyor system. Here the wines are bottled, probably just one of many conveyors in the building. This bottling room was where the bottles were filled with a white wine. The group stopped to watch the personnel dressed in white coats, hats, and face masks similar to surgical masks, working at controls monitoring the system on a gigantic panel of dials and monitors, conveying a certain level of cleanliness is necessary before they're sent for labeling and corking.

Emma thought, *The source of the wine for botting has to come from storage vats piped in here...somewhere else in this building— interesting and very sophisticated!"*

She tried to keep track of the direction they were moving from the point of origin, but it was confusing without seeing any true outside reference point.

*Not one real window scene since we left the main foyer room.*

As their group passed from one room into another corridor, each uniformed guard—with no outward evidence of a firearm—held a portable radio. As the party passed through each door, a guard was stationed on both sides of the door, counting every person in the group as they left one section and another counting them when they entered a new area. Emma bet this information was forwarded to the next station—making certain no one slipped away without being detected.

*What would happen if there was a discrepancy? I'm certain a central alarm from some central security command station would flash...and I'd bet this whole place just shuts down...like a prison! I can't bring attention to myself...but how I'd love to see that happen!"*

Once the entire group was inside each room, Emma noticed the guard radioing information—probably giving a head count to the next station. Clearly, she had no idea what part of the building she was in—but there was a feeling they were going in a circular route.

At the next station they came to, there were heavy metal doors, slowing the group down. The guards were intent on allowing only one visitor in single file to enter this room—as if the process was done deliberately to accomplish some purpose.

*"Now, why does one person enter through the door completely before another...of course! They're taking each person's picture as they enter the room!"*

When it came to Emma to enter, she deliberately lowered her head as if to check the ground footing. Inside, she heard exclamations from individuals as they took in the staggering site before them. The size of the room was colossal. The equipment was gigantic and oversized. Everything was on an enormous scale—more like a warehouse. From the odor, it was actually the Fermentation Aging Storage area.

"I never realized how much security a winery needed," Emma whispered to Dillon.

The massive size of everything in this room was something bordering on gargantuan to see. The fermentation room held colossal over-sized oaken barrels, suspended on chains and stacked on multiple levels above each other up to the ceiling, all tremendously impressive. Most people commented on the smell of damp wood and acrid fermentation permeating the room. It was a smell she knew went with making the wine's characteristics malolactic fermentation that adds to the silky and elegant texture of a wine. For a fleeting second, Emma had a memory of another odor.

**Sharp...bitter...acrid smell...a cold stream of air...odors of laboratory smells...and pain...**

Then the remembrance dissipated...gone!

Shrugging the sinister feeling off, Emma kept taking a visual imprint of the entire room. It was so large she couldn't see the end of the room to count all of the oak vats she saw, and whatever else this room contained beyond her sight. That part of the room was roped off and darkened to keep tourists at a distance from that end. She did manage to count twenty or more wooden barrels reaching ceiling height, maybe twenty-five deep. But in the distant darkness, there were outlines suggesting many more wooden shapes.

*There has to be a way to access the barrels on the upper level, but I don't see how from this vantage point!*

That could only mean there was a corridor or entries behind the vats that accessed the different levels. Unquestionably, this room had its own level of security—someone had to be watching everyone and everything in this place. The room looked rectangular, but with it being so large, Emma had a feeling it was actually a large circular room. If bottling the wine was on the outer portion of the building, and the fermentation was located in a core area, then there could be a hub between the two, too. What else is this innermost area *really* used for? *There's much more than wine fermenting here in these vats than can possibly be bottled at peak ripening! So—what do the vats hold besides wine?* Emma kept posing questions and thoughts to herself.

Dillon and Emma became separated halfway through the tour. Locating sight of him, she made her way over to him through the crowd. "Sean, have you noticed how remarkable all this equipment is in the winery?" Emma asked, hoping he would catch the implied double meaning.

"Aye…Kate, it's all so int'restin' to me. I can see why they would want to guard it all careful'y, with all the expense to it!" She knew he was checking the different kinds of security throughout the floors they passed through—as was she.

At the end of the tour, Gaetana led them into a large, dark, paneled room filled with beautifully upholstered chairs and tables, giving the room an appearance of a large opulently decorated Italian Café. On the perimeter of the room was a circular mahogany bar completely encircling the room replete with shiny brass rails. Behind the bar were beautifully carved individual box cabinets and shelves stocked with wines and champagnes according to color and price reaching up to the vaulted ceiling, accessible only by a movable ladder behind the bar. The selection of wines and champagnes was substantial from the rare Vino Bianco Chardonnay wines to the more popular Vino Rosso Pinot Noir; sparkling champagnes to the sweet Chiantis, to the recently popular Merlots, and the rare Reisling Ice wines—all meant to impress the visitor to buy the best. Here, the large assembly dispersed into smaller groups making their way to the bar to sample the different wines for purchases. The champagnes alone took up one side of the room in the same affluent display.

"Sean, wines may not be your milieu, but we have to sample some of the wines and make purchases so as not to stand out from the rest of the group," Emma said softly.

"I agree, Kate. But I'll leave most of the samplin' and buyin' to you. I'll get a glass and mingle with the seated guests," he said as he asked for a glass of their best Bianco Chardonnay. Another surprise—Dillon did know his vintage *vinos!*

The young maids behind the bar were eager to serve the noisy group. Emma's first choice would be a white wine. A young girl was serving a small group next to her, as she listened to her conversation with the other customers. Seeing Emma's interest, she came over to where she was seated.

"May I help you, *Signora?*" she asked speaking perfect English.

"*Si*, I'd like a glass of a Vino Bianco or a wine nearest to a Pinot Grigio?"

She looked so young, in her early teens. Pouring Emma's wine, she instructed her on how this pinot wine was made, knowing the variety of grapes used to give its unique flavour and the precise fermentation process to give it its unique taste.

"The fruit flavors are refined and enhanced through several different barrel fermentations that contribute to the subtle roasted vanilla aroma that compliments the rich fruity characteristics."

"*Si*, this is an excellent wine! This is one I'll purchase." Hoping to learn more information from the barmaid, Emma decided to taste one other brand and chose a Merlot.

The young server returned and Emma asked, "How does someone get a job here at the winery serving these wines?"

Smiling and hesitating, she said, "It was my father. He has been a friend with the family for a very long time, and because of his long acquaintance, he was able to get this position for me. My father, he has worked in the vineyard for many years."

Emma asked her name.

"Maria de Compo."

"Maria, may I try a Merlot?"

While she was pouring her glass of the deep burgundy-colored wine, Emma asked, "Maria, do you and your family live on the estate here?"

*"Si, Signora.* My family has lived here for many years now, and my whole family is involved in growing the grapes and tending the vineyards."

Noticeably, Maria quickly changed the subject back to her job. "This wine you taste is our finest Merlot. Our Tuscan grapes ripen with notes of bright cherry and ripe raspberries crafted with exotic spices exclusively for this region. This particular Merlot you are sampling has depth and complexity for the serious wine connoisseur. It is expensive, but well worth the price."

"I agree with your appraisal, Maria. This is a fine Merlot. I like your presentation very much!" Emma asked how she could purchase some of the wines to take with her.

"There are agents at those windows across the room ready to take your orders," she said, pointing to a glass room at the farthest end of the bar. Emma caught Dillon's eye and motioned for to him to meet her over at the agent's window.

They made their way to get in line to make their purchases. "I'm going to buy several bottles of wine to take with us. I wish I could send some back home, but I know that's not possible! Do you have a preference, Dillon?" she asked, as they slowly made their way up to the counter.

"Actual'y, the glass of Chardonna'I 'ad was superb! I recommend we get at least one bottle, me dear." Emma purchased four different bottles of the wine, paid in cash, and got her ticket to pick them up when they left the winery. Sales personnel informed their group that once they made their purchases, no one could return to the bar—or any other area. Once the purchase was complete, a guard ushered them out through a different door than the one they entered through—not returning directly back to the foyer where they started.

Walking through the corridor, it felt like they were going around in a circular direction that ended at a bank of lifts. The lifts would probably take them to the ground floor. Inside the lift were front and rear doors.

"I'm almost positive we were walking in a slightly elevated circular direction through the whole winery tour!" Emma said to Dillon.

Their lift was unusually large with beautiful dark mahogany wood accented with a shiny brass panel of "blank" buttons. Emma counted the buttons and saw that there were at least seven or eight buttons, all in a horizontal row—not vertical—none marked. Was that done to confuse which was up or down? Emma was certain Dillon was figuring out how many levels the lifts went to.

She whispered to Dillon, "Once we get outside, look to see if it's possible to identify the different levels of floors in the building—windows usually indicate different floor levels." But this was no ordinary building—with no ordinary windows!

The lift door opened and they exited to a whole different room—not even sure they were on the ground floor. Here uniformed employees assisted the visitors with their purchases. Not only was their purchase ready, but each bottle was beautifully packaged in different fabric bags. A fine gold-like mesh held the Pinot Grigio while the Chardonnay was wrapped in a deep red velvet bag with a gold medallion around it. The medallion appeared to be a miniature Rudolphi family coat of arms, with a large black "R," the initial we saw on the entrance gate.

*The wine delivered to my room in the velvet bag with the "R"! My God...yes! The flowers and wine...but who... sent the violet flowers and the wine—Rudolphi wine—Who knows my favorite rose is the violet rose...and my favorite wine...the Pinot Giorgio? Who? Is it Carlos?*

For a second Emma felt a cold chill. She thought, *I must find out if it was Carlos who sent the gifts or...? But how? These wines are sold everywhere!*

Their four bottles of wine were packaged together in a special canvas valise with the Rudolphi Vineyard logo on the outside. Exiting the winery, they reached their car, not a great distance away despite leaving by another exit. Emma pretended to take a pebble out of her sneaker and bent down to see what the exterior of the building looked like. There were several dozen windows—all slender and randomly spaced in such a way it was impossible to determine any one level. The architectural form deliberately designed to confuse the viewer about the number of levels in the building.

"Are those windows real or dummies?" she asked. Dillon shrugged in uncertainty.

Emma checked her watch—the tour took several hours, and the sun had passed the high point in the sky. When they entered the car, the oppressive heat was intense. Inside the car, Emma remarked, "Dillo…Sean, that place is an education in security!"

He grabbed her arm and pulled her toward him softly saying, "Kate, 'tis like a different car…feels unusual!" Dillon whispered to her to keep her from saying anything more.

"How do you know?" she whispered in his ear.

"The seat's been pushed back from where I left it, and the visor's position changed… among a few other changes!"

"You mean they search every car coming in when the occupants leave it?"

"No, I 'ave a feelin' we may be the on'y car they searched!"

"How did they know…?"

Unexpectedly, Dillon put his hand to her mouth to stop her from blurting out anything more. Instead, he took out a note pad and wrote, "I don't know. Take double care—take nothing for granted – say nothing." He mouthed, "Don't say an'thin' more 'til I tell you." They drove off.

* * *

In the security room inside the winery a monitor was running a tape of the visitor's parking area showing Emma and Dillon entering their car.

"Signore Marcus, do you want me to follow them?"

"No, no. I take it you didn't find anything in the car when you searched it?"

"No. It is a rental car. Clean," the guard replied.

"Then we'll know where to look for them, Edwardo, if we need to locate them. Who's tracking them now?" Marcus asked.

A senior guard answered, "The tracking device we planted has a range of one-hundred twenty-five kilometers. We have a truck in the field with their frequency, and they will call us to keep us informed of their next destination."

"Good!" Marcus took a cigarette out of the gold case and lit up his special Turkish brand. The pungent, sweet-smelling smoke curled upward, as he thought about Emma Llewelyn so close in Milano.

"I hope you enjoyed the wine and flowers, my dear. Violet roses are rare and beautiful—just like you, my dear, charming Emma—just like you." He walked out of the security room toward his private office.

"Baba, I have been reviewing security tapes. It seems we have two new visitors in Milano. Emma Llewelyn and her private investigator, Dillon O'Rourke, just drove away. They were here in the winery with that last tour group," Marcus said, speaking to Giuseppe Rudolphi sitting opposite the desk.

Giuseppe remarked, "I find the timing of their arrival in Milano and now at the winery too coincidental to be benign! I wonder what they are looking for?"

"I will inform Luigi about their presence here today…if he's not aware of it…to make certain he's monitoring their activities at all times. I do not want anything to go wrong before next week for our presentation at Villa Latinestto!" Marcus gave a command to his assistant to locate Luigi Rudolphi.

"*Si!* See that you do! You tell Luigi to do whatever he must to make certain nothing happens to delay our plans!" Giuseppe Rudolphi's command was loud and forceful.

"Baba, I will tell him one of them is expendable if there is trouble! He will know who it is! **The other? Well, she is someone I will take of personally!** Luigi will know exactly what I mean. Nothing for you to worry about, Baba," Marcus Rudolphi reassured his father and helped the elderly Rudolphi with his cane over to the door. "You must be getting tired, Papa. I will call for Dino to take you home now. Lucinda is waiting for my call—to make certain everything is ready for our charity party on Sunday."

"Ah..*si*..your party, *si.*" Marcus knew Giuseppe did not approve of his merrymaking but overlooked it.

"You are a good son, Marcus—not like that other one!" Giuseppe patted Marcus's hand in fatherly consent.

"Now, Baba, don't upset yourself." Giuseppe complimented his oldest son with tender strokes, something he exhibited outwardly only to his eldest son.

"Dino, take Baba directly home and make certain he rests." Marcus waited until the limousine reached the back road to the Villa Tempietto. Shaking his head, Marcus understood why his brother Luigi was such a trial to his father and knew one day he would be the one to do something about it. Something permanent—even if he is his brother by blood!

Marcus sat at his desk quietly smoking. "Emma, what were you looking for here, today?" Pondering his thoughts, he said, "I knew you returned to Milano, but why did you come to the winery?" Marcus's demeanor changed from a calm composure to outward agitation and picked up the phone. "Luigi? Come to my office now!" He didn't wait for a response and hung up.

\* \* \*

Dino drove into the drive at the Villa Tempietto, the grandest villa on the estate. Giuseppe continued to live in the large villa after the death of his wife, Gabriella Rudolphi, who died while giving birth to his youngest son Luigi Rudolphi. Secretly, Giuseppe blamed Luigi for the death of his beloved Gabriella. Without his mother's tender hand to guide him, he became the wild one in the family. Giuseppe had no tolerance for his youngest son! Dino realized Luigi is the unpredictable son—possibly a loose cannon—not like his predictable older brothers Marcus and Dominic. He had to watch out for Luigi—a bad seed!

Once the old man was down for his afternoon rest period, Dino used the opportunity to contact Central Station—it was imperative to pass on the latest information about new password codes—and now he must inform them about the meeting next week at the villa. The latter piece of information was important for Control to know before next week, if a plan was in the making to get an agent inside the complexes. Most importantly, this last piece of new information discovered today at the winery by Marcus—this could change everything and he had to let them know immediately! **"They're on to Emma and Dillon's presence!"**

Luigi was the one Dino took extra precautions to watch carefully; even though Marcus wielded the power, it was Luigi's volatility that was most dangerous for Emma and Dillon! Hearing Marcus's words, "She is someone I will take care of personally." For Emma's safety, Control must know Marcus is Emma's greatest threat here!

* * *

Pulling off to the side of the road, Dillon pretended to check a problem with a tire and opened the boot. In a hidden compartment at the rear of the boot, he took out a small electronic instrument—and cleverly concealing it in his hand, he scanned the outside of the car, but found nothing. Next he checked inside. *It's too easy, no imagination!* He thought. Dillon motioned for Emma to see what he found. Carefully removing the screws from the door handle, the meter jumped to the extreme positive end of the dial. Dillon softly felt inside the handle and removed a minature orb disc. Just as he found it, a car pulled up alongside them and asked if they needed assistance. It was a couple from the tourist group.

"You folks need assistance?"

"No, we're right fine! Though me wheel was makin' too much clatter!" Dillon leaned into their car window and inconspicuously tossed the disc into the rear of the couple's car while distracting them with his witty chatter.

"Thanks, 'preciate yur askin'!"

Watching the couple drive away, he remarked, "Now let 'hem follow 'hem for a while! 'Ope they make it interestin' for whoever!"

"Who planted that device, Dillon?"

"Em, I'd 'ave to say it was someone at the winer' in the Rudolphi family! I guess the questions I'm askin' is, what do they want to find out by 'avin' us followed? That was a powerful new piece of trackin' device! What do they want to learn from us? 'Ow are we a threat to 'hem...so soon?" Dillon's questions were the same for Emma—worrisome.

"I'm glad you're here with me, Dillon."

Knowing they could safely speak now, she asked Dillon, "Why does a winery need *that* level of security? Are they following us because we were at the winery? Why should that be a threatening move...unless the Rudolphis think we know something about them... that's threatening? Does that make any sense to you Dillon? Clearly we know the Rudolphis are behind all these bugging devices! Is it because Lucinda came to me, or is it because of me?" Dillon heard her questions...but before he answered any of them, he was sorting out all of the information they learned that day. Slowly, he made his way back into the line of cars exiting the grounds.

"To answer yur first question, Em, that place is loaded with the most sophisticated securit' I've seen all together in one place in a blood' 'ell of a long time! My question too, is that 'mount of securit' needed 'cause of the winer'—or is there another reason why all that 'lectronic securit' and manpower is concentrated there?"

Dillon clearly felt Emma's connection to the Rudolphi family was more than her association with Lucinda. There was a connection she was not fully aware of, and that's what scared him the most! Not wanting to frighten Emma with his true feelings—more than she already was—he explained, "You mentionin' Lucinda's confidin' in you...that may be a trigger for their surveillance on us—or it may 'ave something to do with yur name in Marcus's library. Then...it could be both!"

*Dillon* gave Emma a reassuring look and squeezed her hand, *"Either way, Em, we'll find all the answers!"*

# CHAPTER TWENTY-THREE

"I know we will! Now, *you* tell *me* what you saw in there… and…what's your opinion for that level of security in a winery?"

With Dillon driving, they exited the Rudolphi Estate onto the public trunk road going south.

"First, Em, I want to drive 'round the perimeter of entire estate to get a good look at the number of Villas on the grounds to get a feel for its dimensions. On the seat next to you is a newspaper with a sketchbook inside. Yur gonna draw what you see on the estate grounds…markin' down an'thin' that appears to look like possible securit' devices. Make notations on the drawin' where there are buildin's and vine'ard terraces on the estate; estimate their location—designate north, south, east, or west on the map."

"How will I know what the special kind of security device looks like?"

"Keep your eye trained on the perimeter for small boxes alon' edges of the road; they'll 'ave camouflage 'round 'hem. They could look black, green, or metallic—they'll blend in with the landscape. If you see an' unusual apparatus, not usual'y seen on a country roadside, point it out to me 'mediately! If I see one, I'll point it out to you. Listen for barkin' dogs, too, and try to pinpoint the direction they're comin' from—mark it down to some reference point on yur drawin'. Most importantl', if you see any uniformed patrols, point them out to me at once!" Dillon had his thoughts well-organized, exactly what he wanted identified.

"One last item, if you see antennae posts stickin' out of the ground, small or big, show me! They could be an ancillar' power sources for transmittin' radio or telephone signals. If we can find one, I can tell what they're used for. It wouldn't surprise me to find the latest fiber optic miniature transmitters out here instead of the large ones atop the ground." Dillon drove at a moderate pace, giving her time to sketch the sights she saw on the land.

"But to answer yur other questions to me back there, let me summarize what I saw." Emma knew Dillon hadn't missed a detail.

"There's 'idden cameras in the ceilin's and in the walls. The walls 'ad very small eyeholes almost undetectable—spaced at intervals— and you'd miss 'hem unless you actuall' knew what to look for. I guess you'd call 'hem 'peepholes' for want of a better name. They probab'y 'ave camera lens be'ind them—maybe even laser lens takin' pictures of every person passin' by 'hem, which means there's a main securit' room somewhere that processes all this information. The floors 'ave motion sensors in them, but don't ask 'ow I know— it's somethin' you learn 'bout in me past particular kind of work. Throughout the 'hole buildin', there's laser alarms built into doors, walls, windows—you name it—it 'as a sensor. The doors are wired to give an electronic signal if touched when they 'ave an electrical alarm turned on—that would be at night most likel'. Inside every door, there's 'idden panels probably where screenin' plates and coded alarms are used to access...they'd 'ave a program set to de-activate the alarms at certain times. Inside those panels—don't know if its palm-prints, voice or eye patterns, or a numerical code—or all of 'hem—that allows certain personnel inside—into certain areas." Dillon kept his eyes on the road as he continued with a descriptive, detailed account of his assessment of security at the winery.

"The fermentation room? Now there's somethin' else to see! First, there's some kind of complicated alarm system with a signal to deliver a lot of 'lectricit' to an' who gets near 'hem—pit' the bloke who gets too close to those vats! He'd feel that zap of 'lectricit'— give 'im a mean burn. I didn't 'ave enough time to figure just 'ow it worked—or *why* the wine vats are alarmed! If there's somethin' other than wine in them vats...whatev'r it is, alarms could be necessar' to keep it secret. The floors in there 'ave timed-spaced laser beam alarms—beams flashin' in a random pattern, probably set to cycle in several predictable patt'ns—they were off when we visited, of course. Its 'arder for an'one to penetrate that kind of settin' than the Tower of London! It's me guess…if the system is breached—could be a dual alarm system—a silent alarm goes to a Central Station while it delivers a stingin' shot to an'one comin' in contact with 'hem!" All the while he explained what he found, he managed to keep his attention on the direction he was driving around the estate.

"Em…what's yur opinion 'bout the wine vats? Do you think the're used for somethin' other than wine fermentation?"

"What else would you put into vats…gigantic containers that needed to be alarmed—to keep others from finding out their contents?" Emma answered Dillon with her own question.

"That's the bloody good question, Em! Another sight of extreme securit' are 'hem lifts. Now why would lifts need to 'ave guards 'round them when visitors are there?"

"I suppose if a visitor strayed and took a lift to another area, they could see something they shouldn't. If there's something there so secret—they could compromise their secrets!" Emma added, "not to mention their life!"

"Each lift has a set of its own sensors and television cameras that gives a three-dimensional view inside the room…which, me lass, is why I said, that place is overkill for securin' a winer'. Now the question is—**what else needs such an elaborate securit' alarm system? Is it to keep someone out? Or is it to keep someone in?"** Dillon looked directly at Emma to see her reaction to his questions. She was amazed at what Dillon saw and how he evaluated it so thoroughly. Actually, what he told her frightened her even more— she thought he read her fear!

Emma wanted to discuss more possible reasons for the high level of security they found, but she needed to concentrate on drawing the sights on the estate and roadside features. At times, the road narrowed and other times it was very wide; the wider areas led to estate gates to different villas located within the estate. On her drawing, Emma mapped out several large villas in relation to the sloping landscapes surrounding them. Many larger residences had terraces in the rear or at the side of the dwelling. Some of the villas had swimming pools with terraced gardens and tall trees fencing them. She was surprised she didn't see more outward signs of life—not unusual for this time of day. With the sun at its hottest point, most people retreated inside to cooler areas. Scattered throughout the vineyards were smaller, plain dwellings, and at times, she did hear dogs barking seeming to come from the smaller homes; most likely the worker's family homes. At one home on the hillside, she saw a few children and women working in the nearby vineyard.

As Dillon instructed, Emma pointed out security features. "Over there, Dillon! Is that a box you warned me about…in front of those several fence posts?" She pointed to it.

"Aye…that it is!" From this point on, they saw some of the boxes were better concealed while others looked as if they were just recently placed in the ground from the fresh loose dirt around them, not as well packed down or overgrown with brush.

"Yeah, that's exact'y what I'm lookin' for, Em." Dillon took pictures of several boxes.

Carefully noting each site on her illustrations, Emma noticed that a pattern appeared. "Dillon, they're all located at equal intervals so far!"

"If it what's I think they are, they'd 'ave to be Em."

"Em, take the camera and get pictures of these antennae and the mounds in front of 'hem as I slow down; I want to check 'hem out."

Dillon took out a handheld radio and dialed a code on it. It gave off several sounds while, simultaneously, different colored lights lit up on the radio dial.

"They're transmitters to link up radio-telephone lines—like sophisticated short wave radios—or remote controlled fiber optic receivers—maybe e'en a laser system. They may e'en 'ave the capacit' to give an 'lectrical shock, or act like a laser beam if someone violates the perimeter—when they'r on."

When they had driven about forty-five kilometers around the property, they came upon an entrance to one of the *villas* that had a tall, heavy, iron-grilled gate and fence. Emma became excited at what they saw. "Dillon! Slow down a little—I want to take pictures!" The grillwork was beautifully scrolled with ornate loops and figures.

It actually had the initials *"R"* formed into the scrolling, *just like the winery's gate!* Next to the gate was a small guardhouse with one man inside. As Dillon slowed down, he waved to the guard; Emma had her camera out to take pictures of the gate and the gatehouse next to the fence.

"Em, don't let 'hem see you takin' pictures—they may confiscate the camera if they catch you!" The guardhouse was about eight meters high against the five meter high fence behind it that was partially concealed with tall well-spaced shrubbery.

"I suspect there's another smaller gate be'ind the guard's 'ouse, too."

"I think I did get a good picture of the gatehouse with some of the area behind the fence."

"Good girl!" Emma was totally unaware Dillon was watching her.

"Who do you think lives ther', Em?" Dillon asked.

"If I have to guess, I'd say it was the patriarch, Giuseppe Rudolphi and his family. I believe they call it the Villa Tempietto—meaning 'small temple.'"

Straining out of the window with binoculars, Emma said, "I can see the house now…it's a huge stone villa—looks like a medieval castle with turrets and towers. I can make out the Italian flag and another one flying atop. Probably the insignia flag of the Rudolphi family! It certainly isn't a small humble home!"

Around a turn, Dillon turned off the road and parked on the opposite side of the road behind a clump of trees. "Let me see those glasses, Em?" She handed him her binoculars. They got out of the car and crossed over the road to get a closer look at the fence and grounds with the binoculars—as close-up as Dillon dared. The sun was dipping lower in the western sky behind the hills, casting deep shadows on the landscape.

Dillon took his time, looking long and carefully in all directions before he said anything. "I'd say for sure the iron fence is electrified. There's e'en some kind of secondar' silent trip wire alarms around the inner shrubs, if someone does penetrate the fence alarm, but I can't be sure. The 'mount of small shrub next to the fence tells me there're 'idden securit' wires. I'd bet they 'ave guard dogs near'r the 'ouse, too, probabl' roam that area at night."

From a crouched position behind a patch of shrubs, they watched a speeding car drive down the serpentine drive inside the grounds, away from the *casa,* with their high-beam headlights on illuminating the Iron Gate. The gate automatically swung open, allowing the car to pass through without stopping with only a wave of the guard's hand to acknowledge them. The black car slowed once through the gates, and then turned in their direction. Suddenly Dillon grabbed her and pushed her down flat on the ground, pretending to be in a romantic clutch in case someone in the car spotted them. His attention was really timing the gates' mechanism to determine how long they stayed open. They barely breathed, trying to stay absolutely still, clutched in each other's arms while he checked his watch and the gate—until it automatically latched shut. "Thirty-eight seconds!"

He saw her gazing up at him and slowly both sat upright after the black car sped off in the distance. It was heading northeast into the hills.

"Couldn't make out who was inside—too dark. But it sure woulda been nice to know where they're goin' tonight! Did you see the faces of an'one inside, Em?"

"No...I was afraid to look for fear someone would see us!" Emma felt vulnerable out in the open field in front of the villa.

"I want to get a look inside that gatehouse, Em, to look for the 'lectrical panel. That'll tell us a lot! Let's drive back past the guard's 'ouse again, and you pretend to ask for directions—maybe I can get a better look inside."

Hurrying back to the car, they drove back toward the gatehouse while Dillon purposely steered close to the gatehouse and stopped. A single guard came out and approached their car. On pretence, Emma asked for directions to Como, possibly the direction the black car sped. The uniformed keeper pointed north telling us in broken English to look for road signs once beyond the crest of the hill to Como. Just as they were about to drive away, a silver convertible sports car sped around the corner of the trunk road raising a dust trail behind it. Intent on watching the car, it turned into the estate gate in front of us. Grabbing the camera, Emma tried to hide behind Dillon to take a get a picture of the driver.

The man driving the car was Italian-looking with dark hair and wore sunglasses, fairly young looking, while the woman sitting next to him had a headscarf around her head and sunglasses. With Emma snapping as many pictures as she could, Dillon slowly drove away. She was hoping the woman was Lucinda. If she were the woman, this would indicate the man might be Marcus Rudolphi.

"That was not Lucinda! That woman had very dark hair blowing out from under her headscarf. Lucinda's hair is brilliant red!" Emma flatly told Dillon.

"Not to change the subject, I do believe our speedin' black car was headin' in the direction of Como." Dillon said in an abstract thought.

"We still 'aven't seen the entire perimeter of the estate, Em, and I need to know just 'ow big it is. So keep on drawin' as I'm going around the last part of it before it gets an' darker. Then we'll start back to Milano."

The sun was dipping the last golden glimmer of light into the western sky. Emma and Dillon made a sharp turn and immediately saw another gated entrance to a second grandiose villa. Only this Iron Gate didn't have a security gatehouse in the front. Slowing down, they stopped to take a picture of the entrance gate, using a night-vision accessory on the camera. This gate had a noticeable logo in the grillwork too, a **"C"!** Dillon took the binoculars to look inside the grounds at the villa perched on the top of the long winding drive. Dusk had deepened, and the lights atop the colonnades on the terrace were all lit up. Lights inside shone in every window, outlining the house brilliantly. A stone patio or balcony surrounded the front and sides of the house as far as they could see. Two cars were parked out front: a small, bright red sports car and the other silver—probably a 'is and 'er set of Jaguar's.

"I wonder if this is the Villa del Christianna? It could be the villa where Lucinda and Marcus Rudolphi live!" The estate grounds surrounding the villa were well landscaped and manicured, sculptured into many garden levels filled with statues. "I'd bet some of these gardens have Lucinda's enhancing touches."

"I can almost make out a pool on the left on a lower level from the 'ouse with a row of cabana 'ouses. There's a large 'ouse adjacent to the pool, might be a pool 'ouse or a garden-room of some sort," Dillon remarked. While Dillon was surveying the estate, Emma was intent on looking for signs of life in or around the house, but now it was too dark—and the villa was too far away. The sun had set and darkness came quickly in the hills and mountains.

"It'll be total darkness in a few minutes, Dillon."

"I can make out one guard armed with an automatic gun and large guard dog on a leash on the patio perimeter. Now that's the first time I've seen security with a firearm!" Dillon remarked. "Em, I 'ave a feelin' yur on the quid! This looks like the 'ome of Lucinda and Marcus Rudolphi—the Villa del Christianna. If it is, then this is where we find the lists! Let's start back to Milano to get these films developed and see what else we found from yur' drawin's!"

"I was thinking the same thing, Dillon—this has to be the Villa del Christianna! This is where we get that list of names!" They took off going north to Como.

"Not to diminish our good work, Dillon, but I'm famished! I'd like to find a place to eat before we drive all the way back to Milano!"

"That's one of yur best ideas yet, Em! I remember seein' a small out-of-the-way ristorante or tav'rn on our way 'ere. I think I can find it on our way 'ome—shouldn't be too long." Dillon looked at Emma with a playful smile to lighten the moment.

"Do you think that couple has discovered the device you tossed into their car?" she asked him amusingly.

He let out a good laugh. "I don't think they'll know anythin' until some armed guard approaches 'hem or stops 'hem to make a search of their car. Imagine the look of incredulit' on the guard's faces when they learn they were trackin' that couple in their car—and not us!" The picture he described made them laugh long and hard out loud.

"What about the look on the faces of the couple when they get pulled over and searched?" Emma put in plain words.

"The best part, Em? The team 'as to go back and tell a Rudolphi they were followin' the wrong car!" Dillon and Emma laughed each time they thought about the expressions on the faces of the guards when they met up with the innocent old couple!

*Oh! t' be a fly on a wheel seein' 'hem drag their tails back to report they lost us! Dillon had his way of lightening the moment. It was just the kind of she relief needed after an intensely challenging day.*

# CHAPTER TWENTY-FOUR

The Cantina del Nonno, a small family-owned café, was located on the Via SS35 back to Milano.

Emma was grateful to be inside a place where no one knew them, and they could speak freely—no suspicious characters lurking around them! Not surprisingly, Dillon located them at a rear table out of sight from the main door. Both of them had ravenous appetites and their choice of dinner was easy—the house special—with Dillon's *burro* and her *vino banco*. She hoped their quick menu decisions would give them time to consider and compare what each discovered inside the winery and the estate. Laying out her lists of sightings and drawings of the terrain of the winery and estate, they examined them and a plan began to develop between them. The Rudolphi Estate was huge—much larger than either of them imagined. It covered many hundreds of acres of land. Dillon knew a successful plan depended on knowing a lot more about the design of the terrain and the occupants of all the villas—that included the hired worker's homes.

Emma's several pages of sketches, when actually laid out next to one another, formed quadrants representing a large map about the size of the estate. "It's a decent representation of what I saw!"

"Nice drawin's, Em!" Dillon commented once he viewed the entire illustration.

"Em, the size of this whole estate is probabl' equal to several thousand kilometers of land, much larger than the 'undred I original'y thought! When we get back to the Manin, I'll check out me map of this region to calculate the actual size with the aid of these drawings. There's no doubt the two estates we got a good look at—along with the winer'—covers a very large area for someone travelin' on foot…" Dillon's comment was more an observation—as if he was formulating some plan.

"What we didn't learn is 'ow man' other Rudolphis live in those other grand 'omes you saw…'ere on yur map!" Pointing to an area, he said, "This one 'ere—'as to be the Villa del Christianna!" Dillon circled that site on the map.

"How can we find out who else lives on the estate?" Emma asked thoughtfully.

"I bet if we inquire at the hotel about this, they'd shed some information about the Rudolphis. This family is well known in Milano."

"That's a good idea, but I have a feelin', Em, the're's some local folk 'ave allegiance to the Rudolphis, and if strangers start askin' 'bout 'hem or the location of their 'omes, it'll fly red flags up the pole—they'd pass that kind of information on, feelin' a duty to the family. For sure it'd alert 'hem to our presence 'ere and what we're interested in—if they don't alread' know it!" Dillon said, casting looks around the cantina checking to see if anyone seemed interested in them.

"No, I think the librar' would 'ave a copy of a map of the *winer'* with locations of 'omes within the estate grounds; maybe ev'n givin' the names of the fam'lies who live on the estate. Better still…I know a friend I can call—'e'll get me some more information. Did ye notice there's no mention of the families' names that're presently runnin' the business—you know, Guiseppe's boys?"

"Yes, I'm certain that's deliberate…not to advertise exactly how many family members are involved in the business…that way they can move people in and out of the organization easier," Emma said.

"Em, after I listened to the tapes last night, I made several calls. I 'ave a reliable source in Roma—someone in me past, and I need 'is kind of skills ag'in in this case. I know I can count on 'im for 'is silence…'e's sendin' me the information I asked 'im to get by way of a relative—'e'll deliver it to me in a day." Their meal came, and they ate hungrily—a real homemade dinner—family owned cantinas had the best food in Italy.

. Dillon continued listing important facts they still had to find out. "We'll need the most recent updated information on each member of the Rudolphi family, and their positions in the family business. 'opin' to figure which one's in charge of runnin' security…It 'as to be a Rudolphi. Got to know even their wives, children, too, and where each of 'hem live, on or off the estate. Once we get this information, we'll revisit yur drawin's to compare it to the 'ouses you drew on this map," Dillon said, pointing to our drawings. "Too much information is never enough! One of me mottos!"

"How can we find out about the routines of Marcus and Lucinda Rudolphi?" Emma asked. "One of our biggest objectives is THE LIST," she emphasized to Dillon.

"We definite'y 'ave to get into that study to find the list of names." Dillon was thinking aloud. "We won't know more 'til we see the complete list of names in the journals Lucinda spoke 'bout. 'Til then we're in the dark to find rhyme or reason why *yur* name is included!" Dillon looked directly at Emma, "'Til me man comes through with me information, we can't make further plans about gettin' our hands on those lists." Dillon set his napkin to the side finishing the last of his meal.

"What we *can* do now, Dillon, is go to Perugia to see if we can find the café in the *piazza* where Lucinda saw the child answering to 'Giorgio'. It sounds like the proverbial needle search, but we may get lucky and see a five-year-old child with dark hair, dark brown eyes, and a chin dimple—the most identifiable feature! Sounds like half the population in this area, doesn't it?" she remarked to Dillon.

"That's still a good idea for tomorr'w, Em! Meantime, I'll 'ave these films developed overnight and get some fresh film for tomor'ow's trip—we need to take pictures in Perugia. We'll need to pass for tourists again, Em," he said smiling at her.

Emma reminded Dillon, "Remember, I have a dinner date tomorrow—I'm meeting Carlos at eight for dinner at the Taverna del Pescatore in Gubbio. I'd rather not change that date, and if I'm to keep my date, we've got to be back from Perugia by six o'clock." As an after thought, she added, "Carlos is returning to Roma on

Monday—tomorrow may be the only day to meet with him. That'll give us Saturday and Sunday for us to plan how and when we get a copy of the contents from that locked box!"

"Wait a minute, Em! Who said **WE** were going to get into the villa?" Dillon queried.

"Dillon, if **WE** are to continue this investigation, then **WE** do it as equal partners! I know you have all the techniques and skills of breaking and entering, but it's **MY** name on that bloody list, and I'll be damned if I let you go alone!"

"Now, now, Emmie, don't get your Welsh temper up," he said calmly. "It's just I don't want an'thin' to 'appen to you, Em. Yur grandfather would never forgive me."

"What do you mean, Papa would never forgive you?"

"Nothin', Em, just a sayin'," Dillon nonchalantly responded.

"I know why you're saying these things…to protect me, Dillon! It's just this feeling I have. This is very important to me Dillon! I *have* to find out the other names on that list to understand how and why the names are grouped together. The explanation has got to be simple. It could be my name is listed as a barrister with other similar names…as simple as that!" Emma said half-heartedly, watching Dillon with downcast eyes. "Sorry, I barked at you. You got to my Welsh temper."

"I know, Em, I know," he said, taking her hand into his to let her know he deeply cared about what happened to her, as she did him. Dillon listened to Emma rationalize for answers to her query, none of which he knew was probably close to the truth. He kept his thoughts to himself, *Em, if you only knew these kinds of feelin's I had in the past always proved true for me! I 'ave no reason to think these ominous feelin's 'bout you would mislead or fail me now.*

With their cappuccinos, they finished dinner. "Dillon, I had Peter arrange an expense account for you in your name in the Tutorio Banco in Milano," she said and handed him the bankcard.

"No need, Em…"

"Never mind," Emma interjected. "It's insurance. Now let's get back to Milano!" she said with a smile. Dillon paid the tick and *camierera,* a young *signorina,* a bonus; he seemed to capture her attention when they walked in. The drive back to Milano felt longer than their trip this morning due to the combination of the late meal and a very long day.

At last, the Via d Manin was in sight! A couple of blocks from the hotel, Dillon stopped the car. "Em, you take the car the rest of the way…I gotta do an errand."

Emma knew he had secret business arrangements he wanted to do alone, referring to them earlier as "getting all the equipments and supplies" ready. He especially needed assurance his calls were untraceable—in case someone was watching his movements or listening to his conversations. Dillon got out at the corner of the Via Venezia.

"Em, you go straight to the hotel and *be careful.*" he cautioned and waved at her as she drove the car the short distance to the hotel alone. The attendant took the car to the garage while she went inside to pick up her key and any messages. The lobby was deserted due to the lateness of the hour.

"Paolo, has anyone left a message or asked for me since this morning?"

"*Si Signora*, an elderly gentle man came by this afternoon to inquire after you, but did not leave any message. I told him you left this morning and had not yet returned." This message totally surprised her.

"What time of day was it?" "

"It was early afternoon, *Signora.*"

"Can you describe this man?"

"He was tall… with gray hair and beard. I did not see his eyes; he wore sunglasses, which he did not remove. He was dressed in a light suit and carried a briefcase. We spoke only a few minutes…and then he went out the front lobby…I did not see him drive away. That is all I remember, *Signora.*"

"*Grazie*, Paolo."

# CHAPTER TWENTY-FIVE

The picture Paolo described fit Papa's description!

But why is Papa here…in Milano asking for her? He *did* say he was leaving for a trip to the Continent for an unspecified time with no set itinerary. Could his trip bring him to Milano so soon? *I know if it was Papa, he'd leave me a message*, she thought, conjuring up all possible reasons why the mystery man could be Papa. *It's probably so simple—he was passing through Milano and made a spur of the moment inquiry! That's what it was!* Dismissing the whole incident from her mind—thinking he would try to contact her again—Emma unlocked the door to her suite and went inside to see the linens turned down and her gown and robe placed on the bed. Switching on the radio softly, she walked outside to the balcony—the jolting ring of the phone distracted her from the tranquil balcony sight.

"*Pronto*–hello."

"Em, I'm back in me room. Just checkin' in to make sure yur fine."

" No problem. Thanks…D…".

"Don't say my name out loud!"

Emma paused before acknowledging Dillon's caution.

"You okay, Em?"

"Yes…yes. While we were out, I had an interesting query from… a friend today. I'll tell you all about it when I see you tomorrow."

"Go to bed! That's me order! We 'ave another long day tomorrow," Dillon said and hung up. Dillon sensed Emma's pensive reaction. *She encountered somethin' troublesome tonight ... Somethin' unexpected 'appened after I left her—just 'ave to wait 'til mornin' to find out what it was.*

"Perugia tomorrow!" Emma said. The mantel clock in the suite chimed midnight, and she quickly showered. "Bed is all I can handle right now!" Dimming the sitting room lamp to the lowest level, she checked one last time around the suite. The last balcony door was ajar the same as last night, with several pieces of furniture rearranged to deter any intruders. Having dried her hair, she slipped into her gown and robe. *I wish I knew who that gray-haired man was who was asking for me. Could it really be Papa? This whole thing about him coming to Milano and looking me up ... It's just not like him not to leave a message if he was here. I'll call him tomorrow instead of waiting until Monday!*

Her final task was to wedge the briefcase between the bed and nightstand, and dim the bedside lamp. The alarm was set for five o'clock. Once under the soft, deep bedcovers, Emma let them envelop her. Putting aside thoughts of her unknown visitor, she felt nothing would keep her awake tonight. The music from the lounge below was soft on the night's gentle breezes. The bed felt so good, so safe, as if...

> *to wait...for what...an identity...sleep comes so easily*
> *...can't fight it...silence...sleep.*
> **No more memor...please...**

* * *

The alarm sounded louder than usual, with Emma fumbling around trying to turn it off. Still feeling the effects of a deep sleep, she opened her eyes. The room's only light was shades of gray, which made it difficult to see shapes. An unexpected feeling overtook her.

*A chilled feeling...a dim distant light...a burning hearth...icy cold air...a girl at the hearth doing something...*

*So many strange flashback memories—why...why those memories again?*

Emma forced her mind to consciously think of the present moment to shrug off the dark, ill-omened thoughts. *They feel so real! Somehow they're from a past that I can't remember!*

"Oh my god...I forgot...Perugia today!"

Seeing the early hour, Emma was glad the alarm rang early; she needed time to clear her thoughts. Walking out on the balcony, she thought, "Tonight I'll see Carlos!"

Taking in the view down in the city, the streetlights were gradually going off. In the distance, a cloud layer shrouded the tops of the mountains conveying a fine murkiness. Across the via, the early morning mist partially obscured the gardens, but she still visualized what sights lay behind the shroud.

"A hot shower is exactly what I need to clear my thoughts!" Donning the Turkish robe, Emma rang room service. *"Questo 'e Llewelyn di signora. La suite tre zero nove. Per favore di inviare un calzone, un succo di arancia ed il caffe alla mia stanza? Ringraziarlo. Si, grazie, caio."*

There was time for a quick coffee before she dressed and got to the café across the way to meet Dillon. The first sun's rays began penetrating the cloud vapor, releasing the mountaintops from the pall. By the time Emma finished dressing, the weather was clear with rays of sun, hinting that there was a possibility the day could turn into a warm spring occasion.

"Comfort is the key for our trek around *Perugia de strata.*" Choosing jeans with a tee shirt and sneakers to appear as a tourist, Emma thought, *No telling how much walking we'll do around Palazzo's shops in Perugia to find the right Café!* A soft rap at the door distracted her.

*"Avanti!"* she said, thinking it was room service. The door opened to reveal Dillon and a stranger standing there.

"Do you always tell an'one to come right in when they knock without askin' who?" Dillon asked in a reprimanding way walking into her room with the stranger.

"Sorry, Dil...I thought you were room service. I telephoned an order ten minutes ago—my coffee?"

In the softest but firmest whisper, he said in admonishment, "Never mind, Em! No matter who you think is knockin', *ask first before* yur open the door!" He was shaking his finger at her.

"I promise! I promise I'll find out who it is first before I open the door! Thanks for reminding me," she whispered back.

"Can ne'er stay mad at you long, Em," he said and leaned to give her a peck on the cheek.

Then a second knock came. Quickly, Dillon and his friend retreated into the loo, out of sight. Emma asked at the door, "*Chi e' alla porta?*"

"Room service, *Signora. Ho la sua colazione.*" Unlocking the door, Emma said, "'*E entrato.*" She signed the slip while the waiter placed the tray in the sitting area.

"*Grazia—Caio.*" Emma closed and locked the door again. The two men came out of the room; turned on the radio and motioned for her to get her coffee, making the natural clatter of noise with the china.

Dillon handed Emma a written note. "This is Biaggio. He brought equipment we need." Emma acknowledged him with a silent nod. The rest of the message read, "Meet me as planned on the Via Venezia in one hour with the car. I'll be alone on the left side of the corner. D." Taking the note back, he tore it into little pieces and lit a match to it in the ashtray.

Emma motioned to Dillon and Biaggio that she understood the plan as they quietly exited the room. Wondering what kind of equipment Dillon asked for, Emma knew it had to do with his plan to get into the Villa del Christianna. Her past experiences with Dillon taught her that some portion of his plans could be illegal—especially now here in Italy. As an officer of the courts, she didn't want to know the illegal details he had already set in motion. Emma finished her Cappuccino, collected her briefcase, a sweater, and her bag and left for the café across the street. Leaving her key at the desk and picking up her passport, Emma stopped to buy several newspapers in the lobby shop—for any local news about the Rudolphis. This morning, the café was bustling busily, and Emma selected a table out front. No sign of Dillon or Biaggio.

"*Buongiorno, Signora, Come sta?*"

*"Si, molto bene, grazie."* Emma ordered breakfast—a frittata, succo and another cappuccino and started reading through the newspapers looking for any news about the Rudolphis. **There it was!** She stared to make certain it was **him!** A large group picture with Marcus Rudolphi among them—naming several other notable Milanese men, too. The caption listed their names for a *"Charity to be held at the Villa del Christianna on Sunday afternoon for the benefit of research."* Emma felt elated.

"Mother of luck!" she said, continuing to examine the rest of the society news. "Yes!" Another picture captured her attention! Only this one was of *Il Signore Marcus and Signora Lucinda Rudolphi*i shown inside their villa! The photograph was large, and in the background of the picture, she saw fresh vases filled with flowers set on what appeared to be a patio, in anticipation of the upcoming charity party. Carefully scrutinizing the picture, Emma made out tall columns with large white-domed lights atop each column. It was exactly the sight Dillon and she saw yesterday at that last villa on the Rudolphi Estate. Excitedly, she said, "Yes, Dillon, our guess was correct! It was the Villa del Christianna we saw last night!"

Hurrying through breakfast, Emma could hardly contain her feelings. "Wait 'til I tell Dillon we were dead on the quid!" The *cameriere* brought her tick, and she quickly left several bonus Euros on the table before grabbing papers, briefcase, and bag to head back to the hotel and her car. All the while, her excitement was growing to tell Dillon her news. Almost lyrically, she thought, *We shall go to the party! We may have a way into the Villa del Christianna!*

Emma had fifteen minutes to get the car and meet Dillon. She used her mobile to call the hotel attendant to ask to have her car at the front of the hotel, *pronto!*

For some reason, Emma glanced back at the café to see a man standing on the opposite side of the street trying to look disinterested in her, but casting frequent glances in her direction while appearing to read his newspaper. At first, Emma thought it coincidental when she first noticed him standing not far from where she sat in the outdoor café. It was not the same man she saw the other night with Dillon.

"He seems too interested in me! Or am I becoming paranoid with Dillon's cautious admonitions to me?"

At the hotel, Emma decided to enter the lobby on pretence it was her purpose to go inside. Once inside the lobby, she hurried into one of the smaller lounges to see if the man in the light suit would follow her inside. She waited a few minutes, saw no one, and then exited. There he was across the lobby inside the gift shop pretending to look at magazines but watching the lounge door. Emma walked—almost ran—out the lobby door and jumped into her car, all the while looking into the rearview mirror. The same man came running out of the hotel door toward a waiting car in the street and raced after her. Emma just knew the waiting car was going to follow her, and she had to lose them before she picked up Dillon.

Driving down the Via d Manin, Emma slowed at the corner of Via Venezia. Dillon was standing there, but she ignored him and drove past him.

*Dillon will catch on to why I'm not stopping to pick him up! I hope he gets a good look at the car behind me!*

Just ahead was an entrance ramp to a parking garage. Emma decided to try and lose them inside the garage if she was fast enough to make a sudden turn onto the ramp. Driving down the street, she circled the block once then quickly turned onto the parking ramp. It was dark inside, making it hard to see if the car behind her was them. Driving up to the second level, Emma parked and waited in a corner slot. No light sedan passed behind her. Emma wasn't even certain the sedan turned into the garage. Waiting about ten minutes, she backed out and drove twice around inside the garage before exiting, tossing the attendant a large bill, and yelling to him to keep the change. The gated arm rose. She raced out, deliberately driving down the wrong way into traffic to the corner, hoping no *policia* saw her. Finally turning into the direction of traffic, Emma checked the mirrors for several blocks—looking back...*Still no sign of the beige sedan!* It wasn't hard finding her way back to the Via Venezia to pick up Dillon. As luck had it, the light turned red. When Emma reached a full stop, Dillon hurriedly jumped inside.

"Go—go, Em... straight ahead 'til I tell you where to turn," Dillon said.

Emma explained what happened while waiting for her car at the hotel.

"Good girl, Em. Let's see if we still 'ave a shadow. Drive 'til we get to the next round'bout and keep on goin' 'round it several times, and I'll keep sight of the cars behind us. It's a good way of keepin' track of a tail—if there's one to catch."

After completely circling the roundabout twice, they turned and headed back toward the Manin. "I'm sure we're clean—no shadows."

"Can you describe the man who was followin' you, Em?" Dillon asked.

"He was tall…muscular build with a tan suit and dark shirt. He wore a light hat with the brim turned down…had sunglasses on, which made it difficult to see his face. The car was a beige four-door make…I'm not certain how many were in the car besides the man in the tan suit and the driver."

"Good 'nough, Em. Now we 'ave to meet Biaggio. He's at an inn on the east side of Milano. Pullover at the next street, and I'll take the wheel. I know where he's stayin', and let's double check…we need to be completely free 'fore I pick 'im up."

At the next corner Dillon and Emma switched positions. Dillon headed toward the east end of Milano, which was the same direction to Perugia.

"Is Perugia still on for today?" Emma asked.

"Oh yes, me girl!"

Feeling safe, she smugly said, "I know how we can get into the *Villa del Christianna* to find the list."

Dillon's look was quizzical with the surprised look on his face. He waited for her to explain! Pointing to the newspaper, Emma said, "Look at this picture in the paper. We now know what Marcus Rudolphi looks like, AND we know that last villa we saw yesterday, without the gatehouse and guard, is the Villa del Christianna—Marcus and Lucinda's home! See, here's a picture of them. Recognize those tall columns with the lights? It says here…they're getting ready for a charity party at the villa on Sunday." Emma showed Dillon the pictures in the paper. "Now all we need to do is get us some invitations to the party!"

"Great work, Em! Leave that to me. O'r invites are in the post! I know a reli'ble source—to get us a couple of duplicate invites! Is this a fancy 'ffair and all? I may 'ave to buy some trend' duds for this part'."

"Not to worry, Dillon, we'll find you something fashionable to blend in with those rich charitable patrons," Emma said laughing.

"Before we start for Perugia, I first need to call a man. He'll get us those invites—by tomor'a."

Feeling more positive and elated, Emma and Dillon drove about thirty minutes and turned into a small inn on the Via Vinncenzo. Biaggio was inside the inn and started out the lobby door as they drove up. He climbed into the back seat without saying a word. He pointed them to a truck parked in the rear of an adjoining parking lot as Dillon drove up to a parked truck. While Emma waited in the car, Biaggio transferred several large cargo bags and a trunk from the van to the car boot. The two men spoke for several minutes outside the car before Biaggio got into the van, and Emma and Dillon drove away.

"Biaggio isn't coming with us to Perugia?" Emma asked.

"No, 'e 'as another job to do today." Handing her his map and pointing out exactly where they were, Dillon said, "Look at the map and find out 'ow far it is to Perugia from 'ere and the best way to get there."

Checking the map, she said, "I calculate we should take the South Coast Autostrada out of Milano heading south directly to the city. It's about 75 kilometers. We should arrive in Perugia around noontime."

"That'll give us severa' good hours to find this *Piazza* and the café where Lucinda saw the boy! I 'ope lady luck is still on o'r side today!" Dillon said.

Emma knew only too well finding this one particular child was going to be a very long shot of a chance—a needle in a rick!

* * *

*"Che noi nono dire Luigi? Se non gli diciamo la verita, scoprira e poi siamo degli uomini morti!"* The driver angrily blurted out.

"We can't tell Luigi we lost her—**again!** That a woman out-maneuvered us? He'd kill us for sure!" The man in the beige suit was speaking to his dark, swarthy companion with fear in his voice.

*"Gesù Christo*, man if we don't tell him the truth—we're good as dead anyway!"

*"Christo no!* We'll tell him she made us and came after us…so we had to lose her in the parking garage to keep her from making us…we felt we needed to protect our identities…for **his sake, too!**

The other man suggested, "First, I say we go back to the garage and check every car there. She may have parked there and had another car pick her up. If that's the case, she'll return to get **her** car some time—and we'll get her! We gotta put some time on this, so he won't think we just gave her up!"

"When we do find her we put two cars on her now! Let me out at the garage while you search, and I'll get the back-up car. **Then we call Luigi and tell him we lost her…and let him know how hard we tried to find her!**"

"Okay…okay…*Si,* that sounds better…*Gesù,* anything is better than facing that *bastardo face to face now!*

"I think someone else is tailing her, too, besides us. I seen another car, a Lamborghini, hanging in the distance each time she took off! Did you make it, too?"

*"Si…L'ho vista!* Luigi will want to know who was tailing her-besides us?"

"If we can get pictures of that other car we saw…maybe, if we can find it again…Luigi will think this information is more important than losing her…and it will save our hides from a beating!"

"You really mean *save our lives!"*

# CHAPTER TWENTY-SIX

The drive to *Perugia* was like going back to a gentler and simpler time.

Perugia is one of Italy's largest and richest cities in the region, positioned on a series of hills, clearly designed to fit the human scale. Approaching the city from the crest of the mountain, Emma saw church steeples peeking out from the treetops, fields of red poppies, and dark green vineyards, expanses of golden green fields dotted with animals contentedly grazing. One pastoral scene after another passed before them. The drive actually did take more than an hour, but the time passed quickly as Dillon and she discussed everything they discovered and what they would do when they arrived in the *Palazzo del Priori* in Perugia.

"We'll start our search at the Palazzo del Priori and play our character roles of Sean and Kate again, friendly tourists, carryin' camera and binoculars, stoppin' at different cafes to see the sights," Dillon explained. It was a good plan, but even with a lot of luck the chance was slim they'd find the same exact child Lucinda saw. At this moment, Emma felt they had to make every effort to come up with some answers for her!

Dillon maneuvered around the narrow streets until he found a good place to park on a *strada* off the Palazzo del Priori. Walking down the hill out onto the large circular *Palazzo*, they first scrutinized the different cafés and boutiques on the *Palazzo* and selected the three largest cafés on the *Palazzo* to explore for evidence of a small boy and girl living on the premises. Three cafes stood out as the most attractive ones to tourists. Lucinda might have stopped at an obviously attractive outdoor café on the *Palazzo*.

"If we fail to find anythin' in these three, then we can look further at another nearby, the Palazzo Via San Francesco, provided there's enough time," Dillon cautioned.

The *Café Sonesta deCaprio* was the first one they approached, and Dillon chose an outside table. The *cameriere* promptly came, and they ordered espressos, acting like tourists delighted with the sights and the view of the large fountain on the *Palazzo* from outside the café. They asked the *cameriere* about the owners of the different cafés on the *Piazzo*. "Are the different cafés owned by different owners?"

He explained in his best broken English that each of the cafés was owned by different *proprietarios* for over the past five or six years. The two explained their story about finding relatives in Perugia; they said they wanted to find the uncle who owned one of the cafés located in Perugia on the Palazzo del Priori.

Emma and Dillon did learn that three known local families operated the three cafés selected on the *Palazzo*. All of the cafés were successful businesses, and each had the same *proprietarios* for several years, all well-known to the locals in the area. During their time at the first café, there were no outward indications that children lived in this particular café so Dillon paid the tick, and they finished their espressos.

"It would be too good to be true to find the child on the first query!" Emma remarked to Dillon.

"I say we look at another place, maybe that one across the square?" Dillon pointed to a smaller café.

Strolling around the town square, they took pictures as tourists and used the binoculars to appreciate the architecture and holiday ambience of the *Palazzo*, all the while really looking for signs of children inside the cafes. Walking toward the Café *Montagne*, Emma continued to focus the camera on the café through the viewfinder when she saw a small boy run out the café's door in her direction. Emma was so startled she just stopped and stared at the unfolding scene!

The very young boy was laughing boisterously, running from a younger girl chasing after him. It looked like they were playing a game of 'tag'n run'. In astonishment, Emma did nothing but stand and stare at the scene for several minutes.

"Impossible!" Dillon quickly took her arm and led her to a table nearest the café door.

"Dillon…do you see the children?" she spoke softly to him. His slight nod told her he was keenly aware of the playful scene at the fountain on the *Palazzo.*

The boy appeared to be about four or five years old with dark brown hair and dark brown eyes. His smile caught Emma's attention. Paying closer attention to his features, she noticed there was the dimple in his chin. *Remembering the photo in this morning's newspaper, the picture of Marcus Rudolphi,—he had what appeared to be a chin dimple and a similar smile!*

"Yes! The newspaper!" Searching her bag for the newspaper, Emma took the paper out and looked at the picture of Marcus Rudolphi with the same wide smile accented with the chin dimple. She kept comparing the features of the small boy with the photo.

*Is it really an uncanny coincidence? But Marcus… he appears dark and swarthy…this boy's coloring is light, the expression in his eyes…like Lucinda's!* Emma handed the paper to Dillon.

Dillon saw her excitement as she handed him the newspaper, pointing to Marcus Rudolphi's picture. His attention turned back to the boy in the distance, laughing and running around the fountain on the *Palazzo* outside the café with the younger girl chasing him in a playful exhibition. Emma heard them calling to one another in Italian. Try as best they could not stop staring at the children, neither Dillon nor Emma could take their eyes off the vision playing out before them. Dillon handed her a menu to distract her.

"I must get a picture of them, Dillon," Emma said softly. Just then, a woman came over and asked for their order. Simply dressed, the woman appeared in her late forties or early fifties with jet-black hair with a single gold band adorning her left hand. She smiled and appeared eager to please them. They decided to get a full lunch to give them more time to spend at the café.

*"Qual'e' la specialitga del giorno?"* The special sounded good, and they ordered prescuitto with a fresh vegetable salad and house wine to go with it—*abbastanza per due persone.* Local *birra* for Dillon. After they gave the woman their order, she turned and called out to the children.

*"Giorgio! Sophia! Qui e ritorni pronto!"* The children pretended not to hear, making the woman walk out to the fountain to bring them back. Approaching the café with the children in tow, Emma went over to her.

*"Signora,* they are beautiful children! *Sono di bei bambini! Ll fratello e la sorella?"* Emma asked, hoping her remark about them being related, maybe tell her something about their ages.

*"Ll figlia—Sophia! Ie mio il figlio—Giorgio! Che sono le loro eta`?* Hesitating with pride, she responded, *"Si. Questa e' Giorgio, un questa e'Sofia. Scuzi. We must go...we prepare your lunch!"*

Afraid she wouldn't get another chance, Emma said, "Please wait! *Poss portare un'immagine di loro...Giorgio, Sophia?"* Showing her enthusiasm, Emma asked again in English, "May I take their picture? They're such lovely children. I want to show my family back home how beautiful the children are in Perugia!"

The woman cast a furtive glance back at the café and then said, *"Si,* if you wish." The three of them posed at the edge of the Café Montague with the cafe's name overhead on the awning. Emma stepped back to make certain she framed the name of the café with the three figures posing in front. Focusing the lens, she called out, *"Chi formaggio—Sorrida!"* Emma could tell the children enjoyed having their pictures taken by their big smiles. She kept snapping several photos in succession taking as many different lens angles as she could, hoping one of them would turn out clear.

*"Grazia, Signora."*

Turning, the woman quickly whisked the children back inside the café.

Sitting down, Emma said softly to Dillon. "Do you think we really found the children Lucinda described to us?" Dillon was deep in his own thoughts.

She spoke her thoughts to him. "Lucinda said the woman called the boy Giorgio—that he had dark brown hair, the color of Marcus's.

This boy's smile is like Marcus's, but the expression in the eyes— it's like Lucinda's! I remember the look in Lucinda's eyes—very expressive and emotional when she spoke about the children. The boy has that very same intense expression! The dimpled chin...Marcus has one, too! His skin coloring is delicate like I remember Lucinda's coloring. Dillon, this is all too coincidental to find another boy who fits her description so well...the description Lucinda gave...and the boy's *name is* the same, *Giorgio*! How can he *not* be the same child Lucinda described?"

"You may be right, Em. The blessin' of the gods may be with us today! But the lit'le girl, she does 'ave some looks like the boy... only red hair, with bright green eyes."

"I tell you, Dillon, the girl is the image of Lucinda; her eyes and her hair coloring, identical to Lucinda's. If you had seen Lucinda *in person*, you would know how much the little girl looks like her—it's like seeing Lucinda when she was a child!"

"Each does 'ave a resemblance to those news pictures, I 'ave to say," Dillon commented. Emma knew he was trying to contain her feelings with his less than animated reaction.

"Dillon, what I'm thinking is too bizarre! Remember in the tape Lucinda said she had a second child two years after the birth of Antonio Rudolphi? She was told the girl child was stillborn, and she never did get to see her. Lucinda named the baby girl Angela Rudolphi and both children are buried in the family plot on the estate. Do you think that little girl...is possibly *Giorgio's* real sister, *Angela Rudolphi*?"

Dillon didn't answer my query. The scenario played out before us was incredible—almost **macabre**!

"How could two children who were to have died at birth come to be alive? And living with another family?" Emma posed her questions with incredulity!

"Now Em...don't jump to conclusions so soon..."

"If Giorgio is the child, Antonio Rudolphi, the baby boy Lucinda delivered, who supposedly died shortly after his birth and the little girl, Sophia, is his sister, Angela, who also was to have died in a stillbirth...then why were her children taken away from her?" Emma's questions were logical and yet... "It's inhuman! Why is someone else raising her children? Dillon…is this some form of kidnapping?" Emma was stunned by where her thoughts were going. "What kind of people do something like this?" Emma asked in disbelief! "It has to be the devil himself to be so cruel!" she said contemplatively. Looking at Dillon, she felt she had touched on a painful nerve from the expression in his eyes! His silence was his answer.

"You know, Em, I 'ave to tell you. When I 'eard the tapes and the story Lucinda told, I found it 'ard to believe she was not sufferin' from some kind of deep depression with imaginin's! Seein' now with me own eyes, I 'ave to believe her story may not be far-fetched. She could be the victim 'ere, too," Dillon said—but more for what he felt…not for what he was thinking.

"What do you mean, 'the victim, too'?" Emma asked.

"*You,* too, are a victim…not knowing 'ow your name fits into this whole Rudolphi situation!" Dillon knew he had to say something truthful to Emma. She would know he was lying if even part of his answer was not truthful. He said what he said to put her off to his real reason for the comment. *His real reason was to find out if Emma had ever been a kidnapping victim.*

"You know, Dillon, I thought Lucinda was a grieving, overwrought mother when she told me that story. As incredible as it sounds, it appears highly possible all of her feelings are real; more than a mother's fantasy!" Trying to outwardly contain her emotions, Emma said, "There's something terribly wrong here, Dillon! I can feel it! We have to find out what it's all about!"

"Em, I don't disagree with an'thing you've said. But me feelin's isn't good 'bout this place. This problem needs lookin' into for sure. But remember, we also 'ave to find out about that list of names in the villa's librar'. We 'ave the pictures you took 'ere to develop. Let's start back to Milano. Remember, you 'ave a dinner date tonight with Carlos. And I have a date with Biaggio. Give me the camera, and I'll see the pictures are developed tonight."

Emma didn't have to tell Dillon know how anxious she felt, he felt it, too.

"How can we find out if these children are really the birth children of that woman in the cafe, Dillon? I'm thinking, how can we do that without making waves to alert anybody around here?" Emma asked.

"It's best not to churn the waters, Em, not 'til after we've attended that charity part'.

Already, someone is followin' us and we don't know who or why! I'll ask Biaggio to take care of gettin' these films developed for us. I'm sure 'e 'as connections to look into the birth records of those two children so as not to set off alarms. That way we won't be tied to them." Dillon already made a mental note to ask Biaggio to check on the background of the couple who owned the café. He had queries of his own—how did this common and simple couple come to own and run one of the finer cafés on the *Palazzo* in Perugia? It takes a lot of Euros to own a nice café like the Café Montague in Perugia.

"Biaggio will know the right contacts to find answers for us 'bout this family without wavin' red flags."

The trip back to Milano was quieter. Both of them were deep with their own thoughts.

At first her thoughts raced with everything that happened that day—so incredible to think what they saw in the *Palazzo* was real! Emma couldn't get the picture of the children out of her mind so she forced her attention to turn to the scenes on the hillsides to distract her. The sun was low, setting over the hills, and the valleys were becoming darker. This time of day, sunset, was the second best time of the day next to the early morning sunrises in the mountains. With the sun dipping low in the west, the fresh mountain breezes quickly changed the city's hot air to cooler temperatures. It already felt considerably cooler than when they left Perugia.

In just a few hours, she'd see *him* again, and she felt ambivalent emotions, dueling with her thoughts of the past. The farther they drove away from Perugia the more her feelings changed to anticipation for what was to come that evening! Driving back through the hills, neither Dillon nor Emma wanted to break the silence of their concentration. The familiar sights of the outskirts of Milano brought back the questionable events happening to them since their arrival at the Hotel Manin: first, discovering someone was following her, then finding a wire tap in her room—so many unexplained things happening! *Why?* Emma was glad Carlos asked to meet her for dinner that night—she needed this distraction tonight!

"Can I handle another rejection if it doesn't work out this time for us? I want so much for our relationship to begin again! *I voli di elaborato—I fremiti ed i sogni—forse puo tutto si e` realizzato?* Emma thought of the words, "Flights of fancy—thrills and dreams—maybe it can all come true?"

Dillon discerned Emma's silence meant she was thinking about Perugia today *and* her meeting with Carlos tonight. This case was becoming much more involved than he anticipated, with the level of danger increasing every day! Dillon was afraid for Emma. But afraid of what...afraid of whom? He had to find out!

"Lucinda and Emma are some'ow tied together in this myster'! Too many facts pointin' the same way. Can't 'elp thinkin' Carlos is involved in these things...without tellin' Emma? Is that why he turned up again...*and now*? 'Ow can he *not know* some of these things goin' on? I need to find a way to reach him...Em says he's goin' to the chari'y par'y Sunda'."

Dillon glanced at Emma deep in her thoughts...but he had his thoughts and questions that needed quick answers! *Is that the real reason why 'e's in Milano—that chari'y par'y? 'e's got to know more 'bout what's 'appening 'ere.*

"*My friend, I'll make certain we 'ave a long talk after that bash tomor'ow to make certain we're all playin' in the same game... ag'in.*"

Dillon looked at the woman sitting next to him and thought, *She is a beautiful woman...*

# CHAPTER TWENTY-SEVEN

In Milano, the church bells were tolling the five o'clock hour.

Reaching the outskirts of the city, Emma and Dillon took a circuitous route back to the hotel. Detecting no shadows of a tail, Dillon wanted to return to the hotel alone so they parted several blocks away, taking no chances someone would see them together. He had plans to contact Biaggio to get the Perugia films developed tonight. Knowing someone had them under surveillance at the hotel, it wouldn't take them long to connect the two of them working together, and that could definitely complicate their plans. Better to keep them second guessing about their movements for as long as possible.

Driving up the hotel's circular drive, Emma looked around for the tan sedan—no sign of it anywhere. The parking attendant waited for her to gather up her things while she deliberately took her time on the pretence to collect her belongings out of the rear to scrutinize the vacant street for loitering pedestrians. Emma saw nothing suspicious and entered the hotel to check for messages or inquiries. There were no messages from Papa!

"I promised Peter I'd call tonight to get an update about the theft!" Checking her watch, she said, "It's too late now...not enough time to talk to him—I have just enough time to get ready for dinner and drive to Gubbio! Even that's going to be close if I'm to meet Carlos on time! I'll have to try Peter at home later tonight when

I return from dinner, if it's not too late, or better still, I'll call first thing in the morning. He should be home Saturday morning."

It was nearly six o'clock, and the drive to the *ristorante* would take almost an hour, and she still had to shower and dress. Once inside her suite, Emma rang Dillon's room but got no answer. She was certain he remembered she had plans to use the car tonight, and Emma didn't want to drive around with that collection of 'equipment' in the boot of the car! He needed to make arrangements to store it elsewhere.

"I'll try calling again after I shower. If necessary, I could call a taxi, I suppose…no, that trip is too long for a taxi ride." Rejecting that possibility, Emma let the warm water pour over her. It seemingly melted away her fatigue and anxiousness. Turning off the shower, she heard a soft rap at the door. Quickly donning a dressing gown to answer it, Emma called, *"Chi e 'li?"*

"It's just me, Em. Sorr' to disturb you, I need the car keys," he said softly, outside the door. "Knowin' yur goin' out, I want to clean the car!"

Emma knew he wouldn't forget! She cracked the door.

"I'll meet you in the lounge to pick up the keys when yur read' to leave." Nodding that she understood, Emma closed and locked the door.

It didn't take her long to choose what to wear…the black silk dress with the black sling shoes. She wanted to impress Carlos tonight, but be simple, too. *Nothing too dressy tonight.* Remembering he asked her to wear her hair down, Emma decided to pull back one side in a casual sweep with the silver hair comb he gave her—it felt dressier. With everything in place, she grabbed the small black bag to hold a few cosmetics and keys. On second thought, she returned to retrieve the silver scarf—there was a chill in the night air already. Looking in the mirror one last time, she said to herself, "This is what he's getting tonight, like it or not." She locked the door and went for the lift.

Dillon was in the Machiavelli Lounge, sitting at the end of the bar. Tonight, the lounge was noisy and filled with patrons celebrating the end of the work week. Emma sidled in between Dillon and a young woman to ask the bartender for a carbonated water. Dillon acknowledged her casually with a glance. With his arms folded next to her bag, he slipped the keys under it.

"Let me *la Signora*? I'd like to pay for this prett' lass' drink."

Smiling, Emma toasted her glass to Dillon. *"Grazie tente."* Picking up the keys with her bag, she walked to a far table, on the pretence of going to the ladies' lounge and instead went out the door. Dillon watched Emma as she left the lounge through the farthest door directly into the lobby. "She's a beautiful woman…'n 'e's a luck' man. I sure 'ope Carlos knows if 'e's got a second chance, he'd better take it. It's a gift that'll ne'er come again."

The night air was still warm with a slight chill in the soft breeze blowing down the mountain. The attendant hurriedly went to get her car, giving Emma a good opportunity to carefully screen the street for signs of lingering men or suspicious sedans. None seen!

*I still must be careful…Can't let my guard down, even though tonight is a social affair and not Rudolphi business.* Her rationalization didn't make her feel safer.

The drive to the Torre del Pescatore kept Emma occupied with thoughts of meeting Carlos: *What would he be like?—Would he act differently?* Emma drove up to the entrance, and the valet took possession of the car to park it while she went inside. The atmosphere was buoyant with laughter.

"The *Signore Esteves* table?"

"*Signore* Esteves is in the bar waiting for you, *Signora*." The waiter escorted Emma through to the bar lounge.

*"Grazie, tente."*

A warm flushed feeling come over her. *God, I hope no one can hear my heart beat!* She felt her heartbeat racing in anticipation of seeing him!

Carlos was seated at the end of the bar next to a vacant seat—at first he didn't see Emma enter. Hesitating, she said, "He looks the same…yet different." Seeing him sitting there alone forced her to acknowledge how much she really missed him. He turned and looked in her direction to see her standing there alone and went to greet her. Emma hoped Carlos wouldn't notice she was trembling when he leaned over and kissed her.

"Emma, you look ravishing! I never fail to realize how beautiful you are...seeing you now...I've truly missed you!"

She felt the warm strength in his hands; smelled his cologne... remembering all the past times she experienced these sensations. It was what Emma saw unspoken in his eyes... "Carlos, it's wonderful to see you." Captivated, they stared silently at each other for a few seconds.

"I hope I haven't kept you waiting long. I was in Perugia today and didn't realize the late hour until I arrived back at the hotel." He seated her next to him at the bar. To fill the void of silence, she said, "I'm really glad you tracked me down and called me."

"I was afraid you wouldn't speak to me when I called you. But never mind that, I'm just glad you're here now! What can I order for you to drink?"

"My usual, *Vino Bianco.*" Just being next to him again, it was as if nothing had changed...he was still everything to her. Carlos gave the bar tender orders for the cocktails as the maitre d' escorted us to a table located in a quiet rear corner of the room.

"Please bring our drinks to the table."

"*Si, signore.*"

Glad to be seated away from the high traffic areas, Emma said, "Can I ask you to order for me tonight, Carlos? I remember the first time we had dinner in Gubbio, and you ordered for me then...it was an excellent selection then. This way I can't go wrong!"

"I have some excellent suggestions. Do you want meat, fowl, or fish?"

"I'd prefer a fish dinner if they have a good one."

"Wise decision for tonight's choice!"

As the moments passed, Emma felt relaxed. She was actually beginning to really enjoy the evening with Carlos, forgetting what happened in Perugia earlier that day.

"Tell me what you have been doing with yourself, Carlos?"

"Well...I've been traveling a lot on the Continent. You know... embassy work. Not very interesting, just mundane political service, and I'm sure I'd bore you with such details." Deliberately changing the direction of the conversation, Carlos asked, "But you, Emma,

I've read you've been involved in several major cases in England with good successes…I'm happy for you," he said softly.

His words were sincere. Their first dinner course came, and she realized she was really very hungry.

"How is your grandfather Cyrus?" Carlos asked.

"Actually, Papa's here on the Continent, too, on business…but I don't have his itinerary. When I called the farm to tell him I was coming to Italy for holiday, he told me about a trip he planned, but he wasn't sure just where it would take him. We left it that we'd speak again this Monday."

"What are *your* plans for holiday here?" Carlos asked.

Not wanting to discuss her real reasons for coming to Milano, Emma said, "I needed some holiday time away from the office and decided to spend it here—in Milano! It's also an opportunity to look up some old friends living in this area that I met several years ago in England." It was a half truth, and she hoped Carlos wouldn't detect anything less.

"Is that why you went to Perugia today?" he queried again. It felt like Carlos had an agenda for all his questions.

"Sort of…in a way, yes," Emma answered briefly, trying to steer the conversation away from that topic.

"Carlos, you've lived in Milano for some time. Do you know of the Rudolphi family?"

"*Si,* they are a very distinguished, influential family in Milano. Everyone knows or has heard of the Rudolphi's. They own and manage a famous winery with their name, exporting large amounts of wine to foreign countries which accounts for a substantial economical export trade for Italy. Why do you ask?" Looking directly at her, his eyes searched for insight about why she asked that specific query.

"No particular reason. Marcus and Lucinda Rudolphi are hosting a charitable event on Sunday to raise money for a local hospital and research, and there's a good possibility I'll be attending the event," Emma said casually.

"That's wonderful, Emma! I had planned to make a brief appearance at that party before I returned to Roma. We can go together then!"

Not wanting to put him off, but knowing she had to tell him about Dillon, Emma remarked, "I wish I could go with you, Carlos. Unfortunately, I've made arrangements to attend the event with a very good friend...from back home." She quickly added, "But we can meet there...at the villa, if that's agreeable with you? My friend won't mind competition," she said laughingly.

"Do I have competition, Emma?" Carlos asked seriously.

"No, Carlos, you have no competition...never have." Emma was sorry she added the last bit...*He has to know now I still care deeply for him.*

"Emma...ever since our last meeting, when we said our good-byes, you've been continually in my mind." His voice softened as he took her hand into his. "So many times I've wanted to call you, but didn't...my work never gave me the opportunities to do it! More than I can tell you now...I've wanted to contact you...see you...to let you know what a fateful mistake I made that last day! I should never have let you go out of my life!" His voice changed. "When I discovered you were here in Italy now, I felt this could be my second chance...This time, if it isn't too late...I'm going to seize the opportunity here and now! You must realize what I'm trying to say, Emma, I want you back in my life...no...*I need you back in my life!* No job should keep someone away from the only one they've ever loved...You must realize you mean everything to me!" Looking pleadingly at her, he asked, "Do I have a second chance, Emma?"

For so long, Emma wanted to hear those words...now that she heard them, she felt overwhelmed. *I can't lose him again...I won't let that happen!* Feeling the tears run down her face, she said, "Carlos, my feelings for you have never changed. When we said goodbye last year, for all of the reasons spoken then, I've felt a terrible void and loss. It was hard for me to get past that time. Tonight, you ask me to start again...where we left off...Has anything changed in your life for you to tell me these things—now—tonight?"

A few seconds passed, but it felt like an eternity to her. Carlos made no attempt to answer.

"I thought we parted because your job and lifestyle were not conducive to a meaningful and lasting relationship between us. Has that changed now? Is your life so different for you to say these things to me tonight?"

"*Si,* Emma...in some ways. These months past, I've come to realize how empty my life has been without you...and no...my job is still at the embassy and some of my work takes me away for various periods of time. Do you think it's possible for each of us to have our jobs in our lives, but have them...together?"

Carlos knew he wanted to tell Emma much more, but he had to be careful. He hated not being completely honest with her.

"Emma, I've missed you so much! I realized too late...it's not the amount of time you spend with someone, but the quality of time spent together that makes relationships work between two people. I can only hope this realization doesn't come too late for me! Our lifestyles could work, if we *both* want it!" Casting his head down, he said, "Maybe all of this is rushing you too fast. We don't have to speak about it more tonight. I'm just so happy you're here with me again!" Taking her hands in his, he kissed them softly. "Let's just enjoy the moment!"

It all felt so good, so right to her, his holding her hands tightly, feeling his strength, hearing him say he wanted her again! They finished their meal with no more talk of their relationship and decided to take a short stroll around the *Palazzo. There will be other nights for us*, Emma promised herself.

The evening air was cool as Emma wrapped her shawl around her shoulders. The lights in the fountain in the *Palazzo* illuminated cascades of water falling in musical tones. Pausing to sit on the edge of the pool, she asked, "Carlos, have you ever heard of a Dr. Ennio Carruchi?" At that instant, Emma sensed that Carlos's body language changed.

"Why do you ask about him, Emma?"

"Oh, I heard someone mention his name and was just inquiring about him. I wanted to find out what kind of medicine he practiced. Do you know what kind of medical practice he has?"

Carlos looked pensively at the ground, not meeting her eyes. "I heard he's in research. His name has been associated with genetics, but I don't know the exact field of his research. How did you learn his name?" Carlos asked again.

"Someone mentioned his name casually to me, related to another matter, and I thought you could shed more light on his field of practice." Emma said it offhandedly to try and put Carlos off. There was much more she wanted to ask, but she could see he was definitely observing her closely to discover more about her reasons for these questions.

"Dr. Carruchi may be at Marcus's charity event on Sunday. He's often included in the Rudolphis' parties, so I've heard," Carlos said, avoiding Emma's vision.

"Have *you* ever met him?" Emma put the question to Carlos.

"No, not personally...never."

*Why does Carlos avoid answering my questions with just half-truths? He definitely isn't being completely truthful! But why would he lie or withhold information from me about this man? He'd have no need to lie to me...unless he knows more about this man than he wants me to believe—and doesn't want me aware of that fact! I've got to find out more about Dr. Carruchi! It'll just have to be another way!* Emma's inner feelings told her to change the subject.

"Is this charity event on Sunday a formal or casual affair? I didn't bring formal clothes with me, and if it is, I'll have to go shopping tomorrow for a dress."

"It's casually informal—suits or dinner jackets—tuxes optional—if that's what you mean," he said laughingly.

"I feel the woman in me wanting an occasion to buy a new dress!"

The night air was much cooler as they started back towards the *taverna*. Behind them, in the distance, a black car was moving slowly in the direction they were walking. Carlos noticed it, too, but neither of them acknowledged its presence. Suddenly, he grabbed her arm and led her into a small side street, as if they were taking a detour back to the *ristorante*. The street was like a "twitten" with an incline leading to the top where it sharply turned into an adjacent alley going back down to the fountain. Putting his arm tightly around her waist to appear as two lovers ambling through the town, Carlos said, "Emma, just act as if we're not aware that black car is following us." But Emma could tell Carlos was keenly aware of its movements as they softly kissed. All the while, he was casting glances back to the car. Reaching the top of the alley, they turned to see the black car parked at the lower entrance to the small twitten-way… the entrance not wide enough for the car to enter. With a sudden motion, Carlos grabbed Emma.

"Run, Emma! Back to the *taverna* now!" Carlos was deeply troubled and suspected some kind of danger.

"Carlos, what's wrong?"

"I'm not sure…I saw that car following us back in the *Palazzo*. It's been watching us ever since we left the *ristorante.* Each new direction we take, the car moves in the same direction! When we entered the small alley, I knew they couldn't follow with the car… They'd have to change their strategy. Whatever they wanted, I didn't want to find out what that was!"

"Do you know who they are? Why would they be interested in us?"

"I'm not certain, Emma. For now you need to get your car and start back for the hotel. I'll find out more about that black car after I see you safely in your car…*and* safely on your way back to Milano. Would you feel better if I drove you back to the Manin?" he asked.

"No, I'll be fine."

"Then I'll follow you to Milano in my car to make certain you reach the hotel safely, before I return to my flat."

They reached the *taverna* when the black car sped past, almost hitting them. Just as the car sped past, Carlos grabbed her by the waist and pushed her aside. The darkened windows gave them no indication who was driving or how many were inside.

At the *taverna*, Carlos gave the valet Emma's ticket stub and checked her car before she got in. Nothing seemed wrong or unusual.

"Emma, I want you to take the Via Proghini road back to your hotel. Do you know that way?"

"Yes, I remember that route."

"I'll follow you to the hotel and then go on to my apartment without stopping. That way, I'll know if they're following you…or me!" Emma didn't want to alarm Carlos that maybe—just maybe—that car *was following her*…not him! Leaning into the car, he held her face in his hand and kissed her gently. Her thoughts, *How I missed his kisses!*

"*Caio, Emma!*"

As Emma put the car into gear, he called to her, "I'll call you tomorrow in the morning." He waved her on. Emma headed for the Via Proghini and drove without incident to the Manin. Looking in her rearview mirror, Emma saw Carlos get into his Gia and follow behind her at a close distance.

\* \* \*

Keeping Emma's rear lights in sight, Carlos picked up his car phone and dialed three digits after he placed his Larson on the seat next to him.

"*Pronto.*"

"Trace *Patente numero—Si,* **8124 K-king—A-Antonio—Q-quatro. *Si –trenta minutos. Caio,***" he said and hung up the phone.

"Emma what have you got yourself into here? Why did you ask about the Rudolphis and Carruchi almost in the same breath tonight? How did you come by that combination of names? I'll make certain we stay together Sunday at that charity party!"

The beeping car phone interrupted his thoughts.

"*Pronto— ah Si. Rudolphi Wineries.*"

*Grazie tenta!* Wait…tell MacEachen I'll not be in Roma on Monday as expected; can't discuss why now. Just tell him I'll call him on Monday. *Caio.*"

Approaching the intersection to the Manin, Carlos watched Emma slow to a stop, exit the car with no problems and give her keys to the valet to park it. With a wave and glance from her, Carlos knew she'd be fine back with Dillon. The black car was nowhere to be seen.

Carlos didn't drive to his flat as he said, but instead, drove southeast to the outskirts of the city, arriving at a drive marked, **"*PRIVATE.*"** Turning into the drive, he stopped, slipped a pass card into the gate lock to gain access, and waited for a red light to flash. Next, he placed his hand on a plate in the machine, while a combination of colored lights flashed on the panel. The heavy gates swung open. The meandering driveway was dimly lit, leading him to a large, darkened three-story house with just a single front light lit. Instead of stopping there, he drove around to the rear of the house where bright lights flashed on, lighting up the parking area. Approaching the rear entry, he stopped by a small box with a screen on the front panel and punched in a code onto a keypad. As he stood directly in front of the keyless door, the small screen snapped open for a millisecond taking his facial impression. He stood waiting. The heavy door unlatched and automatically opened into a large imposing foyer with an ornate staircase up to the second level. Instead of ascending the staircase, Carlos went directly to the end of the hall and entered a study. Walking to a wall case filled with books, he pressed a concealed button, opening a concealed panel. As the panel moved silently aside sounds of high-pitched humming—computers—coming from inside! Passing inside, the wall panel automatically closed behind him. He was very familiar with the large, bright room containing dozens of computers and monitor screens. Along one opposite wall was a bank of telephones—each manned with men and women working amid the humdrum of different bells ringing simultaneously. Carlos walked to the center circular station where a man sat working.

"We have a big problem! Emma is onto the names of some of our 'clients'! Don't ask me how she learned their names! Tonight, she asked me about a name I thought she'd never learn. She asked about Dr. Ennio Carruchi!"

The man at the desk continued to work as Carlos reported his findings—until he heard the name Dr. Ennio Carruchi.

"Carruchi! Bloody hell—Is she in Milano *because of Carruchi?* Christ…now I AM worried!" The gray-haired man slowly rose and stood tall.

"You were on the mark! She's going to attend the Rudolphi charity party on Sunday at the Villa del Christianna with Dillon O'Rourke! She didn't mention him by name, but I have every reason to believe he'll be there with her. Mac…I think they have a definite agenda for attending that affair…. some specific reason for going…*not because of Carruchi*…no…it's something else they want to learn. They've a plan in mind!"

"Aye, of course, I should have known our friend will be there; it has Dillon's signature all over it!" Pushing away from the desk, the gray-haired man paced. "Yes, Emma and Dillon do have a reason to attend that charity party...and I think I know what it is! Lucinda Rudolphi is her client!"

"You're certain of that?"

"Peter told me Emma met with her. So we know they most certainly do have a specific plan in mind for being in Milano and attending that party! *We* need to discover what that reason is, as well as what their plan is. If I know Em, she's here to find information, and it's in everyone's interest to find out as quickly as possible what kind of information she's after...exactly what they are looking for! *You're attending that party too, Carlos?"* The question was more a command.

"*Si*, I told her I'd meet her there. Believe me, I plan to keep a very close eye on her! So don't worry!"

"Good God, how can I *not* worry about both of them?" Carlos knew full well what his words meant.

"I've made arrangements to have another man inside, undercover on Sunday. That will make three of you to watch her—I'm not forgetting the host and hostess will be watching her, too!" The tall man approached Carlos and directly confronted him. "Jesus! Why this now?" We're getting so close...and now this!"

"Mac, remember, I love her too!" Carlos blurted out to calm Cyrus's fears.

"She thinks you're on a farm business trip to the Continent."

Looking directly at Carlos, Cyrus said, "I think I made a bad judgment. When I arrived in Milano, I stopped at the Manin to see her...I wanted to see for myself she was safe. She wasn't there. I needed to know she was all right...I would only know this if *I* saw her...I felt I might learn her reason for the trip...get the truth!"

"Did you leave a message?" Carlos asked.

Cyrus was clearly agitated and walked around. "Hell no! Of course not! Not finding her there was the best thing! But knowing her—my granddaughter—her curiosity will keep her asking questions until she learns who 'that man' was inquiring for her! It's her nature…to be persistent! She never stops asking questions!"

"Wonder where she got that trait?" Carlos asked rhetorically, trying to neutralize their tenseness.

"There's no way she'll learn you're here in Milano, Mac! At least not yet!" Carlos assured him. He weighed whether or not to tell Cyrus about the black car following them tonight at the *Torre del Pescatore* but decided against it at this time—since nothing happened! No…I'll wait until I find out who they were following—Emma or me?

"Oh, by the way, how was your dinner tonight?" Cyrus looked directly at Carlos with his question.

The offhanded question caught Carlos off guard. Does he suspect something happened…is that why he confronted me with his query? Carlos looked directly into Cyrus's eyes.

*"It was everything I hoped for…and more!"*

# CHAPTER TWENTY-EIGHT

Emma unlocked the door to her suite.

The room was lit with just the bedside light, and two of the balcony doors were open to the night air. Everything appeared as she left it...except for the second balcony door—it was closed when she left. "The chambermaid must have opened it when she turned down the bedding," she thought. The mantle clock softly chimed the half hour—twelve thirty—much too late to call London. Undressing, she savored tonight's good feelings spent with Carlos! Dwelling on the night's amazing meeting with Carlos, her feelings became anxiously mixed up with the other baffling events from that whole day!

"Why now Carlos? Why do you want to come back into my life now—amidst all this mystery and uneasiness? This should be happening to me under happy circumstances!" Feeling much too tired to sort it out, she checked the briefcase, saw no suspicious evidence of tampering, and wedged it back into its position next to the bed. Locking all the balcony doors except the last one, she set the dimmer on low and the alarm for six o'clock and crawled into bed. The sheets felt cool and silky and smelled of lavender.

As sleep came, she heard his voice telling her he missed her...at the *Taverna del Pescatore*...

\* \* \*

The alarm rang softly for some time while Emma flailed around the table to turn it off. Still half asleep…suddenly, a different ring sounded. The two different sounds ringing together quickly jarred Emma awake. Picking up the phone, she said, *"Si, Pronto!"*

"Em, meet me at eight o'clock at the same corner I left ye last night!" Emma knew it was Dillon calling—no one else ever called her "Em"!

The shower felt good, and the strong cool spray roused her thoughts back to yesterday's experiences: first Perugia—then Gubbio and Carlo—then the black car!

Outside, the sun was lost in the low gray clouds from which a soft, steady misty rain fell. Even though it was spring in Milano, there was a definite cold chill in the air this morning. Spring in Milano was unpredictable. It was known to change from oppressive heat to freezing rains within a day. Dressing in a heavy sweater, slacks and blouse, she remembered what Carlos said when he left: *"Call you tomorrow."* She kept looking at the phone, willing it to ring.

Dressed and ready to meet Dillon, and still no call, Emma waited a few seconds hoping *not* to miss *his* call. Picking up the phone, she was half wanting him to call when she remembered the bloody listening bug, the "cockroach," Dillon called it, hidden in its niche. Quietly returning the receiver in its cradle, she did a last check to her bag making certain her mobile phone was turned it on and left with the briefcase.

"Carlos knows my mobile number, I'm certain." The hallway was empty. This time the lift door opened immediately and descended directly to the lobby and she headed toward the door. Changing her mind, instead Emma found a quiet place in the lobby and dialed Carlos at his flat. No answer. Neither did an answering machine come on. "That's strange!" Not certain it was the right number she dialed information.

*"Telephono servizio"*…

*"Si prego, il numero di telefono per Esteves, Milano, via Fanti?"*

*"Grazie."*

The number was correct. Emma redialed. This time a machine answered and directed the caller to leave a message.

"Carlos, it's Emma. I'm leaving the hotel…it's nearly eight o'clock now…I've several errands to do this morning, not certain when I'll return. Call me at tea time."

Next dialing Peter's home number, Emma heard the phone ring.

"Good morning, Peter here."

"Peter?"

"Emma? Where are you calling from?"

"I'm calling from the hotel lobby on my mobile. Peter, I can't speak here, because I'm on my way out. Stay close, and I'll call again in exactly fifteen minutes on *your* mobile number, do you understand?"

"Yes, I'll wait for your call," he said and they hung up.

She didn't want to speak to Peter from inside the hotel—not trusting it to be safe—and decided to re-try Peter on his mobile phone from the café across the street to allow her to speak freely, knowing it should be harder to trace the mobile phones.

In a quiet corner inside the café, Emma redialed Peter's cell phone. "Peter, it's me again. What are the police doing to discover who broke into the firm?"

"I've kept in touch with them every day; so far, they have no leads. I did tell them no files were stolen, but an unknown sum of petty cash was gone."

"Peter, are the discs still in the well?"

"Yes, exactly where I placed them." Their code word "well" was for Emma's own personal safe—not the law firm's safe. Everyone at the firm knew the location of the firm's safe. Only Peter and Emma knew she had her own private safe and its location.

"Good job, Peter. If anyone asks you about the Chatelaine files, just act as if you don't know anything—I mean *anything* at all about that case or the contents of the files! I have a feeling my coming to Italy has alerted someone to take notice of something…something that's tied in with that old case. I don't know what that something is all about, but I plan to find out! Someone discovered I went to the Court of Justice and took the files out, and now, whoever they are don't want me to find out what's in those files! So please, Peter, *do not* let on you have done any work on those files!" Emma explicitly emphasized her words to alert Peter he could be in danger!

"Peter, I may need you to send those discs at some future time. When I do, I'll arrange for you to send them to a specific address."

"Emma, what are you involved in?" Peter asked.

"To be honest, Peter, I'm not sure myself—yet, and I can't tell you more at this time. For now, the less you know the safer *you* are! This case may take more time than I realized. Is Olivia handling things at the firm?"

Olivia Grimshaw, Q.C., junior counselor, was very reliable with quick insight to pick up the pace of work when things became backlogged. When Emma first met her, she knew she was perfect for the firm—both had many similar views on critical issues, and both worked zealously on every case they accepted. Though Olivia had many similar characteristics with Emma, they were complete opposites in many other ways. Olivia's bright red, curly hair, freckled features and blue eyes were the opposite of Emma's black-Irish traits. Like Emma, she never missed a nuance of information. When they're together, their distinctive dissimilarity inevitably made people take notice of them. Olivia came to the firm at the most fortunate time, when the firm's cases were overwhelming Emma. Once established in her own standing in the firm, Olivia hired her own private secretary, Hilary Agatha Blair, "Hilly" for short. Hilly and Peter matched up perfectly—interests and work-drive, which made it a simpatico relationship.

"Yes, Liv is picking up the slack nicely, and Hilly is helping me with the extra secretarial work, too. We're managing fine."

"Tell Liv I'll call her in a few days, and I'll decide then what to tell her if I need more time here. The fewer people who know what I'm doing here, the better for now! Remember, Peter, I'm here on holiday! Have to ring off now. If you need to call me, use my cell number and leave a message. Do not use the hotel phone to leave messages, understand?"

"Quite," he said, and he rang off.

Before calling Peter, Emma had asked the valet to bring her car around to the front drive in thirty minutes, thinking this would give her plenty of time to make her calls. She scanned down the block to see if anyone was offhandedly interested in her—no one stood out to her. Just as she drove down the drive and exited onto the *Via di Manin,* she saw the beige sedan come out of the nearby garage and turn behind her.

"Bloody damn! Someone is tailing me again! Only this time I'm sure they'll be harder to lose!" Dialing her cell phone, Emma hoped Dillon had his turned on. "Dillon? I'm on my way to pick you up, but first I have to lose our friends in the beige sedan." Dillon's instructions were precise and rapid.

"Drive 'round the *Piazza* once and then double back—takin' the same route. If they're still with you, pick me up on the northeast corner of the *Via Della Muscova and the Via Appanni.* Just slow up, and I'll approach the car like I'm sellin' you a newspaper and get in when you're at the curb. If they're still with us, I can lose 'hem." The line went dead.

Driving around the *Piazza Princ Cotilde,* Emma circled once, then drove down the *Via San Marco* to the *Piazza* to circle around the roundabout, then headed down the *Via Appanni* to pick up Dillon. The tan car was still following at a close distance along with another unidentified one—in tandem. Speeding up, Emma approached the *Via Della Muscova,* saw Dillon on the corner waving newspapers, and sped over to him. Approaching the car and waving his newspapers, in a flash, he was in the car in the back. Dillon gave instructions, "Go back towards the 'otel but instead, turn onto *Via Turanti* and make a U-turn, doublin' back on *Turanti.*" Emma quickly made the U-turn, passing the beige car and its double, she got a good look at the driver.

"I recognize that man! He's the same man who was watching me that first day—he stood across the street next to the café. Even without the sunglasses, I recognize him!"

The occupants were frantically gesturing to each other with their hands as she sped past them.

"I agree, Emmie…'e's the same bloke!"

"Now I remember! That driver…he's the man I accidentally bumped into in the library in London! He's the one who dropped the antique business card I gave to you…I'm certain of it!" Dillon now understood just how far their surveillance was on Emma—they had her under close surveillence in London. *Why is Emma so important to someone...e'en in London?*

"Take the next right—then a left, Em." Dillon sat upright in the passenger seat. "Go 'bout three blocks and then pull over, so's I can take the wheel."

After quickly exchanging seats, Dillon drove to pick up Biaggio at the *Cimitero Monumentale*. Making several maneuvers into side streets, darting into driveways, all the while watching for the beige sedan, Dillon found the entrance to the *Cimitero Monumentale* and drove in.

"'Ere's where we'll see 'hem comin' in if we 'aven't lost them!" Circling around inside the cemetery, they saw no sign of any beige or black cars behind them or parked outside the cemetery entrance.

In the distance, Biaggio was raking the grounds appearing to be a caretaker. Looking up, he saw Dillon drive past and circle back to him. Biaggio finished his job, picked up his equipment, and got into a truck parked up ahead.

"Where are we heading, Dillon?"

"Biaggio will lead us to a place outside Milano where we'll meet."

As an afterthought, he added, "By the way, we 'ave our invitations to the Rudolphi charit' part' for tomor'ow." With his disarming smile, Dillon handed them to Emma.

"You and I'll be guests of Marcus and Lucinda Rudolphi at their fanc' part'. But first, I need to show Biaggio the lay of the estate; 'e'll be there, too—at the part', not as an invited guest, but o'r driver. More important'y today 'e 'as another reconnaissance job to complete before t'morrow's party. Best to wait 'til we're at the 'ouse to discuss o'r plans, Em." Emma looked at the Charity invitations embossed and scripted in gold relief.

"Very impressive and expensive! I'd expect nothing less!" She nodded.

"Dillon, all this planning we're doing, do you have a specific plan in mind how we'll get into the villa's study to find the list of names Lucinda mentioned?"

"That's exactly what Biaggio will find out for us today. 'Is mission is to get us blueprints of the villa del Christianna. But yes, I 'ave a plan 'ow we'll do it."

"I'm glad to hear you say how '**we'll do it**'!" Looking at Dillon, Emma saw that he caught the real meaning of her words!

They followed Biaggio's truck and turned into a driveway leading up to a small stucco house, drove to the rear, and parked out of site from the road. Making certain their vehicles were somewhat concealed from the road, they entered through the back door.

Dillon disarmed the door alarm. "We're pretty safe in here." They followed Biaggio over to the stairs to a metal door leading down to the basement. When he flipped a switch, the lights revealed a room filled with computer equipment along with other sophisticated electrical equipment: videos, television and projector screens used for viewing, and a dark room for developing films. Dillon and Biaggio were definitely familiar with this place. Emma just looked around while the two men went about collecting equipment and turning on monitors. Split screen images on the monitors came up indicating a sophisticated security system, both inside and outside the house. It was evident this was a kind of safe house—someone had been there at an earlier time. There were dirty coffee cups.

Emma kept looking around…something about the inside of this house triggered a past memory—a *déjà vu* feeling, as if she had been there before.

*Why does this mountain farmhouse have a familiar feeling to it for me?* Emma asked herself, looking carefully around the *paese casa*…

# CHAPTER TWENTY-NINE

"Dillon, I recognize this house!"

She interrupted his task. "Carlos and I stopped here…one day long ago…to get out of the torrential rainstorm!" Memories of that rainstorm…the picnic in the mountain pasture…were so vivid to her again! "An old man lived here then, and we took refuge under the front arbor when he invited us inside to dry off and wait out the storm!" Looking around for something familiar, she had seen before, she continued, "There were paintings on the walls with others stacked one against another on the floor throughout the house. The old man showed us many of his paintings, some he painted and others he collected!" Emma slowly walked around the room, trying to describe how the old man looked. "He had blue eyes, bright blue eyes, and his name…his name was Vittorio! Yes, Giuseppe Vittorio! Does he still live here? Where are all the paintings?" Looking around to a room completely empty of artwork, Emma asked, "Do you know Giuseppe Vittorio?"

"Em, an old man did live here, but not in over a year. He moved and took all his art with him. Biaggio's family owns the house," Dillon answered concisely but avoided looking at her. That didn't keep her from sensing his answer was a "put-off" to her questions. The lack of eye contact always gave him away. Emma knew his eye movements well—always the iris darkened to a deep blue whenever he attempted to conceal the complete truth from her. She knew this answer was only a partial truth to put her off, so she didn't pursue the matter. Somehow, Emma perceived Biaggio had something to do with the old man who once lived here. Clearly, Dillon wasn't going to tell her more, and her inner mindset told her not to pursue it with either Biaggio or Dillon at this moment. They definitely had defenses in place for a specific reason, so she just let the subject drop—for the time being.

After inspecting the basement and changing the security tapes, Emma followed Dillon and Biaggio up to the second floor to a larger room filled with many more tables and computers—all covered with maps and phones; it was more like an office—or better still, more like a headquarters—a control center.

A moment came and Emma had to ask, "Biaggio, why is the basement filled with security tapes and monitors? Were they always here? And has this house always been empty?"

"It's because of all this expensive equipment. If a house looks empty for some time, it becomes a target for the homeless, ruffian gangs, or petty thieves. So we need to keep a high level of security to prevent that from happening," Biaggio said candidly. His answer was partially true—but the security there was definitely overkill for petty thieves. Then too, he never told her the real need for this kind of house.

"Where is the old man who lived here several years ago?" Emma straight out asked Biaggio.

"He's my great-uncle, but when he became too ill to live alone, my brother took him in to live with them, and he's happy where he is now with all his paintings." A partially truthful answer from Biaggio—deliberate but vague.

"Who is responsible for this place? Why is there a need for this place?" He still didn't answer her questions. Was that deliberate? His silence really told her she had no right to pry into his family business. If another opportunity arose, she'd talk to him about purchasing one of his great-uncle's paintings—if his uncle is the artist, Guiseppe Vittorio. Her promise was made long ago—in a completely different life—she still wanted one of his masterful paintings.

"Dillon, I can see you've done a lot of work to maintain the secrecy of our mission. Do you think all of this is overkill, or is there more danger to this trip than I'm aware of?" Emma asked him, walking around a table covered with maps, to get an idea what this trip was about.

"Em, some of the information I've uncovered is raisin' all the 'airs on the back of me neck! I think we've seen the tip of an iceberg, and 'til I know 'ow big that berg is, we 'ave to be extra cautious. I'm hopin' yur fella, Carlos, will 'ave more information 'bout these people—the Rudolphi family."

Turning toward the table of maps, Dillon said, "Em, you and I need to know ev'ry aspect of our plan! Even the smallest element is important if we're to be successful!"

Spreading out the maps of the winery, each identified and drew reference points on the maps. They concentrated on the target in his plan—the Rudolphi library. Biaggio was a man of few words and usually just nodded during a conversation. He took out several maps of his own and laid them next to ours to study and compare. There was something gentle and kind about Biaggio—Emma liked him. One of his peculiarities was that he always kept a toothpick between his teeth—most likely a substitute for a cigarette or cigar.

"Will we know if someone comes to the house, and we're up here?"

"*Si,*—I have a trip switch set. If anyone comes down the drive or opens a door or window, an alarm in the room goes off." Pointing to a screen, he said, "That monitor will show us where they entered the grounds or house." It was a four-way split screen picture of each entrance and the driveway. Biaggio said matter-of-factly, pointing to a bank of computers, particularly one with a split-screen, "Every part of this house is monitored with many different types of alarms—no need to worry." He just smiled at her.

Watching and listening to both men, Emma noticed that Biaggio spoke mostly in broken English interspersed with Italian, yet Dillon knew exactly what he was saying.

"Dillon, when did you learn Italian? You seem to understand Biaggio so well?" Emma interjected into their conversation.

"In one of me other lives, Em, which is one reason I knew I'd enjoy this trip with you," he answered, smiling coyly at her. Studying the map with Dillon, Emma watched him expertly draw markings on the maps from the illustrations she made on their trip to the winery and the Rudolphi estate to set a plan with Biaggio, for canvassing the Rudolphi Estate grounds.

Explaining to Biaggio, he said, "The best—and safes' entrance for you to penetrate the estate is 'ere—between the winer' and the vine'ards", pointing to a spot on the map. Biaggio was going to do a covert assessment of the Rudolphi estate to survey the topography first hand before the charity party on Sunday. Dillon continued briefing him, "The securit' at this point is electrified boundar' fences neares' the perimeter. Bypass the system with these portable computer chips 'til you get over 'hem, then remove the chips to reset 'hem back on. If they're tied to a central station, they can only be off five seconds before a back up kicks in. That's ususall' when the guards will check the system and the area. You'll 'ave yur bag of goodies with you. Once inside the perimeter, you'd better look for lasers—the can of silver talc will take care of that problem. You can see the talc clearl' in daylight too. Do what you 'ave to to get 'round them. Listen for dogs. We did 'ear barkin', but they could be 'ouse pets OR guard dogs! Keep the dart gun in your pocket if you should meet an' dogs or guards—pop 'hem one! Do you have enough darts?"

Biaggio nodded silently. "Good. Bring a bottle of *vino*, if you 'ave to dart an' guards, pour some wine on 'hem. When they wake up they'll smell like they 'ad a good *vino* party! Did you get the proper serum for the darts?"

"*L abbondanza di medicina!* The *doctore* fixed the exact amount of solution for each dose."

"Good."

Dillon went on outlining the plan. "Carry the grape basket for yur disguise. Should you meet some farm'ands—yur' just one of them. Keep headin' due east 'til you come to the main Villa Tempietto," he said, pointing to the spot on the map. "Our guess is the old man, Guisippe Rudolophi, lives at this big main 'ome—The Villa Tempietto. This villa is the only villa with a guard'ouse at the main entrance—we saw one guard. I think there's a pan'l inside the 'ouse that controls the electricit'—maybe e'en the laser system—to the fences." Biaggio intently studied the map without taking any notes, as if this was a routine job for him—something he was used to doing.

"From that villa, make yur way 'round this next villa—without detection of course. 'Ere you'll 'ave to check out the security carefull' and get 'round it 'owever you can. We don't 'ave much information about 'ow secure that villa *is*. You gotta take as man' pictures of the area as you can; we'll need to know 'ow secure the Villa Tempietto is, too. From there, go due north, passin' several workers 'omes and two smaller villas—maybe belongin' to Rudolphis. Once yur past that area, you should come to the Villa del Christiana." Dillon drew a large red circle around the site on the map.

"We know this villa is surrounded by a black iron fence on the outer-most boundary that 'as an ornate grill-iron gate at the entrance. We're assumin' its electrified! Fortunate'y there's no gate'ouse 'ere, but they may still 'ave a guard posted inside the entrance at some point...and they 'ave dogs with 'hem—this we saw! The drive up to the villa from the gate entrance is fair'y long and windin'—goes 'bout a couple of kilometers where it ends at a very large *Piazza*-like drive in front of the villa. In the middle of the *Piazza* is a sculptured fountain. Yesterday, we saw two cars parked there—one red and another silver." Dillon marked the end of the drive with a black **X**. Here his voice changed to reflect the importance of these further instructions.

"**This is the *focus* of our mission**. I need you to find out what kind of securit' is in the 'ouse and 'round the 'ouse, and 'ow 'eavy the grounds are patrolled. Bring some small gardenin' equipment to pose as a gardener—if yur' seen. It's important we learn what rooms and 'ow many are on the first floor in the villa! Of those rooms, 'ow man' lead direct'y out to the balcon'. The balcon' terrace appears to circle the entire first floor with a lot of doors to it from the 'ouse." Dillon's directions took on a greater emphasis. "One important fact—above all else—find the exact location of the main power trunk feedin' the securit' computers. I'm certain they'll 'ave a secondar' back-up system nearby—and you need to find the exact location of that emergenc' back up source! It's probab'y near the main source... but could be complete'y independent at another sight! If o'r plan is to be successful on Sunday, we need to coordinate the moment we deactivate these systems with the exact moment we penetrate the librar'!" Biaggio nodded in understanding.

Dillon then focused on another area on the maps. "Check out the area 'round the pool entrance from the gardens to the pool—and other buildin's beyond the pool." Pointing to the exact area, he said, "Determine if these pool buildin's are accessible from the rear gardens—or pool area—and if they are 'larmed. See if the're tied into the main villa securit' 'larms? **OR** does the 'ouse 'ave its own separate alarm system? Check to see if there's separate servant's quarters in the back away from the main 'ouse. If you find people in the main 'ouse, try and get pictures of 'hem, Marcus Rudolphi or his wife Lucinda, or any others includin' servants, stayin' at the villa. Have you got enough film?"

"Got enough for over couple of hundred," Biaggio said.

"Good. Take yur cell phone. If ye 'ave any trouble at all—I mean **an' trouble at all**—call me immediate'y!" Dillon said to him emphatically. The code for an emergency is *'Sabato'*! We'll send the troops in!" Dillon told him.

"Good to know—but it won't be necessary!" Biaggio said to them, smiling.

"Drive the van to this site. Who's goin' with ye to take the van after ye get in?" Dillon asked.

"Antonio is driving me to the winery. He'll leave me off and then take the van back to his place," Biaggio said. "We set up a signal—a coded *telefono* call—he'll know where and when to pick me up."

Dillon again emphasized to Biaggio, "You must find out exact'y where the librar' is located inside the villa in relation to the front entrance. See if you can tell 'ow man' rooms 'but the librar' and if the librar' is one of the rooms leading out to the balcon'."

"You presuming the library is on the first floor?" Biaggio asked.

"Yeah…I am." Dillon was quiet for a few seconds taking stock of Biaggio's question.

Recalling the lights they saw last night through the windows, Emma interjected, "The windows looked like they may be floor-to-ceiling height…without drapes but maybe shutters on the inside—

too dark last night to see inside. Actually, the lack of drapes may give you a better view into the rooms at a closer distance."

"Good point, Em," Dillon commented.

"Will we see the photos before we go to the villa charity?" Emma asked Dillon.

"Oh, indeed we will, Em! We 'ave our own "speedy developer," he smiled at Biaggio.

Dillon cautioned Biaggio, "Don't get *too* close to the winer'. It's heavil' guarded and for now, I don't want to tip 'm off about this undertakin'! All in good time—all in good time."

Emma found his last remark puzzling as to what Dillon meant by it—he said it almost promisingly. Biaggio folded the maps while Dillon put the rest of the papers into a bucket and burned them. "Nothin' to tip our hand." Before returning downstairs, they each double checked to make certain they had left nothing.

Outside, not detecting anything different from the way they found it, they hurriedly walked out to the cars in the rear. Biaggio was first to drive his truck out the driveway to the road.

Dillon made no move to follow. Instead, he casually leaned on the car. "Need to wait ten minutes, before we leave, Em," he said, taking out a cigarette—not to smoke but to place behind his ear. It was his way of replacing an old chain-smoking habit, a long time routine, with a new one. Emma knew when times were tense, he'd have a pack of cigarettes on him, but instead of smoking, he'd smell the cigarette and place one behind his ear as a ritual anticipating something was about to happen. "Old 'abits die 'ard."

The evening air had a spring chill to it. Gray clouds were in the dusky sky shrouding the mountain tops off to the north. Emma interrupted the silence. "If the sky gets dark and clear tonight, we could see a million stars giving off a spectrum of colors—blue—red—yellow—white. I remember the Milky Way looks so much brighter here in the mountains. It even looks closer here, too. It reminds me of a passage I once read, 'The stars are really tiny atoms constantly bombarding each other to form new planets…but to us it's a field of diamonds to grasp.'"

Dillon enjoyed listening to Emma. He never tired of her company.

Finally, an adequate amount of time had passed, and they slowly drove away from the house out to the main road without headlights on. In the dark, Emma's past memories of Carlos driving this road were happier occasions. No sign of any traffic, Dillon turned and headed back to the city.

"Dillon, you and I have to buy new clothes for the party tomorrow," Emma said half jokingly, but as a reminder.

Remembering she spent last night with Carlos, Emma was waiting for an opportunity to tell Dillon about what happened on the *Palazzo* in Gubbio.

"You're much too kind to ask Dillon, so I'll tell you…I did enjoy dinner with Carlos at the *Taverna del Pescatore* in Gubbio last night. That was the first time I had seen him in almost nine months—it felt as if we hadn't been apart—and the dinner was very good, too! After dinner, we decided to take a walk around the town *Palazzo*—the evening was really nice—like old times. But I digress… Something alarming happened! On our return back to the *ristorante*, a large black car started following us. Carlos saw it and became alarmed! We made some maneuvers, detouring through several streets—alleys—to see if it was really following us. It definitely was! Then on our way back to the ristorante, it just suddenly sped past us and took off down the street! Carlos thought it might be following him! I didn't tell him about the tail we've had since arriving in Milano or about the listening bug in my room. Dillon, I think that car was following me—not Carlos!"

Not wanting to see Dillon's reaction, Emma continued, "When we reached the *ristorante*, Carlos checked my car and followed me back to Milano in his car. As far as I could tell, no one tailed us back to Milano." Dillon silently listened, not interrupting or commenting.

"This morning, before I left the hotel, I called and left Carlos a message to call me this afternoon at the hotel. I haven't heard from him. Dillon, do you think the people in the black car were the same people who have been following us in Milano?"

"Em, they may be the same people—or others are interested in o'r doin's."

"Do you have any idea who they could be?"

249

Emma studied his countenance carefully when he answered, "I may 'ave some idea Em, but fur now, I can't say more. It's best not to get too involved in speculatin'—just yet."

"Dillon, I have every right to know just what's going on here—if you have serious suspicions, then I should know about them! This is *my* case and it's why I asked you to come with me to Milano! Remember?" she queried angrily.

"I know, Em, 'hem's words are all true! 'owever, you must know I've always' been 'onest with you. I'd tell you 'anythin'! But for now yur safet' is the most important thing to me and gettin' the answers you need to find out is the next priorit'. So let's just leave it at that, lass, and get those new duds we need!"

His change of topic was deliberately putting an end to her questions and ending on a lighter note. She knew he mixed truths with deliberate fabrication that didn't let her pin him down where the real truth lay.

"Sorry, Dillon, I didn't mean to jump on you! This whole case... seems to rile me up...the more we learn...the more alarms go off! I know you're thinking about my safety—and thanks." Leaning over, she gave him a hug. Dillon didn't comment any more on the facts she'd just told him, but she knew he was still thinking about it, more than he let on to her.

"Carlos is going to be at the Rudolphis' party tomorrow. I didn't tell him about you, just that I was going with a friend. I think I led him to believe you were a friend from Milano." Dillon made no response for several seconds after learning Carlos would be at the Rudolphis'.

"Then, it will be a very interestin' charit' part' tomorrow! I'll final'y get to meet yur young man! If 'e's all I 'eard 'im to be, 'e'll be a most welcome man," Dillon said, smiling. He's trying to disguise his feelings about something having to do with Carlos!

"It was a nice try, Dillon, but I'm betting you and Carlos have a past together." Making a mental note, Emma would take careful notice how each man reacts when they meet tomorrow at the Rudolphis' party!

With his own thoughts, Dillon was glad to hear Carlos would be at the charity party at the Villa del Christianna. *Is the bloke in*

*Milano just for that reason? If so, why is the Italian Office of the Secret Service interested in the Rudolphis?*

Mentally assuming, *"After the part 'tomor 'ow, Carlos, I'm makin' certain you and I 'ave us a long chat! We need to do some serious talkin'! Me feelin's are we're workin' on the same assignment, matie, and we need to be on the same page! If that's the case...it's been too long a time my friend!"*

**"Now, Em, where do we find some cool fancy duds for this party?"**

# CHAPTER THIRTY

Dillon and Emma separated when they reached the *Via Saint Andrea*—Versace's boutiques would have the exact 'something' for both of them.

They decided each would look for suitable attire to wear for the charity party to blend in with the other ritzy Italian party guests. They needed to appear as if they belonged to the "Milanese society set"—nothing to draw attention to them. It didn't take Emma long to choose the right outfit—a dark, emerald green silk dress, remembering one of Carlos's remarks, "Emeralds play up your Irish/ Welsh charms!" That was a past time long ago...and green was one of her favorite colours.

Emma had forgotten how tedious clothes shopping was, and when she returned to the Manin, she asked the valet to bring her packages up to her suite while she made a stop at Dillon's room.

*"Signore Paolo, my key, per piacere? Grazie!"* Along with her room key, he handed her a message from Carlos. "Call my cell number." Instead of going upstairs to see Dillon, she went into the lounge to make her call to Carlos. The Machiavelli Lounge was already crowded and noisy. Looking around for a quiet place to make the call, Emma saw he was there...sitting at the bar!

**"Carlos, what are you doing here? I just received your message and came in here to call you,"** she said, not telling him her reason for phoning him outside her room.

"Actually, I was waiting for *you,* Emma...I only arrived a few minutes ago." He rose and asked, "What would you like to drink? I'll order for both of us, and we can sit at one of the tables."

"Just tea, and see if they have any tea biscuits or crackers—I'm starved!" Walking over to the corner of the lounge, they consciously chose a table in the rear for privacy with a good view of the doors. "The tea will be ready in a few minutes. How was your day? I can see you've been shopping."

"My trip to Milano didn't include attending a *festa* when I packed, so I needed something to wear tomorrow to blend with the in-crowd in Milano!" After telling him that, she noticed Carlos's attention seemed to be elsewhere; no outward acknowledgement from him that she didn't have the invitation to the Rudolphis' charity party before she left London.

"Carlos, there's something preoccupying you! Is something wrong?" Emma asked, recalling he had the same pre-occupied manner when they left the Taverna Friday night.

"Let's wait for the tea to come." The waiter brought the tea and set it down, and now the lounge was really crowded and much noisier, making it harder to keep their voices low but heard.

"Carlos, tell me what's wrong?" Carlos sipped his drink but his countenance betrayed the seriousness of the moment.

"I need to speak with you, Emma...There are things I said to you last night at the taverna that need explanation now!" Seeing shock on her face, he continued, "Oh, everything I said about us...it's all true! If our relationship is to be built on honesty, then I need to be totally honest with you ...as honest as I possibly can be." Emma watched Carlos struggling to say something important to her.

"Carlos, whatever do you mean?"

"When we agreed last year to go our separate ways because of our different lifestyles, it was because of **my job and lifestyle...not yours!** Emma, there's more to my job than I've led you to believe. Tomorrow, Marcus Rudolphi is giving that charity festa at his villa."

"Yes, I already know that!"

"But what you don't know, Emma, is that I'm here on an assignment that involves Marcus Rudolphi!" Emma tried to contain her astonishment.

"What kind of assignment?" she asked guardedly.

"We've been investigating Marcus…and his family… for some time now for possible criminal operations."

"Why…," Emma started to ask him, but Carlos interrupted her.

"Let me finish first, and then I'll try to answer all your questions."

"I know I told you I work at the embassy in Roma…which is true! My real position there *is* with the Italian government…but with Interpol—in a special division of the Italian Secret Service. My current assignment is highly sensitive and confidential involving Marcus Rudolphi and his family. I can't give you specifics except to say we've had them under investigation for the past two years now—more than that I can't elaborate in detail. But I can tell you it has to do with illegal…criminal…activities!" Emma's eyes were riveted on Carlos, intent on listening to his every word.

"Emma…let me say again—this case has nothing to do with my feelings for you at this moment!" Casting his eyes down, Emma observed him seeing some inner anguish. "When I thought I had lost you last year for a foolish decision I made then…well, I've had a lot of time to think about how lonely my life has been without you…I guess what I'm asking, Em, I want you… no, I *need* you back into my life! I've come to realize if you love someone and they're not part of your life to share it…everything else in life is not important!"

Emma could tell Carlos had a conflict going on inside him… most likely about her…and now his assignment. He was telling her truthfully of his love for her…it was not a maneuver to get her to confide what *she* knew about the Rudolphis!

*Bloody damn…the timing…the events of these last few days… confuses everything. There is another darker reason for Carlos to tell me this! For so long I wanted to hear these words from him… not said in the same sentence with information about his job—it just takes away some of the wonderment of the moment! Still his confession... "he still loves me"...is really what's important to me!* Emma felt warm tears run down her face. "Carlos...."

Putting his finger to her lips, "Please don't say anything now, Emma, let me go on—hear me out first!"

"No! Wait Carlos," Emma said, reaching up to hold his hand. "Carlos, nothing in this world will keep me away from you now... but these things happening here...in Milano...It doesn't seem right our finding each other again should happen in these circumstances! The timing...not knowing what's going to happen here or why! I just feel so confused...please understand." Quietly looking into his eyes, she said, "I do love you! I guess I've never stopped loving you...I've always known that in my heart."

He reached over and gently took her face into his hands and kissed her.

"I understand what you say, Emma, not certain what another day will bring...do you understand why I need to say these things now?" he asked almost pleadingly.

"Yes, I think I do...and I'm glad you're telling me these things! But the timing with the Rudolphis...my client here...I don't want it to diminish this special moment for us! This Rudolphi matter—this case...it's so very important to me!" Emma had to let him know this case was equally important to her as his assignment without telling him why! "Please tell me as much as you can about the Rudolphi family?" she asked urgently. Emma knew Carlos wasn't aware of all the details she learned since coming to Milano about the Rudolphis, and she hated keeping information from him—more so, using him to learn more about Marcus Rudolphi! Rationalizing if they were to be successful in this case, she needed to know *everything* about that family, and if Carlos was the source of information, then she had to get it that way! Emma focused on one fact that Carlos didn't know—Lucinda's visit to her in London—*or did he know*?

"It's true. My job at the Italian Embassy is a screen for my job at Interpol. We've been tracking a certain type of crime for the past several years, kidnappings, taking place in Italy—when we found the same kinds of kidnappings were increasing globally."

Emma listened. *A Kidnapping organization?* she thought, remembering the two children they saw yesterday in Perugia.

"Several years ago, we monitored an increase in kidnappings—unusual kinds of kidnappings—here in Italy, France, and Germany. A common link between them was that money was *not* the object for the return of these victims! In response to this new development, Interpol created a special unit to investigate and confirm if all these kidnappings had something in common—if not money—then we needed to find out what it was. Then the bigger question was—WHY—if not for money then WHAT? Interpol in all these countries worked together—an enormous task—but we learned the scope of the criminal activity was global! We had no idea the extent of this organization's goals or how far this criminal network reached until all the different countries pooled their information into one central database with Interpol. That's when our suspicions were born out! The entire body of evidence confirmed that there was an international kidnapping syndicate of unprecedented proportions reaching into every major country—on all the continents! Persistent investigative sources connected this international syndicate to an underground scientific research group—unbelievable! Supposedly working in the name of science! Emma, these kidnappings were done for the benefit of research science!" The information Carlos was telling her was incredible to hear...knowing what Lucinda confided...and what Dillon and she discovered in Perugia...did make it credible.

"Then about two years ago our persistence paid off! Two facts—kidnapping cases had tripled internationally and those we investigated had a high probability that they were connected to the same scientific research program known to us. These facts coupled together...*ergo*, there's an organization with a diabolical plan in place, with an infinite source of money, under the control of some demented mastermind—working with a medical community of rogue scientists—all for the same common goal! Illegal experimentation! So! Exactly what is that goal? We finally got a break with a group of scientists working in hidden laboratories in western Europe. Our leads led us to discover **one** of these research laboratories is located here in Italy!" Carlos's feelings were anger and concern during his recounting of the facts. "Italy not only has an underground center for subversive research, but we believe it's the center of this global organization and their research!" It was like a brilliant light turning on in Emma's mind when she heard his words.

"Interpol has consulted with legitimate research laboratories to try and better understand certain theories—about the kind of research they could be doing. They confirmed our suspicions about the kind of research we believed the underground scientists are doing. Our hypothesis about their goal...is really possible—no longer speculative! It's in the field of genetics! We believe...the kidnappings are a source of getting genetic material to use for illegal research! Just how the exact genetic product is used in their research—we can only speculate! But trust me...it's on the cutting edge of genetic science!"

"How does this fit in with the Rudolphis?" Emma inquired.

Our information leads us to...the Rudolphi family—more probably they're the money source. We've kept constant surveillance on the entire family for a long time." Carlos did not dare tell her they managed to get an undercover plant inside the Rudolphi family. He hesitated before saying more...taking care not to mention Cyrus's name unconsciously.

"Which brings me to Lucinda Rudolphi." His eyes went downcast.

"I learned Lucinda flew to London several weeks ago and met with you. This was totally unexpected, and we had no idea why she wanted to meet with you!" He was committed to learning more from Emma. "Did she ask to see you or did you ask her to come to London to see her?" *So he did know Lucinda met with me! But he doesn't know the reason for her visit or what she asked me to do!*

"Carlos, you know I can't discuss those issues with you. I can confirm she came to see me."

"Then she is your client?" He looked directly at Emma with his question.

"Why is it so important for you to know what Lucinda wanted to see me about?"

Carlos didn't answer her question, instead he asked, "Does it have something to do with this investigation we're doing?"

"I'm not certain, Carlos." But Emma could tell Carlos had more information to query her about.

"Emma...the most important piece of information came from a reliable source ...linking your name to the Rudolphis!" Carlos was weighing how much he should tell her. "Emma, it's possible you're connected to the Rudolphis...going back a year...we've never confirmed *why* your name is linked to that family!" He watched her reaction to his words closely.

The words totally shocked Emma! It caught her by surprise, "What are you saying, Carlos? How...that I was connected...it's preposterous, Carlos!

"Emma, are you certain you have never met any member of the Rudolphi family?"

Emma paused before answering...thinking, *Does he or doesn't he know I'm aware my name is on a list Marcus keeps locked in his study?*

"Carlos, I have no idea what you're talking about! How can my name be linked to the Rudolphis? Don't you think I would know if I had previously met any of the Rudolphis?" Emma asked, sounding annoyed with his question and trying to hide that she already knew her name was definitely linked to the Rudolphis.

"I was certain you would tell me—if you knew!" he added. *Why the lack of eye contact? He's not telling me something critical!*

"Of course, I would *remember* it, Carlos, why wouldn't I remember it?" Emma asked angrily and irritably. "I would know if I had anything to do with that family in any way in the past! For any reason—legal or personal—and I haven't...a memory of any incident encountered with any of them. I would remember meeting a famous Milanese family!" She reiterated emphatically!

"Emma, I do not doubt your honesty or integrity, please understand!

These people are ruthless and will do anything at any cost to get what they want. We know their operation is global, which makes it difficult for us to find out just how big their organization truly IS!" Carlos was quiet for a few minutes.

"When I learned Lucinda Rudolphi met with you, I did some checking...I'm still not certain why she went to see you. Imagine my surprise when I found out *you* were planning a trip to Milano several weeks later—after that meeting! Coincidental? How could

I *not* have a suspicion it was because of Lucinda Rudolphi's visit to you—that you're here in Milano?"

"Why are you here, Emma?" Carlos blurted out.

"You know, Carlos, I'm bound not to discuss my client's business with you, that's privileged information. I can tell you, it is not about any scientific mission on her behalf." Not wanting to discuss the issue of kidnappings with him, Emma changed the subject.

"Carlos, have you had me followed in Milano?" she asked.

"Yes, I have; more for your safety than anything, Emma. But that black car the other night was not one of ours, which is why I was so alarmed!"

"I've been aware a beige car following me from the hotel for the past three days. You may as well know now, because you'll see him tomorrow, Dillon O'Rourke is here with me. I knew he would help expedite my reason for this trip…faster than if I did it alone…besides I needed a male counterpart with me to get certain information. Both Dillon and I are aware a beige sedan is following us in Milano."

"No, that's not one of ours. AND, we've been aware a beige sedan has been tailing you since your arrival at the hotel. Might I say…I was told you were good at losing them, too?" Carlos didn't want to confide that the beige sedan belonged to the Rudolphis!

"Does that include having my room bugged, too?" Emma asked.

Surprised at her question, he said, "No Emma—we're not the ones listening to conversations in your room! How did you discover the plant?"

"Dillon found it! We left it there, but we've been very careful not to speak about any client's matters in my room—or make any important calls from there. I use my mobile phone to make calls outside the room, which is why I came into the lounge tonight to call you. Dillon checks his room for listening devices every day, and the second day he found a 'cockroach' in his. He moved the device to another hotel room, hoping it would be several days before the culprits realized it was planted elsewhere! His room is still clean… as far as I know."

"Sounds like something Dillon would do—clever *bastardo!*" Carlos commented.

"You didn't see *our* car tail—but the bug plant was not ours!" Carlos became very reflective. "This isn't good! This isn't good at all! If we didn't plant it, then who's interested in you enough to have a bug monitor you so closely? What are they hoping to learn?" Carlos said nothing for several minutes and then checked the time.

"Emma, I have to leave in a couple of minutes to find out exactly who else is interested in your presence here in Milano...besides me."

"Dillon and I have invitations to Marcus's charity party for tomorrow, which is why I told you I couldn't go with you, but I would meet you there."

Looking directly at her, Carlos said, "Dillon O'Rourke is a good man, and he'll take good care of you."

"How is it that you're so familiar with Dillon?" she asked.

"Best not to get into that now, Emma, let's just say I know he does his job very well!"

"Is there anyone in my life you don't know about, Carlos?"

This time Carlos changed the subject. "About that charity party tomorrow...you and Dillon go as planned, and I'll meet you there—as a casual acquaintance." Carlos rose to leave and leaned in close to Emma. "Just why are you going to the Villa del Christianna, my darling? What are you trying to discover?" Emma wanted to tell him the truth at that moment! Maybe half a truth is better than none.

"Lucinda asked me to find out information for her—marital issues, and this maybe one way to get it for her...that's all I can say."

"Carlos—before you go—do you know a case called the Chatelaine case? What exactly is the Chatelaine case about besides kidnappings?" Carlos's eyes went wide and then swept to the right. He clearly knew more facts about the Chatelaine case.

"How did you learn of *that* case, Emma?"

"I came across it while doing research in the Royal Court Justice storage for a case. When I came upon it, I didn't have the time to read the transcripts there, so I signed out the files and brought them back to the office. Before I could review them, someone broke into my firm and stole the whole file of records."

Excitedly, Carlos sat back down close to her and asked, "When was this, Emma?"

"It happened the day I arrived in Milano. Peter called and told me. So far the police have no leads as to who broke into the office, and I can't come up with a reason either." She didn't want to tell Carlos about the transcription discs yet, taking no chances the wrong person would learn of their existence before she scanned them. If they were stolen, she'd never learn first hand what the Chatelaine case was about!

"Yes, I know about the Chatelaine case. It goes back about two or three years. There was a trial here in Italy held in Firenze—for kidnappings. The defendants, seven men and women, disappeared while in custody before the trial ended and were never found. The jury's verdict came, all guilty in absentia of kidnapping. None of the children they kidnapped were ever found." Thinking out loud, Carlos said, "You telling me this now just may enlighten me why that black car was following us the other night!"

"Would that occasion have something to do with the Chatelaine case?"

"Possibly," he said contemplatively. "This explains why I've noticed a lot of activity around you, Emma, since your arrival in Milano, activity that I don't like! I'm going to have one of my men move into the suite next to you in the Manin for extra safety precautions and monitor anyone showing interest in you or your activities while you're in Milano! You can tell Dillon—he'll be glad to know he has help taking care of you. My man's name is Tomas. I know Dillon won't let anything happen to you—you're special to him, and I'm glad he's here with you!" Carlos held her hands in his and kissed them gently.

"I'm glad you're here, too, Carlos."

"Oh, by the way, have you spoken to your grandfather recently?"

"No, but I'm going to call the farm tonight. Carlos, I wish you didn't have to leave now. I *will* see you tomorrow for certain?"

"Absolutely...my love!" There was so much more he wanted to say.

Interrupting his words, Emma said, "I know! When this is all finished...the time will be right for us." Emma had to let him know how much she wanted the time to be right for them.

Checking her watch, she said, "I still need to speak with Dillon and he's probably waiting for my call."

Gently touching her lips, Carlos said, "It's been so long, Emma." His eyes told her he truly loved her!

"You leave first, Em, and I'll follow in a few minutes. There are a few calls I have to make before I leave the hotel. Be extra careful, and remember...call me if you need me at any time! Just leave a message—just say **"Como"**—and I'll know it's you." Picking up her few packages, she walked out the door glancing back to the table. Carlos was nowhere in sight!

\* \* \*

When Emma exited out the door, Carlos went out the farthest lounge door to the street. Dialing a cell number, he said, "It's me. Were you aware Emma took a copy of the transcripts of the Chatelaine Case from the Justice Court to read, that the whole file was stolen from her office the day she left for Milano?" A long silent pause was heard.

"When did this happen?"

"Evidently, the theft occurred the day she left for Milano. She says she never had the opportunity to read the file before she left, so she asked me what the case was about. I told her it had to do with a kidnapping ring. She seemed taken aback by that when I mentioned it...as if she had some additional information related to kidnappings...most likely the reason why she's here in Milano. I don't like her keeping me in the dark, Mac!"

"Christ, neither do I!" Seconds of deadening silence passed before they spoke again. "Do the police think the robbery was to get just that file or was it a random theft?"

"She told the police nothing was stolen, but some petty cash! Why did she lie to the police about the missing case file?"

"Hell, I wish I knew! Don't pursue Chatelaine further with her for now. She's got a stubborn streak in her as hard as a stone wall. If she thinks you're holding something back, it'll provoke her to keep asking questions until she learns the true answers!"

"Now that trait sounds familiar, Cyrus!"

"To answer your very first question, I'd say they wanted just that particular file!"

"She said the office computers were compromised, too; don't know if they found anything there…she's not telling me everything, either., Cyrus, she knows a hell of a lot more than she lets on—about the Chatelaine files *and* the Rudolphis! I know it's all gotta have something to do with Lucinda Rudolphi going to London. Another thing, they planted a cockroach in her room! Dillon found it and left it. They're careful not to speak freely in the room and make all calls outside the hotel."

"Jesus Christ! This means *they* know she's here for reasons that involve them! Bloody hell—they suspect her! And they must know she's trying to get information about them—the Rudolphis! Just what we don't need now…another part of the bloody puzzle missin' to complicate the picture!"

"Mac, I'm stationing Tomas in the room next to her."

"Good decision."

"She knows he's there for her own safety. I had to tell her…a few things, too…I had to be honest with her…there's enough shadow in her life, which is why I told her I'm with Italian branch of Interpol— I had to tell her to get her cooperation! I didn't tell her any concrete specific information. She has no idea about you're involvement."

"**And she mustn't, either!**" he barked. "You do everything possible to keep her safe! You hear me? Watch her like a hawk tomorrow at that party! Don't let her out of your sight at the Rudolphis' tomorrow!" Both men were trying to keep a check on their emotions, shielding their fears from each other.

"By the way, Colin received new satellite data reporting a place on Lake Como that seems to have the specifications we're looking for. He thinks it's the main laboratory that we're searching for… It has all the fingerprints of a large research laboratory in a villa on *Lago di Como*. He's having it checked out daily with updated satellite intelligence reports from several satellite sources. Another thing we found, there are specific scientific heat signatures located in a small area inside the *Lago di Como* villa. This, is in addition to the signature nest of a small army of guards located in and around the grounds of the Villa del Christianna, tells us we may have a second sight to evaluate! I'll keep you updated when I learn more."

"Cyrus, Emma has been trying to call you. She's alarmed you haven't returned her messages. You'd best call her to put her mind at rest."

"Aye, aye, I know it! I hate lying to her—even for her own good! I'll call her tonight. Thanks! You keep me posted. And watch her, you hear?" The line went dead.

* * *

Once inside her suite, Emma's thoughts and emotions were spinning out of control. Recalling the plans she, Dillon, and Biaggio made earlier, now she learns about Carlos and his double life! She felt her life was on a merry-go-round—spinning and never stopping!

Her first task was to put a call through to the farm to speak with Papa! Running a hot tub of water to relax in, she dialed the farm on the mobile phone in the bath and turned the radio on for background noise to muffle her conversation. Bocelli's "Sogno" was playing, and Maggie answered the phone.

"Maggie, it's Emma. It's good to hear your voice," she said, speaking in a light tone.

"Not half as good as to 'ear yurs, me dear."

"Maggie, is Papa there?"

"No, luv 'e isn't. I thought 'e was going to be 'ome two days ago and 'aven't 'eard any news why 'e's not. That's unusual for 'im! He's good 'bout lettin' me know if 'e's goin' to be detained, so I don't send the police out after him," she said laughing.

"Did he tell you where he was traveling to? What places he expected to be in...or who he was meeting?"

"No, luv. Most of the time, 'e just leaves me a number where to call if I need him," she said.

"Maggie can I have that number, please?"

"Wait, it's right 'ere." Maggie wasn't certain she should give Emma that particular private number, thinking, *If I don't she'll keep questionin' me...*

264

"Aye, it's 9989-2134-5555. Cyrus told me when I called to just say 'Maggie' when the machine came on, and 'e would know who to call back. Are you alright, dear?" she asked.

"I'm fine, Maggie, but I do want to speak with Papa so I'll try calling him again tomorrow at that number."

"I 'ope you can get down to the farm when you get home, luv, you must see the two new foals and one of 'hem is the spittin' image of Ddu Kate."

"I promise to take holiday time at the farm as soon as I return. I have to ring off now...say 'hello' to Andrew for me? I love you Magere!" Emma said and hung up.

Emma visualized Maggie at the farm, probably wiping her tears away at that moment.

But Maggie didn't have tears for Emma; rather, she felt fear for her little girl. "I hate lyin' to me little girl!" Softly cradling the phone, she put it down. Truthfully, Maggie knew Cyrus was going to be away for an indefinite time. But she had to lie to Emma as he emphatically told her not to tell her the truth about his trip. Maggie thought, *This Rudolphi case was becomin' all too dangerous and consumin' for him! Best if I put him to notice Emma is questionin' his unknown absence—and she's callin' from Milano.* She dialed the same number immediately, waited for the correct number of rings, disconnected, and then a redialed a different number.

*Mother of God! Take care of me fami'y,* she prayed silently.

"Speak."

"It's Maggie."

\* \* \*

Emma immediately dialed the number Maggie gave her, the call connected through a series of clicks while Bocelli sang in the background, his signature song, *"Con Te Partiro"*—"Time to say Goodbye." The phone rang five rings, then the message machine clicked on. "Papa, it's Emma. I need to speak with you. Maggie gave me this number to reach you. Call me on my cell number. I expect to be in Milano at least several more days!"

Disconnecting the line, she thought, *Why do I have such a bad feeling about Papa? He always lets Maggie know when he's detained.*

265

*What's happened to change his routines like that?* Suddenly, Emma felt an ominous cold feeling—an icy shiver!

> *...shivering cold...silence...so weak...pain—why the pain...*
> *Again another flashback! Why do I keep having these images...feelings...my mind is trying to remember? From when?*

Adding more hot water to the tub, she slid down in the perfumed water to relax. It should have made her feel better, but it didn't. Instead, all her apprehensions persisted as if something was very wrong, though she had no idea why she felt that way. Were these fears for Papa and Carlos? "I'm so glad Carlos told me everything tonight"...*Did he indeed tell me everything? I think not!* "No matter, I have him back."

The ringing phone jarred her dark thoughts away, *"Si, pronto."*

"Em, a meet in thirty minutes—my room? Make certain yur' not followed," a voice said and the phone went dead.

It was Dillon. Emma knew the brevity of his message sounded like he had some information from Biaggio about the party tomorrow. Dressing to meet Dillon, her thoughts were consumed with tomorrow's "play" at the Villa del Christianna.

"What will I say to Lucinda tomorrow when we meet—unexpectedly—at her charity *festa* at the Villa del Christianna? She will certainly realize we were not on the original invitation list!"

Emma's thoughts felt like she was preparing for the drama of a courtroom case, trying to anticipate any and every response from her opponent. Steeling her thoughts for tomorrow's scenario, "I wish I knew where Lucinda stood in this picture! Is she the only unknown factor in our plan? Can I count on her help—if something goes wrong?"

There is one certain, indisputable fact! *"Lucinda wants to learn the truth about her children! Her support may be our ace in this game! Or will it put her in greater danger...the same kind of danger out there for me? How will Marcus Rudolphi react to my presence at the party?"*

A more worrisome thought, *"Is it possible he may already know Lucinda came to me for help?"*

# CHAPTER THIRTY-ONE

Dressed in a black jogging suit, Emma went to meet Dillon.

To avoid attracting attention, she wore her hair up inside a cap, pulling it down low over her eyes. Emptying her briefcase of the maps and tourist information, Emma made certain she had all other important documents with her, not trusting anyone in the hotel! Now was the time to take the stairs down one flight to Dillon's room, once inside the stairwell Emma listened for footsteps above or below her or for any other sounds indicating someone else was in the stairwell—she heard nothing. Dillon's room was on the second floor at the north corner of the hotel overlooking the gardens. Emma knocked softly...

Opening the door slightly, Dillon put his finger to his lips signaling Emma not to speak. Glancing around the hall, she quickly entered.

"I hope yu're up to a long night, Em. It's okay to speak in here. I checked the room—it's clean—no cockroaches! The ones I found yesterda', still re-planted! Let 'em think *they* made the mistake! They still 'aven't discovered what I did, or they would 'ave planted another one!" Dillon chuckled at his own spoof.

"Good, because a lot has happened in the last couple of hours that I need to share with you!" Taking off the cap and shaking her hair loose, Emma was eager to tell Dillon about her meeting with Carlos.

"I just met Carlos in the lounge when I got back from shopping. He's been very helpful…to us…about this case…about the Rudolphis—and you need to hear it, too!" Sitting down, Dillon poured a glass of wine for Emma as she began relating everything that happened since she arrived back from shopping. Dillon saw her eagerness to tell him what just happened, and turned on the radio to a loud station to confuse anyone outside trying to triangulate a listening device!

"When I returned from shopping earlier this evening, there was a message from Carlos to call him—so I went into the lounge to place the call—the thought crossed my mind you might be in the Machiavelli Lounge, too! Inside, I saw Carlos sitting at the bar!" Dillon just quietly watched as she explained. Emma realized it was time to tell him the whole story of the past—why Carlos and she stopped seeing each other.

"I know I never told you why Carlos and I ended our relationship, and being the good friend you are, you never questioned me about it…out of respect for my privacy. But now, Dillon, you need to know everything. It was a mutual agreement between us—to go our separate ways. Truthfully, it was Carlos who felt strongly that our lives took us in different directions that made it difficult to have a strong, lasting, meaningful relationship. Not wanting to stand in his way, I agreed, and we went our separate ways—that was last year. I never spoke to you—or to anyone—not even Papa knew why we stopped seeing each other." Emma walked over to the window and watched the bright neon lights from the traffic below, for several silent minutes.

"Best not to talk by the window…they can 'ave ears, too."

Emma started pacing. "Carlos took more of the blame—saying it was his job! But I didn't *really* understand how his work influenced his decision until tonight!" Emma said, glancing over at Dillon. "He decided his job didn't allow a lot of time to build any permanent relationship…even though we were both very serious in our feelings for each other…Time came to take it to another level. He couldn't make that commitment." Turning to face Dillon, she continued "We said our goodbyes, and it's been almost a year since there was any communication between us. I knew I would have to deal with my past feelings for Carlos when we came to Milano on this case. Never did I dream I would learn he still…loves me…amidst these other mystifying circumstances of our meeting!" Dillon sat on the sofa, listening and watching Emma intently, taking in her body language—seeing her nervousness as she spoke.

Emma sat next to Dillon. She needed to see his reaction close-up as she told him the rest of the story. She had a distinct feeling that Dillon and Carlos worked together at one time.

"Remember when I told you about the black car that followed us in Gubbio? Well, today, I asked Carlos if he was having me followed or watched here in Milano—and he said, yes! He denied the beige sedan was his doing. Neither did he have any idea why that black car was following us in Gubbio! That isn't what I found so surprising tonight…" Emma waited to see Dillon's reaction to her next statement.

"First, I must tell you I knew that Carlos worked in the Italian embassy—but it's a cover position for his real position…in Italian Intelligence! He really works for Interpol in a division of the Italian Secret Service. His present assignment in intelligence involves the Rudolphis!" Emma carefully scrutinized Dillon for his reaction to her information. He took a long sip of beer and maintained his silence with no outward change in his body language—not even a quick glance towards her—no insight there was a past connection between them.

"Carlos related, the whole Rudolphi family has been under surveillance by Interpol for the past several years. Carlos also knew Lucinda came to see me in London last month, but he didn't know why—he asked me…but I couldn't tell him! He's learned my name is associated with the Rudolphis, but didn't elaborate how he found out!" At mention of this last fact, Dillon's countenance changed to vigilance. "Needless to say, this new information was a shock to me but it does answer my question…why he broke off our relationship! He was afraid his job was too dangerous to make our relationship work for us." Emma looked at Dillon. "Surprisingly, Dillon, it doesn't matter to me at all! I love him whatever his job is."

"Did you tell 'im that, Em?"

"No, not in those exact words, I was feeling confused with all the other things he was telling me...but I will, Dillon, the first opportunity I get!"

"See that you do, lass!" Emma saw a part of Dillon she had not seen before—a caring, compassionate—even romantic man.

"So, Carlos's been investigatin' the Rudolphis!" Dillon said in summation of Emma's account.

"Dillon, I think he's aware of the list in Marcus's study! He even asked me if I had ever been associated with the Rudolphi family in any capacity. I told him the truth—I've *never* met any member of the family, or I would have remembered!"

Dillon sat quietly on the sofa holding his hands in a praying position, as was his way when concentrating. He had his own questions about the Rudolphi family, one specifically, how is Emma connected to them? Now this new information confirmed his earlier feelings! Whatever the connection is, she's in extreme danger and doesn't know it. *My man, Carlos, knows it!*

"Tonight I asked Carlos if he knew about the Chatelaine case? He did! He explained it was a case involving international kidnappers on trial in the Firenze courts—about three years ago. The defendants, six men and women, abruptly disappeared before the trial ended! A verdict was rendered in absentia—all guilty. None of the men or woman on trial was ever found. He wanted to know how I learned about that case. I explained I found transcripts from the Chatelaine trial at the Royal Court of Justice in London and took the complete file of transcripts back to my office to study them. Unfortunately, I didn't get to read the files before I left for Milano. I told him the file was stolen from the office the day I left for Italy. What I omitted to tell him was, before they were stolen Peter transcribed the files onto discs and the thieves didn't get them! The Chatelaine discs are in my personal secret vault at the office—not the office safe which is where the original file was stolen from."

Excitedly, Emma said to Dillon, "This case about Lucinda's missing children is beginning to smell like kidnapping! Do you think there's any chance those children—Giorgio and Sofia— are tied to the Chatelaine case? It's seems so bizarre, but there *could* be a connection?" Emma became excited at a possible connection of the two puzzles. What she was omitting to say out loud were her thoughts—*if the Rudolphi babies were kidnapped at birth, Marcus Rudolphi would have to be involved with it to some degree. He had to lie to Lucinda about the babies dying at birth.* This last thought was the most frightening piece of the puzzle! *Why hasn't Dillon posed this question to me?* She thought. *If I came to this conclusion, Dillon must've, too!*

"Dillon, I need to get those discs and find out what exactly is in those transcripts!" My instinct tells me that somehow that Chatelaine case is connected to Milano—even to the Rudolphis—*only I don't know how—yet!* That black car following us in Gubbio may well have been following *me* and not Carlos—which is why he was so alarmed for both of us that night." He must've thought that black car was connected to the Rudolphi family.

"All this is ver' interestin', Em," Dillon said while opening a bottle of beer.

"This news changes things quite a bit, girl." Taking a long drink from the bottle, he began slowly pacing around the room.

"Em, I'm just gettin' back from talkin' to Biaggio. The recon job was very successful today! 'E was able to find out most of the information I asked 'im to get. What we now know for certain is the whole 'illside—all the villas—are 'eavily guarded with all kinds of securit' with the most sophisticated and up-to-date equipment! Not only that, more prob'bly some of the guests tomor'ow will be Rudolphi's own people deliberately planted among the guests! This means we 'ave to be doubl' careful minglin' among the guests—not to give ou'selves away! We 'ave to be on our guard at all times! The securit' systems 'ave their own electrical supply source, and we 'ave a good idea where most of 'em are located—but blood' 'ell—we don't know where all of 'em are! This makes our mission a lit'le more difficult—*but not impossible!*" Sitting down next to Emma, he told her his concerns. "Now, you tell me 'bout Carlos! Em, with Carlos's 'elp, it just became a bit easier for us to do what we came 'ere to do! Get into that librar'—find the list of names, cop' it, and get out! But, I...no, *we* definitely need Carlos in our plan tomorrow if we're to be successful."

"Dillon, have you ever worked with Carlos in the past?"

"Now, why would you be askin' a question like that, Em?"

"I have this persistent feeling Carlos knows more about your background, and you his, than either lets on to me!" Looking directly at Dillon with her question, Emma noticed Dillon didn't seem too surprised to learn Carlos worked for Interpol in Italian intelligence. Somewhere…sometime they shared a past!

"Let's just say—me past lives 'ave taken me to different parts of the world and the cases I've been on—he may well 'ave 'eard me name connected to 'hem! Our two worlds 'aven't been that different, Em—and let's leave it at that!" His vague answer pretty well confirmed her suspicions—He and Carlos had a past together in covert intelligence work—and if it goes back before his family disappeared from Kildarggen, it could be the reason why he refuses to discuss details of that part of his past with anyone.

"What did you and Carlos agree 'bout meetin' at the charit' part'?" Dillon asked.

"Carlos and I agreed we'd all meet tomorrow at the party— pretend to be old friends meeting coincidently—which, in fact, is partially true! Carlos made arrangements to have one of his men move into the suite next to mine, a man named Tomas…I told him about the room being bugged, and he became alarmed."

"Good man, you got ther', Em. Glad to 'ave the 'elp watchin' you," She laughed.

"That's what Carlos said—you'd be glad to have help keeping tabs on me! Am I so difficult that I need two men to keep track of me?" Emma asked glibly!

Taking out notes from an envelope, Dillon said, "'ere's our plan for tomor'ow. Em, we 'ave to know it by 'eart—timin' is critical for success! Let's get started memorizin' ev'ry detail. We'll practice all night if we 'ave to—you up to it, Em?"

"Just show me—I'm a fast learner!" Dillon's instructions were clear and concise. With methodical patience, he explained the plan from beginning to end.

"Biaggio will be our chauffeur tomorrow. He'll pick us up 'ere at the 'otel and drive us to the Villa del Christianna. I'm 'opin' he'll be able to park the car on the grounds to wait for us there—and not be directed away from the 'ouse. If not—I 'ave set up a back-up plan for that change. Describe to me 'bout the kind of outfit you'll wear tomor'ow?"

"That's an odd question coming from you, Dillon! I bought an emerald green two-piece dress—not too much showing anywhere—except my legs! Why do you ask?"

"They're goin' to do some securit screenin' on all the guests without 'hem knowin' it. I 'ave some things I want you to stow in yur purse—a very special purse to go with your dress—a lipstick that's a camera—a very special one; a pair of readin' glasses—made to detect laser beams—a small handheld perfume spray bottle, and a special ladies compact—no lad' goes without her po'der! Now the camera is a three-dimension grid-laser pulse-activated camera...it takes series of pictures in seconds when part of the tube is depressed. There's no aimin' to focus—you just aim it at an'thing, and it'll take continual shots—until you turn it back into a lipstick tube. It's not easil' detectable as a camera if someone 'andles it...so don't worr'. Then you'll 'ave a compact—it's really a radio—both sender and receiver! Depress the floral ornament on top and you send—squeeze the clasp and it'll receive." Dillon showed her with patience and preciseness as she practiced using it.

"Here's a bracelet you'll wear, It'll pick up signals...from me, tellin' you to read the message sent on the radio in yur compact mirror—so stay alert for 'eat changes in temperature of the bracelet—you can't miss feelin' 'hem—that's 'ow it'll alert you! You'll carr' a few old Italian lira coins—special coins—these are the deactivators for laser beams and floor sensors...and the readin' glasses will tell you where they are. All these toys 'ill be in yur purse—things a lad' usual' carries in 'er bag when she goes to a part'!"

"What purse am I to bring?" Emma asked. "Not to worry—I'll 'ave *yur* purse ready for you tomorrow before we set out."

Dillon continued intently, "This part of the plan'll be the most difficult! Before you enter the librar', in yur compact instead of face powder—'ere's silver dust and a pair of readin' glasses. If an'one questions why you're not wearin' 'hem, just tell 'hem 'hey're used just for readin'—and you never go an'where without 'hem! They look ordinar'—but the glass is speciall' treated lens to see the laser beams. First, put the glasses on and then shake out the puff with the silver dust in the doorway before you enter—you'll see the source of each laser beam—a red beam. Place one of the lira-coins over each beam source! This is critical! You must find the light source for each beam emitted and have a coin ready to place over each beam—like a magnate—a COIN on EACH source of each laser beam—all of 'hem got'ta be covered within five seconds! Five seconds!" Emma nodded that she understood.

"To check the floor for motion sensors—take out the small perfume spray and spray the air all around you—inside the room. The molecules of the spray will fall and outline short white beams of light rotatin' through the spray randoml' risin' up from the floor—this means the sensors are turned on! You toss *TWO LIRA* on the floor together!" Dillon held up the two coins. "These two lira will neutralize all the sensors on the floor…it's a special metal that deactivates motion sensors—it freezes them-inactive until the metal is removed. *You'll pick the coins up on your way out, so place them nearest the door within easy reach when you exit!* 'ere you'll 'ave five seconds after you pick them up from the floor…then the sensors are reactivated. So don't dally! *Don't forget! You must pick both coins up before you leave…in less than five seconds!"*

"Got it, Dillon! I'm really very quick and agile—don't worry!"

"I'm certain you'll get in carryin' these things in your purse without detection. Even if they do search you, they're innocent lookin'. I'll 'ave a lighter—that's my radio—and some of the same lira coins, too. Me belt buckle is doublin' as a camera." Dillon said smiling. "Whate'er you do, don't let yur purse out of yur hands while there!" He emphasized everything to impress on Emma the importance of having everything when the exact moment came to make their move.

"I memorized the layout of the house that Biaggio gave to me, and you must do the same!" Opening a map up on the bed to show her the diagram, he pointed out, "'Ere's the study—off the **second floor hall**—no connection to the first floor balcony as I 'oped. This changed things a bit. You need to stud' and memorize this blueprint by 'eart, Em," he said, handing her a reduced size of the floor plans. "Once you've memorized it, completely burn it!" Dillon was taking no chances someone would find any evidence of the Rudolphi estate on them.

"This is 'ow the plan will play out. Once we're safel' inside, we'll mingle in societ's crowd! Exactl' forty-five minutes later, you'll ask to go upstairs to a bedroom to mend a rip in yur skirt—we need you to 'ave a good tear—for this Biaggio's wife, Sienna, will replicate a tear to simulate a real one—and you place that piece of torn material on the dress when the time comes! I'm sure the servants will assist you, gettin' you whatev'r you need to mend yur skirt."

Pointing to a red-circled room on the map, he said, **"This is the LIBRAR'!"**

Drawing her attention to other rooms on the second floor, he said, "These are bedrooms—and this seems to be the largest one—may be Marcus's or Lucinda's—or both", looking over to her for a reaction. "We need you to get into *this* bedroom to mend yur skirt! These are baths ...to the bedroom. The rest of these rooms with black "X's" on 'hem are empty rooms—best me guess probabl' guest rooms. Over in this other wing, on the second floor, is a bank of rooms...either for storage or securit' rooms—Biaggio couldn't be sure...he says 'hey're tied to securit' centers somehow...maybe the area where the CPU's are located—'e wasn't able to find out exactl' what! In a place this big and with this much securit', 'hey'd dedicate a large central area and feed the main power trunk lines to it. Not knowin' this for certain—it's a risky unknown factor! But we'll deal with it! What 'e did find out is large electric trunk lines attach 'ere on the ground floor, " he said, pointing exactly where the lines went into the house on the map, "feed to the second floor into that separate wing—which makes me agree with 'im, that area?" Dillon pointed to the former wing on the blueprints, "that's they're center's power supply for the 'ouse's surveillance systems—*the **main securit' center**!* I'm still fixin' to find out 'ow man' persons man that room...still waitin' on the information."

Changing maps, Dillon continued, "The servants 'ave rooms in the lower level in this farthest wing." Directing her attention to an entrance, he said, "This particular balcon' door from the large main livin' room opens out to the balcon'—leadin' directl' down to an entrance to the swimmin' pool area." Emma watched Dillon methodically define each detail on the map to her.

Pointing to artfully drawn squares, he said, "'Ere are the cabanas for the pool and this 'ouse 'ere—which looks like a garden shed—is most likel' an entrance to some underground buildin'. It's me guess, given this is a wealth' famil' known for its wines, they'd probabl' 'ave an elaborate personal wine cellar as big as parliament's 'ouse! That entrance could be to the personal wine cellar palace! But I doubt it! We've no idea what the underground room is actual'y used for! Me gut says it's an entrance to somethin' far more important than just a wine cellar—no wine cellar needs an army of security to keep it safe...but that's somethin' for me to try and find more 'bout!" Dillon was always planning for the unexpected. "Listen up careful now!"

"Here's 'ow it'll go when you get me signal! You get upstairs to do yur sewin' job, I'll create a diversion at a far point from the librar'—somewhere on the first floor." Picking up a petite toy ball the size of a marble, Dillon explained what it really was, "When I crush this, it'll make some of the guests feel nauseated—dizzy and faint, drawin' everyone's attention to them—hopeful' enough guests will get sick to give us—*you*—the amount of time **we** need! I'll not get sick because I'll take the antidote before I activate it. I'll signal you on the radio compact with the word '**pronto.**' You'll know that's the exact time you must get into the librar'! This is critical, Emma, you'll 'ave exactl' twelve minutes from the time I say 'pronto' to get inside the librar', locate the box, unlock it, and take as many pictures of the contents as you can in that time and **then get the 'ell out with no one seein' you!**" Dillon's look was firmly serious and anticipated Emma's next question.

Dillon opened the compact, "In the compact behind the mirror is a non-metal key—use it to open the box Lucinda described to you on the tape. It's a special key and it'll work easil'. Once you find the journals—take as many pictures of the information as quickl' as you can! Don't stop to read the files—wastes too much time— just take pictures! If there's an'thing else in the box—leave it! You should finish the job in that time—if you haven't finished gettin' ever'thing—just leave and forget the rest! Do you understand, Em?

**Never mind the rest! Just get the 'ell out of the librar'!"** Dillon had commanding words for her. "Time yourself when you **first** enter the room and start the timer on yur bracelet…counting—twelve minutes—and then you leave! **You get out!**" He kept emphasizing the need to leave even if she couldn't get as much as she wanted. His words implied danger if she delayed!

"Return to the bedroom you were original' in mendin' the dress… or come back down to the first floor—whichev'r is safest—all the time checkin' for an' one else on the second floor! You'll probabl' 'ear a commotion on the first floor—so 'ead towards the place w'ere the 'ullabaloo is comin' from…don't worry you won't get sick either! You gotta 'ave immediate exposure to the chemical to come down with symptoms…and it dissipates rapidl'—changes its chemical properties once it's exposed to air in a few minutes…becomes inert! It's most potent when you in'ale the chemical fumes immediatel' after activation—then the effects last longer. So *we* should all 'ave a safet' net of a few extra minutes if somethin' else 'appens." Dillon was thorough and exact as he told her the plan. "Got it, Em?"

"Yes, I have it all memorized to the last detail, Dillon—It all sounds so well planned! Where will Carlos be during this time?"

"I'll clue 'im in 'bout our plan when we meet up. 'E'll be 'elpful as a third man—in case somethin' unforeseen 'appens. 'E needs to watch me back, too—makin' certain no one has a bead on me! 'Is job is to keep everyone under surveillance on that first floor while this is goin' down—makin' sure none of their 'plants' are on to us! The commotion should brin' on chaos and ever'one's attention to that area. More important'y *he* 'as to watch Marcus Rudolphi to make sure 'e's caught by surprise too, and doesn't suspect an'thing! It's a big task—and if necessar', 'e's got to intercept Marcus from goin' upstairs! Carlos will give us more credibil'ty with the 'osts—knowin' we're his friends—at least I think 'e will! Unless they know what his real assignment is at the embassy!"

"God, I hope not!" Emma said.

"Not to worr'—you'll both be in me care! We 'ave to ask Carlos if he can shed more information 'bout the reason yur name is connected to the Rudolphis?"

"Carlos can point out Dr. Ennio Carruchi to us so we can keep an eye on him." she said.

"Yeh, I want to see what that man looks like, too!" Dillon said with angry reprisal in his voice.

"Once we 'ave the pictures of the guests there—which I'll take— and the pictures of the documents in the file—which you'll get—we stay fifteen minutes more **after** the confusion…no longer…find our 'ost and ostess and leave!" Dillon had everything planned out to the precise second.

"We can e'en fake some of the symptoms for an excuse to leave if we 'ave to. Biaggio will 'ave the Mercedes in front when we're ready to leave!" Folding up the maps and notes he used to brief Emma, Dillon walked to the window, standing with his back to her.

"Em, do you 'ave any questions or fears 'bout this plan? If so, now's the time to speak up!"

"No, Dillon. I feel comfortable about the plan—my role—your role—and Carlos's role, too. It does make me feel better knowing you two will be close by!"

"When we leave Rudolphis we return to the 'otel. Now that I know 'bout Carlos, we need to set up a meetin' with him after the part'," Dillon said in an afterthought. "That's somethin' I need to do, Em…It may even be better for us to meet somewhere else other than 'ere. Carlos'll know a safe place for us to meet and discuss our findin's…" he said, turning back to face Emma.

"What's on yur mind, Em? I can see somethin' is botherin' you."

"Dillon, if we find the list and learn the names of the people on the list—and my name is there—will it tell us…do you think it will tell me why these names are listed together and what the common link is between them—and with me?"

"Yeah, I know Em what yur askin'. It maybe time for us to get those discs from yur office and listen to what's on 'hem. They could give us the link we're lookin' for!" Neither spoke for several minutes; each deep into their private thoughts.

"Emma—this case we're on—is dangerous for you—and we 'ave to take our time to get all the facts to see where this is leadin' us, but most of all—to make certain no one gets hurt!" Dillon never called her 'Emma' except when he's really worried…and it's her he's worried about now!

"I know, Dillon…I have a feeling there's a lot more to learn before we get to the bottom of this whole puzzle. Either way, Dillon, I'm committed to finding the answers more than ever now! It just may be that when I find answers around the mystery why my name is associated with Marcus Rudolphi—I'll find answers for Lucinda, too."

Walking over to Dillon, Emma gave him a hug of reassurance. She didn't want him to know how frightened she really felt at that moment…more fearful for what's to come! "It's good to know I have such a good friend like you," she said and kissed him on the cheek.

"None of that stuff, lass. Save 'em for Carlos," he said, but Dillon turned and embraced Emma for a long moment—his strength felt good to her.

"Now! Let's go over the plan again from the very beginning again!" he commanded. Painstakingly, she recited every tiny detail again from beginning to end until they both felt every aspect of the plan and time line was exactly memorized, down to the microsecond…their minds totally in sync!

Dillon's thoughts turned to Carlos. *How much does Carlos reall' know, and would he consent to our plan knowin' how much danger Em will be in? There was great danger in the whole plan. Carlos will 'ave to know the danger we're all takin'. No matter 'ow he feels, we need 'im with us tomorrow. He's vital to the success of our mission!* Dillon silently recalled how well they had worked together in the past—recalling how he owed his life to Carlos that time in Spain—a lifetime ago!

Emma's voice distracted Dillon from his thoughts of the past. "I haven't mentioned this until now—I don't know how Lucinda will react when she sees me tomorrow. I have a feeling she may be a safety net for us, Dillon! She wants answers to her fears and questions as much as I do—so let me handle her—if necessary?"

"If you say so, Em."

"Dillon, it's after two o'clock in the morning! Can we call it a night? We can go over it all again in the morning if you think we need to," she said, picking up her jacket and cap. Emma pushed her hair back up inside and pulled it down tight.

"No need—I think we're ready! I'm followin' you up to yur room, Em. Then I'm goin' down to the lobb' to check it out. See if anyone is stickin' around that shouldn't be."

"Call me in the morning?" Emma asked.

Gathering up all of the papers which had been spread out, Dillon put everything into his valise and set about planting traps around his room to check for intruders when he returned. If his traps were disturbed—he'd know he had a visitor—and they might not like what would happen. They entered the empty lift, first taking Emma up to the third floor. Dillon waited and watched until she entered her suite and then rode the lift down to the lobby while making a call to have an "emerald green purse" ready tomorrow. Walking through the lobby, he casually noted there were very few people around—It was relatively empty.

Music was still coming from several of the lounges including the Machiavelli Lounge.

Entering, he saw it was still half-full of clients laughing and singing with the band. Saturday night was the busiest and noisiest night of the week. Except for one single patron sitting alone at the table next to the entrance door, he was trying to look disinterested in the jovial group when he saw Dillon. Dillon immediately noticed there was no drink or glass on his table. "Strange for a bloke not to be celebratin' on a Saturda' night!" Dillon made his way past him to the bar and ordered a drink, casually turning to look back at the lone patron—he was gone!

*A magician? Let's see who 'as a bigger bag of tricks tomor'ow'!* Dillon sipped his drink slowly and started a conversation with the bartender.

*"La notte accupata, Remo?"*

# CHAPTER THIRTY-TWO

The sound from snooze buzzer sounded louder each time it rang.

The clock read ten past six! Emma had no idea how long the alarm had been ringing, nor did she realize how tired she was when she finally fell asleep last night—that was only four hours ago! Sitting on the edge of the bed to rouse her mind from the murkiness of a deep dream sleep, suddenly the whole memory of last night came rushing back to her.

"Today's Sunday—the Rudolphi's charity!" The sun's brilliant rays streamed through the balcony doors, while the street noise competed for her attention among the echoing sounds of church bells in the distance. No hum of rushing traffic with honking horns this morning on the Via d Manin. Sundays took on a whole different essence in the city. Somewhere in Milano, everyone was going to church this Sunday morning. Looking out across to the gardens, Emma saw spring in its fullest display of colors—everything competing for its freshest vibrancy in the early morning sun.

Putting on her dressing gown, Emma telephoned room service to bring her usual, cappuccino and the *Una Buona Notizia*, the morning newspaper. But first, she tried calling Papa but not before she checked the night button to see if it was flashing phone messages. It was off. Still, she had that uneasy feeling this morning…with no call from Papa!

*Was he the gray-haired man inquiring about me to the concierge the other day?* Looking intently at the phone willing it to ring, Emma thought, *Why hasn't he called me after I left my message at the number Maggie gave me? I wonder if he called Maggie to say when he'd be home.* Reaching for the telephone to make another call to her, Emma thought, *if I call her again, she'll only worry, realizing I wasn't able to reach him. Damn that bug! He's my grandfather, why can't I call him? Would it be so bad if I did talk to him from my room?* Heeding her instincts, instead, she picked up the mobile phone and walked out to the balcony and closed the door to dial his number again. Hearing a series of clicks, the machine requested the caller leave a message.

"Papa, its Emma. I'm here in Milano at the Hotel Manin…I tried to get you at Lyn Brienne but Maggie told me I could reach you at this number…I thought you might be near Milano…we could meet for lunch or dinner if you're in this region…call me when you get this message…I miss you…and send you all my love." Emma pressed 'off' to end the brief conversation, but felt no better after leaving it and went inside.

The lavish engraved invitation sitting on the mantel attracted Emma's attention to read it again. The charity *Festa* starts at three o'clock—more like a cocktail party. A rap came at the door:

*"Chi parla?"*

"Room service—your tray of coffee, *Signora*?"

*"Avanti."* Unlocking the door, Emma immediately noticed this chap was not her usual waiter. Not only was he a different man, there was something singularly wrong about this waiter bringing her morning coffee. Instantly, her senses quickened, something wasn't right—his deportment was so unusual for a waiter…hesitating… not sure of himself…uncertain where to put the tray…he shows too much interest in her. Emma observed him deliberately casting furtive looks at her.

"Just put the tray on the table…anywhere is fine," she stipulated to hurry him along, all the while she remained standing by the open door. He was showing too much interest in the suite, taking his time looking around—he finally handed her the charge slip. Emma signed the tick—knowing he stared long and hard at her—a sneer for a smile. Emma met his look while she signed the slip.

*"Grazia—Caio,"* she said and locked the door quickly. "What a frightening looking man! I must tell Dillon to check on that man! I'm sure he's not one of the hotel's regular room service waiters! There was something different about his uniform...but what?" Emma knew Dillon was an early riser and called his room.

*"Pronto?"*

"It's me. Just checking in with you."

"How was yur evenin'?"

"Very nice—I'm glad I went, making small talk. When can we get together?"

"Let's 'ave breakfast—say in one 'our? Our friend will pick us up at the usual café."

"Sounds great. Is it a working breakfast?"

"You got it right!" The line clicked dead.

Quickly showering, Emma donned slacks and a simple cotton top, for the day was going to be a warm one. Gathering all the materials together in her briefcase along with a few personal items, she grabbed a sweater—eager to get out of the suite. Sunday morning in the lobby was unusually quiet. Regulars were getting Sunday editions of the local papers and heading for the hotel ristorante. The church bells chimed in a beckoning rhythm somewhere out in the city reminding the believers church was the beginning of this day. The aroma of fresh baked bread and coffee stimulated her appetite, but before she made known her choice of brew, a black truck pulled up and stopped outside the café. It was Dillon with Biaggio motioning to her to get in.

"Where are we going for breakfast?" she asked.

"Ah, Biaggio knows this wonderful little place with the best food in Milano— English and Italian foods—where we can eat bang'rs and chips together for breakfast!" Dillon handed her an envelope. "The pictures we took in Perugia."

There must have been about a hundred photos in the stack of pictures, enlarged to make it easy to see every detail. Included in the pile were the films they took on their trip to the winery. Slowly, Emma started viewing each one of them.

"The pictures of the sports car with its occupants came out better than I thought. So this **is** Marcus Rudolphi—but that woman with him isn't Lucinda! Who is she?" Emma's first thought was, *"His mistress? He wouldn't do that to Lucinda in broad daylight? Or would he?"* Dillon just shrugged his shoulders at her questions, not wanting to comment on her observations.

Biaggio drove across town, taking many detours, until they arrived at a large private home off the Via Casantino. Entering from the back of the house, they entered into the kitchen where smells of fresh baked breads, cakes, and coffee overcame them. A small, motherly-looking woman with a spontaneous smile, wiping her hands on her apron, came over to greet them with the usual Italian greeting.

*"Buon giorno, il Signorina. Lei sono piu il benevenuto alla nostra casa. Come sta?"*

*"Si, Bene grazie,"* Emma said.

*"Per favore di sedere e te stesso aiutare,"* she pointed them to a big, bright eating room to a large table set with all kinds of home-baked breads with fruits, cheeses, and coffees—even English bangers!

"Em, this is Biaggio's wife, Sienna."

Nodding, she asked, *"Lei parla l'italiano?"*

*"Si, guisto un poco."* Emma said, gesturing with her fingers—a little bit.

*"Capisco!"* she said laughing—*"Lo capise un piccolo inglese, troppo,"* she said, making the same small gesture with her hand. *"Mangiare adesso!"* She pointed to the food before them. They didn't hesitate to sit down or waste time in filling their plates with hot frittatas, sausages, muffins, and coffee.

*"Teh?"* Sienna asked.

*"No, caffee, grazie."*

"I see you did get your bangers, Dillon."

"You bet! I put my order in to Biaggio last night!" he said, savoring a delicate lasting taste.

"When we finish, we have privacy to look at our pictures," Biaggio told us. Biaggio seldom spoke his thoughts, but here in his home his whole persona changed. He spoke to each child individually at the table with fatherly interest, as if there was no one else present. Emma felt safe! Here with this family, she ate as if it were her last meal, remembering she would not have the opportunity, or desire to eat at the *Festa* this afternoon—knowing what lay ahead for them! Sienna was the perfect hostess, constantly refilling dishes and cups of coffee. She was pleased to have guests in her home; even Biaggio kept encouraging them to 'eat up.' Emma felt such relief being in a safe place—out of the public's scrutiny—to the point of forgetting what was going to take place in several hours. In the distance, children's voices echoed—outside playing games. Happy sounds!

"Biaggio, how many children do you have?" Emma asked.

*"Si, otto."*

"Eight!" she responded.

"Don't ask me to tell you their ages in order—I never remember! One of them changes their age before I learn it!" he said with a chuckle. It was most evident the children enjoyed spending time with their father. Their laughter and interaction was so spontaneous, sincere with no suggestion of fear.

After eating the last morsel of a real Italian breakfast, Biaggio led them to a room in the back of the house set up like a study. On one wall were several computer screens with computer keyboards and a bank of several different colored phones. Emma surmised the different colored phones had to signify a particular dedicated line. Knowing Biaggio's connections to Dillon, she guessed he probably worked for an investigative organization. Biaggio pointed for them to sit at the table, while he picked up the white phone and briefly spoke to someone in Italian and turned several computers on. The screens flashed up different views of the grounds around the perimeter of the house. One of the monitors showed the children playing on a swing in the rear garden. Now Emma had a better understanding of Biaggio's skills and why Dillon wanted him to do surveillance of the Rudolphi estate.

"Em, I want you to look closely at all these pictures we took on Thursday," Dillon said, referring to the trip to the winery and the Rudolphi estate trip. "'Ere's a viewer to put 'em in to enlarge them more. I need you to identify an' person you see in the photos and mark where the photo was taken in relation to some reference point in the picture—a fence, a 'ouse, or an odd-shaped tree, or cluster of trees, or shrubs that's distinguished by sight. Write that information on the back of each picture. We need to learn as much 'bout these people, the layout of the 'ouses, and the lay of the land out to the perimeter fences. Understand?"

"No problem," she replied.

"When you finish with the estate pictures, do the same for the ones we took in Perugia, too. In those pictures, check the buildin's, the windows, doors, e'en the adjoinin' buildin's—to give us as much reference information 'bout the surrounding buildin's near the café where we saw the children as possible—and write the important stuff on the back. If somethin' looks important to you in the picture, circle that spot with this red pen and explain on the back.

"Got it! Is there a special reason why we're doing this?"

"Yeh—but I'll explain later."

"Dillon, before I start—I need to discuss something that happened this morning. I followed my usual routine and ordered my morning cappuccino from room service, only this morning a different waiter delivered it to my room—I don't think he was one of the hired staff at the hotel! All the time he was in the room, he kept watching where I was—leering looks—and he definitely inspected the room—as if he was wanted to remember it—like he was seeing it for the first time. He wore the usual waiter's uniform, but his service was awkward—his whole manner was not like a *cammeriere*." Excitedly, Emma said, "Now I remember what looked so different—it was his shoes! He wore heavy fatigue boots! The boots were so dirty next to the clean uniform! An alarm went off when I first saw him, but I didn't know why I felt so uneasy—until now! His whole behavior was different—anxious—unsure of himself—he could have been a temp—but I doubt it! His boots were lug-soled!"

"What did he look like? Describe him to me," Dillon said.

Concentrating to recall a mental picture of the man, Emma said, "He was about five ten, with wavy black hair brushed back and matted down; dark brown eyes not wanting to make good eye contact with me for any length of time, he kept diverting his eyes from me when he saw me watching him—heavy eyebrows. The left eye was drawn down by a small scar from the brow, heavy five o'clock shadow, and sallow complexion. It was more his shoes—his shoes were heavy—dirty work shoes with lug soles—not worn by any of the other hotel staff. That's what was wrong—he wore boots and a uniform! His hands were big—clumsy—the fingers had dirt ground around the nails…and he had a surly, crooked smile. The look in his eyes was evil—like he was undressing me with his eyes!"

Dillon asked, "Biaggio, you 'eard 'er—Does that description fit an'one you know?"

Slowly, Biaggio walked over to them from the computers. "*Si*, you described Tony Davici perfectly! He's trouble! Does many dirty jobs for anyone who'll pay him—has a long criminal record but always seems to have someone there to bail him out! Let me try to find out who he's working for now—I'll make a few calls," he said and walked over to the bank of phones.

"Good work, Em! Yur instincts were on the quid! But then you have the MacKenna Clan gift!"

"How do you know about the MacKenna Clan trait?" It was as if another door opened for Emma about Dillon. Out of the blue, she blurted out to Dillon, "Dillon, just how well do *you* know Cyrus?"

"Em…I can't get into that with you now." He saw her impatient gesture! "Hold on!" he commanded with his hands raised, as she tried to interrupt him. "Thin's in me past are in the past! Sometimes, it's best to let sleepin' dogs lie—and not wake 'em—unless it's necessar' to prevent bad things from happenin' in yur life…ag'in! Right now is not the time to travel that road ag'in—so please—just trust me, Em! As I said—a'ways rely on yur MacKenna gift!" Emma knew at that moment, Dillon had some kind of connection with Cyrus from the past…but what was it? How long ago? Why doesn't Dillon want to acknowledge he knows Cyrus from his previous life? For the first time, Emma felt Dillon was deliberately hiding something important in his life from her…or *was he hiding something from her about Cyrus's past?*

Biaggio walked over to Dillon and whispered to him.

"Em, Biaggio learned it *was* Tony Davici you saw this morning. He's working for Marcus Rudolphi!" Suddenly, Emma felt a heavy, sick feeling come over her.

"That means... *Marcus Rudolphi* knows I'm here in Milano for some definite reason...and I'm staying at the Manin. Do you think he suspects Lucinda is connected to me? She would never tell him—not willingly! I know she's afraid of him...and her fears have some foundation from the way she described their relationship...she could have been forced to tell him about her visit to me!" Emma looked at Biaggio and Dillon for some reaction.

"Dillon, this doesn't change anything! I'm not backing out from attending that charity party today and getting that information! In fact, I want *him*—and all the rest of the Rudolphis to see me there! I especially want to see *his* reaction to my attendance at his charity *Festa!* If my presence upsets him, I only hope he doesn't take it out on Lucinda—that is, if my being there poses some kind of threat to him!"

Reassuringly, Dillon said, "Em, don't worry! I'm going to ask Carlos to take care of occupying Marcus Rudolphi while you and I do *our* thing! Will Carlos have a problem with that assigment, Em?"

"No, he shouldn't—I know he wants to learn the reason why you and I are going to this affair. In fact, he wants in on all our plans—the information we need—he needs, too!"

"That's good! Let *me* brief him when we meet up. Em, you mingle with as many guests as you can—make mental notes 'bout the names with faces...try to find out a guest's connection to the Rudolphis," Dillon instructed.

"That's fine with me," Emma said in a tone of finality and turned to the viewer and started processing the photographs from the winery and Perugia as Dillon instructed.

Dillon and Biaggio walked to the rear of the room to discuss details of how Biaggio will handle the electrical supply to all the security systems. "Biag, you need to find a way to temporar' interrupt the electric'ty suppl' to the securit' cameras in the main 'ouse that goes to the librar'. Emma's job is to temporari'y neutralize the laser and floor sensors, but the cameras in the librar' must be off for twent' minutes!" Dillon told him emphatically.

Biaggio explained to Dillon his plan for interrupting the security systems.

"*Si*, I know exactly where the main trunk line enters the villa for both systems, but I'm not certain how good their back-up system is. My plan is to short out the whole electrical complex, permanent and back up, located at the back of the house. It's all in the basement, and I should be able to reach it with *no problemo*. I readied the area near the basement so I can access the old cellar quickly! I'll be carrying a spray to use on any guards should I meet them—when I get into the basement. It's quick acting and has no side effects when they come out of it—short-term memory loss! The shutdown of the main power supply may interrupt some electricity to the rooms where the *festa* is held! But when it happens, I think they'll investigate for an immediate source of failure to each room—not thinking it was the main trunk line. We should have the time we need—all of fifteen minutes—for sure…with luck, twenty!" Biaggio was thorough in every detail.

"Then I'll radio you the exact time we start to execute the plan— that's when you'll know we mark those fifteen minutes for Emma to get in and out of the librar'! Once we 'ave secured the information, we'll stick around for another fifteen—no more than thirt' minutes from the time the job is done! That's when you bring the car 'round the drive to the front door and be read' to pick us up—the three of us!" Biaggio knew Dillon planned for any unknown contingency.

"It's good to work with you again, ole comrade!" Dillon commented to his friend. "Sounds like we 'ave every possible phase worked out. I know they're screenin' for firearms when we enter. Is there a place in the car where we can 'ide a piece—just in case?" Dillon asked.

"*No problemo!* Under the driver's seat in the Mercedes, we have a lead-lined box that can't be detected by their equipment. I'll have a self-loading automatic concealed in it. If you need to get it, push the cigarette lighter in three times in quick succession, and the seat slides back to get the gun."

"That's great, Biaggio. I'll feel safer knowin' we 'ave a back-up nearby. I don't expect anythin' to go wrong—it's like a securit' blanket, I guess…" Both men walked back over to where Emma was finishing scanning the photos.

Emma finished reviewing all the pictures, documented the necessary information on the back, and handed them to Dillon. "I knew you'd do a great job. I'm takin' these with me to study when we leave. Em, you need time to set yur mind to the 'plan' before we leave for the Villa del Christianna. Did you commit these pictures and notes to memor' as you viewed 'hem, Em?"

"Yes, all of them! It's my MacKenna gift!" Dillon got the double meaning in her words and checked his watch.

"It's gettin' late, Em. We 'ave to leave and get back to the 'otel. Figure we need to leave for the Villa del Christianna no later than two o'clock—Biaggio will pick us up in a different car. A silver Mercedes will be outside the hotel at two sharp."

Emma was anxious to get back to the hotel to check for a message from Papa! Before the party, she needed a hot bath…a long soak…to go over every detail in her mind…to prepare for any possible event…in case something should go wrong. It was like doing a summation in court. ***Nothing will go wrong—it can't!*** She silently prayed.

"I'll give you yur purse in the car, so don't take any with you—which is why I asked 'bout the color of yur dress. It'll be a perfect match…don't fret." Biaggio was scanning the monitors before they left the house.

"Everything looks fine, we can leave… I'll drive you back to the café." They walked through the house to the car and truck. The house had a strange silence now—absent of sounds from children. Sienna was nowhere in sight.

"My family has gone to visit her *madre,*" Biaggio said as if he were reading Emma's mind.

The trip back to the café across from the hotel seemed shorter than when they came, and it was probably because Biaggio didn't have to take long detours on the trip back—no one was tailing us. It was very evident Biaggio took every precaution to protect his family from any anyone knowing where he lived to prevent any unexpected visitors!

They arrived at the café at one o'clock. Dillon stopped for a paper, while Emma went directly into the hotel. No messages at the desk! Dashing upstairs to check for phone messages, Emma saw that the red light on the phone was flashing—someone had left a message!

Dialing the code to hear the phone message, Emma heard, "Emma, its Papa. Got your messages—sorry I missed you—but I'm not in or near Milano—so we'll have to wait on dinner. I'm traveling and my itinerary changes… I'll be in touch from the farm or in another couple of days—whichever comes first. Please be very careful. Love you, lass." The line went dead. Emma felt a relief when she heard his voice. "He's fine!" She listened again to the message…

*"Be very careful?"* Emma thought, *"Not his usual choice of words to end his message…his message did sound deliberately composed to be vague… to put me off? Cautioning me to be '**very careful**'! Papa…exactly where are you?"*

# CHAPTER THIRTY-THREE

Dillon was waiting in the Mercedes for her.

If she hadn't known to look for a silver Mercedes, she wouldn't have recognized him! Casually dressed in light cream-colored pants, a soft blue shirt, and a slightly darker off-white jacket, he looked so different from the ordinary man she knew.

"Dillon is definitely a very handsome man!" Emma saw facets of Dillon she never imagined! Getting out of the car, he escorted her into the rear seat.

"Dillon, you are a man with impeccable tastes—and all along, I thought you were meant only for denim!"

"I 'ope someone 'as told you emerald green—like the 'ills of Wales—is yur diamond! Em, you look beautiful! I'm proud to be yur escort—at least 'til Carlos arrives." Smiling he handed her a small, dark, emerald-green beaded purse. Biaggio was attending to his chauffeur duties—dressed for the part with uniform, hat, and gloves, he slowly drove them out of Milano. The sun was sinking low on the horizon. With the dark tinted glass, its solar glare was barely perceptible.

"I didn't explain just 'ow special this purse works! Listen up! It's not just a simple purse so you need to know 'ow to op'n it the right way! There's a right way to open it and a **wrong way!**" Dillon took the purse. "**You must always unlatch the purse this way…see…it op'ns with all the contents inside that I mentioned earlier. As you can tell it's not the usual way a woman would open her purse!**"

"What happens if it opens another way?" Emma asked.

"Should an'one op'n the purse an' other way than 'ow I showed you—a clear vapor is activated causin' 'hem to lose consciousness—a momentary faint! This is necessary if someone tries to search yur purse and op'ns it in the usual way, they'll just pass out as if they fainted! We then collect the purse quickl' and leave while the scene is unfoldin' in front of us. *We don't want this purse, and any of its contents, to fall into the wrong hands.*" Emma took the purse back and unlatched it carefully as Dillon instructed her.

"I always knew you're a fast learner, Em!" He next took out the contents to demonstrate exactly how to handle and use each item as it was meant to be, as well as a hidden piece of surveillance equipment.

Inside was a gold lipstick—the color a soft blush crème. Dillon took the cylinder of lipstick and demonstrated the mechanics of the hidden camera. Raising the tube of cream, he turned it and the lip-cream retracted into the gold top. The empty tube became the camera. Focusing the tube on Emma, he said, "This is how you shoot for pictures. Raise the cylinder to your eye—the viewfinder will automatically focus—you press on the end of the cylinder until you hear a slight click. Keep focusin' with yur 'and, pressin' and continuous'y movin' the cylinder around—up or down. Some of the pictures will 'ave duplicate composition—we'll take care of eliminatin' that when the film is processed; we can delete certain duplicate portions when we enlarge the pictures, if necessar'."

Handing her the cylinder, he said, "When you upright the cylinder completel' vertical and turn the bottom, it should raise the stick of crème. *Presto*! It's just a tube of lipstick! I 'ope the color is yours? Now you do it, Em."

Repeating his directions, Emma raised the cylinder, turned, and listened for it to retract. Inside the empty tube was a tiny crystal lens. She aimed at Dillon and pressed to hear a soft click. "I wanted a picture of you—to show all my friends what a handsome man was with me in Milano!" For the first time, Emma saw Dillon blush!

"Do you feel comfortable workin' with it?" he asked.

"Yes, I'm fine with it."

Next he held the compact, a beautiful slender gold square case with a raised sculptured yellow and white gold rose containing a cluster of gemstones on the top. The clasp mechanism was a pressure release mechanism instead of a clasp. Dillon instructed Emma how to open the mirror to get the key behind it, which was made to open the locked box in the study. The loose powder under a puff was silver dust for the lasers! The gemstones were actually radio transmitters and the mirror a receiver. If it became necessary, Dillon would speak and she could see him in the mirror; but this method was only to be used in an emergency, if it became necessary for them to make a quick exit from the house!

"'Ere's the small perfume spray." It was in a metal container. "It's for the motion sensors."

Next, holding a diamond and gold bracelet, he placed it on her wrist. "This is the way I will contact you. You'll feel the bracelet get warm on your wrist from a 'idden 'eat sensor, a signal for you to open the compact and read the message in the mirror."

"How clever!"

Dillon continued, "The mirror will display a message—and if someone is with you, it'll appear it's just a lady adjustin' her make-up! For an emergency, you'll see me face…that'll be the signal we're leavin' *pronto!*" Dillon carefully checked the clasp on the bracelet, making certain it was closed on her wrist. "This is not a piece of jewelry to lose!"

"These are yur readin' glasses—small and grann' lookin' frames for a reason! The glass in 'hem are made to see laser lights. These 'ere are real-looking lira coins with different weights and composition," he said, pointing to several coins in his hand.

"These 'ere are the ones you use on the door lasers, the white metal coins." Next, picking up the copper coins, he said, "Use these four for the floor if you need them—two at a time will do the job. I doubt those beams will be activated today with the 'ouse full of guests."

"Are there cameras in the library?"

"Biaggio will take care of the electric'l supply to the securit' cameras at a specified time—so don't worr' 'bout cameras. The sensors are on an independent system, but he wasn't able to exact'y locate where the power supply to the laser system in the librar'. If both laser and sensor systems are on, *you'll* have to take care of them with yur coins!"

Emphasizing his reason for all this instruction, he said, "I want you to stay focused on gettin' that box opened and the journals photographed—and then get the 'ell out of there safel'! I can't emphasize that enough, Emma! **Do you 'ear me? You do nothin' else in that library!**" Emma heard his admonition and the concern in Dillon's voice—calling her Emma!

"When you get back downstairs, mingle back into the crowd, which may still be gathered at the far end of the house where the commotion is comin' from. Find Carlos or me, dependin' on who is free and meet up. I want you to slip *me* yur lipstick so I can make a switch for a real one as soon as we meet up. When you leave, you'll 'ave the real thing, and I'll deal with gettin' the camera out safe'y. Here's where I may real'y need Carlos's 'elp, if we 'ave a problem leavin'!"

"Carlos will be notin' the names of the guests there and keepin' 'is eye on Marcus and Lucinda—and anyone else he needs to watch! If we need 'im to make a diversion for us, I'll tell him ahead of time. Any questions, Em?"

"No, Dillon. I know it'll all work out for us," Emma said reassuringly. "I want this information more than anything right now! So let's do it!" The last few minutes of the trip were silent as Biaggio pulled up to the front gate. Several men outside the main gate were directing cars and checking invitations. They followed a white Maserati up to the gate and stopped. Biaggio lowered his window and handed the invitations to a guard. He spoke briefly to the man who was dressed entirely in black—suit, tie, and shirt.

*"Buono sera, Signorina—Signore. De dove lo sono?"*

*"Milano, Si."*

*"Sono qui assistere la festa di Rudolphi al Christianna di del de Villa?"* the guard asked.

*"Si!"* Biaggio said. The guard gave instructions to proceed, pointing to the winding drive ahead of them.

*"Per favore di guidare fino all'entrata alla villa guida."*

Biaggio slowly drove up the winding road until they reached an expansive marble-paved drive with a marbled water fountain and pool in the center. The scene all had the ambience of an opulent Italian *Piazza*. Underwater, fountain lights outlined shimmering white flowers floating in the soft whirling waters of the pool. Dillon pointed out to Emma, "There's a camera concealed in the top of the fountain. I just saw the glint of glass off its lens when it flashed; they're takin' pictures of everyone who's comin' to the party! The bastards!" Dillon muttered under his breath as Biaggio parked the car at the front steps. Exiting the car at the grand front entrance, the beckoning steps all had a Cinderella mystique. Tall white topiaries, overflowing with fragrant cascading white roses and green ivy, flanked each step leading up to the enormous century-old wood and iron doors recessed into a parapet.

Dillon and Emma slowly ascended the marble steps leading to the front entrance—deliberately scrutinizing the opened French balcony doors, allowing a view into the lavishly lit and decorated rooms filled with guests. The terrace encircled the entire front and sides of the villa. Taking their time, they casually made their way to the front doors. Tall, gigantic planters overflowing with hibiscus and mountain laurel in different shades of white and pale lilac flanked each side of the open balcony doors. The valets, all dressed completely in black tuxedos, black shirt, and tie, instructed Biaggio to drive the car to the rear of the house and park after leaving them out at the front door. Dillon lingered back to hear where Biaggio was told to park the car. If Biaggio had a problem accessing the cellar, he was to let Dillon know and an alternate plan was to go in place. No signal from Biaggio meant he was clear to carry out his job with the electrical circuitry.

"Biaggio can take care of himself!" Dillon said as he caught up to Emma at the front door.

A young man in a white tuxedo stationed at the front door greeted each guest and gave instructions or offered assistance. With impeccable manners, he directed them into the huge great foyer-hall, more like a great palatial room with its massive crystal chandelier sparkling like a thousand lights.

Following the queue of guests into the main hall, they realized they were in the guests' queue to greet the host and hostess, Marcus and Lucinda Rudolphi. Emma felt her pulse racing, as Dillon softly put his hand around her waist to assure her he was there and gently nudged her out of the queue over to an area off to the side away from Marcus and Lucinda Rudolphi's view—before they saw them. Taking his hand, Emma slowly walked towards a waiter carrying a tray of drinks—probably champagne of their own best vintage—and each picked up a glass.

"I'm glad it's champagne!" Emma knew Dillon was wishing for a beer.

"We should try to avoid meetin' our 'ost and 'ostess just now—and look for Carlos. I'd prefer he be with us for our first introduction."

"There must be hundreds of people here already," Emma remarked while they mingled in the crowd—sipping champagne.

"There's Carlos—walking over toward us." Emma spoke to Dillon in an undertone.

Emma found pleasure in watching Carlos nonchalantly make his way in their direction, unceremoniously acknowledging some of the guests as he passed them. Emma's feelings told her just how much she missed him, and she felt her heart quicken remembering his words to her…, "I need and love you!" His suave aristocratic Italian looks and charm turned several couple's attention. He stopped to speak casually with each of them, all the time working his way toward Dillon and Emma.

*"He fits in with this crowd—like he's one of them!"* she whispered.

Impeccably dressed in a light beige linen suit and brown shirt, he knew how to blend in to work the crowd. Emma's thought, *It doesn't matter what he wears, he portrays the suave continental look at its best and knows exactly how to capture his audience's attention with his eyes and smile, a charismatic disarming magnetism!*

Waiting for Carlos to reach them, Emma couldn't help but notice the lavish surroundings of the Villa del Christianna. The great cathedral room gave definition to a medieval castle with its massive stone hearth flickering with a bright radiant fire. The pink marble mantel rose up to the ceiling. The furniture was old with a feeling of antiquity—not necessarily comfort. The pink marble floor was sparkling and absent of floor coverings. Original artworks were conspicuous—an eclectic selection. The windows were arched and contained both clear and stained glass. The filtering sunlight was like bits of colored glass forming a pattern, as a prism follows exact laws of white light bursting into rainbow's colors—bits of color completing its patterns to disperse light throughout the room. Above the mantle hung an enormous carved Coat of Arms of the Rudolphi family with the large center scrolled **"R"**.

Suddenly, a mental image flashed in Emma's mind…

*a hearth…a picture—an old costumed man…. slender windows…colored light…dancing particles in the sunlight's rays…a door slowly opening…*
*In an instant, the memory is gone!*

*Why would this room trigger a memory from…where? Should I have a memory of this room from the past that I have forgotten? Is it possible I was really here…in a past time…and now have no conscious memory of it…except for a flashback? But how can that be?*

*Is it conceivable…somewhere in my past…I **did** meet a Rudolphi?*

# CHAPTER THIRTY-FOUR

"Em, are you alright?" Dillon asked.

"Yes, yes I'm fine. I have these flashbacks about a past time… or a place…I'm not sure what it means…I get a feeling I should remember something…! When the reflection is gone, I can't remember anything about the image! It's as if something is trying to make me remember a past memory—my mind's picture only lasts for seconds—then a curtain closes in my mind," Emma explained to Dillon. He took note of Emma's comments and the effect it had on her when she experienced the flashback. *Why would this place produce that kind of response in 'er?*

At the far end of the Great Room, doors led to an adjacent banquet room set up with lavishly decorated tables with flowers, elegant ice sculptures, and unimaginable quantities of food! A roasted pig was being carved at one end of the table—at the other end, a chef was skillfully shaving rivulet pieces off a whole side of beef. A delicate glass fountain was set in the middle of the room, with cascades of champagne falling from the tiers—guests filling their glasses from it. Returning to the Great Room from the gilded dining feast, Dillon and Emma walked to the opposite end of the Great Room to the doors leading out on the balcony at the rear of the house, overlooking magnificent sculptured gardens stretching out to a distant wall.

The view of the gardens from the marbled balcony was surreal. The vista captured a serene panoramic theme copied from the Louis XIV gardens in Versailles. Multiple levels of gardens, each with different sculptures and complimentary motif of flowerbeds, shrubs, fountains, and paths circled endlessly among the stone figures, as far as the eye could see! Dillon noted one of the walkways led off in the direction of the swimming pool and cabana houses. Behind the tall trees, flags waved in the breezes, signaling a mid-east Arabian architectural motif in the pool area. On the far side of the balcony, a full orchestral ensemble played softly—it was Mimi's aria from *LaBoheme.*

Suddenly *he* was next to Emma! Leaning over, he kissed her cheek.

"Carlos, I'm so glad you're here! Dillon, I'd like you to meet Carlos Esteves. Carlos, this is Dillon O'Rourke. He's with me on holiday as a friend—really to help me find and look up old friends." Emma watched each man's reply for a hint of familiarity as they greeted each other. Carlos shook Dillon's hand.

"I'm glad to meet you, Carlos. Emma 'as spoken 'bout you to me, and I feel I know you well," he said laughingly.

*A good try, Dillon. You're too damn formal, Dillon...you two have met before!* Emma made the mental note while sipping her champagne.

"Carlos, is there somewhere private we can 'ave a few minutes to speak?" Dillon asked.

"*Si*, let's walk toward the rear of the garden—not too many people there." The three took the least crowded path to the rear gardens not far from where the cabanas' red and gold pennant flags wafted in the breezes.

"I have some idea why you're here tonight, Dillon...You're looking for certain information. And, I'm here to see you get it without getting caught...and to help in any way I can." Carlos spoke evenly as he kept scanning the area.

"Thanks—that's what I needed to know," Dillon said.

"Dillon, when today's assignment is complete, you and I need to talk—we need to clarify a few things...We should all be on the same page! Our 'missions' are probably the same! For now...I'm here to help in any way I can."

*So Carlos does know Emma is tied to the Rudolphis!* Dillon concluded.

"Aye…I totall' agree…we should be workin' together—not against each other!"

"I have a hunch you may not realize the sophistication and size of the Rudolphi organization you're dealing with! So for now—just clue me in how to help you?" Carlos said. "Can you tell me exactly what you're doing here today? What kind of information you're trying to get?" Carlos's questions were direct and clear.

"We're goin' after information Marcus Rudolphis keeps in 'is librar'. Our source is totall' reliable, and we're certain we need to get inside that room! Em knows exactl' where it is and what to look for. 'Er job is to find the object, photograph it, and get out! My job—and yur's—is to create a diversion somewhere away from the librar'. A diversion subt'e enough it won't raise questions to securit' that somethin' else is goin' on in the 'ouse at the same time! What I'd like you to do Carlos is to watch our backs—Emma's and mine! If you get the names of guests—as many as you can—we'll put names to the pictures I'll be takin' of the guests when we need them. I figure some of these guests are really Rudolphi's plants!"

"Most certainly!" Carlos remarked. "So we all need to watch each other's backs! I already see some of Rudolphi's goons, already working the crowd of guests looking for problems!" Carlos remarked to Dillon and Emma.

"With yur embass' connections, it should be no problem for you to give names to faces in this crowd. Em and I can't distinguish guests from Rudolphi's goons, so when you recognize one of 'hem—point 'hem out to me—*pronto*!" Dillon let Carlos know he was depending on him to make his plan a success.

"I'll point out to you anyone I recognize belonging to the Rudolphi family or organization by putting my hand on your shoulder—a sign of familiarity," Carlos instructed.

"When the plan goes down—we need to make certain NO ONE—again, NO ONE— is wise 'bout what's really happenin'!" Dillon stated with authority. "You need to watch me back when the critical count starts! See if an'one is suspicious of a ruse 'appin' and starts a securit' check in the 'ouse!"

"What's the diversion?" Carlos asked.

"It's the argon gas marble. When I activate it in a group of guests, they'll feel ver' nauseous and most will get sick at once. At that moment, we must make certain ever'one's attention is given to those guests reactin' at that time!" All the while Dillon was speaking, he was continually canvassing the gardens and the movements of the guests near them.

"Over there…there's a group of tables and chairs off to the side by that big tree, which is ideal for the diversion." Dillon nodded toward the area, and let out a false laugh to appear that the three of them were enjoying a good conversation.

"You have state-of-the-art equipment, Dillon. I can see you're well prepared for this event!" Carlos said softly, appearing to make small talk to Dillon and Emma.

Dillon explained to Carlos. "The plan is for Em to ask for help repairin' her dress—she'll be upstairs at the time the gas is released. We've had a trick-double of her skirt made to simulate the tear. When there's a good crowd in that area of the garden next to that big tree—that's when I'll activate the gas. At that moment of confusion, she'll slip into the librar', locate the target, get the information, and get out!"

"What is this information you need?" Carlos asked.

"I'd rather not go into detail now, Carlos," Emma answered. "I'll tell you about it after I have it safely in my possession."

Carlos turned to Emma. "Emma, this sounds dangerous! I don't want anything to happen to you…,"

She cut off his sentence. "I know, Carlos. And nothing will if you two do a good job!"

"*No problemo!* I'll do my part to see nothing happens to either of you." Carlos looked around the pool area, making certain no one was showing interest in the three of them. "*Andiamo!*"

"One thing, Carlos…we 'avn't met the host and hostess yet. If we don't, we may be conspicuous for *not* meetin' 'hem! Do you personal'y know the couple?" Dillon asked.

"*Si,* I've met Marcus on several occasions—we both have memberships at the same local clubs in Milano. I'll do the introductions when the time comes. I'll say you're friends of mine from England, when I spent time at Cambridge. Emma you went to law school there, which if they check the facts will be accurate—and Dillon is your escort on your trip to Milano. Whispering to Emma, he said, "I'm already jealous!"

"No contest, Carlos—but it's nice to hear," Emma whispered back.

They made their way back to the Great Room to find Marcus and Lucinda. Emma purposely neglected to tell Carlos about the list with *her* name on it. Since he believed they were there because of Lucinda, she let him think the information was for Lucinda.

The Rudolphis were standing together outside on the balcony mingling with guests when the trio reached the top step.

"They make a very handsome couple!" Emma commented.

Marcus, with the dark swarthy look, dark brown eyes, wide spontaneous smile, and chin dimple, was faultlessly dressed in a white dinner suit that accented his dark Mediterranean features.

Lucinda was dressed in a beautiful strapless, sequined, gold sheath baring her flawless translucent complexion. Her features distinctively Neapolitan, publicized her shimmering golden-red hair worn long to her shoulders, offsetting her emerald-green eyes. She was the epitome of a perfect, beautiful, modern Roman lady. On the arm of her husband, they presented the epitome of beauty and wealth—she ravishingly beautiful—he handsomely continental! Her eyes betrayed her inner self—the smile was genuine—the voice graciously soft, but the deep sadness in her green eyes was inescapable to detect. She appeared almost tearful at times. Approaching the couple, Emma sensed Lucinda saw her from a distance and was trying to remain calmly casual in greeting her guests.

*She is well schooled in control—not giving way to her feelings of astonishment when we drew near.*

"Marcus and Lucinda, I missed seeing you when I first arrived!" Carlos said, walking over to the couple ahead of us to greet Marcus with a firm handshake and Lucinda with a soft kiss on both cheeks. "I'd like you to meet some friends from England. May I present Emma Llewelyn from London and her companion, Dillon O'Rourke."

"Ms. Llewelyn, it's my pleasure to meet you," Marcus raised her hand to kiss it in the gentleman's tradition, all the while keeping his eyes riveted on hers—in an alluring, seductive fashion. Removing her hand from his, he said, "Please meet my beautiful wife, Lucinda." Lucinda took Emma's hand in hers—it felt icy cold, and Emma felt her trembling.

Emma took control, "It's my pleasure to meet you, and to be here for such a worthy cause—your charity for research?" she asked, looking directly at Lucinda.

"*Si,*" Lucinda said softly.

"Research is so important today in curing the many diseases and ills mankind has endured, and it's fortunate I can make a contribution to this worthy cause." Marcus turned the conversation away from Lucinda—it seemed as if he wanted to control the discussion.

Instead, Emma intentionally turned to Lucinda. "Mrs. Rudolphi, you have a lovely home."

"Please call me Lucinda." Marcus stared at both women. Emma wanted Marcus to know she was challenging his attempt to control the encounter—It seemed they were both vying for control of Lucinda's attention!

At once, Lucinda gestured for Emma to go with her toward the gardens—to escape the tension in the group. "This estate has been in the Rudolphi family for many generations, and this area of the estate is particularly beautiful. We are very fortunate our home is in such a magnificent area of Tuscany."

Marcus interjected to show he approved of her maneuver—his way to maintain control. "Lucinda why don't' you take Ms. Llewelyn..."

"Please, call me Emma."

"Take Emma down to the gardens to show her the beauty we care for so meticulously."

"Thank you, I'd like that." Lucinda put her arm into Emma's, appearing to escort her down the steps. Actually, Emma felt she was leaning on her for moral and physical support.

"Gentlemen, please let me get you a drink at the bar." Marcus led the way to a bar outside on the balcony, away from the garden.

"Scotch and water for me," Dillon said.

"Make that two," Carlos echoed.

"My usual Antonio," Marcus said, turning to Carlos. "Now tell me, Carlos, what are you doing in Milano now?"

"On holiday for few days. I just returned from Malaysia with the ambassador. Nice place to spend a few weeks, but it was mostly business. Just returned last week when I decided to take a few days off here in Milano before returning to Roma." Marcus immediately turned to Dillon.

"Mr. O'Rourke, what is it you do?" Both men knew Marcus was skillfully trying to learn their real reasons for being there.

"I'm in the import-export business and 'ave me own business—mainly searchin' out antiques all over the world. There's a lucrative big market for antiques in England and on the continent."

"Now that is something I agree with! Lucinda and I love to visit new places looking for antiques! We have many pieces here in our villa, and one of our favorite pastimes is traveling about keeping our eyes peeled for something more to add to our collection. I especially look for Italian and French Renaissance pieces." Marcus looked around the room. "That sculpture over there," he said, pointing to a mosaic polyptych, "is a Masaccio from the early Italian Renaissance. I believe it is one of a kind—priceless and very rare!" Marcus gestured to the painting on the wall. Dillon walked over to the artwork and took several minutes examining it.

"You're fortunate to own such a rare piece, Mr. Rudolphi. Masaccio's work is not recognized for the polyptych. In fact, that piece of work is in dispute by artistic masters—it's not known exact'y when he painted it—most agree it was done in the seventeenth century." Dillon returned to the group.

"Thank you for your unsolicited expertise. Please call me Marcus."

"Marcus, I've been appreciatin' your collection of origina' pieces of art…I especial'y like the small Raphael piece—sixteenth century if I'm correct—'is only paintin' of Maria d'Avegnon." Dillon pointed to a small picture in a niche near the main door.

"Again, Mr. O'Rourke, your eye is sharp and expert. That piece? It's one is my most prized possessions I own—it's priceless! No value of money can replace it." Clearly, Dillon was captivating his host.

"Mr. O'Rourke, do you have a business card I may have—there may be a time I'd require an evaluation of a piece in England and would appreciate your expertise?" Marcus asked Dillon.

"Indeed I do." Dillon took out his wallet and handed Marcus an engraved business card. "My message center number is there—just leave a message, and I'll get back to you."

Now it was Dillon's chance to ask the questions. "Marcus you have a large vineyard and wine business 'ere. It must keep you very busy overseein' such a well-known international winery."

"You're absolutely correct, Mr. O'Rourke. The responsibility for running the whole business is mine," he said, gesturing to make the point his wealth encompassed his home—all from that successful business." Since my father retired several years ago, and only serves on the Board of Directions in an advisory capacity, I've had to assume more responsibilities. His health was declining...and it was time his sons took over the big task he so successfully started."

*"Scuzi, Mr. Rudolphi, telephono for you."*

"Thank you, *Dino*. I'll be there *pronto!*" Finishing his drink, he said,

"I'm sorry gentlemen, I must leave you. Please continue to enjoy yourselves while you are here, and thank you for coming and making a donation to so worthy a cause." He bowed and walked back toward the Great Room, passing through it to the very end through a door off the dining area.

"Nice work, Mr. O'Rourke!" Carlos said mockingly. "I noticed you made Marcus Rudolphi address you as 'Mr. O'Rourke'...a small way of making him grovel?" Carlos posed to Dillon.

"You bet yur ass! Deliberate, and I enjoyed ev'ry minute of it, too!"

"You still have that uncanny knack and unexpected expertise when it's needed, you bloody limey! You certainly made an impression on that bastard with your artistic tutoring. Did you hear his bloody bull? About traveling looking for antiques! I had all I could do to keep a vacant look on my face when he was speaking!" Carlos said. "He's as dirty as they come in this world, and some day he's going to get his—I only hope I'm the one to give it to him!" Carlos didn't elaborate to Dillon if there was proof Marcus had his hands on Emma—it didn't matter! To Carlos, he was already a dead man walking!

"Sounds like you know more 'bout this man than just a fellow club member, Carlos. We definitel' need to talk after this is over... tonight!" Dillon made his words sound as a command to Carlos. Both men looked at one another while sipping their drinks, knowing exactly what those words meant.

Marcus finished his phone call and slammed the receiver down. *"Just as I thought! Where did they come by invitations to this occasion today? What is their purpose for this visit to the Villa del Christianna? What are they **really after**? First, the winery...then here!"*

Taking out his mobile phone, Marcus dialed Luigi Rudolphi while searching the room for Lucinda. She was nowhere in sight.

*"Luigi—Marcus! It's tonight! Do not fail me!"* Marcus placed the phone back in his breast pocket and walked over to join Dr. Ennio Carruchi.

# CHAPTER THIRTY-FIVE

"Steady, me man," Dillon cautioned Carlos. "Marcus will get what's do 'im—but not yet."

"It's time to find Em—she's with Lucinda—and get started on the reason we came today!" Checking his watch, he said, "It's eighteen-twenty-four hours. Give me fifteen minutes to mingle the crowd and get some pictures. You can do the same...get names of guests," Dillon said to Carlos.

"At exactl' eighteen-forty-five, I'll snap the crystal at the bottom of the balcon' steps in that large group of people on the first level in the garden 'mid those tables and chairs," he said, pointing to the crowd under the cypress tree. The group consisted of twenty or more people gathered down on the next level.

"Clear?" Dillon asked.

"*Si,* I'll be at that bar nearest the door to the main room. I know the bartender and I can look as if I'm talking to him when it happens," Carlos said.

"I 'ave to signal Em now. Be ready, Carlos!"

Dillon started walking slowly toward the selected group of guests in the garden, casually sipping his drink. Carlos returned to the main room, acknowledging and greeting groups of guests he knew, all the while slowly making his way closer to the bar nearest the balcony door.

"Anything yet?" the bartender asked Carlos in an undertone, while he mixed a drink.

"The show begins in fifteen minutes. Be on the look out for Emma—she's wearing an emerald green dress. Make sure she doesn't make you out," Carlos said in a casual manner to the bartender. Picking up his drink, he walked inside the villa in the direction he last saw Marcus.

\* \* \*

Lucinda and Emma walked down the garden paths to a private area in the distant garden. "We can speak safely here. Emma, what are you doing here?" Lucinda asked in a hushed tone, furtively looking around the garden.

"Lucinda, I'm here working on your case—that's all I can tell you now. I may have some important information to tell you soon, but until I have ALL of it, I'm not going to make any premature comments on the matters we discussed." Emma looked to make certain they were alone.

"Lucinda, I need to get upstairs to a room near the library. Is your bedroom near the library?"

"*Si...*"

"Good! When we leave here I have a plan...On pretense my skirt needs mending, I'll ask where I can mend it. You need to make certain I am directed to the second floor—to a bedroom across from the library. You need to see if anyone follows me upstairs—and if someone does—you must distract him or her! If for some reason, I'm discovered upstairs—please corroborate my story for being up there! Whatever I say—any statements or reasons I give for being there—just go along with my explanation! I need you to back up my story for credibility! Can you do that?" she asked pleadingly.

"*Si*, whatever you want me to do, I'll do it! Emma, I know you're trying to find answers for me, and I'm extremely grateful—Count on me to help!" Lucinda took hold of Emma's hands and held them tightly for several minutes—as if to draw strength from her.

At that moment, Emma felt the bracelet warm her wrist. Dillon was trying to contact her. "Lucinda I must return to the house now—it's time. Walk with me back to the Great Room as if you were explaining to me details about your villa and gardens, and then we'll make a gesture to part. You go directly to the Great Room to mingle with the guests there. Ready?"

"*Si, capisco.*" Returning to the balcony, Emma felt Lucinda reach down inside herself to find inner strength. She knew she could count on her if necessary. Despite her appearance of fragility, she was a strong woman with a commitment to finding answers! Before parting, "Remember Lucinda, don't try to contact me! It would be too dangerous.

"I will call you and leave the coded message we agreed upon when the time is right." Squeezing her hand as a signal, Emma started for the stairs, while Lucinda walked over to greet new guests in the Great Room just entering the villa.

* * *

Deliberately taking her time walking down the hall past the circular marble staircase, Emma took out the compact and read the message, Dillon's warning "ten minutes." Pretending to look for the *Toeletto*, Emma walked down a hallway a short distance while working the false tear in the hem to the front of her skirt. A maid came towards her.

"*Scuzi, per favore, filo?*" Pointing to the tear in the skirt, she asked where to go to remove her skirt to mend it? Just at that moment, Lucinda appeared and heard what Emma was asking the maid.

"Melina, take Ms. Llewelyn up to my room and give her whatever she needs to repair her dress."

"*Si signora.*" Melina curtsied to Lucinda and motioned for Emma to follow her up the long, winding staircase.

"*Grazie, Signora* Lucinda.*" Emma followed Melina up the marble staircase to a room exactly where Dillon had identified a bedroom on his map. Emma took her skirt off in the presence of the maid who handed her the sewing materials and left.

"*Grazie, Melina.*"

Watching her close the bedroom door, she quickly checked to see if Melina returned down to the first floor hallway, Emma slipped her skirt back on. The bracelet felt warmer again—Dillon was activating the crystal! *I have twelve minutes to get in and get out of the library with three minutes as a safety net—in case…!*

311

Carefully opening the bedroom door, she listened for any noise in the upper hall—it was empty and silent.

The door at the opposite end of the hall was shut—it should be the door to the library. Taking off her shoes and tucking them into the top of her skirt, she ran barefoot down the corridor hugging the inner wall to avoid attention from the guests in the Great Room below. The heavy oak door had to lead to the library. As Lucinda promised, the door was unlocked. Feeling the recessed doorframe on the outside for any indication of sensors, she felt none—no heat, or indentations, or metal by touch. Checking her watch to set the timer—*eleven minutes*—with two minutes safety to get out! Emma slipped the glasses on; the lens would sense the lasers as soon as she opened the door. Emma had the special coins ready in her hand. Carefully opening the door not to break the laser beam's conduit, she tossed some of the grainy metallic powder from the compact in the air at the doorway.

"I count three laser beams emanating from the right side of the door jam at angles!"

Angling the coins, she methodically placed one on each laser point, all within five seconds! No evidence of an alarm! "So far so good," she said and inhaled a deep breath.

Next, Emma took the perfume spray and sprayed the contents in a wide arc over the hardwood floor, no evidence of white beams circling the room. Taking no chances, she repeated the process in a wider area—still no evidence of white beams seen in the moist particles settling slowly to the floor. Closing the door so as not to disturb the coins, she held her breath when she stepped inside the room—complete silence—no alarms—no rushing footsteps from the hall. Emma scanned the room for cameras and saw several—all darkened and without a signal they were on.

"Biaggio's done his job!"

Checking her watch—seven minutes left—she walked behind the desk. Looking around for a possible place to hide in case she needed it, she saw several places—possibly behind large chairs or behind the heavy drapes at the sides of the windows in the bay.

The library was enormously large; the ceiling was vaulted and painted with pictures of smiling renaissance cherubs. The floor-to-ceiling shelves were filled with books of all sizes; many looked like old manuscripts. Some bindings were covered in plastic to preserve them from decomposition from air and dust. The walls were paneled in dark mahogany with the exception of one wall, which had been renovated with large lead-paned windows to let in great amounts of sunlight. It was exactly as Lucinda described it! The massive mahogany desk was in front of the windows with a green shaded antique lamp set off center, casting a pool of light onto the green-leathered inlaid top. As Lucinda outlined, "Behind the desk on an historic table was a quaint box—locked." Opening the compact, Emma located the key behind the mirror and inserted it into the lock. Nothing happened! Trying not to panic, again she tried the lock. This time—a click and the lid opened! Confirming—six minutes left!

Fixing the tube of lipstick to the camera position, inside she found several handwritten books and a cache of computer discs. Choosing a diary with pages of handwritten names listed first, she began to focus and click with one hand, rapidly turning pages with the other.

*There it was!* **Emma Llewelyn—London—MacKenna**! Emma hesitated making certain she really saw it! There written in the middle of the page was her name with three symbols after it. Emma had to keep taking pictures, focusing on *her* name clearly to show the symbols. Then rapidly snapping pages until she had the whole book completely photographed. Checking the time—*three minutes left*!

The second log was written in Italian with the names of many foreign countries named in alphabetical order. Each country had a file of names listed under it—some even circled. Quickly taking pictures and turning pages as fast as she could, her wrist alarm sounded! **It was a high ping from the bracelet clasp!** Hurriedly, she returned the journals to their original position back inside the box next to the discs, closed and locked it. Running around the desk, she saw—*one minute left!* Emma had one minute to get out of the library and remove any evidence she had been there. Retrieving the laser discs within two seconds, she closed the door and turned to go back downstairs.

**"Oh no, sweet Jesus!"** Emma held her breath! Pressing herself as flat as she could against the door jam…she waited…trying to think what she must do when *he* saw *her!*

Carlos had been watching the upper hall from a position next to the hearth in the Great Room the whole time Emma was upstairs. He saw the flash of her green dress just as Emma closed the library door and immediately he started for the stairs. Ahead of him…**Marcus Rudolphi was walking up the marble staircase to the second floor!**

"Marcus, may I see you for just a minute?" Lucinda called to him from the bottom of the staircase. Nearing the top of the stairs, he heard her request and turned, slowly retreating back down the steps toward her.

**"What is it Lucinda?"** Lucinda was aware Emma was standing concealed against the library door.

"What is it my dear, that can't wait until I returned? I wanted to get some information from the library for Dr. Carruchi. What is so important that it can't wait until I find that information for Ennio?"

Taking Marcus by the arm as he reached the bottom step, Lucinda directed him towards the front door. *"The De Medici's have* just arrived and asked for you. They are some of our best contributors so we shouldn't keep them waiting. Let's see to them now." Emma could see she was leading him to the couple entering the door—latecomers!

"Has Dr. Carruchi taken care of our ill guests yet?" Marcus asked Lucinda.

"Yes, and I have seen to their needs, and they're feeling much better." Lucinda continued to embrace his arm to hold his attention as they went to greet the couple at the door. Carlos took in a deep sigh of relief as he watched the scenario play out in front of him.

Emma let out a deep sigh of relief thinking out loud, "Lucinda you were magnificent! *Grazie!*" Putting her shoes on she removed the false tear in the skirt, straightened her dress, put everything back in the purse—with a deep long breath—she started slowly descending the staircase to give the impression nothing was amiss. When in truth, she wanted to run down as fast as possible to find Carlos and Dillon. Reaching ground level Emma paused and looked to see where any commotion was taking place. Carlos saw her and walked over to put his arm around her.

"Emma, are you alright? I saw what just happened!"

"Yes, I really am fine now…if I could just stop shaking!"

"You are shaking! Here, let me get you a glass of wine." He put his arm around her waist to seat her at one of the sofas in front of the warm hearth and went to the bar for the wine.

"Is Emma alright?" the bartender asked Carlos.

"*Si*…everything's okay…just nerves!" He took the glass of wine from the bartender.

"Here drink this, it will help your nerves."

Sipping the wine, Emma inquired, "Where's Dillon?"

"He should be coming soon," Carlos replied, keeping his eyes on Emma, still trembling from her ordeal.

"I can't ask her…Was she successful locating and retrieving the information she was after in the library?" Instead, he just held her hand tightly.

"Carlos, I want you to point out Dr. Carruchi to me?" Her request alarmed him.

Hearing determination in her voice, he said, "That white-haired, good-looking man talking to Lucinda and Marcus and the other couple nearest the door, that's Dr. Ennio Carruchi."

Emma sipped the wine while observing Lucinda and Dr. Carruchi enjoy a laugh together. Just then, Dillon approached them sitting in front of the fire. As Emma rose to meet Dillon, a bartender passed in front of them carrying a tray of champagne. Emma watched him pass.

"That bartender, Carlos…the one you spoke to earlier." She suddenly grabbed Carlos's arm. "Carlos, who is that bartender carrying that tray of drinks?" she asked without delay.

"Why do you ask, Emma? Do you recognize him?"

Hesitating, she said, "I'm not certain! It's his eyes…I've seen them before—but the rest of his looks don't seem to go with the man I thought he might be…still his height and size… No, that's not possible!" she said aloud. "Did you say you knew his name Carlos?"

"No—if he's not house staff, he may be one of the caterer's employees hired to assist the house staff with the charity affair today. Did you want me to find out his name?" Carlos deliberately asked the question to give validity to his answers—He knew exactly who the man was! Emma stared at the back of the man making his way through the crowd of guests into the dining room.

"No, it's not necessary…he's probably no one I know—it can't be the man I thought it was…he's at Lyn Brienne!"

"Who did he remind you of?" Carlos asked offhandedly.

"He looked like a man who works for my grandfather from Lyn Brienne—Andrew Masters! He's worked with Papa for all the years I know…Papa relies on him to run the farm, especially when he's away on business. Since Papa's away now—Andrew must be at Lyn Brienne. It's just a coincidence! I guess I'm still jittery." Carlos knew exactly whom Emma saw—*it was Andrew Masters*—working undercover as a bartender in disguise for this party—Mac's plant to get additional information about the villa and the guests—with prime directive to look out for Emma's safety! At that moment, Dillon met up with Carlos, who was grateful to distract Emma from the bartender. She could still make him out if she saw him again!

Emma greeted Dillon. "Everything went as planned. I thought I was going to have a problem getting back downstairs without being seen, but Lucinda saw my predicament and played her role marvelously! Marcus was on his way up to the library just as I was leaving! Not to worry—I got out clean—no traces! But I think I'd like to leave," she said, slipping the lipstick into Dillon's pocket. He acknowledged it with a slight nod. Then Dillon deliberately knocked her purse out of her hand—stooping to pick it up, he motioned to her to check the contents to make certain nothing had fallen out and replaced the camera with a real tube of lipstick. If anyone was suspicious and watching them, they could search the purse; it was clean!

"I'll walk out with you, Emma," Carlos said. Instead of walking toward the door, Emma walked over to Marcus and Lucinda who were talking with Dr Ennio Carruchi. Quickly, Carlos caught up with Emma, stepping in front of her!

"Marcus, we have to leave now." Carlos approached him and handed Lucinda a donation in an envelope.

Emma was standing next to Dr. Carruchi. Marcus turned toward Emma. "Dr. Carruchi, I don't believe you've had the pleasure of meeting Ms. Emma Llewelyn from England, and her companion Mr. Dillon O'Rourke?"

"Ah *Si*…" He graciously bowed and kissed her hand. "It's a pleasure to meet such a renowned international criminal barrister—and one with such beauty! I'm sorry I did not have the opportunity to speak earlier with you tonight—I would have liked to learn about your interesting work." How was it he knew her career was in the law? She felt mesmerized by his voice and a flash of a faint memory again…

**something in the voice telling me to lie still…bright lights… the touch of his hands…medicinal odors… pain…**

"Are you alright, Ms. Llewelyn?" Dr. Carruchi asked.

"Oh, yes—yes, I'm fine." Emma was jolted back to the moment.

"Dr. Carruchi, I understand you do research. What kind of research do you do?" Emma asked.

"My field—and love—is in genetics. Specifically, I'm currently exploring specific genes in the DNA component—it's in the field of stem cell research—all very complicated, my dear. However, I will tell you there may be a cutting-edge breakthrough listed in the medical journals in the near future…with all these wonderful donations, we have made startling discoveries, and we hope to let the whole scientific community know of our findings!" He said this as if to impress her but to put an end to her questions.

"Yes, stem cell science is a complicated field in science, but very important today in the research field to identify and treat genetic diseases that have plagued the human race. I will make it a point to look up some of your published studies when I return to England. I'd like to be more knowledgeable about such important work and recent discoveries—in this area." All the while Emma spoke, Dr.

Carruchi kept his eyes riveted on her—analyzing her—trying to detect something hidden!

Dillon interrupted, "Emma, we're runnin' late now." Taking firm hold of her arm in his, he nudged her toward the door.

"Thank you for invitin' us, and I 'ope this donation will go towards that good work." Dillon handed the envelope to Marcus.

"*Grazie,* all of you for coming. I hope we can meet again in a more informal way," Marcus said, shaking hands with Dillon and Carlos.

Lucinda reached over and kissed Emma's cheek. "I'm so glad to have met you, Emma. Maybe when Marcus and I get to London, we can meet for lunch," she said casually and friendly—in a way someone would say good-bye to new friends and guests.

"I'd like that too, Lucinda." Emma moved aside to let other couples behind them leave—not allowing the awkwardness of the moment to linger.

Biaggio was at the front door waiting for them with the Mercedes.

"Em, I can't return with you to the 'otel. Carlos and I need to speak 'bout some things that can't wait. Biaggio will take you back to the Manin," Dillon said. "I'll call you when I get back to the 'otel—it may be late, but I'll call no matter the 'our." He saw her disappointment in her eyes, knowing she was excluded from this meeting.

"Never mind the hour, just call me when you're finished—from wherever you are! I'll be waiting for you when you return to the hotel—or better still, Dillon, stop by my room." Her words spoke her resentment and disappointment for being left out. Emma had some idea what Dillon and Carlos wanted—or needed to discuss, but didn't like being excluded from future plans they made. "There's no bloody way I'll not be counted in any future plans you make!" The two men heard her resolve.

"Emma, please take care! Remember Tomas is in the room next to you—if you have any trouble, just call his name—he'll hear it— got it?" Carlos squeezed her hand—"Call me...." Waving back, he made his way toward Dillon and the Gia.

Before getting into the Gia, Carlos asked, "Dillon, did you notice the way Marcus was looking at Emma all the while she was in his presence? That lascivious, lecherous look! There *is* something in Emma's past somehow connected to that man! If it takes me a lifetime—I'll find out what it is!" Dillon listened to Carlos's description of what he saw but made no comment. He agreed it was all true—there was a horrifying connection!

While waiting for Carlos, Dillon walked over to Biaggio and spoke quietly to him before returning to the Gia. Biaggio drove the Mercedes away from the villa, and Carlos pulled the Gia out behind them.

\* \* \*

"Marcus, I think our subject is beginning to remember certain things! It is imperative we get to her immediately. We cannot afford to have anything go wrong now.

Not when we're so close to our goal!"

"Ennio, do not fret! I have taken steps to have our subject in custody by the morning! She will be taken to the Villa Como laboratory. We can give her more medication." Marcus spoke determined words to Dr. Carruchi. "You must not forget Ennio… nothing is to happen to her! **She is my property**!"

"As long as you make certain she is neutralized so as not to interfere with our plans, you may have her. However, if she is a threat in any way…you know what must be done!" Dr. Carruchi spoke sternly to Marcus Rudolphi then turned and left him standing alone.

Marcus took out one of his cigarettes and lit it with the gold lighter. Inhaling deeply, he slowly let the thick smoke exhale into curls rising upward.

*"She will be neutralized-no threat! She is mine*!"

# CHAPTER THIRTY-SIX

The trip back to Milano alone gave Emma time to think.

Her thoughts were about everything that just happened at the Villa del Christianna. "I thought I'd feel better once we completed this mission! Why do I feel so down?" Seeing her name on that page in the diary sent a definite emotional chill through her. "Clearly, Marcus Rudolphi knows me!" Emma searched her memory to remember something to connect her with *that man*—failing to recall anything only intensified her panicky feelings! Recalling the memories of her first meeting with Lucinda—*doesn't seem possible it happened only a few short weeks ago! How my life has changed since that meeting!*

*I must call Peter to arrange for him to send the discs—but not to the Manin!* Thinking aloud, she said, "Just how can I to get those discs safely from London to Milano?" Biaggio interrupted Emma's concentration to let her know they had arrived back at the hotel. "Don't forget, Ms. Llewelyn, Dillon will contact you when he returns to the hotel."

"*Grazie*, Biaggio, I'll see you tomorrow." Entering the lobby, she had no messages.

During the trip back to Milano, Emma mulled an idea of how to get the discs. First, she'd change into jogging clothes, and then go for a short jog around the block, taking the opportunity to call Peter on her mobile outside the hotel.

Before entering the suite, she knocked on the door next to it. A short, bald-headed man answered. "Tomas?"

"*Si.*"

"I'm Emma Llewelyn—my suite is next door?"

"*Si*, you are returning now?" he asked.

"*Si*, but I'm going out for a jog around the block. I wanted you to know—I won't be long. Dillon is going to call me, but if I'm out when he calls, ask for a number to reach him?"

Tomas became alarmed. "No, *Signora,* I was instructed not to let you go out until Dillon returned! You mustn't go out alone *Signora!*"

"I'm only going around the block...I really need some physical exercise—I'll check in with you when I return."

"*Si*, I will get a message to Dillon. You check with me when you return!"

"Yes! I will. *Grazie.*" She unlocked her suite.

The bedding had been turned down and a clean nightgown lay out on the bed. Quickly changing into her black jogging clothes, sneakers, and cap, she grabbed the phone and keys, slipped out the door and returned to the lobby by way of the stairs. She thought it would be better if she exited from one of the lounge doors out to the street, not to arouse attention if anyone was watching in the lobby.

"I have no choice—I have to call Peter from my mobile phone outside of the hotel." Crossing the street, Emma started jogging toward the entrance into the gardens. Running about quarter of a kilometer inside along the garden path, she came to an isolated bench and sat down. Taking out the phone, Emma dialed Peter's cell number in London.

\* \* \*

Tomas dialed a direct line, "This is Tomas! I need to speak with Carlos—*Pronto!* Is he there with you?"

"Carlos—it's Tomas." Giving Carlos the phone, he said, "Tomas sounds like something's happened!"

Carlos took the phone, "*Si*, what's up?"

"She's gone out by herself."

"What! Why the hell did you let her do that?'

"Carlos…I told her she was to remain in the hotel until Dillon returned, but she said she wanted to take a short jog around the block. I saw her enter the garden grounds across the street alone. Carlos, she's a woman with her own mind! You did not tell me to use physical force—if necessary! Nothing I said would stop her!" Carlos turned to Dillon and relayed the information. "It's Tomas. Emma's gone out alone for a jog despite our warning to her! In the gardens alone, no less!"

"Christ—what the bloody 'ell is she thinkin'?" Dillon said, jumping up from the chair. Just then, Cyrus walked into the conference room and saw Carlos on the phone.

"Who's calling?"

"It's Tomas! He wasn't able to keep Emma in the hotel…She went out alone for a jog around the gardens! Alone!"

"Bloody Christ, get back there and find her! Call Biaggio and tell him to get to the gardens with a few men to find her and watch her—don't intercept—just make certain she gets back to the hotel safely! Tell Biaggio he's to keep a few men on her at all times from now on! She's never to be out of their sight! And I don't care if she knows it!" Carlos called Biaggio while Dillon spoke to Cyrus.

Cyrus turned to see Dillon standing confrontationally in front of him, and the two men looked at one another for several seconds without speaking.

"It's been a 'ell of a long time, Cyrus. But this ain't the time to get caught up! I'm leavin' for the 'otel now to find Emma." Heading out of the room, he called back to Cyrus. Abruptly stopping at the conference room door, Dillon said, "I gave the camera to Andy— 'e's developin' in the lab now, as we speak. It's all the information we found at the villa, along with photos I took of their guests at this charit' gig." Carlos was still on the phone speaking to Biaggio when Dillon walked out of the central station.

"Wait Dillon!" Cyrus called out. "Before you go, do you have those pictures you took of the Rudolphi winery, the estate, and the ones from Perugia?"

"Yeah, th're 'ere," he said and handed Cyrus the folder of pictures.

"Leave these with me and get back to the hotel and find Emma!" Cyrus commanded. **"You call me if there's a problem—you hear? Any problem at all and I want to know about it immediately!"**

"Carlos, pick yur car up tomorr'w." Dillon left central station and drove Carlos's Gia back to the Manin "The same old, Mac!" Dillon remarked to himself.

\* \* \*

Emma jogged around the perimeter of the gardens along the Via d Manin and entered one of the open gates across the street from the Manin. Glad not many people were on the street tonight, she ran down a pedestrian path deeper into the gardens toward an empty bench and slowed up to sit down and make her call. Here, she'd have the privacy to speak with Peter. Knowing it was hours earlier in London, she let the phone ring several times longer. He should be home…

"Hello?"

"Peter, this is Emma."

"How are things going there?" Peter asked.

"Actually good, Peter! We may have found one piece of information we came here for; however, there could be complications—which I can't go into right now. Peter, I need to have the discs sent to me here in Milano! But I'm afraid they could get lost in the mail or someone could intercept my mail here if they learn you're sending them to me. I think I found a way to get them delivered into my hands personally."

"How do we do that?" Peter asked.

"I want you to ask Olivia if Hilly can fly to Milano to bring me the discs—refer to them as Italian Rules of Procedure. Tell Liv I need her for just one day! She can return to London later that same day."

"Emma, I could do that!"

"Yes, I know, Peter, but I need you to remain in the office to keep an eye on things there…to appear as if things are routine there in London while I'm in Milano. Your absence along with mine may tip someone that you could be a courier for me—they'll be less likely to question Hilly's absence. And besides, no one else knows the real reason why the firm was burgled and how to stay on top of that except you! No, I need you there to continue to monitor that situation."

"That is the more sensible thing," Peter remarked.

"I need Liv to spare Hilly for one day. Can you do whatever needs to be done in Hilly's absence for one day? Ask Hilly if her passport is up-to-date. Get tickets for flights directly to and from Milano Internationale Airport in her real name—do not make them from the office. When she arrives here, I will have a man at the airport to meet her. His name is Biaggio, and he'll meet her posing as a limousine driver appearing to pick her up as a tourist. Biaggio will have a name card reading **'BRIENNE,'** and he'll be wearing a white tie on a black shirt!" Hilly is to answer, **'GRAY' in a sentence**—and then she'll give him the discs! Biaggio will drive her to a safe place until it's time for her flight back to London—at which time, he'll make certain she is safely on the return plane. Do you understand, Peter?"

"Yes, I've written all your instructions in my own shorthand language. I'll get right on it when I hang up."

"Tell Liv I'll owe her big time!" Emma looked around thinking she heard something…someone was approaching and her internal alarm signaled caution. Hurriedly she said, "When you know the flight information, call me on my cell phone and just tell me day, time, and airline."

"Understood, I should have that information for you by tomorrow morning," Peter said. There was a long pause on the line. "Are you still there, Emma?" Peter asked.

Emma was intent on listening to some nearby strange sound…a noise coming from the thicket directly behind the bench.

"Peter, I have to go now!" Quickly, she disconnected the call.

Sensing something was wrong, Emma looked around but saw no one in sight. Her internal alarm told her someone was behind her, and she had to get out of the gardens as fast as she could. Leaving the bench, Emma started jogging again, only faster, changing directions down the path off to a grassy area to a thicket of bushes to confuse any pursuer.

Looking back, she thought, *Someone is definitely behind me!* She heard heavy footsteps behind her, this time running down the gravel path. She left the path toward a darker area…running faster! Focusing on finding an exit out of the gardens, she thought, *If I continue in this direction, I should see the exit out to the street!* Deciding to detour again across the path through the grass and flowerbeds, she hoped changing directions would confuse her pursuer—all the while, she kept glancing behind her but still no one in sight!

In a moment's flash, a figure of a man rushed out from behind the bushes, grabbing her in a powerful, vice-like hold around her chest and arms, dragging her back deeper into the gardens. Muffling her screams with his hand across her mouth, he kept her off balance while dragging her away from the lighted pedestrian paths. Emma fought him with all her strength. He kept lifting and carrying her off deeper into the bushes, his vice-like grip tightened.

*Can't breathe…Can't break away! Oh, God, please help me…got to get him off balance!*

With feelings of terror overtaking her, she kept struggling with her attacker and shifted her weight forward—forcing him to stop to get a better hold on her. In that instant, she took advantage of his hesitation and hooked her foot around behind his knee causing him to buckle and trip. Both of them fell to the ground. Quickly breaking out of his grip, she rolled away from him as fast as she could. He kept grabbing at her…trying to reach her! A few inches away—yet far enough to elude his outstretched hands trying to grab hold, she got up on her own and darted into the shrubbery leaving him awkwardly trying to flee after her. In a flash, she saw his face.

"Oh, Jesus! It's him!"

Reaching a heavy thicket of bushes, she quietly knelt inside the wood to hide in the darkest part of the copse. For fear he would hear her breathe, Emma panted in short shallow breaths—not to give her position away. Her lungs felt like they would burst! Every sense in her body was on guard—trying to listen to where *he* was in the gardens.

"I have to keep moving…Can't just wait here!"

Ever so slowly, Emma started crawling on the ground to blend in with the blackness of the night, still not knowing exactly where her assailant was in the gardens. Muffled voices were getting closer! Suddenly, flattening herself on the ground, there a few feet away, directly in front of her—two sets of boots—one pair were heavy lug-soled boots!

"Oh, my God, there's two of them searching for me!"

"*Questa maniera!* She's this way!" one of them cried out, as the noise from crashing bushes and thunderous footsteps came in her direction.

Instinct told Emma to move. Seeing an opening in the thick shrubbery just ahead, she got up and ran as fast as she could. The thick, thorny shrubs tore at her clothes and face as she forced herself through the heavy undergrowth losing her cap in the shrubbery, crouching low. The spiny thicket caught her hair in a tangled grip holding her back, making it harder for her to move swiftly. Again, flattening herself on the ground, listening for the running footsteps, she knew she was vulnerable if she stayed in any one spot too long. She kept searching—listening for street noises and honking car horns—for the nearest exit.

"*Li e laggiu!*" One yelled.

"*Ll Cristo, non lascia la sua portala l'uscital!*" The other voice yelled back.

"*Lei va giustamente dirigerla via da da raggiungere la strada! L'afferrero se viene questa maniera! L'automobile e all'uscita di Manin!*" Emma heard their commands to each other and knew they were splitting up to catch her and take her to their car.

"*Oh God! No! Please no!*" she softly cried out.

# CHAPTER THIRTY-SEVEN

"Please God, no!" she said, fighting back tears!

Emma tried to stay hidden from the men, but kept stumbling forcing herself to scramble to stay on her feet. While running as fast as she could—without warning an arm grabbed her around the waist and a hand went over her mouth to muffle her screams, holding her in a tight grip while pulling her down to the ground. Fiercely fighting back with all her might, they rolled on the ground until she couldn't move.

"Shhh—it's me, Dillon! Stay quiet!"

Looking into her eyes, Dillon saw her terror and fear as she looked up at him with tears spilling out. Feeling her whole body relax under his, he whispered, "When I say run—get up and run with me towards the hotel in that direction." He pointed to a path close to street noises. Emma nodded she understood. Dillon took a firm hold of Emma's hand and with his knife in the other, he waited for the exact second to make their move. The street exit was less than a quarter of a kilometer from their position.

**"Now, Em! Run! Run!"**

The two men were still heard crashing behind them and getting closer. With a tight grasp on Emma, Dillon pulled her up, as they ran through the flowerbeds toward the hotel and the bright street lights. Both heard the pounding of footsteps behind them coming closer. Reaching the exit from the gardens, Dillon abruptly stopped and pushed Emma out of the entrance, calling softly to her, **"Run**

**to the neares' 'otel entrance and get inside and go up to the lobby, girl—wait there for me in the lobby!"** For a split second he watched Emma run toward the hotel. No one was following her.

Detouring stealthily back inside the gardens towards the sounds of running footsteps, he took his gun out of the holster and in a split second screwed the silencer onto the barrel. Dillon heard the oncoming heavy thuds made by lug-soled shoes reach his concealed position. Without any hesitation, never taking his eyes off the sight unfolding—the sounds of swearing were clear and loud coming from the crashing bushes in front of him.

Crouched low, he waited for the approaching thundering footsteps to reach him… he met him face-to-face…a gaze into his shocked eyes…then with one deep gasp…there was a final thud to the ground! *He saw his executioner.*

*SILENCE.*

Without looking back, Emma ran to the nearest lounge door and went inside, panting and breathless. Her loud breathing caused a few heads to turn towards her, while she tried to modulate her loud, heavy breathing. Seeing the jogging clothes, the patrons probably thought she had just finished a good exercise workout, which was the truth—and more. She tried to walk slowly through the lounge out to the lobby to wait for Dillon in an inconspicuous corner of the lobby. It seemed interminably long-waiting. Nearly thirty minutes later, he walked through the front door. Together, they headed for the lift without speaking.

"They won't give you any more trouble, Em," Dillon said pressing the third floor button. Dillon had his usual calmness about him—arms folded across his chest and casually leaning on to the side like nothing had just happened, but his eyes betrayed his real anger. Tomas heard the lift door open and came out of his room.

"No problem, Tomas, we're back safe. Thanks for the call." Dillon tipped his cap to him. Tomas acknowledged Dillon's cue and returned inside. Entering the suite, Dillon locked the door. Emma felt the tears welling up with such relief, but knew she couldn't cry, not in front of Dillon!"

Dillon started pacing. He pointed his finger at her in admonishment for what she had done, while trying to control and hide his extreme concern for what he just encountered.

"What the blood' 'ell were you doin' out in that garden by yur'self, girl?" The ringing phone interrupted his angry tirade.

**"Si, pronto", Emma said.**

**"Emma, its Carlos! Are you all right? I was worried about you when I heard you had gone out alone!"**

**"No...yes! Carlos, I'm okay...now."**

**"Is Dillon with you?"**

**"Yes—he's here."**

**"Put him on the phone?"**

**Emma handed the phone to Dillon and walked into the bathroom to throw cold water on her face and clean up the cuts and bruises on her face and hands. Still trembling from the ordeal, Emma hoped Dillon didn't recognize just how terrified she still felt about what happened back there. She had all she could do to hold back her loud sobs of relief. Staring in the mirror at the dirt and blood on her face, the tears came slowly spilling down her face...her body quietly shaking.**

"Any trouble?"

"Just two—'old on a second." Dillon reached under the nightstand to remove the small disc and dropped it in the glass of water on the stand.

"Yeah! I recognized one as the man Emma described today as the 'odd-looking waiter'—Tony Davici. The other bloke—never saw 'im before. The *Policia* will find both men—Davici's got an extra eye now—''e's dead—the second's dead or unconscious...seriousl' wounded with a cut of a knife! An anonymous caller contacted the *Policia* about the attack in the park—didn't mention who was attacked or what they'd find! I 'eard sirens arrive as I got back 'ere. Since we know Davici was working for Marcus, we can assume 'e—or 'is partners—are tryin' to get 'er! Why Carlos? Why?" Dillon tried to contain his anxiety in low tones to Carlos with Emma in the bathroom.

"Not now, Dillon—not with Emma listening. WE," he said— emphasizing the "we" meant Cyrus was listening—"need to set up a meet now! Biaggio is on his way to the hotel with some men. He'll keep a constant guard around the hotel's perimeter from now on—at least until Emma and you check out! The decision is made…Emma is to go with Biaggio tonight and stay with Sienna at the house. You and Biaggio are to meet us in one hour at the Via Lorenzo—the English Bookstore and bring all the maps you made with you of the estate. Biaggio knows the address. This phone line is scrambled here, but don't say anything on your end—not certain it's clean there. Just tell Emma no luggage—just an overnight bag with essentials. *Caio*."

When Emma heard Dillon hang up the phone, she came out of the bathroom. "You're still very angry with me…" She saw Dillon pace about the room shaking his head, trying to calm down—deliberately keeping his silence. Emma surmised he and Carlos made plans for tonight, intentionally speaking in low tones to keep her from hearing their conversation.

"What's to happen now?" Emma asked, while cleaning her wounds with a towel.

"Em, we're invited to stay with friends tonight—just take yur small bag with a few things—nothin' fanc'–just what yur' wearin' and one change of clothes. Yur ride is on the way."

"What ride?"

"We'll talk on the way down," he told her. Dillon handed Emma her handbag and briefcase. Emma quickly grabbed a few personal things and threw them into the small overnight case. Messing up the bed to appear as if she had slept in it, even throwing her nightgown on the chair, Dillon added a few more touches to the room to make it appear she spent the night there. They took the stairs down to the ground floor and went out a service entrance. A short distance away, Biaggio met them and pointed to a car parked at the end of the alley. Dillon firmly gripped Emma's arm as they walked toward the car.

"I'm not going to bolt!"

"Em, I want you safe and sound in Biaggio's place tonight!"

Prying away from Dillon's grasp, Emma asked. "Dillon, why did those two men grab me? Do you think it was a prearranged attack—or—a random abduction?"

"Is it possible Marcus Rudolphi had anything to do with it?" Her tears still ready to burst out at the thought of what could have happened...and didn't!

Dillon stopped dead in his tracks. "Em, either way—yur in danger—no matter who's behind it! From now on, I'm yur shadow, 'ear?" he said, in tones of admonishment. Then, softly, in the next breath, he added, "I'm goin' to stay closer to you than the skin on yur prett' backside!" Sliding into the seat of the car, he followed and sat next to her.

"I appreciate your concern...don't think I'm not grateful, Dillon! You put your life on the line for me tonight! Thanks...doesn't say enough...but thank you, dear friend."

"Can never stay mad at you, girl! You'll be safe with Sienna and the children tonight. I 'ave business needin' attendin' tonight—need to find answers for us." Emma knew Dillon was right! He could get answers for them without her tagging along tonight.

"But dammit, Dillon, it's MY life—so don't count me out in your plans in this case!" Her anger was out there for not being included in their earlier meeting after the charity party. The ride back to Biaggio's was in silence. *Tomorrow will bring many more answers for me! Emma swore to herself!*

Sienna was waiting with the older children, watching the telly. Dillon turned to her. "Em, I 'ave to find out why someone wants you—but I need to know yur' safe for now. Tonight showed us someone is willin' to go to great lengths to get you! When I know why—yu'll know! Stay with Sienna. PROMISE ME?"

Looking straight at him, she said, "Yes, I promise! When will you return?"

"Plan on Carlos or me pickin' you up in the mornin'."

Sienna came over to Emma, and in her tender way, put her arms around her. *"Lei vienne, Signorina. Avanit. Si accomodi, prego."*

\* \* \*

"Biaggio, we go to *Via Lorenzo*—to the bookstore." Biaggio knew the route to the English Bookstore as well as every back alley in Milano. It was his nature not to take anything or anyone for granted...which is why he was constantly checking and detouring whenever he was on assignment. Biaggio was the best at finding a tracker inside a vehicle—tonight, they were clean.

From the outside, the English Bookstore was dark. Driving down the small alley next to the shoppe, Biaggio dimmed his lights and parked behind a black sedan in the rear courtyard. A single dim light lit up a rear door with a keypad next to it. A green light flashed when Biaggio completed entering the code and the door unlatched automatically.

Walking up to the second floor to a double door, Biaggio said, "*Due di entrare*—a light flashed, exposing a lens taking a photograph of them. Again, the door swung open. They walked into a room filled with a large table, walls covered with maps, and computer stations set-up—it was a command Central station. The equipment was expensive, sophisticated and a number of men and women sat in front of the monitors with earphones, busily entering data on keyboards.

"What happened in the park?" Cyrus asked Dillon with his usual directness.

"Nice to see you, too, Cyrus! I found her runnin' from two men—one I recognized from Emma's earlier description as Tony Davici whose last known employer was Marcus Rudolphi! The other one I didn't recognize—but they're both inactive now. I'm certain I terminated Davici…permanentl'—no way he can recover from his 'ead wound…Good riddance to that bit of scum! The other man reached a car before I could nail him…permanentl'. My knife met its mark in the solar plexus…'e'll bleed out before 'elp arrives. Either way, they'll be not give' us any more problems! They're both dead—the *Policia* will find 'hem in the garden's drive…I didn't see an'one else in the car or aware there was backup for 'hem." Dillon deliberately turned and faced Cyrus, putting his hands on his hips in a stance of direct confrontation. He would have answers to his questions!

"Cyrus…who the 'ell is chasin' Emma? Why does someone want her so badl' to kidnap her? Tell me why she's important to 'hem and just where the 'ell were they goin' to take her?"

Cyrus didn't answer Dillon's questions immediately; instead, he turned and walked to a glassed-in conference room off the main station, signaling Dillon to follow. Carlos was already in the room studying maps spread out on the table. Closing the door, Cyrus stated, "This room is soundproof and safe. We keep anti-surveillance devices in here blockin' outside attempts... In addition, we do daily sweeps of the shoppe below and all the floors and rooms in abuttin' buildin's for new plants...so we know we're clean at all times. Maybe now, I can answer some of your questions, Dillon. I need to start at the beginning to bring you up-to-date—which is what I expect from you when I'm finished!" Cyrus sat down at the head of the conference table as would a teacher facing his pupils.

"I'm not sure you're aware of the scope and gravity of this assignment. This case is about an organization of international proportions. I think of it as a giant octopus with its tentacles reaching out to every part of the globe. What we've been trying to figure out is: *where is the goddamn head of this beast located?*" Cyrus felt it was time for complete honesty—this man was entitled to that much!

"I know you're aware I've been involved with Interpol for the past twenty-five years in a secretive capacity. Emma has *never* had any idea about my work with international crime! She thinks all my trips away from the farm are solely for the business of horses and the farm. *AND THAT'S WHAT I WANT HER TO GO ON THINKING!*" Cyrus loudly commanded and continued with his story. The men were all seated at the conference table ready to listen.

"After you left MI-5, Dillon, we knew you never gave up looking for Maura and Siobhan." Cyrus's voice softened, and he looked Dillon directly in the eye.

"For years, we've had more than a suspicion that international kidnappings were on the increase in many countries—somehow all connected. *But we could never find the common link between them*—until...until we put out questionnaires to as many countries as we knew had kidnappings on the increase. We wanted to form a database of information to pool our resources to see all the similar denominators between the crimes. We got a lot of cooperation from many countries and the process took us a year! Interpol created a central computer program, and a database called 'XYZ,' After we entered the names of every kidnapped person—men, women, and children—from all the cooperating countries, it compared the similiarties of the kidnappings by points. Eventually, category points common to each case gave us a decisive insight into a possibility that a well-systemized organization could be behind *all these kidnappings!* The one dissimilar factor was the reason for diverse ethnic backgrounds of the victims. Then...we realized that the global kidnappings were possibly planned to deliberately get multi-cultural victims! Still no reason *why!* When the list was assembled, I remembered your wife and daughter—and asked myself—'were they victims of this organization, too?' I had no concrete information to say for certain—except the manner of their disappearance was similar to other victims. I entered Maura's and Siobhan's names into XYZ database for unexplained abductions—initially nothing concrete came up. When we kept reviewing all the entries' names, we found a later entry date...a name...Siobhan O. But no Maura O'Rourke. Coincidence?"

Dillon cut off Cyrus's explanation. "First, Mac, I want to know more about the Chatelaine Case? Is it connected to this assignment?"

"The Chatelaine case is a case that came to trial in Italia about three years ago! When that case broke, we thought we had a breakthrough with the information we got out of the defendants about the kidnappings! What facts we did learn were speculative and unproven facts—circumstantial but relative to kidnappings in general. In the Chatelaine case, there was enough evidence to take the defendants to trial, but as you know, ALL the defendants disappeared in the middle of the trial and were never found. That's because we're almost certain they had to be silenced...most likely they're all dead and buried in the mountains across the border in Switzerland. By the way, that case is still open because some of the prosecutors died suspiciously when the trial ended!" Cyrus got up and retrieved a large thick file from a cabinet and sat back down.

"To answer your next question...yes, I think the Chatelaine case is connected to our present case. About one year ago, we got a break when we found two children fitting a description of two children kidnapped in Germany. It came about by a chance meeting with a French couple by one of our operatives when he read an article in a Paris newspaper depicting a family of four selected by a French minister for an award for working with Olympic contestants that year. The French couple arranged for Olympians to live in private homes during the games. Part of this operative's assignment was to find and follow all leads associated with these two specific missing German children. Imagine his chagrin when he saw their pictures in a French newspaper with the names of French parents! He made it his business to get to know the family well. The children were both fair and blond...the newspaper picture showed their parents dark-haired, even Spanish-looking," he said, pointing to an enlarged photograph. "We knew it was always a possibility they could have been adopted! We ran a thorough background check on the children, tracing them back to their birth. What we found were a lot of discrepancies in both their French birth records; in fact, we verified the real documents were changed to duplicate birth records with some factual differences. Unfortunately for us, the hospital with the original birth copies suffered a fire in the medical records department and therefore, no documentary proof of birth was ever confirmed. Most likely the fire was deliberate!" Cyrus was most credible in his presentation of the precise facts.

"The German children were fingerprinted when they started in school in Paris and we obtained copies of those prints. The prints were a perfect match with the two children who were abducted from Essen, Germany two years earlier. To make absolutely certain, we obtained DNA samples from the children's clothes we confiscated and compared this data from the German couple who lost their children—a perfect match!" Carlos spread out some of the files on the table for Dillon to see.

"Once we learned the truth about these children, we kept close surveillance on all of their activities and the whereabouts of these children and their French parents—hoping this was the lead we needed to find the source and reason for their abduction!"

Carlos interjected into Cyrus's story, "One day, the entire French family disappeared! All of them gone! We questioned everyone who knew them but came up empty. The story given was that the family left on a planned holiday—but never returned! Their home was placed for sale at their request when they left, and money from the sale of the house was placed in a bank account. We froze that account…waiting for someone to access it. The money is still there," Cyrus recounted.

"We don't know the fate of those children or the family!" Cyrus's voice changed.

"I suspect they are all dead—or worse!"

"Another dead end!" Carlos echoed.

"What do you mean dead-or worse? What does this 'ave to do with Em's abduction tonight?" Dillon asked.

Cyrus didn't want to answer Dillon's questions. Carlos spoke up.

"We finished developing the film Emma took of the files in Marcus Rudolphi's library and fed the names on *his* lists into XYZ database for cross references and other information. Many names on the lists she photographed appear to match names of people in XYZ lists who are missing still—kidnap victims! There could be as many as a couple of hundred names on those lists matching names of kidnapped victims over the past two to three years!"

"The names of the two German children who were abducted?" Dillon asked.

"We found their names on the lists Emma found!" Carlos knew what Dillon's reaction would be and where his thoughts were going.

"This definitely ties Marcus Rudolphi in with international kidnappings!" Cyrus said.

"Why? What's 'is reason for doing this?" Dillon bellowed out in frustration.

Carlos interrupted, not waiting for Cyrus to answer. "Dillon, I have big questions, too! What are *your* suspicions…or…have *you* learned any reason why Emma's name is on that Rudolphi list with names of people who have disappeared?" Carlos asked him in irritation.

"I 'aven't a clue. It scares me to ask this: Is there any way… that at some time…she was part of their kidnappin's? The research they're doin'—needin' a lot of different people…'Ow could Emma fit that picture?" Dillon asked, looking first to Cyrus and then to Carlos.

Cyrus was standing with his back to the two men looking out into the control station. Carlos knew he was trying to hold it together.

"Or does one of 'er cases 'ave information—maybe facts she's not aware of—that ties 'em to some kind of international crime ring?" Cyrus considered both of these facts many times, but never voiced the words out loud—until he heard Dillon say them. It unnerved him!

"Mac, did you find Maura's and Siobhan's names on the list in Marcus's study?" Dillon asked directly and calmly.

"We think we did," he said hesitantly and turned to look for Dillon's reaction.

"In Marcus's lists we found an entry, 'Maura O/S'…not certain what the symbols after that name means. We're still trying to decipher the meaning of the symbols after each name. The names have coded symbols next to them—some in different colored inks. There's no key in the photographs telling us what the symbols mean."

Without speaking, Dillon rose and stood looking out the glass wall into the control room—seeing only his own reflection. His thoughts were about how his family may be victims of these heinous schemes. In a low, controlled voice, he said, "If I do nothin' else in me life…for the rest of me life…I mean to find out the truth 'bout me famil'! I want justice—no revenge! An eye for an eye…!" He turned back towards the two men seated and walked back to the conference table and sat down again. "Go on, there's more to hear, I know!"

Cyrus continued, "We think the names are grouped together, possibly according to countries—or ages—or backgrounds, but that's not completely clear either. Cryptographers are trying to decipher the meaning of the symbols as we speak. There could be some other meaning for a common category or grouping, which we haven't discovered yet."

"Where does all this lead to, Cyrus?" Dillon asked quietly.

"Dillon, this case is technically very complex, and all of us involved have had a crash course in human physiology and genetics to understand why the kidnappings and what probable experimentation they're doing to them. We know there are rogue scientists experimenting in illegal areas—eager to be the first and to

337

get that recognition. How they fit into the international kidnapping cases...this is the big question mark to us! We don't know *where* all their experimentation is done or *what* the exact kind of research is that they're doing...but we're sure they're here—*in Milano!* To understand those questions you've just asked, it's necessary to understand this new criminal element today!" Cyrus undertook to give Dillon a thumbnail sketch of what they were all up against.

"We first started tracking basic kidnapping crimes reported in Central Europe. What raised the 'red flags' was the number of increased widespread kidnappings in many countries at the same time...where prior kidnapping numbers were not usually high—like small countries. This was our first tip-off something bigger was happening! Our agents discovered many of these kidnappings were not for ransom or used as exchange agents. If you'll hear me out, I'll try and tell you exactly what we're up against in a manner meaningful to you. You've been out of the field for some time now, and there's a new level of criminal en masse we've never encountered in the past! The proportions of this element alone are staggering!" Cyrus commanded the complete attention of the men sitting opposite him.

Dillon rose, started pacing in the room, and asked Cyrus again... Only this time, his questions had greater urgency to it.

*"Does this case 'ave somethin' to do with me missin' wife and daughter? Does it 'ave somethin' to do with Emma?"*

# CHAPTER THIRTY-EIGHT

Cyrus knew Dillon needed to know everything. He could hold nothing back.

"Let me start at the beginning...if I'm to answer your two important questions. Sit down, Dillon, there's something you need to understand before we go anywhere with this case...and before I can honestly answer your first question!" Cyrus wanted Dillon calm to observe his demeanor as he instructed him in certain basic case facts.

"We think these abductions were well planned and for a specific reason—you even mentioned the word 'research' in one of your questions! There is one distinguished researcher we know who has very close connections to the Rudolphis! He's **Dr. Ennio Carruchi!** We've had him under surveillance for over two years now—trying to learn about his research...his subjects, and the location of his laboratories. For certain, Carruchi brags about his successes in stem cell research, which is what this case is about! It's taken us two years, but now we're almost certain there's a place closeby—a laboratory—where he does his work—so well hidden he doesn't have to worry about discovery! Ask yourself! What better place to hide his work than in the midst of local, political, and even the international community right in his own backyard— **In an international wine business owned and managed by an established wealthy family—as his front! Who and what law agency would question the integrity of such a respected family**

**to be involved with something illegal? He hasn't even raised the curiosity of the local police!"** While clarifying the details of the project, Cyrus was pacing the room in an animated manner, and then he walked to a filing cabinet to retrieve a thick folder.

"This is just one of the smaller files we've accumulated on this case—there's stacks of cabinets filled with files on this case that fills a room. We think Marcus Rudolphi—and possibly his father, Giuseppe—and without a doubt, his other sons, Dominic and Luigi—are all some of the big backers for Carruchi's work. We know there's a demand for stem cell research all over the world. There are those questionable scientist's who'll agree to do any research—if the money is there to do it—as well as substantial gratutites for themselves. Information from legitimate researchers instructed us just what's goin' on out there—to give us a better understanding what we're up against—how advances in genetics today depends on a continual source of stem cell material to effectively find credible results. If geneticists did have just such a reliable source of materials for their research, think of what they could do to make remarkable advances in science! Theoretically, the market could be controlled by a single supplier to these prosperous biotechnical laboratories and pharmaceutical companies throughout the world needing this kind of cell material. In legitimate research there is an ongoing search to discover medical remedies for the world's diseases, and they *do use* stem cells in their research—it's a well-known fact today! *But...imagine...*what if the source of the stem cells comes from a *diverse cell bank...*think of the millions of dollars legitimate companies would pay to get this *diverse source of cell material*! A supplier has the potential to make billions—especially, if they think the source is legitimate! Billions of dollars is up for grabs! But let me take a step back."

"Is that what we're facin' 'ere, Mac?" Dillon posed to him, "getting' a pool of donors?" Cyrus cast his eyes down not wanting to answer his queston yet, and raised his hand to stop Dillon from asking more questions.

"To know your enemy, Dillon, it's vital you understand him...and know how dedicated he is!" Cyrus took a few seconds to connect with the two men seated across from him with a strong gaze into each of their eyes.

"Stem cells are liken to a master living cell that has the potential to become any kind of human tissue in the body, and today, this material is the hottest thing in medical research—a cutting edge! Presently, the main source of stem cells comes from embryonic tissue—either from aborted fetuses or fertilized embryos. In the latter case, if a laboratory is successful growing the fertilized egg, called a zygote at this stage, allowing it to grow into the pluripotent cell, you have the source for extracting unknown amounts of stem cells from that fertilized egg. Now, multiply this process performed with millions of different donor eggs, you have an endless supply of cell tissue for future stem cell research projects. Companies and research laboratories will pay handsomely to purchase a never-ending supply—to beat out the other guy and find some cure! Doesn't matter if it was done reputably or not! Simply a turn of the head to shun knowing how they got it. *It's all driven for money!*"

The two men listened intently to a story of how criminal, immoral, and illicit schemes are possible in the minds of twisted psychopathic men! Carlos already knew some of the facts Cyrus was telling them, but now he appreciated learning more since it hit home—with Emma—and it became totally personal for him.

Cyrus continued, "This theory of harvesting stem cells isn't all that new. At one time, scientists tried a method, called parthogenesis, translated, it means virgin origin in Greek—to trick an unfertilized egg into thinking it was fertilized. That process was partially successful and has been tried in many animal groups. The next step was to take it to the human level of experimentation! It failed!" Cyrus paused here to make sure he had the absolute attention of his audience.

"The legitimate scientific community substantiates there are rogue scientists using human ova—not from aborted embryonic tissue—but from fresh human ova and fertilize them…and at the exact time…harvest tissue for stem cells from these human tissues! The rumor is these human ova are harvested from the very young… and old women…the latter seems improbable but the evidence is there! Since the stem cell has the proclivity to become any kind of tissue in the human body, the geneticist can program—or alter—the cell to function differently. He has the potential to change the **DNA structure.** In plain words, *make the cell's function different from what it was originally programmed to do*! When it becomes new parent tissue—**the scientist can take it a step further and make changes to the chromosomes in the cell...permanently**!" Here Cyrus paused to see if his listeners comprehended what he was telling them. "Do you understand what I'm saying?" Looking for questions, neither man said anything.

"In legitimate research, the results of alterning DNA chromosome sets, using human ova, has not been done or published. Worldwide, it's commonplace medicine to treat certain cancers with stem cell transplants, but *these cells haven't been genetically altered*!" All three men were communicating in nonverbal ways—taking in the gigantic nature of the facts.

"If someone did achieve this breakthrough—and modify a DNA gene in a cell—many things can happen. *It's unexplored territory.* Without controlled experimentation, the exact outcome from a genetically altered gene is completely unknown. There's no way of knowing what would happen if this altered DNA cell is introduced into our human species into a new embryo...what would result! There's speculation that if the altered gene was done in a fertilized embryo...possible it could be the beginning of a new species!" Cyrus paused. "I hesitate to think what could happen! Geneticists have no idea what the end result would be, even in the best legitimate controlled experimentation—*what kind of new human species would evolve.*" Silence hung heavily throughout the conference room among the three men.

"Right now banks of stem cells are entirely under the control of private enterprises all over the world. Most governments are without laws to prevent or control the source of stem cells or what kind of research is done with these cells. There is always the potential for the criminal element to do this kind of research for a destructive evil use—terrorists doing it for biological warfare—is one example! This issue is a monumental threat to mankind—as we know it today. If illegal stem cell research is not properly controlled, there's no way to know what the consequences will be! Some countries have *a few* laws governing research, but they're the major powers...many smaller countries have *no* controls on research or experimentaion! **Except...if someone breaks a law to accomplish a scientific purpose-purportrating a crime.**" Neither man interrupted Cyrus's explanation.

"I know that one single stem cell today sells for around twenty-five thousand dollars on the legitimate market...double that on the black market who may have a bigger supply...There's the potential for making billions of dollars here! Gentlemen, *we have us a new class of criminals!*"

"How long does it take to get a big supply of these cells?" Dillon queried.

"That's a very good question. An embryo is grown in the laboratory...on the fourth day of fertilization it reaches the stage where it is called a blastocyst—it's a mass of raw, vague cells that will eventually grow into different kinds of tissue in the body. Researchers harvest the inner portion of the blastocyst, grow the harvested cells, and treat them in a way to program them to become a specific type of tissue the researcher wants. This characteristic of stem cells to divide indefinitely into different kinds of tissue is called **pluripotent**—possessing the ability to become any kind of cell in the body – a source of stem cells. **When stem cells are harvested from the living embryo, it dies—that's the ethical storm...not a prosecutable criminal act!** But to answer your question, Dillon, not long at all."

Here Cyrus's posture changed as he rose tall to continue his instruction. "Here's where we think the criminality lies in our case! If someone wanted to widen the cell families to maximize the most diverse bank of stem cells, what better way than to get an unlimited source of tissue from different ethnic races and cultures—kidnap men and women—take what they wanted from them—use a memory drug on them to inhibit their memory—and maybe, *just maybe*, return them back home to live out their lives! They'd never know what happened to them—unless the memory drug became ineffective at some time! No one would be the wiser to learn a deviant psycho madman performed a form of rape on these innocents—did criminal acts on human bodies as well as with their minds! It's conceivable they had failures! What did they do with these failures? Throw them away?" Cyrus's demeanor changed, hearing his words spoken first in anger change to compassion.

"In legitimate stem cell experimentation, scientists have studied how modification of our DNA code could affect an organism to alter or destroy disease-causing organisms…They do this without human trials in the early stages. **No legitimate researcher has documented that a human being was involved to test an unpredictable outcome!**" Cyrus calculatingly waited for a comment from Dillon or Carlos.

"Yur sayin' this case is 'bout human research…not knowin' 'ow much success or failures they've 'ad…to make money?"

"**I believe the money is no longer their prime purpose, Dillon I believe there is another goal…one goal beyond belief!** My most recent contact with reputable genetic scientists around the world thinks that's what's happening in our own backyard—underground research experimentation and human trial experimentation! Medical research pirating is not new. But our information over the past two years points to *Dr. Ennio Carruchi* as the mastermind…here in Italy!" Cyrus flung a picture of the man on the table. "Word among the scientific community is, *he's isolated the gene that governs the aging process, and he's already performed trials on humans to prove his theory*!" Cyrus paused and took a deep breath before he went on.

"There's great speculation and talk inside the legal scientific community about a breakthrough that Carruchi has achieved and the results will soon be announced, demonstrating the results from his experiments to alter that gene's chromosomes overseein' the aging process! **If this is so…the human DNA helix that governs the aging process in our species—as we kow it today—could forever be changed!**

Dillon hung his head…shaking it in disbief at what he was hearing!

"Aging can't be stopped today! Scientists have published results saying they know of one gene that controls the process of aging in the DNA helix and they think they've isolated it, but there are others. In addition, their research *also* discovered that one gene can govern more than one of our human genetic characteristics. The aging gene they identified is named GENE B53. *In a nutshell, if you remove or alter a gene or a portion of one gene, to make an improvement in that gene to one of its characteristics—it could have an adverse reaction of far greater serious unpredictable proportions in another genetic group! Geneticists believe there is greater potential for an unexpected reaction with much more serious consequences than beneficial outcomes if genes are unnaturally altered! Human life, as we know it today, could be changed forever!"*

Cyrus's voice became emotional and subdued. "I believe Dr. Carruchi has already reached this stage in his research! I believe he's been doing medical research on humans—on young people and on children—to beat out other working scientists in legitimate laboratories! *"I believe he has a specimen...a human specimen that he developed altering a genetic component!"* The two agents looked at Cyrus in astonishment!

"With experimentation, there are always failures first—before successes! One theory how failures could happen—the aging process could speed up instead of slowing down or stopping." Cyrus paused—the room was silent for a long time.

"From everything we've learned in this long investigation, all indications point to this happening in Carruchi's work. His motivations! GREED! POWER! AMBITION! FAME! WEALTH! This is probably what the Chatelaine case was really all about three years ago! We're not certain but we believe that's why those defendants disappeared—to allow the research to go on." Carlos added.

"So this is what the Chatelaine case is REALL' about!" Dillon commented passionately. "Kidnappin's for research! Do you know how they selected their subjects, Mac?" Dillon asked.

"No, not yet, and I won't postulate until we investigate the list of names found in Marcus Rudolphi's home and decipher the codes attached to each name! We have no idea what their master plan is for selection of subject matter, except to hypothesize they wanted a diverse pool of material to achieve their aims. We have no idea how many subjects were used in his experimentation!" Cyrus had no reason to hold back the complete truth. Dillon was silent for a long time—finally understanding why, and what he was up against. He couldn't help but think of his precious Maura and Siobhan as part of this diabolical venture. The men in that room, Cyrus, Carlos, Dillon—and now Emma—all have great personal stakes to uncover this notorious research scheme!

Carlos was the first to break the silence in the room. "Dillon, we've seen a lot of activity going on at the Villa del Christianna on the Rudolphi estate and at a second villa on Lago di Como—at a place called the *Villa Latinestto*. Large refrigerator trucks leave these villas periodically and go into the mountains up north crossing over into Switzerland. We've no idea what these trucks carry into the mountains. We tried tracking them when we learned there was a planned trip, but their trips have been unpredictable—sporadic! First, we followed them by van with a tracker, but lost them once they got inside the mountains—deep into private mountain property. We couldn't enter the property without being seen, and we didn't want to tip our hand! We tried helicopters tracking them, but again… once they entered inside mountain tunnels, the trackers didn't work. GSP surveillance confirmed they leave the mountain road and enter into some kind of underground complex deep in the mountains. It's my opinion they're using the mountain area as burial grounds. Satellite thermal imaging showed sporadic—increased activity in the mountains at certain times, but we're never able to learn ahead of time when a trip is planned or the exact destination." Carlos didn't say more, but Dillon knew exactly what he meant in his unspoken words.

Cyrus interrupted both men's thoughts. "What I need from you, Dillon, is the information you and Biaggio learned about the Rudolphi estate! We have a reason to suspect there may be a laboratory somewhere on the estate, carefully camouflaged by the winery or other buildings on the grounds."

Cyrus asked, "Did you bring the maps and data you gathered when you surveyed the estate?"

Dillon rose and walked to the end of the table, "Yeah. But before I 'and over what I 'ave, some of the information is up 'ere," he said, pointing to his head. "Mac, I need two promises from you—as sacred as a man's word is to a fellow mate! I need to know from 'ere on…first, I'm 'n equal on this team! Nothin' is 'eld back from me! If there's any kind of plan to find these laboratories and bring 'hem bastards to justice, I'm to be a part of it!" He reiterated his last words loudly, "I'm in on ev'rythin'—to the end! The second promise I want from you is when an assault is made at an' of these places Dr. Ennio Carruchi is mine! *Carruchi is mine…just mine*! Otherwise, there's no deal!"

Cyrus knew a man could be pushed so far when it came to his family, and said matter-of-factly, without hesitation, knowing Dillon's exceptional skills and dedication, "Understood and agreed! I'm in charge of this case –the project is called **COMO.** Everything goes through me. No one does anything unless I say so! *Capisce?*" Cyrus looked at both men.

*"Capisco!"* Dillon said. He knew Cyrus's word was a promise in life or death. Carlos nodded in agreement.

"There's one other fact you may already know. Carlos's real job is with the Italian secret service, and he's been assigned to work with my section in Interpol, which I'm sure you already learned from Emma. Jointly, we're working with Colin MacEachen, who represents MI 5 in this matter—thought you ought'a know—he'll be 'ere in a couple of days."

Dillon looked wide-eyed, hearing Colin MacEachen's name. "He's fully aware why you're 'ere and agrees it's time we pooled our resources in this case!" Dillon always felt MacEachen knew more than he let on to Emma when they worked the Dougal MacEachen case.

"What did 'e think Emma or I could do that 'e hadn't alread' done? Does MacEachen think his son, Dougal, could be part of these global kidnappin's?" Dillon asked Cyrus.

"He hasn't spoken outwardly to me about those thoughts, but I think…yes…he thinks Dougal was kidnapped for this purpose. The only question is, why *did he return?*"

Cyrus posed the rhetorical question, but in his mind he asked the same question about Emma, when she disappeared two years ago while on holiday in Tuscany for several weeks. Without a trace in Italy…she turned up in London with no memory of that trip to Tuscany.

Pointing to the map on the table, Cyrus said, "Now show me exactly what you learned about the Rudolphi estate. We have early maps that are updated daily with GPS thermal imaging about activity around the Rudolphi estate, but I want to compare your recent on-sight findings with ours!"

Dillon took out Emma's maps from his pocket, then took some clean drawing paper, and from memory, began to sketch, in fairly good scale, the positions and details of each villa on the estate, the size of the grounds, the workers homes, the different perimeter security system sightings, possible guard dog areas, adjacent pools and cabanas, with roads inside and around the perimeter of the entire Rudolphi estate.

"These cabanas and pool, 'ere at Marcus Rudolphi's Villa del Christianna offer camouflage for somethin' more!" Dillon said, "This area right 'ere? It conceals somethin' else. This 'ouse 'ere—marked with an **X,** gives the impression it's the 'ouse containin' the electrical and plumbin' source for the pool. It's more than that! Biaggio heard muffled whirlin' motors—like ventin' fans—exhaustin' systems or intake ventilator systems extendin' in a wide area with camouflaged open pipes spaced at intervals in the ground in that same area—could be intake sources for a ventilation system or exhaust system. The 'ouse itself is kept locked, but he used a fiber optic-lens to look and saw a second metal door about five feet inside the outer door. The metal door has multiple kinds securit'—what looked like an eye-ground scanner, face identification camera, and a keypad. Who knows?…Could be more! There could be voice recognition devices, too! An'way you look at it, it's overkill in securit' which says somethin' is might' important to keep pryin' eyes out!" Dillon said. "Or is it to keep people IN? It ain't a wine cellar! That's for damn certain!"

"This may be exactly what we're looking for!" Cyrus said excitedly.

Dillon continued, "This 'ere…could be one outside entrance to some underground buildin' or buildin's—possibly laboratories. It's me thinkin' everythin' is reinforced concrete—Could e'en be lead-lined if their usin' somethin' they don't want detected from above!"

348

"You may be right, Dillon," Cyrus said, thoughtfully surveying the drawings.

"Dillon, do you have any information about a villa on Lago di Como—Lake Como?" Carlos put his question to Dillon.

"No. Why?"

Carlos explained. "We have reliable information to believe there may be a place on Lago di Como that's been used in the kidnappings—as a laboratory by Carruchi and his scientific cronies!"

Referencing certain areas on a map, he said, "We need to find a way to look at this particular area on the lake without alerting anyone what we're doing there. On Como, there are a few villas near the Villa Latinessto for rent, and we'd like to get some renters into one of those adjacent villas next to or directly across from the Villa Latinestto. We'd use it as a front for surveillance, covering our operations with some innocent boating on the lake, without raising questions from the locals. It's common for renters from a villa to go boating on the lake—inconspicuous day-trippers—and it'd give us an opportunity to check out all the abutting homes around that one villa. There's a rental villa directly across the lake that fits all the conditions we need; it's the *Villa D'Este.* Some of our surveillance will require underwater work and the Villa D'Este has a boathouse and several boats that go with the villa. Are you up to helping us?" Carlos asked.

"I 'aven't had a pair of lungs on in a long time, but it's like ridin' a two-wheeler—you ne'er forget! Yeah sure! Count on me. I need to know ...if Siobhan and Maura were ever there!" he said pensively.

Cyrus finished studying the maps and drawings. "This reaches to my own family, too, Dillon. You asked why the Rudolphis want Emma? I'll answer your question now. I think Emma is somehow linked to them—which is why they're after her! Only I don't know how or why they want her so desperately *now*! I'm convinced she was a part of their experimentation...at any cost they must not get to her—**at any cost to us here!**" Dillon knew what Cyrus was saying—this project could cost a life!

"Now tell me, why did Lucinda Rudolphi go to London to see Emma?" Cyrus turned and asked Dillon point blank. "I know *she*

349

can't tell me without violating her oath of confidentiality—but *you* can!" Cyrus said loudly.

"Lucinda had two children and both died at birth—ne'er saw either child b'fore they were buried. A couple of months ago, she took a trip to Perugia and stopped at a town café. A boy 'bout four years old came out and ran to her and called her 'Madre'. A woman at the cafe called the boy, 'Giorgio'. Not so much this Giorgio called Lucinda, madre, but she claimed he looked just like Marcus Rudolphi! The color of his hair, his smile and eyes and even the chin dimple were like Marcus. But Giorgio 'ad her features too… Lucinda's fair skin colorin'. It stirred her to think about 'er own son—Antonio Giuseppe Rudolphi, who would probabl' look like this child if 'e were still alive." Dillon stopped his narrative and asked, "Do you have a drink 'ere? I'm really thirsty!"

"In the icebox." Dillon got up, found a cold beer and sat back down at the table. "Lucinda told Em, she found a list in her 'usband's librar'. He keeps this room locked—e'en from 'er, and Marcus is the onl' one with a key. She 'ad an opportunit' to get inside 'is study and into the locked box—out of curiosit'. She was lookin' through a list in a book kept in a locked box and saw Emma's name in it and recognized her as the Barrister Llewelyn in London—and remembered learnin' how successful she'd been in international cases 'bout kidnappin's. It was the initials written alon' side Emma's—a one E. C.—that intrigued Lucinda! Lucinda's real reason for goin' to London was to ask Emma to find and investigate the child she saw in Perugia…to make certain the child was legitimatel' this woman's boy! At the same time she asked Emma why her name was on that list in 'er 'usband's locked stud'." Dillon didn't give anyone a chance to interrupt him until he said what needed saying.

"I can tell you Emma's real reason why she took the case! Foremost to find out why *her name* was on a list in Rudolphi's study! AND of course, to check out Perugia to see if there was an' truth to what Lucinda told her." Dillon went and took out another cold *burro* from the icebox.

"From the pictures we took in Perugia, I think there's some truth to what Lucinda said!" The look of incredulity on Cyrus's face, made Dillon raise his hand to signal there was more.

"Physical'y, these two children in Perugia could be Lucinda Rudolphi's natural children!" Dillon sounded convincing—yet the words were hard to believe!

"Is that what *you* think, Dillon?"

"Mac, I saw the children with me own eyes! I saw Marcus and Lucinda Rudolphi with me own eyes! I saw the woman in Perugia with the children—she can't be their natu'al mother! It's a far reach to say that kind of similarit' is a coincidence! The boy had Marcus Rudolphi's same wide smile with the chin dimple—no doubt about it! If it were not for the light, fair, almost pale complexion—the shape of 'is face—I'd say Marcus could 'ave a mistress there! But it's *the girl—Sophia*! She's the perfect mirror image of Lucinda Rudolphi!" Dillon looked to the two men. "She 'as the red hair, green eyes, and the light colorin'—exactly like Lucinda—e'en the smile!" Dillon spoke with reliability.

"Then you're saying *Marcus* sacrificed his own children for... for experimentation...telling his wife their children died at birth?" Cyrus asked disbelievingly!

"If he's capable of doing something like that, then there's the possibility that Emma was once that son of a bitch's experiment... and he wants her back again now! There's no end to the lengths that man will go to to get what he wants!" Cyrus said in a controlled rage. "If a man would use his own children...saying they were dead to his wife and the world...then he would do anything to anyone... like Emma...*but why Emma*?"

The long silence in the room was pregnant with raging emotions inside the three men. Carlos was silent with inner rage...just hoping someday...when the time was right...Marcus Rudolphi would *be his mission to eliminate*...and his only...at the right time!

"All right! If there's no more questions...we've got work to do now! We find a villa on *Lago di Como* and send two operatives in as a couple on holiday and we set up surveillance there! We need to find that laboratory on *Lago di Como!* But first...first, we find out what lies under the Rudolphi's Villa del Christianna and if it's directly connected to the Winery!" Cyrus walked out to the central station and placed a call.

351

"Colin? Yes I know it's late. We have to move now! Fly in tomorrow—usual flight landing." Cyrus hung up, took a deep breath and returned to the conference room with Andrew Masters.

"Oh…Dillon, you and Emma will check out of the Manin tomorrow. You stay with Carlos at his flat and Emma stays at Biaggio's until I figure out a safer place for her. I want plans made to check out rental villas on Como closest to the Villa Latinestto that are available for immediate occupancy! Andrew, you'll pick up Sir Colin tomorrow at the usual place? I need you to devise a list of what we'll need for surveillance on the lake when we move into the rental." Checking his watch, he said, "We'll all meet here tomorrow at twenty hundred hours with all the arrangements completed. At that time, we'll go over the fine details of the two plans." Cyrus turned and started out the door, but stopped when Dillon asked, "Two plans?"

*"Aye, the Villa del Christianna and the Villa Latinestto on Como. The immediate job? Get inside the Villa del Christianna!"*

# CHAPTER THIRTY-NINE

Emma had no trouble sleeping in the safety of Sienna and Biaggio Giambetti's home.

Elena, the oldest daughter, graciously gave up her room to Emma for the night while she doubled up with one of her sisters.

At first light, Emma roused to hear voices in the hall outside her door and abruptly sat up. The luminous clock dial said five thirty. Through the window curtain, the first glimpse of dawn was breaking in the distance. Shades of black gave way to gray clouds. The shifting first light of dawn had moved down the mountains to lift the black blanket to one of muted browns and greens. Putting on the outsized sweater over her pajamans Elena lent her, Emma went into the hall and down the staircase toward the sound of voices. Sienna's voice was clear and came from the kitchen. It sounded like she was quizzing Biaggio, but without any replies. There was a third person in the room whom Biaggio was speaking to saying, "The best way to check out Lago di Como villas is a tour boat trip. There're scheduled tours down the lake every day—some even stopping at certain villas along the way." Emma was surprised to see Dillon standing at the window in the kitchen when she walked in.

"I thought I heard your voice. What kind of meeting did you have last night that I was not invited to attend—again?" Emma looked directly at Dillon who made no attempt to answer her question.

"What's this boat tour about?" Emma poured a cup of tea and asked, turning to Biaggio with her question.

"Now, Em, before you get yur dander up, it was best to keep you safe under wraps last night 'til we found out why an attempt was made on you in the gardens!" Dillon said to her.

"Okay—I agree with that! But from now on I'm to be included in any future plans! *I will learn* why this is all happening to me, why the Rudolphis are interested in me, and why my name is on a secreted list! I do have a client I gave my word to that I'd find answers to her queries. I can't help thinking everything that's happened since we arrived in Milano…is somehow all connected!" Giving feeling to her words showed her raw frustration.

"Understood, Em!"

"Did *you* learn why someone was after me—and exactly who it is?" she asked.

Dillon didn't want to alarm Emma unnecessarily with the truth, "Carlos is workin' on that at this very moment, Em. I'm certain 'e'll tell us when he knows somethin'!"

Dillon was dealing with his own personal frustrations and empathathized with Emma, remembering his Maura and Siobhan; Siobhan would be almost seven years old now. His thoughts conjured up what she would look like at seven. He was thinking, *Most like'y, she'd be the image of Maura.* Setting his personal thoughts aside, he returned to the present moment…and put his arm around Emma.

"You asked about a boat trip?"

"Yes, I heard Biaggio say a boat tour was the best way to see some villas?"

Biaggio returned to the room. "Did you explain about the boat plan?" Biaggio asked.

"Not yet. I need to speak with Carlos first."

"Before anybody makes *any* plans, I want to shower—be back shortly. Don't make any decisions until I return," she yelled back assertively, directing her remarks to Dillon to make her point heard!

"We need to change Emma's appearance so she won't be easily recognizable…a different hair color and cut…some glasses will help and different clothes, too. Any ideas, Biaggio?"

"That's a job Sienna and the girls can do." Biaggio said. "Let me ask them."

Dillon rang Carlos's cell phone.

"*Si, pronto,*"

"It's me. I take it we're makin' arrangements for a boat tour up Lake Como today? Emma's comin', too. I'm seein' to it she makes some temporary changes to her looks."

"Good thinking! We should all meet at ten o'clock in Como at the Duomo to get tour tickets. We'll be four. *Caio.*" Carlos rang off.

Emma walked into the room. Dillon gave the catcall whistle. "I see Sienna and the girls did a good job! Not a semblance of the Welsh girl. I'd say she's a Tuscan beaut'!" Emma was wearing a short reddish-blond wig, tortoise shell glasses, dark red lipstick, and vivid eye make-up to look like a young girl—a Neapolitan girl! The trim-tight jeans and oversized shirt were the costume of a young girl trying to look good for the boy's eye without revealing anything!

"Good choice, girls," Dillon said to the two teenagers giggling in the background.

"Is this really necessary?" Emma asked.

"Absolutely! Now grab some breakfast—we go to Como to meet Carlos. Tell you more on the way. Biaggio do we have a car ready to go to Como?" Dillon asked.

"*Si*—the VW wagon is gassed up and ready."

On their way to Como, Emma told Dillon the reason she went outside alone last night was to call Peter, and then she discovered someone was after her in the gardens.

"I called Peter to ask him to send the Chatelaine discs to me ASAP. We devised a plan. Hilly is going to fly over directly to Milano Internationale Airport with the discs, and Biaggio will meet her, identifying himself to her by holding a placard with the name BRIENNE. She'll reply to him 'GRAY' and hand him the discs. Biaggio can take her to a safe place until her return flight home that evening and see her safely aboard the plane for London. Peter will call me today with the flight information to and from Milano. Will it be a problem for you to pick up my secretary, Biaggio?"

"*No Signora* Emma, just let me know the flight time, and a description of the woman to meet. I will do the rest."

"Thanks, Biaggio. When I learn the flight information, I'll let you know."

Turning to Dillon, she said, "Now tell me about Lake Como."

\* \* \*

Carlos was at Duomo waiting when the VW wagon pulled up. "I called ahead and reserved tickets for the noon boat tour on Lago di Como for four." He stopped speaking and stared at Emma for a few minutes. "Good transformation! I had to take a second look to make sure it was you," he said to Emma. "My first choice? I prefer the raven-haired girl," he said smiling.

"You're on safe ground, Carlos...and your preference is understood!" Emma said, playing with Carlos's remarks. They both got into the rear seat and the VW wagon headed up the SS340 route for Lago di Como.

The tour-boat office was easy to reach in the middle of the city. The ticket lines were already forming for the morning tour scheduled. This tour was a four-hour excursion that included one stop at one of the rental villas. Dillon and Carlos had narrowed possible rental sites to three villas, in close proximity to the Villa Latinesetto. The tour passed by each one of the rental villas, and even made a stop at one of them. Carlos knew two of the villas were currently empty, and the third one would be available within a few days.

"Emma take this camera and get as many pictures of the shoreline and homes as you can around the three villas we named. When we pass the Villa Latinesetto, if you make out someone on the grounds, use the zoom lens to take a picture. The villas we're particularly interested in are located here, here and here," he said, pointing to three different sites on a map. Use the zoom lens at this villa for close-ups of the buildings and grounds; get scenes from the water, boathouses, docks—anything around the waterline." Carlos handed Emma the loaded camera and a pair of binoculars.

Boarding the boat with the crowd of tourists, each of them went in a different direction on the boat to get different views of the shore and land. It appeared many of the tourists had the same intention—to view the estates.

"I concentrate on taking pictures, and viewing the sites close-up with binoculars," Emma told herself. Dillon, Carlos, and Emma blended in easily with the group of tourists while Biaggio went up into the pilothouse—he knew the *Capitano*.

* * *

Cyrus arrived in Firenze at a large warehouse and drove slowly up to the doors. They automatically opened for him to drive inside.

"How was your trip, Colin?"

"Good—easy flight—the weather was good for once."

"What did you learn from Dillon?" Colin asked immediately.

"What we thought all along! Dillon's facts corroborated what we suspected! There's probably a complex of underground laboratories under the Villa del Christianna, as we suspected from the heat signatures we've been getting, definitely indicating activity! Our thought is, there's a multi-level complex of tunnels under or around the pool with an entrance through a pool house. It won't be easy to penetrate! A high level of security IDs will be needed to get inside that door to access the tunnels and underground chambers. I'm certain there're other entrances, too, elsewhere on the grounds, or most likely, inside the Villa del Christianna. Maybe our contact can find that out for us. It's my belief the pool entrance is our most likely place to successfully penetrate without being discovered! Biaggio's opinion is multiple identifications are needed—eye-ground scanners or facial recognition machines—or both—even voice codes along with a coded key pad."

"We know all access codes are changed daily, and if we are to get inside, we'll need to get the code used for the day we go in!"

Colin commented, "Our undercover chap will give us the code for that day if we get word to him in time."

"I'll inform him when I know that date!

Now do we have a duplicate eye lens for Marcus Rudolphi yet?"

"I gave the measurements to Andrew, and he's having the lens made as we speak," Cyrus said.

"There's more than a possibility we'll need face recognition masks, disguises that will pass for the real thing. We can try for all the Rudolphis—Marcus, Dominic, and Luigi, if necessary."

"That shouldn't be a problem if we have enough notice to make the facial impressions at the special ops lab, we have plenty of photos and videos to draw from," Colin remarked.

"We have only ONE day, Colin! If we delay, we could miss our window of opportunity, so get your labs working now!" Cyrus cautioned Colin.

"One day is awfully short notice, Mac!"

"I know! But we no longer have the choice to delay. There's more activity now that Emma's in Milano! I have a feeling something big is going to come down. No! We have to make our moves now if we're to locate those laboratories! Did you bring the latest voice altering apparatus with you? We'll need them to get inside, and if our men unexpectedly meet an employee, they've got to sound like the real Rudolphis."

"Yes, ever'thing is being unloaded as we speak. What did Andrew learn at the villa Sunday?" Colin asked.

"He was able to find an entrance in the cellar at the villa—head source, I suspect. It comes out in the basement behind the wine cellar wall which suggests it leads to an underground tunnel; possibly a tunnel from a main complex running under the pool to the villa. He wasn't able to explore the tunnel to see exactly where it goes. Could be from the Villa del Christianna to some labs or to the winer' building or both! A stroke of luck came when he was sent down for boxes of wines. He saw Dominic Rudolphi closing a false wall in the wine cellar while hiding in the shadows. Dominic was talking to Marcus, and Andrew overheard Dom say, 'Everything was set in Triple A Laboratory.' The leak in # 15 storage vat was sealed—which means he had just come from the winer' or the underground complex. This is something we need to be absolutely certain of before the assaults go down there! We just ratchet up our timetable."

"The evidence is overwhelming...the number of underground tunnels. From the basement in the *villa* some go directly to the *winery* building, and there could be other tunnels according to the satellite scanners. All the recent heat imagery reports picks up heat sources moving in unilateral directions indicating halls or corridors with rooms—maybe laboratories—around a series of hollow space-tunnels. Now that's some distance for several complexes to tie in to one another! With tunnels and hallways, you have rooms off these tunnels—laboratories or living quarters—who knows what else is down there! Which is why we must get someone into the Villa del Christianna complex to find out what the bloody hell goes on inside! The sooner the better! It's my opinion we should go in within the next forty-eight hours," Cyrus said with conviction.

"Do you have any ideas how we can do it?" asked Colin.

"Yes, I have a plan in mind, but we need to run it by Dillon and Carlos! Biaggio's reconnaissance found an area in the gardens at the Villa del Christianna with multiple vents in one particular area! Most likely an intake or outtake system associated with underground air systems. If we contaminate the intake system with a noxious gas, they would have to empty that area of the complex of personnel. And if we do it at night, most likely, it's the shift with the fewest number of personnel; we'd lessen our chances of detection. Once the complex is cleared out, our men slip inside. It's easier than breaking into the complex in an outright skirmish and having them on to us!"

"It could work. Aye—it could work, Mac!" Colin said excitedly.

"It's doable," Cyrus said cautiously.

Cyrus gathered the reports, "You and I need to review this information about this area *pronto!* Let me talk to Carlos and see what we can arrange. Dillon is on the team, Colin—he's a good man and I owe him," Cyrus said.

Colin gave Cyrus a look. "I don't disagree...I 'ated to lose Dillon in MI 5—'e was one of my best operatives at the time. But given what 'e had on his plate, it made 'im too vulnerable, and 'e knew it. 'E did the right thing to resign. Never did find another like 'im—bloody damn shame, too!" Colin said.

"Right now, they're checking out Lake Como. We're going to have two agents pose as a couple renting a villa on Como—gives us the opportunity to check out the Villa Latinestto. Dillon, Carlos, Biaggio, and Emma are checking out rental villas near the Villa Latinestto as we speak. Public information is that the Rudolphis have a long time association with the Villa Latinestto, but they're not listed as owners."

"No, it's probably a dummy corporation name listed as owner for them," Colin commented. Cyrus showed Colin the map of the Como and the area currently considered for rentals.

"What I need from you, Colin, are several good underwater teams for surveillance. We'll need to do a water survey of the lake around the Villa Latinestto as well as the grounds around the villa, approaching from the water. No doubt there's thick securit' at the beach and around the beach houses leading up to the villa."

"If that's the right villa we're lookin' for, the securit' may even be 'eavier than the winery estate villas," Colin retorted.

"We'll survey the Villa Latinestto by water—get the information—without alerting anyone!" Cyrus replied.

"That shouldn't be a problem by water. I 'ave two teams available that I'll notify 'hem at once and 'ave them 'ere in twenty-four hours."

"Tell them to bring extra sets of lungs—at least for Dillon and Carlos to go with your men. We must know every bit of the area—by land and water!" Cyrus said emphatically.

"There are large formal gardens between the lake and the house—that's about all we know from architectural plans of the estate—besides the usual old floor plans. I wouldn't count on them being accurate either! If the villa's been updated, and we know it has—these newer modifications could be laboratories. Local rumor from a few men who worked in the new areas seems to suggest they were going to be used as laboratories."

"You'll 'ave your teams! Where will they be staying?" Colin asked.

"Right in our rental villa on Como. We'll finalize the rental contract for Como in a day and get two operatives to move in immediately—set up housekeeping—surveillance of the Latinestto. Your men will be guests at the villa. Andrew is getting together the equipment we'll need for security and surveillance at the Como rental as we speak." Colin left to make his call.

"The teams will be 'ere within two days with all their gear and with extras tanks, too."

"When Carlos returns today from Lake Como—I'm meeting tonight with him and Dillon to finalize a plan to infiltrate the Villa del Christianna complex. I think the two of them can do the job! They're already familiar with the grounds, and they know what they're up against and what to look for! None more knowledgeable on short notice."

Cyrus hesitated before speaking. "My main concern is Emma... she's got herself deeply involved... more vulnerable just being here! There was an attempt last night to kidnap her...luckily Dillon prevented it...and she's safe for now. Yet, I know she'll never leave Milano until she finds answers for herself and her client...may be just as well! If they're after her—I can keep her safe, here—but there's more the threat for her to find out about me!" Cyrus spoke as if he were trying to convince himself not Colin.

"You know, my friend—someday, you're goin' to 'ave to tell her the whole truth! She's your flesh and blood—she'll understand! Better to 'ear it all from you than from someone else!" Colin walked over to Cyrus and put his hand on his shoulder.

"From what I've seen of 'er—she's steel all the way through. The kind of steel that made the MacKenna Clan one of the strongest clans in Welsh history!"

Colin walked to the door to leave. "Don't underestimate her strengths, Cyrus."

"Thanks, Colin. You know how to reach me. We'll talk again when the team gets back." Cyrus walked out to the waiting car. Andrew came down the steps from the upper floor in the hanger.

"Everything is packed, Mac. I have Aldo loading the van with equipment we need for Como to take back to the station."

"What kind of firepower have you packed?" Cyrus asked.

"Sweet Jesus, Mac—both heavy and light-enough ammo to destroy a castle-fortress...enough to last for weeks! When it's time to take out **PROJECT COMO**, we'll be ready!" Andrew said with zeal.

"I'm heading back to the station in Milano—meeting Carlos and Dillon tonight."

"Where's Emma staying?" Andrew asked.

"For now, at Biaggio's with his family. But I need to move her out of there tomorrow. I don't want to put his family in danger—no telling what someone would do to get Emma! I'm hoping she can stay at the rental villa on Como—we'll have plenty of guards there to watch her. Whatever you do—*don't let her see you, Andy*!" Walking towards the door, he said, "Carlos tells me she almost made you out at the charity last Sunday—so be forewarned!" Cyrus said to Andrew, driving out slowly as the overhead door swung open.

\* \* \*

The boat tour had proven successful. Emma used all of her film to get good shots of the Villa Latinestto. It was an old pictorial castle-like villa with magnificent formal gardens sloping from the water up to the sprawling stone *casa*. With binoculars, she did make out movement on the terraces, but too far away to make out if they were men or women. Docking back at Como, Dillon and Carlos joined her. The tour provided a small lunch in a basket to each tourist with a small bottle of wine. Grateful this would save them time on the way back to Milano, no one was interested in stopping to eat.

"You first, *Signora*," Carlos said to Emma, helping her onto the gangplank from the boat to the dock.

"I'd like an opportunity to live in one of those beautiful homes for a short while. It all looks so serenely peaceful!" she said for the benefit of anyone leaving the boat to hear. Biaggio and Dillon caught up to them as they reached the parked car.

Carlos called Cyrus on his cell phone. "We just finished the boat tour, and we're on our way to meet with the rental agent for the *Villa D' Este* near Tremezzo. It's the closest, but more importantly, it's directly across the lake with a clear view of the Villa Latinestto," he said, implying surveillance, accessibility, and easy to access the Villa Latinestto from the Villa D' Este.

"Then do it!" Cyrus instructed. Dillon caught the gist of the telephone conversation.

"Biaggio, we go to the realtor in Como to take rental of the Villa D'Este."

Carlos completed all the arrangements for the rental of the Villa D'Este to take immediate occupancy until further notice, making it an indefinite length for renting—suggesting a possible sale of the property. This kind of arrangement would keep rental agents away.

"Everything is set—we go in tomorrow!"

For now, only Carlos and Cyrus knew the importance of finding the main laboratory site for Dr. Carruchi's experiments. When this is uncovered, victims will be found!

"Emma, when we return to Milano, you and Dillon have to check out of the hotel. For now, you must stay with Sienna! Dillon is coming with me," Carlos said.

"Why do we have to be separated? Why can't we all stay with you?" Emma asked begrudgingly.

"We want people to think you two are returning to London when you check out of the hotel. We've booked flights for you and Dillon today for London and two operatives will take your places on the flight. You have to maintain the disguise at least until you get to Milano—and not be seen together. Dillon is less conspicuous than you, my sweet—doesn't come near to your beauty," Carlos said jokingly.

"For now, you two shouldn't be seen together—too many people know you two by sight together. Staying at Sienna's is the best short-term solution. Biaggio will drive you to the hotel while you check out and then to the airport. Once at the airport, you'll be Emma Llewelyn, but a switch will take place and your double will board in your place. The same goes for Dillon. Leaving the airport, you'll wear your Milanese disguise and return to Milano with Biaggio. I'll catch up with you then," Carlos said.

The ride back was in companionable silence. Occasionally, they compared what each had seen and remembered about Lago di Como. Emma removed the red wig, the glasses, and the make-up in the car. By the time they reached the Manin, she was the raven-haired Emma Llewelyn again.

"Each time I see you, my darling—you're more beautiful that my memory recalls," Carlos whispered to her as she exited the car and started up the steps. Turning, she blew him a kiss.

*"Eight o'clock,"* Dillon remarked to Carlos as he closed the car door and entered the hotel.

# CHAPTER FORTY

Checking out of the hotel went without difficulty.

Emma informed the desk concierge she was called back to London unexpectedly and had to cut short her holiday. Dillon settled his account earlier and was nowhere in sight when Biaggio greeted Emma and deposited her bags in the car boot.

"Where's Dillon?" she asked.

"We'll pick him up at Carlos's flat," he said. At that moment, Emma's cell phone rang.

"*Pronto.*"

"Emma—it's Peter."

"Yes Peter…the arrangements…what flight? Let me write this down…Hilly leaves on Air Italia and arrives in Milano tomorrow at two-twenty in the afternoon. Return flight is same day at eight-fifteen from Milano Internationale—arriving in London at eleven-tomorrow night. Peter, that's great! Biaggio will pick her up—remember the recognition signal is the chauffeur holding the large placard with the name **Brienne** on it; she'll approach him and acknowledge saying 'Gray' in a sentence. That's the signal for Hilly to give Biaggio the package. Any questions?"

"No. I've already briefed her. Discs of 'court protocols' will be inside a sleeve in a package of documents. Hilly knows you're interested in two discs and to make certain nothing happens to them! The two discs you need are a different color from the others."

"Good thinking, Peter. I have to make a change in residence here. I had to check out of the hotel, and I can't tell you where I'll be staying at the moment. If you need, you can always reach me on my cell phone."

"I hope you're not in any danger, Emma. Is Dillon still with you?"

"Yes—he's with me," she said, crossing her fingers while speaking with Peter.

"Tell Liv—many thanks for me! And I owe her big time!"

"One more thing, have you spoken to Cyrus yet?" Peter interjected.

"Yes, he left me a message saying he was traveling on the continent and wasn't able to give me his travel itinerary. I don't expect to see him until I get to Lyn Brienne. Why do you ask?"

"No reason…I knew you were trying to contact him. There's nothing new with the police…I haven't heard anything more from them…and don't expect to either!"

"Have to ring off now, Peter—I'll call again—not certain when."

"Stay safe and be careful, Emma!" Peter said in a loud afterthought to assure him, "As long as Dillon's with her—she'll be fine."

"Biaggio, I need you to pick up that delivery tomorrow at two-twenty on Air Italia at Milano airport. You'll look for a woman with short curly red hair and blue eyes. She always wears a hat—something with green in it—her personal insignia! She has a delivery for you."

"*Si Signora*. I'll bring the delivery to you at my home," Biaggio said, continuing his route to pick up Dillon for the trip to the Milano International Airport. Everything went as planned—the doubles took off for London—and by the time Emma reached Sienna's, it was almost seven o'clock.

"Don't forget! Someone will pick you up tomorrow to go to the Villa D'Este…Can't say who that will be or what time, but you'll get a call to let you know the details," Dillon said to Emma. Giving her a high five wave, he drove away. Everything was ready for the eight o'clock meeting with Cyrus.

"Oh, for a long hot soak tonight!" Emma said walking into Sienna's kitchen.

* * *

Dillon went directly to Carlos's flat on the *Via Lepotinno* where earlier he deposited his bags inside the private foyer. He had the code information to enter the apartment. Apollo and Zeus met him inside the door. Just as Carlos instructed, he gave the dogs each a glove as a signal for the dogs to let him inside. They just sniffed the glove and let out a friendly bark. He then gave the hand signal to the dogs to stay at the front entrance and they relaxed their sentry posture.

*This place is too much for just one person,* Dillon thought, walking to the small balcony off the bedroom overlooking the city. "Can't blame you for livin 'ere—great view!" The dogs watched Dillon's every move. "Okay, you two… nice to meet you, too. I'll feed you, and then we'll take a short run—we all need some exercise!" Carlos had a state-of-the-art complicated security system installed and instructed Dillon how to alter its mode while he was there. If he didn't do it immediately, it would alarm back in central control and armed operatives would check for intruders with *firepower!* Once inside the apartment, he made certain the security system was back online in the modification mode …just in case any unwanted visitors came calling. Checking the exits, the balcony entrance was secured from below and hidden cameras and sensors were installed on the roof, picking up movements and weight. "Good thinkin', me man." Walking around the flat to get a feel for the physical layout, he noticed the apartment was geared more for convenience rather than comfort or decoration. Dillon remembered Carlos liked his *burros* too, and found a cold beer on ice. There were actually two bedrooms, but the second one served as a study with sophisticated computer equipment, radio scanners, and several differently colored telephones. From the balcony, he saw the city lights off in the distance playing with the neon colored lights from the cars.

"Ain't life funny…we've come almost full circle, ole friend."

Finishing the beer, he leashed the dogs and went for a jog around the immediate area. The dogs knew a familiar route to take, and he let them lead. It felt good to get some real exercise, and the dogs were eager for a good run. It was dark when he returned to the apartment. First, he fed the dogs then showered and grabbed his small bag to take with him. Stashing his large case in the rear of a closet, he dialed in the surveillance mode for the security system. With a final check to see if everything was as he found it, he hoped he didn't set off the silent alarm and would meet control on their way there!

\* \* \*

Cyrus was sitting in the conference room waiting for him. "Everything go as planned at the airport?"

"No problems. Emma is checked out of the Manin and with Sienna tonight. I parked my gear with Carlos." Carlos walked into the room.

"Nice digs, Carlos. Yur down one beer, and the dogs were fed and exercised."

"Biaggio told me Em's made arrangements for the discs to arrive tomorrow afternoon with a courier at the airport," Dillon said.

Cyrus interjected, "I want to see what's on those discs first! He's to bring them here, and we'll make copies and then return the originals to Emma. She can view them at Biaggio's place."

"The Chatelaine case may give 'er the link she's lookin' for in this matter," Dillon said.

"I know it! But I want to be the *first* to know if the discs hold the key, and since she's not yet privy to all of the facts *we know*—she may not yet make a connection to her involvement to the case—*and to* Carruchi!" Cyrus said. "At least not yet," he added, in afterthought!

"Now about Como," he said, shifting everyone's concentration to the table illustrating a large oversized map of Lago di Como.

Cyrus spoke, "The rental arrangements are complete. Andy has the equipment all ready to go into the villa. It'll appear a van is moving the client's private belongings—suitcases, trunks—into the villa. He'll have men set the electronic equipment up for the whole place before we go in. We're taking extra precautions that Emma isn't aware Andrew will be in the villa—or me for that fact! **I can't afford to change that...not at this time!** Colin is arranging for underwater seal teams to come in to scout and explore the lake area leading to the beach to detect security from that point—and how to neutralize it. They'll be responsible for deactivating all systems by the lake access and beach area leading up to and including the grounds of the Villa Latinestto, as well as the two beaches abutting the villa's property—when the time comes. He's also packed additional underwater firepower in case we need it," Cyrus said.

"Who's the lucky couple hostin' all these people as their guests?" Dillon asked.

Carlos had this information. "The Villa D'Este is rented in the name of *Signore* and *Signora* Josepi and Maria Rosetti, from Boston, Massachusetts. The Rosetti's are owners of a restaurant chain in the United States, and they're in Italia vacationing for an extended period of time in the Villa D'Este, entertaining friends! I have two Italian operatives—Giovanni and Alma—to pose as the Rosetti's. When everything's in place, Emma will be taken there, but she is to remain out of sight! And she must wear the disguise if she goes outside or in public! Biaggio will have local men doing outside security day and night."

Cyrus moved to the filing cabinet. "Now there's a more urgent mission we need to take care of first. We need to get into that small storage house located next to the pool on Marcus Rudolphi's estate and see what's so important beneath that spot!" Cyrus flicked on several switches, displaying large laser-colored maps on the table.

"Our GPS surveillance is sending continual data, and the Helix satellite is sending thermal images of those areas every six hours. These are the most recent series downloaded," he said, pointing to a progression of topographical maps on the table—he handed each still photographs.

"You'll see the dark red areas are consistently seen in the same planes; it's the same degree of heat signatures every twenty-four hours in the same areas, indicating thermal patterns for a twenty-four hour period, apparently identical over a week's time. Our interpretation is, these here are a series of tunnels and underground complexes where people are working and moving about in. During daylight hours, there's the greatest detection of heat sources—the darker red. Conversely, at night, there's a minimum of heat signals. This translates that the night hours have the least number of people inside the complex. You two are to get yourselves into that underground facility...here." Cyrus pointed to the small house in the pool area on the Villa del Christianna estate.

Carlos and Dillon looked at one another, not uttering a word.

"This is our first objective...to find out what it's used for—could be just one entrance to the underground complex. It's going to be tricky! *We can't tip our hand!* We can't leave footprints! And for God's sake—they can't find us in there! We're so close...so close to cutting off the bloody beast's head!" At times, Cyrus couldn't hide his passion in this case.

"I take it there'll be more to this mission than just takin' a look at this complex?" Dillon queried both Carlos and Cyrus. Cyrus looked intently at Dillon. Silence was his answer.

"Once we know the purpose of this complex, we'll next focus on the laboratory in the Villa Latinestto. General opinion is Lago Como is the place where the most important experimentation and research was—and is done, and that may be tougher to penetrate! For one thing, it'll be much bigger! It's conceivable a place that large could be outfitted for the most important scientific surgical experimentation—rather than the limited underground facility on the Rudolphi estate." Cyrus wanted to impress on them the importance of this first mission without giving away his whole plan.

"But to get back to the matter at hand, if they learn or even suspect we're close to uncovering their organization...they'll just move everything out and start somewhere else...and we'll 'ave lost all this work and time—for nothing! We CANNOT fail—and we'll 'ave only one chance at this!" Cyrus emphasized his words with passion in his voice.

"I agree our chances are best to go in at night. I also agree they'll 'ave a minimum of people at night—and if we 'ad to force 'em out—we could slip back in with 'em *or* take two of 'em out and go back inside as workers." Dillon took out a cigarette and placed it behind his ear, his signature of serious reflection.

Carlos explained, "What we need first is a way to get on the grounds undetected! The information Biaggio learned when he took his tour of the estate has this information we need about security in the vicinity of those vent-pipes. I'm thinking the pipes are both intake and outflow vents from a ventilation system. If we can determine which ones are inflow vents, we'll know which ones to contaminate—we'll infect intakes and if necessary, block off some of the outflow tubes to maximize the effects."

Cyrus said, "I'd suggest you use an inert gas for a sudden but short-lived effect. If they don't speed up the exhaust system—it'll take time to be vented out but hopefully not too soon! This should give you the time you need—if you work quickly! If this plan fails—and we can't pollute the ventilation system—we need a back-up plan. Any ideas?"

Dillon listened to everything. "Think about this for back-up... we use the gas to contaminate the complex...and enter the complex through the pool entrance. We'll need all the different kinds of security IDs to fool the systems! We know they'll 'ave eye-ground checks... and I'd bet Marcus and brother Dominic would 'ave eye-ground IDs programmed into this security system. If our IDs don't work...we'll take out two workers and return inside posing as the workers and leave with their IDs when we're finished. If we 'ave to, we take the two workers back with us and keep 'hem out of circulation, to keep secrecy—we'll do it. What do you think, Carlos?" Dillon asked.

"I think it's a good alternate plan, in case...! Either way we get inside! Cyrus, you mentioned Andy was finishing the ID retinal lenses...are they finished?"

"Yes, he's completed Marcus's and is working on Dominic's now." Cyrus walked out to the central station and made several phone calls.

"What do you think, Carlos? Think we can pull it off?" Dillon asked.

"It'll be like ole times..."

Just then Cyrus returned. "Andy's finished the retinal lenses and has started with your facial disguises. The materials are totally adaptable to the features we mold, and we'll have tinted lenses to go with them. You'll each have a voice-alteration system that will modulate your voices to sound like your intended Rudolphi. The voice systems were developed by MI 5 and they're reliable without any failures. Carlos, you'll be Marcus and Dillon we've chosen

Dominic Rudolphi for you—he is more your size. Flesh-like-skin gloves with each Rudolphi's fingerprints are ready. All means of sensory identification are ready. We're working on getting the daily coded message. I think we've covered all possibilities unless you have any further suggestions?" Cyrus asked. The two men shook their heads no.

"Good! That's our plan." Cyrus looked long and hard at each man to sense any disapproval. He sensed complete agreement.

Carlos gave further instructions to Dillon. "When we get inside the underground complex, first we look for laboratories; note the number you find and how they're set up. Then look for offices where we can access files and documents to get information. We'll each have a laser camera for high-speed takes. Check out for other exits to other tunnels...possibly to the villa and winery—that's if we have time. I'll have the advantage of knowing and speaking Italian, so let me do the talking if we meet any employees," Carlos said.

"Do we take an' materials with us or do we just photograph?" Dillon asked.

Cyrus retorted, "You take *nothing* from there this time! We can't afford to tip our hand! Use your photographic minds and take mental pictures of the layout and use the camera for any other important information—I leave that up to your judgment!"

The conference room phone rang and Cyrus answered. "Good. Bring them to the conference room when you're done. That was Andy—he's finished Dominic Rudolphi's eye-ground lens. That means we have everything for the mission. You'll both have to do a dry run with your disguises...Check the lens, the fingerprints, and face masks and modulators," Cyrus said.

"This *mission* is to learn exactly what kind of research is done there—and anything else you can! If you find research journals, take pictures for evidence—but leave them as you found them. We must learn what's going on in the underground complex before we can plan for Lago di Como. If there's evidence experimentation was done—or you see any...subjects in the complex, get a picture— understand?" Cyrus said with disgust. "This is the kind of evidence we need for convictions!"

"Our early discoveries showed us they've done 'experimental trials' to test formulas. We're hypothesizing human experimentation was performed to see what happened to subjects when a modified genetic formula was introduced…we surmise it was something to do with aging. Needless to say, such experiments had to be performed on young people. Some of our information suggested…they had many failures. Bits of data supported that the process actually had the opposite effect. It accelerated old age! That could only mean the failures were premature deaths of the young…children—dying the deaths of old men and women! We need concrete evidence of this…nothing better than a picture telling a thousand words…for convictions! See if these secret labs are the place where the formulas are made for the experiments!" Cyrus recounted with constraint. Dillon listened impassively outwardly, but inside his passion for revenge was raging—thinking of his lost family!

"You two be ready tomorrow night. We'll have all the equipment you'll need checked and ready for you. The weather report is fair and clear with a new moon—lunar darkness. Any change of opinions?" Cyrus asked the two men.

"It's a go with me," Dillon said.

"No objections—*si,* I'm ready," Carlos echoed.

"Not a word to Emma about this job. Biaggio will take charge of her safety until we're ready to go into the villa." Cyrus walked out the door and disappeared into the outer station.

"What kind of firepower do we take?" Dillon asked.

"Are you comfortable with a Magnum or a Larson?" Carlos opened a wall cabinet and took out several different brands and handed them to Dillon.

"I'd prefer the Larson—I use to 'ave one of me own in…Saved me life many times then!"

"We'll each have some fast-acting scopolamine darts—if it's necessary to silence dogs or humans! They'll wake up without remembering what happened…none the wiser…decay of any evidence of the darts starts almost immediately—neither does it leave any chemical trace of a drug in the body. But if we get close enough to guards, use pressure-point techniques to drop them. If not—it's the darts," Carlos said to Dillon.

"A doable plan!

"So let's do it!" Dillon stated with finality, and both men went out to the central station.

Before leaving control, Cyrus instructed them, "Be here at eight sharp! I want to go over every aspect of the plan one last time. We'll have the latest satellite imaging to know exactly what to expect inside for tomorrow night. Our source will provide us with tomorrow's password, too!"

"Then, we'll be seein' you when it's over, Mac." Dillon's eyes conveyed his message to Cyrus—they would not fail. The two men left the building together.

Once outside, Dillon said, 'I'm glad to be workin' with you again, friend."

Dillon's words held a world of memories for the two men.

"We never really parted, *il mio amico.*"

Inside, Cyrus was seated alone in the conference room with his thoughts.

*"Be **my** eyes and ears tomorrow night!"*

# CHAPTER FORTY-ONE

Marcus Rudolphi drove away from the Villa del Christianna.

At the gate, he turned north toward Lago di Como speeding into the night—alone.

The drive from the Villa del Christianna to the Villa Latinestto at Verrano took just over an hour at night; a shorter trip than during daylight hours. Tonight, the ride gave him the time to think...*I will have Emma Llewelyn soon!*

Marcus slowed to a stop outside the gate to the Villa Latinestto, the uniformed guard dressed in black fatigues recognized him and walked over to the car.

"*Milano contra Torino.*" Marcus gave the daily pass phrase and the guard released the gate mechanism opening the gates to let the silver Maserati silently and slowly drive up the dimly lit driveway to the front of the villa. A young man opened the door.

"*Buono sera, Signore Marcus,* we've been expecting you. Everyone is in the study."

"*Grazie,* Dino." Marcus walked straight down the long hall into the study. "Always the polite one—but the cunningest, too!" Dino thought.

"*Buono sera Baba, come sta lei?*" Marcus leaned over to kiss his father seated next to the warm hearth.

"*Sono buono come un vecchil puo'essere!*" Giuseppe Rudolphi, head of the Rudolphi family, muttered. He liked to be seated next to the warm fire. He no longer tolerated the cold damp air in the villa..

*"Miei fratelli cari"* Marcus acknowledged Dominic and Luigi both standing in front of the fireplace, his glance purposely meant to interrupt their conversation with each other.

"Any trouble getting here Marcus," Giuseppe asked.

"No, Lucinda is with her *madre* tonight; she is not feeling well today. She needs to see a doctor, but refuses to see Carruchi anymore."

"Then *you* take her to see Doctore Franco Dinardi in Firenze! He's a good man and will be honest and tell you everything, too! If there is something you should know—he will tell you!" Giuseppe Rudolphi was telling his son to take control of his wife. "Let's get started—it's already late." The elder Rudolphi held the power in the family despite his aging years, and his sons acknowledged it.

"Dominic, what has Carruchi done about completing the last set of trials? Has he completed a sufficient amount of the formula for the meeting, and has he administered the last injections? We need that last set of data." Giuseppe said.

"*Baba,* he finished the last injection on the Chinese children last week. He will finish with the French boy and girl sometime this week. The new batch of serum from the laboratory will be ready in another day," Dominic told his father.

"I hope all the documentation will be completed by the time the presentation starts!" Giuseppe stated as a command.

"What arrangements did you make for the Llewelyn woman?" he asked his youngest son, Luigi.

"We have not yet been successful in getting her… and right this moment we're not sure exactly where she is." Luigi's voice softened with his last words. "However, my informer learned she and that investigator flew back to England from Milano on a flight to London this very evening. My man in London is waiting at the airport to follow her and he's set up a twenty-four hour surveillance team on her London home and office. He has instructions to report to me every twelve hours…or as necessary!" Luigi said.

"Luigi, if *you* can't get this woman…then I'll send a man who can!" Giuseppe shouted to his youngest son, who was feeling the sting of his father's words, not to mention his humiliation in front of his brothers.

"There will be no more blunders, *Baba*! If I must...*I* will get her myself!"

"Then DO IT! And no more slip-ups—Dr. Carruchi wants her back here now! She's a liability to this whole operation! If we're to proceed and go public, marketing the formula to Biotechnical and Pharmaceutical companies, we need to dispose of her before this phase of the operation!" Giuseppe's words were adamant with no flexibility.

"*Si Baba, capisco.*" Luigi acknowledged his father's command. Though he was aging and frail, he still feared his power within the family.

"We will have her within the next several days, I promise, *Baba*," Luigi told his father, setting down his wine glass.

"I'm going to London myself—tomorrow—to see that nothing goes wrong! I assure you there will be no more complications in this matter!" To change the subject away from his failures to detain Emma, Luigi looked directly at Marcus with his statement.

"It's too bad what happened to Davici in Milano. I understand Remo is no longer with us either!"

"He was stupid and careless...neither of them could overcome one woman? We have no proof who was responsible for their deaths. But when I find out...they will pay a heavy price!"

"Do not mourn the likes of their passing...Tony was a pig and Remo no better, big brother!" Luigi said to Marcus.

"I do not mourn the likes of that scum, you fool! It is the problems they created for us...by failing to do the job!" Marcus stared at his brother, Luigi, hoping he understood the real implication behind his chosen words. Marcus was more worried about Emma than he would let on to the family! His father wanted her dead. He wanted her alive!

"*Baba,* I have taken steps to dispose of our failures—several trucks are ready to come in tomorrow night...for their trip to the Ober Engadin in Switzerland. Unfortunately—or fortunately, as you look at it, we had two more failures last week. They succumbed to complications earlier than we expected. Franco has already taken care of the remains—cremation in a Firenze crematorium," Marcus addressed the group.

"Is Ennio coming here tonight?" Giuseppe asked Marcus.

"*Sì Baba,* but not until later. He's finishing the last of his data tonight in the villa complex. He's quite excited about what his data has proven. I expect we'll know tomorrow the percentage of our successes."

"Then, I'll not wait up for him tonight. When he comes, tell him I will see him in the morning at breakfast at the usual time." Giuseppe slowly walked out the door to the stairs. Dino was waiting to assist him up the staircase to his suite on the second floor.

"Dino, you should be my son! You do more for me than any one of them back there does! Except Marcus, of course."

"*Baba* Rudolphi I like doing for you! There is nothing more I should want...here lean on me these stairs are steep and slippery." Slowly, Dino took the old man up the stairs to his room to prepare him for bed.

"Dino, give me my pills with the wine tonight. I want to make sure I get a good sleep. Tomorrow is a big day here, and I want to be ready!" Dino prepared Giuseppe's pills, as usual with the wine. To make certain he would sleep soundly, he added another half dose of sleeping medication. The man looked old but still had the body of a bull. Dino had to be certain Guiseppe would sleep through the night and not interrupt his work tonight.

"I still have to contact Control tonight to tell them the new password for the mission tomorrow night. More importantly, they must know Emma Llewelyn is still a target in London!"

Returning to the old man sitting on the bed, he said, "Drink, *Baba,* it is as you like it!"

"When do you leave for London, Luigi?" Marcus asked his brother.

"My plane is ready to go at a moment's notice—most likely, I'll leave tomorrow evening. I have to make certain Michala is all right...she has only two more weeks and then the baby could come anytime. *La madre* is with her for the next several months or even longer, since this is our first child! *La Madre,* Ophelia is more concerned for her than I am, but then, isn't that how *le madri* are supposed to be?" Luigi asked with a cynical laugh.

"As long as you accomplish your primary mission with no more complications…or failures, that's what matters now! Remember, Luigi, *deliver her to me alive!"* Marcus retorted viciously. He didn't allow Luigi time for a reply, and turned to Domimic with a question.

"Dominic, you say the new formula is almost completed. Does this mean it can be mass produced or is it just the trial sample?"

"It is just one of the many samples we are making in the winery. What we will do is take a sample to the approved Pharmaceutical Company for mass production only *after* the trials are completed. Of course, we will explain our mandates to them; we'll carry out the trial procedures on a species—our choice—in their labs—mice or whatever subject they suggest—the companies will oversee and document the results—making it very legitimate. Neither will they have any chance to duplicate the chemical formula for themselves before we get our money!" Dominic explained. "While these trials are going on, we will produce the serums in great quantities for our clients—once the prices are agreed to! When the trial results are final, then we sell the companies the rights to produce the serum only at a specified date in the future. This gives us the lion's share of that income, too!"

"Does this include the AC-1 formula as well as the AC-5 formula? Or would it be to our advantage to keep the latter formula on the gene mutation until we're absolutely certain the preliminary trials are as successful as ours?" Marcus asked his brother.

"They must first trial the **AC-1 formula** and document the results from that formula. Not until we're certain they are going to buy from us will we offer the **AC-5 gene formula** to them for a second series of testing to their satisfaction! All the while, we have complete control of the formula. The latter formula is Dr. Carruchi's formula, and he still controls it and has the final say when and how it will be handled—he keeps the formula locked in his head. This is the formula that will make us rich beyond our dreams! We can selectively choose who gets the formula for the highest price!"

Dominic Rudolphi was the most intelligent of the Rudolphis. He understood the technical and financial aspects of the research and was the one to work closely with Dr. Carruchi in his experiments.

"Then we need to discuss the specifics with Ennio tomorrow to find out the quantity we will need when the time comes, and how much stock we'll keep, when the date to go public is decided," Marcus told his two brothers.

At that moment Dr. Ennio Carruchi opened the door.

"*Avanti Ennio*—good to see you at last!" Marcus greeted him with a strong show of affection.

"Let me fix you a drink, Ennio. What would you like?" Dominic asked.

"Bourbon with a splash of water, *grazie*. It's as good as a sleeping potion for me," Ennio Carruchi laughed with confidence as he accepted the drink.

"Do we have the Llewelyn woman yet?" the doctor asked in a serious tone to the three men in the room.

"Not exactly, Ennio," Luigi Rudolphi said.

"I understand she has returned to London just today, and I have my plane ready to leave at any time for London…I'm personally going to London to oversee her return to Milano with me! There will be no failures!" Luigi said trying to impress upon the group that he had the situation under his complete control.

"I know in the past, you always got your man, Luigi. I hope this translates the same for the woman!" Carruchi said in a derogatory lecture.

"I don't think I should have to say more about this now. But to clarify how critical it is we have her in hand, so to speak, she is the only uncertain linkage—the weakest link in our master plan, and we must deal with that weakness BEFORE we start our negotiations! **I think we all know what happens to failures, don't we?**" He looked sternly at all three men in the room.

Changing the conversation to ease the chilling reaction permeating the room, Carruchi asked, "Dominic, have the laboratories completed the samples we need for our summit meeting with the pharmaceutical companies, three days away?"

"*Si*, I have seen to it that we have enough serum produced already! But each pharmaceutical rep will do secret bidding for the right to test subjects, and the two highest bidders will be chosen for the trials in outside laboratories—each will have to compete with each other for the final contract." Dominic explained for the benefit of his brothers.

Carruchi interjected, "I have handpicked our two scientists who will do the work with the pharmaceutical companies. They will oversee their experiments in their labs AND make certain nothing goes wrong!" Carruchi instructed.

"Tomorrow, a general meeting in the conference complex for ten o'clock is planned. Be there, gentlemen. We have already sent out the invitations to the pharmaceutical companies who will be invited to attend the first seminar I am giving on stem cell research and genetics at Firenze tomorrow evening," Carruchi said.

"After this seminar, I will speak with the companies' representatives to determine which ones will be chosen for the testing." Carruchi looked at each man in the room.

"I take it Giuseppe has retired already?"

"*Si*. Ennio. He will be with us tomorrow at the morning conference," Marcus said.

Dominic made a move to leave, "Ennio, I must return to Milano. There is still some last minute work in the Complex to insure we have enough serum produced and packaged. I will be here tomorrow with all the information you will need for the conference meeting. *Caio*—Ennio, Marcus, Luigi!" Dominic nodded to each man and walked out to the foyer.

"I, too, will have everything you need completed for tomorrow's meeting, Ennio," Marcus echoed with complacency.

"I know you will, Marcus—It is your signature. You have always been the meticulous one." Dr. Carruchi finished his drink and set his glass on the mantel.

"I'm very tired now and will retire for the night. And may I suggest you men do the same? Marcus, see me to the door?" The two men walked over to the door speaking in low tones.

"When we get the woman, what are your plans for her, Marcus?"

"I haven't decided yet! Guiseppe wants her terminated. But that decision is for **me to make!** I will have to see how she reacts to… learning about Carina."

"Do you think it is wise to tell at this time?"

"Ennio, I've taken great care to arrange a place outside of Italy to take her…a place that's a good opportunity to tell her…The Swiss mountains are quiet and desolate…and the chalet is not easy to get to or away from…She will enjoy the beauty of the mountains, too, especially after she learns about Carina! I still have to make a decision about Lucinda."

"You'd best not wait too long, Marcus! Mistakes are made with procrastination. So I leave you…we'll talk more about this in the morning!" After Dr. Carruchi left the Library, Marcus turned to his brother, Luigi.

"The only loose and weak link in this whole matter is Emma Llewelyn! Bring her to me alive, brother! Do not fail this time, Luigi!" Marcus spoke to him in angry reproach and set his wine glass down with purpose and walked out the door. Luigi understood exactly what his brother's rebuke implied!

"Do not worry big brother—you will have your woman!" Luigi poured another glass of wine and turned on the television and sat down alone to watch the television show. He loved the late night shows.

"*Bellisomo – magnifico.*" Luigi laughed out loud in the study amused by the program.

Marcus quietly peered through the slightly opened door studying his brother's behavior of enjoyment with the comedy show. He knew Luigi was the weak link in the organization—and someday he would have to do something about it.

"*Do not fail me little brother, **your very life** depends on success this time!*" Marcus softly muttered, and shut the door tightly to silence the noise from the television.

# CHAPTER FORTY-TWO

Concealed behind a pillar at the top of the stairs, Dino observed Marcus's behavior standing outside the study.

"Why is he spying on Luigi? He doesn't trust Luigi! And with good reason not to…he's the erratic conniving one of the three!" Inaudibly, Marcus mumbled something while watching Luigi. Dino knew it was Luigi's job to watch Emma Llewelyn. Careful to avoid detection, he quietly slipped back into his small adjoining quarters next to Giuseppe's suite before Marcus came upstairs. Safe in his room, he heard the sounds of the old man's deep sonorous breathing and knew he was asleep for the night. But he had to wait until Marcus and Luigi retired, too, before he attempted to contact control. Too dangerous—either one could walk into his room while he was sending his message to control! No, he'd wait until everyone in the house was asleep. Luigi was the last to finally retire to his room. Dino heard the bedroom door close, but waited another hour, making certain no one was stirring inside the villa. The house was eerily quiet. Dominic returned to Milano, Marcus and Luigi retired for the night, Giuseppe was still deep in sleep…Dino opened his watch lens. Using a code, he sent a message to control in Milano.

**Tomorrow's password—La bambini—the children! Carruchi scheduled most important meeting at Latinestto ten/twenty-one! Emma's capture planned for London by L.R.**

\* \* \*

Andrew and Aldo worked all night at the Villa D' Este, installing the communications, surveillance, and security systems. The sun was rising over the treetops on the east side of the Lake—a beautiful sight from the terrace. Biaggio walked into the Grand Room and saw Aldo setting up the telescope and camera in the corner window to view the Villa Latinestto directly across the lake.

"Can I have a look?" Biaggio asked Aldo.

"Sure—try it out. See if you can see the picture on the wall in the Villa Latinestto? I made out a Bonard of the Virgin Mary hanging— early Renaissance, probably worth millions of Euros. Do you see it?" Aldo asked Biaggio, intently focusing the scope's lens.

Biaggio took his time looking through the lens. "There's a painting on the wall on the right…it's the Holy Mother, but I can't make out the signature."

"You're half right, old man! But it's on the left wall. Could be the lens' fault. Should I put in a stronger lens…What do you think, old man?" Aldo amusingly toyed with Biaggio.

"Leave it, Aldo! These old eyes saw the Bonard you did, but YOU missed the Raphael on the other wall across from it worth three times more!" Biaggio chuckled and walked down the hallway leaving Aldo looking intently through the scope across the lake.

"*Jesu Christo*, he's right!"

Andrew chose the largest room in the basement to set up the central command station. Actually, it was the garden room with three walls of glass windows covered on the inside with sheer translucent blinds allowing light into the room, but nothing inside was visible from the outside. The room easily held all the computers and monitors. Besides, the ground floor was easy to feed all the special lines required for the different types of security planned inside and outside. The villa's original private security system was too accessible to anyone with a computer to figure out the codes. A good computer hack could figure out all the possible code combinations even if the code was changed and get inside. Interpol had far superior and almost impassable systems—proven over many times.

The perimeter alarm was uniquely set up with a system of lasers— when breached, a series of alarms went off. If someone passed one meter away from the heat-oriented beam, the broken beams would signal a silent alert in the Control center, identifying exactly the site of the breach while simultaneously delivering an electrical shock that would neutralize an intruder leaving him helpless for several minutes. The double kind of response was a backup to make certain no intruder could get into the villa's grounds without some form of security violation. This was Andrew's first level of security.

The second level of security inside the house was much more sophisticated; each room, door and window was electronically wired with a combination laser/motion sensor originating from central control which continually monitored with three-dimensional cameras. Likewise, an electrical impulse would deter an intruder for several seconds—a unique system Andrew installed throughout the villa. An Interpol agent was to be assigned at Control station twenty-four hours monitoring the monitors in every room, every exit door and the immediate grounds. On the roof of the villa, marksmen were assigned to inspect all activity around the Villa Latinestto—night and day.

The site chosen for Emma's bedroom suite was the north side, facing the Lepontine Alps—out of view of the Villa Latinestto. Andrew explained to Biaggio, "If *we* have sophisticated systems surveying the Villa Latinestto, they could do the same to us if they knew we were here …Emma must never be in direct vision from across the lake—in any room! The Rosetti's will occupy the front suite, directly in sight of the Villa Latinessto, since it is their vacation—you'd expect them to be in the master suite!"

Lakeside, two boathouses belonged to the villa—each with an inside dock with several boat slips in the basement. The larger boathouse housed the large power cruiser in a basement slip, while the smaller boathouse had slips for other smaller boats with outboard engines. The large cruiser was allocated to stow underwater paraphernalia—as the special ops teams would need the cruiser for their underwater excursions. The second and third floors of the large boathouse were apartment complexes for the teams to stay in—along with their weapons cache. The smaller boathouse, closer to the water's edge, stored additional munitions. The seal teams took care of the special water security system to the two boathouses, so no unexpected visitors could approach from the lake.

Andy was finishing the final connections in the garden room when the door opened.

"Mac—didn't expect you so back so soon."

"Needed to check everything with you before our special guests move in...*before Emma gets here*. Did you get a chance to put a tap on the phone lines across the lake yet?"

"Aldo is doin' that as we speak. I expect he'll be back with his report in an hour."

"Then, let's you and I check the boathouse." Cyrus and Andrew walked down the path through the gardens to the large stone boathouse and entered the front door.

"Lyn Brienne would fit inside this place—and this is just a boathouse!" Cyrus remarked, taking in the surrounding shrubbery and access from the beach. In the basement, they boarded the forty-foot cruiser, inspecting all the cabins.

"This is doable! Should be able to take it out for a trip with snorkeling gear during the day—innocent activity—tanks by night."

"We stored munitions upstairs in the apartment. The Special Teams will bunk here, and if they're out doing surveillance two operatives will be here at all times. The diving tanks can be refilled here, too, if we need to do several consecutive dives," Andy said.

"Then let's get a look upstairs." Cyrus and Andrew went up two flights of stairs to the top apartment. "I guess the Milanese think anything smaller than a *villa* is a flat," Cyrus noted, observing the far side of the room. Stacks of small and large stocks of munitions were carefully arranged.

"We'll stock the food larder well while the guests are here—no need to go to town," Andrew said.

"Anna Morena is assigned the villa maid and Aldo, the butler. Both are excellent marksmen and both know our security systems well. We can all pitch in to do the cooking," Andrew stated.

"No one will hold a candle to Biaggio's cooking!" Cyrus said. Closing the door, both men started back to the *casa*.

Voices greeted them inside the spacious foyer…Anna and Aldo met the Rosettis at the door. "All the bags go to the large front bedroom," Anna informed Aldo.

"She's always telling me what to do!" Aldo winked at Cyrus as he started up the circular staircase loaded with suitcases.

"Good to see you, Mac," Anna said with an embrace. "It's been too long!"

"Anna, you never change. Can't imagine why someone hasn't snatched you away from us," Cyrus said greeting her with a fatherly embrace.

"Don't be too sure someone hasn't already, Mac," Anna remarked with a wink.

"Anna have you ever met my granddaughter, Emma Llewelyn?"

"No, I haven't had the pleasure."

"Well you're about to do that. Only there's one important wrinkle here…Emma has no idea I work with Interpol, and therefore, doesn't have any knowledge I'm here on this mission. It's vital she doesn't learn this information about me—or about Andrew's presence here either, or his involvement with the company! There can be no slip-ups with her *about us*! Most of the time, I will be at Central Control in Milano, and Andrew will be here in this Control center, but there may be times when I'll have to be here, too. The door to the garden room will be locked at all times! Emma believes I'm away from Lyn Brienne somewhere on the Continent on farm business, so we all go along with that story…if the topic arises. If Emma asks about the locked room—it's classified personnel only—and she's not! She has a way of finding out things, the truth. Can't blame her for that—she gets it from me!"

"Any questions?"

"No, Mac. There'll be no problems here."

A second unmarked van drove up the drive to the front door. Anna scrutinized the two couples carrying several cases. "Mornin' folks…you're expectin' us…Colin's blokes from Manchester-Ivy. Where do we stow our stuff?"

"I take it that translates you're MI 5 teams?" Cyrus asked.

"Aye—that be us! I'm called Joe, and this here's Amy—call us the Littletons for propriety's sake. That bloke followin' behind is Kevin and his misses, Casey Kirkland."

"This is Anna the maid—and Aldo is the butler. Biaggio will be the chauffeur and the renters are Josepi and Maria Rosetti—here on holiday from Boston, Massachusetts. I'm Cyrus MacKenna—call me Mac." Cyrus explained.

"There will be another houseguest, Emma Llewelyn. She will be here… in cognito! This directive concerning her is Priority One. I want all of you to keep a close eye on her at all times with one catch…none of you know me or saw me here! Cyrus MacKenna has nothing to do with this mission, and you've never heard the name nor met the man! Andrew Masters, in charge of Control quarters here, his is another name you've never come by! Any questions? Biaggio will show you to your quarters in the boathouse. I'm leaving for Milano headquarters now."

"Got it all, Mac. We ne'er 'eard of Cyrus MacKenna or Andrew Masters!"

Biaggio drove the van to the rear of the *villa* and down to the boathouse to unload and store the underwater tanks, wetsuits, and the other water paraphernalia—including the cache of weaponry. As Colin promised, there were extra diving tanks and suits, including night vision water-equipment, charting supplies, underwater spots, and cameras. Biaggio watched the team of men and women carry up the three trunks of equipment to one of the apartments.

"I hope that's top-shelf brands!" Biaggio said to the group.

"You better believe it, chief! Taxes pay for nothin' but the very best with us!" Biaggio was referring to the weapons equipment ordered for the assault on the Villa Latinestto—when that time came. Colin's teams carefully stowed the diving equipment inside the cruiser, while Biaggio and Andy carried the trunks of munitions upstairs to the first flat, carefully checking firing mechanisms and laying them out with all the other firearms.

Andy gave instructions. "Here's a rotation watch-list for the waterfront—two men posted outside the house—one at the front of this boathouse by the water, and the other is between the villa and the upper boathouse. Everyone will have radio communication. If there's any problem, sound the alarm immediately! Carry a holster piece on you at all times...every man in the villa is to be armed at all times—with whatever he's comfortable with. This boathouse is never to be left empty...with its munitions. We don't want any surprises—especially if word leaks out Emma is staying here!"

"Gov—I take it Emma is a prime target?"

"Yeah! She is...by the very people in the villa across the lake! It's everyone's job here to see she's protected at all costs! They've already made unsuccessful attempts to abduct her in Milano, and if they discover she's here, they're sure to try again! Emma has no idea what's going to go down from here—not yet! So watch what you say in front of her. Any more questions?" Andy made it clear everyone had to be mentally alert when Emma was with them.

"No questions, yet, Johnny! That's our code name for you...so no slipups?"

Andy and Biaggio walked back to the villa. "You like her, too, huh, Biaggio? You know, I've seen her grow from a tiny babe into a beautiful successful woman...There's nothin' I wouldn't do to keep her safe! She's like me own...!" Andrew just let the words trail off.

*"Si capisco, `e la famiglia!"*

# CHAPTER FORTY-THREE

Carlos and Dillon returned to the English Bookstore.

"Are you two set for tonight?" Cyrus greeted them.

"*Si*—we're waiting for Andy to bring us the equipment." At that moment, Andy walked into the conference room carrying two leather cases.

"I suggest you try out all the equipment…We need to check everything for precision. You won't get a second chance to fix a mistake in the field!" Andy counseled them. Carlos and Dillon donned the facemasks and the tinted eye lenses. "Phenomenal! Now the voice modulators."

"*Si, sono Marcus Rudolphi*—and my brother," Carlos said.

"*Dominic Rudolpi. Si, come sta lei?* Did that come out right?" Dillon asked his partner in disguise.

"You'll pass for now," Carlos retorted. Removing the disguises to pack them back into the black bags, Andy added the necessary facial creams to go under the masks to mold them perfectly to their facial contours.

"Here are your white lab coats and the special gloves with the fingerprints of Marcus and Dominic. Both of you wear good presentable clothes under the lab coats to look like there's money in your pockets; shoes, pants, shirts—the works!" Andy finished marking off his checklist.

"Biaggio should be here shortly to drive you to the Villa del Christianna. He knows the best spot to access the pool area with the fewest security devices. Do you have the target area in the grounds mapped out and memorized?" Cyrus questioned them.

"Yeah, we double checked with Biaggio, and we think the best way to get into the grounds is at the farthest point north in the gardens," he said, pointing to a spot on the map. "There's a lot of ground cover there good for 'iddin', and we'll be wearin' black fatigues over our good duds," Dillon said.

"Once we neutralize the security points and come to the pool house entrance, we'll check out those ground pipes to distinguish 'intake' from 'outflow' ducts."

"We have the gas pellets for the pipes and darts for emergencies and each of us has our handgun with several rounds and silencers—just in case," Carlos said, looking at Dillon who was securing his Larson in the shoulder holster.

"I can't caution you enough! This mission must be absolutely secret! No one in the Rudolphi organization must even suspect we penetrated that complex. If anyone learns we breached their security system, they'll most likely shut down and investigate thoroughly how it happened—thwarting our time table. We can't afford to tip our hand and have them change their plans—not at this delicate juncture—just when we're ready to make our moves! *We're so close now...!* If they suspect we're on to them, they'll move somewhere else—so time is critical to us now!"

Both men heard the urgency in Cyrus's cautions to them. Moving towards Carlos and Dillon, Cyrus reached out and shook hands with each man.

"I wish I was going with you...I know you'll both do a good job tonight...**for God's sake—be bloody careful!**" Cyrus's last admonition was more from the heart than a command. He saw himself in these young men twenty years ago—dedicated, strong, and committed.

"One last instruction, the password for today is *La Bambino*—the children! You'll need it to get past the security checks. When the mission's completed, Biaggio will bring you back here directly! Andy and I will be here waiting for the films, and we'll do the debriefing then. Any questions?"

"None—*Caio,* Mac!" Carlos waved.

"*Arrivederci!*" Dillon echoed as they picked up the leather cases, checked their holsters once more, and left without looking back.

\* \* \*

Night had fallen, and the new moon provided total blackness—the darkest of nights—no moon shadows. Biaggio drove around to the back of the Villa del Christianna's gardens to the most distant point from the *casa.* The car barely moving, with its lights out, coasted to a pre-selected spot, and the motor was turned off. Biaggio knew this area well from his past surveillances—exactly where to drive with lights out and avoid any collisions in the dark. He chose a spot close to the seven-foot stone wall for quick and easy access over it. Without anyone moving, the three men listened to the silence around them. Carlos and Dillon painstakingly donned the disguises—facemasks, lenses, gloves, and voice modulators without wasting time. Each wore a black ski cap over their disguises to keep reflections off their faces from the dim garden lights until they reached the target entrance. The last piece of equipment was a hidden earpiece that allowed them to communicate with one another by microphones inside their shirt collars.

"Everything is ready, *Signores!*" Biaggio whispered and gave the thumbs-up sign.

The two men quietly opened the door and latched it closed by feel. Climbing atop the hood of the car up to the roof, Dillon pressed a pad that released a grappling hook over the stone wall snagging a secure grip the first time and scaled the rest of the way up the wall to the top, dropping silently on the other side. Carlos followed. A low stacotto whistle told Biaggio they were safely over as Dillon pressed the pad and the grappler hook retracted. Dillon pointed to a large bush with shallow roots to hide the grappler in a shallow grave. They heard the hum of the car motor getting distant. It wasn't difficult to determine the right direction—the pool lights lit up the cabanas and flags wafting in the night breezes.

"Check—it's exactly twenty-three zero four."

"Check!" Dillon whispered.

"We make our way over in that direction." Carlos pointed to the pennant flags flying in the wind.

"Check for the trip wires or laser cameras. Biaggio found the wires startin' fifty meters from the wall; the cameras at fifty, seventy-five, and one hundred-meter intervals. Carlos, you attach the false lens to each camera goin' in, and I'll remove them on our way out," Dillon said.

"Here's the first trip wire." Carlos pointed to the ground in front of them. Both carefully stepping widely around the area. Dillon lay flat using the night vision binoculars to see what was ahead.

"I see a camera…it's directly to your left." Carlos made his way over to the bushes housing the camera, and in an instant, he had the false lens in place.

"Sure hope the monitor tunes it in correctly!" he said in a whisper.

"'ave faith boy—Andy's a genius!"

Slowly, they made their way towards the pool area, listening for any approaching sounds of security patrols. "It's a night just for o'ls." Finally passing all the security cameras and trip lines, they reached the back of the pool house—a few feet away were the cabanas.

"Now's the time to confirm if we're alone or if we 'ave compan'!" Dillon whispered to Carlos. They stopped and listened for sounds of voices or radios; no noise—no voices—no movement from the pool area as seen in the monochromatic green night-vision binoculars.

With infrared goggles sensitive to darkness and heat, the ground pipes were quickly located, showing various degrees of heat by the reddish-orange colors at the tops of outflow vents. Crawling over to them, each listened to the din from the pipes and held feathery-like material light enough to twist in the direction of the airflow. All the outlets were tested this way.

"Here's an outflow tube, and I can feel the hot air coming from it," Carlos said.

Dillon crawled over to a farther pipe and put his ear next to it and then held the wispy material over the tube.

"This is intake—I'm pretty certain." Dillon heard his remark.

"Carlos, you get ready to enter the pool house, and I'll drop the pellets down this pipe and meet you at the door." Carlos signaled with the thumbs-up signal, and Dillon slowly and deliberately dropped the pellets into the pipe then made his way to the pool house door.

Quickly undressing out of the black fatigues, they arranged their disguises, stashing their fatigues behind the thickest shrubs. A final check of each other's appearances—Marcus and Dominic Rudolphi were ready to enter the complex! The disguises were made to fool the security cameras from a distance throughout the complex. The plan was that Marcus and Dominic Rudolphi were there investigating the cause of the noxious fumes. The last piece of equipment in place was the tiny microphone inside the necks of their shirts, with the hidden earpiece to communicate with each other when they separated.

"It's a piece of cake!" Carlos whispered.

"Clear!" Dillon responded.

"Let's roll!" *Marcus said to Dominic.*

The outer door of the small house was easy to breach with a master duplicate key that turned off the door's alarms. The inner door was the final checkpoint. Wearing the duplicate handprint gloves, they pressed the keypad and spoke what they hoped was the latest code—"*La bambino.*" It should be correct if their inside source sent the right code for this date. The next security step—the hand scanner for each man—then the eye-ground scanner; lastly, the computer asked for voice identification.

"*Marcus Rudolphi, la bambino,*" said Carlos.;

"*Dominic Rudolphi, la bambino,*" said Dillon.

The inner door unlatched automatically with a loud thud. Dillon opened the door wider to see a spotlessly clean hallway brightly lit up all the down to the steps at the farthest end. Closing the door quickly, Carlos motioned for Dillon to follow him. "You take the right—I'll take the left."

Quickly making their way down the corridor, Carlos and Dillon tried every door on each side, moving rapidly to the end of corridor—all locked! But each door had a small window allowing them to view the room and contents—storage rooms.

"No sign of cameras mounted exteriorly—most likely they're in the ceiling with three hundred sixty degree surveillance," Carlos said and took out a small aerosol can concealed in his hand and started spraying in the direction of the ceiling, hoping to fog any camera lenses behind the glass tiles. Finally reaching the far end of the corridor, the steps opened to an empty stairwell.

Reaching the next level, Carlos said, "Crack the door a bit to see if the gas is working."

Dillon whispered, "Yeah...I see a few men and women runnin' out of the rooms...That gas is workin' fine! They're coughin' and tryin' to hold their breaths, runnin' down the far end of the hall out to another exit. The hall's clear!"

Dillon motioned to Carlos to enter the rooms on the left, and he would stay on the right side.

Watching the last worker disappear out the door at the far end, Carlos entered the first door to find a large well-lit laboratory with all kinds of scientific equipment used for chemical testing. Taking as many pictures of the room as possible, he came upon a journal on the counter. Focusing the camera, he turned each page and completed copying the book in two minutes.

"Dillon, you finding anything?"

"You bet yur ass! But just keep movin' and lookin'!"

Carlos moved through the connecting doors to a lab with a green sign reading **"Clean Room"** between them. The next room was a second laboratory with a logo for universal contamination on the door! Disregarding the sign, he entered inside.

"Jesus! What is this place?" Dillon heard his exclamation.

"Pay dirt, *amico*?" Carlos didn't answer his question.

On one wall were several large individual, horizontal, numbered refrigerator stalls with glass outer doors. Carlos peered inside one of the doors.

"My God! It's a morgue in here," he spoke to Dillon softly.

Carlos approached several compartments with bodies inside. Hesitantly opening one, he choked at the sight of what lay on the slab.

"You okay?" Dillon asked.

"Yeah...no problem," Carlos said staring at a small child-like figure. The sight of the face and withered body appeared to be that of an old man—wrinkled, white-haired, long white beard, and sunken facial features. The vision startled and stunned him into silence. Looking away to catch his breath and not let Dillon know the gravity of his find, Carlos quickly snapped pictures of the body and returned the tray back inside the cubicle, fighting every fiber in his body to stay focused and emotionless.

"This is incredible—they're murderers, Dillon! They were only children!" Carlos said.

"Don't go soft now—still a lot to do!" Dillon retorted.

Carlos knew this was the kind of evidence they needed to get convictions. It was real, hard evidence needed to show a jury to convict and seek the death penalty. He took pictures of each specimen in each cubicle.

The last refrigerator cubicle had a label and name on the cold metal tray that he thought he recognized. For what seemed like long minutes, he just stared...deliberately not taking any pictures of what was lying in front of him. Knowing Dillon was listening to all his comments or sounds, he clenched his jaw tight to keep from making a noise. Taking in a deep breath, he raised the sheet and swallowed hard. Slowly—almost reverently—he replaced the sheet and pushed the metal tray back into the darkness and closed the door. Taking in one deep breath to cleanse away what he had just seen, he needed to continue the mission. Silently, his thoughts rang in his mind, *Now it's become my personal war! I swear by everything good ...they'll all die...!* It touched him more than he realized.

In the laboratory on the opposite side of the hallway, Dillon found several desks at one end of the room with shelves of containers marked with coded labels. The counters extended the length of the room and the shelves were filled two deep with coded flasks of all sizes. Seeing several empty syringes lying on the counter...he picked one up.

"One for you...one for me..." Pointing to the flasks, he quickly chose one of the flasks, opened it, and drew up the syringe...he filled it with the serum from the flask, capped the syringe, and placed it in his pocket. Making certain to place the flask back in its original position, he made a mental note, **AC-5** was written on the flask's label. Next, seeing stacks of journals on the desks, Dillon started photographing pictures of the lab and then turned to the different journals, snapping film as fast as he could. Hurrying into the connecting laboratory, he found cages of animals and mice. Some looked young and others aged—all alive.

A sudden rush of air came from the corridor. The laboratory door opened and startled Carlos.

"*Signore* Marcus, I did not know you would be here tonight. We had a fright when a terrible odor came in, and we had to evacuate the laboratories! Did you not smell it?" the laboratory technician asked.

"*Si! Certo ho fatto, che `e perche' sono venuto!* I'm here to make certain nothing in the complex was damaged! I have almost completed my check in here and in those other rooms; I've not found anything permanently damaged by the foul smell. *Signore* Dominic is looking into the cause of the annoyance as we speak. I think the worst has passed and you can all return to your stations. I must locate *Signore* Dominic to see if he located the source of the problem in the ventilation systems." Carlos said duplicating Marcus Rulolphi's voice. He quickly left the laboratory and crossed the hall to the last room to look for Dillon.

"I can't let Dillon stumble into an employee; if they speak Italian, he may be a dead giveaway—even with Dominic's voice!"

Carlos found Dillon exiting the farthest room at the end of the corridor. Dillon motioned to Carlos he was going up to the next level.

The door at the end of the hall from the stairwell opened, and several more employees entered.

Carlos spoke to the group. "It's clear down here! I'm going upstairs to check. If any of you have anymore problems, let me know!"

Dillon was aware of the complications happening to Carlos. Both men heard the change in a high-pitched hum coming from the on-site underground generators boosting the exhaust systems to clear the complex of the noxious fumes.

Taking the same stairs the employees did, they went up and opened a door on another level. Hurrying down the corridor, they continued checking rooms on each side of the hall.

"Private offices with lavish decorations!" Carlos added.

"Clearl' belongin' to the chiefs," Dillon said.

The doors were locked—except for one. Carlos entered the office and went directly to the desk. A nameplate sat on the desk—Dr. Ennio Carruchi.

"Pay dirt!" Carlos said. Rifling through the appointment book, there was a notation of a meeting with, *"Genrad and Phisto—10 A.M"* on the twentieth of this month. *"Finish tests and copy reports."* Carlos photographed that page and the next several pages. "Something big is going to go down in two days, Dillon. I have to get all this information before we leave!"

"Carlos, its time to get out—now! The gas is almost completel' exhausted! We need to 'ead down to the lowest level to get out before someone from the villa comes down to investigate more thorough'y—like the real Marcus Rudolphi!"

Carlos took one last check, making certain nothing looked disturbed and met up with Dillon on the stairs to the lowest level. They needed to find the same exit out to the pool house. The stairwells were empty as well as the ground corridor. Running towards the exit door, they heard a sound of a heavy thud. The two men stopped abruptly. The noise came from the exit door at the end of the hall. In an instant, Carlos and Dillon darted into one of the locked storerooms that Dillon opened with his lock-pick in an instant just as two guards entered the hallway. Inside, they pressed against the wall out of direct sight from the glass door panel. Dillon held the dart gun in readiness; Carlos had the Larson with the silencer in place.

"Nothing's open here! The guards checked each storeroom, peering through the glass window in the door. "It's all locked down...just as we left it!" the guard said to his companion.

"Something must have gone wrong in one of the laboratories! Those people are always making foul-smelling solutions! Just last week, I just about passed out from the smell from **Laboratory A!** We had best check there to report to *Signore* Marcus—he's particular and will ask if we checked every lab for the cause of the evacuation."

Hearing the voices trail off in the distance, Dillon said, "It looks clear, Carlos—let's get the 'ell out of 'ere now!" They made their way out through the pool-house exit to the fresh air of the night. Quickly donning their black fatigues and woolen masks, they carefully retraced the exact route back to the penetration point in the rear wall, taking every precaution to find the trip wires and remove each false lens planted over the cameras. Finally, they reached the garden wall.

Carlos radioed Biaggio. "The picture show is over. Coming home!" The coded message for Biaggio translated to pick them up in five minutes at the same site.

In the distance, near the villa patio, sounds of dogs barking and men's voices were getting louder. They seemed a fair distance away but were checking the gardens—getting closer to the rear garden.

"The guards and dogs must be comin' from the villa. It won't take long for 'em to reach this area—let's move it!" Dillon said.

Dillon directed the grappling hook over the top of the wall. "Dillon, you go—if someone finds me, I might have a chance with Marcus's disguise to give you time to intervene with the dart guns—if necessary! Go—*pronto!*" Carlos urged.

Dillon scaled the wall to the top but stayed flat on his belly. Biaggio was parked several meters away and saw Dillon flatten himself out on the top of the wall. Quietly he ran along the side of the wall to the area directly under Dillon and squatted—with gun and silencer ready. He knew there was trouble. Dillon silently scanned the *villa* and gardens. Biaggio heard the dogs and men getting closer—there could be complications! Carlos saw the guards reach the garden one tier away with the leashed dogs straining to go on toward the back of the garden—only fifty meters away from the wall!

Atop the wall, Dillon readied the dart gun loaded with two darts and took up a position to fire—making out the two dogs in the night-vision scope, he took aim at the dogs sniffing the ground and quickly and noiselessly fired the darts at the two dogs.

"Bulls-eye!"

Within seconds, the dogs dropped to the ground confusing the guards who went over to them to see what happened. Both guards were prodding the dogs with their rifles, thinking they were dead.

"Now, Carlos! The dogs are down and the guards 'ave stopped! Now's your chance," he said and tossed him the rope to scale the wall. Both men reached the top and dropped quietly to the ground on the outside of the wall where Biaggio motioned for them to follow him. Dillon retrieved the grappling hook from its anchor on the far side of the wall, picked up the bag of equipment, and ran after Biaggio and Carlos. Once inside the car, Biaggio started the car in lowest gear and without lights, slowly drove down the road before deliberately turning off the road into an open field. He knew exactly where it would lead them out onto a trunk road, a fair distance away from the Villa del Christianna.

"Better to go through the fields—they may be watching the perimeter road if they suspect someone has breached the estate," Biaggio whispered.

"Whate'er you say, Biaggio—you're the driver!"

"Take us 'ome, Jeeves!" Carlos let out a good laugh.

*Dillon smiled and put a cigarette behind his ear.*

# CHAPTER FORTY-FOUR

Cyrus checked his watch again! Four twenty-five.

"Don't worry, Mac—they'll be here anytime now," Andrew told Cyrus. "Pacing won't 'urry them any faster, either!"

Just then, an alarm sounded in the room alerting the two men that someone had driven to the rear of the shoppe. Cyrus switched the monitor screen on to view the rear door.

"It's them—they're back!" Cyrus said to Andrew with the sound of relief in his voice. The door to Central control opened, and the three men entered the room.

"Well?" Cyrus turned in his chair and walked over to the men. "Well?" Repeating his one-word question again, confronting them with his eagerness to hear a response.

"I need a good drink! What's in the box that's cold?" Dillon asked.

"Make that *due*," echoed Biaggio.

"No *tre*!" Carlos said. The five men walked into the conference room together.

"We did it, Mac! We got the information we need...and then some...we didn't expect to find!" Carlos said, after taking a long sip of beer and wiping the sweat from his face with his sleeve. Cyrus saw a different look on Carlos's face. Not a picture of triumph, but an incredible look of shock, horror, and anxiety in Carlos's eyes. Cyrus's reading of Carlos's face told him he found something totally unexpected. What would shock a man to show such fear in his eyes? Cyrus knew he had to be patient—Carlos would tell him in time.

"Where are the films? I want Andy to start developing them immediately!" Carlos and Dillon handed their cameras to Andrew Masters. Biaggio followed him to the dark room. "I 'stimate we took 'bout two, maybe three 'undred pics between us, so you'll be a while gettin' them done." Dillon sat down opposite Cyrus at the conference table.

Cyrus showed restraint in his words. "I can see you're both exhausted, but we need to go over everything now while it's fresh in your minds! The debriefing may take the rest of the night, so let's get started. I'm taping each of your reports!" Cyrus put a clean tape in the machine in front of the two men.

"Each of you will give a thorough description of what happened and what you saw from the moment you arrived at the estate until you left. Once we've completed taping, I'll want each of you to draw a blueprint map of the underground complex—mark each floor in the structure and identify the rooms you entered—listing the contents of each room to the best of your memory. More importantly, do you think anyone detected your presence there?" Cyrus directed his question to both men. Both men shook their heads no.

"Not if you don't' count dogs! To make our escape clean I 'ad to dart two security guard dogs. The dogs dropped cleanly! Without evidence of a dart found, they can't tie the events at the complex with a break-in, 'specially since the dogs dropped after the gas cleared the complex. We didn't take an'thing!" At that moment, Dillon reached into his pocket.

"Oh—wait! I lied! I did take somethin', but I doubt they'll notice it's gone!"

"What in God's name are you talking about?" Cyrus bellowed out at Dillon with incredulity and leaned over the table toward him, looking at what he was slowly taking from his jacket pocket.

Gingerly taking the syringe filled with the solution out of his pocket, Dillon held it in the palm of his hand for Cyrus to see.

"'Ave this analyzed to find out its formula. There were some empty syringes on the counter next to all these flasks of solutions. So I randoml' chose a flask...drew up the syringe full...placed the flask exactl' back where I found it! This…" he said, pointing to the syringe, "***HAS TO BE IMPORTANT!*** I remember the label on the flask said **AC-5**. So, let's see what we got 'ere?" Dillon passed the syringe across the table to Cyrus.

Cyrus was silent for a few seconds—looking disbelievingly at the syringe on the table. "Bloody Jesus…," he said, picking up the phone to the dark room. "Andy, is Biaggio still with you?"

"Yeah, he's here."

"Can you spare him? I have another job I need him to do immediately," he said and hung up. In minutes, Biaggio entered the conference room.

"Take this syringe to the chemistry lab—you know where it is and ask Dr. Ricci to analyze it immediately to determine the contents. Wake him up if you have to—tell him we need to know the formula of its contents—yesterday! Tell him… even if he has to work the next several days and nights, we must have the formula's analysis! And tell him to call me when he has any kind of results—no matter the time—whatever he can discover to let me know *pronto!* Day or night! Nothing else is important!" Cyrus placed the syringe into a metal cylinder and handed it to Biaggio.

"Now let's start with the debriefing." Cyrus saw an unsettled anxiousness about Carlos. He kept pacing around the room as if he was trying to hold something inside.

"Carlos, tell me what you saw?" Cyrus kept his eyes trained on him to detect him withholding some facts—sensing he found something so unexpected, it deeply affected him. Finally sitting down next to the recorder, Carlos started his report.

"We did everything exactly as planned. No problem entering the grounds; we located all the trip wires, the cameras, and had no problems applying the false lens on the cameras. We heard no alarms or saw any change in security activity, so everything was going as planned. We took our time determining what pipes were intakes and tossed a few gas balls into the intake vents. Within a few minutes, we entered the complex by the pool house door, using all the security checks. The three different security IDs, from what we could tell, accepted our duplicates—we passed inside successfully," Carlos said.

Dillon interjected, "Yeah, once inside, we found ourselves on the ground floor—or basement—where supplies were stored in large rooms. Everythin' was locked up tighter than a drum down 'here. We did 'ave to open one of the rooms comin' out, but that's gettin' ahead of our report," Dillon said and took another drink of beer. "Sorry, Carlos, go on."

Carlos was deep in thought when Cyrus asked, "Carlos, you found something important. What was it?" Carlos took a minute to answer, trying to avoid eye contact, all the while looking away from the gaze of both men.

"On the first floor, where all the laboratories are located, I entered one room, which seemed to be a...morgue...and a laboratory with all the usual paraphernalia. This room was larger than the others, and there were eight refrigerator wall cubicles...Each door had a glass panel on the front of the door and a name written on the outside. I checked cubicle #1...and saw a sheet-covered object on a sliding tray—like a body...and opened the door. The cold air confirmed my suspicion of refrigeration...a morgue. Lifting the sheet, I saw a small body on the slab." Carlos took a long drink of beer to pause speaking.

"It was the body of a child—a boy! Only the child looked like an old man...with white hair...wrinkled skin, and shriveled limbs... like an old man ninety years old! There was a name on a wrist tag, Gunter G." Carlos looked directly at Cyrus. "Mac...if you check our records I'd bet we have a Gunter G. listed in the list of missing children!"

It was evident the scene Carlos came upon deeply affected him, and he started pacing around the room again. His emotions finally broke—he slammed his drink down on the table. With fire and anger in his eyes and voice, he said, "He's a modern beast—another *Josef Mengele!*" Walking to the front of the room, he avoided meeting the eyes of the two men.

"I quickly looked inside several more cubicles; each contained bodies. They all seemed to be children—in different stages of aging! They had tags on them...one read "Naomi R.," another read "Françoise T.," and then...the third cubicle had the body of a girl..."

403

It was clear Carlos was having trouble relating objectively to what he saw.

"The tag on the last child said…it said…*Siobhan O.,*" Carlos whispered the name and stopped speaking.

He looked immediately to see Dillon's reaction. He knew there would be a reaction—maybe slow or quick…but it would come. Carlos waited, not taking his eyes off Dillon. No one spoke or moved in the room. The silence was an ominous anticipation of a foreboding emotional outburst of disbelief…anger…rage…pain! At the moment Dillon heard Carlos's words, he dropped his beer on the floor, smashing the bottle.

In a soft tone, he asked, "Say 'gain, Carlos? What was that last name you mentioned?"

"The tag read…*Siobhan O.*" Again…the long silence.

"Did you examine the bod'?" Dillon asked in a soft tone.

"Only to notice it was a small girl—about seven or eight years old." Never daring to speak out loud what kind of horror he saw!

"Did she look normal or…different… than an eight year old?" Dillon asked as he slowly walked towards Carlos.

"Dillon, this isn't going to help you…"

Before Carlos finished the sentence, in a livid outburst, Dillon yelled, **"Tell me what she looked liked? You knew all the while we were comin' back 'ere and didn't say a word to me? You dirt' rotten bastard! You saw 'er and didn't tell me—I could 'ave seen her…she could 'ave been me bab' girl! I could 'ave touched her just once more…!"** Dillon yelled grabbing Carlos by his jacket throwing him to the floor on his back, pummeling his head to the floor with his fists! When there was no resistance from Carlos, except to put his hands up defensively, Dillon pulled him up close to his face, shaking him violently in a rage—**"Why? Why didn't you tell me?"**

Carlos made no attempt to stop Dillon's assault. Then he felt Dillon's slow release of him, and Carlos grabbed Dillon's shoulders firmly to let him know…he understood the unfathomably deep pain he was feeling…and he was okay. Cyrus started toward the two men on the floor when slowly Dillon stopped shaking Carlos. Carefully, he removed his hands from Carlos's jacket, rose and walked out the door of the conference room; his body hunched over—shaking his head. His hands clenched and face distorted, fighting the pain of his silent sobs! Cyrus started after him.

"No, Mac—let him go! He needs to be alone. Dillon will be back when he's ready. He's a professional."

Carlos faced Cyrus squarely. "There was no way in hell I was going to let him see what I saw...if that child was his..." Carlos's voice broke and trailed off in a whisper. The two men left in the room were each coping with their emotions and thoughts about what had been described.

Cyrus slowly rose from his chair. "You're right. Dillon can handle this. We'll get his report later. Even Cyrus's deportment had changed...more subdued... his voice showed more determination and commitment. "Tell me what else you saw there, Carlos." Carlos continued taping every detail he recalled.

"Mac, one thing I did find was Carruchi's office! I was going through his desk and found his appointment book with an entry underlined and circled. Day after tomorrow—in forty-eight hours— there's some kind of meeting going down. There were two names written on the page—most likely pharmaceutical companies, *Genrade and Phisto!* They must be the names of outside companies attending that big meeting. Next to the names was written, '**Finish tests and copy reports.**'" Carlos anxiously related this information to Cyrus. "Maybe some of the pictures I took from the lab's journals will give us more information about what kind of tests the memo is referring to!"

"A meeting in two days...this confirms what Dino reported to us! We don't know for certain where this meeting will be held...Dino thinks it's going to be at the Villa Latinestto...It's possible it could be at the underground complex...or at the Villa del Christianna. Though, I doubt it would be there—too open with Lucinda and too many servants around. No! I agree and bet anything it will be held at the Villa Latinestto on Lago di Como! A perfect place for entertaining potential so-called clients without raising questions for anyone's curiosity." Cyrus stood up. "Yes, I'm sure they'll all be at the villa for this meeting. What time did you say the meeting was scheduled?"

"Ten o'clock."

"I'll get word to Dino to confirm—again—when the meeting goes down at the Villa Latinestto." Cyrus had to let Carlos know the rest of Gino's message.

"Carlos, there was more information in Dino's message. As we suspected...they want Emma kidnapped in London by the time this meeting goes down. We have to get her to the Villa D'Este and keep her there under tight wraps. Dino reported Luigi believes she returned to London and he's personally going to London to get her and bring her back here, which is why we have to get her to the villa and keep her under close guard without alarming her! Right now the Rudolphis have no idea where she is in London—which is our trump card! But for how long?"

"Bloody hell, Mac—she's in more danger now than before!" Carlos said angrily.

"Christ, don't you think I know that!" Cyrus stood up in a sudden move knocking his chair over.

"Is the Villa D'Este ready for us?" Carlos asked.

"Everything is in place at the Villa D'Este—Andy has seen to that—the seal teams are ready and the equipment's in place. Andy and Biaggio finished tapping the phone lines into the Villa Latinestto. We have a truck hidden near the property recording all phone calls in and out of the *casa*. It's set up with fiber optic wiring in the major trunk line, monitoring all incoming and outgoing calls and phones acting as microphones transmitting conversations from any room through the phone lines. We're taping all conversations in that villa over the next two days! I'm sure we'll hear more about this important meeting! There's a phone in every room on the first floor and in each of the bedrooms. This covers about eighty percent or more of the house we can listen to."

"The special operational teams have already started surveillance on the lake! I'll call ahead and make arrangements for an excursion with the cruiser within the next two hours for the divers to survey the lakefront side," Cyrus said.

"One thing, Mac...how long do you think you can keep your presence a secret from Emma?"

"Jesus, at least until the assault is over! I'll not tell her anything until then!" Cyrus said defensively, knowing what he was risking should Emma learn the truth now.

"Then I'm leaving to get her and bring her to the Villa D'Este myself as soon as we're finished here. I want to make certain they don't learn she's still in Milano. I only hope they're fooled for the next several days thinking she's somewhere in London!"

Before Carlos left control, Cyrus said, "Don't forget! You and Dillon must make those drawings of the complex from memory. They're vital to the assault team for that mission!"

"Don't worry, Mac—you'll have them today."

"Before you leave…Andy has set up special security in the north bedroom for Emma. There's no easy access from the outside to that room for unexpected intruders!" Cyrus explained some of security measures at the villa.

"I take it Biaggio gave her the discs?" Carlos asked.

"Yes, she has them now. And if I know my granddaughter, she's aware of everything on those tapes by now!"

At that very moment, Dillon walked back into the conference room, as Carlos was about to leave. "Sorry, Carlos…you did the right thin' back there. I would've done the same thin' in yur shoes." Dillon was in command of himself again.

"No need for apologies, *il mio amico*." Carlos put his hand on Dillon's arm as he left.

Calmly, Dillon said, "Mac, bring me up to speed now…but first before anything else 'appens, you 'ave to know somethin': I'm in this mission 'til the end. We 'ave to take down the Rudolphi family and Carruchi! **When it goes down—no matter what else 'appens Carruchi is mine! Understand? He's all mine—and he ain't comin' out of there alive!**" Dillon made known his attitude with determination, looking squarely at Cyrus. Cyrus knew there was no way he could order him to take 'that principal' alive under these circumstances. That decision would have to be an immediate judgment at the time of capture by his captor. Both men knew Carruchi was a dead man walking.

"Wouldn't have it any other way! You're an integral part of this mission now…you're vital to the success of this whole operation, Dillon," Cyrus said and motioned for Dillon to sit.

"Just a few questions, Dillon, and then you can leave. I want you to head out to the Villa D' Este when you leave here, stop at the apartment if necessary. We have a lot to do if the meeting Dr. Carruchi has scheduled is to be held at the Villa on Lago di Como! But now I need your input from tonight's mission; a schematic drawing of the underground complex and what you saw there. This is vital to us before we can formulate a final plan for a simultaneous multi-pronged assault on that complex and two others! We can do the rest of the debriefing later."

"Just as you say, Mac!" Dillon showed he was in complete command of his emotions.

Carlos stuck his head in the door. "Dillon, I'm leaving to get Emma at Biaggio's and bring her to the Villa D'Este myself. No telling when they'll catch on to the 'double act' and figure out she's not in London! When they do, they'll send out feelers here in Milano, suspecting her flight was a false trail. They'll do everything to locate her! I've got to make certain she can't be a target here. Catch you later—call me when you're done."

"I may see you back at the apartment," Dillon told Carlos. Carlos left the center and headed to Biaggio's to get Emma.

"Dillon, let's get the most vital part of your report of the mission taped now." Dillon gave his detailed account of the past night's operation to Cyrus.

"That was smart thinking to take that sample from the lab for us to analyze. That sample just may give us the answer—to understand just what they're doing in the laboratories with human experimentation—What kind of drug they discovered? With the evidence we get from the pictures and these first-hand accounts, that single piece of evidence you took may be the defining portion of this whole puzzle—come time to convict!"

"Yeah, Mac. If there's any one left to convict! It may tell me what 'appened to me wife and baby girl, too!" Dillon rose…he paused before leaving.

*"Mac...they say Lady Justice is blind...maybe that's so someone can tip those scales she's holdin' in the right direction!"*

# CHAPTER FORTY-FIVE

Dillon left Control and headed straight for Lago di Como.

The sun was just rising and the spring day was going to be clear and sunny. Dialing the car phone, he left the message, "Carlos. I'm on my way to Como, bypassing the flat."

At that same time Carlos was trying to reach Emma on her cell phone. "*Si pronto? E buono per sentire la sua voce la sua prima cosa nella mattina. Sembra come un angelo.*"

"Carlos? It's so good to hear your voice!"

Playing with her, "Did I ever tell you how lovely you look when you first wake up?"

"Carlos—where are you? And when did you get televised phone service in your car?"

"Right this moment!" He laughed. "I'm on my way to Biaggio's. I should be there in about… fifteen minutes. Can you be dressed and packed by then?"

"Of course. Where are we going?"

"I'll tell you everything when I see you. I've missed you, Emma, and I'll tell you in person exactly how much when I see you in a few minutes! *Caio.*"

Emma felt the same eagerness to see Carlos. "I've missed you too, my darling," she commented to herself. Dressing in slacks and sweater, she finished packing her small bag and headed downstairs to the kitchen where she knew Sienna would be preparing breakfast.

The sounds of singing and laughter and the good smell of food came from the rear of the house as Carlos drove up and parked the car in the back. Emma ran out to meet him and into his arms. Oh! He felt so good in her arms—so strong and yet so tender. He didn't hesitate to kiss her—and she him.

"I miss you more each time I'm away from you! Every time I see you, I find you're even more desirable than the last time I remembered you...I really do love your beautiful, soft dark hair." He slowly caressed it with his fingers. "But there is something I forgot to tell you, *il mia amore*, when I called."

"And what was that?" Emma asked.

"You need to wear your disguise Sienna and Elena made for you—until this whole business is over." A frown came over Emma's face.

"I know...I know... it's not you! But people are out there looking for you, *mia cara,* and we must do everything to keep them far from you for as long as we need to!" Carlos told her, still holding her close in his arms, not wanting to let her go.

"Yes, I know it's necessary, Carlos! You're right—I can do it until we end this madness! Is there any more information about the Rudolphis?" Emma asked.

"*Si* let's go inside. We shouldn't be so visible out here." Turning, they walked back into the Giambrettis. Carlos was extra cautious not to let Emma detect his morbid feelings from the night's mission at the Villa del Christianna and turned to her with a smile and a soft caress.

Once inside, Sienna met them, gesturing for them to sit down for breakfast. *"Buongiorno, signore and signorina. Avanti, si, per favore 'e venito e voi piacerstessi."*

Her homemade breakfast consisted of dishes of eggs, fresh sausages, and homemade baked breads with her sauces.

*"Il suo cappuccino 'e il magliore, terra, di Siena,"* Carlos said to make light conversation with Sienna. Sienna had a certain sparkle of lightheartedness and made everyone in her presence feel comfortable, especially in her home. She definitely had the secret to a happy family. Carlos enjoyed spending time with this family and wondered if he would ever have something similar to what

Biaggio and Sienna had together. He looked at Emma and his smile met hers…hoping some day they would have a happy home—his one dream. It was as if they were experiencing the same wishful thoughts.

"*Mi scusi ma dobbuani abdare, Sienna,*" Carlos told Sienna. "Biaggio will be here soon."

Emma excused herself. "I need to finish packing," she said and left the kitchen to get her things. "*Grazie infinite per la vostra hospitalita.*" While Carlos bid goodbye to Sienna, Emma donned the wig with the rest of her disguise, checking the mirror once more. It really did change her whole persona. They started out for Lago di Como—the Villa D'Este.

Alone, Emma told Carlos. "I listened to the Chatelaine tapes last night. It all came back to me. I do remember a criminal trial in Italy where there were seven defendants on trial for international kidnappings. They were charged with multiple kidnappings of children and adults without actual evidentiary proof the kidnappings were for profit. The evidence presented was mostly circumstantial. I remember following the trial in the *London Times*, until news of the trial dried up. In the transcripts, it alluded to kidnappings from five different countries, but most of them occurred in Germany, France, and Italy. The defendants were not considered the masterminds in the case—not the brains behind the schemes—none gave up knowledge who they were really working for. They were just the people who cared for the victims over a period of time—and I'm sure they profited doing it!" Emma's excitement about the tapes heightened.

"There was one piece of information—a document found which gave a list of names of some of the kidnapped victims—those who were returned to their real families. I listened carefully to this part of the transcript to find out who and where these more fortunate victims came from—it was hard to tell because there was no mention in the transcript I had—which is very strange…for a trial transcription…to be incomplete! To protect some of the victims, this point may have been purposely excluded from the transcripts. **But this could be THE most revealing part of evidence—if specifics can be found to determine just who these people are today—we might locate these same people to question them about what happened to**

**them—see if they have any memory!** The statute of limitations may still apply to some of these cases—it's a thought! I'll have Peter do some research for me when I return to London to find out how we can discover who these particular victims are." Carlos realized how thorough Emma was and how she wouldn't let this fact lie—until she had the answers she wanted to find.

"What was the final outcome? Did they ever find any of the defendants' remains?" Emma queried Carlos.

"No. More the tragedy…we never had a final count of the number of people they kidnapped. Sadly, we never found any victims alive before the trials—*except one*. A child who ran away from her foster parents was found unharmed without memory of what happened to her. She never gave any significant information to the police except to tell them she remembered living in a small town in Sweden, but ran away from people in Italy. The police were able to reunite her with her real parents in Sweden two years after her abduction. The last I heard, that Swedish family dropped out of sight. Probably took on a new identification fearing another abduction!" Carlos gave this reasonable fact to Emma to hide the real possibility the whole family could have been abducted by the organization—the Rudolphi family!

"What did happen to the defendants?" Emma asked and closely observed Carlos as he kept driving, keeping his eyes on the road and deliberately not making eye contact with her.

"The defendants were all held in the same prison when there was a jailbreak and a number of prisoners escaped—including our seven defendants. The authorities caught all the escapees—except our seven kidnappers, which makes us believe the jailbreak was deliberately planned and executed to eliminate the seven defendants. Any other prisoners who happened to get away with the seven were a bonus—depending on which side you were on. Information on the defendants' kidnappers led to the mountains in Switzerland—then went cold," Carlos said.

"To my knowledge, we assume they were all killed and buried in the mountains to keep the identity of the real brains of the organization from being discovered. The court found all seven *guilty in absentia.*

"Am I correct to say, two of the prosecutors died mysteriously the year following the trial? Were their deaths ever tied to the Chatelaine trial?" Emma asked.

Carlos was taken aback with Emma's question put so pointedly. She was learning more than he realized about the Chatelaine Case, and he knew he had to answer her question with a modicum of truth or she would catch him in a lie. "I heard the local authorities were investigating the similarities in the two deaths. The last I knew their deaths were never tied together—or solved. And yes, the cases are still open," Carlos said matter-of-factly to Emma.

Everything he said was true, Emma sensed. What he didn't say was there was evidence showing the two deaths were revenge killings for the guilty verdict. To warn other prosecutors what would happen if another case like that came to trial. Emma realized the information Carlos had confided to her was true, but there was much more he wasn't telling her. She acknowledged his answers to let him know she believed what he told her. The facts he *didn't tell her*...she would discover another way.

"I'll have Peter do some research for me on the death of those two prosecutors the next time I speak to him," she said to let Carlos know the subject was not closed. "My last question—why were the case transcripts in the basement of the London Court of Justice? But more importantly—why were the transcripts stolen from my office?"

"That, my darling, are my questions, too! I'll be very honest, Emma...somehow the Rudolphis have deeply involved you in this troubling scheme. I don't know how yet—but you are vital to them and their plans—which is why they are pursuing you now!"

"But, Carlos—I have no memory of any dealings with that family or anyone associated with the family! Not until Lucinda Rudolphi came to me did the name Rudolphi mean anything to me! I took the case on primarily because I wanted to find out why my name is on a list in Marcus's private papers. Secondly, I do want to find out how and why Lucinda's children died. I have a sixth sense about this case now...her children *may not* be dead! I'm going to find the truth to both of these questions!" Emma said with conviction.

"What I find alarming since returning to Italy is the frequency of the memory flashes I get at odd times. Something triggers these sudden seconds of memory from somewhere—when I think I can understand the meaning of them—it's gone...My mind becomes blank! It's almost as if there's a familiarity to a moment in time from somewhere in my past...that connects with the present moment—but I can't find the missing link!" Emma spoke her thoughts. Carlos believed Marcus did have her at some time! The flashbacks are the beginning of those memories returning.

*Marcus, if it's the last thing I do on this earth you will pay...for what you did to her!* Carlos promised silently.

"Now, tell me what you have learned about the Rudolphis since we last spoke," she next asked Carlos.

Carlos began telling Emma about some of the information they discovered about an underground facility on the Rudolphi estate where research is done—excluding that he had any knowledge about the kind of research done there. He had to be careful and filter out certain facts he didn't want Emma to learn—at least not yet—and do it credibly.

"We learned there, there is to be a big meeting—most likely at the Villa Latinestto at Como in two days. It appears they are at the stage where they want to present their research findings to some companies—most likely for further studies and production. Two specific companies are considered at this moment. We've installed a sophisticated system to monitor the telephone lines at the Villa Latinestto through non-detectable microphones throughout the villa. We have long-range cameras set up at the Villa D'Este to screen anyone entering or leaving the premises across the lake. Our underwater surveillance teams are taking the cruiser out on the lake today—looking like vacationers scuba diving and snorkeling for fun and relaxation! What we plan to do is underwater surveillance." Carlos turned to Emma who was listening intently.

"I want to be on that boat, Carlos. I want to go with the scuba teams."

"Now wait a minute..."

"No, you wait, Carlos! I will be on that boat today with or without you!"

415

Carlos heard the determination in her voice and thought maybe it would be a safe place for her to be at that time.

"I'll have to check it out with my Control Chief. I hope you brought a swimsuit along?"

"Don't worry about that—I'll blend in with the rest of you!" Emma said. It wasn't long before they drove up the drive to the Villa D'Este. Anna met Emma while Carlos brought in her bags.

"You must be Emma Llewelyn from London."

"Yes, and I see you speak perfect English. I'm glad for that—my Italian is not the best," Emma commented to Anna.

"I'm Anna. Let me show you to your room," Anna said leading the way up to the second floor. "Our vacationing host and hostess, Josepi and Maria, have the large suite on the front side of the house. Your room is the next best one on the north side of the house— but you do have a view of the lake from that side. Each room is a complete private suite."

As Anna led Emma upstairs, Carlos headed directly downstairs to the Control center. Andy was at the computers watching the security monitors.

"Where's Mac?" Carlos asked.

"He's back at Milano control. Why?"

"I need to speak to him about the surveillance team going out this morning on the lake. Emma has made it known she's going, too."

"You'd better call him before he leaves for here—let him know she's here, and he's to come in the far side entrance. I've locked the passageway from upstairs down to this entrance. He's got a key to get in. Here's your key, don't let Emma get a hold of it and for God's sake, don't lose it!" Pointing to the far door, he said, "That door will be kept locked at all times!"

"Understood," Carlos commented and dialed the number to Milano control.

"*Pronto?*"

"The lake is very blue today."

"Carlos? What's the trouble?"

"Mac—Emma is here in her disguise. There's a catch! She's informed me she's going with the surveillance team out on the boat this morning."

"Bloody Damn!"

"I didn't try to discourage her too strongly! If she's with us, I'll know she's safe."

"Then inform the divers they'll have another diver to go with them—besides you and Dillon. She's a good diver, Carlos—but all of you watch what you say in her presence. I don't want her privy to any facts about the assault teams. Dillon should be arriving there any time now. He's okay for now. Just keep your other eye on him! He's a man with a definite mission." The conversation ended and the line went dead.

"So am I, Mac—so am I! Only Marcus Rudolphi will be mine—just mine!" Carlos muttered to himself and returned back upstairs.

Dillon walked through the door into the Drawing Room.

"Catch any shuteye?" Carlos asked him.

"The cappuccino here is the best stimulant you'd want in place of sleep! I'm headin' downstairs. Is Emma upstairs?" Dillon asked.

"Yes. By the way, she's coming with us on the boat this morning." Dillon rolled his eyes in a negative response.

"I already informed Control. He's coming here shortly and will be downstairs. We have enough scuba gear for six people, but some of us should be snorkeling to attract any interested observers to keep eyeing the snorkelers near the boat."

"It's me opinion the women should be doin' the snorkelin'! That'll entice 'hem to watch—if they have any testosterone in 'hem!"

"You're saying I should try and keep Emma from diving? Be one of the snorklers?" Carlos posed the question as a joke.

"Good luck, matie, and then some!" Dillon said with half a smile to Carlos. Dillon was becoming his old witty self again, Carlos noticed.

Carlos, Dillon, and Emma walked down to the boathouse and met the two dive couples checking out their scuba gear. Emma disguised in the red wig and large sunglasses, gave a totally different look from her real appearance to the teams. As the boat slowly left its water birth under the house and the diving equipment was stowed below in the cabins, the cruiser headed out for the predetermined location in the middle of Lago di Como to drop anchor. The spot chosen directly in front of the Villa Latinestto—but halfway out on the lake—at least two kilometers away from the Villa Latinesetto's waterfront. Everyone on board had a camera, pretending a holiday manner, taking pictures of the party-goers with the women striking poses purposely in front of the villa grounds. The photographers, with long-range lenses, got good shots of the Villa Latinestto. Below, in the cabins were high-powered telescopes with cameras zooming in on specific areas on the grounds and waterfront, taking pictures of any person seen.

Emma had a swimsuit under the wetsuit that completely covered her, and the cap hid her hair, no longer covered with the red wig. Most of the scuba divers were on the far side of the boat out of sight from the Villa Latinestto donning their diving gear. The two women from the dive teams were doing the snorkeling while the four men and Emma made the scuba teams to map and scan the lake bottom.

"Glad to have you all with us. I'm Joe and this here is Kevin. Any questions about the equipment?" All three shook their heads no. Joe, the captain of the divers, explained the plan to Emma, Carlos, and Dillon.

"Once we submerge, we split into two groups—a group of two and a group of three. The bottom depth here is estimated at sixty meters. The two groups will swim together toward the shore, marking the distance from this point to the shoreline. At fifty meters depth near the shore, there's a sudden change in the lake bottom; it rises quickly to about twenty meters. At this point, one team will go north and the other will go south down the lake, mapping out the lake bottom on the drawing boards you each were given. The two teams will swim one hundred meters in each direction using no more than fifteen minutes of air and then return to the boat from that point—underwater."

The directions were clear and concise, and no one had questions.

The five divers entered the water one by one. Dive Team One would be the two seal divers, and Dive Team Two was Carlos, Emma, and Dillon. The weather was cooperating with a warm, bright sun and soft breezes. The sun's rays provided good light almost to the bottom of the lake. Emma was glad she wore the wetsuit—the water was cold at this depth. The five divers slowly made their way into shore with no detection of air bubbles on the lake surface. The lake breezes were just strong enough to keep the surface water slightly choppy, dissipating the air bubbles. At the twenty-five meter mark from shore, Captain Joe indicated his team would go up the lake and motioned for Carlos and the others to go down the lake as originally directed. Checking her watch, Emma noted the time—fifteen minutes of air for the survey and five minutes left to return to the boat.

The sunlight filtering through the water made it easy to sketch certain unique shapes seen on the bottom. Using large objects—boulders, a small sunken boat, and even a piece of machinery half buried in the sand as a reference points, Emma sketched a representation of the ever-changing lake bottom—making additional orientation points at intervals for her own reference. Recalling how her father, Michael, taught her to always have a back up water trail to follow—if she became confused or water currents drastically changed her position—she memorized the bottom topography in a matter of minutes—still diligently sketching reference sites on her slate for the captain.

Carlos pointed out to Dillon and Emma beams radiating out from the waters near the distant shore. The men recognized the beach had underwater laser sensor security! Both were familiar with these kinds of sensors randomly intersecting one another—each high intensity beam would deliver static powerful bolts of heat into anything caught in the beams—even killing small fish. To a man the beams would give stacotto jolts of electricity, similar to an electrical charge causing considerable pain. The villa's security was meant to be impregnable from all sides—even swimmers approaching the beach from the lake. Any boats coming close to the beach from the lake would interrupt the laser beams and alarm security there was a breach at the waterfront, before any boat reached the boat docks. Dillon motioned to Carlos and Emma; they had gone one hundred meters down the lake and it was time to start back to the cruiser. The divers set their watches to measure the underwater distance from this farthest point back to the boat. The timing was perfect—both teams arrived back at the anchored boat simultaneously.

"Great work, you three! You can be on my team anytime!" Joe collected the underwater charts from everyone. "Now we need to interpret everyone's graphic representation to make a master chart of the bottom. Get a hot drink and meet me in the main cabin in thirty minutes. We need to debrief what each of us saw down there."

"I agree with 'im, we do make a good team," Dillon said, wiping down with the towel.

"I need a hot shower! Meet you in twenty minutes in the cabin," Emma said and went below to one of the cabins and stowed her wet suit in a cabinet out of sight.

"Let's get a drink, Dillon. It's been a long two days!" Carlos and Dillon headed down to the main cabin. Neither had slept in two days and now was not the time to make any mistakes.

"What does Control 'ave in mind next?"

Carlos took a long drink of beer before answering. "After we get today's information processed, he'll decide when the units will commence incursions on the Villa Latinestto, the complex, the winery, the Villa del Christianna, and all the other major villas on the estate—synchronized attacks at all the sites."

"Me? I'm goin' to find and meet up with Dr. Ennio Carruchi! You, my friend, must find and take out Marcus Rudolphi!" Dillon said.

"You read my mind, Dillon." Both men raised their drinks in a toast.

"*Alle victorio!*

# CHAPTER FORTY-SIX

The cruiser arrived back at the Villa D'Este boathouse five hours later.

The sun's warm rays were competing with the cool air blowing stronger from the distant mountains. The daily weather phenomenon of hot rising air mingling with the cooler winds blowing down the steep slopes of the Lepontine Mountains in the north frequently produced large puffy fair weather clouds in the late afternoon that often kept the sun's rays hidden at day's end. Cyrus observed the teams going upstairs in the boathouse through the binoculars. Emma returned to her disguise of the red wig and tortoise glasses, again.

"It does change her looks dramatically!" he thought out loud.

"Mac, they'll be here anytime with their information. I'll make sure the films get back to control as soon as they deliver them. Have you heard anything from Dr. Ricci yet?" Andy asked.

"No, not yet," Cyrus remarked, still watching the scene at the beach house.

"I'll make a call to Ricci when I get to Control Milano...and try to find out what he's learned from the syringe of serum we sent." Andy explained to Cyrus, "Ricardo can relieve me here...Martin is manning the telescope in the front tonight."

"So, where will you spend the night, Mac?"

"Right here when I get back. In the back room, there's a bed and phone, and I can lock the door. When I get all the information from today's dive, I'm calling for a meeting to finalize our plans. I expect

Colin and Tony Serrano will be here to give me their input for their objectives. Right now, Colin takes down the winery; Tony takes down the Rudolphi villas, and I will take down *that villa* across the way—the Villa Latinestto!" All the while Cyrus kept looking out the window through the binoculars. Turning to Andy, he said, "So get as much rest as possible and be back here early tomorrow no later than 0600 hours. I'll have Anna bring me dinner down here later," Cyrus said.

"Mac, I take it you'll be going with the assault team on the Villa Latinestto?"

"Nothing in this world could keep me away when we take down the Rudolphi Empire!" Cyrus said quietly and firmly. "Andy I've not told you this…but it is my belief they had Emma at one time. I don't know what they did to her, but if it's the last thing I do on this earth, I'll make them all pay for that! Every last one of them! Yes, I will be going with the team when it's time! Now, not a word to anyone about this—you hear?"

"Mac—have I ever let you down in the all the years we've been together?"

"I know Andy—I know…" At that moment, the outer door opened, and Carlos and Dillon walked in.

"Glad your back. There's still a lot to do from here on in—so let's get busy!" Cyrus said to the men. "I've been in touch with MacEachen and with the Italian International Crime Agency—the IICA. Both these agencies have been in constant communication with Interpol, sharing the latest satellite and communication information and setting up plans to coordinate the simultaneous objectives. I've assigned you two to assist in planning the assault of the Villa Latinestto here on Como," he said, pointing at Carlos and Dillon who sat down opposite him.

"MacEachen's team will move on the Rudolphi Winery. Security seems to be the heaviest at this facility, with the most sophisticated equipment. The IICA will be under Tony Serrano, a smart man with a long history of working with Italian crime syndicates has been with us since the beginning of this case for two years now. He'll be in charge of the assault team on the Villa del Christianna and Guiseppe Rudolphi's Villa… the major land estates. He'll handle the rest of the Rudolphis' homes on the estate and off the estate grounds. There will be a team in Firenze at several different locales that we know are linked to the organization." Checking his watch, Cyrus said, "I have a meeting with MacEachen and Serrano in Milano in two hours and probably won't get back here until very late. When I return, I want to be certain Emma has retired." Cyrus looked at the two men silently conveying his message…*Emma should retire early.*

"What exactly do you want us to do about the plans for now? Should we wait until you return from Milano to update us about the other objective sites?" Carlos asked.

"No need for you to wait. You two lay out how you'll coordinate the move from all sides—the lakefront will be special operations job along with the lateral perimeters close to the beaches! Before you make firm plans, check out the two villas on either side of the Villa Latinestto to get the occupants of those villas moved out… on some pretense…use sewage contamination…that'll get them out! Determine how many men are needed to penetrate, secure, and surround the entire villa. We'll use all four of the divers for the approach from the lakeside with additional men from Tony. If they need more back up, we need to decide how many now! Andy and myself with a predetermined number will be going in the front way for the frontal attack."

"You?" Dillon asked surprised.

"You have a problem with that, Dillon?" Cyrus asked curtly.

"Yeah, I do, Mac! This is a major undertakin' and people are gonna get 'urt—some terminal'y! We need you 'ere…"

Before Dillon could finish, Cyrus interrupted him. "You mean… you're afraid something will happen to me, or are you afraid I can't pull my weight? Well, I have every intention of going in and seeing for myself just what happened in there! And I can still use a weapon as good as any man on this team! So get used to the idea—**I'm going to be with the frontal team!** Now! You already have one member on that team—and I suggest you count Andy as another man on the frontal assault. And get busy finding out exactly how many more you'll need in total!"

"Mac—I know it's goin' to be dangerous, and if anythin' 'appened to you—well Emma would be devastated…that's all I meant!" Dillon explained.

"Then I suggest you get yourself a 9 mm laser Makarov with a silencer—and an Italian infrared Uzi. There's nothing better for assassinations these days! If you haven't used one before—check with Andy—he'll have one of each for you, I'm sure." Cyrus took his Makarov pistol from the holster and handed it to Dillon. "That's the piece you need with you—it's never let me down yet!"

"Mac, you may not want to hear this, but Emma has every intention of going with us on this move, though she hasn't said it out loud—I know she has it in her mind!" Carlos said.

**"The bloody hell she is NOT! If we have to lock and tie her up here—then we will!** There's no way she's going to be near the Villa Latinestto," Cyrus bellowed loudly with anger in his eyes. Pointing his finger at Dillon and Carlos, he said, "It's up to you two to convince her she is to remain here until the whole ordeal if over! That's a prime order!"

"That's no easy task—she's a MacKenna—through and through!"

"I don't care how you do it—it must be done! Just do it! Is that clear to everyone in this room?" Cyrus enunciated in clear words, commanding the attention of every person in the room. Their silence was a positive acknowledgement to his commands.

"I leave for Milano now. When I return later tonight, we'll meet here again at 0600 hours tomorrow to finalize our plans with the others. We'll coordinate the exact time everybody moves. That final meeting tomorrow will give us the best opportunity to pick the exact time to capture most of the company in one place. At least—all of the main characters should be in one place. I'll propose to Colin and Tony we make the assaults some time tomorrow between ten and eleven o'clock in the morning. It's that soon!"

Packing his briefcase and replacing the laser Makarov back in his holster, Cyrus checked with Andy who was walking into the room reading a report.

"Mac, this report just came from Dr. Ricci—the analysis of that syringe we asked him to analyze…its several pages long."

Andy scanned the pages and read out loud, **"I concluded the syringe contained a formula with specific properties with the potential to act on certain chromosomal cells in the body."** Looking at the group, he read, **"The contents are very complex chemical groupings of unknown substances with the potential to affect certain DNA components...possibly stem cells, most likely by inhibiting or altering cells from producing certain enzymes in tissues that normally effectuate an anabolic or catabolic effect. A single isolated chemical component in the serum has the potential to allow tissues to continue to produce cells in a static growth pattern...may even eventually slow down the cell's catabolic cycle. One of the components in the serum can affect certain cells ability to regenerate cells to replace the dying cells... or possibly-slowly inhibit them. This is just a provisional report until the final analysis has been done. With just this information it appears the serum can affect the aging factor in a particular set of gene's chromosomes. This report is based on non-tested and unproven theoretical assumptions, based solely on a partial analysis of the compound. Final report to follow. Ricci."**

Andy looked at the three men. "Sounds like we hit the mother load!"

"Yeah—and 'ow many lives did it take for 'hem to develop this product—I know of two!" Dillon got up and walked out to the back garden leading down to the boathouse.

"Carlos, keep an eye on him. He needs a clear head and no baggage for this assignment."

"He's okay, Mac...He's first a professional! Nothing will keep him from performing his job in this mission."

Cyrus checked the monitor to find where Emma was in the villa—her room monitor showed her coming out of her bath. The radio was playing soft music—something she liked to listen to when she had a difficult problem. Cyrus left for Milano.

He stowed the briefcase in the car boot under the spare tire, not taking any chances it would be easily found if he was stopped and then got into the BMW. Checking his watch, he decided the ride back to control headquarters should take about an hour—if the traffic stays light heading away from Lago di Como towards Verrena. His route was in the direction of Verrena with the lighter traffic. Lost in his thoughts, he said, "We're so close…so close."

*The black van was careful to stay two cars behind the BMW at all times for several kilometers, making it hard to detect in the black night.*

# CHAPTER FORTY-SEVEN

Suddenly, the black van pulled out of the lane passing the two cars and BMW.

Speeding to get ahead of Cyrus, the driver swerved sharply in front of the oncoming BMW forcing Cyrus to veer off the road onto the soft dirt shoulder to avoid a collision—slamming on his brakes. "What the bloody hell…" Cyrus cried out. Three men jumped out of the black van dressed in black fatigues and masks, wielding Uzi machine guns, and ran to the BMW and opened the door.

"*Uscire!* The man yelled. "Get out! I said, GET OUT!" The other man shouted, while another grabbed Cyrus just as a burst of fire came from one of the Uzi's hitting the back of the BMW causing an instant burst of flames in the rear. Cyrus quickly shifted his weight out of the opened door drawing his gun. Rolling out of the car on the ground ready to fire the Makarov, a foot smashed down kicking his arm, forcing him to drop the gun before he could fire a round. The second man had the butt of his gun raised to hit his head while the third man knelt on his chest and pinned him squarely on the ground. Cyrus saw the butt of the gun coming down at him and instinctively tried to turn his head away—too late—pain and darkness!

\* \* \*

Slowly, the feeling was beginning to return back into his arms and legs—but it was painful to move them…something held him frozen in position…unable to move any extremity. Feeling his restraints, the tight ropes and chains digging into his arms and legs, he opened his eyes. The light shown brilliantly as if a hundred suns lit the room—emitting an intense white heat just on him. The concentrated beam of light blinded him, forcing him to painfully squint just to try and focus on his surroundings. Seeing his restraints attached to a stone wall with chains bracketed to it, he followed the other end of the chains shackled tightly to his body, forcing him to stand upright. Chains tightly clamped his outstretched arms and hands over his head to the wall and his feet together making it difficult to keep his balance standing. He realized if he lost his balance the pain increased—any movement to cause his weight to hang from his shoulders was unbearable. Then—a splash of cold water cascaded down his face! Shaking his head against the force of the second bucket of water, he wanted to cry out in anger at his captors. No! First listen—he needed to listen to hear voices before he spoke. *Who were his captors?*

"Ah, Commander MacKenna. Is that not your title in Interpol?" The voice was Italian but spoke English fluently. The lights were so bright Cyrus couldn't see the face of the man who spoke. The voice came from the far side of the room behind the lights.

"I know you can hear me—so let's not delay this any longer than we have to."

Hearing soft footsteps approach, Cyrus noticed the voice was clearer and closer to him.

"Commander MacKenna, I am going to tell you a story. Then when I'm finished with my story I expect YOU to tell me YOUR story. That's only fair isn't it?" *The voice sounded familiar—but who?* Cyrus thought.

"Let's see… you have been with Interpol for almost twenty-five years now—and with a very impressive record, I must say! I understand you have a flourishing stable of prized Arabian horses, with a prosperous breeding business—for which I have even tried to purchase one of your mares for my own stables. I'm still waiting to hear you will sell one to me."

Remembering instantly, Cyrus thought, *I know that voice! That's who it is! A horse breeder wanted to make a deal with me for a mare from Cymru's lineage. Of course! Marcus Rudolphi—himself.*

Marcus was speaking again, "But that's neither here nor there. I was most disappointed to hear you have this other occupation—with Interpol—and that you have been investigating my family and business for quite some time." The soft footsteps were pacing faster.

"I don't like that, Commander MacKenna. You have caused me many delays and much money by interfering in my business dealings! So! That is why we are meeting here tonight." Pounding the table with his fists, he shouted, "I WANT TO KNOW HOW MUCH YOU LEARNED ABOUT OUR RESEARCH IN HUMAN GENETICS?"

"Is that what you call it? 'Research in human genetics'—for the betterment of mankind, I presume? Well, I call it murder—not for mankind—but murder for personal gain! Usually first meetings warrant introductions…I presume I'm speaking with Marcus Rudolphi?"

**"Why you DO know me! I'm flattered! Yes!** We have been making great strides in finding certain DNA genes that will allow future generations to sustain their youth for a greater period of time! You are wrong to accuse me of murder! Our research is like other research work done to prevent the diseases that promote the aging process—heart diseases…kidney diseases…all kinds of brain tumors and many, many more that I haven't mentioned, I'm sure you're aware of!" Marcus sounded his accolades pompously

"But at what great price have you paid to reach this important stage? How may innocent human beings have been your guinea pigs to find this 'serum of youth'?" Cyrus thought here might be a time to challenge his feeling of control and accuse him of insensitive acts to rile the calm Marcus Rudolphi to brag about the research, hoping to learn more facts.

"Tell me, Marcus. Did you use your own two children in this experiment?" Going out on a limb without evidence but a gut hunch, Cyrus continued, "Your children didn't die at birth—you stole them from your own wife—for this maniacal scheme of yours! Were they guinea pigs or were they some of the successful few?" Cyrus knew he was reaching—but he needed to know. No sound. Cyrus was prepared for anything.

Marcus made a silent motion to the two men waiting in the shadows. Suddenly, Cyrus felt a crushing blow to his face—and then his gut—repeated blows causing intense pain.

"Two against one isn't fair, especially if the...one...is...ti..."The beating continued relentlessly.

**"Do not kill him, you fools! I need him alive! But he is to feel pain—just not die from it—yet!"**

The pain was becoming more excruciating in every part of his body! Then another blow to the head—this time his head hit the wall with a hard thud and for a few seconds—the pain diminished and blackness came. Blood trickled into his eyes from open gashes on his face and head. Cyrus barely felt the repeated punches to his body. He knew when the body is assaulted repeatedly beyond the level of enduring pain—the pain actually begins to diminish—as if something in the body turns off the receptors of pain in the brain. Soon, the beating went on without pain—only touch was sensed. Then...complete and total blackness. He felt the cold water thrown on him. This time the bright lights went out, and a door slammed shut. A heavy bolt latched the door.

*SILENCE.*

His eyes burning from the blood and sweat pooling in them from his head gashes, he could make out only a dim light over the door, barely giving evidence what kind of room he was left in. Was he alone? Or was someone still back in the shadows, watching... waiting?"

The pain was returning with increasing intensity everywhere in his body, as he fully realized he was still standing and chained to the wall, his legs barely supporting his weight upright. *How long can I go on?* "Is anyone...there...?" Cyrus moaned out loud.

*SILENCE!*

*I...must overcome...this pain. I...must think...of something more...important. How much time...before they return?* He remembered Marcus said... *I was to tell him a story—no doubt he'll be back to hear it. How long can I hold out...before he learns everything? I know Colin and Tony will wonder where I am... when I don't show up... They'll start making calls...to find out what happened to me. They'll search...sure to find my car torched—and then what? At least...they didn't get the contents of the briefcase...in the fire... or Marcus wouldn't be trying to get it out of me here—I only hope everything burned with the rest of the car! I need a plan... a plan...for when they return...how to press for time...I need time! Make time for Control to realize something happened to me—and to act! Got to buy time...for them!* Cyrus felt the cold and dampness. Numbness was replacing the pain in his feet and hands. *It's got to be several hours since I left Como! When I don't show up for the meeting at 0600, they'll know something's wrong—how long does that give me 'til then? One thing the bastard doesn't know...we have a sample of the serum. If worse comes to worse, I can use that as leverage to stall for time! But that could backfire and make Rudolphi head straight to Milano control and the Villa D'Este. If he did that— he'd find Emma! No! I can't let that happen!*

*Emma! Yes! That could be his Achilles' heel! Emma...is the weak point!*

Maybe that's the way I can gain time—find out his connection to Emma! Feed his ego! Must...stay alert! I must keep Marcus second-guessing...his kind always has an Achilles' heel! Just why...does he want her bad enough to order her abduction in a public garden? Was that his only attempt to kidnap her...or were there other times... in Tuscany? If I feed his egomaniacal psyche...he'll fall prey to questions! Yes! Allow his ego to exploit his successes...and learn the truth...gain time...need more time! I know I can do it...I must stay conscious!

Cyrus didn't know how much longer before the guards would return and keep up the beatings. He knew he had to keep remembering happy thoughts about his life on the farm...with Emma and Maggs... trying to overcome the pain...trying to stay conscious.

Fatigue...pain...thirsty...oh, for a good drink...God please don't let me fail...so many people have been victims...please let me stop them...no more...no more victims.

*Patricia E. Peterson*

**The door opened with a loud bang!**

# CHAPTER FORTY-EIGHT

"Where's Mac?

Colin asked Tony Serrano. "He should have arrived at Milano Control an hour ago! Call the villa to find out when he left!"

Tony called the direct line to the basement at the Villa D'Este. Andy answered the phone. "The Lake is very blue today."

"And clear," Andy said in response.

"This is Milano Control—is Cyrus there?"

"No. He left a couple of hours ago. Why? Hasn't he arrived yet?" Tony nodded to Colin that Cyrus wasn't at the Villa D'Este, and Colin grabbed the phone from him.

"No! He never arrived here! Somethin' must've 'appened on the way. I can't raise him on his private line either! Is Carlos or Dillon there?"

"Wait a minute—here's Carlos." Andy handed the phone to Carlos.

"Are you saying Mac never reached Milano Control?" Carlos asked.

"That's right! He's not 'ere!"

"Colin, Dillon, and I will leave now to retrace the route Mac planned to travel back to Milano…usually by way of Verrena to Milano. Stay put, and I'll be in touch as soon as we find anything!" Carlos handed the phone back to Andy.

"Carlos, I'm coming with you and Dillon!" Andy said. "Ricardo can manage here! He's upstairs now…I'll find him and meet you at

433

the front entrance in ten minutes. I'll have Anna keep Emma busy while we leave." Andy called upstairs and spoke to Ricardo in a short curt message. Then he rang the kitchen and Anna answered.

"Occupy Emma for the next twenty minutes—an emergency's come up and three of us have to leave by way of the front. **Do not**—repeat—**do not** let Emma see us exit from the front! Just serve dinner as planned. We'll keep in touch." Andy headed upstairs and out the front door as soon as he saw Anna talking to Emma on the monitor screen.

Driving down the Via di Verrena road slowly, the three men scanned the roadside for signs of a parked car or an accident—allowing the cars behind to pass them.

"I know this is the route Mac usually drove! If he had a breakdown, he would have called...No something's happened to him!" Andrew said convincingly.

Up ahead the traffic was slowing down, seemingly interested in a roadside accident near the open Autostrada leading out of Verrena.

"There—on the right! Pull over! It's a burned out car!" Andy pointed to a blackened shell. "It looks like a BMW. Mac drove a BMW!"

All three men got out of the van and walked over to the shell of the burned car.

"Yes—it was a black BMW! This is his license plate!" Andy brushed off charred ash from most of the plate's numbers. Dillon looked around to see if anyone was watching them, while Carlos and Andy looked inside for evidence of a body.

"There's no one inside—thank God! Look here." Carlos flashed his light and pointed to a set of tire tracks near the burned car. It looks as if they dragged something—or someone—from this point next to the BMW over to another waiting car."

Carlos followed a trail of deep gouges in the dirt leading to tire tracks—evidence of a car parked perpendicular to the front of the BMW.

"There was another car parked here in front of Mac that looks as if it forced him off the road—a hijacking!" Andy proposed.

"Look what I found—shells from an Uzi. This was no accident! Mac was deliberately ambushed!" Dillon said.

"Do you think he made it out of the car before it burned?" Andy posed the question.

"It's me feelin' they forced him off the road. Then fired into the car causin' it to burst into flames. If Mac wasn't injured by the gunfire, he must 'ave got out, and they took him back to their car.

"I know Mac is alive—they wanted him alive!" Carlos said.

"Then…it's my guess they took him to the Villa Latinestto—if he was forcibly abducted here. It's the closest place from here…too far back to Milano…no, he was taken to the Villa Latinestto!" Andy postulated.

"He had his briefcase with him when he left. Check the car to see if it was burned in the fire, or did they get that, too?" Andy and Carlos began searching the car.

"Mac had a habit of putting his briefcase and important papers under the spare tire in a hidden well he had made for just that purpose," Andy told them.

Dillon opened the boot with a hammer blow to the lock—the metal was still warm. In the tire well next to the spare tire, securely in place but only partially burned was the locked briefcase. Dillon grabbed hold of the tire and yanked hard, forcing parts of it to crumble in his hands. Carlos flashed a light into the well. There was the partially burned briefcase with the lock intact!

"They didn't get it! The jackasses didn't find it! If they had 'alf a brain, they'd know to check for documents first before torchin' the car," Dillon said, and the three men hurried back to the van with the remnants of the briefcase.

Carlos dialed Control in Milano. "Carlos here. We found the BMW on the highway—burned but no evidence of a body inside. We also found a briefcase—it's Mac's! From the lay of things here, it looks like they forced him off the road and out of the car—fired into the car setting it on fire and then took Mac with them—probably a van from the size of the tire marks found nearby. Shell casings from an Uzi were found on the ground where the cut-off vehicle was parked according to tire tracks. I'd say Mac was dragged to a van—so he may have been injured or unconscious—but no signs of blood from what we can tell in the dark. The briefcase was still locked, too."

435

"Where do you think they took him?" Colin asked.

"We think he's been taken to the Villa Latinestto. It's the nearest place to the abduction area. Too risky taking him clear back to Milano or to the winery or the complex...No—he's at the Villa Latinestto—where the best security is. This has all the signs of a planned kidnapping! They had to be watching Mac's movements in this area for some time, which means they know about the Villa D'Este...maybe even Central Control Headquarters! Getting him outside the Milano station wasn't possible, so they planned the capture here—when he was alone. I'm certain they'll take him to a place with high security, too, for interrogation!" Carlos said.

Tony Serrano put emphasis on his command. "This changes everything now! We've got to get Mac back...before we lose him and everything we've worked for these past two years! Carlos, you and Dillon go back to the Villa D'Este and wait for my call there. We have things pretty well worked out here. We can't pick the time for our battle now—it's been picked for us!"

*"The Villa D'Este takes out the Villa Latinestto tonight!"* The line went dead.

# CHAPTER FORTY-NINE

*The door opened and the bright intense white lights exploded on!*

Brilliant lights focused directly on Cyrus who was barely able to support his weight upright against the wall. The illumination was so great he couldn't open his eyes for several minutes, and when he did, he couldn't see anything—or anybody. Everything was a blur—blinding! There was no way of knowing who entered the room. How many were there? Three different sets of footsteps…he thought he heard three different kinds of footsteps. Unexpectedly, out of the bright light a hand grabbed his head and slammed it back against the wall. The pain jarred his senses.

"Wake him up!"

*"Si. Signore* Marcus."

"You don't have to—I'm awake!" Cyrus said in a low tone.

"Good. Mr. MacKenna. May I call you Cyrus—since we are on first name basis here? You have had time to think about what I was telling you—when you so rudely interrupted me with some far-fetched notion about my poor dead children.Tsk…tsk.That made me very angry, Cyrus! I have decided to forgive you for your shortsightedness. We have more important things to discuss now!" Marcus was taking time to carefully pose his questions. Cyrus was beginning to understand how this man's mind worked.

"Just why have you and your organization rented the Villa D'Este? I am aware you have several agents there with you. Now, tell me what your mission is?"

"Don't you think agents ever take vacations? What better place to meet old friends than on a beautiful lake and in a villa? Actually… that's precisely what we're doing!

Milano and the lake region…is one of the most beautiful areas in Italy…one I like to return to often…but before I tell you anything more…Marcus…I want these shackles removed first! Then maybe… just maybe…we can have that mutual discussion. I am only one… you are…three? Surely, I'm no threat…to you or your goons!" There was a long pause of silence.

Marcus motioned to the two men in the shadows to remove the chains holding Cyrus to the wall, taking for granted Cyrus was too weak to cause any problems about escaping. Motioning the men to bring him to the table in the center of the room, the men dragged Cyrus to the middle of the room where a single bright spotlight shone on a table and chair and forcefully seated him into it.

"Cuff him to the chair—legs and hands—securely but carefully."

The two men pushed Cyrus down into the chair and bound leather straps to his wrists, his chest lashed to the chair's back, and his ankles tied to the feet of the chair.

"Is all this really necessary, Marcus? There's three strong men here and just one of me—and I'm not in very good condition at that!" Cyrus calculated each response to Marcus, scheming to take up time—while hoping to create a false security in his bastard opponent.

"If you cooperate with me Cyrus, then we can see if we can remove some of those tethers. Now! Again, why have you been investigating my family and my businesses?" Marcus took out a cigarette from a gold case and lit it. The smoke curled upward and floated towards Cyrus.

*Yes!* Cyrus thought—*complacency.* "Marcus, before I spin my story, there're a few facts I need to know. I understand you had a certain man in your employ—a Tony Davici. Now, I've learned this man tried to abduct my granddaughter in Milano not too long ago. Fortunately…he failed! Unfortunately, for Tony, a friend was with her and upset his plans! I heard Tony met an untimely demise. Now, why did one of your men want to kidnap my granddaughter? Why's…that? Why's that, Marcus?" Cyrus repeated, demonstrating anger in his voice while rhetorically repeating his question.

That scent of smoke! A Turkish tobacco Cyrus recognized as Marcus's special brand.

"You have a very beautiful granddaughter—and a very intelligent and internationally esteemed granddaughter, and may I add she's a very desirable woman."

Cyrus listened intently taking care not to fall prey to Marcus's confident, cool manner. He knew he was deliberately baiting him to anger—to lose control and say something unexpected…or unplanned. Each man was calculating their response…to control the stage in the stinking dungeon.

"I have followed Emma's career for some time now. It is unfortunate one of my employees made a bad judgment, and it cost him his life. But I cannot be held accountable for his actions he made independently without my knowledge! In fact, it was fortunate for me that he was killed. It saved me a lot of aggravation. No! I would not harm her…she is important to me…I would not do any harm to your granddaughter, Barrister Emma Llewelyn."

"I don't believe that for one second, Marcus! It's a known fact when Emma was on vacation here—in Tuscany two years ago—she went missing for over two weeks! In fact, when I asked the Italian police to investigate her whereabouts—they could not locate her or find any evidence…she was ever there! What they *did learn* was the villa she rented was vacant—with no trace of her ever being there. After intensive weeks of searching the continent and England…she turns up in London with no recollection of what had happened during her trip to Tuscany. The Italian police searched to find out where she had been those two weeks. Eventually…a single lead led them to the hospital in San Remo…where a record was found describing treatment to an English tourist for a head injury during that period. Only this record was found weeks after the police had checked all area hospitals! Imagine! Weeks later! We knew whoever was involved in her disappearance deliberately forged that record…to satisfy the investigators and get the case closed. Is that how *you* threw the *Policia* off the trail?"

Marcus finished his cigarette, but did not respond to the question. Cyrus remained silent, hoping to feed into Marcus's ego and maniacal alter ego to get some kind of response or explanation.

"We are straying from MY question, Cyrus! Why are you investigating my family and me? How much have you learned?" This time there was great impatience in his voice.

"I told you, Marcus—you answer me why you want Emma—and then we talk about the answer to YOUR questions! Why is Emma so important to you?"

Marcus walked toward Cyrus slowly. Now Cyrus could see him though his bloody and swollen eyes. "Are you sure you want to hear that story now, Cyrus?" Marcus was standing next to Cyrus with a victor's smirk on his face. Leaning over the table toward Cyrus to impress his response, "Sometimes, it's better *not* to know the whole truth—if you have a choice! The truth can be more painful to hear— than not to hear!" Cyrus remained silent almost afraid to hear the truth from Marcus Rudolphi's lips.

"Very well, I'll tell you what you want to hear! It doesn't matter if you hear it now or later, it won't matter…we have the ways and the means of getting the truth out of you—if you do not cooperate. Besides you will never remember this story…should you live!" Marcus walked behind Cyrus.

*"When I finish telling you my story, you will tell me everything I want to know, and it will be the truth too, Cyrus!"* Standing behind him, he leaned down close to his ear, *"Your mind and body are mine now…and there is no other choice left for you!"*

‘

# CHAPTER FIFTY

The three men arrived back at the Villa D'Este.

Immediately entering Control Central in the basement, Andy walked over to view the monitor to Emma's room. "Ricardo, anything important happen while I was gone?" Andy asked.

"Nothing—why?"

"Where's Emma?"

"Everyone is where they're supposed to be—in the dining room finishing dinner. What's happened?" Ricardo asked Andy anxiously.

"Mac is missing! We think he's been kidnapped by the Rudolphis and taken to the Villa Latinestto. I need you to go upstairs and relieve Martin at the telescope and do a sweep of the Latinestto—the entire estate grounds for any unusual activity...Concentrate on activity inside to see who's there...and who's not there! While you're doing this, ask Martin to alert the communication's truck to carefully monitor every bit of conversation heard throughout the villa and record every word...every phone call in and out of that place! Take notice of any references to unusual conversations about a new houseguest...or something unexpectedly going on in the villa!" Andy called the boathouse to alert security to add extra patrols.

"If they learn Emma is here, they could make an attempt to get at her here, as they did Mac!" Andy made the statement for everyone present. Carlos and Dillon knew there was no time to waste now that Cyrus had disappeared. It was crucial to move on the Rudolphi organization—if they were going to find him alive!

"Dillon, I'm going upstairs to divert Emma's attention while you go down to the boathouse and talk to Special Teams. Inform them to get ready to go—with minutes' notice. When Colin and Tony get here, we'll have to be ready to move. Meanwhile, I'll deal with Emma. Wish me luck! It's no easy business keeping truths from her!" Carlos went out the door and locked it again.

"I 'ave the easier job than Carlos! How did you ever fool her Andy when she was growin' up?" Dillon asked.

"I didn't!" Andy remarked.

With dinner finished, Anna was in the kitchen cleaning. "There's a new development," Carlos said in hushed tones.

Anna stopped working. "What's happened?"

"It's Mac—he was abducted on his was back to Milano. We're not certain, but we think he's at the Villa Latinestto. We need to double security here immediately! Where's Emma?" Carlos asked, pausing before entering the dinning room.

"The last time I saw her she was heading toward the Great Room wearing her disguise. Is she aware something happened?"

"God no! She's not to hear about it either! Keep your eyes fixed on the monitors! If there's any questionable outside movements on this place—sound the alarm!" Anna pulled out a keypad panel and switched channels to view split-screen images of the villa from the rear, front, and sides of the villa. From the drawer, she took out a handgun, loaded it, checked the safety, and placed it under a towel on the counter. Continuing her business of cleaning the kitchen, Anna keenly listened to the sounds of different noises inside and outside the villa, while constantly viewing the movements on the screen. Carlos went directly to the Great Room.

"Carlos—it's so good to see you. I've missed you," Emma said in a quiet tone. Immediately meeting his eyes, she knew something had happened. "What's happened?"

"There's a change of plans… Let's you and I take a walk up to your room." Carlos took hold of her arm to emphasize his need to speak to her privately. He knew her room was free of audio listening devices and the visual security cameras didn't pose a problem.

"I've missed you," he said and gently took her in his arms and kissed her tenderly. "I need to talk to you about our plans—which at this moment are not entirely complete. We've learned its imperative we move on the Rudolphis as soon as possible—things are happening faster than we anticipated and time is extremely important from now on! The general plan includes synchronous assaults on the winery and on the Villa del Christianna, as well as the whole Rudolphi estate… and the Villa Latinestto."

"I want to be included in the team going into the Villa Latinestto!"

"For God's sake, no! Absolutely no way! Emma! It's too dangerous for you!" Recalling Cyrus's intense reaction and forceful command to him when he heard these same words, Carlos took a stance of authority.

"You know there are people out there who want to kidnap you, and we know it's someone in the Rudolphi family—most likely Marcus Rudolphi or Carruchi. This is the safest place for you now!" Carlos was trying to control his anxiety in front of Emma and yet remain firm without alarming her instincts to question some of the facts he withheld.

"Then all the more reason for me to go with you! I can use a gun…and I want to find out if the Villa Latinestto…is the place from my past—my connection to the Rudolphi's!"

Emma listened and analyzed all the facts and objections Carlos presented. "Carlos…these flashbacks of memories…from somewhere…where I'm in this stone-walled room—cold—trying to find out who brought me there and why? I always see a woman dressed in old-world dress…bringing me food…each time I wake up there…she is the only one I remember in detail. How long ago did this happen? I thought I must have been in some kind of accident…suffered amnesia to have these memories come and go! Then…when I met Dr. Carruchi…I knew I heard that voice in my… dreams…and I think…no…I KNOW he has something to do with my amnesia dreams! I need to find out answers…*I need to know the truth*! Is Dr. Carruchi responsible for me having these frightening memories? Carlos I need to know…about that Villa for ME…you have to let me go with you!"

443

"There's no way in hell, Emma, I'm going to put you in harm's way…as much as I want you to find out answers to rid you of these demons…I can't let you go to the Villa Latinestto!" Carlos said emphatically, not looking directly at her, but making his point heard.

"Please trust me, my darling, when the attack is over…and it is safe…I promise I will take you there myself for you to see! I need you to promise me you will remain here at this villa—where it is secure and you're safe! Emma, please promise me?"

Emma walked away from Carlos, feeling he was letting her down. His voice and arguments were convincing to a point…*He's not telling me everything…He's hiding something important from me…about the Villa Latinestto!*

Turning she faced him, "Very well, Carlos. I'll do as you ask—with a condition! I want to go with the Special Scuba Teams on the boat…I'll stay on the boat moored out on the lake, while the teams go in from the lakeside. I can be of some help that way! I can man the radio—if necessary! Surely that's an important position as a back-up for the men!" Emma pleaded with Carlos with as much sincerity she could find in herself. She knew she was deliberately lying to him…but rationalized his arguments didn't completely make sense about her safety, and she wouldn't make any moves to jeopardize their plans for the attack on the Villa Latinestto.

Shaking his head in disbelief, Carlos said, "Very well, on ONE CONDITION! You can go on the cruiser with the dive teams but remain on the boat!" Carlos said with firm instruction, **"You are to remain on board and monitor the radio! Do you understand—just that Emma?** *You are to remain on the boat until I come for you!* **That is a flat out order! We do need to have someone on board with Biaggio to assist with the radio and anyone needing to be taken back to the Villa D'Este. Emma…you do promise me to do just that?"** Carlos said emphatically while looking directly into her eyes to see her sincerity.

"Yes! Yes, I promise you—I will do just as you ask!"

"Then why do I feel I'm being manipulated?" he asked her.

"Yes—my darling, I promise to follow your orders," she said and kissed him lightly. "But then, after it is over…you will take me inside the villa? I need to see if there is a place in the villa like the place in my dream memories!"

"Absolutely! I want those demons exorcised from you, too!" he said, softly kissing her again and again. "When this is over... I know we can make a fresh new beginning with no more fears!" Giving her one last tender kiss, he walked over to the phone and dialed an extension.

"Dillon? Carlos! Is it a go with everybody?"

"Everythin's set with the dive teams. They're up-to-date and know what their job is from the lake approach. Colin and Tony are downstairs—meet you there now!" Carlos hung up the phone without further comment to Dillon.

"Emma, I have to leave now. Get dressed in dark black clothing for the boat ride, and I'll meet you at the boathouse in thirty minutes," he said, checking his watch. "Keep your disguise on!"

Colin MacEachen and Tony Serrano were in the villa's Control room studying maps with Andy, Dillon, and Ricardo. The Special Underwater Operatives, from MI5, were the Blue and Red Teams. They were intent on studying photos of the Villa Latinestto two boathouses showing exact details of the beach and boathouses in relation to the several terraced gardens, as well as the placement of the underwater laser sensors and alarms around the beach. The commander of Special Teams outlined the route to the villa they would take—the first direct assault was from the beach. Tony was standing in front of the table of maps with a small contingent of men garbed in black.

"Every man in this room must listen carefully! This plan is called—**Sonata**! Its important Sonata goes down at the same exact moment at all three locations simultaneously. Success is based on the three strikes happening at the same time—not allowing any place a chance to alert the other areas." Each man in the room nodded and listened.

"This is a three-pronged assault—the code name is SONATA— for the three parts of this operation! ALPHA team under the command of Colin is assigned the WINERY. BETA team under my command is assigned ALL THE RUDOLPHI VILLAS on and off the estate. OMEGA team under Carlos and Dillon is assigned the

VILLA LATINESTTO. I don't need to tell any man here—Mac's life depends on our success tonight!" Tony was a seasoned cop with experience planning and executing many successful covert operations in IICA. Each man knew how important this operation was and the years of hard work gone into this case—not to mention the number of lives it had already cost!

"Our first objective is to get Mac back alive! Equally important? Take down the whole Rudolphi organization!" Besides these two prime priorities, each man had his own agenda to annihilate this deadly criminal organization with so much riding on the success of tonight's actions! Everyone's attention was riveted on Tony Serrano's explanation of the assaults.

"Colin's team—the **ALPHA TEAM**—make's the first prong attack on the winery. We know this will be extremely difficult—the winery is heavily fortified, and we don't know the extent of their resistance—but it will be heavy! The security there is **OVERKILL** for just a winery. His team consists of well-trained elite MI-5 forces, and they're in position and primed to go. I needn't say there will be casualties!" Changing the maps, Tony continued.

"My men and I are the **BETA TEAM** and our target is the complex on the Villa del Christianna, which includes the underground chambers as well as all the villas on the property and to secure the entire Rudolphi Estate. On **Beta's** team there are five groups assigned to take down a different place at the precise time—Villa Tempietto is Giuseppe Rudolphi's villa, the Villa del Chrisitianna-Marcus Rudolphi's home, and Dominic Rudolphi's villa. Additional teams of men are stationed outside Luigi Rudolphi's residence in Milano ready to go in with my word. Our last information was that Luigi was seen in London. Scotland Yard has located him in London and has continual surveillance on him until it's time for the assault to go down. Then they'll move to pick him up and detain him there. They have the private airfield under surveillance where he keeps his private plane—if he eludes them in London, they'll get him if he tries to get back to Milano by private plane! We have agents stationed at the Milano Internationale Airport around the clock-in case... Also there's a team stationed outside Isabella Rudolphi Liguori's home, Giuseppe's sister in Firenze, waiting for my word to go in. That's to be on the safe side no one alerts the family to flee once this starts to go down!"

Pointing to the third map, he said, "Here's the third prong of the assault—the **OMEGA TEAM**—headed up by Carlos and Dillon—they take the Villa Latinestto! **We have no definite confirmation—but we all believe Mac is being held captive in that villa!**"

Tony presented clear, precise, essential data to every member of the teams, covering the smallest details, delegating certain responsibilities to the men in the room, answering all questions and covering all contingencies to make the night a complete success. Acknowledging the Blue and Red Seal team's captains, he said, "These teams include the two MI-5 Seal teams, Blue and Red—they'll make the primary assault from the water, shut down beach front security installations and secure the gardens down to the water. They will be deployed from the cruiser, which will be anchored offshore until it's all over. If necessary, the seriously injured can be ferried out to the cruiser and then brought back here for immediate treatment."

Changing maps, he continued, "Andy, Ricardo, Martin, Carlos and Dillon will command different sections of the *Primo* Omega team with two squads from IICA SWAT teams. A *Due* Omega team with a full contingent of forces from IICA will enter directly through the front entrance! Once inside the *Primo* Omega will move through the main house toward the rear of the villa including the first, second, and other upper floors. Once inside, *Primo* Omega splits—Dillon, Martin, and Ricardo with the rest of the squad will start for the basement.

Once *Due* Omega is inside the front door—this team unites with Carlos securing the entire villa—*excluding the basement*! Dillon's team spearheads the basement, and the *Due* Omega is back up for them. I think the heaviest fortifications will be in the basement! That part is new, and we don't know how large or how much security there will be. Therefore, once the upper villa is completely secure, *Primo* Omega will back up Dillon's men in the basement. It's our guess if Mac is inside he'll probably be located in an area not easily accessible from the outside—most likely somewhere in the basement! Any questions so far?" Everyone listening shook their heads 'no' in agreement.

"Munitions, both light and heavy, are being loaded in the vans as we speak. There's special equipment for the underwater assault teams. Become very familiar with your equipment! Your lives—and the lives of every other man with you, will depend on knowing how to use each piece of equipment. Every man will be equipped with this two-way radio and speaker. It's an earpiece with a tiny fiberoptic microphone attached. Voice vibrations are translated by the fiberoptic piece and sent out. So every man on the team can hear your call! This tiny dial on the ear piece can tune to the frequency of the three teams as well to each member of your squad at all times." Tony looked to Carlos. "Carlos will give you more details about **OMEGA TEAMS.**"

Carlos's voice was calm and clear. Referencing the map, he said, "We leave here and drive around the lake to the other side in two separate unmarked trucks to these points." Carlos pointed to the two marked '**X's**' on the map near the Villa Latinestto circled in red. The dive teams will leave by boat with their equipment and munitions from the underwater slip. Biaggio is manning the cruiser." At this point, his voice changed another decibel. **"We're not exactly sure Mac is inside the Villa Latinestto, but we feel it's the most likely a place for them to keep him hidden for an indefinite time.**

We have blueprints of the villa—but there's a good chance they're not totally accurate. I understand part of the basement in the villa was renovated a couple of years ago. More basement rooms were added—we think these additions are rooms—or laboratories— where most of the experimentation is done." Tony walked over to post a rough print, and Carlos continued with his instructions pointing to the print.

"This new basement area may be as large as the whole villa itself! We have no actual construction prints of that area; these are reports from some of the workers who were involved in the construction. All original copies of the blueprints were destroyed. The *Due* Omega team joins with Dillon and gets into the basement to find Mac! When he's located his objective and has him safely out of the basement, he will radio one of the dive teams, and they will take him to the cruiser and then back here. Dr. Ricci and his medical team will be here in Villa D'Este to take care of any wounded. One last thing—there may be hidden exits from that new basement area leading directly outside—probably exiting somewhere in the gardens or the beach area. Blue Team will keep a constant lookout around the beach area to make certain no one—I repeat—NO ONE—escapes from a concealed exit. I suspect when they built it, they purposely made hidden exit routes for escape—they'll use these to escape to the beach. Red Team will neutralize all the boats on or near the beach so they can't be used!"

Carlos knew he had to inform the teams about Emma. Pointing to a wall map of Como, he said, "Biaggio is going to drive the boat to the prearranged spot for the divers to enter the water and then he'll proceed to this area on the lake and drop anchor." He pointed to a red circle on the map. There's one change in the plans." Carlos made certain he had the attention of everyone in the room. **"Emma Llewelyn is going on the boat with Biaggio!"**

"What the hell…she can't go…no way…it's too dangerous for all of us!" Several voices called out.

"Hear me out!" Carlos cried out. "She has no idea Cyrus MacKenna is in the Villa Latinestto. Nor does she know about his or Andy's role in Interpol in this case. The Rudolphis desperately want her and will do anything to get their hands on her! This is one way we will know where she is, and they won't! Biaggio will take care of her and see to it she remains on the boat with him." Carlos had to elicit their support for his decision.

"She is an unknown factor here, I know! Make no mistake, she is a liability—but part of our objective is her safety. **Her safety is as paramount to this mission as it is to rescue Mac!** Therefore, to make certain we know where she is at all times—having her on the boat with Biaggio is probably the least dangerous to her and to the success of this mission!"

"When all of this is over, she'll be told everything—but not until then! That was Mac's last command!" he said in an afterthought.

Dillon finally vented his frustration. "What! Are you crazy?— We can't protect her out there, Carlos! What if they make an attempt to sink the boat?"

449

"It's a very remote possibility…and you and I can't protect her out there, Dillon! But the safest place for her is on the water with Biaggio—and I trust him—he's always done his job well! You think I want her anywhere near the Villa Latinestto? Hell no! I don't want her anywhere near the raid on the villa or near any part of the Rudolphi estates! At least Biaggio will be with her! **HE WILL DO WHAT HE HAS TO DO IF NECESSARY!**" Carlos looked to Biaggio to see his reaction to his statement.

"Biaggio—you're to keep her on the boat! Drug her if you have to to keep her there—tie her up…whatever it takes to keep her safe!" Carlos said with authority. *"Farò il cosa di qualunque Porta!"* Biaggio said with his sternest look..

While Tony and Carlos were laying out the plans to their commanders on their assault teams in Control, Colin MacEachen had been on the telephone with the two teams in Milano and Firenze, readying them to move on the targets there. "Tony—it's a go from **ALPHA** team at the winery and your **BETA** team is set outside the Villa del Christianna—waiting for our word!"

Tony commanded, "We need one hour for everyone here to get back to their designated sites. Everyone check your watches! It is now nineteen-twenty-five hours. The squad-teams leave to get in place at twenty-one-thirty hours. Everyone moves on the objectives at twenty-two hundred hours. Does anyone have any questions? Now's the time to ask! We'll all be in touch at all times with the talkies—they'll pick up a whisper." Tony finished looking around into the faces of the men who knew what lay ahead for them.

"Do we try to take captives or is it a dead or alive command?" Dillon asked deliberately.

"If we can take captives, they'll be helpful to interrogate to get information from them. But no man's life on the team is an exchange for a live captive!" Tony said in a monotone with finality.

"All of us have a stake in this mission—we've invested so much of our personal lives over these past years—but the objectives are to find Mac alive and put the organization out of business and bring those bastards to trial—so records and information are vital to a successful prosecution!" Colin said.

"Most important top priority—*get Mac out alive*!" Dillon looked firmly at Carlos, Andy, Colin, and Tony.

"You best remember! Dr. Ennio Carruchi is MINE." Dillon said matter-of-factly for the benefit of the four men, but loud enough for the rest of the team to hear.

"That big important meetin' of 'is is scheduled for tomorrow—and 'e's most likely at the villa right now!" Carlos and Andy knew exactly what Dillon was saying to the group. None of the men challenged a hidden meaning in his words.

**"Essere salvo!"** Each man echoed silently.

# CHAPTER FIFTY-ONE

Cyrus, you are a disappointment to me, but I understand your concern for your granddaughter!"

Marcus came out of the shadows and sat down at the table opposite Cyrus smoking. Despite the physical beating Cyrus endured, the sickly smell of the Turkish tobacco from across the table pervaded his sense of smell in a nauseous way—a smell he associated with Marcus Rudolphi from the past!

"Your information about Emma's disappearance is correct when you say she suffered an amnesiac event in her past. The very fact that she still has no memory of those events today is testimonial of one of our medical successes! We did have her in our care—here in this very villa." Marcus indicated he meant in this very area with a gesture of his hand. Cyrus felt repulsion and anger rise inside him, and he knew why men killed without remorse! But he had to remain calm and in control. He had to play the game…gain time…more time…play his game! *Jesus…give me what it takes…!* he prayed.

"Emma Llewelyn has certain qualities we are looking for in our subjects—and when we discovered she was in this region two years ago on holiday, we decided to make our move at that time."

"What do you mean, 'she has certain qualities'?

"I'm certain you're intimately knowledgeable about your history of the Clan of MacKenna going back a thousand years to the very origins of the Celtic people. I, too, am fully aware the MacKenna's are 'royal descendants' with pure and unusual characteristics of

Celtic-Welsh traits. I know about this telepathic ability to see truth—a *Cymry* trait! I know Emma possesses this trait in its highest developed and purest form! We…I should say *I*, chose her for the purity of her lineage—for her pure *Cymry* traits! We've been studying her for a much longer time from a distance, determining exactly what characteristics she drew from her ancestors! We obtained material to do a full DNA profile of her, proving she has some of the rarest genetic qualities important in developing an especially strong stem cell with the kinds of qualities needed to encourage a successful process in isolating a particular gene! Yes! The human gene that will give youth and longevity in a new human species! I particularly liked what I saw in the results of our early research! All our investigations indicated she was a specimen we needed to add to our pool of donors. The purity of these characteristics made her a prime donor and Dr. Carruchi wanted to grow her stem cells and use them in his research." Marcus rose and started pacing slowly.

"When did you make your move on her?"

"*Si*! Two years ago we successfully and secretly seized her from her rental villa and brought her here. Of course, she was under special sedation all the time—amnesiac drugs and memory altering drugs removed any memory of what happened to her. Under the most sterile conditions, Dr. Carruchi surgically removed some unfertilized eggs—ova they're called—to fertilize and bring them to maturation level where we could harvest the stem cells from the embryos. We tried 'parthogenesis' on her—but nothing came of it. So we knew we had to have a male donor to do a test-tube fertilization. Of course we had to be equally selective of the male donor, someone with many of the same superior qualities to form a perfect embryo for the stem cells!" All the while Marcus smugly told his story, Cyrus listened with great physical and psychological pain, but with absolute raging hatred toward the bastard across from him taking pride in his tale. *Time…I need more time…keep him talking,* Cyrus kept repeating.

"We had the perfect donor sperm to fertilize the ova, and it was successful on the first attempt! We had the embryonic tissue we wanted! You see Cyrus it was my own sperm used to fertilize her ova—a perfect union of two pure specimens of mankind—to be used toward the development of a more perfect human species—

and destined to live together for a very long time in the name of molecular science! This specimen was needed to show the world how we achieved the brilliant breakthrough for a long and near perfect life!" Cyrus was listening silently to Marcus telling his story with the pleasure and self-gratification of a maniacal, twisted mind! With all his willpower it took, Cyrus remained silent—as he listened to the story of horror this man related so powerfully with demoniac smugness and pride.

With control and firmness in his voice, Cyrus asked, "Marcus, why doesn't she remember what happened to her? How do you know for certain—sometime in the future she will not remember everything and come to hate you for what you did to her?"

"I don't!" Marcus snapped. A calmer Marcus said, "I am told the more time passes without recollection of what happened, the less chance she will ever recall that time and those events!" Marcus rose and walked closer to Cyrus as if his nearness would gain him an understanding from Cyrus. His voice changed to almost tenderness as he continued his tale.

"You see, Cyrus, I wanted to take the fertilization further…only this time we *did not destroy* the fertilized embryo for research tissue! No, I realized we achieved a perfect union and allowed it to reach maturity! Of course with Carruchi's expertise and medical supervision, the viable embryo grew into a perfectly duplicate child until it completed nine months gestation. We produced the first living fetus to mature, possessing all the qualities we worked so hard to find! We had a new baby—a new species—one *free from the process of aging with superior mental talents!"*

Cyrus listened to the words, disbelieving what he was hearing… fearful Marcus was going to say what he already concluded, conception through a demoniac rape!

"You should see this outcome as something precious for both of us—now we have something very precious to each of us—something in common between us now that can't be denied!" Cyrus knew this was not the end of his story. He felt completely drained of all physical and emotional energy. What he heard was so heartbreaking—so heartrending, he willed his senses to experience the physical pain to block out his greater mental anguish. Marcus was basking in his success recounting his crowning achievement!

*"We actually took one of the cells—a single ova of Emma's and fertilized it with my sperm to make a perfect test tube child of ours. Yes! We have a child together! She is absolutely beautiful and so perfect in every way—just like her mother!"*

The words kept ringing over and over in Cyrus's mind—a child…together—despite the bloody swollen eyes, the stinging tears rolled down his face, as his head hung down on his chest.

"I know when Emma learns she is the mother of such a beautiful and privileged child she will become completely mine!" With assurance and pride, Marcus placed his hand on Cyrus's shoulder. The tears stinging his eyes, he slowly raised his head to face the demon. All the while, cringing at the touch of this devil's hand on his shoulder, thinking how to keep control of the situation for as long as possible to gain more time.

"I named our daughter CARA ROSINA! ROSE OF THE HEART!"

Marcus took great pleasure in saying these words. "I have taken great pains to make certain she is safe…well cared for… and wants for nothing. No one in my family knows about Cara, our love child—except Dr. Carruchi, who will keep my confidence. He has a stake in this match, too! He is a great man, and I am privileged to work with him. But I deviate!" Cyrus heard the smugness return in his tone of self-praise.

"Our beautiful daughter is in a safe place, and I see her whenever I can. She knows me as her father and calls me *Baba*…I hope someday she will come to know her mother…but that is enough for you to know now!"

Cyrus raised his head to ask, "Why would you think I believe one word you're telling me Marcus? You're capable of any kind of lie to get what you want…and can't have! How do I know you're not lying now to get me to tell you more information…information that I do not have?"

"No, Cyrus—I am not lying about this! Cara Rosina is alive and is a child of yours and mine! If you saw her—you would think you were looking into the eyes of Emma at the age of two years!"

As incredible as it sounded, there was truth in Marcus's demeanor. Cyrus heard truth spoken and fought hard to disbelieve it all. There is truth to this whole fiendish story!

"Why, Marcus, why did you go to such lengths to have this child born?"

"You must know, Cyrus, I'm in love with Emma Llewelyn and have been for a very long time!"

"But you're married to Lucinda?"

"Ah—*Si*! I will have to make a decision about Lucinda soon. Accidents are always happening…who's to know! That is no concern of yours!"

"So, it is you who's been trying to kidnap Emma in Milano!"

"Your granddaughter has greater things waiting for her—here with me! I can give her so much more than a life back in England or Wales! Unfortunately, you, Cyrus—may or may not—be a part of that life with her. But that issue is not to be decided yet." Marcus walked and stood behind Cyrus's chair. "Now! It is your turn to tell me all you have learned and who else knows about my…businesses!" He grabbed Cyrus's hair and jerked his head back and glared down to meet his eyes. Suddenly Marcus looked away.

Loud bursts of gunfire in the distance echoed in the room. Everyone in the room was listening to the sporadic sounds of turmoil heard out in the corridor. Again…another rapid series of gun bursts! Marcus released his hold on Cyrus then quickly walked over to speak with one of the guards. Giving an abrupt command to the guard in Italian, the guard immediately exited the room. Marcus returned to Cyrus taking out a cigarette to light up again. That unmistakable odor of sweet smoke was intense. Cyrus watched him closely. Visibly, an unexplainable tenseness took over that calm facade in his enemy! He did not pursue his questioning of Cyrus but became silent—anxious—pacing in the room. Cyrus knew Marcus was disturbed…worried!

"What do you think that noise is, Marcus?" Knowing full well it was the sound of gunfire getting closer—the sound he had been waiting to hear! *The assault had begun on the villa.*

"It is no concern of yours! Sometimes animals come onto the property and set off alarms—we have our ways of scaring them away.

I'm certain that is all it is!" Cyrus heard a worrisome uneasiness in the voice not there before. He hoped his instincts were right! Marcus walked over to the other guard impatient to hear what was happening and sent him to find out. Now Cyrus and Marcus were alone.

"You cannot think someone has come looking for you here, Cyrus? No one knows you are here! Even if they did, no one can breach this villa and live to tell about it! Tell me what you know about my organization?" A frightened and impatient Marcus slapped Cyrus so hard his head snapped backwards almost causing him to lose consciousness for a few seconds.

"Marcus...I detect fear in you! You have every right to be frightened! We know all about your mad schemes...all the people your henchmen kidnapped all over the world—for your experimentation! How many failures did it take to reach the success you claim you found?"

Marcus's anger was increasing—almost out of control! "Every brilliant man suffers many failures before great successes! What did it take to trial all those vaccines to eradicate those dreaded diseases of the past—the black plague, small pox, tuberculosis, the newest implants, heart machines to keep people alive—all those organ transplants and the drugs needed to keep their organs alive! EXPERIMENTATION WAS NECESSARY IN ALL THOSE INSTANCES! We are no different now!"

"Don't hide behind all those decent scientists—life was important to those men—and one loss was one too many! But you...you are the lowest of the beasts to take the most precious beings we have— our children—and use them for such devious experiments—when you knew there was little chance of success in the early stages! I know...about the bodies on the morgue slabs! The children who were turned into old men and women when the experiment failed!" Cyrus shouted at him as best he could.

"No NEVER!" An unexpected blow came down on Cyrus, causing him to almost lose consciousness again.

At that moment, the door opened and a guard rushed in summoning Marcus out of the room. Voices outside the door were getting louder in the hall...Marcus screamed out an order before returning inside, slamming and bolting the door! Again, rapid gunfire! Now louder and constant! With a knock, he opened the door to let the guard in holding a needle and syringe. Cyrus sensed something was about to happen to him! Maybe, this too, is a failure Marcus Rudolphi will hide—the death of Cyrus MacKenna. The drug stung his arm as he felt the plunger pushing the medication into his flesh while the guard held him tightly. Fighting his tethers, a rush of blackness quickly overtook his thoughts and mind...must fight to keep control... Caitlyn...Caitlyn...take care of her...her... baby...Cara...

**"It's too bad Cyrus you will not survive...if you do make it... either way you will have no recollection of my story!"**

# CHAPTER FIFTY-TWO

Running without lights, the cruiser's motors slowed and stopped.

Biaggio and Emma stayed in the pilot's cabin while the dive teams were readying for submersion. The two teams slipped silently into the dark waters each carrying a munitions pack. Once the divers submerged out of sight, Biaggio waited five extra minutes then continued running silently without lights to a second chosen sight further up the lake, deploying the forward and aft anchors with barely a splash. This was the designated spot to wait until word came the assault was over. Within several minutes, they felt the boat tugging from the currents. The cruiser was lost in total darkness. Only tiny distant lights from the shore blinked through the blackness.

"Biaggio, how long do you think we'll be here before the teams return?" she asked.

"I can't say. It could be hours—more like six or…eight hours! They have a lot to accomplish before the frontal teams can take over the entire Villa. Emma, I need you to make sure the outboard dinghy is well secured in case we need to go ashore to get anyone." Emma knew exactly what Biaggio meant. The dinghy would pick up the injured or anyone found at the Villa Latinestto and ferry them back to the cruiser then to the Villa D'Este.

"I've stowed extra rope in the forward cabin with other supplies. Can you get them and bring them up on starboard deck? I'm going to double tie the anchor—we're drifting more than I expected!"

459

Following Biaggio's instructions, she went below to the cabins, but not to get the equipment. Emma devised a plan of her own. This was her fight, too! Maybe even more her fight to find answers to her terrorizing dreams for the past two years...

**Always...a dark cold stone room...alone...and pain...a familiar voice!**

Instead of going to the forward cabin to get the supplies, she went to the aft storage area where she hid a wetsuit and scuba tank. Removing the wig and the rest of her disguise, she donned the insulated wetsuit and strapped the scuba equipment on securely. Cautiously making her way up the stern steps to the aft deck to a hidden blind spot behind the cabin, she slowly lowered herself over the side of the boat without a splash.

"I'm sorry, Biaggio, but this is my fight, too," she whispered as she put the mouthpiece in and silently submerged under the boat heading toward the Villa Latinessto.

Diving to a safe depth with the night-vision mask and underwater torch, Emma headed toward land looking for the markers she left on the bottom when she surveyed the area yesterday. Recognizing familiar underwater sights she had deliberately marked, the water depth rose quickly—becoming shallower at a much faster rate. Extinguishing the torch, she felt the sandy bottom and gradually surfaced to take a bearing on the lights from the villa. The boathouse was less that fifty meters away; she scanned for signs of the laser alarms in the shallower water. The Special Operational Teams must have neutralized them—no sign of laser beams rising from the lake bottom. Listening and scanning, her night-field mask saw signs of some of the scuba teams located in the gardens. "Damn! I see only three of them! Where's the fourth?"

Slowly descending again into the dark water, she started swimming north for another fifty meters, this time surfacing at the farthest boundary of the beach. Silently gliding into shore with the ebbing of the waves until she could go no farther with the scuba gear, she crawled the rest of the distance on her belly to the closest bush in front of a stone wall. Lying very still and listening for sounds of voices, there were only loud rapid bursts of gunfire coming from the villa. She chose her spot to go deeper into the gardens and quietly ran to the outer perimeter—behind the Special Teams sites.

Here, she took off the scuba pack, helmet, and fins and took out a pair of rubber slippers from inside her wetsuit. Checking the gun stowed inside her waist—it was dry and fully loaded— removing the safety latch she readied it and felt for the additional clips of bullets inside the suit. The gunfire was definitely getting louder and more rapid from inside the villa.

Biaggio radioed the **OMEGA TEAM**. "Dillon! Carlos come in!"

"Carlos here—what's up Biaggio?"

**"Emma's gone! She must have gone into shore. I think she has a tank and gear—can't be certain—there's her disguise clothes here!"**

"How long ago do you think she left the boat?" Carlos interrupted Biaggio trying to remain calm.

"No longer than fifteen or twenty minutes ago! I searched the boat—no sign of her anywhere on the boat! I'm sorry, Carlos! I let her out of my sight when I asked her to bring me extra equipment from the forward cabin. When she didn't return, I went looking for her!"

"You stay there at the controls, Biaggio—we'll keep watch for her here! Dillon did you hear?"

"Jesus Christ! Yeah! I heard!" Dillon yelled dejectedly.

"Where are you now, Dillon?" Carlos asked.

"The three of us are forward of the squad making our way down toward the new section of corridor; we're outside the door leading from the old basement into a newer section. We've taken out about half a dozen guards—permanently. No other way to do it. Casualties of war!" Dillon quoted.

Carlos explained, "We're still securing the first floor! Andy's just about cleaned the nest and secured the first floor…only house servants left, and they're neutral and locked in the pantry. I'm on my way up to the second floor. The guards took off for the upper level…must be where important guests or owners have retreated to—gotta go for now!"

461

Carlos heard the Uzi machines guns going off at the top of the staircase and signaled to his men to take up positions around the ground floor marble columns and pointed to the positions above them where the guards were firing on them! Each acknowledged his instructions with a nod. Suddenly, with a cue from Carlos, a barrage of guns fired from behind each column simultaneously aimed at the whole second floor. Within seconds, several men from the Omega team started up the long, wide marble staircase hugging the wall firing continuously as they ascended—taking out all of the guards visible in the upper hallway. The upper hall was quiet without movement.

Before ascending the staircase, Carlos paused and made his way back out through the Great Hall to the terrace searching the gardens with night-vision binoculars. Suddenly, a flash of light on something and then it was gone! No movement! **"Damn it, Emma! Where the bloody hell are you? You promised me…!"** Instantly, a sting in his left shoulder threw him off balance and knocked him to the floor! Carlos grabbed his shoulder and saw blood. Checking the shoulder—nothing broken—a bleeding flesh wound, he stuffed a piece of his torn shirt into the shoulder wound placing his holster strap over the area to apply pressure to stop the bleeding. Grabbing his Uzi, he ran back through the Great Room keeping low, he saw the guard who fired at him from the window. "Too late, *Amico*! Now it's my turn!—*Caio*!" The guard spun around too late. Carlos fired first with exact accuracy. Inspecting the dead guard, he took his Uzi gun and clips and ran up the steps to the second floor. Andy was taking fire from the rooms down the north wing.

"Hold it, Andy—I have the gas gun!" Carlos fired the gas pellets into several rooms' doors with intense velocity shattering the doors. In minutes, the gunfire stopped inside the rooms. Andy signaled to Carlos to take the rooms on the right and he'd go down the left side of the hall into each room looking for survivors—guards or Rudolphis! Carlos carefully opened the first door, peering in to see Giuseppe Rudolphi lying in a large bed appearing asleep—or dead. Checking for a pulse, he said, "Ah yes! A faint one. Good old man! I want you alive to have your day in court to feel some of the pain you're *responsible* for!" he shackled him to the bed—both hands and feet to make certain any escape was not going to be easy!

"Dino should be near!" Continuing into the next room, he abruptly stopped. "Dino! No Dino!" On the floor next to the telephone lay Dino. Carlos felt for a pulse, there was none. "You did well my dear friend... he must've tried to contact us...and *they* discovered him! We'll get them my friend—for you!" Closing his sightless eyes, Carlos covered him with a sheet.

"Dillon! Where are you now?"

"I'm still in the front part of the new complex in the main corridor. I'd like to use a grenade to take down some of these guards fast—but I'm afraid Mac could be near in a room here."

"Andy is finishing up on floors one and two. I found Dino—he's dead! I'm coming down to meet you! See you, *amico,* in a few minutes!" Carlos started down toward the basement with caution and stealth, checking all the rooms for any other members of the Rudolphi family.

"Where are you, Marcus? You can't hide deep enough from me!"

"Any sign of Emma?" Dillon called on the mike.

"No! I looked for her, but I'll take another look on my way down to the basement." Carlos ran silently back out onto the front balcony terrace and again scanned the gardens with night-vision binoculars. He saw several members of the Blue and Red teams still in their positions in the gardens. "Where the hell are you Emma?" Carlos asked himself. "Come in Blue team!" Carlos called on his mike.

"Yeah man! We're on the lookout for her! She hasn't passed us! If she's still outside the villa 'ole chap, we'll find her. I have all my men watchin' for her. I doubt she can get past us! We'll find her and hold her here! Out!"

"*Essere salvo, Emma!*"

# CHAPTER FIFTY-THREE

Emma crawled along the exterior perimeter of the garden up to the rear terrace undetected.

The gunfire inside the villa became more intense and louder the closer she came to the villa. The rapid and sporadic bursts outside the villa were even more frightening. Staying well concealed among the thick shrubs, she slowly scanned the entire terrace and grounds, deliberately looking for something. There it was! Emma remembered old villas were built with outside subterranean accesses leading to underground storage rooms, usually located under the terraces for the servants to use. "Yes! Just as I hoped!" Afraid of detection with her penlight, instead she felt around the old decaying wooden door in the corner of the terrace foundation in the dark making a mental image map of it.

"This has to be it! It's covered with clinging vines and embedded shrubs and probably its bolts are rusted shut! Maybe its old rusty lock is weak, and with a bit of luck, I can dig away at the rotting wood around it!" Taking the knife out of her ankle sheath, she silently pulled away the thicket of vines off the door.

With most of the entangled vines removed, she examined the entrance more closely to determine if was still a semblance of a door. "It's a single rotting wooden door with iron grillwork and can't be that strong!" When she pulled the rest of the vines away, some of the rusted ironwork came off imbedded with the vine roots, which meant it hadn't been opened for eons. Persistently digging around the bolts of the grillwork with her knife, the stone crumbled and the rotting wood fell away. Finally the stone released the iron grill and gave up its prison security. With one good kick to push the door open without much noise, Emma was able to squeeze through the small, slim opening wider at the bottom. Now, using her penlight, she scanned inside to find a damp, dirty crypt, thick with moss and compost with hanging roots and vines creeping up the walls. "No one's disturbed or seen this place for a century. There's got to be an entrance from the inside to this place—but where!" Emma started searching the walls of the subterranean vault, looking for any evidence of an inside entrance—a door, or grillwork or gate. Feeling around the walls for a latch, her hand caught hold of an old iron pull handle. Holding the pen light in her mouth to examine the latch, it felt the handle was attached to a single iron gate grill encased with centuries of dirt, roots and vines that netted it permanently shut and felt as solid as wood. Pulling and yanking as hard as she could, it didn't move.

"A door is made to open!" she said in frustration. Again, with all her strength and force, she repeatedly pulled and pushed her weight against it. Slowly, it began to give up its secret and opened a few centimeters inward. Repeatedly slashing away at the thick growth, she dug at the composted roots—with one final tug, it finally opened a wedge wide enough for her to slither through.

Fearful of what she'd find on the other side, Emma hesitated, listening before flashing the light through the opening. Beyond the iron grill was a narrow stone corridor devoid of the growth of vines and roots. Clearly, the sporadic bursts of gunfire sounded much closer inside from that corridor. Taking out her Larson three-eighty, she removed the safety and started down the corridor with gun raised ready to fire, and with the penlight in her mouth guiding her toward the end. Voices with the gunfire! "Italian—men yelling—must be the villa's security."

The door at the end of the stone corridor had been recently replaced—the wood was clean and new. Turning off her torch, she said, "I can't come this far and quit! How do I find out what and who's on the other side?" Overcoming her fear, she fired several rounds at close range into the bolt and lock. The door sprang ajar.

"Oh God!" Emma stepped back into the darkness of the corridor. Kicking the door open she raised the Larson ready to fire, the light from the other side of the door outlined a figure. Aiming the gun steady to pull the trigger a light flashed on her with a voice behind it!

"Em? It's Dillon! For God sakes drop that gun! It does fire real bullets! 'ow the 'ell did you get 'ere, girl? Ne'er mind! I'm just glad to see you alive!" Dillon grabbed her from the narrow opening and quickly pushed her to the ground next to him. Feeling her body next to his, he felt a great relief she was safe here with him.

"Carlos—I've got 'er with me!" Dillon spoke into the mike.

"Repeat that?" ·

"I'm in the new section of the basement...in a storage room. Emma is 'ere with me!"

"Still 'aven't found the target yet. I need your 'elp to take her to a safe spot upstairs before I go on. Our target is close—I feel and sense it!" Dillon said, all the while constantly scanning around for something unexpected to happen.

"I'm on my way down...keep your mike on me—so I can locate you."

Sudden and furious hails of gunfire erupted just outside the door in the corridor beyond where Dillon and Emma crouched low. Volleys of bullets ricocheted off the stone walls in the hall, splintering the door next to them. Dillon pushed Emma down completely under him shielding her with his body. Glancing up, he saw his two partners in the hall outside the door flail in anguished convulsions as bullets smashed them backwards against the wall until they fell slowly lifeless to the floor. The onslaught of bullets kept raining down on all of them for several more minutes.

With a moment of silence, Dillon called out, "Dann'...Luis—can you 'ear me?" Dead silence! Dillon knew the two men were lifeless. He was alone with Emma. Another barrage of bullets started ricocheting off the walls next to them inside the room. Whoever was firing was coming toward them and into this storage room!

"Em—stay close and follow me! Do EXACT'Y as I tell you—no questions asked and keep your gun read'!" Emma saw the anger and fear in his eyes and voice and nodded. Slowly, they crept to the other side of the large room staying behind large wooden vats and boxes as shields.

"You're to stay 'ere, Em! For no reason are ye to move! **Do ya 'ear?** If an'one comes near without speakin', you shoot to kill!" Dillon spoke specific instructions to her.

"Where are you going, Dillon?"

"I want to draw their fire away from this spot. I can cause more damage just with this MAG 'ere—pointing to a bag of grenades. "I need to make certain you're in 'ere when I use 'hem—got it?" Emma nodded. Dillon crawled over toward the doorway to the main corridor where the automatic gun continued firing.

Observing the direction the bursts of fire came from, Dillon pulled out the grenade pin and with an overhand toss threw a grenade down to the end of the hall and then another. Immediately tossing several more grenades to the opposite end of the hall just beyond the doorway, he threw himself on the floor back inside the room. Loud... continuous explosions—another—and another almost shattering the walls! The gunfire stopped! He yelled out, "Em! Stay put!"

Dillon stayed low and made his way out into the corridor, all the while firing his Uzi and running down the corridor until he reached the last room at the end of the corridor without any return fire. He saw the door.

"PRIVATE LABORATORY"—locked. "Damn!" Ducking into doorways, "Bloody 'ell! Locked, too! There's nowhere to 'ide you fuckin' devils!" Firing at the lock to this last room, he pushed open the door with the butt of his gun and quickly stepped back into the corridor leaning against the wall, expecting a return of gunfire from within the room. Nothing! Taking rapid glances into the room, it was dark with only a small dim overhead light on. Checking the room perimeter for someone concealed—nothing-no one! The dim light drew his eyes to a man sitting slumped down, chained to a chair beside a table in the middle of the room—looking more dead than alive—showing no signs of any life. Thinking this a trap—a decoy—he took no chances and stayed crouched by the walls. When his eyes became accustomed to the darkness he saw no movement inside the room. Slipping over to the chained man, he knelt next to the man, turning to see his face.

"Sweet Jesus—Mac!" Laying down the Uzi next to him, Dillon worked as fast as he could trying to free him while glancing out the door expecting a guard to come in at any moment. "Mac—Mac! Jesus—Mac, you gotta hear me now! Sorry ole chap, this'll 'urt me more than you." Dillon fired at the locks of the chains, smashing them open. Feeling a fast and faint pulse, he pulled Cyrus up onto his feet and saw his eyelids fluttering to open as if he was in pain.

"Mac—it's me—Dillon! Don't you let me down now, you big bastard!"

* * *

Carlos made his way down from the second floor to locate Andy. "Andy? Dillon found Emma! She's with him in the new section of the cellar—I'm going down to get her! Still no sign of Mac yet! You stay here and secure it. When Em's safe out of here, I'll let you know. You're in charge here so get Blue Team up here to help secure these floors if you need them. I'm taking two men to go with me to help Dillon—he's in trouble down there!" Running down the steps, he yelled to Andy, "Have Blue team continue up to the loft and roof—check every room on the upper floors, too! Keep any live ones locked in one of the rooms shackled together—blindfold them first!"

Carlos and two IICA men made their way down into the old cellar without encountering any resistance. The door to the new section of the basement wing was open with the far corridor partially lit.

"Dillon—where the hell are you? You've changed position!"

"Yeah, get Em! She's in the third room on the left behind the vats—safe! I just found Mac! He's alive—barely!"

Carlos and his two-man team started down into the new section, when more gunfire erupted from rooms off to the right. Carlos signaled to his two companions to take out the rooms on the right while he made his way down to the third left room. Hugging the wall and making his way down the passage, he saw the bodies of Danny and Luis outside the third room on the left. Pausing to check for a pulse…nothing.

"Emma—it's me—Carlos!" he called inside the room.

"Carlos? Is it really you? Dillon and I were pinned down in here! He went down the hall to find the source of the gunfire! I think he's killed the guards, but he hasn't returned yet!" she shouted out to Carlos.

Carlos made his way into the storage room and met up with Emma. "You okay, *mia cara?*" he asked tenderly.

"I'm okay."

"You and I need to get the hell out of here now! Dillon can take of himself! Keep your gun ready at all times!" Emma grabbed Carlos's arm. "Wait! Smells I remember...musty walls and the smells... Carlos, I was here at some time—I know it!"

"Bloody hell of a time to remember it!" Carlos said.

"This place...Yes, I remember this place...faint memories of this part of the villa from a past!" Emma's words confirmed what Carlos suspected—at one time the Rudolphis held her captive in the villa.

"You may be right, Emma, but right now we need to get the bloody hell out of here alive! It's still not safe for either of us!" Emma followed Carlos to the door where a dim light lit only the distant end of the corridor.

"Carlos, you're injured!" Emma said with alarm, seeing his bloody jacket.

"It's a flesh wound; the bullet went straight through the shoulder without much damage. It looks worse than it is! Let's go now!" Carlos grabbed Emma and led her out to the corridor, crouching low until he knew it was clear to try for the stairs.

"Keep your gun ready—fire if you have to! Then ask questions!"

\* \* \*

"Mac? Can you hear me?" Dillon kept shaking Cyrus firmly but gently. He saw the extent of his injuries and understood his pain, but if there was life in him, he had to respond to the pain.

"Christ—aye! Man, I hear you ...and...it's good hearing your corny, sweet brogue!" Cyrus grimaced trying to open his eyes despite the pain and swelling.

"Where is he?" Cyrus asked.

"Who?"

"That bastard…maniac—Marcus Rudolphi!"

"He wasn't 'ere when I found you! Not to worry…we'll get him, Mac. There's no way he's goin' to get out of 'ere alive!" Cyrus was dead weight and could not help Dillon get him out of the room.

"Mac, lean on me to get out of 'ere! We need to get you to the boat'ouse and out to the cruiser anchored off shore and back to Villa D'Este, me ole man!" As tough as Dillon portrayed himself to be, his touch was tender and comforting. Dillon carried and dragged Cyrus. Halfway down the corridor, sudden bursts of fire came from the rear of the corridor throwing Mac against the wall out of Dillon's arms. Dillon fell to the floor simultaneously turning and firing a constant barrage of bullets, spraying the whole end of the hall emptying the clip in the Uzi. The lone gunman fell backwards in an onslaught of bullets blowing his body apart against the wall.

Carlos heard the hail of bullets spraying the walls just outside the door and threw Emma on the floor, shielding her with his body. Taking aim at the doorway, he shot the lights out. "Ssh!" Carlos said to Emma, crawling back behind the door to listen. Moans from the hall…Carlos crawled to the edge of the door and saw Dillon and Mac. Quickly scrambling to his feet, he ran to the two men lying on the floor. Mac's leg was pumping blood out fast! His whole body was covered in blood over his tattered clothes!

"Dillon? Mac? It's Carlos!"

"Carlos—no more time for secrets now!" Dillon said concealing his own pain.

"You 'ave to take Mac out with Emma! I 'ave one more job to do 'ere! She's strong and will 'elp Mac more now!" At that very moment, Emma ran out the door in a crouched position and stopped suddenly next to them.

"Oh Sweet Mother! Oh my God!" Crawling over to Cyrus, Emma tenderly cradled his head in her lap, "Papa—it's me, Emma!" Trying to contain her tears, she said, "Papa—what have they done to you—who did this to you?" She was afraid to touch his bloodied face distorted and swollen.

"Emma… you're safe…thank God!" Cyrus looked up at the sound of her voice…reaching out to touch her.

"Papa, did someone do this to you because...of ME?" Emma fought hard to conceal her tears, seeing his bloody, broken, and bruised body and swollen-almost unrecognizable face. He could barely open his eyes to see her.

"Emma—I know...you will learn everything...but now...not the time...no questions! We must get out...alive—all of us," he said, barely mouthing the words. As Cyrus tried to stand, he grabbed his leg bleeding profusely.

"You've been shot, Papa! Here let me see it! Can you stand on it?"

"Yeah—I think I can...the bone isn't broken—we'll make it, lass!" Emma tore her shirt under the wetsuit and dressed the leg in a tourniquet to stay the bleeding.

"You three get goin'!" Dillon said decisively, concealing his own wound.

"Carlos will take you safel' back to the beach and out to the cruiser." Quickly turning away, Dillon shouted at them, "My job 'ere isn't finished—not yet! Now...GET THE 'ELL OUT...GO!"

Dillon yelled and ran back down the corridor, trying to hide the bleeding coming out faster from under his jacket—faster than he wanted anyone to see.

The room marked PRIVATE LABORATORY was located next to Mac's torture chamber. This has got to be Carruchi's private laboratory! First Dillon checked the lateral hall for exits from the PRIVATE LABORATORY. Three!

"Time to do a little dirty work!" Dillon took out a grenade, partially removed the pin and then reattached the live grenade to each door in such a way that if someone opened the door from the inside, the pin would completely pull out and everything—or everyone—would blow with the door. Making certain there were no other exits, he returned to the main door. "Jesus...why this now?" he said, looking down at the wound in his stomach. "No way! Don't worry...I'll get 'im, Maura...me love!" Dillon blew open the locked door with bullets. Taking the necessary precautions before entering the room, he saw it was an operating room—fully equipped with several anterooms off the big surgical theater.

"Carruchi—you're 'ere! I know it! Let me see your face! There's no way out of these rooms...'cept through this room!" Dillon yelled out, all the while looking around for a sign of movement. Now the pain was trying to overtake him. *First...my job...no pain.*

"Carruchi...can you 'ear me? I've been bus'—all the exits from the anterooms, they'e all wired with explosives to go off if the door opens from the inside. So you...and me...we're locked in 'ere now! My specialt' is death, too! Don't be shy now—show me yur face!" Dillon knew he had to find his mark soon—the light seemed dimmer and objects blurred. Making it to the last room, it was an office...and there... sitting behind a large glass-topped desk was Carruchi with a gun cradled in his lap. "Mother luck!" Dillon spoke softly.

"Don't be stupid, Dr. Carruchi, I can pull my trigger three times fast'r than you! That is...if that's the way you want to go...then go for it! Put the gun on the desk—I just want to talk to you!" Dillon watched Carruchi calmly seated behind the desk with the gun in his lap.

"On the desk—not the lap!" Dillon yelled and watched him place the gun on the desk as he walked in.

"You're injured! Let me take a look—I may be able to help you," Dr. Carruchi spoke to Dillon.

"That's iron' fur ya! You 'elp me! Stay where you are for now Carruchi!" Dillon moved to the end of the room away from the desk and climbed atop boxes giving him a clear view and advantage of the desk and door, never taking his eyes off of Carruchi.

"You surprise me Carruchi! I'da thought a clever man like you would 'ave an escape plan in case somethin' just like this 'appened! Instead, I find you sittin' 'ere in your office! What did you think? You would win this war?" Dillon grabbed his abdomen tightly.

"The bigger they are the 'arder for 'hem to think 'bout failure!"

Taking in a deep breath to stay focused, he said, "Dr. Carruchi, I'm short on time...tell me, did you know all of the names of the victims you worked on? Or were they just a number in one of your logs—given a symbol of a success or a failure? Did you 'elp me wife, Maura, or me baby daughter, Siobhan? What did you do to 'elp make their lives better? When did my Maura die? 'Ow did she die? Me bab'...she's on a slab because of you! Do you e'en remember who they were—you bastardl' monster?" Dillon felt the tears stinging for the very first time…the light fading. He was grabbing his stomach tighter to stave off the pain.

"No answer? I'll tell you 'ho they were! They were me 'hole life and soul! They were everythin' I 'ad that mattered in this world. And *you* took them from me. Why 'hem Carruchi? Why 'hem?"

"I—I can't recall those names exactly…I didn't pick out all of our subjects…It was important we had good subjects…Marcus Rudolphi did most of the selecting of material…he…he's the one you should be asking these questions to…not me!"

"Then tell me… 'ho did the actual experiments on 'hem? Was that Marcus Rudolphi, too? Did he inject 'hem with your death serum? Did he watch 'hem ever' day turn into old men and women—not knowin' what was happenin' to 'hem? You are the worst kind of evil monster, preyin' on innocent children! A bloody fuckin' monster! If there's a God in hea'en…he could not 'ave made you! No! You were made by the devil 'imself! My only…regret is that I can't make you die the same way me Maura and Siobhan died! Or like…all those other babies…**But 'here is justice Carruchi—and I'm 'ere to see it's done!**"

"No—please…have mercy…what I did…I did for the betterment of mankind! We are on the cutting edge of a great breakthrough…it was all…necessary…"

"We all 'have our reasons…for our actions…Carruchi. We all gotta pay the piper for ou' actions…" Dillon realized he was becoming weaker, and it was more difficult to see clearly. He wanted Carruchi to suffer like his Siobhan and Maura—but time was running out.

"Stand up, Dr. Carruchi! STAND UP, I said!" Yelling at him in a quiet, controlled rage, Dillon fired a round of bullets into the glass desk shattering it to make his point. Dr. Carruchi shielded his face from the flying shards of glass and slowly stood up.

"Now walk over and stand in from of me—and do it quickly!"

Dr. Ennio Carruchi slowly walked out from behind the desk to stand in front of Dillon. "Closer Carruchi—I want you to see my eyes!" Dillon was mustering every bit of strength inside him.

"Yur're goin' to die, Dr. Carruchi, in a few minutes. How does it feel to know you are goin' to die? I 'ad…a plan to do it slow…one bullet at a time. I want you to see me eyes...the last ones you'll see...and the 'atred in 'hem for you! You took the one precious thing from me...me famil'. Now...I'm takin' the one precious thing you 've left...your life! How does...it feel? But you see...I don't 'ave an' more time...precious time."

Dr. Ennio Carruchi just stood and looked directly at Dillon...no more begging...

Raising his gun, Dillon fired one bullet—it hit its target squarely in the center.

\* \* \*

Carlos heard the one shot. "Stay here! Emma, stay with Mac. I have to find out where that shot came from!" Carlos quickly ran down the corridor. Looking into the room marked PRIVATE LABORATORY, he saw the door lock shattered and the operating room empty! Continuing cautiously through the small anterooms, he finally reached the PRIVATE OFFICE. Peering through the back of the door, Carlos saw Carruchi lying on his back staring at the ceiling—lifeless. Entering in a crouched position, Carlos stopped, checking for a pulse—nothing! Thinking there may still be a sniper, he swung around quickly, not expecting to see Dillon bloodied and slouched on top of the boxes.

"Dillon—Dillon! It's Carlos!" Carlos saw Dillon's jacket saturated with his blood, his eyes barely open and sweat dripping. Carefully lifting his friend down off the boxes where he sat clenching his side—his blood dripping into a pool beneath him—breathing very slowly and gasping, he laid him down gently on the floor.

"Carlos...I got my target...he did kill...me Maura and Siobhan!" Dillon was struggling to speak. Carlos cradled Dillon's head in his arms.

"The rest...is up to you, frien...keep Em and Mac safe...but it's Marcus you want...Marcus...'e's the real brains be'ind this...'e's the one who chose the...victims...Emmie's...victim..."

Dillon, trying to look around, grasped Carlos's hand tightly. *"They'll ne'er...ne'er...be safe...get...hi..."*

# CHAPTER FIFTY-FOUR

Carlos cradled Dillon in his arms for as long as he dared, his eyes burning with his tears.

Emma and Mac were still in the basement, and Marcus was somewhere out there—still alive and maybe in the villa, too. He had to move quickly! Marcus Rudolphi was uppermost in his mind. "Knowing the devil...his obsession about details...he'll have a backup plan ready in case something like this goes down! "No, Marcus will make certain he's got a way out of here no matter who dies!" Carlos spoke to his friend as if he were alive. Remembering Dillon's words, *Emma is a victim...it was true...*Marcus Rudolphi will not stop his fanatical zealousness until he had his hands on Emma! Tears blurring his eyes, he looked into the lifeless face of his longtime friend. "I promise...my friend...I will not let you down... Marcus Rudolphi will pay with his life...for you...for Maura and Siobhan...Emma...for Mac." Tenderly, he laid Dillon down behind the remnants of the desk out of sight from the door.

"*Requiem in pace, Amico.* I'll be back for you." There was no time to grieve for his friend now! There would a proper day and time for that. Turning off the lights to the office, he made is way back to the corridor to the area where he left Emma and Mac.

"Andy, can you hear me? I found Mac and Emma." A long pause, he was expecting Carlos to tell him where they were.

"Carlos, are you still there?—I can't hear you!"

"Yeah—I'm here, Andy! It's Dillon! He's in the last room on the left...in an office beyond the operating theater...behind the desk. He's dead...but not before he took out Carruchi! Get some men down here to bring him out, but with back up! It's still not secure down here! Copy?"

"I copy. We'll take him to the Villa D'Este. Are you getting Mac and Emma out?"

"I'll see they get help from Blue Team to get them to the cruiser. We got Carruchi—but not the bastard himself, not Marcus Rudolphi—yet! Have you spoken to Colin or Tony?"

"Yeah briefly! The Villas del Christianna and Tempietto are secure. The winery is not. That's all I know now!"

Carlos met up with Mac and Emma inside the storage room. Mac's gaping wound in his leg was still bleeding despite the tourniquet. "Can you walk on that leg, Mac?"

"I'll...make do...just get us...out ...!" Cyrus was trying to put on a strong front for the benefit of Emma, but it was clear he was getting weaker.

"Follow me closely. I'll take you up to the first floor and then Blue team will take you back to the cruiser and across the lake to the Ville D'Este to Dr. Ricci. I can't go back with you just yet. There's still some unfinished business here I have to take care of first!"

"Carlos...make sure... you have...enough...men...with you." Mac grabbed Carlos's arm knowing he was still searching for Marcus Rudolphi.

The three of them made their way back down the dimly lit hall into the old basement section of the villa cellar; sporadic gunfire was still heard at a distance.

"Mac here's my automatic! It's got a full clip! Emma keep your Larson ready at all times." It was slow going up the stairs; Cyrus's wound and weakened condition prevented him walking as he tried crawling up each step. Carlos saw him struggle almost collapsing with each step, he moved Emma aside and grabbed Cyrus and threw him over his good shoulder carrying him the rest of the way up the stairs.

"Emma watch my back...no one is safe here yet!" Once on the first floor Carlos told Emma, "I need to leave you here until Blue team comes for you, laying Cyrus down in a secure area. "Do not leave this spot...you'll be safe here until Blue team transports you down to the boathouse and out to the cruiser! I have to return downstairs and make certain that area is completely secured. Don't leave this position! Hear me?"

Mac grabbed Carlos's arm again, "Carlos...when you get... target...bring me...everything...on the package...ALL...contents in target's package...understand? Every...last thing!"

"Yeah—I understand Mac. Watch your backs for God's sake!"

"Carlos...be careful!" Emma pleaded.

"Take care of Mac now…" Carlos reached over and quickly kissed her, then turned and silently retraced his steps down to the old basement cautiously expecting gunfire to erupt at any time. He had only his handgun now, and he checked it to make certain there was a full clip in it. Passing over dead guards in the hallway, he was looking for one of their automatic weapons to use, not knowing how well-armed Marcus would be when he found him. Carlos knew if he could find prints or plans of the new basement's layout, he would have an idea where Marcus would go to hide or where he'd try to escape from inside the villa.

"Carruchi's office!"

Carlos spied Andy in one of the storage rooms. "Andy?" Andy turned, signaling him there were guards hidden in the nearby storage room along the darkened corridor. Carlos gave the sign Emma and Cyrus were out of the basement. Deploying his men two to a room, Andy signaled for them to use the grenades in the rooms to flush out the rest of the guards. The men threw gas grenades into the rooms then slammed the doors, allowing Carlos to run back down the hall to enter the PRIVATE LABORATORY again…looking away from the bloodied sheet in the corner. He needed to find a hidden exit… thinking the operating room would make a good place for a hidden escape point. Checking exits, he saw Dillon's explosive traps on the three doors—and warned Andy. There was one other door at the very end of the hall with the lock blown off. Pushing the door wide open with his foot he saw the dirty cell with wall chains and bloodied ropes. Cyrus's bloody, torn jacket was on the floor, and Carlos knew here is where they tortured him. The blood and sweat was still moist on the walls and floor. A stale, sickly odor…a smoky smell…Turkish tobacco mixed with the stench of blood and human sweat hung heavy in the air. No one else smoked that brand—it had to be Marcus Rudolphi's smell that dominated the odors.

Looking slowly around the stonewalled cell, he said, "I bet you enjoyed seeing him in agony—feeling your power over him— enjoying every minute you tortured him, you son of a bitch! But you didn't get squat out of him either! You misjudged your opponent this time! Now *you* are the hunted!" Carlos returned to the office and started searching for maps, floor plans, blueprints…anything to tell him where Marcus would run to escape!

"Ah *Si*—here is what I'm looking for," he said as he moved a file cabinet to drag out a large book of blueprints from behind it. Turning pages, he found "Operating Suite. Section B."

"I knew that bastard would have holes to run and hide in, like the animal he is!" Carlos carefully traced an exit…a passage…from the operating suite to a far point near the beach. "It's an underground exit from the operating room leading out to the garden!" Looking around at the walls for something unusual, instead, he spied an oddly-shaped stone on the floor next to the surgical table. It was a circular stone, not fixed permanently in place with mortar like the adjacent ones. Standing by the table and pressing different combinations of buttons on a panel, Carlos heard a grinding noise start, and the section of concrete began to rotate open to form a circular stone stairway leading down to a shallow dark passageway.

Creeping softly down the darkened steps, feeling the walls and floor with his hands, all the time Carlos kept his automatic ready. Ahead was total blackness with no light except for the dim light from the operating room above. The air was thick with damp, musty smells. Feeling the wall ahead of him with his hand, Carlos found a pole. He lit a match to see a kerosene tuff and lit up the torch. The passageway was very narrow with a low ceiling, meant only for one person to pass through, while the floor inclined downwards. Periodically, Carlos stopped and listened for some kind of movement coming from inside the passage behind or ahead of him.

*SILENCE.*

The narrow passage twisted sharply. He heard sounds of rushing water in the distance…then ripples of waves slapping on a beach. He was nearing the lake.

"Of course, what better way to get away unseen than by water and the bastard probably had underwater gear stowed here for a quick escape!" Reaching the end of the opening, Carlos found himself out in the garden approaching the water's edge. No sign of Marcus Rudolphi!

"I will find you Marcus! This world is too small for you to hide in! I have the one thing you want most, and you'll try, again, to get her! Only, now to get her—you go through me! You're a dead man walking, *Signore* Marcus Rudolphi!" Carlos yelled, running down the sandy beach toward the villa's boathouse.

\* \* \*

Cyrus and Emma waited for ten minutes for the Blue Team to come, but there was no sign of them. Emma started crawling toward the terrace door, half pushing, half pulling Cyrus. Cyrus was so gravely weakened from the loss of blood he could no longer move on his own. There was still no sight of the Blue Team. Bursts of gunfire were still coming from different areas outside the villa—somewhere in the gardens!

"Papa, we need to try and get outside the villa by ourselves. We can't stay here any longer!" Emma started dragging Cyrus toward the front terrace. With his arm around her shoulders, she managed to get him to his feet to guide him. She could feel his weight becoming heavier—dragging him more than he was walking. His leg wound still oozing freely—he was losing his strength faster each minute. She gently placed him down by the edge of the terrace.

"I've got to see if I can stop that bleeding, Papa. Stay here, I'll find something to stop the bleeding."

"Emma—no—we must...keep going," Cyrus whispered to her in a weakened voice. The cover of night was lifting—streaks of light were penetrating the blackness.

Emma turned to go back inside the villa when she stumbled upon a young girl hiding near the terrace entrance. It was not so much finding the young girl as to see who she was and what she was wearing: an old-world dress with a long apron! It was as if a trance came over Emma as she remembered,

**...a costume showing only her hands...the eyes so young under a headscarf...with a large-brimmed hat concealing**

**her features…except for her eyes…handing her a hot drink…**

"COMPANGNIA?"

"*Si, per favore non dolerme!* Do not hurt me!" The young girl called cowering away in fright as Emma reached out to her.

"I remember you! Compangnia, I won't hurt you! You were the one who took care of me…brought me food…comforted me…I'm not here to hurt you! You are called Compangnia?"

"*Si, sono…*I am!"

"Compangnia, I need your help again now! My grandfather is seriously hurt…please get me some clean cloths to cover his wounds to stop his bleeding…I'm not here to hurt you." Emma gestured toward Cyrus trying to explain what she needed from her. Compangia made no sign to help her. Seeing the fear in her eyes, Emma shook her to get her full attention and to allay her fears. "Compangnia, my name is Emma, and I need your help again!"

"Emma, *Chiedo come lei, risultare me.* I can help you…what you need." She followed Compangnia to a small closet and found towels and sheets. Tearing a sheet, Compangnia and Emma ran back to Cyrus who was barely conscious. Tying up Cyrus's wounds tightly with the clean cloths, she asked, "Is there another way I can get to the boathouse without going through the gardens…a…*Ci 'e una maniera segreta albraverso I da qui?*" Gunfire erupted from the next level close to the three—Emma knew Cyrus could no longer move quickly through the gardens. Compangnia was overwhelmed by the gunfire and hid her head.

"Is there a way to get to a boat from here…a back way around the gardens to the water?" Emma pleaded with her.

"*Si! Mi mostri?*" Both women helped Cyrus to his feet, holding his weight on their shoulders. Compangnia led them through the kitchen area and down a stairwell to a storage room—a root cellar. Pointing to a door, the two women together forced it open to find a passage.

"*Senorita*, this passage…*via all' acqua…spiaggia..a casa!* Here…*qui luce!*"

"I'm grateful to you, Compangnia, you are very kind…I think I can manage from here! *Grazie—grazie!* You go now! Run out the front villa door up to the road…away from the *casae' spiaggia!* You will meet men there in the road…they will not hurt you! Tell the men—'Emma sent me'! Tell them I'm taking this man—*Nonno*—with me to a boat back to the cruiser on *Lago di Como*! Now hurry—get out now! *Corra! Corra!*"

Emma watched Compangnia run upstairs and silently close the root cellar door.

"Papa…Papa, lean on me! We're almost at the water and the boat! Please help me…we can do it…I'll get you back to the cruiser and Biaggio!" Cyrus heard her words but could not mouth a response. He could only nod his head gently. Struggling to stay conscious, he knew he must follow her directions. He was fighting with all his strength to stay conscious.

*"I must…must…help her…."*

# CHAPTER FIFTY-FIVE

Carlos carefully scanned the shoreline and the lake for signs of swimmers, divers, boats…any unusual movement on the *lago* at this early hour.

The surrounding silence of first dawn light was deafening, broken only by the sound of each wave lapping on the beach as if it was carried through a microphone. It seemed sound carried farther over the water in the early morning hours—distorting the origin. No sounds of gunfire! No sounds of running feet—just a vacuum! *He had to have a back-up plan by way of the lake…and it would have to include a boat,* Carlos thought. In the distance, he saw where Biaggio anchored the cruiser.

"Biaggio…can you hear me? This is Carlos!"

*SILENCE.*

"Biaggio…come in! `E entrato! `E entrato, la copia?"

*He's not answering! He wouldn't leave the boat unattended to come ashore!* Carlos scanned through the binoculars looking for activity on the cruiser. The dinghy was still moored behind it. No sight of anyone or any movement on the boat—searching the water again for signs of a swimmer or diver, "If *Marcus* used scuba gear to escape, he may still be in the water!

"Biaggio…*Dove l'inferno lo sono, l'uomo! `E entrato, Carlos, qui, la copia?"*

*SILENCE.*

"Where are you, Biaggio…What the hell's going on out there?"

An eerie light from the east was advancing through the different cloud layers in the sky. Darkness was receding toward the western end of the lake. Carlos was undecided if he should return to the villa to finish the carnage and take count of losses, or stay to try and raise Biaggio to alert him to be on the look out for Marcus. Seeing no evidence of anyone in the water, Carlos started back toward the Villa Latinestto careful not to take chances in case a lone gunman was still free. Occasional sporadic gunfire was heard outside the villa in the front cleaning out pockets of resistance. He tried one more time to raise Biaggio on the cruiser. Still no reply from the cruiser! Running through the gardens, he suddenly heard the loud distant motors of the cruiser revving its engines. Turning, Carlos saw the cruiser slowly move from the anchored spot with the engines at full throttle with a heading north.

"Biaggio—come in! Where the hell are you going?"

"Sorry, Carlos! I need your boat! You may have won this battle but you have not won the war! *Caio!*"

"Marcus! You bastard!"

*He's taken over the boat!*

"What's happened to Biaggio? Tell me what's happened to Biaggio?" Carlos's fear was overcome by anger, watching through the binoculars—the cruiser moving at full speed straight up the lake—directly north!

"If you've killed Biaggio, you *bastardo,* you'll never get away, if that's what you're planning!" Carlos could only think of one way Marcus overtook the cruiser. But if Biaggio were valuable to him— he'd have a chance to stay alive.

"Marcus—hear this you piece of scum! *You're a dead man walking*! You'll know how it feels to be the hunted now! And guess what? I'm your hunter! *Lei sono un uomo morto che camminando! Caio per adesso!*"

Carlos ran to the Villa to make certain Emma and Mac reached safety.

\* \* \*

483

Emma and Cyrus made it down to the beach through the root cellar away from the Villa Latinestto. It was still dark, but the black of night was fading to a gray light in the east. Emma lay Cyrus down next to a clump of bushes near the water. His breathing was labored and shallow. Searching for her scuba tanks, she dragged them over to Cyrus, placing the mask on his face. "Breathe Papa! Take deep breaths!" There was still some oxygen and gas in the tanks to help him breathe. The bleeding had slowed down and began to clot.

"Papa, I need to find a boat to take us back out to the cruiser. Don't move and stay quiet!" Cyrus barely heard Emma's voice.

Approaching the boathouse silently and slowly, with her gun raised and ready, not knowing what she'd find inside, Emma found several small boats moored in the boat alley, only one had a small outboard motor. Checking the gas tanks in the small outboard, she saw one tank was half filled. Cautiously checking the rest of the underground alley for someone hiding, she heard nothing. Returning to where she left Cyrus, she managed to drag him to a standing position, and placed herself under his shoulder and arm to steady his weight on hers. Now his weight was heavier, and it was almost impossible to hold him up to walk any distance.

"Papa...Papa! Can you hear me? I found a boat! You have to help me get you into the boat!" Cyrus heard what she was asking him to do...it sounded so distant. His physical weakness was so overpowering he was unable to speak but nodded to let her know he understood. "I'll...try..." Stumbling down the steps of the boathouse to the basement landing, Emma barely had a hold on Cyrus to keep him from falling in the water while trying to steady the boat, too. Unable to control his weight, Cyrus fell into the boat bottom and lay there unconscious. Exhaustion was overcoming her, too. Putting aside her fatigue, she placed the scuba gear in the rear of the boat and the Larson at her side and quietly paddled out of the water alley onto the lake, taking care not to make any noise to alert anyone of their presence. Checking to make sure she was far enough from shore, she started the outboard with the first pull of the engine. "Thank God! I needed that piece of luck!" Emma steered the outboard towards the cabin cruiser anchored on the lake—still moored off the point where she left it.

* * *

Outside the front of the villa, Andy met up with Tony. They were watching the men carry out the dead and wounded. "We lost three. One of them…Dillon O'Rourke," Andy told Tony.

"That's three fuckin' too many!" Tony turned and walked back up the road to the command van.

Andy answered his mobile. "Is Mac safe?" Colin queried.

"Yeah! But he's badly injured. He's with Emma on their way back to the *Villa D'Este*. When they get there, have Mac seen immediately. He needs a medic—wounds look serious. I only 'ope it's not too late!"

"Did you secure the winery yet, Colin?"

"Most of it is secure—still a few pockets of resistance. All the villas are secure in Milano and Firenze. We lost several men, too," Colin said.

"Colin, I'm driving back to the Villa D'Este with Tony. We'll all meet later! Brief Carlos up to speed when you hear from him!"

At that moment Carlos ran out of the villa. "Did the Blue team get Emma and Mac back to the Villa D'Este?"

Andy looked surprised at his question. "Hell no! Were they supposed to?"

"Then, where the bloody hell are they?" Carlos yelled as he ran back inside the villa to see a young girl run out the door toward him screaming, "Emma…Emma…she send me! She…take *il nonno…a spiaggia…a barca!* Hide me?" she said, pointing to the dead guards with tears and fear in her eyes.

Calming her, Carlos said, "Not to worry. You're safe now. You said Emma took grandpapa to water to boat?"

"*Si! Il nonno* very bad—bleeding! I show her…a passage to water…Emma tells me to leave villa to tell you!" Carlos called Tony over to ask him to take the girl back with him to a safe place and told him what he just learned.

"Emma took Mac out through an underground passage to the beach—alone! She thinks the cruiser is waiting to ferry them to the Villa D'Este, and she'll head for the cruiser to get Biaggio's help! Christ almighty! Marcus Rudolphi seized the cruiser from Biaggio!" Carlos yelled out!

Andy saw a look of horror on Carlos's face. "What the 'ell are you sayin', Carlos?"

"I was trying to raise Biaggio when Marcus answered from our cruiser anchored off the point! He escaped through a hidden tunnel from the villa basement leading down to the beach and must have had scuba tanks hidden! He got out to the cruiser. Somehow he overtook the boat...I saw him driving the cruiser going due north at full speed! I don't know what happened to Biaggio!"

"Jesus—no! Not Biaggio!" Andy yelled in anger.

"It's worse! I told Mac and Emma to go with Blue Team to the boathouse to get a boat out to the cruiser to take them back to the Villa D'Este. The Blue Team never met up with them!"

"Fuckin no!" Andy said and the two men raced out of the villa, through the gardens and down to the boathouse. Quickly scanning the beach and boathouse, they saw a small launch was missing out of its mooring in the water alley.

Both men scanned the lake and horizon with binoculars looking for signs of the small launch. "There!" Andy pointed out to Carlos.

"At two o'clock...a small outboard heading out on the lake! I can only make out one person handling the outboard! It's Emma—no sign of Mac. He's probably down in the boat!" Carlos took out his cell phone and dialed.

"Martin—Martin, for Christ's sake answer! The blue lake has turned red!"

"What's happened?"

"Be on the lookout for a small outboard launch heading toward the Villa D'Este from the Villa Latinestto. Emma and Mac are in it! Get some men down to the boat ramp to get them safely inside! Send a boat out from there to meet them if they're not in sight in the next few minutes!" Carlos was shouting with anxiety. "They're not safe on the lake! Marcus Rudolphi commandeered the cruiser and is somewhere on the lake, too, most likely heading north—he may just miss her! Emma knows nothing about this—she may be trying to reach the cruiser in the outboard, thinking Biaggio is on it! If the light stays dim for another half hour, they'll be okay! I have a feeling he's going to *Novate Mezzola* at the north end of Como—maybe making his way to Switzerland and the mountains! Alert IICA to get a team up to Novate Mezzola to check all public-docking areas. PICK HIM UP—repeat PICK HIM UP—DO NOT KILL!"

"Understood. Keep your phone handy. Will call again when we site the small launch!"

Afraid to take their eyes off the skiff in the middle of the lake, the two men kept their eyes trained on the small launch with Cyrus and Emma in it trying to catch up with the cruiser, but losing distance in the boat's giant wake. The small launch was tossed about in the cruiser's ever-widening turbulent wake. Emma kept steering the boat to cut straight across the choppy waters at a right angle to keep her heading…towards the cruiser…going further away from the Villa D'Este. The cruiser was moving faster…putting greater distance between the cruiser and the small launch. Marcus didn't see the small outboard launch behind him with Emma in it!

"She can't catch the cruiser—she's lagging farther behind! She's realized she missed it, and she's turning back toward the Villa D'Este! Sweet Jesus—*deo gratias*—thank God!" Carlos said prayerfully.

"Andy, you and I have to get back to the Villa D'Este now!" Carlos said commandingly.

"Carlos, that shoulder need's lookin' after! It's still oozing a lot of blood—you've lost a lot of blood from the exit wound in your back. Dr. Ricci is at the villa now; he's tending to the injured and triaging them for hospital care for those who need it. You're one of them, Carlos!" Andy said decisively.

"I'm in command now—you and Mac are injured and … and…. Dillon is…! Just get in the fuckin' van, and I'll drive us to the other side!" Andy was forceful and commanding in his instructions.

\* \* \*

Emma couldn't understand why Biaggio left the anchored spot prematurely. She watched the cruiser speeding north, and with no means of communication, she couldn't signal him she was nearby, trying to return with Cyrus. Finally realizing she wasn't going to catch up with the cruiser, she checked the gas gauge to see if there was enough fuel to cross the lake to the Villa D'Este.

"Why did Biaggio just take off? Surely someone must have radioed I was trying to get Papa to the cruiser for help! I just hope I have enough petrol to get to the Villa D'Este!"

Cyrus lay unconscious in the bottom of the boat. Emma had both guns ready on the seat next to her. The morning sun was breaking through the layer of clouds with an eerie golden luminescence. Como was known for its unexpected squalls coming down from the mountains without warning! Seeing the far shoreline, she searched to find the outline of the Villa D'Este sitting on the hill with its lights all lit up. Her fears were calming slightly, but she wouldn't feel safe until she reached the villa.

"Papa, Papa! Can you hear me? We're almost at the villa! Please hang on for me! Please—I need you with me, Papa! Please hang on a little longer!" Emma said, keeping her voice strong to keep his attention focused on her and to stay conscious.

With the outboard motor open at full throttle, the launch glided toward the boat landing. Clearly, she could see Anna and Martin on the deck of the landing. Reducing speed, she slowly steered the boat into the underground slip in the boathouse.

"Emma, throw me that line next to you then cut your motor!" Anna commanded. Martin jumped into the boat as she turned off the motor.

"I'll take Mac!" Heaving him onto his shoulder, he stepped out of the boat and carried him upstairs to the apartment. Emma followed.

"Keep your gun with you, Emma! I'm going to get Dr. Ricci up at the house! Stay with Mac and Martin!" Anna quickly ran out towards the villa.

*"Martin, where was Biaggio speeding to in the cruiser? Why didn't he wait for me to get Cyrus back to the Villa D'Este?"*

# CHAPTER FIFTY-SIX

Marcus slowly maneuvered the boat into an empty slip at the private marina on the northern most end of *Lago di Como*.

Surveying the docks for signs of *Policia* or *gli agenti Italiani* before he cut the engines, everything looked benign and quiet at this early hour. Removing his wetsuit inside the cabin, Marcus climbed down the starboard side of the cruiser, first anchoring the bow of the boat to the dock cleat then casually heading for the upper landing to find a *telephono*. Careful not to attract attention to himself, he approached the marina next to the *Pubblica Telephono* scanning the area. Using his calling card, he dialed long distance.

"Marcus here. Let me speak to Günter!"

"This is Gunter, *Herr* Marcus—is something wrong? It is so early!"

"Gunter? Has there been any unusual activity or visitors at the mountain this week?"

"*Nien, Herr* Marcus. No one has been here. We had no visitors!"

"Good! I want you to wake up Katya and tell her to pack for a long trip. She and Cara will be taking a long trip with me. Have their passports ready."

"*Ya*, I understand *Herr* Marcus. When will you be here?"

"I'll be there in one day or sooner. Everything must be ready to leave as soon as I arrive. You will remain at the chalet, Gunter, to close it up, and then I'll send for you from the new address."

"I understand, *Herr* Marcus."

"Good. Gunter, if anyone asks about me—do not tell them or say you have spoken to me! Do not acknowledge you even know me— as I cautioned you before! Tell no one I'm coming there or that I'll be taking Cara and Katya on a trip with me! Do you understand?"

"Yes! You can count on me, *Herr* Marcus!"

"If Katya asks questions…tell her we are taking holiday— but that's all! Do as I say and you will be handsomely rewarded, Gunter!"

"I do everything you ask, *Herr* Marcus!"

Without any delay, Marcus dialed a second number and a woman answered.

"*Si* Nina?" Not waiting for her to answer his question, he said, "Is Bruno there? This is Marcus Rudolphi—do not waste time. I need to speak with Bruno now!"

"Signore Rudolphi?" A man's voice asked.

"*Si*, is this Bruno Tomasini?"

"I'm sorry, *Signore* Rudolphi, Bruno Tomasini is not here. Can I help you?"

"Who am I speaking with?" Marcus asked angrily.

"My name is Roberto Ceruso. I can help you."

"Why can't Bruno speak to me—what is going on there?" Marcus said, showing more agitation in his voice!

"You can speak to me…Bruno can't come to the phone. I may be able to help you, *Signore*. Are you calling for a specific reason?"

"*Si*, I want to know where his family is NOW? Where are his children, Giorgio and Sofia?"

"They are away at present, as are Nina and Bruno. But if you tell me why you are calling, I may be able to help you?"

"When will the family be back?" Marcus asked.

"I cannot say. They did not tell me when they left when they would return…it may be some time…"

Marcus crashed the phone down. "It can't be…they can't know…I'll call Lucinda to see if the villa is safe."

Dialing the Villa del Christianna, Marcus Rudolphi heard a series of clicks and then a voice, "*Si, la residenza di Rudolphi.*"

"Lucinda Rudolphi *pronto!*"

490

"I'm sorry, *Signora* Lucinda is not available at this time, may I take a message?"

"This is Signore Marcus, where is Ricardo?"

*"Signore* Marcus, Ricardo is very busy at this moment...I can help you..." Marcus quickly disconnected the line! He knew what the delay meant.

"They have the children and they have taken over the Villa del Christianna and Lucinda! Damn you, Cyrus MacKenna...I should have killed you! *They will not get what they want most ...Marcus Rudolphi... and my Cara!"*

Quickly making one last call, Marcus dialed a local car rental service and requested a car be delivered to the private marina club and gave his credit card number for payment. Now, he had to be patient and wait a little longer. Entering the marina clubhouse, no one was around. He sat down at a table in the rear to wait for the rental car to arrive.

* * *

"Tony here." Agent Ceruso related to Tony that Marcus just called Perugia.

"Marcus Rudolphi just called the Tomasini's home in Perugia, asking about the children and the Tomasinis. I checked—he also called the Villa del Christianna asking for Lucinda Rudolphi!"

"Get a trace on all calls made on Marcus Rudolphi's calling cards—and all credit card charges he makes! This is Red Priority One! Immediate notification to all banks and to telephone companies to telefax that information to the IICA—*pronto*, when it's recorded at real time! He's going to need a car—maybe a rental, and we'll track his movements if he rent's a car by credit! Should he call again, tell him he can speak with Lucinda and ask him to hang on until you get her...then get out a satellite fix!"

"It's done!" Tony Serrano updated Colin while waiting for Emma and Mac to return to the Villa D'Este.

Anna rushed in. "Where's Ricci?"

"He's upstairs."

"Mac needs him now! He's in a bad way down in the boathouse—get him down there, *pronto!"*

491

Martin and Emma placed Mac on the bed upstairs in the boathouse. His breathing was labored, rapid, and shallow!

"Papa—Papa can you hear me?" Emma pleaded.

"Here, Emma, let me see to him," Dr. Ricci said and moved her aside and quickly assessed his wounds and vital signs.

"We need to get him to hospital now! He's lost too much blood! I have a van outside we can use with flashers to make speedy time to the clinic for an E-MED-airlift to a trauma center. I'll take him to *Chiasso* clinic for immediate treatment and air flight him out from there. I want several men to carry him out to the van, but first I'll dress his wounds and start intravenous fluids. Anna, go and get the van and drive it down here to the back entrance." Dr. Ricci carefully and methodically assessed Cyrus's wounds—still no response to pain from him. Emma watched Ricci work rapidly, holding her Papa's hand—cold and icy to touch.

Dr. Ricci took Emma aside. "Emma, I know you want to go with him..."

"Yes—please? I must!"

"Not yet...you must stay here, at least for now. When everything has been sorted out, Carlos or Andy can bring you to see Mac after I have him airlifted to the hospital where thy have the best facilities to treat his wounds. We must move quickly!"

Emma understood through her tears. Shaking her head through her sobs, she said, "I understand, Dr. Ricci—you won't let him die...please...don't let him die!"

Andy walked over to the van and Emma. "Andy—you and Papa... you were in on this all along? You and Papa? Why?" she asked disbelievingly.

He put his arm around her. "Emmie, it was Mac's wishes. He did it his way because he loves you more than anything else in this world. And so do I!" The two watched the van drive out the long circular driveway toward Chiasso with blue flashing lights on. "We'll go to him as soon as we can! He'll tell you everything you want to know."

Andy walked with Emma inside the villa with his arms around her, feeling her body shaking with sobs...recalling all the past times he quieted her fears and tears.

There was no reason to keep Emma out of the Villa D'Este security room now. Tony and Colin were inside as they entered the basement Control room.

"Emma, Colin MacEachen represents MI-5, and Tony Serrano is head of the Italian Secret Service—he's Carlos's boss. Both sections were in on the assaults against the Rudolphi Organization!" Tony Serrano approached Emma.

"Ms. Llewelyn—can I call you, Emma?" She nodded trying to keep herself in control.

"I need to ask you some questions. You and Dillon O'Rourke made a trip to Perugia to investigate children Lucinda Rudolphi wanted you to learn about their background?"

"Yes, we found two children—a boy and girl living in Perugia with a family who owns a café on the Piazza there. We took pictures of the children and the mother. I gave the film to Dillon…he should have the pictures…Biaggio may have prints. Why do you ask?"

"I sent agents to Perugia to find these children. Time is important! Can you tell me the name of the café?"

"Yes it was… *Café Montague.*"

"You're certain?"

"Yes! Dillon and I sat outside and the building next to the café was a stone building with a tailor shop in the basement, directly facing the Piazza, too."

"That's good enough!" Tony walked over to Colin and gave a nod to several men. Colin MacEachen finished his telephone call and approached Emma.

"I'm sorr' we meet again under these circumstances, Ms. Llewelyn. But we need to know if you 'ave spoke' to Lucinda Rudolphi since your first meetin' with her several weeks ago in London?"

"No. Not until we met at the charity party last Sunday at the Villa del Christianna! I didn't want to tell her about the two children we found in Perugia until we had hard evidence there was a connection between the children and the Rudolphis. Why are you all asking me these questions?"

"We 'ave Lucinda Rudolphi in our custod'. We know she saw you in London, and we learned that the nature of that visit was to find out about a child she saw only once in Perugia. We believe we 'ave those same children in custod' now. What we wanted from you is confirmation we 'ad the right children. Our information unofficial'y indicates there may be a connection between these children and Marcus Rudolphi! The Italian couple, the Tomasinis, we 'ave them in our custody, too, and they claim these two children are their own—a boy named Giorgio and a daughter named Sophia. We needed confirmation from you the Tomasini children are actual'y the children you and Dillon O'Rourke found in Perugia. We 'ad to act quickl' before they disappeared!"

"Disappear? Why would they disappear?" Emma asked.

"If this boy and girl are related to Lucinda Rudolphi, if they are her children who were taken from her at birth, we 'ad to find them immediate'y before Marcus Rudolphi arranged for their disappearance. If they are his and Lucinda's natural children, then he would make e'ery attempt to 'ide 'hem again—this time it could be permanent!"

Emma was astonished by what Colin said to her. His questions told her Marcus Rudolphi was not captured or killed...Is that why they were being so cautious with me?

"Where is Dillon O'Rourke? And where is Carlos Esteves?" Emma asked in a firm voice. Andy took her by the arm and led her upstairs. "I'll take you to him." Colin issued an order to an IICA agent on the phone.

"I need to speak to Lucinda Rudolphi. Put her on the phone."

* * *

Carlos was in the Great Hall receiving medical attention to his shoulder wound from a medic.

"Carlos!" Emma ran over to him. "Are you alright?" she asked, seeing the clean dressing on his shoulder.

"I'm fine," he said and kissed her gently.

"Papa is on his way to the clinic in *Chiasso* with Dr. Ricci. He looked...so bad, oh, Carlos...he looked so ashen...so lifeless...I need to get to him...somehow! Please help me find a way?" Carlos saw more tears on the already dirty stained face but knew more would come. Putting on a clean shirt Andy gave him, he put the shoulder holster and gun back under his jacket.

"Emma—let's go into the study next door. There's a lot of chaos going on here." Taking her in his arms, he gently caressed her. "God—you feel so good to me... at this moment! Oh, my Emma... my Emma! I was so afraid I would lose you, again!" The feeling of relief holding her close to him again, was calming amidst the inner turmoil he felt knowing what he had to do. He knew a day would come when he'd never have to let her go again. But first...there was Marcus!

Emma had much the same feeling at the moment. *This feels so good to be close to him again—safe in his arms. Will there ever be a time for us?* Their eyes meeting, she saw the fear in his eyes and heard it in his voice.

"Emma, come sit with me. Right now you have to concentrate on two things. First—Marcus Rudolphi was not captured! He managed to escape and stole the cabin cruiser from Biaggio and was last seen heading north. We think he's going to Novate Mezzola and then flee into Switzerland...or...he could return to Milano! Tony Serrano is taking care of tracking his whereabouts as I speak. That means until we catch him, you're not safe!"

Emma pulled away from Carlos with frustration and anger in her voice.

"I'm not afraid of that man! I will not allow him to rule my life anymore!"

"Not rule your life, Emma—*he wants your life*! This is why you must stay here for now until we know his whereabouts! We think he may be trying to get to Switzerland, but he could double back to Milano to take care of any unfinished business! YOU! We have essentially destroyed his operation, but...we have not destroyed the man...the brains behind the organization." Carlos saw Emma withdraw again into herself listening to his words.

"The second thing you must concentrate on is Lucinda Rudolphi!"

"Why Lucinda now?" Emma asked surprised.

"Tony sent a squad of men to pick up those two children you saw in Perugia and the parents as well. If those are Lucinda and Marcus's children, then Marcus Rudolphi may attempt to get them and hide them somewhere else—or kill them all! He's a hunted man now— and hunted men are infinitely more dangerous and unpredictable! What we need you to do is talk to Lucinda and tell her why we raided the Villa del Christianna, that we're investigating the true identities of the children in Perugia. Be honest with her! Tell her we have to keep these children in custody to determine if they are indeed her own...dead...children! That's going to be a great shock to her, Emma. This information coming from you may make it easier for her to hear and accept."

"Yes—I agree! I wouldn't be surprised if she feels relieved to be out of Marcus's control as well as the whole Rudolphi family!" Emma reassured Carlos.

"She will have to go into hiding, too, until we catch Marcus. She'll be taken to a safe house out of this area until Marcus is no longer a threat to her...or those children!"

Right now, Colin MacEachen has her in custody in Milano. I will ask him to keep her there until you speak to her...You must go to Milano as soon as possible! Then we'll make plans to get you to Mac." Holding her close, not wanting to let her go, Carlos knew he had to tell her everything now.

"How long have you known Papa was involved with this Rudolphi case?"

"*Si*, I have known for some time. Mac made it clear to all of us—his life in Interpol was *his* business, and it was his decision to choose the time and place, he would confide that part of his life to you. I had to honor his wishes! Emma...his directive had no bearing on my feelings for you. The very first time we met? I didn't know you were...his granddaughter, his Emma Llewelyn! When this is all over, I will answer all your questions truthfully—no more holding back...I promise." Carlos held her—each taking comfort in the other's arms.

"After you speak to Lucinda, I'll fly you to Mac wherever he is but that may take a day or so. He'll get the very best care possible... and he'll need your strength and love to get through this ordeal... with all his injuries. It's going to take him some time to recover."

Emma sat curled up on the sofa listening to Carlos without interruptions. Carlos rose from the sofa, taking in a long deep breath for what he was going to tell her next.

"Emma…there's something more I have to tell you." The words sounded cutting and ominous. Carlos knew there was no easy way to tell her…but to say the words outright. "It's Dillon." Carlos stopped speaking for several seconds and took in a deep breath.

"What about Dillon?" she asked, looking directly into his eyes.

"Dillon…is…Dillon is dead!"

"What did you say? Dillon isn't dead! You made a mistake! Dillon is a man who can take care of himself in any situation…he…can't…die?" Her voice softly trailed off. Her eyes just stared into Carlos's, asking him to say it was all a mistake. Suddenly, Emma reached out and grabbed Carlos's jacket and started pummeling him with her fists…crying out loudly.

"Tell me Dillon isn't dead…you made a mistake!" she yelled at him. "Tell me!" she kept hitting his chest repeatedly, crying louder, not remembering his painful shoulder wound. " No…not…hi… please not Dil…" Soon, her fight gone…only her head rested on his chest. She was sobbing uncontrollably for everything that happened and the changes in everyone's life—from the past night. Carlos just held her in his arms…supporting her…and loving her all the more.

Her unfathomable grief was the same kind of pain inside Carlos. He made no effort to stop her fists jabbing him, though the pain in his shoulder was ever-increasing! He heard her sobs quieting, felt her body stop trembling. Then—she just sat on the sofa in a curled position—retreating to a place in her mind.

"No…please no…not Dillon…he's always there for me…" Carlos just sat next to her—to be close to her—*he needed to feel her closeness now*—his loss overcame his fatigue as the tears spilled down his face.

"Every man I love…could die, too…I may lose…You're going after Marcus, aren't you?" she asked Carlos knowing his answer.

"I have no choice, Emma. You will never be safe in this world as long as that man lives! Your life is my life!"

*Saying it again softly,* he repeated, *"La sua vita `e la mia vita."*

# CHAPTER FIFTY-SEVEN

Emma now understood the depth of Dillon's passion for revenge for what he once had and lost!

She, too, wanted revenge for what she once had and lost! "Where can I change before I meet with Lucinda?" she asked Carlos. "My things are upstairs…can I go upstairs and change? I need to clean up before I speak with Lucinda," she said, speaking in a composed monotonic voice. Carlos walked with her up to her room.

"Take a shower, Emma, and change. I'll wait here for you." Not wanting to let her out of his arms, he kissed her tenderly on the forehead then on her nose and then her lips—tasting the salt from her tears.

\* \* \*

Lucinda arrived at Control headquarters in Milano with Colin MacEachen who ushered her into the conference room. Alone, she sat down and waited. Out of sight, Emma watched her for several minutes from outside the conference room—seeing a woman lost and despondent. She thought about how she was going to tell her about last night's incursion on the villa. Lucinda would understand some of it… but could she handle the worst of it? Emma searched for answers to her own thoughts before moving towards the glassed conference room. Lucinda caught sight of her and rushed out to meet her. This was not the woman Emma remembered from the charity party, a few days ago, or her meeting with her in London—rather, she saw a frightened, frail, plain woman dressed in jeans, shirt and sweater, her hair pulled back in a pony tail. The lack of make-up gave her a sickly, transparent look; with no likeness to the elegantly coiffed, coutured Milanese *Signora* from the Villa del Christianna.

"Emma, what has happened? Men rushed into the villa tonight and brought me here! No one will tell me why?" Her eyes pleaded with Emma to speak.

"Lucinda, I need to talk to you about last night. Please come over and sit with me."

Emma knew there was no easy way to start. "Let me start at the beginning and tell you the whole story and then… if you have any questions, I'll try to answer them for you."

"Tonight, there were many assaults on the Rudolphi Empire. They took place at the winery, the Villa del Christianna, the Villa Tempietto, the homes of Dominic, Luigi, and your sister-in-law and at a villa on Lago di Como called Villa Latinestto. The reason for this action is the result of years of work by many investigative groups here in Italy…in England…and Interpol. These international anti-crime organizations combined their resources to break up an international crime organization—a very highly sophisticated organization! The *Rudolphi family directed this crime organization!*" Lucinda's eyes showed her innocent astonishment.

Emma continued, "Several years of investigation discovered a global kidnapping business…taking victims for the sole purpose of biological research. This kidnapping organization had a single goal—medical research. It appears they wanted a diverse source of human donors for a new kind of research called stem-cell research, to research a human gene to find how to impede our normal aging process. These scientists wanted to be the first to find and alter the human genetic make-up—even possibly perfect a new human species. If this could be accomplished—control the process to alter a part of the human genetic code—this organization would stand to make millions of dollars!"

"Is this what Dr. Carruchi was doing with the research donations I helped him to get?"

499

"I would have to say, yes—but without your knowledge! The kidnappings gave him a diverse source of genetic material...with their research ending in hundreds of innocent victims' deaths...all for the purpose of...finding and changing molecular genetics. The records seized in the raids pointed out a small percentage of the kidnapped victims were *returned to their families*...with no memory of what had been done to them. We don't understand why, but these few victims have no memory of what happened to them and at this time, they could be anywhere in the world! A hypothetical consideration is... these victims were returned for a definite reason...possibly they're still part of their experiments. It's possible their DNA was altered, and then these victims were returned to lead normal lives...under close observation to see what kind of response they would have to this alteration in their genetic make-up in years to come. In other words, they are still human guinea pigs! The deaths resulting from the failures in this research occurred in a most cruel and inhuman manner...Most of the victims appear to have been...children!"

"*Oh, Madre Dei...no..no!*" Lucinda cried out softly with tears, listening to the account of these heinous crimes, hiding her face in her hands.

"Let me finish..." *More for me to hear this, too,* thought Emma. "Those journals you found in Marcus's library contained the names of victims...with names of some of the research scientists involved in the research. When the Interpol force decodes and interprets everything in them, we will know more. We do know Dr. Ennio Carruchi was the chief researcher in this mission. He is dead, Lucinda."

"Emma...your name was on that list..."

"Yes...I know. Please understand...I can't talk about that now!" Composing herself to continue, "All the crime agencies have rounded up most of the major players in the European organization—except one. Lucinda...Marcus was the person in command of this whole project—next to Carruchi! Marcus escaped the assault last night and his whereabouts are unknown—he's a hunted man!"

"*Il mio dio...I lived with a devil...and didn't know it!* I could have done something to stop it!" She said, as if she shared some blame.

"No, Lucinda. None of this is your fault! Marcus duped you, too!" Emma took hold of Lucinda's hands in hers. "You are as much a victim here as I am. The devil is clever...someone who follows him is clever, too! We will find Marcus, Lucinda...we will find him before he can do any more harm...to you...or anyone else!" Emma was thinking about Carlos out there tracking someone who was more a devil than a man!

"Lucinda, there is more. I did see that child you found in Perugia and couldn't help but observe the similarities you saw. What you didn't see that day was that Giorgio has a sister—her name is Sofia. It is our belief at this time...these children may well be...the children you gave birth to, then for some macabre reason, Marcus told you they died!" Emma held Lucinda's hands tightly in hers, as her tears became shuddering sobs.

"The *Policia* have Giorgio and Sophia in custody now. They are safe. What we did learn was that after the attacks ended and Marcus escaped, one of the agents in Perugia received a telephone call from Marcus asking for the children...He knew about them living in Perugia. The agent duped him and told him they were away, and he had no idea when they would return. Marcus seemed very angry learning this, which brings me to this point. Lucinda we believe he will try to get to *you*—as leverage to get to the children—as he tried to get to the children after he escaped the police net! We feel you are in great danger, and we need to keep you safe...until Marcus is caught!"

"When can I see the children?"

"I'm not sure. The agents are questioning the man and woman caring for them now. I'm sure within a day or so, we can unite you with the children—at least for a visit. DNA tests will be performed on all three of you to confirm you are their real mother."

"I was not crazy...imagining my children were not dead! All the time, I thought I was losing my sanity!"

"No, Lucinda, your motherly instincts probably saved those two children."

"I feel so badly for all those people who died because of the Rudolphi family! But I have such happiness, too, knowing my babies did not die! Can you understand that, Emma?" Emma embraced her and understood her conflicting emotions of pain and joy…losing someone you loved…and saving another loved one.

"Lucinda, you must listen carefully to what the agents tell you to do! I must leave you now… I still have much to do…This will not be over for both of us until Marcus is caught!" Emma started out of the conference room.

"Emma. I knew at the time we first spoke, you would find answers for me. *Grazie…grazie* with all my heart. You are a very brave woman!" The two women just held each other silently for several more minutes.

Emma thought, *"You lost one family, but may have found your real family—your children. I lost a much-loved friend…Will I lose my family, too?"*

# CHAPTER FIFTY-EIGHT

Biaggio woke and felt the sting of pain in his arm and shoulder from the rocking motion of the boat.

*"Che è successo?* Before moving, he took notice he was lying in a cramped galley in the forward section of the cruiser—when he felt a sharp pain to his head. His arm and shoulder were stiff, almost numb with throbbing pain trying to move it. Examining it in the cramped quarters, he saw the dried blood on his jacket. Slowly opening his shirt he saw a hole in his arm and remembered feeling the hot stinging bullet—it shattered the upper arm bone. Looking around for something to support the broken bones, he found a piece of a wood and slipped it into his shirtsleeve and tied a piece of cord around it to support his arm while gently putting his jacket back on—all with great pain!

His thoughts cleared! *He slipped through their nets!* "It was Marcus Rudolphi who climbed aboard the cruiser in his wetsuit and burst into the cabin. I never even heard him until he was inside pointing a gun at me! We struggled on deck…a shot went off." Biaggio thought. "Evidently Marcus thought I fell overboard when he shot me, instead I *was lucky and* landed on the tarpaulin and must've rolled or crawled into the forward bay."

Biaggio listened for several minutes for any sounds. Not aware of any human movements on the boat, he wedged himself out of the tight quarters into the light above him. It was a sunny, bright day. Looking around the boat, he saw the forward line moored to the cleat on a dock in a marina slip. In the distance, there were voices and noises, and took notice which direction they came from. Checking the other boat slips on either side of the cruiser, he saw no signs of life and quietly slid over the side and headed up the ramp to the marina office, fighting off the stabbing pain in his arm with each step he took.

Walking inside the office, he said, *"Pronto, scuzi...telephono?"*

*"Si."* The attendant pointed to the phone on the desk.

*"Grazie!"* Biaggio said. Dialing Control's safe line, "Biaggio here—who's this? Andy?"

"Biaggio? Man, is it good to hear your voice! Where the bloody 'ell are you?"

"I'm not sure...wait a second...*Scuzi, signore* what is the name of this marina, and where is it located exactly?" The proprietor explained where the marina was located.

"Andy, I'm calling from the marina at the north end of Como at Novate Mezzalo—the *Marina del Aqi*. Send a car for me...it's too far to walk back!"

"Funny man—be there in twenty!"

Biaggio looked around but saw no other customers. If Marcus came in here, someone must have seen him. "*Scuzi, signore*, did a man come in here earlier today—alone?"

"*Si,* a man came and waited for a car to come—about one hour ago."

"Do you remember what kind of car it was?"

"Didn't *see it*, no...I'm pretty sure it was a rental car. An attendant came in and handed him keys, and he signed some papers, then left in a hurry. But I have this ear to know motors!" The attendant pointed to his ear to emphasize his skills. "It's my job...to *know every kind of motor* out there! I can tell the make of the motor by listening to its purring revolutions—the car your man drive away in? It had a Volvo motor—a high tram motor! Like the ones in wagons, you know..."

"*Grazie* for your help." Biaggio walked to the rear of the room to wait for Andy. His arm and shoulder were throbbing, but the bleeding stopped. Forcing himself to think about something else instead of the pain, he thought of his Sienna. He took out a toothpick and placed it between his teeth…listened… watched the attendants's movements inside and kept an eye on the docks outside.

The door opened, and Andy and Martin walked inside. Andy looked at Biaggio sitting there. *"Che è questo?"* Martin said. "You didn't tell me you were 'urt! Come on me man—we'll get you fixed up, and you'll be good as new." The three men walked out to the BMW.

"What 'appened on the cruiser?" Andy asked

"It was Marcus Rudolphi! He got away from the villa with scuba gear and managed to sneak on board the cruiser and surprised me in the cabin. Before I could draw my gun, he took a couple of shots at me, throwing me over the rail outside the cabin. He must've thought I went into the water; fortunately, I landed on the tarpaulin and rolled into the forward galley out of his sight. I guess I passed out. When I woke, I found I had this hole in my arm—and my head hurts, too!" Biaggio rubbed his bruised head.

"Marcus was here ahead of me—only about an hour ago! He arranged for a rental car to be delivered to him. The marina's attendant said the rental car was a 'Volvo'—with a high-powered motor. We can track the rental down and find out how many Volvo's were rented today from the surrounding towns—probably an all-terrain wagon. The closest rental agency to the marina is in *Bellinzona.* He'd go to the nearest rental place to get transportation away from here fast!" Biaggio commented.

"That narrows it down and saves us time looking in a wide region. I'll call Tony and the *Internationale Policia* when we get back and give them this information."

"He might be headed for Switzerland!" Biaggio said.

"Good work, Biaggio! We're just glad you're alive!"

Biaggio asked, "Now, tell me the final report!"

"We got Mac out alive—barely. He's critically wounded and was airlifted to hospital. They didn't break him either! Emma is safe for the moment at the Villa D'Este! We have the two children from Perugia in custody. It seems they just may be Lucinda and Marcus Rudolphi's natural children. All the objectives have been neutralized as planned!" Andy stopped speaking at this point.

"Was Marcus the only one to get away? Did we get the rest of those bastardos?" Biaggio asked.

"Yeah—we won, Biaggio! Ennio Carruchi's dead." Andy said despondently.

"How many losses?" Biaggio asked.

"All total—six men. All the best!" Andy found it hard to go on. Biaggio knew Andy's hesitation told him there was more to hear about the casualties.

"Anyone I know?" Biaggio was afraid to ask for a specific name.

"Yeah… *yeah…Dillon O'Rourke.*"

"Ah, *Gesu Cristo! No!*" Biaggio said out loud, shaking his head in disbelief when he heard the name. The rest of the way back to the villa, he couldn't stop thinking about the last few days he spent with Dillon before the attacks…the breakfasts they had together at his home…the days they spent planning every detail of their missions together…his peculiar way he took care of Emma…how his eyes lit up when he saw her!

"Dillon did get *his* man…He took out Carruchi at the Villa Latinestto," Andy said.

"Then he's found his Maura and Siobhan."

The rest of the ride back to the Villa D'Este was silent and long. In their thoughts, each man was remembering the fighter who wouldn't give up.

*Essere alla pace, il mio amico!*

# CYMRU—BEDD

# CHAPTER FIFTY-NINE

Emma was helping Magere in the kitchen with the preparations for the buffet meal after the service.

Each woman worked silently with her thoughts about what was going to happen in a few hours. These past days, Maggie kept herself busier than usual preparing a large feast for the guests, assuming most of the mourners would return to Lyn Brienne after the services. The day started early with a low, overcast gray sky. Now, the gray clouds were ascending—always a sign the storm front was passing. The *Cymry* knew the sun always followed the passing of storm fronts in the *Rhiws of Tywi*.

"Magere, if you don't need me any more here, I'd like to check on Papa, he still needs help getting downstairs these mornings," Emma said.

"You go a'ead, luv. Everythin' is fine 'ere. Mary and Tess will be 'ere soon to 'elp me with the rest of the preparations." Emma wanted time with Cyrus to go over certain details of the service. Anna and Andy were staying at Lyn Brienne as full-time company, an arrangement purported for security purposes, but rather their presence provided a distraction from what lay ahead. Not to mention, they kept depressing thoughts at bay.

"Anna there's fresh coffee in the kitchen, and Maggie's serving all the fixings to go with it, too." Greeting Anna on the stairs, Emma continued up to Cyrus's room and knocked on the door.

"Come."

"I see you're getting faster every morning, Papa, dressed already?" Emma walked over to Cyrus and greeted him with her affectionate kiss and made a small adjustment to his tie.

"I miss seeing you in MacKenna's tartan dress for this occasion!" Cyrus let the remark pass.

"I've made it a goal to shave off two minutes every day until I get back to me usual time for morning ablutions. Still have a bit to go, lass. I don't think it will happen this week!" Cyrus leaned over and gave Emma a kiss.

"Are you ready for today, Em?" She nodded her answer. Looking into Cyrus's eyes, Emma knew he had taken care of every detail of the service…no need for questions. She couldn't help but wonder if it would be just the final tribute planned…or was there more to it?

"Then let's go downstairs! I'm in need of some of Magg's breakfast delights."

Emma held one arm; Cyrus held the rail, steadily making his way downstairs to the dining room. His wounded leg was healing well from the gunshot wound, but stairs were still troublesome. It was the brutal beating that caused the more serious injuries; this he kept to himself. Since his return to the farm, his level of strength was noticeably better, evidenced by the way he walked with more confidence, but he was still in need of a cane.

Cyrus and Emma entered the dining room to see Anna and Andy already seated. Taking his usual place at the head of the table, he said, "I hope you all slept well." Andy and Anna were glad to see the take-command Mac back again.

"Now that we're all here, I want us to go over the service arrangements again, taking into consideration—all contingencies!" Cyrus said to the group as he started with Maggie's special breakfast fixings.

Andy checked with Control for the most recent information and presented the final details of the plan. "The cars are ready and assigned. There are eight cars of mourners, and our car will be the last one. Once the contingent of mourners is in place, the immediate family will form the closed circle directly 'round the casket. E'ery agent is assigned a designated position in an outer circle be'ind the family, and they're armed! This next line of mourners will be a circle of agents, there are about two-dozen agents from IICA and MI-5 posing as mourners 'just attending the funeral of a friend' and spread out at strategic distances to cover every angle within the groups of mourners and out to the 'illside. Be'ind this group are pre-positioned sharp shooters positioned at certain tactical vantage points on the surrounding berns with scopes constantly scanning the whole cemeter'. Our group will be the last to approach the casket once every mourner is in place. A canopy over'ead will make it 'arder for anyone to see the positions of the individual family mourners from a distance under its darker undersides. Except you—Mac—you'll be more detectable with your cane and Emma on your arm. I'll be with Anna next to you. The good'y 'illside is well covered!"

"Emma, do you and Anna have your mourning clothes ready?" Cyrus asked.

"Yes. We're all ready, Papa."

"We're about the same size so it was easy to choose what we needed," Anna said.

"Can any of you think of anything we've missed? Something we haven't thought about?" Cyrus looked at each individual seated at the table.

"I have," Emma said. "Has anyone heard from Carlos?"

Each one at the table looked at the other to answer. It was Cyrus who spoke.

"Emma, he's doing a job. I know he'll be somewhere at the cemetery today—near us—but not with us. He'll get word to you soon...I know Carlos, too." Cyrus looked directly at her knowing she was examining his behavior while he spoke for a sign of disinformation.

"We all have our job to do...and we know he'll do his today... wherever he is," Cyrus said this for Emma's benefit.

"Then I'll get dressed for the service, Papa. See you in a short while." Emma rose and returned upstairs to dress for the service. Sitting on the bed, she kept thinking about Dillon...knowing he'd want no part of this elaborate ceremony today...but it was so deserved. *I miss you partner...wherever you are...*she thought and deliberately roused herself from past memories to concentrate on the present event about to start. She changed into her black suit. *"Somehow this isn't Dillon's color...no...green is his color."* Thinking out loud, she smiled.

*"Emeralds...like the hills of Wales... are yur diamonds, Em, giving me the matching purse..."*

When Emma left the dining room, Andy made a call and returned to the Great Room to speak with Cyrus. "Mac—Control said the two children's DNA matched Lucinda Rudolphi. They are her children. We are still keeping the foster parents separated and under guard... until Marcus is captured. Lucinda had a visit with the children already...she wants to gain their trust first before she tries to tell them some kind of truth."

"Emma will be happy to hear that news...to think if she hadn't persevered to find those children, they could've disappeared permanently...even be dead!" Cyrus's words trailed off silently.

**A child born...a rose...sharp pains...blackness!**

"Why do I feel there is something in the back of my mind I should remember?" Cyrus said, fighting a feeling of ominous foreboding when he tried to remember...something.... Andy took notice of the trance-like look Cyrus had on his face.

"Mac, are you all right?"

"Aye...aye, I'm fine! Anymore news from Control?"

"A brief, cryptic message was sent to Colin yesterday, **'Target in sight. Date confirmed.'**"

"Then everything is ready here, Andy. It's a go now."

Maggie finished dressing in her best mourning dress and was putting on her hat and coat, giving last instructions to Tess and Mary about setting out the food on the tables while she attended the services. Cyrus walked into the kitchen. Maggie saw that look in Cyrus's face she knew so well.

"Maggs...let's take a walk outside for a bit. They walked out into the garden together to the ivy-covered wall. The two sat on the stone bench.

"It's been a while since we've had a chance to be together...you and me...to be as we should...with one another...since I've been on the mend. I felt your gentle touch when me mind was sleeping.

Without that touch and care, I'd not have made it, Maggs dear." He looked tenderly at her.

"I've had nothing but time…and I've done a lot of thinkin' about what's important to me…about us, Maggs! You've been so patient with me all these years… and more's the thought how much I've missed you, Maggs, when I was so close to death. It was you I felt drawin' me back…" He took hold of her and held her close. "I took you for granted for all these years…I counted on you'd always be there for me. I now know, with no more qualms, I want you—need you with me as my soulmate—that you've already been…but I want it out there for all to see…I need you, Margaret Mack…me dearest. I think when this is finally over, we need to speak of things…things about us…to Emma. It's time for us to be family…again."

Meeting his eyes Maggie Mack said, "I know, Cyrus, we will be famil', again, when it's over. I ne'er doubted this time would come." Cyrus gently kissed her; each held the other tenderly for a long moment. For a lifetime, she understood and loved this strong man of deep feelings and few words.

Andy finished and walked into the Great Room dressed in his black suit instead of traditional tartan dress for the service. Traditional tartan clan attire was always worn at weddings and funerals. Today's service required conservative clothes for obvious reasons. Cyrus was already seated in front of the fire—quiet and contemplative. The sun was beginning to lighten the room with soft rays from the east, penetrating the dark room with streaks of light.

"Has there been any further word from Carlos?" Andy asked Cyrus.

"No—he's made no contact with us here. I feel he's in deep cover and not taking any chances a leak will get back to his target—not knowing who his sympathizers are—or where they are!" Cyrus said in confidence to Andy. "That cryptic message to Colin was his only communication."

"Then you think he saw the notice in the paper and will be at the cemetery today?" Andy gestured in exasperation to his own question. "I know the answer to my question, Mac! I guess I just wanted to hear someone tell me out loud!" Andy remarked anxiously.

"That is exactly what that last coded message said. He'll be there!" Cyrus repeated his own words, "He'll be there—not a doubt in me mind, Andy!"

Cyrus rose and walked with his cane over to the large desk at the end of the Great Room and unlocked the bottom drawer. Taking out the wooden box, he removed the 9mm Makarov, the silencer, and several clips of ammunition and placed the gun in his shoulder holster. It was the first time he had it on since he was taken prisoner and was more aware of its weight at his side, something he hadn't felt in a long time. The weight was definitely palpable now! The silencer went into his pocket. Replacing the box, he locked the drawer, and put his suit coat on before Emma and Anna came down. "I doubt I will need it...but I won't feel dressed for today's service without it," Cyrus commented to Andy.

"For that fact, I'm dressed, too, Cyrus," Andy stated.

At that moment, Emma and Anna entered the room together wearing black suits with hats and veils. Anna's golden blond hair was covered with the large black-brimmed hat and veil. Emma's long ebony hair was seen under the small black pillbox faille hat covered with sheerer netting—the veils concealing their facial characteristics.

"May I say you ladies look fine in your mourning attire?" Cyrus commented.

"The cars are ready and waiting out front. Maggie is going to go the cemetery with her brother—best she not be involved in this scenario too closely," Andy informed Cyrus.

"It's all so unreal!" Emma commented.

"Are you sure, Anna, you want to do this?" Emma asked.

"I know what I'm doing, Emma, so stay close at all times. We'll be on the arms of Cyrus and Andy, guiding us to our places under the canopy." Anna gave Emma's hand a squeeze.

The procession of cars left Lyn Brienne and drove slowly to the cemetery—"The Goodly Ground." Meeting up with the hearse, the lesser cars in the procession of mourners were the first to enter the cemetery in slow formation. No one spoke inside the limousine car, each one carefully watching the scene unfold. Martin was driving their limousine car directly behind the black hearse carrying the casket and flowers. Attendants guided each car to park in tandem. All eyes watched the funeral attendants slide the casket from the platform inside the hearse onto their shoulders. Slowly they marched up the slight hill in step with the pipes playing up to the hallowed ground on the hilltop, the canopy fluttering in the breeze, they placed the casket on the covered bier under the canopy. Everything was ready for the procession of mourners and the attendant signaled the mourners to start the march up the knoll, directing the occupants from the last car to go first. The cars emptied one by one. With everyone in place, the signal was given to the last car. Martin opened the door for Cyrus and Emma and Andy and Anna. Emma gave Cyrus a last hug and got out of the car first. Slowly, the four of them started up the rise. With Cyrus's weak leg it was a slow deliberate walk. He was determined not to use his cane at the last minute. Each scanned the crowds and hillsides for the sight of the man indelibly imprinted in their minds.

Cyrus stopped abruptly. "What's wrong, Papa?" Emma asked.

"That smell…the smell…Turkish tobacco! He's near!" Without showing alarm, the group of four proceeded to their places under the canopy next to the casket adorned with flowers and messages of "Goodbye—*Hwyl.*"

Emma scanned the crowd of mourners. There was Peter and Mrs. Tibitts, Olivia and Hilly, and Jonathan Kavanaugh standing in the crowd of gatherers. Nearby, she saw a small group of men gathered…somehow familiar? But from where? Oh! The 'members' from Black Swan Pub.

"Dillon, you may have been alone in this world without your family—but you were never lonely…so many wonderful friends!"

The vicar started the service with words for the mourners gathered to bid farewell to a trusted friend…a loving friend who gave his life for every man and woman here today. "For Dillon's legacy to every one here…we take a bit of Dillon O'Rourke within us for knowing the man he was…with that bit of him in us, he can make us a better person for knowing what he did in his life to make ours better." Emma felt Dillon's presence near her…just as she had so many times in their past together. *One last time dear friend, be with me one last time…* Emma reflected.

The breeze was blowing stronger now, coming from the east carrying curls of smoke out to the nearby hillsides from a nearby knoll. "He's close by—heads up everyone!" Cyrus said in a quiet tone, appearing to give words of comfort to "Emma." His body more rigid and taut, Cyrus loosened his jacket, as did Andy. Then both men deliberately took a step sideways, away from Emma and Anna. Anna took a step closer to Emma, standing almost in front of her. All the agents on the hillside heard the message over their microphone and responded accordingly.

*Except for one man! He didn't hear those words of warning or detect the shift among the mourners!*

# CHAPTER SIXTY

Kneeling on the grave next to the mausoleum he appeared as a disinterested mourner at a graveside on a nearby Bern.

The solitary mourner closely observed each figure in the unfolding pageant across the mount. He readied everything atop his own hillside long before the distant burial procession began. Now rising to stand, ending in prayer over his private burial crypt, he took out a cigarette from his gold case and lit it with a brief spurt of flame, never losing concentration or sight of the large group assembling across the next Bern. He studied each mourner as they took a position near the canopied coffin. The slowly curling smoke from the cigarette floated away on the breeze. Marcus walked slowly back towards the mausoleum and stood behind it out of site of the funeral service. He was modestly dressed to blend in with the country folk, telling himself, "Appear like a country farmer and you become a country farmer." Even for the sake of his mission, he disliked dressing like common folk and felt uncomfortable in his farmer's garb; he'd rather be seen as a gentleman, impeccably attired in his Armani or a Versace suit as he was at his last charity party. Removing the special gun from his shoulder holster, made just for this mission with precision that included a mini infrared laser scope and silencer, he made certain it was ready—and concealed it inside his jacket. Flicking the cigarette away into an arc across the grass, he watched it give off a shower of tiny red coals. Sounds from the bagpipes drifted over to him playing their eerie notes over and over on the distant Bern...he waited until the music stopped before he took up his position.

Marcus chose this particular spot in the cemetery long before the contingent of mourners arrived there today and took up his position before dawn. He purposely made a trip to the cemetery days before to learn where the newly dug gravesite was located and to scout out the best and most undetectable site to execute his plan. He knew exactly how to carry out his final plan after reading the obituary notice about the funeral service for Sean Dillon O'Rourke in Llandrindod Wells' papers. Even the newspaper in Andermatt, Switzerland as well as the local paper in Aix les Bains, France carried an account of the funeral service planned for today to honor an important Irishman, not giving too many details surrounding his death. Marcus decided it happened at the Villa Latinestto. But he could have died later from wounds received that day. It didn't matter when he died—he was glad the man was dead! "That man was a bad influence on Emma," Marcus told himself.

\* \* \*

The morning after the attack, when Marcus failed to find Giorgio and Sofia, learning Nina and Bruno Tomasini were not in Perugia with the children, he panicked and decided to stay away from Perugia—get out of Italy! If they were away on a legitimate holiday, he would find them later. Marcus concluded, "It's not possible for anyone to discover those children are really mine!" Justifying his decisions to himself, he said, *"Cara is the one I must care for now*—never mind Perugia! She is the most important one to protect!"

Fleeing Italy that morning after the attack, Marcus was focused on reaching Andermatt to take Cara and Katya to a safe place no one knew about—except him! From the marina, he traveled day and night to reach the Chalet late the following day. Gunter had them packed and ready to leave. Once the car was packed, he planned to drive to the secure house in France, settle them in and then return the Volvo for another rental. There was one final mission for him to accomplish—before they all disappeared!

The trip from Andermatt was going to be a long one. "Herr Rudolphi, where will Cara and I be staying?" Katya asked.

Katya was the young Dutch girl Marcus hired as au pair for Cara. She was well educated in childcare and came with excellent credentials. The only rule Marcus made was that she was never to question him about decisions he made. This was not the first time Kaya questioned him! Not wanting to answer her question directly, he thought it best to give some answer to satisfy her curiosity and not arouse suspicions about his urgency to leave Switzerland.

"It's a good time for us to take this trip and see different places for a while! Certain people are bothersome…no longer trustworthy, and I don't want Cara or you upset by them. Gunter will join us in a few days after he closes the chalet." Marcus realized this didn't answer Katya's question, and he had no intention of telling her exactly where they were going! Katya knew Marcus's retort was deliberately said to put her off—and she wouldn't pursue the question again, knowing Marcus's penchant for unpredictable behavior!

The three of them drove all night crossing the border into France. Letting Katya and Cara sleep most of the trip made it easy for Marcus. He was glad they slept when they crossed the border into France—Katya would not know how far they traveled to the exact destination. At daylight, they reached a private drive leading to a French country chateau. What pleased him most with the new house, it was situated some distance from the closest neighboring farm and very private—a distance from town. Driving up the graveled drive to the front entrance, an elderly woman opened the door to escort them into the front sitting room. Marcus carried their bags inside and placed them in the large foyer.

"Cara Rosina, this is your new home and Katya's, too. Baba has to take care of some business then I will return to spend more time with you. Will you like that?" he asked and knelt next to the small dark-haired child. The child remained close to her young au pair, but nodded yes to his question. Marcus gave instructions to Eloise emphasizing she was to tell no one about Cara or Katya taking up residence there.

"Eloise, Gunter, my caretaker will be joining us in several days. He will be responsible for the garden grounds and help in the care of the house—and he knows how to keep unnecessary visitors away."

Eloise was glad to have tenants in the house again and listened carefully to her new employer's instructions.

Marcus turned to the child. "Come here, Cara. Baba must leave now to go to work...I want you to be a good girl for Katya and Eloise while I'm away." Cara slowly walked over and stood in front of Marcus. When he bent down to kiss her, she suddenly turned and ran back to Katya crying and hid behind her. "She'll get use to me again when I return," Marcus told Katya.

"If you should need to reach me, you can call this number," he said, handing her a mobile telephone number.

"I will call you daily to check on things," Marcus instructed the au pair and returned to his car out the front door.

"I don't like Baba! Baba does not tell us the truth...he makes things up," Cara looked up into the eyes of Katya.

"I know what you mean, Cara, but don't you worry! I will always be with you, and I will always tell you the truth." She hugged and tickled Cara to distract her and make her smile. She loved to see Cara laugh—her dark brown eyes lit up whenever she showed that pixie smile. Katya had to hide her own fears from Marcus Rudolphi.

A week passed, and Marcus saw no evidence Interpol or the IICA had followed him to France. No unusual activity around him. He returned the Volvo to a rental agency in *Luc du Bourget* in exchange for a silver Mercedes. His next task—the trip to Germany to pick up his special package, and then on to Wales.

Katya kept him updated daily. No one made inquires at the chateau in *Aix les Bains*, and no one visited them. Katya remembered Marcus's instructions to her that he would be away for a week or two, but would call her daily—his way of keeping a tight control over them—until this new job was over. Each conversation ended with his constant warning *not to venture into town or take Cara out to play anywhere, but on the Chateau's private grounds.* Knowing Marcus's penchant for discovering disobedience, Katya felt like a prisoner—as did her charge.

\* \* \*

He felt her closeness even a hilltop away, remembering how happy he was to see her at their charity party that Sunday. Recalling his feelings when he looked up to see her standing next to him, remembering how his thoughts and feelings quickened when she spoke. Now he felt that same excitement—the emotional surge again, seeing Emma standing under the canopy.

"You are as beautiful as I remember you, my darling. I have tried to tell you about our secret love, but they wouldn't let it happen. I am sorry, my love...I have no recourse, my darling, but to do this! I know if you saw her—your baby—you would be so happy...she is so much like you! I think she has the same MacKenna traits as you...your bright dark eyes...but you will never come to know this, my darling. If only I had the opportunity to talk to you in Milano... things would be different now!" Looking past Emma, he said, "I need to make certain Cyrus never finds her... He must die, too!" He mouthed the last words with passion.

Marcus had gone over his preparations many times in his mind, making contingency arrangements for any unexpected development that could happen today! First—he had to silence Cyrus! When he fell, Emma would be next to him in a vulnerable position—easy to single out next! From what he could see through the scope, she was dressed in black with a small black pillbox hat and veil standing next to Cyrus with his arm in hers as if he needed her support.

"Good! His wounds still give him trouble!" Marcus mumbled.

The procession passed slowly and reverently before the casket. Taking careful aim in preparation, he flashed the infrared beam to locate and focus the laser beam on its first target to lock in the coordinates. Concealing himself as much as possible behind the great oak tree, he was careful not to let the mourners see the red laser beam seeking out its victim. Next, he made the corrections on the range finder, screwed the silencer in place, and permanently focused on Cyrus. Turning on the laser-tracking beam fixed at Cyrus's forehead, his finger lightly rested on the firing pin...

*"I wouldn't pull the trigger if I were you, Marcus!"* Marcus attempted to spin around to see who spoke those words behind him, when he felt the barrel of a gun slam into the back of his head with such force it pressed and locked his head against the bark of the great oak. His firing arm was wrenched and twisted in a painful

vice-like grip behind his back until there was a crack—making him drop his gun.

"ACH! YOU! *Come lei me ha trovato?* How did you find me here?" He spit out the words feeling great pain.

"I've been following you for the past two weeks! *Si*, I've tracked every movement you made day and night! I commend you on your choice of position here to take out your marks! I think I would have chosen this same place!" Toying with his foe, all the while tightening the pressure on Marcus's head against the tree.

"I knew you would turn up at Llandrindod Wells for this service. *We* purposely choreographed this whole funeral—*just for you, Marcus*! YOU ARE A PREDICTABLE MAN, Marcus! I knew Emma is the one person who would draw you out of hiding! And we counted on that!" Carlos whispered.

"How...do you know that?"

"Because I know what you did to her two years ago at the Villa Latinesstto! Because I know you had your henchman, Carruchi perform surgical procedures on her without her knowledge! Because I know you gave her mind-altering drugs to mask your rape of her!"

"You can't prove...any of those accusations!"

"I don't intend to prove them to anyone, Marcus." Marcus's eyes widened fearing what could happen to him.

"You see, Marcus, today's funeral is nothing more than an empty coffin down there. No one is inside that wooden box! Unless you say...no one is inside *at this present moment*...but that will change! *This service is for you!*" Carlos's words turned Marcus's face pale with a terrified look, his eyes darting around furtively looking for any opportunity to seize a chance to distract Carlos, who had not taken his eyes off his captive anticipating an attempt to break free. Carlos's gaze was permanently fixed on his target without a flinch or blink of an eye.

"But I delay! Yes...the man Dillon O'Rourke did die but not before he finished his mission."

"What...was...HIS mission?" Marcus mouthed.

"He was to terminate Dr. Ennio Carruchi. He did just that! Your doctor Mengele is dead! We buried Dillon in a beautiful service befitting a brave man in a secret place where we know he is at rest with his wife and child, Maura and Siobhan—two of your victims you destroyed in your research! You see Marcus, this service was planned JUST FOR YOU! See all those people over there? They're here to say good-bye to you!"

Marcus was thinking…*let him talk…buy time to make a move against him!* Carlos knew exactly what he was thinking and planning and anticipated every flinch!

"No…no…Marcus—no sudden moves! Time is not on your side!" Marcus tested his strength to break the lock-wrenching hold on him…thinking if he could try a fast dart away from him and break his hold on him, he'd have a chance!

"In this hand I hold a gun to your head." Carlos pushed the barrel down harder into the base of his skull forcing his face painfully deeper into the ragged bark of the oak tree.

"In this OTHER hand, I hold a stiletto laced with a fast acting neurotoxin poison that paralyzes in seconds! The poison first attacks pain centers slowly causing pain to intensify to an excruciating degree! Then, at the same time you become totally helpless— paralyzed—unable to move or speak—all the while your muscles writhing motionless in unbearable pain! You can't move or even blink an eye! *Tortured and still alive—just like all those victims you murdered!* If you dare flinch now, I'll not have that choice of my first weapon! You see, Marcus, I still have a choice to make! Which do you think I will choose first? What is YOUR preference?" Carlos put the question to his captive. It was clear Marcus believed Carlos, as beads of perspiration trickled down his temples and his eyes widened, pleading in a desperate look.

"I'm telling you these things, because I want you to know just how badly you failed at everything you wanted in this world! You see… Lucinda is united with her children—Antonio and Angela—*your children*, at this very moment as we stand here! Yes, we know they are her birth children! She has Giorgio and Sophia—your Antonio and Angela—with her in a safe place and when this is all past, she will start a new life with her son and daughter that you denied her! You failed there too!" The rest of the Rudolphis are either dead or in jail. We have collected more than enough evidence needed to prosecute every man and woman involved in your organization—starting with Giuseppe! For *il padre?* We will ask for the death penalty and will certainly get it! And for each Rudolphi that we prosecute!" Marcus listened but all the while his mind searched for a way out.

"They're singing the final hymn down there, Marcus. I promised my friend...I would not stop searching until I had completed my mission. *YOU are MY mission, Marcus*! Best look down there... Marcus...that's YOUR burying ground. They call it the 'Goodly ground' here in Wales."

"What...*Che significa les*—my...burying ground?"

"That casket over the open grave on the next hill will be the final resting place for Marcus Rudolphi! There will be no outward evidence who lies in that grave! No! No marker to clue history to the name of the man buried there." Marcus strained to see what was taking place on the next Bern.

"The curious will read the epitaph—"**A TRAVELER MET HIS JUDGE!**" You see Marcus, **I AM THE JUDGE!**"

Using the hardest grip he could muster, Carlos jammed Marcus against the tree in a final painful vice-hold.

"No...no wait...you don't know...yet...the ba...!" Marcus's face was wedged so hard against the tree it was hard to speak his pleading words.

"If you kill...me...you will ne'er...find the...truth...the ba...!"

"No! I already know all the truth! There is no more truth from the mouth of a devil!" Carlos angrily mouthed the words in Marcus's face. A moment he worked so hard towards...was now here!

"NOW! For Emma...Cyrus...Dillon...his Maura and Siobhan... Lucinda and her Antonio and Angela...and the hundreds that have no voice today..." Carlos fired one shot with the silencer into Marcus directly between the third and fourth cervical spinal space. The bullet felt like a collision inside the man rendering him immediately helpless in seconds—thrusting his body to flaccidly rest against the great oak tree with no further need of outward force to hold him. Rather he appeared as a tired man resting on the tree in front of him. Marcus's breathing was becoming slow and shallow. His eyes still followed Carlos when a sudden convulsion erupted from his torso as the stiletto found its mark into his neck at the base of the skull directly into the brain stem, and immediately a horrific look of revulsion and surprise came over Marcus's face—a look frozen in time.

Staring fixedly…no eye movements…no blinking…no tears… no breathing…he slowly collapsed little by little slumping down to the ground in a heap at the base of the great oak tree. A passerby might take notice of a traveler in a restful sleep next to a tree—only this traveler was unable to close his eyes in rest.

\* \* \*

The procession of mourners began to make their way back to the motorcade of cars. Bagpipes continued playing. Eerie tones plied with the wind sending them off to the farthest distant mount giving testimony of finality. Once inside the car, Anna removed the small black pillbox hat and veil, then the dark ebony wig and looked at Emma.

"Was it all for nothing, Mac?" She asked.

"No, we accomplished what we set out to do today! Emma you can remove your disguise. I much prefer you the black-Irish beauty." Emma took off the large black brimmed hat and blond wig.

"There will be no need for disguises anymore," Cyrus said to her.

"Papa, how do you know for certain? How can you be so sure it is finished?"

"Carlos was there among us too, Emma. Marcus Rudolphi is dead."

"How do you know this, Papa? I didn't see you speak to anyone at the service?"

"The MacKenna gift is to know, my lass."

No one spoke in the car on the trip back to Lyn Brienne, still thinking…*is it really, finally over?*

# CHAPTER SIXTY-ONE

The mourners returned to Lyn Brienne to commiserate and share more intimate moments about the precious life of a friend.

With everyone gathered in the Great Room and sated on Maggie's special delicacies, Cyrus rose from his chair and walked over to stand in front of the hearth with its softly crackling, dying embers echoing as a hushed spirit came over the room. He saw before him a gathering of friends, family, and faces from a lifetime ago—save one…one was missing. One face seen in his mind and heart. A quiet whisper came over the assemblage in the Great Room.

"I think the time is fitting to say a few words now…though Dillon would not allow it if he were here today! He would definitely find a way to keep me from saying what is in my heart." The deep voice thick with the Welch brogue was commanding with emotion.

"This service today was dedicated to a man, a man who made the ultimate sacrifice without asking the cost—his life—for what he saw as the devil incarnate destroying our species of mankind. Each one of us, here in this room, has a memory of Dillon and how his unselfish acts touched our personal lives making each of us a better person today than we were yesterday. Without his wise and unselfish dedication, some of us would not be here today!" Cyrus paused to take a deep breath to compose himself for what he wanted to, and felt he must, say. "I…for one…would be one of those lost…"

Gaining his composure, "What I'm trying to say to each of you is…he touched many of our lives…and because of that unique

527

experience we each had with him—it's the reason we gathered here now! We speak what is in our hearts today, but we should have said it long ago…but didn't." Emma knew Papa was speaking about his feelings…to her, too.

"Because of him, this world is a much safer place today…but a much sadder one! I, for one, will never forget the gift this man gave to me—*my life*! So raise your glasses to a mighty warrior…to Sean Dillon O'Rourke…thank you dear friend! *Diolch*…my friend!"

"To Sean Dillon O'Rourke…to Dillon…to Dillon…*Diolch*!" The name resounded mightily in the Great Room.

Emma silently toasted her glass with tears running down her cheeks. Her feelings were myriad… something was missing… a test of her faith…insecurity. Was it gone for good? Will I ever again find what Dillon and I had? Maybe a poor imitation—it can never be the real thing, again! In her heart, she said, "To you my dear friend…I will always remember you…and love you…"

The crowd slowly began dispersing into small groups, eventually leaving Lyn Brienne to just a few lingering mates. A few lagging— trying to hold on to the feeling of camaraderie among a special group of men—for one last time—to celebrate the life of a first-class comrade. Emma went upstairs and changed into riding clothes and returned to find Cyrus sitting alone in the Great Room before the flickering hearth.

"Papa, I'm going for a ride with Ddu Kate. I won't be long." She leaned down and kissed him.

"Be careful, lass! Test her first before taking those stone walls!" Cyrus cautioned her. Watching her run out to the stable and pasture looking for her spirit mate, he fully realized how lucky he was to have her back with him today…the past is dead and buried!

***Then why do I keep having these ominous feelings…something I should be remembering…about Emma?*** Cyrus could not rid himself of these dark, macabre feelings.

Emma found Ddu Kate in the paddock pasture next to the barn, darting and running in the pasture in anticipation of something about to happen. Seeing Emma climb the paddock's fence, the mare stopped and gazed at her. Emma held out her hand with her morsel, and the black mare trotted over to the fence. "It's been a long time, girl, but I'm back now. How about a ride?" Emma led her out of the pasture and saddled her. Mounting Ddu Kate, she immediately felt the mare start her quickening gallop. "Let's go, girl!" The sun found its way out of the overcast clouds to reveal bright blue skies with a south wind blowing. Ddu Kate and rider started racing faster toward the east pasture at a full gallop. Emma's hair blowing as freely as the ebony mane. Unexpectedly, Emma felt the reins pull and Ddu Kate took her head. Emma knew where she was taking her and gave her free rein heading to the farthest north pasture, jumping stone walls, circling around the great oaks. The mare knew every step of the way without guidance from the rider's reins. Gradually, Ddu Kate slowed to a leisurely trot, climbing the last rise to the crest before stopping.

Below, in the distance was Kittery Cottage. Emma stared at the cottage for a long time without moving forward. Prodding the mare to walk down the hill…they reached the overgrown stone path, long disappeared in the last three decades. Dismounting and leaving Ddu Kate to graze, Emma walked along the remnants of the stone path up to the fenced cottage. The gate was permanently ajar as if beckoning the wayfarer inside. She slowly pushed it open all the way. Remnants of wild flowers were blooming and waving in the breeze in the small garden. Clumps of bright spring flowers darted to and fro with the wind in a game of tag in the semblance of a garden. "Flowers mother planted."

Finding the large plantar next to the door fractured into pieces and spilling its contents of dirt, she started digging feeling for…"Yes… the key!" Inserting the key into the door, she found it opened easily in anticipation of this day…for someone to unlock its secrets—to open and find its history inside! Emma had never set foot inside the cottage before this moment, and little by little, she walked into a past that should have been her life. Was this the reason she felt her life was beginning again—here in this cottage?

"Mother, I've come home."

It was as if time stood still inside the cottage. The *grib* at the hearth stood readied for the child it never held. *Needlework…mother was working on when…never finished.*

The kitchen had the teakettle next to the teapot and cups in preparation for sharing teatime with someone...never more shared.

The bedroom...the nightgown hanging...the cover thrown back on the bed still with the impression of someone having just left there...and never returned. "Why...oh why? Mother...you were happy here...such a loving home...do you think it could ever become a loving home...again for me...with the right man...as you found in father?" Emma spoke softly as if she was there to listen, touching and holding the quilt cover close to her face to capture a lost moment...trying to seize a moment of time past...a person... lost...a love never felt...

* * *

A bell rang at the front door of Lyn Brienne. Maggie went to answer it.

"Good day to you, young man, how can I 'elp you?" she asked the stranger.

"Is Emma or Cyrus at home?"

"Yes, Cyrus is in the Great Room. Emma is out riding with Ddu Kate. Please come in, and I'll tell Cyrus you're 'ere." Carlos followed Maggie inside, walking slowly, seeing Lyn Brienne for the first time!

"Carlos! Come in! Cyrus walked with cane in hand and greeted him with a warm embrace.

"Welcome to Lyn Brienne!" Carlos didn't expect this show of emotion from Cyrus, who always took great effort to keep his emotions hidden.

"Come! We can talk in the Great Room by the fire," he said, motioning Carlos to a dark green leathered chair appearing black in the shadows from the glow of the fire. Cyrus sat down in his own worn chair well contoured and broken to fit his big stature.

"Warm yourself by the fire!" he said, taking notice of Carlos's tense conduct sitting on the edge of the chair.

"Maggie? Fetch us tall drinks of Scotch!"

"Do you want to talk about it now?" Cyrus asked him.

"Yeah...Mac, I do. I understand Emma is out riding—I better do it without her hearing." Maggie brought the bottle of Scotch and two glasses and placed them on the table.

"*Grazie.*" Carlos motioned to her lifting the glass to drink. Carlos was clearly exhausted, dirty, and intensely saddened.

"Then tell me...where was he?"

*SILENCE.*

"He was on the hilltop near the mausoleum, one hilltop distant—in direct vision of the grave site—a full view of everything. I won't go into detail how I picked out the exact site I knew he'd choose...I just knew he'd pick the best site in the cemetery, and I waited there all night hidden inside the mausoleum. He arrived at dawn and was in position early and well prepared before the funeral procession arrived. Watching him from inside the Mausoleum, I let him play out his charade, until I knew exactly what he was going to do. He was totally predictable with absolute concentration on the events playing out over at burial hill. He had a heat-seeking laser pistol raised, with trigger finger ready...I caught him off guard—his 'pride' was his undoing and made him overconfident! His biggest mistake! He never heard me approach! He was ready to take you and Emma out!" Carlos relived the hilltop scenario again.

"I chose the small snub-nosed twenty-two gun—it would maim...not kill immediately...and ...may God forgive me...the neurotoxin on the stiletto, too! But first...I wanted him to know how he failed at everything he tried to accomplish! I held nothing back and told him how he failed with Emma...you...Dillon...Lucinda and his own two children! I made certain he knew the Rudolphi organization was completely demolished and the rest of his family—those who survived and were captured will be prosecuted with the death penalty! I made certain he knew he failed at everything!"

Carlos rose and walked over to the windows, looking out to the pastures. Cyrus didn't interrupt or prod him to continue but let him take his time, knowing the pain he was reliving. Carlos picked up his glass and poured another drink and raised his glass in a silent toast to Cyrus.

"I...first shot him in the fourth cervical disc...paralyzing him to a point...but still breathing...motionless...then...I used the stiletto...I wanted him to suffer the way he made so many human beings suffer...without conscience!"

Carlos's voice quivered and he hesitated in speaking his tale of death. Cyrus saw the psychological torment Carlos was living from the ordeal he experienced. He had to impress on Carlos how absolutely necessary it was to openly discuss his actions and feelings in order to understand why his emotions are controlling him now.

"Carlos...the difference between Marcus and you is...he did the killing without conscience...you had to do it with a conscience! He took great pride in killing...you feel only remorse in killing! This is the difference between a devil in human form and a man of our human species. If you did not have a conscience to stop the murdering...you could never have carried out your mission! Right now...there's someone important to both of us who needs you more at this moment than anyone else!"

Cyrus motioned Carlos's attention out to the pastures.

"Mac, you asked me to bring you everything on the 'target' when I found it. I searched him completely! He had no papers of identification or personal items except this one thing...a cigarette case and lighter...engraved with 'MAR' with several Turkish cigarettes inside. No watch...no keys...nothing. I was in place all night when I saw him walking a distance to the cemetery...he didn't drive." Carlos laid the gold case and lighter on the table next to Cyrus and walked to the window to hide the tears...a release it was finally over. Cyrus rose and walked slowly over to the window next to Carlos.

"I want to say how grateful I will always be to you for what you gave back to me today—my granddaughter's life! Thank you!"

"You would have done the same for me, Mac...Is there somewhere I can clean up? I'd like to see Emma."

"Maggie! Maggs!" Maggie came rushing into the room.

"Take Carlos upstairs to my room and give him whatever he needs." Carlos followed Maggie up the winding stone stairs. A short time later he came back down. "Borrowed one of you shirts, Mac—thanks."

"I've had Aur Cymru saddled for you. Take him and find Emma. Head toward the farthest northeast pasture. If I know Ddu Kate she's there. She'll be at the cottage—the Kittery Cottage."

"Thanks, Mac—for everything!"

"Go now! Be careful the old steed still likes to take those stone walls! Thinks he's a young buck!"

Cyrus watched Carlos ride out to the far field, letting the stallion set the pace. Picking up the gold lighter and case, he opened it. The aroma of Turkish tobacco was strong...no pictures. Snapping it closed he placed it in a false bottom of the desk drawer and locked it. "Caitlyn...Katherine...you'd approve of Emma's young man!"

Just then Andy walked in. "Mac? The burial is complete. The inscription on the stone...just as you ordered, **"A TRAVELER MET HIS JUDGE."**

"Thanks, Andy." The only sound in the Great Room was the crackling of the flickering flames from the hearth.

*SILENCE.*

* * *

The sun was deep in the western sky when Carlos saw the darkened cottage from atop the Bern and the black mare grazing down below. Ddu Kate sensed the duo on the hilltop and slowly trotted over as Carlos walked Aur Cymru down the hillside and dropped the reins next to Ddu Kate. "You are as beautiful as she is," he said, stopping to stroke the black mare before walking down the path to the partially opened door of the cottage. At the door, he listened for a sound from inside...soft footsteps?

"Emma?"

Emma was sitting on a window seat by the kitchen hearth looking out over the small brook, when she heard her name called from inside the cottage. Rising to follow the sound of the voice, she stopped. He was there...standing casually in the darkened doorway with the bright light at his back silhouetting and outlining his dark hair and tall stature. Reflections from the back-light cast a shadowy luminosity on his tired face.

Another moment flashed in Emma's memory, *"A silhouette of a curly, dark-haired man looking up at her from the road on a warm spring day on a Tuscan hilltop…in jeans and a shirt opened at the collar…his sunglasses hooked into the shirt collar."*

Carlos remembered a scene on a Tuscan hillside when he looked up the hill to see a dark-haired goddess of beauty among the leaves and trees. *"Signorina, you look like you are in need of help!"*

Emma stood motionless in the hall. Dare she hope the man she loved with all her heart was standing there…at this very moment?

*"E realmente lei mio e l'amore?"* Emma asked running to him, he swept her up into his arms. For a long unending moment—each held the other tightly in a long, silent embrace! The fresh perfumed scent of her hair permeated his sense of smell. The softness of her skin next to his cold face told him this moment was real. The fullness of her breasts pressed against him with the warmth of her body reminded him how much he longed to have her close in his arms—to show her the complete depth of his love.

His strong but gentle sinewy body in her arms emanated authority, strength, gentleness, and affection. The physical strength of his arms around her gave her a sense of sanctuary where her past fears and pains vanished. Her tears mingled with blissful feelings of joy, not wanting to let go of him…*her petition to the gods to stop the pendulum of time in Kittery cottage.*

*"Now time is ours…together! Time for laughter! Time to share our days and nights! Time to let go of the past! Time to dream of our future…together!"*

*"Non pensare al passato!* Do not think of the past," Carlos whispered to her.

"I love you, Emma Llewelyn…and I want you with me forever!"

Sobbing almost uncontrollably and not caring, Emma nodded. "Yes…my darling…it's just the beginning…of our lifetime… together!"

There was no need to rush back to Lyn Brienne. Kittery Cottage felt warm and right in the shadows of evening twilight, like a feeling of coming home.

*"L'Amo siamo l'inizio di giusti il nostro viaggio insieme,"* Carlos whispered to Emma. "Our journey is beginning...," he said, kissing her passionately, and she him.

# EPILOGUE

## *CARA ROSINA RUDOLPHI*

Cyrus finished packing his bag.

Checking his briefcase he made certain he had packed all the documents downloaded from the computer, together with the packet of information from Colin, he sat at the desk to write a note to Emma. Not certain where in France he would be staying, he made the note short and casual. She was expected at Lyn Brienne in a few days.

"In France for a few days—a journey for myself. Love, Papa."

The same memory over and over…started again…

**the child…a rose…Cara…a baby…**

Cyrus knew these flashes of memory were bits and pieces of information Marcus Rudolphi bragged to him in that dark, foul-smelling dungeon. Remembering how he injected the drug-filled syringe into his arm…the stinging feeling…then everything vanished—every memory gone. It had to be a mind-altering drug! A drug given to create amnesia—to erase his memory of something! Only something is different now, a flash of memory…from those hours spent in the subterranean room…tightly strapped in the chair… experiencing numbing pain all over again. Cyrus was reliving that same traumatic experience…the beatings…the pain…the anxiety, as if it was all really happening to him, again. Intermingled with the terrorizing thoughts, there's a voice somewhere in the dark room speaking. "Marcus confided a secret to me…what was it? How is it connected to Emma?"

Emma was his Achilles' heel! "I used that weakness to make him reveal…**WHAT?**"

Cyrus requested a report from Interpol about Marcus Rudolphi's last days of travels from Lago di Como at Novate Mezzelo to Andermatt, Switzerland. From all reports, he traveled straight to *Andermatt,* Switzerland in the rented Volvo from *Novate Mezzola.* Agents followed the trail of petrol charges to *Andermatt* and a mountain chalet that was leased to a client under the name of Count Majioli over two years ago. When Interpol agents arrived at the chalet, they found it vacant. Evidence pointed to a woman and child living there, and went missing only a few days earlier.

Town's people recalled seeing a young woman with a baby living in the chateau with an old man, a caretaker. Interpol issued a request to the French, Austrian, German, English and Swiss National Police to immediately contact the Italian IICA, if this couple with a child was seen traveling in these countries.

Property rental agents in a radius of five hundred kilometers from *Andermatt* were instructed to report any new requests for immediate occupancy by a young woman with a small child, in the company of an old man. Most likely, the couple preferred renting a house in an out-of-the-way place—probably a private country house somewhere outside a town.

A break came in the case when a young woman named Katya left a hurried message for her boyfriend, Franz Hanniken in *Andermatt,* telling him she had to leave Andermatt unexpectedly with her charge, Cara, and would let him know where she was staying when she arrived at their new destination. Luck had it; Franz Hanniken worked at a rental car company in *Andermatt* at the Central Office as an accountant for the Swiss International Auto-rental Company. When the communiqué went out to all car rental agencies mandating them to report to the police all Volvos, rented or returned, it was Franz who notified Interpol about the Volvo wagon returned to an affiliate office in *Aix les Bains, France.* Not realizing his girlfriend was one member of the couple the agents were trying to locate, Franz readily provided the agency's rental information to Interpol agents.

A second piece of good fortune came when Franz casually mentioned to the agents his girlfriend, Katya, left *Andermatt* and had to relocate to a small town in France—*Aix les Bains*!

Together, these two pieces of information confirmed they were on the trail to Marcus Rudolphi's whereabouts! Interpol agents reviewed the company's ledgers and found the entry, "**Marcus Rudolphi's return destination of Volvo—***Aix les Bains***, France; originated—***Novate Mezzola***, Italy.**" Further data indicated when Marcus Rudolphi returned the Volvo, he exchanged it for a Mercedes—*a silver Mercedes*—just a short time after the assault raids took place in Milano. Cyrus spoke first hand with the agent who investigated, and confirmed that the man who rented the Mercedes in *Aix les Bains* was the same Marcus Rudolphi who returned the Volvo, with payment charged to the same credit card bank number. *He had him!*

Months after the burial service, the silver Mercedes with French license plates was found abandoned in Llandrindod Wells in a private rented garage barn. It had been parked and hidden in the same garage stall for several months. When the renter didn't return to pay his rent, the landowner notified the police, and they impounded it.

"It's too much information for *all of it* to be coincidences! *I* need to confirm that all these facts have a connection to *something* in my subconscious...I've got to go to the field office in *Aix les Bains*, France! If there are answers, they will be there for me!" Cyrus made *his decision to go to Lyons, France alone.*

Colin MacEachen put out queries to his agents in MI 5 to ask about any couple taking up a rental residence within hundred-fifty kilometers of *Aix les Bains* near *Luc du Bourget*, France. Response was almost immediate! Four names came up matching that description of new renters. Colin called Cyrus.

"I may 'ave a lead for you. There's a slim chance, that an old man and a young woman with a small child—a girl—were seen in *Aix les Bains*, not far from the Switzerland boarder, near *Luc du Bourget* rather recently. It appears they've been livin' in the area for many months or longer at a place called, the *Chateau de Villiers*."

"Thanks, old friend."

"No use me askin' why the need for this information, Mac?" Moments of deafening silence passed. "Then I 'ope you find what you're lookin' for, Mac." Cyrus's silence told Colin the Chatelaine Connection was still not over!

"If it turns out to be a false lead or nothing at all—then I've wasted nothing! *One chance in a million...*", Cyrus spoke.

"*Lwc dda,* old friend," Colin rang off.

Emma remained at Lyn Brienne for several days after the "Goodly Ground" burial service before returning to London. Carlos stayed on at Lyn Brienne for a few days—they were days they all needed to spend together!

Work no longer kept Emma in London for long periods of time. After Carlos returned to Milano, she spent more time at Kittery Cottage. No definite plans were announced, but Cyrus knew there was talk between them about renovating the cottage. Emma's plans were to return to Lyn Brienne this very weekend to oversee the beginning of new architectural construction at Kittery Cottage. Cyrus had seen a transformation in her; the joy she took in spending more time at Kittery each trip home. He had much to be happy about! Still, there were moments when he saw Emma struggling with the loss of Dillon in her life. Though she returned to her law practice, the type of legal cases she accepted were different—no more cases dealing with children. His wish for her—she would return to the type of law she loved most, international law.

"Then why do I still have such fears for her...frightening imaginings...dreams of the torture in the dungeon room? I remember Marcus Rudolphi's last words...

**"'Rose of the heart...Cara Rosina!'"**

*Can I believe the words of such an evil man? Or was it his way of bragging to feed his ego? What is the significance of Marcus Rudolphi kidnapping Emma...bragging about his research on her... and returning her to London? Is she still being victimized by him? Was he telling me...**Cara Rosina** is connected to Emma?*

Cyrus and Emma found the time to speak about his past secret life, discussing his Interpol position and years of work in a clandestine existence. Neither confronted one another, it just happened one night and surprisingly it was easy for both to speak about it. The timing was right for total honestly, to share what his life's work is all about with her—about his first position with MI 5 and then with Interpol. Cyrus confided to Emma how his secret service work started after her grandmother, Caitlyn died, and how it helped him to find a reason to live again, when he was thrust into a life without Caitlyn and left with Katherine to rear. Years later, when he lost Katherine…he had *her*. It had always been his wish to confide completely that secret part of his life with her, but the right time never came…until that day.

"Keeping my secret was my way of protecting my family…first Katherine, then you…from the taint of a sordid, dangerous life that I never wanted to touch you!" Still with reservation, he felt he must hold back certain facts, for her safety, about the 'torture room'. Cyrus had to keep certain secrets from her…secrets he still had to search out answers until he knew everything! Would there ever be a time when he could be completely honest with Emma? For so long, so much of his life was a spent *alone*!

"Maggs knew…she always accepted the job…she had to know about my other life…in case something happened to me…she had to know what she must do—for you."

"What was she to do, Papa?"

"Maggie was to see that no harm would come to you…It's no longer important now, we know that can never happen!" But, would Emma understand why I keep secrets from her now?

At the present moment, he removed the gold cigarette case with the initials MAR from the hidden compartment in the desk and studied it for a few minutes. He hadn't looked or touched it since that day Carlos gave it to him. Fingering the etched initials…it almost felt like Marcus Rudolphi was still alive. Without further reflection, he slid the case into his pocket.

Calling Andy into the Great Room, "Andy, have the plane checked and ready for a trip to France in the morning. Find out the earliest departure time I can leave for *Lyons,* France. This journey I must make alone. No questions, please!" Cyrus's final words stopped Andy from arguing the matter.

Andy didn't like Mac flying the plane without a co-pilot, aware he still suffered lingering effects from his ordeal at the Villa Latinestto—the thought of him alone at the controls disturbed him. There was no use arguing—once Mac made up his mind—there was no changing it! Whatever Mac's reasons were for going to France alone, Andy knew it was something he discovered…something Marcus Rudolphi told him…"Whatever it is, it's consumin' 'is thoughts since 'is return to Lyn Brienne." His only conclusion, "If it were somethin' involvin' only Mac, I know 'e'd confide 'is thoughts to me. No, this passion 'as to do with Emma! But what's terrorizin' 'im so completely 'e 'as to make this trip alone?"

*　*　*

Alone in flight, with only the drone of the motors heard, haunting questions plagued Cyrus MacKenna.

"If I do discover what I'm searching for…will it be just *my secret* to keep hidden?"

*"Has the Chatelaine Connection really ended?"*

Printed in the United States
31727LVS00002B/300

9 781420 818642